THE OXF[...]
BOOK O[...]
ENGLISH GHOST
STORIES

MICHAEL COX is Senior Commissioning Editor, Reference Books, at OUP and is currently compiling *The Oxford Chronology of English Literature* on a freelance basis. His previous books for the Press include *A Dictionary of Writers and Their Works*, *Victorian Ghost Stories* (with R. A. Gilbert), and *Victorian Detective Stories*.

R. A. GILBERT is a well-known antiquarian bookseller and a world authority on the historiography of esoteric thought in general, and on the occult currents of the nineteenth century in particular.

THE OXFORD
BOOK OF
ENGLISH GHOST
STORIES

Chosen by
MICHAEL COX
and
R. A. GILBERT

OXFORD
UNIVERSITY PRESS

OXFORD
UNIVERSITY PRESS

Great Clarendon Street, Oxford OX2 6DP

Oxford University Press is a department of the University of Oxford.
It furthers the University's objective of excellence in research, scholarship,
and education by publishing worldwide in

Oxford New York

Auckland Bangkok Buenos Aires Cape Town Chennai
Dar es Salaam Delhi Hong Kong Istanbul Karachi Kolkata
Kuala Lumpur Madrid Melbourne Mexico City Mumbai Nairobi
São Paulo Shanghai Singapore Taipei Tokyo Toronto

with an associated company in Berlin

Oxford is a registered trade mark of Oxford University Press
in the UK and in certain other countries

First published 1986
First issued as an Oxford University Press paperback 1989
Reissued 2002

British Library Cataloguing in Publication Data

Data available

Library of Congress Cataloging in Publication Data

The Oxford book of English ghost stories / chosen
by Michael Cox and R. A. Gilbert.
p. cm.
1. Ghost stories. I. Cox, Michael, 1948- .
II. Gilbert, R. A.
PR1309.G5904 1989 823'.0873308—dc20 89-9243

ISBN 0-19-284085-1

2

Printed in Great Britain by
Clays Ltd, St Ives plc

ACKNOWLEDGEMENTS

Two individuals deserve special mention: Richard Dalby for his generous advice and help, particularly in compiling and checking bibliographical details; and Glen Cavaliero, for several valuable suggestions regarding both the selection of stories and the Introduction. Our thanks are also due to Robert Booth, Esmé Cogdon, Dr M. H. Coleman, Michael Gill, Warwick Gould, and George Locke.

CONTENTS

INTRODUCTION

I

WHATEVER we do with the dead they will not go away. Whether we entomb and isolate them or scatter their ashes, they remain as ghosts in our memories and faced with their continuing presence we have no option but to learn to live with them. Our most effective way of accommodating them is, perhaps, to encapsulate them in stories, either as the vengeful or grateful dead of folklore, as the dull prosaic phantoms of psychical research, or as the less predictable revenants of fiction.

Strictly, a ghost is 'the soul of a deceased person . . . appearing to the living' (*OED*), but in both folklore and fiction the meaning is often less precise. Supernatural beings of a decidedly non-human kind and of a most unpleasant nature—like the evil spirits in Ecclesiasticus 'created for vengeance'—may wander furiously if imprecisely in lore and legend and at will in the literary tale of terror, which has its own conventions; but in the ghost story proper, with a handful of notable exceptions, they have no place. Which leads us to a more immediately important question: what is a ghost story?

In essence it is, as M. R. James said, 'only a particular sort of short story',[1] but a short story possessing features unique to itself. The ghostly protagonists must act with a deliberate intent; *their* actions—or the consequences of their actions—rather than those of the living must be the central theme; and, most important of all, each ghost, whether human or animal phantom or reanimated corpse, must unquestionably be dead. From this it follows that there can be no rationalization of the ghost, no explanation of events by natural causes. Not all supernatural stories involve ghosts, but every ghost story must be supernatural.

L. P. Hartley described the ghost story as 'certainly the most exacting form of literary art, and perhaps the only one in which there is almost no intermediate step between success and failure. Either it comes off or it is a flop.'[2] But what determines that one story shall 'come off' while another flops? In keeping with the ghost story's many and necessary enigmas, only partial reasons can be advanced. A high degree of purely technical skill is essential, both in plotting and in handling description.

[1] M. R. James, introduction to V. H. Collins (ed.), *Ghosts and Marvels* (Oxford, 1924), p. v.

[2] L. P. Hartley, introduction to Lady Cynthia Asquith (ed.), *The Third Ghost Book* (1955).

Hyperbole lays the literary ghost with deadly finality: it gathers strength through obliquity and operates most powerfully on us, in Elizabeth Bowen's words, 'through series of happenings whose horror lies in their being just, *just* out of the true'.[3] To bring off this kind of effect successfully calls for fine literary judgement; and never is an ear for *le mot juste* more in need than when the reader's attention is focused squarely on the supernatural intruder: 'There was a slow, heavy tread, characterized by the emphasis and deliberation of age . . . and, what made the sound more singular, it was plain that the feet which produced it were perfectly bare, measuring the descent with *something between a pound and a flop, very ugly to hear*'[4] (emphasis added). We must not become alienated from the fictional world by gross unlikelihood of incident or character, but drawn inexorably into it by an insidious sense of *probability*. We must feel this imagined world to be in its essentials a reflection of our own, making us anxious witnesses to a sudden and often fatal violation of everyday reality by the supernatural. It follows that a good ghost story must exhibit internal consistency and observe a certain decorum of manner and tone; which is not at all the same thing as conforming either to the conventional patterns of behaviour deman-ded from the ghosts of oral tradition or to the pseudo-scientific theories of occultists. As M. R. James again observed, stories that bring in the technicalities of folklore or occultism (as several of Algernon Black-wood's later tales did) are virtually assured of failure in this peculiarly demanding literary form.

Circumstantial detail, believable living characters, economy of style, and the power of suggestion all create the necessary atmosphere for a successful ghost story. Just as essential is a due regard for dramatic strategy. The story must be exactly paced and the narrative energy firmly under the writer's control. Although we know from the outset that the ghost's appearance is inevitable, that appearance should be climactic rather than unexpected. The most effective ghosts are those who intrude gradually but insistently and who, when they come, prove to be far from pleasant. Some fictional ghosts, of the innocent and the just, enlist our sympathy; but they are exceptions. As Montague Summers admitted in his classic anthology *The Supernatural Omnibus* (1931), the 'good and kindly ghost' has 'little or no place' in fiction.

There is, of course, Oscar Wilde's 'The Canterville Ghost', and there are other stories whose ghosts are incompetent or frivolous; but these

---

[3] Elizabeth Bowen, introduction to Lady Cynthia Asquith (ed.), *The Second Ghost Book* (1952).

[4] J. S. Le Fanu, 'An Account of Some Strange Disturbances in Aungier Street' (*Dublin University Magazine*, December 1853).

are not what the present collection understands as true ghost stories. The implicit consensus amongst ghost-story writers, with which most of their readers would undoubtedly agree, is that the aim of such stories should be to make us afraid, or at the very least less sure of ourselves and our condition. In general the success of a story may be judged by what the American Edith Wharton called its 'thermometrical quality; if it sends a cold shiver down one's spine, it has done its job and done it well'. Thus the fictional ghost succeeds best when it fulfils M. R. James's condition and appears to us as 'malevolent or odious'. Most satisfying of all is the story that impresses us with a horror of the spirit that is the hallmark of real fear—not by a repellent excess of blood and corruption, but by a subtle and suggestive tone of mystery and malevolence, the 'vague we know not what' of Vernon Lee, in comparison with which 'no reality of dreadfulness could seem aught but paltry, bearable and easy to face'.[5]

Whether, to achieve this, an author must 'believe' in ghosts is a ticklish and perhaps unresolvable critical question. Montague Summers was in no doubt: 'Can an author "call spirits from the vasty deep" if he is very well satisfied that there are, in fact, no spirits to obey his conjurations? I grant that by some literary *tour de force* he may succeed in duping his readers, but not for long. Presently his wand will snap short . . . the glamour dissipates, and the spell is broken!' Summers was reacting here to M. R. James's magisterial avoidance of the issue in the Preface to his *Collected Ghost Stories*, published in the same year (1931) as *The Supernatural Omnibus*. 'Do I believe in ghosts?' James had written. 'To which I answer that I am prepared to consider evidence and accept it if it satisfies me.' As Summers remarked, 'This leaves us, I venture to think, very much in the same position as we were before the question was asked and the reply returned.' But if belief of a kind can nevertheless be inferred from James's stories *in toto*, we belittle the power of human imagination if we deny it the ability to convince and alarm us in spite of an author's personal agnosticism or even downright scepticism on the question of ghosts: H. G. Wells's 'The Red Room' (included here) is a fine instance of the triumph of skill over cold reason, while H. P. Lovecraft even maintained that it was the 'materialists' who wrote the most frightening ghost stories: for them, the supernatural represented 'an absolute and stupendous violation of the natural order'.[6] Perhaps most writers of ghost stories simply belong to the class described by Edith Wharton as 'ghost-feelers', as opposed to 'ghost-seers'—people,

---

[5] Vernon Lee, preface to *Hauntings* (1890).
[6] H. P. Lovecraft, *Supernatural Horror in Fiction* (1945; repr. NY, 1973), p. 82.

that is, who are 'sensible of invisible currents of being in certain places and at certain hours'.[7]

II

As all roads lead to Rome, so all ghost stories may be said to stem from her. The first literary ghosts, as opposed to legendary or allegedly true ('veridical') tales, occur in Apuleius, Petronius, and the younger Pliny; but they are rare instances. In medieval and renaissance Europe ghosts were largely confined to legend and popular tradition: they might be recorded by chroniclers, sung of in ballads, or employed occasionally by dramatists and moralists, but they had no place in overt fiction. Nor did they make much impact before the eighteenth century. Defoe's 'True Relation of the Apparition of one Mrs Veal' (prefixed to Drelincourt's *The Christian's Defence Against the Fears of Death*, 1706) was no more than an embellished account of a reported haunting of the time. Ghosts did not fully enter fiction until the coming of the Gothic novel, which began its flamboyant career in England, under German influences, with Horace Walpole's *The Castle of Otranto* (1764); but even then the ghost generally played a secondary role, serving a moral purpose by bringing retribution upon the villain, or fulfilling the more basic function of shocking the ladies.

It was not until the 1820s that the ghost story as we now know it began to mature into a distinct form. The genre's earliest masterpiece is usually considered to be Scott's 'Wandering Willie's Tale', inset into *Redgauntlet* (1824). Scott, a connoisseur of the supernatural in folklore and the ballad, was also responsible for one of the earliest self-contained ghost stories (the first story in the present collection), 'The Tapestried Chamber', from *The Keepsake* (1829). First elegant and fashionable annuals like *The Keepsake*, then the literary magazines and their Christmas supplements provided a vehicle for the proliferation of ghost stories. The tales of J. S. Le Fanu—who in M. R. James's opinion 'stands absolutely in the first rank as a writer of ghost stories'—began to appear in magazines from the late 1830s, beginning in January 1838 with 'The Ghost and the Bone-Setter' in the *Dublin University Magazine*, which Le Fanu purchased in 1861. The magazines owned and edited by Charles Dickens (*Household Words*, 1850–9, and its successor *All the Year Round*, 1859–70) regularly carried ghost stories and encouraged a flock of imitators, such as *Temple Bar*, *Belgravia*, *Tinsley's Magazine*, and *London Society*, that helped to satisfy the growing

---

[7] Edith Wharton, preface to *The Ghost Stories of Edith Wharton* (1973).

public demand for such stories over the next half century. As S. M. Ellis put it, Dickens 'consolidated the modern taste and appreciation for the supernatural story'.[8] The golden age of Empire was also the golden age of the English ghost story. Interestingly, women writers came to the fore: Amelia Edwards, Mary Elizabeth Braddon, Rhoda Broughton, Mrs Gaskell, Mrs Riddell, Mrs Molesworth, Rosa Mulholland, Mrs Oliphant, and later E. Nesbit and Violet Paget ('Vernon Lee') in England, Edith Wharton and Mary Wilkins in America. Why so many women were—and are—attracted to the form is another question that has received little critical attention. Perhaps women, being on the margins of society—politically speaking—during the nineteenth century, were especially impelled to write about the margins of the visible, for the ghost story (as Dorothy Sayers observed) deals with power and thus might be expected to appeal to those who felt the absence of self-determination in their own lives. From a more technical point of view, it has been suggested by Julia Briggs that 'a taste for romance and sensitivity to mood and atmosphere made [women] well-suited to this particular form', and she compares this with their contribution to the Gothic novel.[9]

Such speculations of course raise more questions than they answer; but whatever the reasons, women played a key role in the development of the English ghost story, and were also prominent in a phenomenon that has some bearing on the popularity of ghost stories during the nineteenth century. In 1848, a year of political revolution in Europe, spiritualism arrived in England from Hydesville, NY, and the exchanging of platitudes with the dead became something of a national obsession, stimulating a general interest in all matters pertaining to the 'Beyond'. But a deeper malaise, that of theological doubt, was also prevalent and continued when spiritualism had ceased to be fashionable. It may be that ghost stories, with their necessary insistence on the reality of life after death (however perverted and unfathomable), provided a buttress of sorts against materialism. A story like Mrs Oliphant's 'The Open Door' (*Blackwood's Magazine*, January 1882) can certainly be read in this light: ' "I told you it was human agency," he said, triumphantly. He forgets, I suppose, how he and I stood with our lights seeing nothing, while the space between us was audibly traversed by something that could speak, and sob, and suffer. There is no argument with men of this kind.' There is something, too, in the idea that ghost stories were a way of confronting contemporary taboos regarding death

---

[8] S. M. Ellis, 'The Ghost Story and its Exponents', *Fortnightly Review* (December 1923); repr. in *Mainly Victorian* (1925), p. 326.

[9] Julia Briggs, *Night Visitors. The Rise and Fall of the English Ghost Story* (1977), p. 44.

and (more particularly in stories, like Le Fanu's 'Carmilla', 1871–2, that developed the vampire theme), sex.

By the end of the century the ghost story had firmly established itself with both readers and writers—the latter ranging from Grant Allen and 'Dick Donovan' (J. E. Preston-Muddock) to Kipling, Robert Louis Stevenson, and Henry James. But the 1890s brought a change of style. Magazines like the *Pall Mall* (a particularly rich repository of ghost stories) and the *Strand* were more highly illustrated than their predecessors and demanded shorter stories. With less room for their activities, ghosts became more urgently and inventively malevolent. Refinement of style and more careful handling gave a sharper edge to the fear they could inspire, and as the new century opened collections of short stories by individual authors became increasingly popular: a selection at random from this period includes volumes by Richard Marsh (*The Seen and the Unseen*, 1900), Barry Pain (*Stories in the Dark*, 1901), W. W. Jacobs (*The Lady of the Barge*, 1902), M. R. James (*Ghost Stories of an Antiquary*, 1904—the year that also saw the publication of Kipling's 'They'), Algernon Blackwood (*The Empty House*, 1906), and R. H. Benson (*A Mirror of Shalott*, 1907), among many others.

The unspeakable horrors of the First World War ought to have brought a revulsion against death, but there was to be no diminution in the demand for fictional ghosts and the ghost story enjoyed its second flowering with the work of H. Russell Wakefield, A. M. Burrage, L. P. Hartley, May Sinclair, E. F. Benson, Marjorie Bowen, Walter de la Mare, W. F. Harvey, and Margaret Irwin. The list of writers taking up the challenge of the ghost-story form continued after the Second World War (it includes Cynthia Asquith, L. T. C. Rolt, Elizabeth Bowen, Robert Aickman, Rosemary Timperley, and Elizabeth Jane Howard), and the appeal of the literary ghost story continues today, eclipsed somewhat by both science fiction and crude horror. Susan Hill's *The Woman in Black* (1983), though a full-length novel, successfully exploits characteristics of the traditional ghost story. Its publication in an era of video violence is curiously comforting.

III

No one has ever counted the total number of fictional ghosts; there are certainly several thousand, but there are by no means as many plots as stories. No full typological analysis of the literary ghost story has yet been undertaken, though Dickens listed some of the traditional types in his delightful essay 'A Christmas Tree' (*Household Words*, 1850; included in *Christmas Stories*). In essence they come down to two:

unconscious ghosts doomed perpetually to re-enact some past wickedness of their own or another's, and conscious ghosts. The latter may appear only to a specific person, seeking him out to bid farewell, to right some ancestral wrong, or to seek redress and retribution; but equally purposeful ghosts abound who have more promiscuous intentions, who are not confined to a particular spot or percipient, who come, willingly or unwillingly, when called up, wittingly or unwittingly, by the living.

The returning dead are traditionally at home in mists and shadows, and we expect to meet them, if not in their native churchyards, then at least somewhere equally gloomy and isolated: in ruinous or long-empty houses, on lonely roads, wild moorlands, or dreary estuaries; among monastic ruins and other sites of ancient worship, in disused churches, overgrown gardens, decaying canals, and vanished railways; and we do not expect them before twilight. Yet more disquieting are the ghosts permitted by their authors to intrude upon mundane concerns in broad daylight in hotels, suburban bungalows, or country houses, utilizing—when it suits them—our telephones and modes of transport. The critic Edmund Wilson, writing in 1944, expressed surprise that the ghost story was still alive and well in the age of the electric light: a decade later literary ghosts were still thriving. This adaptability was memorably described by L. P. Hartley: 'Like women and other depressed classes, [ghosts] have emancipated themselves from their disabilities, and besides being able to do a great many things that human beings can't do, they can now do a great many things that human beings can do. Immaterial as they are or should be, they have been able to avail themselves of the benefits of our materialistic civilization.'[10] While this is true, the ghost story remains a conservative form. It is not usually those who die peacefully who wander, and we who feel ourselves to be blameless and wish only to live in peace do not expect the phantom consequences of murder, suicide, or nameless crime to sit down with us at dinner.

That is not to say that our fictional counterparts are necessarily bad. Some do receive their just deserts for past wickedness, but most encounter ghosts through incautious enthusiasm, folly, or sheer bad luck. And who are these unfortunates? Usually (in the English ghost story) they are middle-class persons of independent, if modest, means: academics, writers, retired professionals, all of them people who might be expected to have leisure enough for the story to develop. The working class and those in trade are generally too busy to concern themselves with ghosts.

[10] L. P. Hartley, op. cit.

Except, of course, to read about them. The appeal of ghosts is universal, as is enthusiasm for the ghost story. With enthusiasm goes the demand for ghost stories to be made available; but the best stories of the best authors have not always been kept in print, while anthologies have all too often inserted stories that are neither good stories in themselves nor even ghost stories. The opinions of some anthologists as to what constitutes a ghost story can be imprecise and contradictory. There is, to be sure, a persistent critical dilemma: the difficulty, perhaps impossibility, of imposing order on the tradition of ghost fiction in English. The many writers to whom the ghost story has appealed cannot easily be gathered under a single convenient heading: for example, what set of critical co-ordinates could comfortably encompass the short, sharply-focused stories of M. R. James and the shifting delicate surfaces of those of his more famous namesake, Henry James?

Even so, an anthology of the English ghost story offers a means of directly experiencing the genre's range and vitality, once certain obvious limits have been set. In the present collection we have tried to hold five broad criteria in mind: each story should reveal to the reader a spectacle of the returning dead, or their agents, and their actions; there must be a dramatic interaction between the living and the dead, more often than not with the intention of frightening or unsettling the reader; the story must exhibit clear literary quality (not as subjectively vague a condition as it might sound); there must be a definable Englishness about the story, by which we generally understand English settings, English characters and institutions, and qualities (both stylistic and thematic) representative of the English ghost-story tradition as a whole; and finally, for not entirely practical reasons, the story must be relatively short.

We have tried to strike a balance between the expectations of the enthusiast, to whom several of the stories will be familiar, and the needs of the reader coming fresh to the genre. Unlike many anthologies of ghost stories, this collection has been arranged chronologically, the aim being to give the reader a sense of the historical development of the form since the 1820s, and in particular to illustrate the half century from 1890 to 1940 when the writing of ghost stories was at its peak. Some will say that we have stuck too rigidly to definitions of the fictional ghost story that are in any case open to debate. In fact our criteria leave few, if any, classic stories out of the reckoning, and as far as drawing our stories solely from the English tradition is concerned, that tradition is richer than any other in a genre it has made peculiarly its own. There is no inconsistency in selecting stories from Scottish, Irish, and American authors: the British stories have no Celtic element and are part of the mainstream of English literature, while the American stories—by Henry James, Edith Wharton, and Mary Wilkins—display quite clearly their English roots. Nor are all our ghosts malevolent (or even physically apparent). Some indeed, as in E. G. Swain's 'Bone to His Bone' or Mary Wilkins's 'The Lost Ghost', touchingly engage our sympathy; but all of them fulfil their separate purposes through relationships with the living and are, beyond question, dead. Whatever the ghost's motivation—be it one of menace or emotional hunger—it is the intensity of this relationship, bridging the chasm between life and death, that provides a link between such disparate stories as John Buchan's 'Fullcircle' (in which no ghost is seen) and L. P. Hartley's 'A Visitor From Down Under' (in which one most certainly is).

Virginia Woolf, in 1918, pondered the enigma of 'the strange human craving for the pleasure of feeling afraid which is so much involved in our love of ghost stories' and concluded that 'It is pleasant to be afraid when we are conscious that we are in no kind of danger.'[11] Pleasure, indeed, is to be had from a well-crafted ghost story, though it is pleasure (in M. R. James's phrase) 'of a certain sort'. Perhaps in the end it all comes down to what Edith Wharton called 'the fun of the shudder'; for as the critic Jack Sullivan wisely remarked: 'As for the ultimate reasons why we read these stories, that tiresome, unanswerable question has already been raised too many times. That we enjoy them is enough. The reasons remain as perverse and mysterious as the stories themselves.'[12]

Michael Cox

Robert Gilbert

[11] 'The Supernatural in Fiction' (review of Dorothy Scarborough, *The Supernatural in Modern English Fiction*), *Times Literary Supplement*, 31 January 1918; repr. in *Collected Essays* (1966), vol. 1, 293–6.

[12] Jack Sullivan, *Elegant Nightmares. The English Ghost Story From Le Fanu to Blackwood* (Ohio University Press, 1978), p. 135.

The ghost . . . reminds us that death is the one thing certain and the thing most uncertain; the bourn from which no traveller returns, except this one.

ROBERT AICKMAN

The Tapestried Chamber

SIR WALTER SCOTT

＿

About the end of the American war, when the officers of Lord
Cornwallis's army which surrendered at York-town, and others, who
had been made prisoners during the impolitic and ill-fated controversy,
were returning to their own country, to relate their adventures and
repose themselves after their fatigues, there was amongst them a general
officer of name of Browne. He was an officer of merit, as well as a
gentleman of high consideration for family and attainments.

Some business had carried General Browne upon a tour through the
western counties, when, in the conclusion of a morning stage, he found
himself in the vicinity of a small country town, which presented a scene
of uncommon beauty and of a character peculiarly English.

The little town, with its stately old church whose tower bore testimony
to the devotion of ages long past, lay amidst pasture and corn-fields of
small extent, but bounded and divided with hedge-row timber of great
age and size. There were few marks of modern improvement. The
environs of the place intimated neither the solitude of decay, nor the
bustle of novelty; the houses were old, but in good repair; and the
beautiful little river murmured freely on its way to the left of the town,
neither restrained by a dam, nor bordered by a towing-path.

Upon a gentle eminence, nearly a mile to the southward of the town,
were seen amongst many venerable oaks and tangled thickets the turrets
of a castle, as old as the wars of York and Lancaster, but which seemed
to have received important alterations during the age of Elizabeth and
her successors. It had not been a place of great size; but whatever
accommodation it formerly afforded, was, it must be supposed, still to be
obtained within its walls; at least, such was the inference which General
Browne drew from observing the smoke arise merrily from several of the
ancient wreathed and carved chimney-stalks. The wall of the park ran
alongside of the highway for two or three hundred yards; and through
the different points by which the eye found glimpses into the woodland
scenery, it seemed to be well stocked. Other points of view opened in
succession; now a full one, of the front of the old castle, and now a side
glimpse at its particular towers; the former rich in all the bizarrerie of the
Elizabethan school, while the simple and solid strength of other parts of

the building seemed to show that they had been raised more for defence than ostentation.

Delighted with the partial glimpses which he obtained of the castle through the woods and glades by which this ancient feudal fortress was surrounded, our military traveller was determined to inquire whether it might not deserve a nearer view, and whether it contained family pictures or other objects of curiosity worthy of a stranger's visit; when, leaving the vicinity of the park, he rolled through a clean and well-paved street, and stopped at the door of a well-frequented inn.

Before ordering horses to proceed on his journey, General Browne made inquiries concerning the proprietor of the chateau which had so attracted his admiration, and was equally surprised and pleased at hearing in reply a nobleman named whom we shall call Lord Woodville. How fortunate! Much of Browne's early recollections, both at school and at college, had been connected with young Woodville, whom, by a few questions, he now ascertained to be the same with the owner of this fair domain. He had been raised to the peerage by the decease of his father a few months before, and, as the general learned from the landlord, the term of mourning being ended, was now taking possession of his paternal estate in the jovial season of merry autumn, accompanied by a select party of friends to enjoy the sports of a country famous for game.

This was delightful news to our traveller. Frank Woodville had been Richard Browne's fag at Eton, and his chosen intimate at Christ Church; their pleasures and their tasks had been the same; and the honest soldier's heart warmed to find his early friend in possession of so delightful a residence, and of an estate, as the landlord assured him with a nod and a wink, fully adequate to maintain and add to his dignity. Nothing was more natural than that the traveller should suspend a journey, which there was nothing to render hurried, to pay a visit to an old friend under such agreeable circumstances.

The fresh horses, therefore, had only the brief task of conveying the general's travelling carriage to Woodville Castle. A porter admitted them at a modern Gothic Lodge, built in that style to correspond with the castle itself, and at the same time rang a bell to give warning of the approach of visitors. Apparently the sound of the bell had suspended the separation of the company, bent on the various amusements of the morning; for, on entering the court of the chateau, several young men were lounging about in their sporting dresses, looking at, and criticizing, the dogs which the keepers held in readiness to attend their pastime. As General Browne alighted, the young lord came to the gate of the hall, and for an instant gazed, as at a stranger, upon the countenance of his friend, on which war, with its fatigues and its wounds, had made a great alteration. But the uncertainty lasted no longer than till the visitor had spoken, and the hearty greeting which followed was such as can only be exchanged betwixt those who have passed together merry days of careless boyhood or early youth.

'If I could have formed a wish, my dear Browne,' said Lord Woodville, 'it would have been to have you here, of all men, upon this occasion, which my friends are good enough to hold as a sort of holiday. Do not think you have been unwatched during the years you have been absent from us. I have traced you through your dangers, your triumphs, your misfortunes, and was delighted to see that, whether in victory or defeat, the name of my old friend was always distinguished with applause.'

The general made a suitable reply, and congratulated his friend on his new dignities, and the possession of a place and domain so beautiful.

'Nay, you have seen nothing of it as yet,' said Lord Woodville, 'and I trust you do not mean to leave us till you are better acquainted with it. It is true, I confess, that my present party is pretty large, and the old house, like other places of the kind, does not possess so much accommodation as the extent of the outward walls appears to promise. But we can give you a comfortable old-fashioned room; and I venture to suppose that your campaigns have taught you to be glad of worse quarters.'

The general shrugged his shoulders, and laughed. 'I presume,' he said, 'the worst apartment in your chateau is considerably superior to the old tobacco-cask, in which I was fain to take up my night's lodging when I was in the Bush, as the Virginians call it, with the light corps. There I lay, like Diogenes himself, so delighted with my covering from the elements, that I made a vain attempt to have it rolled on to my next quarters; but my commander for the time would give way to no such luxurious provision, and I took farewell of my beloved cask with tears in my eyes.'

'Well, then, since you do not fear your quarters,' said Lord Woodville, 'you will stay with me a week at least. Of guns, dogs, fishing-rods, flies, and means of sport by sea and land, we have enough and to spare: you cannot pitch on an amusement, but we will pitch on the means of pursuing it. But if you prefer the gun and pointers, I will go with you myself, and see whether you have mended your shooting since you have been amongst the Indians of the back settlements.'

The general gladly accepted his friendly host's proposal in all its points. After a morning of manly exercise, the company met at dinner, where it was the delight of Lord Woodville to conduce to the display of the high properties of his recovered friend, so as to recommend him to his guests, most of whom were persons of distinction. He led General Browne to speak of the scenes he had witnessed; and as every word marked alike the brave officer and the sensible man, who retained possession of his cool judgement under the most imminent dangers, the company looked upon the soldier with general respect, as on one who had proved himself possessed of an uncommon portion of personal courage—that attribute, of all others, of which everybody desires to be thought possessed.

The day at Woodville Castle ended as usual in such mansions. The hospitality stopped within the limits of good order; music, in which the young lord was a proficient, succeeded to the circulation of the bottle: cards and billiards, for those who preferred such amusements, were in readiness: but the exercise of the morning required early hours, and not long after eleven o'clock the guests began to retire to their several apartments.

The young lord himself conducted his friend, General Browne, to the chamber destined for him, which answered the description he had given of it, being comfortable, but old-fashioned. The bed was of the massive form used in the end of the seventeenth century, and the curtains of faded silk, heavily trimmed with tarnished gold. But then the sheets, pillows, and blankets looked delightful to the campaigner, when he thought of his mansion, the cask. There was an air of gloom in the tapestry hangings, which, with their worn-out graces, curtained the walls of the little chamber, and gently undulated as the autumnal breeze found its way through the ancient lattice-window, which pattered and whistled as the air gained entrance. The toilet too, with its mirror, turbaned, after the manner of the beginning of the century, with a coiffure of murrey-coloured silk, and its hundred strange-shaped boxes, providing for arrangements which had been obsolete for more than fifty years, had an antique, and in so far a melancholy, aspect. But nothing could blaze more brightly and cheerfully than the two large wax candles; or if aught could rival them, it was the flaming bickering faggots in the chimney, that sent at once their gleam and their warmth through the snug apartment; which, notwithstanding the general antiquity of its appearance, was not wanting in the least convenience that modern habits rendered either necessary or desirable.

'This is an old-fashioned sleeping apartment, General,' said the young lord; 'but I hope you will find nothing that makes you envy your old tobacco-cask.'

'I am not particular respecting my lodgings,' replied the general; 'yet were I to make any choice, I would prefer this chamber by many degrees, to the gayer and more modern rooms of your family mansion. Believe me that when I unite its modern air of comfort with its venerable antiquity, and recollect that it is your lordship's property, I shall feel in better quarters here, than if I were in the best hotel London could afford.'

'I trust—I have no doubt—that you will find yourself as comfortable as I wish you, my dear General,' said the young nobleman; and once more bidding his guest good night, he shook him by the hand and withdrew.

The general again looked round him, and internally congratulating himself on his return to peaceful life, the comforts of which were endeared by the recollection of the hardships and dangers he had lately sustained, undressed himself, and prepared himself for a luxurious night's rest.

Here, contrary to the custom of this species of tale, we leave the general in possession of his apartment until the next morning.

The company assembled for breakfast at an early hour, but without the appearance of General Browne, who seemed the guest that Lord Woodville was desirous of honouring above all whom his hospitality had assembled around him. He more than once expressed surprise at the general's absence, and at length sent a servant to make inquiry after him. The man brought back information that General Browne had been walking abroad since an early hour of the morning, in defiance of the weather, which was misty and ungenial.

'The custom of a soldier,'—said the young nobleman to his friends; 'many of them acquire habitual vigilance, and cannot sleep after the early hour at which their duty usually commands them to be alert.'

Yet the explanation which Lord Woodville thus offered to the company seemed hardly satisfactory to his own mind, and it was in a fit of silence and abstraction that he awaited the return of the general. It took place near an hour after the breakfast bell had rung. He looked fatigued and feverish. His hair, the powdering and arrangement of which was at this time one of the most important occupations of a man's whole day, and marked his fashion as much as, in the present time, the tying of a cravat or the want of one, was dishevelled, uncurled, void of powder, and dank with dew. His clothes were huddled on with a careless negligence, remarkable in a military man, whose real or supposed duties are usually held to include some attention to the toilet; and his looks were haggard and ghastly in a peculiar degree.

'So you have stolen a march upon us this morning, my dear General,' said Lord Woodville; 'or you have not found your bed so much to your mind as I had hoped and you seemed to expect. How did you rest last night?'

'Oh, excellently well! remarkably well! never better in my life'—said General Browne rapidly, and yet with an air of embarrassment which was obvious to his friend. He then hastily swallowed a cup of tea, and neglecting or refusing whatever else was offered, seemed to fall into a fit of abstraction.

'You will take the gun today, General;' said his friend and host, but had to repeat the question twice ere he received the abrupt answer, 'No, my Lord; I am sorry I cannot have the honour of spending another day with your lordship; my post-horses are ordered, and will be here directly.'

All who were present showed surprise, and Lord Woodville immediately replied, 'Post-horses, my good friend! what can you possibly want with them, when you promised to stay with me quietly for at least a week?'

'I believe,' said the general, obviously much embarrassed, 'that I might, in the pleasure of my first meeting with your lordship, have said something about stopping here a few days; but I have since found it altogether impossible.'

'That is very extraordinary,' answered the young nobleman. 'You seemed quite disengaged yesterday, and you cannot have had a summons today; for our post has not come up from the town, and therefore you cannot have received any letters.'

General Browne, without giving any further explanation, muttered something of indispensable business, and insisted on the absolute necessity of his departure in a manner which silenced all opposition on the part of his host, who saw that his resolution was taken, and forbore further importunity.

'At least, however,' he said, 'permit me, my dear Browne, since go you will or must, to show you the view from the terrace, which the mist that is now rising will soon display.'

He threw open a sash window, and stepped down upon the terrace as he spoke. The general followed him mechanically, but seemed little to attend to what his host was saying, as, looking across an extended and rich prospect, he pointed out the different objects worthy of observation. Thus they moved on till Lord Woodville had attained his purpose of drawing his guest entirely apart from the rest of the company, when, turning round upon him with an air of great solemnity, he addressed him thus:

'Richard Browne, my old and very dear friend, we are now alone. Let me conjure you to answer me upon the word of a friend, and the honour of a soldier. How did you in reality rest during last night?'

'Most wretchedly indeed, my lord,' answered the general, in the same tone of solemnity;—'so miserably, that I would not run the risk of such a second night, not only for all the lands belonging to this castle, but for all the country which I see from this elevated point of view.'

'This is most extraordinary,' said the young lord, as if speaking to himself; 'then there must be something in the reports concerning that apartment.' Again turning to the general, he said, 'For God's sake, my dear friend, be candid with me, and let me know the disagreeable particulars which have befallen you under a roof, where, with consent of the owner, you should have met nothing save comfort.'

The general seemed distressed by this appeal, and paused a moment before he replied. 'My dear lord,' he at length said, 'what happened to me last night is of nature so peculiar and so unpleasant, that I could hardly bring myself to detail it even to your lordship, were it not that, independent of my wish to gratify any request of yours, I think that sincerity on my part may lead to some explanation about a circumstance equally painful and mysterious. To others, the communications I am about to make, might place me in the light of a weak-minded, superstitious fool who suffered his own imagination to delude and bewilder him; but you have known me in childhood and youth, and will not suspect me of having adopted in manhood the feelings and frailties from which my early years were free.' Here he paused, and his friend replied:

'Do not doubt my perfect confidence in the truth of your communication, however strange it may be,' replied Lord Woodville; 'I know your firmness of disposition too well, to suspect you could be made the object of imposition, and am aware that your honour and your friendship will equally deter you from exaggerating whatever you may have witnessed.'

'Well then,' said the general, 'I will proceed with my story as well as I can, relying upon your candour; and yet distinctly feeling that I would rather face a battery than recall to my mind the odious recollections of last night.'

He paused a second time, and then perceiving that Lord Woodville remained silent and in an attitude of attention, he commenced, though not without obvious reluctance, the history of his night's adventures in the Tapestried Chamber.

'I undressed and went to bed, so soon as your lordship left me yesterday evening; but the wood in the chimney, which nearly fronted my bed, blazed brightly and cheerfully, and, aided by a hundred exciting recollections of my childhood and youth which had been recalled by the unexpected pleasure of meeting your lordship, prevented me from falling immediately asleep. I ought, however, to say, that these reflections were all of a pleasant and agreeable kind, grounded on a sense of having for a time exchanged the labour, fatigues, and dangers of my profession, for the enjoyments of a peaceful life, and the reunion of those friendly and affectionate ties which I had torn asunder at the rude summons of war.

'While such pleasing reflections were stealing over my mind, and gradually lulling me to slumber, I was suddenly aroused by a sound like that of the rustling of a silken gown, and the tapping of a pair of high-heeled shoes, as if a woman were walking in the apartment. Ere I could draw the curtain to see what the matter was, the figure of a little woman passed between the bed and the fire. The back of this form was turned to me, and I could observe, from the shoulders and neck, it was that of an old woman, whose dress was an old-fashioned gown which, I think, ladies call a sacque; that is, a sort of robe, completely loose in the body, but gathered into broad plaits upon the neck and shoulders, which fall down to the ground, and terminate in a species of train.

'I thought the intrusion singular enough, but never harboured for a moment the idea that what I saw was anything more than the mortal form of some old woman about the establishment, who had a fancy to dress like her grandmother, and who, having perhaps (as your lordship mentioned that you were rather straitened for room) been dislodged from her chamber for my accommodation, had forgotten the circumstance, and returned by twelve to her old haunt. Under this persuasion I moved myself in bed and coughed a little, to make the intruder sensible of my being in possession of the premises.—She turned slowly round, but gracious heaven! my lord, what a countenance did she display to me! There was no longer any question what she was, or any thought of her being a living being. Upon a face which wore the fixed features of a corpse, were imprinted the traces of the vilest and most hideous passions which had animated her while she lived. The body of some atrocious criminal seemed to have been given up from the grave, and the soul restored from the penal fire, in order to form, for a space, a union with the ancient accomplice of its guilt. I started up in bed, and sat upright, supporting myself on my palms, as I gazed on this horrible spectre. The hag made, as it seemed, a single and swift stride to the bed where I lay, and squatted herself down upon it, in precisely the same attitude which I had assumed in the extremity of horror, advancing her diabolical countenance within half a yard of mine, with a grin which seemed to intimate the malice and the derision of an incarnate fiend.'

Here General Browne stopped, and wiped from his brow the cold perspiration with which the recollection of his horrible vision had covered it.

'My lord,' he said, 'I am no coward. I have been in all the mortal dangers incidental to my profession, and I may truly boast that no man ever knew Richard Browne dishonour the sword he wears; but in these horrible circumstances, under the eyes, and as it seemed, almost in the grasp of an incarnation of an evil spirit, all firmness forsook me, all manhood melted from me like wax in the furnace, and I felt my hair individually bristle. The current of my life-blood ceased to flow, and I sank back in a swoon, as very a victim to panic terror as ever was a village girl or a child of ten years old. How long I lay in this condition I cannot pretend to guess.

'But I was roused by the castle clock striking one, so loud that it seemed as if it were in the very room. It was some time before I dared open my eyes, lest they should again encounter the horrible spectacle. When, however, I summoned courage to look up, she was no longer visible. My first idea was to pull my bell, wake the servants, and remove to a garret or a hay-loft, to be ensured against a second visitation. Nay, I will confess the truth, that my resolution was altered, not by the shame of exposing myself, but by the very fear that, as the bell-cord hung by the chimney, I might, in making my way to it, be again crossed by the fiendish hag, who, I figured to myself, might be still lurking about some corner of the apartment.

'I will not pretend to describe what hot and cold fever-fits tormented me for the rest of the night, through broken sleep, weary vigils, and that dubious state which forms the neutral ground between them. A hundred terrible objects appeared to haunt me; but there was the great difference betwixt the vision which I have described, and those which followed, that I knew the last to be deceptions of my own fancy and over-excited nerves.

'Day at last appeared, and I rose from my bed ill in health, and humiliated in mind. I was ashamed of myself as a man and a soldier, and still more so, at feeling my own extreme desire to escape from the haunted apartment, which, however, conquered all other considerations; so that, huddling on my clothes with the most careless haste, I made my escape from your lordship's mansion, to seek in the open air some relief to my nervous system, shaken as it was by this horrible rencounter with a visitant, for such I must believe her, from the other world. Your lordship has now heard the cause of my discomposure, and of my sudden desire to leave your hospitable castle. In other places I trust we may often meet; but God protect me from ever spending a second night under that roof!'

Strange as the general's tale was, he spoke with such a deep air of conviction, that it cut short all the usual commentaries which are made on such stories. Lord Woodville never once asked him if he was sure he did not dream of the apparition, or suggested any of the possibilities by which it is fashionable to explain supernatural appearances, as wild vagaries of the fancy or deceptions of the optic nerves. On the contrary he seemed deeply impressed with the truth and reality of what he had heard; and, after a considerable pause, regretted, with much appearance of sincerity, that his early friend should in his house have suffered so severely.

'I am the more sorry for your pain, my dear Browne,' he continued, 'that it is the unhappy, though most unexpected, result of an experiment of my own! You must know, that for my father and grandfather's time, at least, the apartment which was assigned to you last night had been shut on account of reports that it was disturbed by supernatural sights and noises. When I came, a few weeks since, into possession of the estate, I thought the accommodation which the castle afforded for my friends was not extensive enough to permit the inhabitants of the invisible world to retain possession of a comfortable sleeping apartment. I therefore caused the Tapestried Chamber, as we call it, to be opened; and without destroying its air of antiquity, I had such new articles of furniture placed in it as became the modern times. Yet as the opinion that the room was haunted very strongly prevailed among the domestics, and was also known in the neighbourhood and to many of my friends, I feared some prejudice might be entertained by the first occupant of the Tapestried Chamber, which might tend to revive the evil report which it had laboured under, and so disappoint my purpose of rendering it a useful part of the house. I must confess, my dear Browne, that your arrival yesterday, agreeable to me for a thousand reasons besides, seemed the most favourable opportunity of removing the unpleasant rumours which attached to the room, since your courage was indubitable and your mind free of any preoccupation on the subject. I could not, therefore, have chosen a more fitting subject for my experiment.'

'Upon my life,' said General Browne, somewhat hastily, 'I am infinitely obliged to your lordship—very particularly indebted indeed. I am likely to remember for some time the consequences of the experiment, as your lordship is pleased to call it.'

'Nay, now you are unjust, my dear friend,' said Lord Woodville. 'You have only to reflect for a single moment, in order to be convinced that I could not augur the possibility of the pain to which you have been so unhappily exposed. I was yesterday morning a complete sceptic on the subject of supernatural appearances. Nay, I am sure that had I told you what was said about that room, those very reports would have induced you, by your own choice, to select it for your accommodation. It was my misfortune, perhaps my error, but really cannot be termed my fault, that you have been afflicted so strangely.'

'Strangely indeed!' said the general, resuming his good temper; 'and I acknowledge that I have no right to be offended with your lordship for treating me like what I used to think myself—a man of some firmness and courage.—But I see my post-horses are arrived, and I must not detain your lordship from your amusement.'

'Nay, my old friend,' said Lord Woodville, 'since you cannot stay with us another day, which, indeed, I can no longer urge, give me at least half an hour more. You used to love pictures, and I have a gallery of portraits, some of them by Vandyke, representing ancestry to whom this property and castle formerly belonged. I think that several of them will strike you as possessing merit.'

General Browne accepted the invitation, though somewhat unwillingly. It was evident he was not to breathe freely or at ease until he left Woodville Castle far behind him. He could not refuse his friend's invitation, however; and the less so, that he was a little ashamed of the peevishness which he had displayed towards his well-meaning entertainer.

The general, therefore, followed Lord Woodville through several rooms, into a long gallery hung with pictures, which the latter pointed out to his guest, telling the names, and giving some account of the personages whose portraits presented themselves in progression. General Browne was but little interested in the details which these accounts conveyed to him. They were, indeed, of the kind which are usually found in the old family gallery. Here was a cavalier who had ruined the estate in the royal cause; there a fine lady who had reinstated it by contracting a match with a wealthy Roundhead. There hung a gallant who had been in danger for corresponding with the exiled Court of St Germain's; here one who had taken arms for William at the Revolution; and there a third that had thrown his weight alternately into the scale of Whig and Tory.

While Lord Woodville was cramming these words into his guest's ear, 'against the stomach of his sense', they gained the middle of the gallery, when he beheld General Browne suddenly start, and assume an attitude of the utmost surprise, not unmixed with fear, as his eyes were caught and suddenly riveted by a portrait of an old lady in a sacque, the fashionable dress of the end of the seventeenth century.

'There she is!' he exclaimed; 'there she is, in form and features, though inferior in demoniac expression to the accursed hag who visited me last night!'

'If that be the case,' said the young nobleman, 'there can remain no longer any doubt of the horrible reality of your apparition. That is the picture of a wretched ancestress of mine, of whose crimes a black and fearful catalogue is recorded in a family history in my charter-chest. The recital of them would be too horrible; it is enough to say, that in yon fatal apartment incest and unnatural murder were committed. I will restore it to the solitude to which the better judgement of those who preceded me had consigned it; and never shall any one, so long as I can prevent it, be exposed to a repetition of the supernatural horrors which could shake such courage as yours.'

Thus the friends, who had met with such glee, parted in a very different mood; Lord Woodville to command the Tapestried Chamber to be unmantled and the door built up; and General Browne to seek in some less beautiful country, and with some less dignified friend, forgetfulness of the painful night which he had passed in Woodville Castle.

The Phantom Coach

AMELIA B. EDWARDS

The circumstances I am about to relate to you have truth to recommend them. They happened to myself, and my recollection of them is as vivid as if they had taken place only yesterday. Twenty years, however, have gone by since that night. During those twenty years I have told the story to but one other person. I tell it now with a reluctance which I find it difficult to overcome. All I entreat, meanwhile, is that you will abstain from forcing your own conclusions upon me. I want nothing explained away. I desire no arguments. My mind on this subject is quite made up, and, having the testimony of my own senses to rely upon, I prefer to abide by it.

Well! It was just twenty years ago, and within a day or two of the end of the grouse season. I had been out all day with my gun, and had had no sport to speak of. The wind was due east; the month, December; the place, a bleak wide moor in the far north of England. And I had lost my way. It was not a pleasant place in which to lose one's way, with the first feathery flakes of a coming snowstorm just fluttering down upon the heather, and the leaden evening closing in all around. I shaded my eyes with my hand, and stared anxiously into the gathering darkness, where the purple moorland melted into a range of low hills, some ten or twelve miles distant. Not the faintest smoke-wreath, not the tiniest cultivated patch, or fence, or sheep-track, met my eyes in any direction. There was nothing for it but to walk on, and take my chance of finding what shelter I could, by the way. So I shouldered my gun again, and pushed wearily forward; for I had been on foot since an hour after daybreak, and had eaten nothing since breakfast.

Meanwhile, the snow began to come down with ominous steadiness, and the wind fell. After this, the cold became more intense, and the night came rapidly up. As for me, my prospects darkened with the darkening sky, and my heart grew heavy as I thought how my young wife was already watching for me through the window of our little inn parlour, and thought of all the suffering in store for her throughout this weary night. We had been married four months, and, having spent our autumn in the Highlands, were now lodging in a remote little village situated just on the verge of the great English moorlands. We were very much in love, and, of course, very happy. This morning, when we parted, she had implored me to return before dusk, and I had promised her that I would. What would I not have given to have kept my word!

Even now, weary as I was, I felt that with a supper, an hour's rest, and a guide, I might still get back to her before midnight, if only guide and shelter could be found.

And all this time, the snow fell and the night thickened. I stopped and shouted every now and then, but my shouts seemed only to make the silence deeper. Then a vague sense of uneasiness came upon me, and I began to remember stories of travellers who had walked on and on in the falling snow until, wearied out, they were fain to lie down and sleep their lives away. Would it be possible, I asked myself, to keep on thus through all the long dark night? Would there not come a time when my limbs must fail, and my resolution give way? When I, too, must sleep the sleep of death. Death! I shuddered. How hard to die just now, when life lay all so bright before me! How hard for my darling, whose whole loving heart——but that thought was not to be borne! To banish it, I shouted again, louder and longer, and then listened eagerly. Was my shout answered, or did I only fancy that I heard a far-off cry? I halloed again, and again the echo followed. Then a wavering speck of light came suddenly out of the dark, shifting, disappearing, growing momentarily nearer and brighter. Running towards it at full speed, I found myself, to my great joy, face to face with an old man and a lantern.

'Thank God!' was the exclamation that burst involuntarily from my lips.

Blinking and frowning, he lifted his lantern and peered into my face.

'What for?' growled he, sulkily.

'Well—for you. I began to fear I should be lost in the snow.'

'Eh, then, folks do get cast away hereabout fra' time to time, an' what's to hinder you from bein' cast away likewise, if the Lord's so minded?'

'If the Lord is so minded that you and I shall be lost together, friend, we must submit,' I replied; 'but I don't mean to be lost without you. How far am I now from Dwolding?'

'A gude twenty mile, more or less.'

'And the nearest village?'

'The nearest village is Wyke, an' that's twelve mile t'other side.'

'Where do you live, then?'

'Out yonder,' said he, with a vague jerk of the lantern.

'You're going home, I presume?'

'Maybe I am.'

'Then I'm going with you.'

The old man shook his head, and rubbed his nose reflectively with the handle of the lantern.

'It ain't o' no use,' growled he. 'He 'ont let you in—not he.'

'We'll see about that,' I replied, briskly. 'Who is He?'

'The master.'

'Who is the master?'

'That's nowt to you,' was the unceremonious reply.

'Well, well; you lead the way, and I'll engage that the master shall give me shelter and a supper tonight.'

'Eh, you can try him!' muttered my reluctant guide; and, still shaking his head, he hobbled, gnome-like, away through the falling snow. A large mass loomed up presently out of the darkness, and a huge dog rushed out, barking furiously.

'Is this the house?' I asked.

'Ay, it's the house. Down, Bey!' And he fumbled in his pocket for the key.

I drew up close behind him, prepared to lose no chance of entrance, and saw in the little circle of light shed by the lantern that the door was heavily studded with iron nails, like the door of a prison. In another minute he had turned the key and I had pushed past him into the house.

Once inside, I looked round with curiosity, and found myself in a great raftered hall, which served, apparently, a variety of uses. One end was piled to the roof with corn, like a barn. The other was stored with flour-sacks, agricultural implements, casks, and all kinds of miscellaneous lumber; while from the beams overhead hung rows of hams, flitches, and bunches of dried herbs for winter use. In the centre of the floor stood some huge object gauntly dressed in a dingy wrapping-cloth, and reaching half way to the rafters. Lifting a corner of this cloth, I saw, to my surprise, a telescope of very considerable size, mounted on a rude movable platform, with four small wheels. The tube was made of painted wood, bound round with bands of metal rudely fashioned; the speculum, so far as I could estimate its size in the dim light, measured at least fifteen inches in diameter. While I was yet examining the instrument, and asking myself whether it was not the work of some self-taught optician, a bell rang sharply.

'That's for you,' said my guide, with a malicious grin. 'Yonder's his room.'

He pointed to a low black door at the opposite side of the hall. I crossed over, rapped somewhat loudly, and went in, without waiting for an invitation. A huge, white-haired old man rose from a table covered with books and papers, and confronted me sternly.

'Who are you?' said he. 'How came you here? What do you want?'

'James Murray, barrister-at-law. On foot across the moor. Meat, drink, and sleep.'

He bent his bushy brows into a portentous frown.

'Mine is not a house of entertainment,' he said, haughtily. 'Jacob, how dared you admit this stranger?'

'I didn't admit him,' grumbled the old man. 'He followed me over the muir, and shouldered his way in before me. I'm no match for six foot two.'

'And pray, sir, by what right have you forced an entrance into my house?'

'The same by which I should have clung to your boat, if I were drowning. The right of self-preservation.'

'Self-preservation?'

'There's an inch of snow on the ground already,' I replied, briefly; 'and it would be deep enough to cover my body before daybreak.'

He strode to the window, pulled aside a heavy black curtain, and looked out.

'It is true,' he said. 'You can stay, if you choose, till morning. Jacob, serve the supper.'

With this he waved me to a seat, resumed his own, and became at once absorbed in the studies from which I had disturbed him.

I placed my gun in a corner, drew a chair to the hearth, and examined my quarters at leisure. Smaller and less incongruous in its arrangements than the hall, this room contained, nevertheless, much to awaken my curiosity. The floor was carpetless. The whitewashed walls were in parts scrawled over with strange diagrams, and in others covered with shelves crowded with philosophical instruments, the uses of many of which were unknown to me. On one side of the fireplace, stood a bookcase filled with dingy folios; on the other, a small organ, fantastically decorated with painted carvings of medieval saints and devils. Through the half-opened door of a cupboard at the further end of the room, I saw a long array of geological specimens, surgical preparations, crucibles, retorts, and jars of chemicals; while on the mantelshelf beside me, amid a number of small objects, stood a model of the solar system, a small galvanic battery, and a microscope. Every chair had its burden. Every corner was heaped high with books. The very floor was littered over with maps, casts, papers, tracings, and learned lumber of all conceivable kinds.

I stared about me with an amazement increased by every fresh object upon which my eyes chanced to rest. So strange a room I had never seen; yet seemed it stranger still, to find such a room in a lone farmhouse amid those wild and solitary moors! Over and over again, I looked from my host to his surroundings, and from his surroundings back to my host, asking myself who and what he could be? His head was singularly fine; but it was more the head of a poet than of a philosopher. Broad in the temples, prominent over the eyes, and clothed with a rough profusion of perfectly white hair, it had all the ideality and much of the ruggedness that characterises the head of Louis von Beethoven. There were the same deep lines about the mouth, and the same stern furrows in the brow. There was the same concentration of expression. While I was yet observing him, the door opened, and Jacob brought in the supper. His master then closed his book, rose, and with more courtesy of manner than he had yet shown, invited me to the table.

A dish of ham and eggs, a loaf of brown bread, and a bottle of admirable sherry, were placed before me.

'I have but the homeliest farmhouse fare to offer you, sir,' said my entertainer. 'Your appetite, I trust, will make up for the deficiencies of our larder.'

I had already fallen upon the viands, and now protested, with the enthusiasm of a starving sportsman, that I had never eaten anything so delicious.

He bowed stiffly, and sat down to his own supper, which consisted, primitively, of a jug of milk and a basin of porridge. We ate in silence, and, when we had done, Jacob removed the tray. I then drew my chair back to the fireside. My host, somewhat to my surprise, did the same, and turning abruptly towards me, said:

'Sir, I have lived here in strict retirement for three-and-twenty years. During that time, I have not seen as many strange faces, and I have not read a single newspaper. You are the first stranger who has crossed my threshold for more than four years. Will you favour me with a few words of information respecting that outer world from which I have parted company so long?'

'Pray interrogate me,' I replied. 'I am heartily at your service.'

He bent his head in acknowledgment; leaned forward, with his elbows resting on his knees and his chin supported in the palms of his hands; stared fixedly into the fire; and proceeded to question me.

His inquiries related chiefly to scientific matters, with the later progress of which, as applied to the practical purposes of life, he was almost wholly unacquainted. No student of science myself, I replied as well as my slight information permitted; but the task was far from easy, and I was much relieved when, passing from interrogation to discussion, he began pouring forth his own conclusions upon the facts which I had been attempting to place before him. He talked, and I listened spellbound. He talked till I believe he almost forgot my presence, and only thought aloud. I had never heard anything like it then; I have never heard anything like it since. Familiar with all systems of all philosophies, subtle in analysis, bold in generalisation, he poured forth his thoughts in an uninterrupted stream, and, still leaning forward in the same moody attitude with his eyes fixed upon the fire, wandered from topic to topic, from speculation to speculation, like an inspired dreamer. From practical science to mental philosophy; from electricity in the wire to electricity in the nerve; from Watts to Mesmer, from Mesmer to Reichenbach, from Reichenbach to Swedenborg, Spinoza, Condillac, Descartes, Berkeley, Aristotle, Plato, and the Magi and mystics of the East, were transitions which, however bewildering in their variety and scope, seemed easy and harmonious upon his lips as sequences in music. By-and-by—I forget now by what link of conjecture or illustration—he passed on to that field which lies beyond the boundary line of even conjectural philosophy, and reaches no man knows whither. He spoke of the soul and its aspirations; of the spirit and its powers; of second sight; of prophecy; of those phenomena which, under the names of ghosts, spectres, and supernatural appearances, have been denied by the sceptics and attested by the credulous, of all ages.

'The world,' he said, 'grows hourly more and more sceptical of all that lies beyond its own narrow radius; and our men of science foster the fatal tendency. They condemn as fable all that resists experiment. They reject as false all that cannot be brought to the test of the laboratory or the dissecting-room. Against what superstition have they waged so long and obstinate a war, as against the belief in apparitions? And yet what superstition has maintained its hold upon the minds of men so long and so firmly? Show me any fact in physics, in history, in archæology, which is supported by testimony so wide and so various. Attested by all races of men, in all ages, and in all climates, by the soberest sages of antiquity, by the rudest savage of today, by the Christian, the Pagan, the Pantheist, the Materialist, this phenomenon is treated as a nursery tale by the philosophers of our century. Circumstantial evidence weighs with them as a feather in the balance. The comparison of causes with effects, however valuable in physical science, is put aside as worthless and unreliable. The evidence of competent witnesses, however conclusive in a court of justice, counts for nothing. He who pauses before he pronounces, is condemned as a trifler. He who believes, is a dreamer or a fool.'

He spoke with bitterness, and, having said thus, relapsed for some minutes into silence. Presently he raised his head from his hands, and added, with an altered voice and manner,

'I, sir, paused, investigated, believed, and was not ashamed to state my convictions to the world. I, too, was branded as a visionary, held up to ridicule by my contemporaries, and hooted from that field of science in which I had laboured with honour during all the best years of my life. These things happened just three-and-twenty years ago. Since then, I have lived as you see me living now, and the world has forgotten me, as I have forgotten the world. You have my history.'

'It is a very sad one,' I murmured, scarcely knowing what to answer.

'It is a very common one,' he replied. 'I have only suffered for the truth, as many a better and wiser man has suffered before me.'

He rose, as if desirous of ending the conversation, and went over to the window.

'It has ceased snowing,' he observed, as he dropped the curtain, and came back to the fireside.

'Ceased!' I exclaimed, starting eagerly to my feet. 'Oh, if it were only possible—but no! it is hopeless. Even if I could find my way across the moor, I could not walk twenty miles tonight.'

'Walk twenty miles tonight!' repeated my host. 'What are you thinking of?'

'Of my wife,' I replied, impatiently. 'Of my young wife, who does not know that I have lost my way, and who is at this moment breaking her heart with suspense and terror.'

'Where is she?'

'At Dwolding, twenty miles away.'

'At Dwolding,' he echoed, thoughtfully. 'Yes, the distance, it is true, is twenty miles; but—are you so very anxious to save the next six or eight hours?'

'So very, very anxious, that I would give ten guineas at this moment for a guide and a horse.'

'Your wish can be gratified at a less costly rate,' said he, smiling. 'The night mail from the north, which changes horses at Dwolding, passes within five miles of this spot, and will be due at a certain cross-road in about an hour and a quarter. If Jacob were to go with you across the moor, and put you into the old coach-road, you could find your way, I suppose, to where it joins the new one?'

'Easily—gladly.'

He smiled again, rang the bell, gave the old servant his directions, and, taking a bottle of whisky and a wineglass from the cupboard in which he kept his chemicals, said:

'The snow lies deep, and it will be difficult walking tonight on the moor. A glass of usquebaugh before you start?'

I would have declined the spirit, but he pressed it on me, and I drank it. It went down my throat like liquid flame, and almost took my breath away.

'It is strong,' he said; 'but it will help to keep out the cold. And now you have no moments to spare. Good night!'

I thanked him for his hospitality, and would have shaken hands, but that he had turned away before I could finish my sentence. In another minute I had traversed the hall, Jacob had locked the outer door behind me, and we were out on the wide white moor.

Although the wind had fallen, it was still bitterly cold. Not a star glimmered in the black vault overhead. Not a sound, save the rapid crunching of the snow beneath our feet, disturbed the heavy stillness of the night. Jacob, not too well pleased with his mission, shambled on before in sullen silence, his lantern in his hand, and his shadow at his feet. I followed, with my gun over my shoulder, as little inclined for conversation as himself. My thoughts were full of my late host. His voice yet rang in my ears. His eloquence yet held my imagination captive. I remember to this day, with surprise, how my over-excited brain retained whole sentences and parts of sentences, troops of brilliant images, and fragments of splendid reasoning, in the very words in which he had uttered them. Musing thus over what I had heard, and striving to recall a lost link here and there, I strode on at the heels of my guide, absorbed and unobservant. Presently—at the end, as it seemed to me, of only a few minutes—he came to a sudden halt, and said:

'Yon's your road. Keep the stone fence to your right hand, and you can't fail of the way.'

'This, then, is the old coach-road?'

'Ay, 'tis the old coach-road.'

'And how far do I go, before I reach the cross-roads?'

'Nigh upon three mile.'

I pulled out my purse, and he became more communicative.

'The road's a fair road enough,' said he, 'for foot passengers; but 'twas over steep and narrow for the northern traffic. You'll mind where the parapet's broken away, close again the sign-post. It's never been mended since the accident.'

'What accident?'

'Eh, the night mail pitched right over into the valley below—a gude fifty feet an' more—just at the worst bit o' road in the whole county.'

'Horrible! Were many lives lost?'

'All. Four were found dead, and t'other two died next morning.'

'How long is it since this happened?'

'Just nine year.'

'Near the sign-post, you say? I will bear it in mind. Good night.'

'Gude night, sir, and thankee.' Jacob pocketed his half-crown, made a faint pretence of touching his hat, and trudged back by the way he had come.

I watched the light of his lantern till it quite disappeared, and then turned to pursue my way alone. This was no longer matter of the slightest difficulty, for, despite the dead darkness overhead, the line of stone fence showed distinctly enough against the pale gleam of the snow. How silent it seemed now, with only my footsteps to listen to; how silent and how solitary! A strange disagreeable sense of loneliness stole over me. I walked faster. I hummed a fragment of a tune. I cast up enormous sums in my head, and accumulated them at compound interest. I did my best, in short, to forget the startling speculations to which I had but just been listening, and, to some extent, I succeeded.

Meanwhile the night air seemed to become colder and colder, and though I walked fast I found it impossible to keep myself warm. My feet were like ice. I lost sensation in my hands, and grasped my gun mechanically. I even breathed with difficulty, as though, instead of traversing a quiet north country highway, I were scaling the uppermost heights of some gigantic Alp. This last symptom became presently so distressing, that I was forced to stop for a few minutes, and lean against the stone fence. As I did so, I chanced to look back up the road, and there, to my infinite relief, I saw a distant point of light, like the gleam of an approaching lantern. I at first concluded that Jacob had retraced his steps and followed me; but even as the conjecture presented itself, a second light flashed into sight—a light evidently parallel with the first, and approaching at the same rate of motion. It needed no second thought to show me that these must be the carriage-lamps of some private vehicle, though it seemed strange that any private vehicle should take a road professedly disused and dangerous.

There could be no doubt, however, of the fact, for the lamps grew larger and brighter every moment, and I even fancied I could already see the dark outline of the carriage between them. It was coming up very fast, and quite noiselessly, the snow being nearly a foot deep under the wheels.

And now the body of the vehicle became distinctly visible behind the lamps. It looked strangely lofty. A sudden suspicion flashed upon me. Was it possible that I had passed the cross-roads in the dark without observing the sign-post, and could this be the very coach which I had come to meet?

No need to ask myself that question a second time, for here it came round the bend of the road, guard and driver, one outside passenger, and four steaming greys, all wrapped in a soft haze of light, through which the lamps blazed out, like a pair of fiery meteors.

I jumped forward, waved my hat, and shouted. The mail came down at full speed, and passed me. For a moment I feared that I had not been seen or heard, but it was only for a moment. The coachman pulled up; the guard, muffled to the eyes in capes and comforters, and apparently sound asleep in the rumble, neither answered my hail nor made the slightest effort to dismount; the outside passenger did not even turn his head. I opened the door for myself, and looked in. There were but three travellers inside, so I stepped in, shut the door, slipped into the vacant corner, and congratulated myself on my good fortune.

The atmosphere of the coach seemed, if possible, colder than that of the outer air, and was pervaded by a singularly damp and disagreeable smell. I looked round at my fellow-passengers. They were all three, men, and all silent. They did not seem to be asleep, but each leaned back in his corner of the vehicle, as if absorbed in his own reflections. I attempted to open a conversation.

'How intensely cold it is tonight,' I said, addressing my opposite neighbour.

He lifted his head, looked at me, but made no reply.

'The winter,' I added, 'seems to have begun in earnest.'

Although the corner in which he sat was so dim that I could distinguish none of his features very clearly, I saw that his eyes were still turned full upon me. And yet he answered never a word.

At any other time I should have felt, and perhaps expressed, some annoyance, but at the moment I felt too ill to do either. The icy coldness of the night air had struck a chill to my very marrow, and the strange smell inside the coach was affecting me with an intolerable nausea. I shivered from head to foot, and, turning to my left-hand neighbour, asked if he had any objection to an open window?

He neither spoke nor stirred.

I repeated the question somewhat more loudly, but with the same result. Then I lost patience, and let the sash down. As I did so the leather strap broke in my hand, and I observed that the glass was covered with a thick coat of mildew, the accumulation, apparently, of years. My attention being thus drawn to the condition of the coach, I examined it more narrowly, and saw by the uncertain light of the outer lamps that it was in the last stage of dilapidation. Every part of it was not only out of repair, but in a condition of decay. The sashes splintered at a touch. The leather fittings were crusted over with mould, and literally rotting from the woodwork. The floor was almost breaking away beneath my feet. The whole machine, in short, was foul with damp, and had evidently been dragged from some outhouse in which it had been mouldering away for years, to do another day or two of duty on the road.

I turned to the third passenger, whom I had not yet addressed, and hazarded one more remark.

'This coach,' I said, 'is in a deplorable condition. The regular mail, I suppose, is under repair?'

He moved his head slowly, and looked me in the face, without speaking a word. I shall never forget that look while I live. I turned cold at heart under it. I turn cold at heart even now when I recall it. His eyes glowed with a fiery unnatural lustre. His face was livid as the face of a corpse. His bloodless lips were drawn back as if in the agony of death, and showed the gleaming teeth between.

The words that I was about to utter died upon my lips, and a strange horror—a dreadful horror—came upon me. My sight had by this time become used to the gloom of the coach, and I could see with tolerable distinctness. I turned to my opposite neighbour. He, too, was looking at me, with the same startling pallor in his face, and the same stony glitter in his eyes. I passed my hand across my brow. I turned to the passenger on the seat beside my own, and saw—oh Heaven! how shall I describe what I saw? I saw that he was no living man—that none of them were living men, like myself! A pale phosphorescent light—the light of putrefaction—played upon their awful faces; upon their hair, dank with the dews of the grave; upon their clothes, earth-stained and dropping to pieces; upon their hands, which were as the hands of corpses long buried. Only their eyes, their terrible eyes, were living; and those eyes were all turned menacingly upon me!

A shriek of terror, a wild unintelligible cry for help and mercy, burst from my lips as I flung myself against the door, and strove in vain to open it.

In that single instant, brief and vivid as a landscape beheld in the flash of summer lightning, I saw the moon shining down through a rift of stormy cloud—the ghastly sign-post rearing its warning finger by the wayside—the broken parapet—the plunging horses—the black gulf below. Then, the coach reeled like a ship at sea. Then, came a mighty crash—a sense of crushing pain—and then, darkness.

It seemed as if years had gone by when I awoke one morning from a deep sleep, and found my wife watching by my bedside. I will pass over the scene that ensued, and give you, in half a dozen words, the tale she told me with tears of thanksgiving. I had fallen over a precipice, close against the junction of the old coach-road and the new, and had only been saved from certain death by lighting upon a deep snowdrift that had accumulated at the foot of the rock beneath. In this snowdrift I was discovered at daybreak, by a couple of shepherds, who carried me to the nearest shelter, and brought a surgeon to my aid. The surgeon found me in a state of raving delirium, with a broken arm and a compound fracture of the skull. The letters in my pocket-book showed my name and address; my wife was summoned to nurse me; and, thanks to youth and a fine constitution, I came out of danger at last. The place of my fall, I need scarcely say, was precisely that at which a frightful accident had happened to the north mail nine years before.

I never told my wife the fearful events which I have just related to you. I told the surgeon who attended me; but he treated the whole adventure as a mere dream born of the fever in my brain. We discussed the question over and over again, until we found that we could discuss it with temper no longer, and then we dropped it. Others may form what conclusions they please—I *know* that twenty years ago I was the fourth inside passenger in that Phantom Coach.

Squire Toby's Will

A Ghost Story

J. S. LE FANU

Many persons accustomed to travel the old York and London road, in the days of stage-coaches, will remember passing, in the afternoon, say, of an autumn day, in their journey to the capital, about three miles south of the town of Applebury, and a mile and a half before you reach the old Angel Inn, a large black-and-white house, as those old-fashioned cage-work habitations are termed, dilapidated and weather-stained, with broad lattice windows glimmering all over in the evening sun with little diamond panes, and thrown into relief by a dense background of ancient elms. A wide avenue, now overgrown like a churchyard with grass and weeds, and flanked by double rows of the same dark trees, old and gigantic, with here and there a gap in their solemn files, and sometimes a fallen tree lying across on the avenue, leads up to the hall-door.

Looking up its sombre and lifeless avenue from the top of the London coach, as I have often done, you are struck with so many signs of desertion and decay,—the tufted grass sprouting in the chinks of the steps and window-stones, the smokeless chimneys over which the jackdaws are wheeling, the absence of human life and all its evidence, that you conclude at once that the place is uninhabited and abandoned to decay. The name of this ancient house is Gylingden Hall. Tall hedges and old timber quickly shroud the old place from view, and about a quarter of a mile further on you pass, embowered in melancholy trees, a small and ruinous Saxon chapel, which, time out of mind, has been the burying-place of the family of Marston, and partakes of the neglect and desolation which brood over their ancient dwelling-place.

The grand melancholy of the secluded valley of Gylingden, lonely as an enchanted forest, in which the crows returning to their roosts among the trees, and the straggling deer who peep from beneath their branches, seem to hold a wild and undisturbed dominion, heightens the forlorn aspect of Gylingden Hall.

Of late years repairs have been neglected, and here and there the roof is stripped, and 'the stitch in time' has been wanting. At the side of the house exposed to the gales that sweep through the valley like a torrent through its channel, there is not a perfect window left, and the shutters but imperfectly exclude the rain. The ceilings and walls are mildewed and green with damp stains. Here and there, where the drip falls from the ceiling, the floors are rotting. On stormy nights, as the guard described, you can hear the doors clapping in the old house, as far away as old Gryston bridge, and the howl and sobbing of the wind through its empty galleries.

About seventy years ago died the old Squire, Toby Marston, famous in that part of the world for his hounds, his hospitality, and his vices. He had done kind things, and he had fought duels: he had given away money and he had horse-whipped people. He carried with him some blessings and a good many curses, and left behind him an amount of debts and charges upon the estates which appalled his two sons, who had no taste for business or accounts, and had never suspected, till that wicked, open-handed, and swearing old gentleman died, how very nearly he had run the estates into insolvency.

They met at Gylingden Hall. They had the will before them, and lawyers to interpret, and information without stint, as to the encumbrances with which the deceased had saddled them. The will was so framed as to set the two brothers instantly at deadly feud.

These brothers differed in some points; but in one material characteristic they resembled one another, and also their departed father. They never went into a quarrel by halves, and once in, they did not stick at trifles.

The elder, Scroope Marston, the more dangerous man of the two, had never been a favourite of the old Squire. He had no taste for the sports of the field and the pleasures of a rustic life. He was no athlete, and he certainly was not handsome. All this the Squire resented. The young man, who had no respect for him, and outgrew his fear of his violence as he came to manhood, retorted. This aversion, therefore, in the ill-conditioned old man grew into positive hatred. He used to wish that d——d pippin-squeezing, humpbacked rascal Scroope, out of the way of better men—meaning his younger son Charles; and in his cups would talk in a way which even the old and young fellows who followed his hounds, and drank his port, and could stand a reasonable amount of brutality, did not like.

Scroope Marston was slightly deformed, and he had the lean sallow face, piercing black eyes, and black lank hair, which sometimes accompany deformity.

'I'm no feyther o' that hog-backed creature. I'm no sire of hisn, d——n him! I'd as soon call that tongs son o' mine,' the old man used to bawl, in allusion to his son's long, lank limbs: 'Charlie's a man, but that's a jack-an-ape. He has no good-nature; there's nothing handy, nor manly, nor no one turn of a Marston in him.'

And when he was pretty drunk, the old Squire used to swear he should never 'sit at the head o' that board; nor frighten away folk from Gylingden Hall wi' his d——d hatchet-face—the black loon!'

'Handsome Charlie was the man for his money. He knew what a horse was, and could sit to his bottle; and the lasses were all clean *wad* about him. He was a Marston every inch of his six foot two.'

Handsome Charlie and he, however, had also had a row or two. The old Squire was free with his horsewhip as with his tongue, and on occasion when neither weapon was quite practicable, had been known to give a fellow 'a tap o' his knuckles'. Handsome Charlie, however, thought there was a period at which personal chastisement should cease; and one night, when the port was flowing, there was some allusion to Marion Hayward, the miller's daughter, which for some reason the old gentleman did not like. Being 'in liquor', and having clearer ideas about pugilism than self-government, he struck out, to the surprise of all present, at Handsome Charlie. The youth threw back his head scientifically, and nothing followed but the crash of a decanter on the floor. But the old Squire's blood was up, and he bounced from his chair. Up jumped Handsome Charlie, resolved to stand no nonsense. Drunken Squire Lilbourne, intending to mediate, fell flat on the floor, and cut his ear among the glasses. Handsome Charlie caught the thump which the old Squire discharged at him upon his open hand, and catching him by the cravat, swung him with his back to the wall. They said the old man never looked so purple, nor his eyes so goggle before; and then Handsome Charlie pinioned him tight to the wall by both arms.

'Well, I say—come, don't you talk no more nonsense o' that sort, and I won't lick you,' croaked the old Squire. 'You stopped that un clever, you did. Didn't he? Come, Charlie, man, gie us your hand, I say, and sit down again, lad.' And so the battle ended; and I believe it was the last time the Squire raised his hand to Handsome Charlie.

But those days were over. Old Toby Marston lay cold and quiet enough now, under the drip of the mighty ash-tree within the Saxon ruin where so many of the old Marston race returned to dust, and were forgotten. The weather-stained top-boots and leather-breeches, the three-cornered cocked hat to which old gentlemen of that day still clung, and the well-known red waistcoat that reached below his hips, and the fierce pug face of the old Squire, were now but a picture of memory. And the brothers between whom he had planted an irreconcilable quarrel, were now in their new mourning suits, with the gloss still on, debating furiously across the table in the great oak parlour, which had so often resounded to the banter and coarse songs, the oaths and laughter of the congenial neighbours whom the old Squire of Gylingden Hall loved to assemble there.

These young gentlemen, who had grown up in Gylingden Hall, were not accustomed to bridle their tongues, nor, if need be, to hesitate about a blow. Neither had been at the old man's funeral. His death had been sudden. Having been helped to his bed in that hilarious and quarrelsome state which was induced by port and punch, he was found dead in the morning,—his head hanging over the side of the bed, and his face very black and swollen.

Now the Squire's will despoiled his eldest son of Gylingden, which had descended to the heir time out of mind. Scroope Marston was furious. His deep stern voice was heard inveighing against his dead father and living brother, and the heavy thumps on the table with which he enforced his stormy recriminations resounded through the large chamber. Then broke in Charles's rougher voice, and then came a quick alternation of short sentences, and then both voices together in growing loudness and anger, and at last, swelling the tumult, the expostulations of pacific and frightened lawyers, and at last a sudden break up of the conference. Scroope broke out of the room, his pale furious face showing whiter against his long black hair, his dark fierce eyes blazing, his hands clenched, and looking more ungainly and deformed than ever in the convulsions of his fury.

Very violent words must have passed between them; for Charlie, though he was the winning man, was almost as angry as Scroope. The elder brother was for holding possession of the house, and putting his rival to legal process to oust him. But his legal advisers were clearly against it. So, with a heart boiling over with gall, up he went to London, and found the firm who had managed his father's business fair and communicative enough. They looked into the settlements, and found that Gylingden was excepted. It was very odd, but so it was, specially excepted; so that the right of the old Squire to deal with it by his will could not be questioned.

Notwithstanding all this, Scroope, breathing vengeance and aggression, and quite willing to wreck himself provided he could run his brother down, assailed Handsome Charlie, and battered old Squire Toby's will in the Prerogative Court and also at common law, and the feud between the brothers was knit, and every month their exasperation was heightened.

Scroope was beaten, and defeat did not soften him. Charles might have forgiven hard words; but he had been himself worsted during the long campaign in some of those skirmishes, special motions, and so forth, that constitute the episodes of a legal epic like that in which the

Marston brothers figured as opposing combatants; and the blight of law-costs had touched him, too, with the usual effect upon the temper of a man of embarrassed means.

Years flew, and brought no healing on their wings. On the contrary, the deep corrosion of this hatred bit deeper by time. Neither brother married. But an accident of a different kind befell the younger, Charles Marston, which abridged his enjoyments very materially.

This was a bad fall from his hunter. There were severe fractures, and there was concussion of the brain. For some time it was thought that he could not recover. He disappointed these evil auguries, however. He did recover, but changed in two essential particulars. He had received an injury in his hip, which doomed him never more to sit in the saddle. And the rollicking animal spirits which hitherto had never failed him, had now taken flight for ever.

He had been for five days in a state of coma—absolute insensibility—and when he recovered consciousness he was haunted by an indescribable anxiety.

Tom Cooper, who had been butler in the palmy days of Gylingden Hall, under old Squire Toby, still maintained his post with old-fashioned fidelity, in these days of faded splendour and frugal house-keeping. Twenty years had passed since the death of his old master. He had grown lean, and stooped, and his face, dark with the peculiar brown of age, furrowed and gnarled, and his temper, except with his master, had waxed surly.

His master had visited Bath and Buxton, and came back, as he went, lame, and halting gloomily about with the aid of a stick. When the hunter was sold, the last tradition of the old life at Gylingden disappeared. The young Squire, as he was still called, excluded by his mischance from the hunting-field, dropped into a solitary way of life, and halted slowly and solitarily about the old place, seldom raising his eyes, and with an appearance of indescribable gloom.

Old Cooper could talk freely on occasion with his master; and one day he said, as he handed him his hat and stick in the hall:

'You should rouse yourself up a bit, Master Charles!'

'It's past rousing with me, old Cooper.'

'It's just this, I'm thinking: there's something on your mind, and you won't tell no one. There's no good keeping it on your stomach. You'll be a deal lighter if you tell it. Come, now, what is it, Master Charlie?'

The Squire looked with his round grey eyes straight into Cooper's eyes. He felt that there was a sort of spell broken. It was like the old rule of the ghost who can't speak till it is spoken to. He looked earnestly into old Cooper's face for some seconds, and sighed deeply.

'It ain't the first good guess you've made in your day, old Cooper, and I'm glad you've spoke. It's bin on my mind, sure enough, ever since I had that fall. Come in here after me, and shut the door.'

The Squire pushed open the door of the oak parlour, and looked round on the pictures abstractedly. He had not been there for some time, and seating himself on the table, he looked again for a while in Cooper's face before he spoke.

'It's not a great deal, Cooper, but it troubles me, and I would not tell it to the parson nor the doctor; for, God knows what they'd say, though there's nothing to signify in it. But you were always true to the family, and I don't mind if I tell you.'

' 'Tis as safe with Cooper, Master Charles, as if 'twas locked in a chest, and sunk in a well.'

'It's only this,' said Charles Marston, looking down on the end of his stick, with which he was tracing lines and circles, 'all the time I was lying like dead, as you thought, after that fall, I was with the old master.' He raised his eyes to Cooper's again as he spoke, and with an awful oath he repeated—'I was with him, Cooper!'

'He was a good man, sir, in his way,' repeated old Cooper, returning his gaze with awe. 'He was a good master to me, and a good father to you, and I hope he's happy. May God rest him!'

'Well,' said Squire Charles, 'it's only this: the whole of that time I was with him, or he was with me—I don't know which. The upshot is, we were together, and I thought I'd never get out of his hands again, and all the time he was bullying me about some one thing; and if it was to save my life, Tom Cooper, by —— from the time I waked I never could call to mind what it was; and I think I'd give that hand to know; and if you can think of anything it might be—for God's sake! don't be afraid, Tom Cooper, but speak it out, for he threatened me hard, and it was surely him.'

Here ensued a silence.

'And what did you think it might be yourself, Master Charles?' said Cooper.

'I han't thought of aught that's likely. I'll never hit on't—*never*. I thought it might happen he knew something about that d—— humpbacked villain, Scroope, that swore before Lawyer Gingham I made away with a paper of settlements—me and father; and, as I hope to be saved, Tom Cooper, there never was a bigger lie! I'd a had the law of him for them identical words, and cast him for more than he's worth; only Lawyer Gingham never goes into nothing for me since money grew scarce in Gylingden; and I can't change my lawyer, I owe him such a hatful of money. But he did, he swore he'd hang me yet for it. He said it in them identical words—he'd never rest till he *hanged* me for it, and I think it was, like enough, something about *that*, the old master was troubled; but it's enough to drive a man mad. I *can't* bring it to mind—I can't remember a word he said, only he threatened awful, and looked—Lord a-mercy on us!—frightful bad.'

'There's no need he should. May the Lord a-mercy on him!' said the old butler.

'No, of course; and you're not to tell a soul, Cooper—not a living soul, mind, that I said he looked bad, nor nothing about it.'

'God forbid!' said old Cooper, shaking his head. 'But I was thinking, sir, it might ha' been about the slight that's bin so long put on him by having no stone over him, and never a scratch o' a chisel to say who he is.'

'Ay! Well, I didn't think o' that. Put on your hat, old Cooper, and come down wi' me; for I'll look after that, at any rate.'

There is a bye-path leading by a turnstile to the park, and thence to the picturesque old burying-place, which lies in a nook by the roadside, embowered in ancient trees. It was a fine autumnal sunset, and melancholy lights and long shadows spread their peculiar effects over the landscape as 'Handsome Charlie' and the old butler made their way slowly toward the place where Handsome Charlie was himself to lie at last.

'Which of the dogs made that howling all last night?' asked the Squire, when they had got on a little way.

' 'Twas a strange dog, Master Charlie, in front of the house; ours was all in the yard—a white dog wi' a black head, he looked to be, and he was smelling round them mounting-steps the old master, God be wi' him! set up, the time his knee was bad. When the tyke got up a' top of them, howlin' up at the windows, I'd a liked to shy something at him.'

'Hullo! Is that like him?' said the Squire, stopping short, and pointing with his stick at a dirty-white dog, with a large black head, which was scampering round them in a wide circle, half crouching with that air of uncertainty and deprecation which dogs so well know how to assume.

He whistled the dog up. He was a large, half-starved bull-dog.

'That fellow has made a long journey—thin as a whipping-post, and stained all over, and his claws worn to the stumps,' said the Squire, musingly. 'He isn't a bad dog, Cooper. My poor father liked a good bull-dog, and knew a cur from a good 'un.'

The dog was looking up into the Squire's face with the peculiar grim visage of his kind, and the Squire was thinking irreverently how strong a likeness it presented to the character of his father's fierce pug features when he was clutching his horsewhip and swearing at a keeper.

'If I did right I'd shoot him. He'll worry the cattle, and kill our dogs,' said the Squire. 'Hey, Cooper? I'll tell the keeper to look after him. That fellow could pull down a sheep, and he shan't live on my mutton.'

But the dog was not to be shaken off. He looked wistfully after the Squire, and after they had got a little way on, he followed timidly.

It was vain trying to drive him off. The dog ran round them in wide circles, like the infernal dog in 'Faust'; only he left no track of thin flame behind him. These manoeuvres were executed with a sort of beseeching air, which flattered and touched the object of this odd preference. So he called him up again, patted him, and then and there in a manner adopted him.

The dog now followed their steps dutifully, as if he had belonged to Handsome Charlie all his days. Cooper unlocked the little iron door, and the dog walked in close behind their heels, and followed them as they visited the roofless chapel.

The Marstons were lying under the floor of this little building in rows. There is not a vault. Each has his distinct grave enclosed in a lining of masonry. Each is surmounted by a stone kist, on the upper flag of which is enclosed his epitaph, except that of poor old Squire Toby. Over him was nothing but the grass and the line of masonry which indicate the site of the kist, whenever his family should afford him one like the rest.

'Well, it does look shabby. It's the elder brother's business; but if he won't, I'll see to it myself, and I'll take care, old boy, to cut sharp and deep in it, that the elder son having refused to lend a hand the stone was put there by the younger.'

They strolled round this little burial-ground. The sun was now below the horizon, and the red metallic glow from the clouds, still illuminated by the departed sun, mingled luridly with the twilight. When Charlie peeped again into the little chapel, he saw the ugly dog stretched upon Squire Toby's grave, looking at least twice his natural length, and performing such antics as made the young Squire stare. If you have ever seen a cat stretched on the floor, with a bunch of Valerian, straining, writhing, rubbing its jaws in long-drawn caresses, and in the absorption of a sensual ecstasy, you have seen a phenomenon resembling that which Handsome Charlie witnessed on looking in.

The head of the brute looked so large, its body so long and thin, and its joints so ungainly and dislocated, that the Squire, with old Cooper beside him, looked on with a feeling of disgust and astonishment, which, in a moment or two more, brought the Squire's stick down upon him with a couple of heavy thumps. The beast awakened from his ecstasy, sprang to the head of the grave, and there on a sudden, thick and bandy as before, confronted the Squire, who stood at its foot, with a terrible grin, and eyes that glared with the peculiar green of canine fury.

The next moment the dog was crouching abjectly at the Squire's feet.

'Well, he's a rum 'un!' said old Cooper, looking hard at him.

'I like him,' said the Squire.

'I don't,' said Cooper.

'But he shan't come in here again,' said the Squire.

'I shouldn't wonder if he was a witch,' said old Cooper, who remembered more tales of witchcraft than are now current in that part of the world.

'He's a good dog,' said the Squire, dreamily. 'I remember the time I'd a given a handful for him—but I'll never be good for nothing again. Come along.'

And he stooped down and patted him. So up jumped the dog and looked up in his face, as if watching for some sign, ever so slight, which he might obey.

Cooper did not like a bone in that dog's skin. He could not imagine what his master saw to admire in him. He kept him all night in the gun-room, and the dog accompanied him in his halting rambles about the place. The fonder his master grew of him, the less did Cooper and the other servants like him.

'He hasn't a point of a good dog about him,' Cooper would growl. 'I think Master Charlie be blind. And old Captain (an old red parrot, who sat chained to a perch in the oak parlour, and conversed with himself, and nibbled at his claws and bit his perch all day),—old Captain, the only living thing, except one or two of us, and the Squire himself, that remembers the old master, the minute he saw the dog, screeched as if he was struck, shakin' his feathers out quite wild, and drops down, poor old soul, a-hangin' by his foot, in a fit.'

But there is no accounting for fancies, and the Squire was one of those dogged persons who persist more obstinately in their whims the more they are opposed. But Charles Marston's health suffered by his lameness. The transition from habitual and violent exercise to such a life as his privation now consigned him to, was never made without a risk to health; and a host of dyspeptic annoyances, the existence of which he had never dreamed of before, now beset him in sad earnest. Among these was the now not unfrequent troubling of his sleep with dreams and nightmares. In these his canine favourite invariably had a part and was generally a central, and sometimes a solitary figure. In these visions the dog seemed to stretch himself up the side of the Squire's bed, and in dilated proportions to sit at his feet, with a horrible likeness to the pug features of old Squire Toby, with his tricks of wagging his head and throwing up his chin; and then he would talk to him about Scroope, and tell him 'all wasn't straight', and that he 'must make it up wi' Scroope', that he, the old Squire, had 'served him an ill turn', that 'time was nigh up', and that 'fair was fair', and he was 'troubled where he was, about Scroope'.

Then in his dream this semi-human brute would approach his face to his, crawling and crouching up his body, heavy as lead, till the face of the beast was laid on his, with the same odious caresses and stretchings and writhings which he had seen over the old Squire's grave. Then Charlie would wake up with a gasp and a howl, and start upright in the bed, bathed in a cold moisture, and fancy he saw something white sliding off the foot of the bed. Sometimes he thought it might be the curtain with white lining that slipped down, or the coverlet disturbed by his uneasy turnings; but he always fancied, at such moments, that he saw something white sliding hastily off the bed; and always when he had been visited by such dreams the dog next morning was more than usually caressing and servile, as if to obliterate, by a more than ordinary welcome, the sentiment of disgust which the horror of the night had left behind it.

The doctor half-satisfied the Squire that there was nothing in these dreams, which, in one shape or another, invariably attended forms of indigestion such as he was suffering from.

For a while, as if to corroborate this theory, the dog ceased altogether to figure in them. But at last there came a vision in which, more unpleasantly than before, he did resume his old place.

In his nightmare the room seemed all but dark; he heard what he knew to be the dog walking from the door round his bed slowly to the side from which he always had come upon it. A portion of the room was uncarpeted, and he said he distinctly heard the peculiar tread of a dog, in which the faint clatter of the claws is audible. It was a light stealthy step, but at every tread the whole room shook heavily; he felt something place itself at the foot of his bed, and saw a pair of green eyes staring at him in the dark, from which he could not remove his own. Then he heard, as he thought, the old Squire Toby say—'The eleventh hour be passed, Charlie, and ye've done nothing—you and I 'a done Scroope a wrong!' and then came a good deal more, and then—'The time's nigh up, it's going to strike.' And with a long low growl, the thing began to creep up upon his feet; the growl continued, and he saw the reflection of the up-turned green eyes upon the bed-clothes, as it began slowly to stretch itself up his body towards his face. With a loud scream, he waked. The light, which of late the Squire was accustomed to have in his bedroom, had accidentally gone out. He was afraid to get up, or even to look about the room for some time; so sure did he feel of seeing the green eyes in the dark fixed on him from some corner. He had hardly recovered from the first agony which nightmare leaves behind it, and was beginning to collect his thoughts, when he heard the clock strike twelve. And he bethought him of the words 'the eleventh hour be passed—time's nigh up—it's going to strike!' and he almost feared that he would hear the voice reopening the subject.

Next morning the Squire came down looking ill.

'Do you know a room, old Cooper,' said he, 'they used to call King Herod's Chamber?'

'Ay, sir; the story of King Herod was on the walls o't when I was a boy.'

'There's a closet off it—is there?'

'I can't be sure o' that; but 'tisn't worth your looking at, now; the hangings was rotten, and took off the walls, before you was born; and there's nout there but some old broken things and lumber. I seed them put there myself by poor Twinks; he was blind of an eye, and footman afterwards. You'll remember Twinks? He died here, about the time o' the great snow. There was a deal o' work to bury him, poor fellow!'

'Get the key, old Cooper; I'll look at the room,' said the Squire.

'And what the devil can you want to look at it for?' said Cooper, with the old-world privilege of a rustic butler.

'And what the devil's that to you? But I don't mind if I tell you. I don't want that dog in the gun-room, and I'll put him somewhere else; and I don't care if I put him there.'

'A bull-dog in a bedroom! Oons, sir! the folks 'ill say you're clean mad!'

'Well, let them; get you the key, and let us look at the room.'

'You'd shoot him if you did right, Master Charlie. You never heard what a noise he kept up all last night in the gun-room, walking to and fro growling like a tiger in a show; and, say what you like, the dog's not worth his feed; he hasn't a point of a dog; he's a bad dog.'

'I know a dog better than you—and he's a good dog!' said the Squire, testily.

'If you was a judge of a dog you'd hang that 'un,' said Cooper.

'I'm not a-going to hang him, so there's an end. Go you, and get the key; and don't be talking, mind, when you go down. I may change my mind.'

Now this freak of visiting King Herod's room had, in truth, a totally different object from that pretended by the Squire. The voice in his nightmare had uttered a particular direction, which haunted him, and would give him no peace until he had tested it. So far from liking that dog today, he was beginning to regard it with a horrible suspicion; and if old Cooper had not stirred his obstinate temper by seeming to dictate, I dare say he would have got rid of that inmate effectually before evening.

Up to the third storey, long disused, he and old Cooper mounted. At the end of a dusty gallery, the room lay. The old tapestry, from which the spacious chamber had taken its name, had long given place to modern paper, and this was mildewed, and in some places hanging from the walls. A thick mantle of dust lay over the floor. Some broken chairs and boards, thick with dust, lay, along with other lumber, piled together at one end of the room.

They entered the closet, which was quite empty. The Squire looked round, and you could hardly have said whether he was relieved or disappointed.

'No furniture here,' said the Squire, and looked through the dusty window. 'Did you say anything to me lately—I don't mean this morning—about this room, or the closet—or anything—I forget—'

'Lor' bless you! Not I. I han't been thinkin' o' this room this forty year.'

'Is there any sort of old furniture called a *buffet*—do you remember?' asked the Squire.

'A buffet? why, yes—to be sure—there was a buffet, sure enough, in this closet, now you bring it to my mind,' said Cooper. 'But it's papered over.'

'And what is it?'

'A little cupboard in the wall,' answered the old man.

'Ho—I see—and there's such a thing here, is there, under the paper? Show me whereabouts it was.'

'Well—I think it was somewhere about here,' answered he, rapping his knuckles along the wall opposite the window. 'Ay, there it is,' he added, as the hollow sound of a wooden door was returned to his knock.

The Squire pulled the loose paper from the wall, and disclosed the doors of a small press, about two feet square, fixed in the wall.

'The very thing for my buckles and pistols, and the rest of my gimcracks,' said the Squire. 'Come away, we'll leave the dog where he is. Have you the key of that little press?'

No, he had not. The old master had emptied and locked it up, and desired that it should be papered over, and that was the history of it.

Down came the Squire, and took a strong turn-screw from his gun-case; and quietly he reascended to King Herod's room, and, with little trouble, forced the door of the small press in the closet wall. There were in it some letters and cancelled leases, and also a parchment deed which he took to the window and read with much agitation. It was a supplemental deed executed about a fortnight after the others, and previously to his father's marriage, placing Gylingden under strict settlement to the elder son, in what is called 'tail male'. Handsome Charlie, in his fraternal litigation, had acquired a smattering of technical knowledge, and he perfectly well knew that the effect of this would be not only to transfer the house and lands to his brother Scroope, but to leave him at the mercy of that exasperated brother, who might recover from him personally every guinea he had ever received by way of rent, from the date of his father's death.

It was a dismal, clouded day, with something threatening in its aspect, and the darkness, where he stood, was made deeper by the top of one of the huge old trees overhanging the window.

In a state of awful confusion he attempted to think over his position. He placed the deed in his pocket, and nearly made up his mind to destroy it. A short time ago he would not have hesitated for a moment under such circumstances; but now his health and his nerves were shattered, and he was under a supernatural alarm which the strange discovery of this deed had powerfully confirmed.

In this state of profound agitation he heard a sniffing at the closet-door, and then an impatient scratch and a long low growl. He screwed his courage up, and, not knowing what to expect, threw the door open and saw the dog, not in his dream-shape, but wriggling with joy, and crouching and fawning with eager submission; and then wandering about the closet, the brute growled awfully into the corners of it, and seemed in an unappeasable agitation.

Then the dog returned and fawned and crouched again at his feet.

After the first moment was over, the sensations of abhorrence and fear began to subside, and he almost reproached himself for requiting the affection of this poor friendless brute with the antipathy which he had really done nothing to earn.

The dog pattered after him down the stairs. Oddly enough, the sight of this animal, after the first revulsion, reassured him; it was, in his eyes, so attached, so good-natured, and palpably so mere a dog.

By the hour of evening the Squire had resolved on a middle course; he would not inform his brother of his discovery, nor yet would he destroy the deed. He would never marry. He was past that time. He would leave a letter, explaining the discovery of the deed, addressed to the only surviving trustee—who had probably forgotten everything about it—and having seen out his own tenure, he would provide that all should be set right after his death. Was not that fair? at all events it quite satisfied what he called his conscience, and he thought it a devilish good compromise for his brother; and he went out, towards sunset, to take his usual walk.

Returning in the darkening twilight, the dog, as usual attending him, began to grow frisky and wild, at first scampering round him in great circles, as before, nearly at the top of his speed, his great head between his paws as he raced. Gradually more excited grew the pace and narrower his circuit, louder and fiercer his continuous growl, and the Squire stopped and grasped his stick hard, for the lurid eyes and grin of the brute threatened an attack. Turning round and round as the excited brute encircled him, and striking vainly at him with his stick, he grew at last so tired that he almost despaired of keeping him longer at bay; when on a sudden the dog stopped short and crawled up to his feet wriggling and crouching submissively.

Nothing could be more apologetic and abject; and when the Squire dealt him two heavy thumps with his stick, the dog whimpered only, and writhed and licked his feet. The Squire sat down on a prostrate tree; and his dumb companion, recovering his wonted spirits immediately, began to sniff and nuzzle among the roots. The Squire felt in his breast-pocket for the deed—it was safe; and again he pondered, in this loneliest of spots, on the question whether he should preserve it for restoration after his death to his brother, or destroy it forthwith. He began rather to lean toward the latter solution, when the long low growl of the dog not far off startled him.

He was sitting in a melancholy grove of old trees, that slants gently westward. Exactly the same odd effect of light I have before described— a faint red glow reflected downward from the upper sky, after the sun had set, now gave to the growing darkness a lurid uncertainty. This grove, which lies in a gentle hollow, owing to its circumscribed horizon on all but one side, has a peculiar character of loneliness.

He got up and peeped over a sort of barrier, accidentally formed of the trunks of felled trees laid one over the other, and saw the dog straining up the other side of it, and hideously stretched out, his ugly head looking in consequence twice the natural size. His dream was coming over him again. And now between the trunks the brute's ungainly head was thrust, and the long neck came straining through, and the body, twining after it like a huge white lizard; and as it came striving and twisting through, it growled and glared as if it would devour him.

As swiftly as his lameness would allow, the Squire hurried from this solitary spot towards the house. What thoughts exactly passed through his mind as he did so, I am sure he could not have told. But when the dog came up with him it seemed appeased, and even in high good-humour, and no longer resembled the brute that haunted his dreams.

That night, near ten o'clock, the Squire, a good deal agitated, sent for the keeper, and told him that he believed the dog was mad, and that he must shoot him. He might shoot the dog in the gun-room, where he was—a grain of shot or two in the wainscot did not matter, and the dog must not have a chance of getting out.

The Squire gave the gamekeeper his double-barrelled gun, loaded with heavy shot. He did not go with him beyond the hall. He placed his hand on the keeper's arm; the keeper said his hand trembled, and that he looked 'as white as curds'.

'Listen a bit!' said the Squire under his breath.

They heard the dog in a state of high excitement in the room—growling ominously, jumping on the window-stool and down again, and running round the room.

'You'll need to be sharp, mind—don't give him a chance—slip in edgeways, d'ye see? and give him both barrels!'

'Not the first mad dog I've knocked over, sir,' said the man, looking very serious as he cocked the gun.

As the keeper opened the door, the dog had sprung into the empty grate. He said he 'never see sich a stark, staring devil.' The beast made a twist round, as if, he thought, to jump up the chimney—'but that wasn't to be done at no price,'—and he made a yell—not like a dog—like a man caught in a mill-crank, and before he could spring at the keeper, he fired one barrel into him. The dog leaped towards him, and rolled over, receiving the second barrel in his head, as he lay snorting at the keeper's feet!

'I never seed the like; I never heard a screech like that!' said the keeper, recoiling. 'It makes a fellow feel queer.'

'Quite dead?' asked the Squire.

'Not a stir in him, sir,' said the man, pulling him along the floor by the neck.

'Throw him outside the hall-door now,' said the Squire; 'and mind you pitch him outside the gate tonight—old Cooper says he's a witch,' and the pale Squire smiled, 'so he shan't lie in Gylingden.'

Never was man more relieved than the Squire, and he slept better for a week after this than he had done for many weeks before.

It behoves us all to act promptly on our good resolutions. There is a determined gravitation towards evil, which, if left to itself, will bear down first intentions. If at one moment of superstitious fear, the Squire had made up his mind to a great sacrifice, and resolved in the matter of that deed so strangely recovered, to act honestly by his brother, that resolution very soon gave place to the compromise with fraud, which so conveniently postponed the restitution to the period when further enjoyment on his part was impossible. Then came more tidings of Scroope's violent and minatory language, with always the same burthen—that he would leave no stone unturned to show that there had existed a deed which Charles had either secreted or destroyed, and that he would never rest till he had hanged him.

This of course was wild talk. At first it had only enraged him; but, with his recent guilty knowledge and suppression, had come fear. His danger was the existence of the deed, and little by little he brought himself to a resolution to destroy it. There were many falterings and recoils before he could bring himself to commit this crime. At length, however, he did it, and got rid of the custody of that which at any time might become the instrument of disgrace and ruin. There was relief in this, but also the new and terrible sense of actual guilt.

He had got pretty well rid of his supernatural qualms. It was a different kind of trouble that agitated him now.

But this night, he imagined, he was awakened by a violent shaking of his bed. He could see, in the very imperfect light, two figures at the foot of it, holding each a bed-post. One of these he half-fancied was his brother Scroope, but the other was the old Squire—of that he was sure—and he fancied that they had shaken him up from his sleep. Squire Toby was talking as Charlie wakened, and he heard him say:

'Put out of our own house by you! It won't hold for long. We'll come in together, friendly, and stay. Forewarned, wi' yer eyes open, ye did it; and now Scroope'll hang you! We'll hang you together! Look at me, you devil's limb.'

And the old Squire tremblingly stretched his face, torn with shot and bloody, and growing every moment more and more into the likeness of the dog, and began to stretch himself out and climb the bed over the foot-board; and he saw the figure at the other side, little more than a black shadow, begin also to scale the bed; and there was instantly a dreadful confusion and uproar in the room, and such a gabbling and laughing; he could not catch the words; but, with a scream, he woke, and found himself standing on the floor. The phantoms and the clamour were gone, but a crash and ringing of fragments was in his ears. The great china bowl, from which for generations the Marstons of Gylingden had been baptized, had fallen from the mantelpiece, and was smashed on the hearth-stone.

'I've bin dreamin' all night about Mr Scroope, and I wouldn't wonder, old Cooper, if he was dead,' said the Squire, when he came down in the morning.

'God forbid! I was adreamed about him, too, sir: I dreamed he was dammin' and sinkin' about a hole was burnt in his coat, and the old

master, God be wi' him! said—quite plain—I'd 'a swore 'twas himself—
"Cooper, get up, ye d——d land-loupin' thief, and lend a hand to hang
him—for he's a daft cur, and no dog o' mine." 'Twas the dog shot over
night, I do suppose, as was runnin' in my old head. I thought old master
gied me a punch wi' his knuckles, and says I, wakenin' up, "At yer
service, sir"; and for a while I couldn't get it out o' my head, master was
in the room still.'

Letters from town soon convinced the Squire that his brother
Scroope, so far from being dead, was particularly active; and Charlie's
attorney wrote to say, in serious alarm, that he had heard, accidentally,
that he intended setting up a case, of a supplementary deed of
settlement, of which he had secondary evidence, which would give him
Gylingden. And at this menace Handsome Charlie snapped his fingers,
and wrote courageously to his attorney; abiding what might follow with,
however, a secret foreboding.

Scroope threatened loudly now, and swore after his bitter fashion,
and reiterated his old promise of hanging that cheat at last. In the midst
of these menaces and preparations, however, a sudden peace proclaimed itself: Scroope died, without time even to make provisions for a
posthumous attack upon his brother. It was one of those cases of disease
of the heart in which death is as sudden as by a bullet.

Charlie's exultation was undisguised. It was shocking. Not, of course,
altogether malignant. For there was the expansion consequent on the
removal of a secret fear. There was also the comic piece of luck, that only
the day before Scroope had destroyed his old will, which left to a
stranger every farthing he possessed, intending in a day or two to
execute another to the same person, charged with the express condition
of prosecuting the suit against Charlie.

The result was, that all his possessions went unconditionally to his
brother Charles as his heir. Here were grounds for abundance of savage
elation. But there was also the deep-seated hatred of half a life of mutual
and persistent aggression and revilings; and Handsome Charlie was
capable of nursing a grudge, and enjoying a revenge with his whole
heart.

He would gladly have prevented his brother's being buried in the old
Gylingden chapel, where he wished to lie; but his lawyers doubted his
power, and he was not quite proof against the scandal which would
attend his turning back the funeral, which would, he knew, be attended
by some of the country gentry and others, with an hereditary regard for
the Marstons.

But he warned his servants that not one of them were to attend it;
promising, with oaths and curses not to be disregarded, that any one of

them who did so, should find the door shut in his face on his return.

I don't think, with the exception of old Cooper, that the servants cared for this prohibition, except as it baulked a curiosity always strong in the solitude of the country. Cooper was very much vexed that the eldest son of the old Squire should be buried in the old family chapel, and no sign of decent respect from Gylingden Hall. He asked his master, whether he would not, at least, have some wine and refreshments in the oak parlour, in case any of the country gentlemen who paid this respect to the old family should come up to the house? But the Squire only swore at him, told him to mind his own business, and ordered him to say, if such a thing happened, that he was out, and no preparations made, and, in fact, to send them away as they came. Cooper expostulated stoutly, and the Squire grew angrier; and after a tempestuous scene, took his hat and stick and walked out, just as the funeral descending the valley from the direction of the 'Old Angel Inn' came in sight.

Old Cooper prowled about disconsolately, and counted the carriages as well as he could from the gate. When the funeral was over, and they began to drive away, he returned to the hall, the door of which lay open, and as usual deserted. Before he reached it quite, a mourning coach drove up, and two gentlemen in black cloaks, and with crapes to their hats, got out, and without looking to the right or the left, went up the steps into the house. Cooper followed them slowly. The carriage had, he supposed, gone round to the yard, for, when he reached the door, it was no longer there.

So he followed the two mourners into the house. In the hall he found a fellow-servant, who said he had seen two gentlemen, in black cloaks, pass through the hall, and go up the stairs without removing their hats, or asking leave of anyone. This was very odd, old Cooper thought, and a great liberty; so upstairs he went to make them out.

But he could not find them then, nor ever. And from that hour the house was troubled.

In a little time there was not one of the servants who had not something to tell. Steps and voices followed them sometimes in the passages, and tittering whispers, always minatory, scared them at corners of the galleries, or from dark recesses; so that they would return panic-stricken to be rebuked by thin Mrs Beckett, who looked on such stories as worse than idle. But Mrs Beckett herself, a short time after, took a very different view of the matter.

She had herself begun to hear these voices, and with this formidable aggravation, that they came always when she was at her prayers, which she had been punctual in saying all her life, and utterly interrupted them. She was scared at such moments by dropping words and sentences, which grew, as she persisted, into threats and blasphemies.

These voices were not always in the room. They called, as she fancied, through the walls, very thick in that old house, from the neighbouring apartments, sometimes on one side, sometimes on the other; sometimes they seemed to holloa from distant lobbies, and came muffled, but threateningly, through the long panelled passages. As they approached they grew furious, as if several voices were speaking together. Whenever, as I said, this worthy woman applied herself to her devotions, these horrible sentences came hurrying towards the door, and, in panic, she would start from her knees, and all then would subside except the thumping of her heart against her stays, and the dreadful tremors of her nerves.

What these voices said, Mrs Beckett never could quite remember one minute after they had ceased speaking; one sentence chased another away; gibe and menace and impious denunciation, each hideously articulate, were lost as soon as heard. And this added to the effect of these terrifying mockeries and invectives, that she could not, by any effort, retain their exact import, although their horrible character remained vividly present to her mind.

For a long time the Squire seemed to be the only person in the house absolutely unconscious of these annoyances. Mrs Beckett had twice made up her mind within the week to leave. A prudent woman, however, who has been comfortable for more than twenty years in a place, thinks oftener than twice before she leaves it. She and old Cooper were the only servants in the house who remembered the good old housekeeping in Squire Toby's day. The others were few, and such as could hardly be accounted regular servants. Meg Dobbs, who acted as housemaid, would not sleep in the house, but walked home, in trepidation, to her father's, at the gatehouse, under the escort of her little brother, every night. Old Mrs Beckett, who was high and mighty with the make-shift servants of fallen Gylingden, let herself down all at once, and made Mrs Kymes and the kitchen-maid move their beds into her large and faded room, and there, very frankly, shared her nightly terrors with them.

Old Cooper was testy and captious about these stories. He was already uncomfortable enough by reason of the entrance of the two muffled figures into the house, about which there could be no mistake. His own eyes had seen them. He refused to credit the stories of the women, and affected to think that the two mourners might have left the house and driven away, on finding no one to receive them.

Old Cooper was summoned at night to the oak parlour, where the Squire was smoking.

'I say, Cooper,' said the Squire, looking pale and angry, 'what for ha' you been frightenin' they crazy women wi' your plaguy stories? d—— me, if you see ghosts here it's no place for you, and it's time you should pack. I won't be left without servants. Here has been old Beckett, wi' the cook and the kitchen-maid, as white as pipe-clay, all in a row, to tell me I must have a parson to sleep among them, and preach down the devil! Upon my soul, you're a wise old body, filling their heads wi' maggots! and Meg goes down to the lodge every night, afeared to lie in the house—all your doing, wi' your old wives' stories—ye withered old Tom o' Bedlam!'

'I'm not to blame, Master Charles. 'Tisn't along o' no stories o' mine, for I'm never done tellin' 'em it's all vanity and vapours. Mrs Beckett 'ill tell you that, and there's been many a wry word betwixt us on the head o't. Whate'er I may *think*,' said old Cooper, significantly, and looking askance, with the sternness of fear in the Squire's face.

The Squire averted his eyes, and muttered angrily to himself, and turned away to knock the ashes out of his pipe on the hob, and then turning suddenly round upon Cooper again, he spoke, with a pale face, but not quite so angrily as before.

'I know you're no fool, old Cooper, when you like. Suppose there was such a thing as a ghost here, don't you see, it ain't to them snipe-headed women it 'id go to tell its story. What ails you, man, that you should think aught about it, but just what *I* think? You had a good headpiece o' yer own once, Cooper, don't be you clappin' a goosecap over it, as my poor father used to say; d—— it, old boy, you mustn't let 'em be fools, settin' one another wild wi' their blether, and makin' the folk talk what they shouldn't, about Gylingden and the family. I don't think ye'd like that, old Cooper, I'm sure ye wouldn't. The women has gone out o' the kitchen, make up a bit o' fire, and get your pipe. I'll go to you, when I finish this one, and we'll smoke a bit together, and a glass o' brandy and water.'

Down went the old butler, not altogether unused to such condescensions in that disorderly and lonely household; and let not those who can choose their company, be too hard on the Squire who couldn't.

When he had got things tidy, as he said, he sat down in that big old kitchen, with his feet on the fender, the kitchen candle burning in a great brass candlestick, which stood on the deal table at his elbow, with the brandy bottle and tumblers beside it, and Cooper's pipe also in readiness. And these preparations completed, the old butler, who had remembered other generations and better times, fell into rumination, and so, gradually, into a deep sleep.

Old Cooper was half awakened by some one laughing low, near his head. He was dreaming of old times in the Hall, and fancied one of 'the young gentlemen' going to play him a trick, and he mumbled something in his sleep, from which he was awakened by a stern deep voice, saying, 'You wern't at the funeral; I might take your life, I'll take your ear.' At the same moment, the side of his head received a violent push, and he started to his feet. The fire had gone down, and he was chilled. The candle was expiring in the socket, and threw on the white wall long shadows, that danced up and down from the ceiling to the ground, and their black outlines he fancied resembled the two men in cloaks, whom he remembered with a profound horror.

He took the candle, with all the haste he could, getting along the passage, on whose walls the same dance of black shadows was continued, very anxious to reach his room before the light should go out. He was startled half out of his wits by the sudden clang of his master's bell, close over his head, ringing furiously.

'Ha, ha! There it goes—yes, sure enough,' said Cooper, reassuring himself with the sound of his own voice, as he hastened on, hearing more and more distinct every moment the same furious ringing. 'He's fell asleep, like me; that's it, and his lights is out, I lay you fifty——'

When he turned the handle of the door of the oak parlour, the Squire wildly called, 'Who's *there*?' in the tone of a man who expects a robber.

'It's me, old Cooper, all right, Master Charlie, you didn't come to the kitchen after all, sir.'

'I'm very bad, Cooper; I don't know how I've been. Did you meet anything?' asked the Squire.

'No,' said Cooper.

They stared on one another.

'Come here—stay here! Don't you leave me! Look round the room, and say is all right; and gie us your hand, old Cooper, for I must hold it.' The Squire's was damp and cold, and trembled very much. It was not very far from day-break now.

After a time he spoke again: 'I 'a done many a thing I shouldn't; I'm not fit to go, and wi' God's blessin' I'll look to it—why shouldn't I? I'm as lame as old Billy—I'll never be able to do any good no more, and I'll give over drinking, and marry, as I ought to 'a done long ago—none o' yer fine ladies, but a good homely wench; there's Farmer Crump's youngest daughter, a good lass, and discreet. What for shouldn't I take her? She'd take care o' me, and wouldn't bring a head full o' romances here, and mantua-makers' trumpery, and I'll talk with the parson, and I'll do what's fair wi' everyone; and mind, I said I'm sorry for many a thing I 'a done.'

A wild cold dawn had by this time broken. The Squire, Cooper said, looked 'awful bad', as he got his hat and stick, and sallied out for a walk, instead of going to his bed, as Cooper besought him, looking so wild and distracted, that it was plain his object was simply to escape from the house. It was twelve o'clock when the Squire walked into the kitchen, where he was sure of finding some of the servants, looking as if ten years had passed over him since yesterday. He pulled a stool by the fire, without speaking a word, and sat down. Cooper had sent to Applebury for the doctor, who had just arrived, but the Squire would not go to him. 'If he wants to see me, he may come here,' he muttered as often as Cooper urged him. So the doctor did come, charily enough, and found the Squire very much worse than he had expected.

The Squire resisted the order to get to his bed. But the doctor insisted under a threat of death, at which his patient quailed.

'Well, I'll do what you say—only this—you must let old Cooper and Dick Keeper stay wi' me. I mustn't be left alone, and they must keep awake o' nights; and stay a while, do *you*. When I get round a bit, I'll go and live in a town. It's dull livin' here, now that I can't do nout, as I used, and I'll live a better life, mind ye; ye heard me say that, and I don't care who laughs, and I'll talk wi' the parson. I like 'em to laugh, hang 'em, it's a sign I'm doin' right, at last.'

The doctor sent a couple of nurses from the County Hospital, not choosing to trust his patient to the management he had selected, and he went down himself to Gylingden to meet them in the evening. Old Cooper was ordered to occupy the dressing-room, and sit up at night, which satisfied the Squire, who was in a strangely excited state, very low, and threatened, the doctor said, with fever.

The clergyman came, an old, gentle, 'book-learned' man, and talked and prayed with him late that evening. After he had gone the Squire called the nurses to his bedside, and said:

'There's a fellow sometimes comes; you'll never mind him. He looks in at the door and beckons,—a thin, hump-backed chap in mourning, wi' black gloves on; ye'll know him by his lean face, as brown as the wainscot: don't ye mind his smilin'. You don't go out to him, nor ask him in; he won't say nout; and if he grows anger'd and looks awry at ye, don't ye be afeared, for he can't hurt ye, and he'll grow tired waitin', and go away; and for God's sake mind ye don't ask him in, nor go out after him!'

The nurses put their heads together when this was over, and held afterwards a whispering conference with old Cooper. 'Law bless ye!— no, there's no madman in the house,' he protested; 'not a soul but what ye saw,—it's just a trifle o' the fever in his head—no more.'

The Squire grew worse as the night wore on. He was heavy and delirious, talking of all sorts of things—of wine and dogs, and lawyers; and then he began to talk, as it were, to his brother Scroope. As he did so, Mrs Oliver, the nurse, who was sitting up alone with him, heard, as she thought, a hand softly laid on the door-handle outside, and a stealthy attempt to turn it. 'Lord bless us! who's there?' she cried, and her heart jumped into her mouth, as she thought of the hump-backed man in black, who was to put in his head smiling and beckoning—'Mr Cooper! sir! are you there?' she cried. 'Come here, Mr Cooper, please—do, sir, quick!'

Old Cooper, called up from his doze by the fire, stumbled in from the dressing-room, and Mrs Oliver seized him tightly as he emerged.

'The man with the hump has been atryin' the door, Mr Cooper, as sure as I am here.' The Squire was moaning and mumbling in his fever, understanding nothing, as she spoke. 'No, no! Mrs Oliver, ma'am, it's impossible, for there's no sich man in the house: what is Master Charlie sayin'?'

'He's saying *Scroope* every minute, whatever he means by that, and—and—hisht!—listen—there's the handle again,' and, with a loud scream, she added—'Look at his head and neck in at the door!' and in her tremor she strained old Cooper in an agonizing embrace.

The candle was flaring, and there was a wavering shadow at the door that looked like the head of a man with a long neck, and a longish sharp nose, peeping in and drawing back.

'Don't be a d—— fool, ma'am!' cried Cooper, very white, and shaking her with all his might. 'It's only the candle, I tell you—nothing in life but that. Don't you see?' and he raised the light; 'and I'm sure there was no one at the door, and I'll try, if you let me go.'

The other nurse was asleep on the sofa, and Mrs Oliver called her up in a panic, for company, as old Cooper opened the door. There was no one near it, but at the angle of the gallery was a shadow resembling that which he had seen in the room. He raised the candle a little, and it seemed to beckon with a long hand as the head drew back. 'Shadow from the candle!' exclaimed Cooper aloud, resolved not to yield to Mrs Oliver's panic; and, candle in hand, he walked to the corner. There was nothing. He could not forbear peeping down the long gallery from this point, and as he moved the light, he saw precisely the same sort of shadow, a little further down, and as he advanced the same withdrawal, and beckon. 'Gammon!' said he; 'it is nout but the candle.' And on he went, growing half angry and half frightened at the persistency with which this ugly shadow—a literal shadow he was sure it was—presented itself. As he drew near the point where it now appeared, it seemed to collect itself, and nearly dissolve in the central panel of an old carved cabinet which he was now approaching.

In the centre panel of this is a sort of boss carved into a wolf's head. The light fell oddly upon this, and the fugitive shadow seemed to be breaking up, and re-arranging itself as oddly. The eye-ball gleamed with a point of reflected light, which glittered also upon the grinning mouth, and he saw the long, sharp nose of Scroope Marston, and his fierce eye looking at him, he thought, with a steadfast meaning.

Old Cooper stood gazing upon this sight, unable to move, till he saw the face, and the figure that belonged to it, begin gradually to emerge from the wood. At the same time he heard voices approaching rapidly up a side gallery, and Cooper, with a loud 'Lord a-mercy on us!' turned and ran back again, pursued by a sound that seemed to shake the old house like a mighty gust of wind.

Into his master's room burst old Cooper, half wild with fear, and clapped the door and turned the key in a twinkling, looking as if he had been pursued by murderers.

'Did you hear it?' whispered Cooper, now standing near the dressing-room door. They all listened, but not a sound from without disturbed the utter stillness of night. 'God bless us! I doubt it's my old head that's gone crazy!' exclaimed Cooper.

He would tell them nothing but that he was himself 'an old fool', to be frightened by their talk, and that 'the rattle of a window, or the dropping o' a pin' was enough to scare him now; and so he helped himself through that night with brandy, and sat up talking by his master's fire.

The Squire recovered slowly from his brain fever, but not perfectly. A very little thing, the doctor said, would suffice to upset him. He was not yet sufficiently strong to remove for change of scene and air, which were necessary for his complete restoration.

Cooper slept in the dressing-room, and was now his only nightly attendant. The ways of the invalid were odd: he liked, half sitting up in his bed, to smoke his churchwarden o' nights, and made old Cooper smoke, for company, at the fire-side. As the Squire and his humble friend indulged in it, smoking is a taciturn pleasure, and it was not until the Master of Gylingden had finished his third pipe that he essayed conversation, and when he did, the subject was not such as Cooper would have chosen.

'I say, old Cooper, look in my face, and don't be afeared to speak out,' said the Squire, looking at him with a steady, cunning smile; 'you know all this time, as well as I do, who's in the house. You needn't deny— hey?—Scroope and my father?'

'Don't you be talking like that, Charlie,' said old Cooper, rather sternly and frightened, after a long silence; still looking in his face, which did not change.

'What's the good o' shammin', Cooper? Scroope's took the hearin' o' yer right ear—you know he did. He's looking angry. He's nigh took my life wi' this fever. But he's not done wi' me yet, and he looks awful wicked. Ye saw him—ye know ye did.'

Cooper was awfully frightened, and the odd smile on the Squire's lips frightened him still more. He dropped his pipe, and stood gazing in silence at his master, and feeling as if he were in a dream.

'If ye think so, ye should not be smiling like that,' said Cooper, grimly.

'I'm tired, Cooper, and it's as well to smile as t'other thing; so I'll even smile while I can. You know what they mean to do wi' me. That's all I wanted to say. Now, lad, go on wi' yer pipe—I'm goin' asleep.'

So the Squire turned over in his bed, and lay down serenely, with his head on the pillow. Old Cooper looked at him, and glanced at the door, and then half-filled his tumbler with brandy, and drank it off, and felt better, and got to his bed in the dressing-room.

In the dead of night he was suddenly awakened by the Squire, who was standing, in his dressing-gown and slippers, by his bed.

'I've brought you a bit o' a present. I got the rents o' Hazelden yesterday, and ye'll keep that for yourself—it's a fifty—and give t' other to Nelly Carwell, tomorrow; I'll sleep the sounder; and I saw Scroope since; he's not such a bad 'un after all, old fellow! He's got a crape over his face—for I told him I couldn't bear it; and I'd do many a thing for him now. I never could stand shilly-shally. Good-night, old Cooper!'

And the Squire laid his trembling hand kindly on the old man's shoulder, and returned to his own room. 'I don't half like how he is. Doctor don't come half often enough. I don't like that queer smile o' his, and his hand was as cold as death. I hope in God his brain's not a-turnin'!'

With these reflections, he turned to the pleasanter subject of his present, and at last fell asleep.

In the morning, when he went into the Squire's room, the Squire had left his bed. 'Never mind; he'll come back, like a bad shillin',' thought old Cooper, preparing the room as usual. But he did not return. Then began an uneasiness, succeeded by a panic, when it began to be plain that the Squire was not in the house. What had become of him? None of his clothes, but his dressing-gown and slippers, were missing. Had he left the house, in his present sickly state, in that garb? and, if so, could he be in his right senses; and was there a chance of his surviving a cold, damp night, so passed, in the open air?

Tom Edwards was up to the house, and told them, that, walking a mile or so that morning, at four o'clock—there being no moon—along with Farmer Nokes, who was driving his cart to market, in the dark, three men walked, in front of the horse, not twenty yards before them, all the way from near Gylingden Lodge to the burial-ground, the gate of which was opened for them from within, and the three men entered, and the gate was shut. Tom Edwards thought they were gone in to make preparation for a funeral of some member of the Marston family. But the occurrence seemed to Cooper, who knew there was no such thing, horribly ominous.

He now commenced a careful search, and at last bethought him of the lonely upper storey, and King Herod's chamber. He saw nothing changed there, but the closet door was shut, and, dark as was the morning, something, like a large white knot sticking out over the door, caught his eye.

The door resisted his efforts to open it for a time; some great weight forced it down against the floor; at length, however, it did yield a little, and a heavy crash, shaking the whole floor, and sending an echo flying through all the silent corridors, with a sound like receding laughter, half stunned him.

When he pushed open the door, his master was lying dead upon the floor. His cravat was drawn halter-wise tight round his throat, and had done its work well. The body was cold, and had been long dead.

In due course the coroner held his inquest, and the jury pronounced, 'that the deceased, Charles Marston, had died by his own hand, in a state of temporary insanity.' But old Cooper had his own opinion about the Squire's death, though his lips were sealed, and he never spoke about it. He went and lived for the residue of his days in York, where there are still people who remember him, a taciturn and surly old man, who attended church regularly, and also drank a little, and was known to have saved some money.

The Shadow in the Corner

M. E. BRADDON

Wildheath Grange stood a little way back from the road, with a barren stretch of heath behind it, and a few tall fir-trees, with straggling wind-tossed heads, for its only shelter. It was a lonely house on a lonely road, little better than a lane, leading across a desolate waste of sandy fields to the sea-shore; and it was a house that bore a bad name among the natives of the village of Holcroft, which was the nearest place where humanity might be found.

It was a good old house, nevertheless, substantially built in the days when there was no stint of stone and timber—a good old grey stone house with many gables, deep window-seats, and a wide staircase, long dark passages, hidden doors in queer corners, closets as large as some modern rooms, and cellars in which a company of soldiers might have lain perdu.

This spacious old mansion was given over to rats and mice, loneliness, echoes, and the occupation of three elderly people: Michael Bascom, whose forebears had been landowners of importance in the neighbourhood, and his two servants, Daniel Skegg and his wife, who had served the owner of that grim old house ever since he left the university, where he had lived fifteen years of his life—five as student, and ten as professor of natural science.

At three-and-thirty Michael Bascom had seemed a middle-aged man; at fifty-six he looked and moved and spoke like an old man. During that interval of twenty-three years he had lived alone in Wildheath Grange, and the country people told each other that the house had made him what he was. This was a fanciful and superstitious notion on their part, doubtless, yet it would not have been difficult to have traced a certain affinity between the dull grey building and the man who lived in it. Both seemed alike remote from the common cares and interests of humanity; both had an air of settled melancholy, engendered by perpetual solitude; both had the same faded complexion, the same look of slow decay.

Yet lonely as Michael Bascom's life was at Wildheath Grange, he would not on any account have altered its tenor. He had been glad to exchange the comparative seclusion of college rooms for the unbroken solitude of Wildheath. He was a fanatic in his love of scientific research, and his quiet days were filled to the brim with labours that seldom failed to interest and satisfy him. There were periods of depression, occasional moments of doubt, when the goal towards which he strove seemed unattainable, and his spirit fainted within him. Happily such times were rare with him. He had a dogged power of continuity which ought to have carried him to the highest pinnacle of achievement, and which perhaps might ultimately have won for him a grand name and a world-wide renown, but for a catastrophe which burdened the declining years of his harmless life with an unconquerable remorse.

One autumn morning—when he had lived just three-and-twenty years at Wildheath, and had only lately begun to perceive that his faithful butler and body servant, who was middle-aged when he first employed him, was actually getting old—Mr Bascom's breakfast meditations over the latest treatise on the atomic theory were interrupted by an abrupt demand from that very Daniel Skegg. The man was accustomed to wait upon his master in the most absolute silence, and his sudden breaking out into speech was almost as startling as if the bust of Socrates above the bookcase had burst into human language.

'It's no use,' said Daniel; 'my missus must have a girl!'

'A what?' demanded Mr Bascom, without taking his eyes from the line he had been reading.

'A girl—a girl to trot about and wash up, and help the old lady. She's getting weak on her legs, poor soul. We've none of us grown younger in the last twenty years.'

'Twenty years!' echoed Michael Bascom scornfully. 'What is twenty years in the formation of a strata—what even in the growth of an oak—the cooling of a volcano!'

'Not much, perhaps, but it's apt to tell upon the bones of a human being.'

'The manganese staining to be seen upon some skulls would certainly indicate——' began the scientist dreamily.

'I wish my bones were only as free from rheumatics as they were twenty years ago,' pursued Daniel testily; 'and then, perhaps, I should make light of twenty years. Howsoever, the long and the short of it is, my missus must have a girl. She can't go on trotting up and down these everlasting passages, and standing in that stony scullery year after year, just as if she was a young woman. She must have a girl to help.'

'Let her have twenty girls,' said Mr Bascom, going back to his book.

'What's the use of talking like that, sir. Twenty girls, indeed! We shall have rare work to get one.'

'Because the neighbourhood is sparsely populated?' interrogated Mr Bascom, still reading.

'No, sir. Because this house is known to be haunted.'

Michael Bascom laid down his book, and turned a look of grave reproach upon his servant.

'Skegg,' he said in a severe voice, 'I thought you had lived long enough with me to be superior to any folly of that kind.'

'I don't say that I believe in ghosts,' answered Daniel with a semi-apologetic air; 'but the country people do. There's not a mortal among 'em that will venture across our threshold after nightfall.'

'Merely because Anthony Bascom, who led a wild life in London, and lost his money and land, came home here broken-hearted, and is supposed to have destroyed himself in this house—the only remnant of property that was left him out of a fine estate.'

'Supposed to have destroyed himself!' cried Skegg; 'why the fact is as well known as the death of Queen Elizabeth, or the great fire of London. Why, wasn't he buried at the cross-roads between here and Holcroft?'

'An idle tradition, for which you could produce no substantial proof,' retorted Mr Bascom.

'I don't know about proof; but the country people believe it as firmly as they believe their Gospel.'

'If their faith in the Gospel was a little stronger they need not trouble themselves about Anthony Bascom.'

'Well,' grumbled Daniel, as he began to clear the table, 'a girl of some kind we must get, but she'll have to be a foreigner, or a girl that's hard driven for a place.'

When Daniel Skegg said a foreigner, he did not mean the native of some distant clime, but a girl who had not been born and bred at Holcroft. Daniel had been raised and reared in that insignificant hamlet, and, small and dull as it was, he considered the world beyond it only margin.

Michael Bascom was too deep in the atomic theory to give a second thought to the necessities of an old servant. Mrs Skegg was an individual with whom he rarely came in contact. She lived for the most part in a gloomy region at the north end of the house, where she ruled over the solitude of a kitchen, that looked like a cathedral, and numerous offices of the scullery, larder, and pantry class, where she carried on a perpetual warfare with spiders and beetles, and wore her old life out in the labour of sweeping and scrubbing. She was a woman of severe aspect, dogmatic piety, and a bitter tongue. She was a good plain cook, and ministered diligently to her master's wants. He was not an epicure, but liked his life to be smooth and easy, and the equilibrium of his mental power would have been disturbed by a bad dinner.

He heard no more about the proposed addition to his household for a space of ten days, when Daniel Skegg again startled him amidst his studious repose by the abrupt announcement:

'I've got a girl!'

'Oh,' said Michael Bascom; 'have you?' and he went on with his book.

This time he was reading an essay on phosphorus and its functions in relation to the human brain.

'Yes,' pursued Daniel in his usual grumbling tone; 'she was a waif and stray, or I shouldn't have got her. If she'd been a native she'd never have come to us.'

'I hope she's respectable,' said Michael.

'Respectable! That's the only fault she has, poor thing. She's too good for the place. She's never been in service before, but she says she's willing to work, and I daresay my old woman will be able to break her in. Her father was a small tradesman at Yarmouth. He died a month ago, and left this poor thing homeless. Mrs Midge, at Holcroft, is her aunt, and she said to the girl, Come and stay with me till you get a place; and the girl has been staying with Mrs Midge for the last three weeks, trying to hear of a place. When Mrs Midge heard that my missus wanted a girl to help, she thought it would be the very thing for her niece Maria. Luckily Maria had heard nothing about this house, so the poor innocent dropped me a curtsey, and said she'd be thankful to come, and would do her best to learn her duty. She'd had an easy time of it with her father, who had educated her above her station, like a fool as he was,' growled Daniel.

'By your own account I'm afraid you've made a bad bargain,' said Michael. 'You don't want a young lady to clean kettles and pans.'

'If she was a young duchess my old woman would make her work,' retorted Skegg decisively.

'And pray where are you going to put this girl?' asked Mr Bascom, rather irritably; 'I can't have a strange young woman tramping up and down the passages outside my room. You know what a wretched sleeper I am, Skegg. A mouse behind the wainscot is enough to wake me.'

'I've thought of that,' answered the butler, with his look of ineffable wisdom. 'I'm not going to put her on your floor. She's to sleep in the attics.'

'Which room?'

'The big one at the north end of the house. That's the only ceiling that doesn't let water. She might as well sleep in a shower-bath as in any of the other attics.'

'The room at the north end,' repeated Mr Bascom thoughtfully; 'isn't that——?'

'Of course it is,' snapped Skegg; 'but she doesn't know anything about it.'

Mr Bascom went back to his books, and forgot all about the orphan from Yarmouth, until one morning on entering his study he was startled by the appearance of a strange girl, in a neat black and white cotton gown, busy dusting the volumes which were stacked in blocks upon his spacious writing-table—and doing it with such deft and careful hands that he had no inclination to be angry at this unwonted liberty. Old Mrs Skegg had religiously refrained from all such dusting, on the plea that she did not wish to interfere with the master's ways. One of the master's ways, therefore, had been to inhale a good deal of dust in the course of his studies.

The girl was a slim little thing, with a pale and somewhat old-fashioned face, flaxen hair, braided under a neat muslin cap, a very fair complexion, and light blue eyes. They were the lightest blue eyes Michael Bascom had ever seen, but there was a sweetness and gentleness in their expression which atoned for their insipid colour.

'I hope you do not object to my dusting your books, sir,' she said, dropping a curtsey.

She spoke with a quaint precision which struck Michael Bascom as a pretty thing in its way.

'No; I don't object to cleanliness, so long as my books and papers are not disturbed. If you take a volume off my desk, replace it on the spot you took it from. That's all I ask.'

'I will be very careful, sir.'

'When did you come here?'

'Only this morning, sir.'

The student seated himself at his desk, and the girl withdrew, drifting out of the room as noiselessly as a flower blown across the threshold. Michael Bascom looked after her curiously. He had seen very little of youthful womanhood in his dry-as-dust career, and he wondered at this girl as at a creature of a species hitherto unknown to him. How fairly and delicately she was fashioned; what a translucent skin; what soft and pleasing accents issued from those rose-tinted lips. A pretty thing, assuredly, this kitchen wench! A pity that in all this busy world there could be no better work found for her than the scouring of pots and pans.

Absorbed in considerations about dry bones, Mr Bascom thought no more of the pale-faced handmaiden. He saw her no more about his rooms. Whatever work she did there was done early in the morning, before the scholar's breakfast.

She had been a week in the house, when he met her one day in the hall. He was struck by the change in her appearance.

The girlish lips had lost their rose-bud hue; the pale blue eyes had a frightened look, and there were dark rings round them, as in one whose nights had been sleepless, or troubled by evil dreams.

Michael Bascom was so startled by an undefinable look in the girl's face that, reserved as he was by habit and nature, he expanded so far as to ask her what ailed her.

'There is something amiss, I am sure,' he said. 'What is it?'

'Nothing, sir,' she faltered, looking still more scared at his question. 'Indeed, it is nothing; or nothing worth troubling you about.'

'Nonsense. Do you suppose, because I live among books, I have no sympathy with my fellow-creatures? Tell me what is wrong with you, child. You have been grieving about the father you have lately lost, I suppose.'

'No, sir; it is not that. I shall never leave off being sorry for that. It is a grief which will last me all my life.'

'What, there is something else then?' asked Michael impatiently. 'I see; you are not happy here. Hard work does not suit you. I thought as much.'

'Oh, sir, please don't think that,' cried the girl, very earnestly. 'Indeed, I am glad to work—glad to be in service; it is only——'

She faltered and broke down, the tears rolling slowly from her sorrowful eyes, despite her effort to keep them back.

'Only what?' cried Michael, growing angry. 'The girl is full of secrets and mysteries. What do you mean, wench?'

'I—I know it is very foolish, sir; but I am afraid of the room where I sleep.'

'Afraid! Why?'

'Shall I tell you the truth, sir? Will you promise not to be angry?'

'I will not be angry if you will only speak plainly; but you provoke me by these hesitations and suppressions.'

'And please, sir, do not tell Mrs Skegg that I have told you. She would scold me; or perhaps even send me away.'

'Mrs Skegg shall not scold you. Go on, child.'

'You may not know the room where I sleep, sir; it is a large room at one end of the house, looking towards the sea. I can see the dark line of water from the window, and I wonder sometimes to think that it is the same ocean I used to see when I was a child at Yarmouth. It is very lonely, sir, at the top of the house. Mr and Mrs Skegg sleep in a little room near the kitchen, you know, sir, and I am quite alone on the top floor.'

'Skegg told me you had been educated in advance of your position in life, Maria. I should have thought the first effect of a good education would have been to make you superior to any foolish fancies about empty rooms.'

'Oh, pray, sir, do not think it is any fault in my education. Father took such pains with me; he spared no expense in giving me as good an education as a tradesman's daughter need wish for. And he was a religious man, sir. He did not believe'—here she paused, with a suppressed shudder—'in the spirits of the dead appearing to the living, since the days of miracles, when the ghost of Samuel appeared to Saul. He never put any foolish ideas into my head, sir. I hadn't a thought of fear when I first lay down to rest in the big lonely room upstairs.'

'Well, what then?'

'But on the very first night,' the girl went on breathlessly, 'I felt weighed down in my sleep as if there were some heavy burden laid upon my chest. It was not a bad dream, but it was a sense of trouble that followed me all through my sleep; and just at daybreak—it begins to be light a little after six—I woke suddenly, with the cold perspiration pouring down my face, and knew that there was something dreadful in the room.'

'What do you mean by something dreadful. Did you see anything?'

'Not much, sir; but it froze the blood in my veins, and I knew it was this that had been following me and weighing upon me all through my sleep. In the corner, between the fire-place and the wardrobe, I saw a shadow—a dim, shapeless shadow——'

'Produced by an angle of the wardrobe, I daresay.'

'No, sir; I could see the shadow of the wardrobe, distinct and sharp, as if it had been painted on the wall. This shadow was in the corner—a strange, shapeless mass; or, if it had any shape at all, it seemed——'

'What?' asked Michael eagerly.

'The shape of a dead body hanging against the wall!'

Michael Bascom grew strangely pale, yet he affected utter incredulity.

'Poor child,' he said kindly; 'you have been fretting about your father until your nerves are in a weak state, and you are full of fancies. A shadow in the corner, indeed; why, at daybreak, every corner is full of shadows. My old coat, flung upon a chair, will make you as good a ghost as you need care to see.'

'Oh, sir, I have tried to think it is my fancy. But I have had the same burden weighing me down every night. I have seen the same shadow every morning.'

'But when broad daylight comes, can you not see what stuff your shadow is made of?'

'No, sir: the shadow goes before it is broad daylight.'

'Of course, just like other shadows. Come, come, get these silly notions out of your head, or you will never do for the work-a-day world. I could easily speak to Mrs Skegg, and make her give you another room, if I wanted to encourage you in your folly. But that would be about the worst thing I could do for you. Besides, she tells me that all the other rooms on that floor are damp; and, no doubt, if she shifted you into one of them, you would discover another shadow in another corner, and get rheumatism into the bargain. No, my good girl, you must try to prove yourself the better for a superior education.'

'I will do my best, sir,' Maria answered meekly, dropping a curtsey.

Maria went back to the kitchen sorely depressed. It was a dreary life she led at Wildheath Grange—dreary by day, awful by night; for the vague burden and the shapeless shadow, which seemed so slight a matter to the elderly scholar, were unspeakably terrible to her. Nobody had told her that the house was haunted, yet she walked about those echoing passages wrapped round with a cloud of fear. She had no pity from Daniel Skegg and his wife. Those two pious souls had made up their minds that the character of the house should be upheld, so far as Maria went. To her, as a foreigner, the Grange should be maintained to be an immaculate dwelling, tainted by no sulphurous blast from the under world. A willing, biddable girl had become a necessary element in the existence of Mrs Skegg. That girl had been found, and that girl must be kept. Any fancies of a supernatural character must be put down with a high hand.

'Ghosts, indeed!' cried the amiable Skegg. 'Read your Bible, Maria, and don't talk no more about ghosts.'

'There are ghosts in the Bible,' said Maria, with a shiver at the recollection of certain awful passages in the Scripture she knew so well.

'Ah, they was in their right place, or they wouldn't ha' been there,' retorted Mrs Skegg. 'You ain't agoin' to pick holes in your Bible, I hope, Maria, at your time of life.'

Maria sat down quietly in her corner by the kitchen fire, and turned over the leaves of her dead father's Bible till she came to the chapters they two had loved best and oftenest read together. He had been a simple-minded, straightforward man, the Yarmouth cabinet-maker—a man full of aspirations after good, innately refined, instinctively religious. He and his motherless girl had spent their lives alone together, in the neat little home which Maria had so soon learnt to cherish and beautify; and they had loved each other with an almost romantic love. They had had the same tastes, the same ideas. Very little had sufficed to make them happy. But inexorable death parted father and daughter, in one of those sharp, sudden partings which are like the shock of an earthquake—instantaneous ruin, desolation, and despair.

Maria's fragile form had bent before the tempest. She had lived through a trouble that might have crushed a stronger nature. Her deep religious convictions, and her belief that this cruel parting would not be for ever, had sustained her. She faced life, and its cares and duties, with a gentle patience which was the noblest form of courage.

Michael Bascom told himself that the servant-girl's foolish fancy about the room that had been given her was not a matter of serious consideration. Yet the idea dwelt in his mind unpleasantly, and disturbed him at his labours. The exact sciences require the complete power of a man's brain, his utmost attention; and on this particular evening Michael found that he was only giving his work a part of his attention. The girl's pale face, the girl's tremulous tones, thrust themselves into the foreground of his thoughts.

He closed his book with a fretful sigh, wheeled his large arm-chair round to the fire, and gave himself up to contemplation. To attempt study with so disturbed a mind was useless. It was a dull grey evening, early in November; the student's reading-lamp was lighted, but the shutters were not yet shut, nor the curtains drawn. He could see the leaden sky outside his windows, the fir-tree tops tossing in the angry wind. He could hear the wintry blast whistling amidst the gables, before it rushed off seaward with a savage howl that sounded like a war-whoop.

Michael Bascom shivered, and drew nearer the fire.

'It's childish, foolish nonsense,' he said to himself; 'yet it's strange she should have that fancy about the shadow, for they say Anthony Bascom destroyed himself in that room. I remember hearing it when I was a boy, from an old servant whose mother was housekeeper at the great house in Anthony's time. I never heard how he died, poor fellow—whether he poisoned himself, or shot himself, or cut his throat; but I've been told that was the room. Old Skegg has heard it too. I could see that by his manner when he told me the girl was to sleep there.'

He sat for a long time, till the grey of evening outside his study windows changed to the black of night, and the war-whoop of the wind died away to a low complaining murmur. He sat looking into the fire, and letting his thoughts wander back to the past and the traditions he had heard in his boyhood.

That was a sad, foolish story of his great-uncle, Anthony Bascom: the pitiful story of a wasted fortune and a wasted life. A riotous collegiate career at Cambridge, a racing-stable at Newmarket, an imprudent marriage, a dissipated life in London, a runaway wife; an estate forfeited to Jew money-lenders, and then the fatal end.

Michael had often heard that dismal story: how, when Anthony Bascom's fair false wife had left him, when his credit was exhausted, and his friends had grown tired of him, and all was gone except Wildheath Grange, Anthony, the broken-down man of fashion, had come to that lonely house unexpectedly one night, and had ordered his bed to be got ready for him in the room where he used to sleep when he came to the place for the wild duck shooting, in his boyhood. His old blunderbuss was still hanging over the mantelpiece, where he had left it when he came into the property, and could afford to buy the newest thing in fowling-pieces. He had not been to Wildheath for fifteen years; nay, for a good many of those years he had almost forgotten that the dreary old house belonged to him.

The woman who had been housekeeper at Bascom Park, till house and lands had passed into the hands of the Jews, was at this time the sole occupant of Wildheath. She cooked some supper for her master, and made him as comfortable as she could in the long untenanted dining-room; but she was distressed to find, when she cleared the table after he had gone upstairs to bed, that he had eaten hardly anything.

Next morning she got his breakfast ready in the same room, which she managed to make brighter and cheerier than it had looked overnight. Brooms, dusting-brushes, and a good fire did much to improve the aspect of things. But the morning wore on to noon, and the old housekeeper listened in vain for her master's footfall on the stairs. Noon waned to late afternoon. She had made no attempt to disturb him, thinking that he had worn himself out by a tedious journey on horseback, and that he was sleeping the sleep of exhaustion. But when the brief November day clouded with the first shadows of twilight, the old woman grew seriously alarmed, and went upstairs to her master's door, where she waited in vain for any reply to her repeated calls and knockings.

The door was locked on the inside, and the housekeeper was not strong enough to break it open. She rushed downstairs again full of fear, and ran bare-headed out into the lonely road. There was no habitation nearer than the turnpike on the old coach road, from which this side road branched off to the sea. There was scanty hope of a chance passer-by. The old woman ran along the road, hardly knowing whither she was going or what she was going to do, but with a vague idea that she must get somebody to help her.

Chance favoured her. A cart, laden with sea-weed, came lumbering slowly along from the level line of sands yonder where the land melted into water. A heavy lumbering farm-labourer walked beside the cart.

'For God's sake, come in and burst open my master's door!' she entreated, seizing the man by the arm. 'He's lying dead, or in a fit, and I can't get to help him.'

'All right, missus,' answered the man, as if such an invitation were a matter of daily occurrence. 'Whoa, Dobbin; stond still, horse, and be donged to thee.'

Dobbin was glad enough to be brought to anchor on the patch of waste grass in front of the Grange garden. His master followed the housekeeper upstairs, and shattered the old-fashioned box-lock with one blow of his ponderous fist.

The old woman's worst fear was realised. Anthony Bascom was dead. But the mode and manner of his death Michael had never been able to learn. The housekeeper's daughter, who told him the story, was an old woman when he was a boy. She had only shaken her head, and looked unutterable things, when he questioned her too closely. She had never even admitted that the old squire had committed suicide. Yet the tradition of his self-destruction was rooted in the minds of the natives of Holcroft: and there was a settled belief that his ghost, at certain times and seasons, haunted Wildheath Grange.

Now Michael Bascom was a stern materialist. For him the universe, with all its inhabitants, was a great machine, governed by inexorable laws. To such a man the idea of a ghost was simply absurd—as absurd as the assertion that two and two make five, or that a circle can be formed of a straight line. Yet he had a kind of dilettante interest in the idea of a mind which could believe in ghosts. The subject offered an amusing psychological study. This poor little pale girl, now, had evidently got some supernatural terror into her head, which could only be conquered by rational treatment.

'I know what I ought to do,' Michael Bascom said to himself suddenly. 'I'll occupy that room myself tonight, and demonstrate to this foolish girl that her notion about the shadow is nothing more than a silly fancy, bred of timidity and low spirits. An ounce of proof is better than a pound of argument. If I can prove to her that I have spent a night in the room, and seen no such shadow, she will understand what an idle thing superstition is.'

Daniel came in presently to shut the shutters.

'Tell your wife to make up my bed in the room where Maria has been sleeping, and to put her into one of the rooms on the first floor for to-night, Skegg,' said Mr Bascom.

'Sir?'

Mr Bascom repeated his order.

'That silly wench has been complaining to you about her room,' Skegg exclaimed indignantly. 'She doesn't deserve to be well fed and cared for in a comfortable home. She ought to go to the workhouse.'

'Don't be angry with the poor girl, Skegg. She has taken a foolish fancy into her head, and I want to show her how silly she is,' said Mr Bascom.

'And you want to sleep in his—in that room yourself,' said the butler.

'Precisely.'

'Well,' mused Skegg, 'if he does walk—which I don't believe—he was your own flesh and blood; and I don't suppose he'll do you any hurt.'

When Daniel Skegg went back to the kitchen he railed mercilessly at poor Maria, who sat pale and silent in her corner by the hearth, darning old Mrs Skegg's grey worsted stockings, which were the roughest and harshest armour that ever human foot clothed itself withal. 'Was there ever such a whimsical, fine, lady-like miss,' demanded Daniel, 'to come into a gentleman's house, and drive him out of his own bedroom to sleep in an attic, with her nonsenses and vagaries.' If this was the result of being educated above one's station, Daniel declared that he was thankful he had never got so far in his schooling as to read words of two syllables without spelling. Education might be hanged for him, if this was all it led to.

'I am very sorry,' faltered Maria, weeping silently over her work. 'Indeed, Mr Skegg, I made no complaint. My master questioned me, and I told him the truth. That was all.'

'All!' exclaimed Mr Skegg irately; 'all, indeed! I should think it was enough.'

Poor Maria held her peace. Her mind, fluttered by Daniel's unkindness, had wandered away from that bleak big kitchen to the lost home of the past—the snug little parlour where she and her father had sat beside the cosy hearth on such a night as this; she with her smart work-box and her plain sewing, he with the newspaper he loved to read; the petted cat purring on the rug, the kettle singing on the bright brass trivet, the tea-tray pleasantly suggestive of the most comfortable meal in the day.

Oh, those happy nights, that dear companionship! Were they really gone for ever, leaving nothing behind them but unkindness and servitude?

Michael Bascom retired later than usual that night. He was in the habit of sitting at his books long after every other lamp but his own had been extinguished. The Skeggs had subsided into silence and darkness in their dreary ground-floor bed-chamber. Tonight his studies were of a peculiarly interesting kind, and belonged to the order of recreative reading rather than of hard work. He was deep in the history of that mysterious people who had their dwelling-place in the Swiss lakes, and was much exercised by certain speculations and theories about them.

The old eight-day clock on the stairs was striking two as Michael slowly ascended, candle in hand, to the hitherto unknown region of the attics. At the top of the staircase he found himself facing a dark narrow passage which led northwards, a passage that was in itself sufficient to strike terror to a superstitious mind, so black and uncanny did it look.

'Poor child,' mused Mr Bascom, thinking of Maria; 'this attic floor is rather dreary, and for a young mind prone to fancies——'

He had opened the door of the north room by this time, and stood looking about him.

It was a large room, with a ceiling that sloped on one side, but was fairly lofty upon the other; an old-fashioned room, full of old-fashioned furniture—big, ponderous, clumsy—associated with a day that was gone and people that were dead. A walnut-wood wardrobe stared him in the face—a wardrobe with brass handles, which gleamed out of the darkness like diabolical eyes. There was a tall four-post bedstead, which had been cut down on one side to accommodate the slope of the ceiling, and which had a misshapen and deformed aspect in consequence. There was an old mahogany bureau, that smelt of secrets. There were some heavy old chairs with rush bottoms, mouldy with age, and much worn. There was a corner washstand, with a big basin and a small jug—the odds and ends of past years. Carpet there was none, save a narrow strip beside the bed.

'It is a dismal room,' mused Michael, with the same touch of pity for Maria's weakness which he had felt on the landing just now.

To him it mattered nothing where he slept; but having let himself down to a lower level by his interest in the Swiss lake-people, he was in a manner humanised by the lightness of his evening's reading, and was even inclined to compassionate the weaknesses of a foolish girl.

He went to bed, determined to sleep his soundest. The bed was comfortable, well supplied with blankets, rather luxurious than otherwise, and the scholar had that agreeable sense of fatigue which promises profound and restful slumber.

He dropped off to sleep quickly, but woke with a start ten minutes afterwards. What was this consciousness of a burden of care that had awakened him—this sense of all-pervading trouble that weighed upon his spirits and oppressed his heart—this icy horror of some terrible crisis in life through which he must inevitably pass? To him these feelings were as novel as they were painful. His life had flowed on with smooth and sluggish tide, unbroken by so much as a ripple of sorrow. Yet to-night he felt all the pangs of unavailing remorse; the agonising memory of a life wasted; the stings of humiliation and disgrace, shame, ruin; a hideous death, which he had doomed himself to die by his own hand. These were the horrors that pressed him round and weighed him down as he lay in Anthony Bascom's room.

Yes, even he, the man who could recognise nothing in nature, or in nature's God, better or higher than an irresponsible and invariable machine governed by mechanical laws, was fain to admit that here he found himself face to face with a psychological mystery. This trouble, which came between him and sleep, was the trouble that had pursued Anthony Bascom on the last night of his life. So had the suicide felt as he lay in that lonely room, perhaps striving to rest his wearied brain with one last earthly sleep before he passed to the unknown intermediate land where all is darkness and slumber. And that troubled mind had haunted the room ever since. It was not the ghost of the man's body that returned to the spot where he had suffered and perished, but the ghost of his mind—his very self; no meaningless simulacrum of the clothes he wore, and the figure that filled them.

Michael Bascom was not the man to abandon his high ground of sceptical philosophy without a struggle. He tried his hardest to conquer this oppression that weighed upon mind and sense. Again and again he succeeded in composing himself to sleep, but only to wake again and again to the same torturing thoughts, the same remorse, the same despair. So the night passed in unutterable weariness; for though he told himself that the trouble was not his trouble, that there was no reality in the burden, no reason for the remorse, these vivid fancies were as painful as realities, and took as strong a hold upon him.

The first streak of light crept in at the window—dim, and cold, and grey; then came twilight, and he looked at the corner between the wardrobe and the door.

Yes; there was the shadow: not the shadow of the wardrobe only— that was clear enough, but a vague and shapeless something which darkened the dull brown wall; so faint, so shadowy, that he could form no conjecture as to its nature, or the thing it represented. He determined to watch this shadow till broad daylight; but the weariness of the night had exhausted him, and before the first dimness of dawn had passed away he had fallen fast asleep, and was tasting the blessed balm of undisturbed slumber. When he woke the winter sun was shining in at the lattice, and the room had lost its gloomy aspect. It looked old-fashioned, and grey, and brown, and shabby; but the depth of its gloom had fled with the shadows and the darkness of night.

Mr Bascom rose refreshed by a sound sleep, which had lasted nearly three hours. He remembered the wretched feelings which had gone before that renovating slumber; but he recalled his strange sensations only to despise them, and he despised himself for having attached any importance to them.

'Indigestion very likely,' he told himself; 'or perhaps mere fancy, engendered of that foolish girl's story. The wisest of us is more under the dominion of imagination than he would care to confess. Well, Maria shall not sleep in this room any more. There is no particular reason why she should, and she shall not be made unhappy to please old Skegg and his wife.'

When he had dressed himself in his usual leisurely way, Mr Bascom walked up to the corner where he had seen or imagined the shadow, and examined the spot carefully.

At first sight he could discover nothing of a mysterious character. There was no door in the papered wall, no trace of a door that had been there in the past. There was no trap-door in the worm-eaten boards. There was no dark ineradicable stain to hint at murder. There was not the faintest suggestion of a secret or a mystery.

He looked up at the ceiling. That was sound enough, save for a dirty patch here and there where the rain had blistered it.

Yes; there was something—an insignificant thing, yet with a suggestion of grimness which startled him.

About a foot below the ceiling he saw a large iron hook projecting from the wall, just above the spot where he had seen the shadow of a vaguely defined form. He mounted on a chair the better to examine this hook, and to understand, if he could, the purpose for which it had been put there.

It was old and rusty. It must have been there for many years. Who could have placed it there, and why? It was not the kind of hook upon which one would hang a picture or one's garments. It was placed in an obscure corner. Had Anthony Bascom put it there on the night he died; or did he find it there ready for a fatal use?

'If I were a superstitious man,' thought Michael, 'I should be inclined to believe that Anthony Bascom hung himself from that rusty old hook.'

'Sleep well, sir?' asked Daniel, as he waited upon his master at break-fast.

'Admirably,' answered Michael, determined not to gratify the man's curiosity.

He had always resented the idea that Wildheath Grange was haunted.

'Oh, indeed, sir. You were so late that I fancied——'

'Late, yes! I slept so well that I overshot my usual hour for waking. But, by-the-way, Skegg, as that poor girl objects to the room, let her sleep somewhere else. It can't make any difference to us, and it may make some difference to her.'

'Humph!' muttered Daniel in his grumpy way; 'you didn't see anything queer up there, did you?'

'See anything? Of course not.'

'Well, then, why should she see things? It's all her silly fiddle-faddle.'

'Never mind, let her sleep in another room.'

'There ain't another room on the top floor that's dry.'

'Then let her sleep on the floor below. She creeps about quietly enough, poor little timid thing. She won't disturb me.'

Daniel grunted, and his master understood the grunt to mean obedient assent; but here Mr Bascom was unhappily mistaken. The proverbial obstinacy of the pig family is as nothing compared with the obstinacy of a cross-grained old man, whose narrow mind has never been illuminated by education. Daniel was beginning to feel jealous of his master's compassionate interest in the orphan girl. She was a sort of gentle clinging thing that might creep into an elderly bachelor's heart unawares, and make herself a comfortable nest there.

'We shall have fine carryings-on, and me and my old woman will be nowhere, if I don't put down my heel pretty strong upon this nonsense,' Daniel muttered to himself, as he carried the breakfast-tray to the pantry.

Maria met him in the passage.

'Well, Mr Skegg, what did my master say?' she asked breathlessly. 'Did he see anything strange in the room?'

'No, girl. What should he see? He said you were a fool.'

'Nothing disturbed him? And he slept there peacefully?' faltered Maria.

'Never slept better in his life. Now don't you begin to feel ashamed of yourself?'

'Yes,' she answered meekly; 'I am ashamed of being so full of fancies. I will go back to my room tonight, Mr Skegg, if you like, and I will never complain of it again.'

'I hope you won't,' snapped Skegg; 'you've given us trouble enough already.'

Maria sighed, and went about her work in saddest silence. The day wore slowly on, like all other days in that lifeless old house. The scholar sat in his study; Maria moved softly from room to room, sweeping and dusting in the cheerless solitude. The mid-day sun faded into the grey of afternoon, and evening came down like a blight upon the dull old house.

Throughout that day Maria and her master never met. Anyone who had been so far interested in the girl as to observe her appearance would have seen that she was unusually pale, and that her eyes had a resolute look, as of one who was resolved to face a painful ordeal. She ate hardly anything all day. She was curiously silent. Skegg and his wife put down both these symptoms to temper.

'She won't eat and she won't talk,' said Daniel to the partner of his joys. 'That means sulkiness, and I never allowed sulkiness to master me when I was a young man, and you tried it on as a young woman, and I'm not going to be conquered by sulkiness in my old age.'

Bed-time came, and Maria bade the Skeggs a civil good-night, and went up to her lonely garret without a murmur.

The next morning came, and Mrs Skegg looked in vain for her patient hand-maiden, when she wanted Maria's services in preparing the breakfast.

'The wench sleeps sound enough this morning,' said the old woman. 'Go and call her, Daniel. My poor legs can't stand them stairs.'

'Your poor legs are getting uncommon useless,' muttered Daniel testily, as he went to do his wife's behest.

He knocked at the door, and called Maria—once, twice, thrice, many times; but there was no reply. He tried the door, and found it locked. He shook the door violently, cold with fear.

Then he told himself that the girl had played him a trick. She had stolen away before daybreak, and left the door locked to frighten him. But, no; this could not be, for he could see the key in the lock when he knelt down and put his eye to the keyhole. The key prevented his seeing into the room.

'She's in there, laughing in her sleeve at me,' he told himself; 'but I'll soon be even with her.'

There was a heavy bar on the staircase, which was intended to secure the shutters of the window that lighted the stairs. It was a detached bar, and always stood in a corner near the window, which it was but rarely employed to fasten. Daniel ran down to the landing, and seized upon this massive iron bar, and then ran back to the garret door.

One blow from the heavy bar shattered the old lock, which was the same lock the carter had broken with his strong fist seventy years before. The door flew open, and Daniel went into the attic which he had chosen for the stranger's bed-chamber.

Maria was hanging from the hook in the wall. She had contrived to cover her face decently with her handkerchief. She had hanged herself deliberately about an hour before Daniel found her, in the early grey of morning. The doctor, who was summoned from Holcroft, was able to declare the time at which she had slain herself, but there was no one who could say what sudden access of terror had impelled her to the desperate act, or under what slow torture of nervous apprehension her mind had given way. The coroner's jury returned the customary merciful verdict of 'Temporary insanity'.

The girl's melancholy fate darkened the rest of Michael Bascom's life. He fled from Wildheath Grange as from an accursed spot, and from the Skeggs as from the murderers of a harmless innocent girl. He ended his days at Oxford, where he found the society of congenial minds, and the books he loved. But the memory of Maria's sad face, and sadder death, was his abiding sorrow. Out of that deep shadow his soul was never lifted.

The Upper Berth

F. MARION CRAWFORD

I

Somebody asked for the cigars. We had talked long, and the conversation was beginning to languish; the tobacco smoke had got into the heavy curtains, the wine had got into those brains which were liable to become heavy, and it was already perfectly evident that, unless somebody did something to rouse our oppressed spirits, the meeting would soon come to its natural conclusion, and we, the guests, would speedily go home to bed, and most certainly to sleep. No one had said anything very remarkable; it may be that no one had anything very remarkable to say. Jones had given us every particular of his last hunting adventure in Yorkshire. Mr Tompkins, of Boston, had explained at elaborate length those working principles, by the due and careful maintenance of which the Atchison, Topeka, and Santa Fé Railroad not only extended its territory, increased its departmental influence, and transported live stock without starving them to death before the day of actual delivery, but, also, had for years succeeded in deceiving those passengers who bought its tickets into the fallacious belief that the corporation aforesaid was really able to transport human life without destroying it. Signor Tombola had endeavoured to persuade us, by arguments which we took no trouble to oppose, that the unity of his country in no way resembled the average modern torpedo, carefully planned, constructed with all the skill of the greatest European arsenals, but, when constructed, destined to be directed by feeble hands into a region where it must undoubtedly explode, unseen, unfeared, and unheard, into the illimitable wastes of political chaos.

It is unnecessary to go into further details. The conversation had assumed proportions which would have bored Prometheus on his rock, which would have driven Tantalus to distraction, and which would have impelled Ixion to seek relaxation in the simple but instructive dialogues of Herr Ollendorff, rather than submit to the greater evil of listening to our talk. We had sat at table for hours; we were bored, we were tired, and nobody showed signs of moving.

Somebody called for cigars. We all instinctively looked towards the speaker. Brisbane was a man of five-and-thirty years of age, and remarkable for those gifts which chiefly attract the attention of men. He was a strong man. The external proportions of his figure presented nothing extraordinary to the common eye, though his size was above the average. He was a little over six feet in height, and moderately broad in the shoulder; he did not appear to be stout, but, on the other hand, he was certainly not thin; his small head was supported by a strong and sinewy neck; his broad, muscular hands appeared to possess a peculiar skill in breaking walnuts without the assistance of the ordinary cracker, and, seeing him in profile, one could not help remarking the extraordinary breadth of his sleeves, and the unusual thickness of his chest. He was one of those men who are commonly spoken of among men as deceptive; that is to say, that though he looked exceedingly strong he was in reality very much stronger than he looked. Of his features I need say little. His head is small, his hair is thin, his eyes are blue, his nose is large, he has a small moustache, and a square jaw. Everybody knows Brisbane, and when he asked for a cigar everybody looked at him.

'It is a very singular thing,' said Brisbane.

Everybody stopped talking. Brisbane's voice was not loud, but possessed a peculiar quality of penetrating general conversation, and cutting it like a knife. Everybody listened. Brisbane, perceiving that he had attracted their general attention, lit his cigar with great equanimity.

'It is very singular,' he continued, 'that thing about ghosts. People are always asking whether anybody has seen a ghost. I have.'

'Bosh! What, you? You don't mean to say so, Brisbane? Well, for a man of his intelligence!'

A chorus of exclamations greeted Brisbane's remarkable statement. Everybody called for cigars, and Stubbs, the butler, suddenly appeared from the depths of nowhere with a fresh bottle of dry champagne. The situation was saved; Brisbane was going to tell a story.

I am an old sailor, said Brisbane, and as I have to cross the Atlantic pretty often, I have my favourites. Most men have their favourites. I have seen a man wait in a Broadway bar for three-quarters of an hour for a particular car which he liked. I believe the bar-keeper made at least one-third of his living by that man's preference. I have a habit of waiting for certain ships when I am obliged to cross that duck-pond. It may be a prejudice, but I was never cheated out of a good passage but once in my life. I remember it very well; it was a warm morning in June, and the Custom House officials, who were hanging about waiting for a steamer already on her way up from the Quarantine, presented a peculiarly hazy and thoughtful appearance. I had not much luggage—I never have. I mingled with the crowd of passengers, porters, and officious individuals in blue coats and brass buttons, who seemed to spring up like mushrooms from the deck of a moored steamer to obtrude their unnecessary services upon the independent passenger. I have often noticed with a certain interest the spontaneous evolution of these fellows. They are not there when you arrive; five minutes after the pilot has called 'Go ahead!' they, or at least their blue coats and brass buttons, have disappeared from deck and gangway as completely as though they had been consigned to that locker which tradition unanimously ascribes to Davy Jones. But, at the moment of starting, they are there, clean shaved, blue coated, and ravenous for fees. I hastened on board. The *Kamtschatka* was one of my favourite ships. I say was, because she emphatically no longer is. I cannot conceive of any inducement which could entice me to make another voyage in her. Yes, I know what you are going to say. She is uncommonly clean in the run aft, she has enough bluffing off in the bows to keep her dry, and the lower berths are most of them double. She has a lot of advantages, but I won't cross in her again. Excuse the digression. I got on board. I hailed a steward, whose red nose and redder whiskers were equally familiar to me.

'One hundred and five, lower berth,' said I, in the business-like tone peculiar to men who think no more of crossing the Atlantic than taking a whisky cocktail at down-town Delmonico's.

The steward took my portmanteau, greatcoat, and rug. I shall never forget the expression of his face. Not that he turned pale. It is maintained by the most eminent divines that even miracles cannot change the course of nature. I have no hesitation in saying that he did not turn pale; but, from his expression, I judged that he was either about to shed tears, to sneeze, or to drop my portmanteau. As the latter contained two bottles of particularly fine old sherry presented to me for my voyage by my old friend Snigginson van Pickyns, I felt extremely nervous. But the steward did none of these things.

'Well, I'm d——d!' said he in a low voice, and led the way.

I supposed my Hermes, as he led me to the lower regions, had had a little grog, but I said nothing, and followed him. 105 was on the port side, well aft. There was nothing remarkable about the state-room. The lower berth, like most of those upon the *Kamtschatka*, was double. There was plenty of room; there was the usual washing apparatus, calculated to convey an idea of luxury to the mind of a North American Indian; there were the usual inefficient racks of brown wood, in which it is more easy to hang a large-sized umbrella than the common tooth-brush of commerce. Upon the uninviting mattresses were carefully folded together those blankets which a great modern humorist has aptly compared to cold buckwheat cakes. The question of towels was left entirely to the imagination. The glass decanters were filled with a transparent liquid faintly tinged with brown, but from which an odour less faint, but not more pleasing, ascended to the nostrils, like a far-off sea-sick reminiscence of oily machinery. Sad-coloured curtains half closed the upper berth. The hazy June daylight shed a faint illumination upon the desolate little scene. Ugh! how I hate that state-room!

The steward deposited my traps and looked at me, as though he wanted to get away—probably in search of more passengers and more fees. It is always a good plan to start in favour with those functionaries, and I accordingly gave him certain coins there and then.

'I'll try and make yer comfortable all I can,' he remarked, as he put the coins in his pocket. Nevertheless, there was a doubtful intonation in his voice which surprised me. Possibly his scale of fees had gone up, and he was not satisfied; but on the whole I was inclined to think that, as he himself would have expressed it, he was 'the better for a glass'. I was wrong, however, and did the man injustice.

II

Nothing especially worthy of mention occurred during that day. We left the pier punctually, and it was very pleasant to be fairly under way, for the weather was warm and sultry, and the motion of the steamer produced a refreshing breeze. Everybody knows what the first day at sea is like. People pace the decks and stare at each other, and occasionally meet acquaintances whom they did not know to be on board. There is the usual uncertainty as to whether the food will be good, bad, or indifferent, until the first two meals have put the matter beyond a doubt; there is the usual uncertainty about the weather, until the ship is fairly off Fire Island. The tables are crowded at first, and then suddenly thinned. Pale-faced people spring from their seats and precipitate themselves towards the door, and each old sailor breathes more freely as his sea-sick neighbour rushes from his side, leaving him plenty of elbow-room and an unlimited command over the mustard.

One passage across the Atlantic is very much like another, and we who cross very often do not make the voyage for the sake of novelty. Whales and icebergs are indeed always objects of interest, but, after all, one whale is very much like another whale, and one rarely sees an iceberg at close quarters. To the majority of us the most delightful moment of the day on board an ocean steamer is when we have taken our last turn on deck, have smoked our last cigar, and having succeeded in tiring ourselves, feel at liberty to turn in with a clear conscience. On that first night of the voyage I felt particularly lazy, and went to bed in 105 rather earlier than I usually do. As I turned in, I was amazed to see that I was to have a companion. A portmanteau, very like my own, lay in the opposite corner, and in the upper berth had been deposited a neatly-folded rug, with a stick and umbrella. I had hoped to be alone, and I was disappointed; but I wondered who my room-mate was to be, and I determined to have a look at him.

Before I had been long in bed he entered. He was, as far as I could see, a very tall man, very thin, very pale, with sandy hair and whiskers and colourless grey eyes. He had about him, I thought, an air of rather dubious fashion; the sort of man you might see in Wall Street, without being able precisely to say what he was doing there—the sort of man who frequents the Café Anglais, who always seems to be alone and who drinks champagne; you might meet him on a racecourse, but he would never appear to be doing anything there either. A little over-dressed—a little odd. There are three or four of his kind on every ocean steamer. I made up my mind that I did not care to make his acquaintance, and I went to sleep saying to myself that I would study his habits in order to avoid him. If he rose early, I would rise late; if he went to bed late, I would go to bed early. I did not care to know him. If you once know people of that kind they are always turning up. Poor fellow! I need not have taken the trouble to come to so many decisions about him, for I never saw him again after that first night in 105.

I was sleeping soundly when I was suddenly waked by a loud noise. To judge from the sound, my room-mate must have sprung with a single leap from the upper berth to the floor. I heard him fumbling with the latch and bolt of the door, which opened almost immediately, and then I heard his footsteps as he ran at full speed down the passage, leaving the door open behind him. The ship was rolling a little, and I expected to hear him stumble or fall, but he ran as though he were running for his life. The door swung on its hinges with the motion of the vessel, and the sound annoyed me. I got up and shut it, and groped my way back to my berth in the darkness. I went to sleep again; but I have no idea how long I slept.

When I awoke it was still quite dark, but I felt a disagreeable sensation of cold, and it seemed to me that the air was damp. You know the peculiar smell of a cabin which has been wet with sea-water. I covered myself up as well as I could and dozed off again, framing complaints to be made the next day, and selecting the most powerful epithets in the language. I could hear my room-mate turn over in the upper berth. He had probably returned while I was asleep. Once I thought I heard him groan, and I argued that he was sea-sick. That is particularly unpleasant when one is below. Nevertheless I dozed off and slept till early daylight.

The ship was rolling heavily, much more than on the previous evening, and the grey light which came in through the porthole changed in tint with every movement according as the angle of the vessel's side turned the glass seawards or skywards. It was very cold—unaccountably so for the month of June. I turned my head and looked at the porthole, and saw to my surprise that it was wide open and hooked back. I believe I swore audibly. Then I got up and shut it. As I turned back I glanced at the upper berth. The curtains were drawn close together; my companion had probably felt cold as well as I. It struck me that I had slept enough. The state-room was uncomfortable, though, strange to say, I could not smell the dampness which had annoyed me in the night. My room-mate was still asleep—excellent opportunity for avoiding him, so I dressed at once and went on deck. The day was warm and cloudy, with an oily smell on the water. It was seven o'clock as I came out—much later than I had imagined. I came across the doctor, who was taking his first sniff of the morning air. He was a young man from the West of Ireland—a tremendous fellow, with black hair and blue eyes, already inclined to be stout; he had a happy-go-lucky, healthy look about him which was rather attractive.

'Fine morning,' I remarked, by way of introduction.

'Well,' said he, eyeing me with an air of ready interest, 'it's a fine morning and it's not a fine morning. I don't think it's much of a morning.'

'Well, no—it is not so very fine,' said I.

'It's just what I call fuggly weather,' replied the doctor.

'It was very cold last night, I thought,' I remarked. 'However, when I looked about, I found that the porthole was wide open. I had not noticed it when I went to bed. And the state-room was damp, too.'

'Damp!' said he. 'Whereabouts are you?'

'One hundred and five——'

To my surprise the doctor started visibly, and stared at me.

'What is the matter?' I asked.

'Oh—nothing,' he answered; 'only everybody has complained of that state-room for the last three trips.'

'I shall complain too,' I said. 'It has certainly not been properly aired. It is a shame!'

'I don't believe it can be helped,' answered the doctor. 'I believe there is something—well, it is not my business to frighten passengers.'

'You need not be afraid of frightening me,' I replied. 'I can stand any amount of damp. If I should get a bad cold I will come to you.'

I offered the doctor a cigar, which he took and examined very critically.

'It is not so much the damp,' he remarked. 'However, I dare say you will get on very well. Have you a room-mate?'

'Yes; a deuce of a fellow, who bolts out in the middle of the night, and leaves the door open.'

Again the doctor glanced curiously at me. Then he lit the cigar and looked grave.

'Did he come back?' he asked presently.

'Yes. I was asleep, but I waked up, and heard him moving. Then I felt cold and went to sleep again. This morning I found the porthole open.'

'Look here,' said the doctor quietly, 'I don't care much for this ship. I don't care a rap for her reputation. I tell you what I will do. I have a good-sized place up here. I will share it with you, though I don't know you from Adam.'

I was very much surprised at the proposition. I could not imagine why he should take such a sudden interest in my welfare. However, his manner as he spoke of the ship was peculiar.

'You are very good, doctor,' I said. 'But, really, I believe even now the cabin could be aired, or cleaned out, or something. Why do you not care for the ship?'

'We are not superstitious in our profession, sir,' replied the doctor, 'but the sea makes people so. I don't want to prejudice you, and I don't want to frighten you, but if you will take my advice you will move in here. I would as soon see you overboard,' he added earnestly, 'as know that you or any other man was to sleep in 105.'

'Good gracious! Why?' I asked.

'Just because on the last three trips the people who have slept there actually have gone overboard,' he answered gravely.

The intelligence was startling and exceedingly unpleasant, I confess. I looked hard at the doctor to see whether he was making game of me, but he looked perfectly serious. I thanked him warmly for his offer, but told him I intended to be the exception to the rule by which every one who slept in that particular state-room went overboard. He did not say much, but looked as grave as ever, and hinted that, before we got across, I should probably reconsider his proposal. In the course of time we went to breakfast, at which only an inconsiderable number of passengers assembled. I noticed that one or two of the officers who breakfasted with us looked grave. After breakfast I went into my state-room in order to get a book. The curtains of the upper berth were still closely drawn. Not a word was to be heard. My room-mate was probably still asleep.

As I came out I met the steward whose business it was to look after me. He whispered that the captain wanted to see me, and then scuttled away down the passage as if very anxious to avoid any questions. I went toward the captain's cabin, and found him waiting for me.

'Sir,' said he, 'I want to ask a favour of you.'

I answered that I would do anything to oblige him.

'Your room-mate has disappeared,' he said. 'He is known to have turned in early last night. Did you notice anything extraordinary in his manner?'

The question coming, as it did, in exact confirmation of the fears the doctor had expressed half an hour earlier, staggered me.

'You don't mean to say he has gone overboard?' I asked.

'I fear he has,' answered the captain.

'This is the most extraordinary thing——' I began.

'Why?' he asked.

'He is the fourth, then?' I exclaimed. In answer to another question from the captain, I explained, without mentioning the doctor, that I had heard the story concerning 105. He seemed very much annoyed at hearing that I knew of it. I told him what had occurred in the night.

'What you say,' he replied, 'coincides almost exactly with what was told me by the room-mates of two of the other three. They bolt out of bed and run down the passage. Two of them were seen to go overboard by the watch; we stopped and lowered boats, but they were not found. Nobody, however, saw or heard the man who was lost last night—if he is really lost. The steward, who is a superstitious fellow, perhaps, and expected something to go wrong, went to look for him this morning, and found his berth empty, but his clothes lying about, just as he had left them. The steward was the only man on board who knew him by sight, and he has been searching everywhere for him. He has disappeared! Now, sir, I want to beg you not to mention the circumstance to any of the passengers; I don't want the ship to get a bad name, and nothing hangs about an ocean-goer like stories of suicides. You shall have your choice of any one of the officers' cabins you like, including my own, for the rest of the passage. Is that a fair bargain?'

'Very,' said I; 'and I am much obliged to you. But since I am alone, and have the state-room to myself, I would rather not move. If the steward will take out that unfortunate man's things, I would as lief stay where I am. I will not say anything about the matter, and I think I can promise you that I will not follow my room-mate.'

The captain tried to dissuade me from my intention, but I preferred having a state-room alone to being the chum of any officer on board. I do not know whether I acted foolishly, but if I had taken his advice I should have had nothing more to tell. There would have remained the disagreeable coincidence of several suicides occurring among men who had slept in the same cabin, but that would have been all.

That was not the end of the matter, however, by any means. I obstinately made up my mind that I would not be disturbed by such tales, and I even went so far as to argue the question with the captain. There was something wrong about the state-room, I said. It was rather damp. The porthole had been left open last night. My room-mate might have been ill when he came on board, and he might have become delirious after he went to bed. He might even now be hiding somewhere on board, and might be found later. The place ought to be aired and the fastening of the port looked to. If the captain would give me leave, I would see that what I thought necessary were done immediately.

'Of course you have a right to stay where you are if you please,' he replied, rather petulantly; 'but I wish you would turn out and let me lock the place up, and be done with it.'

I did not see it in the same light, and left the captain, after promising to be silent concerning the disappearance of my companion. The latter had had no acquaintances on board, and was not missed in the course of the day. Towards evening I met the doctor again, and he asked me whether I had changed my mind. I told him I had not.

'Then you will before long,' he said, very gravely.

III

We played whist in the evening, and I went to bed late. I will confess now that I felt a disagreeable sensation when I entered my state-room. I could not help thinking of the tall man I had seen on the previous night, who was now dead, drowned, tossing about in the long swell, two or three hundred miles astern. His face rose very distinctly before me as I undressed, and I even went so far as to draw back the curtains of the upper berth, as though to persuade myself that he was actually gone. I also bolted the door of the state-room. Suddenly I became aware that the porthole was open, and fastened back. This was more than I could stand. I hastily threw on my dressing-gown and went in search of Robert, the steward of my passage. I was very angry, I remember, and when I found him I dragged him roughly to the door of 105, and pushed him towards the open porthole.

'What the deuce do you mean, you scoundrel, by leaving that port open every night? Don't you know it is against the regulations? Don't you know that if the ship heeled and the water began to come in, ten men could not shut it? I will report you to the captain, you blackguard, for endangering the ship!'

I was exceedingly wroth. The man trembled and turned pale, and then began to shut the round glass plate with the heavy brass fittings.

'Why don't you answer me?' I said roughly.

'If you please, sir,' faltered Robert, 'there's nobody on board as can keep this 'ere port shut at night. You can try it yourself, sir. I ain't a-going to stop hany longer on board o' this vessel, sir; I ain't, indeed. But if I was you, sir, I'd just clear out and go and sleep with the surgeon, or something, I would. Look 'ere, sir, is that fastened what you may call securely, or not, sir? Try it, sir, see if it will move a hinch.'

I tried the port, and found it perfectly tight.

'Well, sir,' continued Robert triumphantly, 'I wager my reputation as a A1 steward that in 'arf an hour it will be open again; fastened back, too, sir, that's the horful thing—fastened back!'

I examined the great screw and the looped nut that ran on it.

'If I find it open in the night, Robert, I will give you a sovereign. It is not possible. You may go.'

'Soverin' did you say, sir? Very good, sir. Thank ye, sir. Good-night, sir. Pleasant reepose, sir, and all manner of hinchantin' dreams, sir.'

Robert scuttled away, delighted at being released. Of course, I thought he was trying to account for his negligence by a silly story, intended to frighten me, and I disbelieved him. The consequence was that he got his sovereign, and I spent a very peculiarly unpleasant night.

I went to bed, and five minutes after I had rolled myself up in my blankets the inexorable Robert extinguished the light that burned steadily behind the ground-glass pane near the door. I lay quite still in the dark trying to go to sleep, but I soon found that impossible. It had been some satisfaction to be angry with the steward, and the diversion had banished that unpleasant sensation I had at first experienced when I thought of the drowned man who had been my chum; but I was no longer sleepy, and I lay awake for some time, occasionally glancing at the porthole, which I could just see from where I lay, and which, in the darkness, looked like a faintly-luminous soup-plate suspended in blackness. I believe I must have lain there for an hour, and, as I remember, I was just dozing into sleep when I was roused by a draught of cold air, and by distinctly feeling the spray of the sea blown upon my face. I started to my feet, and not having allowed in the dark for the motion of the ship, I was instantly thrown violently across the state-room upon the couch which was placed beneath the porthole. I recovered myself immediately, however, and climbed upon my knees. The porthole was again wide open and fastened back!

Now these things are facts. I was wide awake when I got up, and I should certainly have been waked by the fall had I still been dozing.

Moreover, I bruised my elbows and knees badly, and the bruises were there on the following morning to testify to the fact, if I myself had doubted it. The porthole was wide open and fastened back—a thing so unaccountable that I remember very well feeling astonishment rather than fear when I discovered it. I at once closed the plate again, and screwed down the loop nut with all my strength. It was very dark in the state-room. I reflected that the port had certainly been opened within an hour after Robert had at first shut it in my presence, and I determined to watch it, and see whether it would open again. Those brass fittings are very heavy and by no means easy to move; I could not believe that the clamp had been turned by the shaking of the screw. I stood peering out through the thick glass at the alternate white and grey streaks of the sea that foamed beneath the ship's side. I must have remained there a quarter of an hour.

Suddenly, as I stood, I distinctly heard something moving behind me in one of the berths, and a moment afterwards, just as I turned instinctively to look—though I could, of course, see nothing in the darkness—I heard a very faint groan. I sprang across the state-room, and tore the curtains of the upper berth aside, thrusting in my hands to discover if there were any one there. There was some one.

I remember that the sensation as I put my hands forward was as though I were plunging them into the air of a damp cellar, and from behind the curtains came a gust of wind that smelled horribly of stagnant sea-water. I laid hold of something that had the shape of a man's arm, but was smooth, and wet, and icy cold. But suddenly, as I pulled, the creature sprang violently forward against me, a clammy, oozy mass, as it seemed to me, heavy and wet, yet endowed with a sort of supernatural strength. I reeled across the state-room, and in an instant the door opened and the thing rushed out. I had not had time to be frightened, and quickly recovering myself, I sprang through the door and gave chase at the top of my speed, but I was too late. Ten yards before me I could see—I am sure I saw it—a dark shadow moving in the dimly lighted passage, quickly as the shadow of a fast horse thrown before a dog-cart by the lamp on a dark night. But in a moment it had disappeared, and I found myself holding on to the polished rail that ran along the bulkhead where the passage turned towards the companion. My hair stood on end, and the cold perspiration rolled down my face. I am not ashamed of it in the least: I was very badly frightened.

Still I doubted my senses, and pulled myself together. It was absurd, I thought. The Welsh rare-bit I had eaten had disagreed with me. I had been in a nightmare. I made my way back to my state-room, and entered it with an effort. The whole place smelled of stagnant sea-water, as it had when I had waked on the previous evening. It required my utmost strength to go in, and grope among my things for a box of wax lights. As I lighted a railway reading lantern which I always carry in case I want to read after the lamps are out, I perceived that the porthole was again open, and a sort of creeping horror began to take possession of me which I never felt before, nor wish to feel again. But I got a light and proceeded to examine the upper berth, expecting to find it drenched with sea-water.

But I was disappointed. The bed had been slept in, and the smell of the sea was strong; but the bedding was as dry as a bone. I fancied that Robert had not had the courage to make the bed after the accident of the previous night—it had all been a hideous dream. I drew the curtains back as far as I could and examined the place very carefully. It was perfectly dry. But the porthole was open again. With a sort of dull bewilderment of horror I closed it and screwed it down, and thrusting my heavy stick through the brass loop, wrenched it with all my might, till the thick metal began to bend under the pressure. Then I hooked my reading lantern into the red velvet at the head of the couch, and sat down to recover my senses if I could. I sat there all night, unable to think of rest—hardly able to think at all. But the porthole remained closed, and I did not believe it would now open again without the application of a considerable force.

The morning dawned at last, and I dressed myself slowly, thinking over all that had happened in the night. It was a beautiful day and I went on deck, glad to get out into the early, pure sunshine, and to smell the breeze from the blue water, so different from the noisome, stagnant odour of my state-room. Instinctively I turned aft, towards the surgeon's cabin. There he stood, with a pipe in his mouth, taking his morning airing precisely as on the preceding day.

'Good-morning,' said he quietly, but looking at me with evident curiosity.

'Doctor, you were quite right,' said I. 'There is something wrong about that place.'

'I thought you would change your mind,' he answered, rather triumphantly. 'You have had a bad night, eh? Shall I make you a pick-me-up? I have a capital recipe.'

'No, thanks,' I cried. 'But I would like to tell you what happened.'

I then tried to explain as clearly as possible precisely what had occurred, not omitting to state that I had been scared as I had never been scared in my whole life before. I dwelt particularly on the phenomenon of the porthole, which was a fact to which I could testify, even if the rest had been an illusion. I had closed it twice in the night, and the second time I had actually bent the brass in wrenching it with my stick. I believe I insisted a good deal on this point.

'You seem to think I am likely to doubt the story,' said the doctor, smiling at the detailed account of the state of the porthole. 'I do not doubt it in the least. I renew my invitation to you. Bring your traps here, and take half my cabin.'

'Come and take half of mine for one night,' I said. 'Help me to get at the bottom of this thing.'

'You will get to the bottom of something else if you try,' answered the doctor.

'What?' I asked.

'The bottom of the sea. I am going to leave this ship. It is not canny.'

'Then you will not help me to find out——'

'Not I,' said the doctor quickly. 'It is my business to keep my wits about me—not to go fiddling about with ghosts and things.'

'Do you really believe it is a ghost?' I enquired, rather contemptuously. But as I spoke I remembered very well the horrible sensation of the supernatural which had got possession of me during the night. The doctor turned sharply on me.

'Have you any reasonable explanation of these things to offer?' he asked. 'No; you have not. Well, you say you will find an explanation. I say that you won't, sir, simply because there is not any.'

'But, my dear sir,' I retorted, 'do you, a man of science, mean to tell me that such things cannot be explained?'

'I do,' he answered stoutly. 'And, if they could, I would not be concerned in the explanation.'

I did not care to spend another night alone in the state-room, and yet I was obstinately determined to get at the root of the disturbances. I do not believe there are many men who would have slept there alone, after passing two such nights. But I made up my mind to try it, if I could not get any one to share a watch with me. The doctor was evidently not inclined for such an experiment. He said he was a surgeon, and that in case any accident occurred on board he must be always in readiness. He could not afford to have his nerves unsettled. Perhaps he was quite right, but I am inclined to think that his precaution was prompted by his inclination. On enquiry, he informed me that there was no one on board who would be likely to join me in my investigations, and after a little more conversation I left him. A little later I met the captain, and told him my story. I said that, if no one would spend the night with me, I would ask leave to have the light burning all night, and would try it alone.

'Look here,' said he, 'I will tell you what I will do. I will share your watch myself, and we will see what happens. It is my belief that we can find out between us. There may be some fellow skulking on board, who steals a passage by frightening the passengers. It is just possible that there may be something queer in the carpentering of that berth.'

I suggested taking the ship's carpenter below and examining the place; but I was overjoyed at the captain's offer to spend the night with me. He accordingly sent for the workman and ordered him to do anything I required. We went below at once. I had all the bedding cleared out of the upper berth, and we examined the place thoroughly to see if there was a board loose anywhere, or a panel which could be opened or pushed aside. We tried the planks everywhere, tapped the flooring, unscrewed the fittings of the lower berth and took it to pieces— in short, there was not a square inch of the state-room which was not searched and tested. Everything was in perfect order, and we put everything back in its place. As we were finishing our work, Robert came to the door and looked in.

'Well, sir—find anything, sir?' he asked, with a ghastly grin.

'You were right about the porthole, Robert,' I said, and I gave him the promised sovereign. The carpenter did his work silently and skilfully, following my directions. When he had done he spoke.

'I'm a plain man, sir,' he said. 'But it's my belief you had better just turn out your things, and let me run half a dozen four-inch screws through the door of this cabin. There's no good never came o' this cabin yet, sir, and that's all about it. There's been four lives lost out o' here to my own remembrance, and that in four trips. Better give it up, sir— better give it up!'

'I will try it for one night more,' I said.

'Better give it up, sir—better give it up! It's a precious bad job,' repeated the workman, putting his tools in his bag and leaving the cabin.

But my spirits had risen considerably at the prospect of having the captain's company, and I made up my mind not to be prevented from going to the end of the strange business. I abstained from Welsh rarebits and grog that evening, and did not even join in the customary game of whist. I wanted to be quite sure of my nerves, and my vanity made me anxious to make a good figure in the captain's eyes.

IV

The captain was one of those splendidly tough and cheerful specimens of seafaring humanity whose combined courage, hardihood, and calmness in difficulty leads them naturally into high positions of trust. He was not the man to be led away by an idle tale, and the mere fact that he was willing to join me in the investigation was proof that he thought there was something seriously wrong, which could not be accounted for on ordinary theories, nor laughed down as a common superstition. To some extent, too, his reputation was at stake, as well as the reputation of the ship. It is no light thing to lose passengers overboard, and he knew it.

About ten o'clock that evening, as I was smoking a last cigar, he came up to me, and drew me aside from the beat of the other passengers who were patrolling the deck in the warm darkness.

'This is a serious matter, Mr Brisbane,' he said. 'We must make up our minds either way—to be disappointed or to have a pretty rough time of it. You see I cannot afford to laugh at the affair, and I will ask you to sign your name to a statement of whatever occurs. If nothing happens tonight we will try it again tomorrow and next day. Are you ready?'

So we went below, and entered the state-room. As we went in I could see Robert the steward, who stood a little further down the passage, watching us, with his usual grin, as though certain that something dreadful was about to happen. The captain closed the door behind us and bolted it.

'Supposing we put your portmanteau before the door,' he suggested. 'One of us can sit on it. Nothing can get out then. Is the port screwed down?'

I found it as I had left it in the morning. Indeed, without using a lever, as I had done, no one could have opened it. I drew back the curtains of the upper berth so that I could see well into it. By the captain's advice I lighted my reading lantern, and placed it so that it shone upon the white sheets above. He insisted upon sitting on the portmanteau, declaring that he wished to be able to swear that he had sat before the door.

Then he requested me to search the state-room thoroughly, an operation very soon accomplished, as it consisted merely in looking beneath the lower berth and under the couch below the porthole. The spaces were quite empty.

'It is impossible for any human being to get in,' I said, 'or for any human being to open the port.'

'Very good,' said the captain calmly. 'If we see anything now, it must be either imagination or something supernatural.'

I sat down on the edge of the lower berth.

'The first time it happened,' said the captain, crossing his legs and leaning back against the door, 'was in March. The passenger who slept here, in the upper berth, turned out to have been a lunatic—at all events, he was known to have been a little touched, and he had taken his passage without the knowledge of his friends. He rushed out in the middle of the night, and threw himself overboard, before the officer who had the watch could stop him. We stopped and lowered a boat; it was a quiet night, just before that heavy weather came on; but we could not find him. Of course his suicide was afterwards accounted for on the ground of his insanity.'

'I suppose that often happens?' I remarked, rather absently.

'Not often—no,' said the captain; 'never before in my experience, though I have heard of it happening on board of other ships. Well, as I was saying, that occurred in March. On the very next trip—— What are you looking at?' he asked, stopping suddenly in his narration.

I believe I gave no answer. My eyes were riveted upon the porthole. It seemed to me that the brass loop-nut was beginning to turn very slowly upon the screw—so slowly, however, that I was not sure it moved at all. I watched it intently, fixing its position in my mind, and trying to ascertain whether it changed. Seeing where I was looking, the captain looked, too.

'It moves!' he exclaimed, in a tone of conviction. 'No, it does not,' he added, after a minute.

'If it were the jarring of the screw,' said I, 'it would have opened during the day; but I found it this evening jammed tight as I left it this morning.'

I rose and tried the nut. It was certainly loosened, for by an effort I could move it with my hands.

'The queer thing,' said the captain, 'is that the second man who was lost is supposed to have got through that very port. We had a terrible time over it. It was in the middle of the night, and the weather was very heavy; there was an alarm that one of the ports was open and the sea running in. I came below and found everything flooded, the water pouring in every time she rolled, and the whole port swinging from the top bolts—not the porthole in the middle. Well, we managed to shut it, but the water did some damage. Ever since that the place smells of sea-water from time to time. We supposed the passenger had thrown himself out, though the Lord only knows how he did it. The steward kept telling me that he cannot keep anything shut here. Upon my word—I can smell it now, cannot you?' he enquired, sniffing the air suspiciously.

'Yes—distinctly,' I said, and I shuddered as that same odour of stagnant sea-water grew stronger in the cabin. 'Now, to smell like this, the place must be damp,' I continued, 'and yet when I examined it with the carpenter this morning everything was perfectly dry. It is most extraordinary—hallo!'

My reading lantern, which had been placed in the upper berth, was suddenly extinguished. There was still a good deal of light from the pane of ground glass near the door, behind which loomed the regulation lamp. The ship rolled heavily, and the curtain of the upper berth swung far out into the state-room and back again. I rose quickly from my seat on the edge of the bed, and the captain at the same moment started to his feet with a loud cry of surprise. I had turned with the intention of taking down the lantern to examine it, when I heard his exclamation, and immediately afterwards his call for help. I sprang towards him. He was wrestling with all his might with the brass loop of the port. It seemed to turn against his hands in spite of all his efforts. I caught up my cane, a heavy oak stick I always used to carry, and thrust it through the ring and bore on it with all my strength. But the strong wood snapped suddenly and I fell upon the couch. When I rose again the port was wide open, and the captain was standing with his back against the door, pale to the lips.

'There is something in that berth!' he cried, in a strange voice, his eyes almost starting from his head. 'Hold the door, while I look—it shall not escape us, whatever it is!'

But instead of taking his place, I sprang upon the lower bed, and seized something which lay in the upper berth.

It was something ghostly, horrible beyond words, and it moved in my grip. It was like the body of a man long drowned, and yet it moved, and had the strength of ten men living; but I gripped it with all my might— the slippery, oozy, horrible thing—the dead white eyes seemed to stare at me out of the dusk; the putrid odour of rank sea-water was about it, and its shiny hair hung in foul wet curls over its dead face. I wrestled with the dead thing; it thrust itself upon me and forced me back and nearly broke my arms; it wound its corpse's arms about my neck, the living death, and overpowered me, so that I, at last, cried aloud and fell, and left my hold.

As I fell the thing sprang across me, and seemed to throw itself upon the captain. When I last saw him on his feet his face was white and his lips set. It seemed to me that he struck a violent blow at the dead being, and then he, too, fell forward upon his face, with an inarticulate cry of horror.

The thing paused an instant, seeming to hover over his prostrate body, and I could have screamed again for very fright, but I had no voice left. The thing vanished suddenly, and it seemed to my disturbed senses that it made its exit through the open port, though how that was possible, considering the smallness of the aperture, is more than any one can tell. I lay a long time upon the floor, and the captain lay beside me. At last I partially recovered my senses and moved, and instantly I knew that my arm was broken—the small bone of the left forearm near the wrist.

I got upon my feet somehow, and with my remaining hand I tried to raise the captain. He groaned and moved, and at last came to himself. He was not hurt, but he seemed badly stunned.

Well, do you want to hear any more? There is nothing more. That is the end of my story. The carpenter carried out his scheme of running half a dozen four-inch screws through the door of 105; and if ever you take a passage in the *Kamtschatka*, you may ask for a berth in that state-room. You will be told that it is engaged—yes—it is engaged by that dead thing.

I finished the trip in the surgeon's cabin. He doctored my broken arm, and advised me not to 'fiddle about with ghosts and things' any more. The captain was very silent, and never sailed again in that ship, though it is still running. And I will not sail in her either. It was a very disagreeable experience, and I was very badly frightened, which is a thing I do not like. That is all. That is how I saw a ghost—if it was a ghost. It was dead, anyhow.

A Wicked Voice

VERNON LEE

To M. W.

IN REMEMBRANCE OF THE LAST SONG
AT PALAZZO BARBARO,
Chi ha inteso, intenda.

They have been congratulating me again today upon being the only composer of our days—of these days of deafening orchestral effects and poetical quackery—who has despised the new-fangled nonsense of Wagner, and returned boldly to the traditions of Handel and Gluck and the divine Mozart, to the supremacy of melody and the respect of the human voice.

O cursed human voice, violin of flesh and blood, fashioned with the subtle tools, the cunning hands, of Satan! O execrable art of singing, have you not wrought mischief enough in the past, degrading so much noble genius, corrupting the purity of Mozart, reducing Handel to a writer of high-class singing-exercises, and defrauding the world of the only inspiration worthy of Sophocles and Euripides, the poetry of the great poet Gluck? Is it not enough to have dishonoured a whole century in idolatry of that wicked and contemptible wretch the singer, without persecuting an obscure young composer of our days, whose only wealth is his love of nobility in art, and perhaps some few grains of genius?

And then they compliment me upon the perfection with which I imitate the style of the great dead masters; or ask me very seriously whether, even if I could gain over the modern public to this bygone style of music, I could hope to find singers to perform it. Sometimes, when people talk as they have been talking today, and laugh when I declare myself a follower of Wagner, I burst into a paroxysm of unintelligible, childish rage, and exclaim, 'We shall see that some day!'

Yes; some day we shall see! For, after all, may I not recover from this strangest of maladies? It is still possible that the day may come when all these things shall seem but an incredible nightmare; the day when *Ogier the Dane* shall be completed, and men shall know whether I am a follower of the great master of the Future or the miserable singing-masters of the Past. I am but half-bewitched, since I am conscious of the spell that binds me. My old nurse, far off in Norway, used to tell me that were-wolves are ordinary men and women half their days, and that if, during that period, they become aware of their horrid transformation they may find the means to forestall it. May this not be the case with me? My reason, after all, is free, although my artistic inspiration be enslaved; and I can despise and loathe the music I am forced to compose, and the execrable power that forces me.

Nay, is it not because I have studied with the doggedness of hatred this corrupt and corrupting music of the Past, seeking for every little peculiarity of style and every biographical trifle merely to display its vileness, is it not for this presumptuous courage that I have been overtaken by such mysterious, incredible vengeance?

And meanwhile, my only relief consists in going over and over again in my mind the tale of my miseries. This time I will write it, writing only to tear up, to throw the manuscript unread into the fire. And yet, who knows? As the last charred pages shall crackle and slowly sink into the red embers, perhaps the spell may be broken, and I may possess once more my long-lost liberty, my vanished genius.

It was a breathless evening under the full moon, that implacable full moon beneath which, even more than beneath the dreamy splendour of noontide, Venice seemed to swelter in the midst of the waters, exhaling, like some great lily, mysterious influences, which make the brain swim and the heart faint—a moral malaria, distilled, as I thought, from those languishing melodies, those cooing vocalisations which I had found in the musty music-books of a century ago. I see that moonlight evening as if it were present. I see my fellow-lodgers of that little artists' boarding-house. The table on which they lean after supper is strewn with bits of bread, with napkins rolled in tapestry rollers, spots of wine here and there, and at regular intervals chipped pepper-pots, stands of tooth-picks, and heaps of those huge hard peaches which nature imitates from the marble-shops of Pisa. The whole *pension*-full is assembled, and examining stupidly the engraving which the American etcher has just brought for me, knowing me to be mad about eighteenth-century music and musicians, and having noticed, as he turned over the heaps of penny prints in the square of San Polo, that the portrait is that of a singer of those days.

Singer, thing of evil, stupid and wicked slave of the voice, of that instrument which was not invented by the human intellect, but begotten of the body, and which, instead of moving the soul, merely stirs up the dregs of our nature! For what is the voice but the Beast calling, awakening that other Beast sleeping in the depths of mankind, the Beast which all great art has ever sought to chain up, as the archangel chains up, in old pictures, the demon with his woman's face? How could the creature attached to this voice, its owner and its victim, the singer, the great, the real singer who once ruled over every heart, be otherwise than wicked and contemptible? But let me try and get on with my story.

I can see all my fellow-boarders, leaning on the table, contemplating the print, this effeminate beau, his hair curled into *ailes de pigeon*, his sword passed through his embroidered pocket, seated under a triumphal arch somewhere among the clouds, surrounded by puffy Cupids and crowned with laurels by a bouncing goddess of fame. I hear again all the insipid exclamations, the insipid questions about this singer:— 'When did he live? Was he very famous? Are you sure, Magnus, that this is really a portrait,' &c. &c. And I hear my own voice, as if in the far distance, giving them all sorts of information, biographical and critical, out of a battered little volume called *The Theatre of Musical Glory; or, Opinions upon the most Famous Chapel-masters and Virtuosi of this Century*, by Father Prosdocimo Sabatelli, Barnalite, Professor of Eloquence at the College of Modena, and Member of the Arcadian Academy, under the pastoral name of Evander Lilybæan, Venice, 1785, with the approbation of the Superiors. I tell them all how this singer, this Balthasar Cesari, was nicknamed Zaffirino because of a sapphire engraved with cabalistic signs presented to him one evening by a masked stranger, in whom wise folk recognised that great cultivator of the human voice, the devil; how much more wonderful had been this Zaffirino's vocal gifts than those of any singer of ancient or modern times; how his brief life had been but a series of triumphs, petted by the greatest kings, sung by the most famous poets, and finally, adds Father Prosdocimo, 'courted (if the grave Muse of history may incline her ear to the gossip of gallantry) by the most charming nymphs, even of the very highest quality.'

My friends glance once more at the engraving; more insipid remarks are made; I am requested—especially by the American young ladies—to play or sing one of this Zaffirino's favourite songs—'For of course you know them, dear Maestro Magnus, you who have such a passion for all old music. Do be good, and sit down to the piano.' I refuse, rudely enough, rolling the print in my fingers. How fearfully this cursed heat, these cursed moonlight nights, must have unstrung me! This Venice would certainly kill me in the long-run! Why, the sight of this idiotic engraving, the mere name of that coxcomb of a singer, have made my heart beat and my limbs turn to water like a love-sick hobbledehoy.

After my gruff refusal, the company begins to disperse; they prepare to go out, some to have a row on the lagoon, others to saunter before the *cafés* at St Mark's; family discussions arise, gruntings of fathers, murmurs of mothers, peals of laughing from young girls and young men. And the moon, pouring in by the wide-open windows, turns this old

Vernon Lee

palace ballroom, nowadays an inn dining-room, into a lagoon, scintillating, undulating like the other lagoon, the real one, which stretches out yonder furrowed by invisible gondolas betrayed by the red prow-lights. At last the whole lot of them are on the move. I shall be able to get some quiet in my room, and to work a little at my opera of *Ogier the Dane.* But no! Conversation revives, and, of all things, about that singer, that Zaffirino, whose absurd portrait I am crunching in my fingers.

The principal speaker is Count Alvise, an old Venetian with dyed whiskers, a great check tie fastened with two pins and a chain; a threadbare patrician who is dying to secure for his lanky son that pretty American girl, whose mother is intoxicated by all his mooning anecdotes about the past glories of Venice in general, and of his illustrious family in particular. Why, in Heaven's name, must he pitch upon Zaffirino for his mooning, this old duffer of a patrician?

'Zaffirino,—ah yes, to be sure! Balthasar Cesari, called Zaffirino,' snuffles the voice of Count Alvise, who always repeats the last word of every sentence at least three times. 'Yes, Zaffirino, to be sure! A famous singer of the days of my forefathers; yes, of my forefathers, dear lady!' Then a lot of rubbish about the former greatness of Venice, the glories of old music, the former Conservatoires, all mixed up with anecdotes of Rossini and Donizetti, whom he pretends to have known intimately. Finally, a story, of course containing plenty about his illustrious family:— 'My great grand-aunt, the Procuratessa Vendramin, from whom we have inherited our estate of Mistrà, on the Brenta'—a hopelessly muddled story, apparently, full of digressions, but of which that singer Zaffirino is the hero. The narrative, little by little, becomes more intelligible, or perhaps it is I who am giving it more attention.

'It seems,' says the Count, 'that there was one of his songs in particular which was called the "Husbands' Air"—*L'Aria dei Mariti*—because they didn't enjoy it quite as much as their better-halves . . . My grand-aunt, Pisana Renier, married to the Procuratore Vendramin, was a patrician of the old school, of the style that was getting rare a hundred years ago. Her virtue and her pride rendered her unapproachable. Zaffirino, on his part, was in the habit of boasting that no woman had ever been able to resist his singing, which, it appears, had its foundation in fact—the ideal changes, my dear lady, the ideal changes a good deal from one century to another!—and that his first song could make any woman turn pale and lower her eyes, the second make her madly in love, while the third song could kill her off on the spot, kill her for love, there under his very eyes, if he only felt inclined. My grand-aunt Vendramin laughed when this story was told her, refused to go to hear this insolent dog, and added that it might be quite possible by the aid of spells and infernal pacts to kill a *gentildonna*, but as to making her fall in love with a lackey—never! This answer was naturally reported to Zaffirino, who piqued himself upon always getting the better of any one who was wanting in deference to his voice. Like the ancient Romans, *parcere subjectis et debellare superbos.* You American ladies, who are so learned, will appreciate this little quotation from the divine Virgil. While seeming to avoid the Procuratessa Vendramin, Zaffirino took the opportunity, one evening at a large assembly, to sing in her presence. He sang and sang and sang until the poor grand-aunt Pisana fell ill for love. The most skilful physicians were kept unable to explain the mysterious malady which was visibly killing the poor young lady; and the Procuratore Vendramin applied in vain to the most venerated Madonnas, and vainly promised an altar of silver, with massive gold candlesticks, to Saints Cosmas and Damian, patrons of the art of healing. At last the brother-in-law of the Procuratessa, Monsignor Almorò Vendramin, Patriarch of Aquileia, a prelate famous for the sanctity of his life, obtained in a vision of Saint Justina, for whom he entertained a particular devotion, the information that the only thing which could benefit the strange illness of his sister-in-law was the voice of Zaffirino. Take notice that my poor grand-aunt had never condescended to such a revelation.

'The Procuratore was enchanted at this happy solution; and his lordship the Patriarch went to seek Zaffirino in person, and carried him in his own coach to the Villa of Mistrà, where the Procuratessa was residing. On being told what was about to happen, my poor grand-aunt went into fits of rage, which were succeeded immediately by equally violent fits of joy. However, she never forgot what was due to her great position. Although sick almost unto death, she had herself arrayed with the greatest pomp, caused her face to be painted, and put on all her diamonds: it would seem as if she were anxious to affirm her full dignity before this singer. Accordingly she received Zaffirino reclining on a sofa which had been placed in the great ballroom of the Villa of Mistrà, and beneath the princely canopy; for the Vendramins, who had intermarried with the house of Mantua, possessed imperial fiefs and were princes of the Holy Roman Empire. Zaffirino saluted her with the most profound respect, but not a word passed between them. Only, the singer inquired from the Procuratore whether the illustrious lady had received the Sacraments of the Church. Being told that the Procuratessa had herself asked to be given extreme unction from the hands of her brother-in-law, he declared his readiness to obey the orders of His Excellency, and sat down at once to the harpsichord.

'Never had he sung so divinely. At the end of the first song the Procuratessa Vendramin had already revived most extraordinarily; by the end of the second she appeared entirely cured and beaming with beauty and happiness; but at the third air—the *Aria dei Mariti*, no doubt—she began to change frightfully; she gave a dreadful cry, and fell into the convulsions of death. In a quarter of an hour she was dead! Zaffirino did not wait to see her die. Having finished his song, he withdrew instantly, took post-horses, and travelled day and night as far as Munich. People remarked that he had presented himself at Mistrà dressed in mourning, although he had mentioned no death among his relatives; also that he had prepared everything for his departure, as if fearing the wrath of so powerful a family. Then there was also the extraordinary question he had asked before beginning to sing, about the Procuratessa having confessed and received extreme unction. . . . No, thanks, my dear lady, no cigarettes for me. But if it does not distress you or your charming daughter, may I humbly beg permission to smoke a cigar?'

And Count Alvise, enchanted with his talent for narrative, and sure of having secured for his son the heart and the dollars of his fair audience, proceeds to light a candle, and at the candle one of those long black Italian cigars which require preliminary disinfection before smoking.

. . . If this state of things goes on I shall just have to ask the doctor for a bottle; this ridiculous beating of my heart and disgusting cold perspiration have increased steadily during Count Alvise's narrative. To keep myself in countenance among the various idiotic commentaries on this cock-and-bull story of a vocal coxcomb and a vapouring great lady, I begin to unroll the engraving, and to examine stupidly the portrait of Zaffirino, once so renowned, now so forgotten. A ridiculous ass, this singer, under his triumphal arch, with his stuffed Cupids and the great fat winged kitchenmaid crowning him with laurels. How flat and vapid and vulgar it is, to be sure, all this odious eighteenth century!

But he, personally, is not so utterly vapid as I had thought. That effeminate, fat face of his is almost beautiful, with an odd smile, brazen and cruel. I have seen faces like this, if not in real life, at least in my boyish romantic dreams, when I read Swinburne and Baudelaire, the faces of wicked, vindictive women. Oh yes! he is decidedly a beautiful creature, this Zaffirino, and his voice must have had the same sort of beauty and the same expression of wickedness. . . .

'Come on, Magnus,' sound the voices of my fellow-boarders, 'be a good fellow and sing us one of the old chap's songs; or at least something or other of that day, and we'll make believe it was the air with which he killed that poor lady.'

'Oh yes! the *Aria dei Mariti*, the "Husbands' Air," ' mumbles old Alvise, between the puffs at his impossible black cigar. 'My poor grand-aunt, Pisana Vendramin; he went and killed her with those songs of his, with that *Aria dei Mariti.*'

I feel senseless rage overcoming me. Is it that horrible palpitation (by the way, there is a Norwegian doctor, my fellow-countryman, at Venice just now) which is sending the blood to my brain and making me mad? The people round the piano, the furniture, everything together seems to get mixed and turn into moving blobs of colour. I set to singing; the only thing which remains distinct before my eyes being the portrait of Zaffirino, on the edge of that boarding-house piano; the sensual, effeminate face, with its wicked, cynical smile, keeps appearing and disappearing as the print wavers about in the draught that makes the candles smoke and gutter. And I set to singing madly, singing I don't know what. Yes; I begin to identify it: 'tis the *Biondina in Gondoleta,* the only song of the eighteenth century which is still remembered by the Venetian people. I sing it, mimicking every old-school grace; shakes, cadences, languishingly swelled and diminished notes, and adding all manner of buffooneries, until the audience, recovering from its surprise, begins to shake with laughing; until I begin to laugh myself, madly, frantically, between the phrases of the melody, my voice finally smothered in this dull, brutal laughter. . . . And then, to crown it all, I shake my fist at this long-dead singer, looking at me with his wicked woman's face, with his mocking, fatuous smile.

'Ah! you would like to be revenged on me also!' I exclaim. 'You would like me to write you nice roulades and flourishes, another nice *Aria dei Mariti,* my fine Zaffirino!'

That night I dreamed a very strange dream. Even in the big half-furnished room the heat and closeness were stifling. The air seemed laden with the scent of all manner of white flowers, faint and heavy in their intolerable sweetness: tuberoses, gardenias, and jasmines drooping I know not where in neglected vases. The moonlight had transformed the marble floor around me into a shallow, shining pool. On account of the heat I had exchanged my bed for a big old-fashioned sofa of light wood, painted with little nosegays and sprigs, like an old silk; and I lay there, not attempting to sleep, and letting my thoughts go vaguely to my opera of *Ogier the Dane,* of which I had long finished writing the words, and for whose music I had hoped to find some inspiration in this strange Venice, floating, as it were, in the stagnant lagoon of the past. But Venice had merely put all my ideas into hopeless confusion; it was as if there arose out of its shallow waters a miasma of long-dead melodies, which sickened but intoxicated my soul. I lay on my sofa watching that pool of whitish light, which rose higher and higher, little trickles of light meeting it here and there, wherever the moon's rays struck upon some polished surface; while huge shadows waved to and fro in the draught of the open balcony.

I went over and over that old Norse story: how the Paladin, Ogier, one of the knights of Charlemagne, was decoyed during his homeward wanderings from the Holy Land by the arts of an enchantress, the same who had once held in bondage the great Emperor Cæsar and given him King Oberon for a son; how Ogier had tarried in that island only one day and one night, and yet, when he came home to his kingdom, he found all changed, his friends dead, his family dethroned, and not a man who knew his face; until at last, driven hither and thither like a beggar, a poor minstrel had taken compassion of his sufferings and given him all he could give—a song, the song of the prowess of a hero dead for hundreds of years, the Paladin Ogier the Dane.

The story of Ogier ran into a dream, as vivid as my waking thoughts had been vague. I was looking no longer at the pool of moonlight spreading round my couch, with its trickles of light and looming, waving shadows, but the frescoed walls of a great saloon. It was not, as I recognised in a second, the dining-room of that Venetian palace now turned into a boarding-house. It was a far larger room, a real ballroom, almost circular in its octagon shape, with eight huge white doors surrounded by stucco mouldings, and, high on the vault of the ceiling, eight little galleries or recesses like boxes at a theatre, intended no doubt for musicians and spectators. The place was imperfectly lighted by only one of the eight chandeliers, which revolved slowly, like huge spiders, each on its long cord. But the light struck upon the gilt stuccoes opposite me, and on a large expanse of fresco, the sacrifice of Iphigenia, with Agamemnon and Achilles in Roman helmets, lappets, and knee-breeches. It discovered also one of the oil panels let into the mouldings of the roof, a goddess in lemon and lilac draperies, foreshortened over a great green peacock. Round the room, where the light reached, I could make out big yellow satin sofas and heavy gilded consoles; in the shadow of a corner was what looked like a piano, and farther in the shade one of those big canopies which decorate the anterooms of Roman palaces. I looked about me, wondering where I was: a heavy, sweet smell, reminding me of the flavour of a peach, filled the place.

Little by little I began to perceive sounds; little, sharp, metallic, detached notes, like those of a mandoline; and there was united to them a voice, very low and sweet, almost a whisper, which grew and grew and grew, until the whole place was filled with that exquisite vibrating note, of a strange, exotic, unique quality. The note went on, swelling and swelling. Suddenly there was a horrible piercing shriek, and the thud of a body on the floor, and all manner of smothered exclamations. There, close by the canopy, a light suddenly appeared; and I could see, among the dark figures moving to and fro in the room, a woman lying on the ground, surrounded by other women. Her blond hair, tangled, full of diamond-sparkles which cut through the half-darkness, was hanging dishevelled; the laces of her bodice had been cut, and her white breast shone among the sheen of jewelled brocade; her face was bent forwards, and a thin white arm trailed, like a broken limb, across the knees of one of the women who were endeavouring to lift her. There was a sudden splash of water against the floor, more confused exclamations, a hoarse, broken moan, and a gurgling, dreadful sound. . . . I awoke with a start and rushed to the window.

Outside, in the blue haze of the moon, the church and belfry of St George loomed blue and hazy, with the black hull and rigging, the red lights, of a large steamer moored before them. From the lagoon rose a damp sea-breeze. What was it all? Ah! I began to understand: that story of old Count Alvise's, the death of his grand-aunt, Pisana Vendramin. Yes, it was about that I had been dreaming.

I returned to my room; I struck a light, and sat down to my writing-table. Sleep had become impossible. I tried to work at my opera. Once or twice I thought I had got hold of what I had looked for so long. . . . But as soon as I tried to lay hold of my theme, there arose in my mind the distant echo of that voice, of that long note swelled slowly by insensible degrees, that long note whose tone was so strong and so subtle.

There are in the life of an artist moments when, still unable to seize his own inspiration, or even clearly to discern it, he becomes aware of the approach of that long-invoked idea. A mingled joy and terror warn him that before another day, another hour have passed, the inspiration shall have crossed the threshold of his soul and flooded it with its rapture. All day I had felt the need of isolation and quiet, and at nightfall I went for a row on the most solitary part of the lagoon. All things seemed to tell that I was going to meet my inspiration, and I awaited its coming as a lover awaits his beloved.

I had stopped my gondola for a moment, and as I gently swayed to and fro on the water, all paved with moonbeams, it seemed to me that I was on the confines of an imaginary world. It lay close at hand, enveloped in luminous, pale blue mist, through which the moon had cut a wide and glistening path; out to sea, the little islands, like moored black boats, only accentuated the solitude of this region of moonbeams and wavelets; while the hum of the insects in orchards hard by merely added to the impression of untroubled silence. On some such seas, I thought, must the

Paladin Ogier have sailed when about to discover that during that sleep at the enchantress's knees centuries had elapsed and the heroic world had set, and the kingdom of prose had come.

While my gondola rocked stationary on that sea of moonbeams, I pondered over that twilight of the heroic world. In the soft rattle of the water on the hull I seemed to hear the rattle of all that armour, of all those swords swinging rusty on the walls, neglected by the degenerate sons of the great champions of old. I had long been in search of a theme which I called the theme of the 'Prowess of Ogier'; it was to appear from time to time in the course of my opera, to develop at last into that song of the Minstrel, which reveals to the hero that he is one of a long-dead world. And at this moment I seemed to feel the presence of that theme. Yet an instant, and my mind would be overwhelmed by that savage music, heroic, funereal.

Suddenly there came across the lagoon, cleaving, chequering, and fretting the silence with a lace-work of sound even as the moon was fretting and cleaving the water, a ripple of music, a voice breaking itself in a shower of little scales and cadences and trills.

I sank back upon my cushions. The vision of heroic days had vanished, and before my closed eyes there seemed to dance multitudes of little stars of light, chasing and interlacing like those sudden vocalisations.

'To shore! Quick!' I cried to the gondolier.

But the sounds had ceased; and there came from the orchards, with their mulberry-trees glistening in the moonlight, and their black swaying cypress-plumes, nothing save the confused hum, the monotonous chirp, of the crickets.

I looked around me: on one side empty dunes, orchards, and meadows, without house or steeple; on the other, the blue and misty sea, empty to where distant islets were profiled black on the horizon.

A faintness overcame me, and I felt myself dissolve. For all of a sudden a second ripple of voice swept over the lagoon, a shower of little notes, which seemed to form a little mocking laugh.

Then again all was still. This silence lasted so long that I fell once more to meditating on my opera. I lay in wait once more for the half-caught theme. But no. It was not that theme for which I was waiting and watching with bated breath. I realised my delusion when, on rounding the point of the Giudecca, the murmur of a voice arose from the midst of the waters, a thread of sound slender as a moonbeam, scarce audible, but exquisite, which expanded slowly, insensibly, taking volume and body, taking flesh almost and fire, an ineffable quality, full, passionate, but veiled, as it were, in a subtle, downy wrapper. The note grew stronger and stronger, and warmer and more passionate, until it burst through that strange and charming veil, and emerged beaming, to break itself in the luminous facets of a wonderful shake, long, superb, triumphant.

There was a dead silence.

'Row to St Mark's!' I exclaimed. 'Quick!'

The gondola glided through the long, glittering track of moonbeams, and rent the great band of yellow, reflected light, mirroring the cupolas of St Mark's, the lace-like pinnacles of the palace, and the slender pink belfry, which rose from the lit-up water to the pale and bluish evening sky.

In the larger of the two squares the military band was blaring through the last spirals of a *crescendo* of Rossini. The crowd was dispersing in this great open-air ballroom, and the sounds arose which invariably follow upon out-of-door music. A clatter of spoons and glasses, a rustle and grating of frocks and of chairs, and the click of scabbards on the pavement. I pushed my way among the fashionable youths contemplating the ladies while sucking the knob of their sticks; through the serried ranks of respectable families, marching arm in arm with their white frocked young ladies close in front. I took a seat before Florian's, among the customers stretching themselves before departing, and the waiters hurrying to and fro, clattering their empty cups and trays. Two imitation Neapolitans were slipping their guitar and violin under their arms, ready to leave the place.

'Stop!' I cried to them; 'don't go yet. Sing me something—sing *La Camesella* or *Funiculì, funiculà*—no matter what, provided you make a row;' and as they screamed and scraped their utmost, I added, 'But can't you sing louder, d——n you!—sing louder, do you understand?'

I felt the need of noise, of yells and false notes, of something vulgar and hideous to drive away that ghost-voice which was haunting me.

Again and again I told myself that it had been some silly prank of a romantic amateur, hidden in the gardens of the shore or gliding unperceived on the lagoon; and that the sorcery of moonlight and sea-mist had transfigured for my excited brain mere humdrum roulades out of exercises of Bordogni or Crescentini.

But all the same I continued to be haunted by that voice. My work was interrupted ever and anon by the attempt to catch its imaginary echo; and the heroic harmonies of my Scandinavian legend were strangely interwoven with voluptuous phrases and florid cadences in which I seemed to hear again that same accursed voice.

To be haunted by singing-exercises! It seemed too ridiculous for a man who professedly despised the art of singing. And still, I preferred to believe in that childish amateur, amusing himself with warbling to the moon.

One day, while making these reflections the hundredth time over, my eyes chanced to light upon the portrait of Zaffirino, which my friend had pinned against the wall. I pulled it down and tore it into half a dozen shreds. Then, already ashamed of my folly, I watched the torn pieces float down from the window, wafted hither and thither by the sea-breeze. One scrap got caught in a yellow blind below me; the others fell into the canal, and were speedily lost to sight in the dark water. I was overcome with shame. My heart beat like bursting. What a miserable, unnerved worm I had become in this cursed Venice, with its languishing moonlights, its atmosphere as of some stuffy boudoir, long unused, full of old stuffs and pot-pourri!

That night, however, things seemed to be going better. I was able to settle down to my opera, and even to work at it. In the intervals my thoughts returned, not without a certain pleasure, to those scattered fragments of the torn engraving fluttering down to the water. I was disturbed at my piano by the hoarse voices and the scraping of violins which rose from one of those music-boats that station at night under the hotels of the Grand Canal. The moon had set. Under my balcony the water stretched black into the distance, its darkness cut by the still darker outlines of the flotilla of gondolas in attendance on the music-boat, where the faces of the singers, and the guitars and violins, gleamed reddish under the unsteady light of the Chinese-lanterns.

'*Jammo, jammo; jammo, jammo jà,*' sang the loud, hoarse voices; then a tremendous scrape and twang, and the yelled-out burden, '*Funiculì, funiculà; funiculì, funiculà; jammo, jammo, jammo, jammo, jammo jà.*'

Then came a few cries of '*Bis, Bis!*' from a neighbouring hotel, a brief clapping of hands, the sound of a handful of coppers rattling into the boat, and the oar-stroke of some gondolier making ready to turn away.

'Sing the *Camesella*,' ordered some voice with a foreign accent.

'No, no! *Santa Lucia.*'

'I want the *Camesella.*'

'No! *Santa Lucia.* Hi! sing *Santa Lucia*—d'you hear?'

The musicians, under their green and yellow and red lamps, held a whispered consultation on the manner of conciliating these contradictory demands. Then, after a minute's hesitation, the violins began the prelude of that once famous air, which has remained popular in Venice—the words written, some hundred years ago, by the patrician Gritti, the music by an unknown composer—*La Biondina in Gondoleta.*

That cursed eighteenth century! It seemed a malignant fatality that made these brutes choose just this piece to interrupt me.

At last the long prelude came to an end; and above the cracked guitars and squeaking fiddles there arose, not the expected nasal chorus, but a single voice singing below its breath.

My arteries throbbed. How well I knew that voice! It was singing, as I have said, below its breath, yet none the less it sufficed to fill all that reach of the canal with its strange quality of tone, exquisite, far-fetched.

They were long-drawn-out notes, of intense but peculiar sweetness, a man's voice which had much of a woman's, but more even of a chorister's, but a chorister's voice without its limpidity and innocence; its youthfulness was veiled, muffled, as it were, in a sort of downy vagueness, as if a passion of tears withheld.

There was a burst of applause, and the old palaces re-echoed with the clapping. 'Bravo, bravo! Thank you, thank you! Sing again—please, sing again. Who can it be?'

And then a bumping of hulls, a splashing of oars, and the oaths of gondoliers trying to push each other away, as the red prow-lamps of the gondolas pressed round the gaily lit singing-boat.

But no one stirred on board. It was to none of them that this applause was due. And while every one pressed on, and clapped and vociferated, one little red prow-lamp dropped away from the fleet; for a moment a single gondola stood forth black upon the black water, and then was lost in the night.

For several days the mysterious singer was the universal topic. The people of the music-boat swore that no one besides themselves had been on board, and that they knew as little as ourselves about the owner of that voice. The gondoliers, despite their descent from the spies of the old Republic, were equally unable to furnish any clue. No musical celebrity was known or suspected to be at Venice; and every one agreed that such a singer must be a European celebrity. The strangest thing in this strange business was, that even among those learned in music there was no agreement on the subject of this voice: it was called by all sorts of names and described by all manner of incongruous adjectives; people went so far as to dispute whether the voice belonged to a man or to a woman: every one had some new definition.

In all these musical discussions I, alone, brought forward no opinion. I felt a repugnance, an impossibility almost, of speaking about that voice; and the more or less commonplace conjectures of my friend had the invariable effect of sending me out of the room.

Meanwhile my work was becoming daily more difficult, and I soon passed from utter impotence to a state of inexplicable agitation. Every morning I arose with fine resolutions and grand projects of work; only to go to bed that night without having accomplished anything. I spent hours leaning on my balcony, or wandering through the network of lanes with their ribbon of blue sky, endeavouring vainly to expel the thought of that voice, or endeavouring in reality to reproduce it in my memory; for the more I tried to banish it from my thoughts, the more I grew to thirst for that extraordinary tone, for those mysteriously downy, veiled notes; and no sooner did I make an effort to work at my opera than my head was full of scraps of forgotten eighteenth-century airs, of frivolous or languishing little phrases; and I fell to wondering with a bitter-sweet longing how those songs would have sounded if sung by that voice.

At length it became necessary to see a doctor, from whom, however, I carefully hid away all the stranger symptoms of my malady. The air of the lagoons, the great heat, he answered cheerfully, had pulled me down a little; a tonic and a month in the country, with plenty of riding and no work, would make me myself again. That old idler, Count Alvise, who had insisted on accompanying me to the physician's, immediately suggested that I should go and stay with his son, who was boring himself to death superintending the maize harvest on the mainland: he could promise me excellent air, plenty of horses, and all the peaceful surroundings and the delightful occupations of a rural life—'Be sensible, my dear Magnus, and just go quietly to Mistrà.'

Mistrà—the name sent a shiver all down me. I was about to decline the invitation, when a thought suddenly loomed vaguely in my mind.

'Yes, dear Count,' I answered; 'I accept your invitation with gratitude and pleasure. I will start tomorrow for Mistrà.'

The next day found me at Padua, on my way to the Villa of Mistrà. It seemed as if I had left an intolerable burden behind me. I was, for the first time since how long, quite light of heart. The tortuous, rough-paved streets, with their empty, gloomy porticoes; the ill-plastered palaces, with closed, discoloured shutters; the little rambling square, with meagre trees and stubborn grass; the Venetian garden-houses reflecting their crumbling graces in the muddy canal; the gardens without gates and the gates without gardens, the avenues leading nowhere; and the population of blind and legless beggars, of whining sacristans, which issued as by magic from between the flagstones and dust-heaps and weeds under the fierce August sun, all this dreariness merely amused and pleased me. My good spirits were heightened by a musical mass which I had the good fortune to hear at St Anthony's.

Never in all my days had I heard anything comparable, although Italy affords many strange things in the way of sacred music. Into the deep nasal chanting of the priests there had suddenly burst a chorus of children, singing absolutely independent of all time and tune; grunting of priests answered by squealing of boys, slow Gregorian modulation interrupted by jaunty barrel-organ pipings, an insane, insanely merry jumble of bellowing and barking, mewing and cackling and braying, such as would have enlivened a witches' meeting, or rather some medieval Feast of Fools. And, to make the grotesqueness of such music still more fantastic and Hoffmannlike, there was, besides, the magnificence of the piles of sculptured marbles and gilded bronzes, the tradition of the musical splendour for which St Anthony's had been famous in days gone by. I had read in old travellers, Lalande and Burney, that the Republic of St Mark had squandered immense sums not merely on the monuments and decoration, but on the musical establishment of its great cathedral of Terra Firma. In the midst of this ineffable concert of impossible voices and instruments, I tried to imagine the voice of Guadagni, the soprano for whom Gluck had written *Che farò senza Euridice,* and the fiddle of Tartini, that Tartini with whom the devil had once come and made music. And the delight in anything so absolutely, barbarously, grotesquely, fantastically incongruous as such a performance in such a place was heightened by a sense of profanation: such were the successors of those wonderful musicians of that hated eighteenth century!

The whole thing had delighted me so much, so very much more than the most faultless performance could have done, that I determined to enjoy it once more; and towards vesper-time, after a cheerful dinner with two bagmen at the inn of the Golden Star, and a pipe over the rough sketch of a possible cantata upon the music which the devil made for Tartini, I turned my steps once more towards St Anthony's.

The bells were ringing for sunset, and a muffled sound of organs seemed to issue from the huge, solitary church; I pushed my way under the heavy leathern curtain, expecting to be greeted by the grotesque performance of that morning.

I proved mistaken. Vespers must long have been over. A smell of stale incense, a crypt-like damp filled my mouth; it was already night in that vast cathedral. Out of the darkness glimmered the votive-lamps of the chapels, throwing wavering lights upon the red polished marble, the gilded railing, and chandeliers, and plaqueing with yellow the muscles of some sculptured figure. In a corner a burning taper put a halo about the head of a priest, burnishing his shining bald skull, his white surplice, and the open book before him. 'Amen' he chanted; the book was closed with a snap, the light moved up the apse, some dark figures of women rose from their knees and passed quickly towards the door; a man saying his prayers before a chapel also got up, making a great clatter in dropping his stick.

The church was empty, and I expected every minute to be turned out by the sacristan making his evening round to close the doors. I was leaning against a pillar, looking into the greyness of the great arches, when the organ suddenly burst out into a series of chords, rolling through the echoes of the church: it seemed to be the conclusion of some service. And above the organ rose the notes of a voice; high, soft, enveloped in a kind of downiness, like a cloud of incense, and which ran through the mazes of a long cadence. The voice dropped into silence; with two thundering chords the organ closed in. All was silent. For a moment I stood leaning against one of the pillars of the nave: my hair was clammy, my knees sank beneath me, an enervating heat spread through my body; I tried to breathe more largely, to suck in the sounds with the incense-laden air. I was supremely happy, and yet as if I were dying; then suddenly a chill ran through me, and with it a vague panic. I turned away and hurried out into the open.

The evening sky lay pure and blue along the jagged line of roofs; the bats and swallows were wheeling about; and from the belfries all around, half-drowned by the deep bell of St Anthony's, jangled the peal of the *Ave Maria*.

'You really don't seem well,' young Count Alvise had said the previous evening, as he welcomed me, in the light of a lantern held up by a peasant, in the weedy back-garden of the Villa of Mistrà. Everything had seemed to me like a dream: the jingle of the horse's bells driving in the dark from Padua, as the lantern swept the acacia-hedges with their wide yellow light; the grating of the wheels on the gravel; the supper-table, illumined by a single petroleum lamp for fear of attracting mosquitoes, where a broken old lackey, in an old stable jacket, handed round the dishes among the fumes of onion; Alvise's fat mother gabbling dialect in a shrill, benevolent voice behind the bullfights on her fan; the unshaven village priest, perpetually fidgeting with his glass and foot, and sticking one shoulder up above the other. And now, in the afternoon, I felt as if I had been in this long, rambling, tumble-down Villa of Mistrà—a villa three-quarters of which was given up to the storage of grain and garden tools, or to the exercise of rats, mice, scorpions, and centipedes—all my life; as if I had always sat there, in Count Alvise's study, among the pile of undusted books on agriculture, the sheaves of accounts, the samples of grain and silkworm seed, the ink-stains and the cigar-ends; as if I had never heard of anything save the cereal basis of Italian agriculture, the diseases of maize, the peronospora of the vine, the breeds of bullocks, and the iniquities of farm labourers; with the blue cones of the Euganean hills closing in the green shimmer of plain outside the window.

After an early dinner, again with the screaming gabble of the fat old Countess, the fidgeting and shoulder-raising of the unshaven priest, the smell of fried oil and stewed onions, Count Alvise made me get into the cart beside him, and whirled me along among clouds of dust, between the endless glister of poplars, acacias, and maples, to one of his farms.

In the burning sun some twenty or thirty girls, in coloured skirts, laced bodices, and big straw-hats, were threshing the maize on the big red brick threshing-floor, while others were winnowing the grain in great sieves. Young Alvise III (the old one was Alvise II: every one is Alvise, that is to say, Lewis, in that family; the name is on the house, the carts, the barrows, the very pails) picked up the maize, touched it, tasted it, said something to the girls that made them laugh, and something to the head farmer that made him look very glum; and then led me into a huge stable, where some twenty or thirty white bullocks were stamping, switching their tails, hitting their horns against the mangers in the dark. Alvise III patted each, called him by his name, gave him some salt or a turnip, and explained which was the Mantuan breed, which the Apulian, which the Romagnolo, and so on. Then he bade me jump into the trap, and off we went again through the dust, among the hedges and ditches, till we came to some more brick farm buildings with pinkish roofs smoking against the blue sky. Here there were more young women threshing and winnowing the maize, which made a great golden Danaë cloud; more bullocks stamping and lowing in the cool darkness; more joking, fault-finding, explaining; and thus through five farms, until I seemed to see the rhythmical rising and falling of the flails against the hot sky, the shower of golden grains, the yellow dust from the winnowing-sieves on to the bricks, the switching of innumerable tails and plunging of innumerable horns, the glistening of huge white flanks and foreheads, whenever I closed my eyes.

'A good day's work!' cried Count Alvise, stretching out his long legs with the tight trousers riding up over the Wellington boots. 'Mamma, give us some aniseed-syrup after dinner; it is an excellent restorative and precaution against the fevers of this country.'

'Oh! you've got fever in this part of the world, have you? Why, your father said the air was so good!'

'Nothing, nothing,' soothed the old Countess. 'The only thing to be dreaded are mosquitoes; take care to fasten your shutters before lighting the candle.'

'Well,' rejoined young Alvise, with an effort of conscience, 'of course there *are* fevers. But they needn't hurt you. Only, don't go out into the garden at night, if you don't want to catch them. Papa told me that you have fancies for moonlight rambles. It won't do in this climate, my dear fellow; it won't do. If you must stalk about at night, being a genius, take a turn inside the house; you can get quite exercise enough.'

After dinner the aniseed-syrup was produced, together with brandy and cigars, and they all sat in the long, narrow, half-furnished room on the first floor; the old Countess knitting a garment of uncertain shape and destination; the priest reading out the newspaper; Count Alvise puffing at his long, crooked cigar, and pulling the ears of a long, lean dog with a suspicion of mange and a stiff eye. From the dark garden outside rose the hum and whirr of countless insects, and the smell of the grapes which hung black against the starlit, blue sky, on the trellis. I went to the balcony. The garden lay dark beneath; against the twinkling horizon stood out the tall poplars. There was the sharp cry of an owl; the barking of a dog; a sudden whiff of warm, enervating perfume, a perfume that made me think of the taste of certain peaches, and suggested white, thick, wax-like petals. I seemed to have smelt that flower once before: it made me feel languid, almost faint.

'I am very tired,' I said to Count Alvise. 'See how feeble we city folk become!'

But, despite my fatigue, I found it quite impossible to sleep. The night seemed perfectly stifling. I had felt nothing like it at Venice. Despite the injunctions of the Countess I opened the solid wooden shutters, hermetically closed against mosquitoes, and looked out.

The moon had risen; and beneath it lay the big lawns, the rounded tree-tops, bathed in a blue, luminous mist, every leaf glistening and trembling in what seemed a heaving sea of light. Beneath the window was the long trellis, with the white shining piece of pavement under it. It was so bright that I could distinguish the green of the vine-leaves, the dull red of the catalpa-flowers. There was in the air a vague scent of cut grass, of ripe American grapes, of that white flower (it must be white) which made me think of the taste of peaches all melting into the delicious freshness of falling dew. From the village church came the stroke of one: heaven knows how long I had been vainly attempting to sleep. A shiver ran through me, and my head suddenly filled as with the fumes of some subtle wine; I remembered all those weedy embankments, those canals full of stagnant water, the yellow faces of the peasants; the word malaria returned to my mind. No matter! I remained leaning on the window, with a thirsty longing to plunge myself into this blue moon-mist, this dew and perfume and silence, which seemed to vibrate and quiver like the stars that strewed the depths of heaven. . . . What music, even Wagner's, or of that great singer of starry nights, the divine Schumann, what music could ever compare with this great silence, with this great concert of voiceless things that sing within one's soul?

As I made this reflection, a note, high, vibrating, and sweet, rent the silence, which immediately closed around it. I leaned out of the window, my heart beating as though it must burst. After a brief space the silence was cloven once more by that note, as the darkness is cloven by a falling star or a firefly rising slowly like a rocket. But this time it was plain that the voice did not come, as I had imagined, from the garden, but from the house itself, from some corner of this rambling old villa of Mistrà.

Mistrà—Mistrà! The name rang in my ears, and I began at length to grasp its significance, which seems to have escaped me till then. 'Yes,' I said to myself, 'it is quite natural.' And with this odd impression of naturalness was mixed a feverish, impatient pleasure. It was as if I had come to Mistrà on purpose, and that I was about to meet the object of my long and weary hopes.

Grasping the lamp with its singed green shade, I gently opened the door and made my way through a series of long passages and of big, empty rooms, in which my steps re-echoed as in a church, and my light disturbed whole swarms of bats. I wandered at random, farther and farther from the inhabited part of the buildings.

This silence made me feel sick; I gasped as under a sudden disappointment.

All of a sudden there came a sound—chords, metallic, sharp, rather like the tone of a mandoline—close to my ear. Yes, quite close: I was separated from the sounds only by a partition. I fumbled for a door; the unsteady light of my lamp was insufficient for my eyes, which were swimming like those of a drunkard. At last I found a latch, and, after a moment's hesitation, I lifted it and gently pushed open the door. At first I could not understand what manner of place I was in. It was dark all round me, but a brilliant light blinded me, a light coming from below and striking the opposite wall. It was as if I had entered a dark box in a half-lighted theatre. I was, in fact, in something of the kind, a sort of dark hole with a high balustrade, half-hidden by an up-drawn curtain. I remembered those little galleries or recesses for the use of musicians or lookers-on which exist under the ceiling of the ballrooms in certain old Italian palaces. Yes; it must have been one like that. Opposite me was a vaulted ceiling covered with gilt mouldings, which framed great time-blackened canvases; and lower down, in the light thrown up from below, stretched a wall covered with faded frescoes. Where had I seen that goddess in lilac and lemon draperies foreshortened over a big, green peacock? For she was familiar to me, and the stucco Tritons also who twisted their tails round her gilded frame. And that fresco, with warriors in Roman cuirasses and green and blue lappets, and knee-breeches— where could I have seen them before? I asked myself these questions without experiencing any surprise. Moreover, I was very calm, as one is calm sometimes in extraordinary dreams—could I be dreaming?

I advanced gently and leaned over the balustrade. My eyes were met at first by the darkness above me, where, like gigantic spiders, the big chandeliers rotated slowly, hanging from the ceiling. Only one of them was lit, and its Murano-glass pendants, its carnations and roses, shone opalescent in the light of the guttering wax. This chandelier lighted up the opposite wall and that piece of ceiling with the goddess and the green peacock; it illumined, but far less well, a corner of the huge room, where, in the shadow of a kind of canopy, a little group of people were crowding round a yellow satin sofa, of the same kind as those that lined the walls. On the sofa, half-screened from me by the surrounding persons, a woman was stretched out: the silver of her embroidered dress and the rays of her diamonds gleamed and shot forth as she moved uneasily. And immediately under the chandelier, in the full light, a man stooped over a harpsichord, his head bent slightly, as if collecting his thoughts before singing.

He struck a few chords and sang. Yes, sure enough, it was the voice, the voice that had so long been persecuting me! I recognised at once that delicate, voluptuous quality, strange, exquisite, sweet beyond words, but lacking all youth and clearness. That passion veiled in tears which had troubled my brain that night on the lagoon, and again on the Grand Canal singing the *Biondina*, and yet again, only two days since, in the deserted cathedral of Padua. But I recognised now what seemed to have been hidden from me till then, that this voice was what I cared most for in all the wide world.

The voice wound and unwound itself in long, languishing phrases, in rich, voluptuous *rifiorituras*, all fretted with tiny scales and exquisite, crisp shakes; it stopped ever and anon, swaying as if panting in languid delight. And I felt my body melt even as wax in the sunshine, and it seemed to me that I too was turning fluid and vaporous, in order to mingle with these sounds as the moonbeams mingle with the dew.

Suddenly, from the dimly lighted corner by the canopy, came a little piteous wail; then another followed, and was lost in the singer's voice. During a long phrase on the harpsichord, sharp and tinkling, the singer turned his head towards the dais, and there came a plaintive little sob. But he, instead of stopping, struck a sharp chord; and with a thread of voice so hushed as to be scarcely audible, slid softly into a long *cadenza*. At the same moment he threw his head backwards, and the light fell full upon the handsome, effeminate face, with its ashy pallor and big, black brows, of the singer Zaffirino. At the sight of that face, sensual and sullen, of that smile which was cruel and mocking like a bad woman's, I understood—I knew not why, by what process—that his singing *must* be cut short, that the accursed phrase *must* never be finished. I understood that I was before an assassin, that he was killing this woman, and killing me also, with his wicked voice.

I rushed down the narrow stair which led down from the box, pursued, as it were, by that exquisite voice, swelling, swelling by insensible degrees. I flung myself on the door which must be that of the big saloon. I could see its light between the panels. I bruised my hands in trying to wrench the latch. The door was fastened tight, and while I was struggling with that locked door I heard the voice swelling, swelling, rending asunder that downy veil which wrapped it, leaping forth clear, resplendent, like the sharp and glittering blade of a knife that seemed to enter deep into my breast. Then, once more, a wail, a death-groan, and that dreadful noise, that hideous gurgle of breath strangled by a rush of blood. And then a long shake, acute, brilliant, triumphant.

The door gave way beneath my weight, one half crashed in. I entered. I was blinded by a flood of blue moonlight. It poured in through four great windows, peaceful and diaphanous, a pale blue mist of moonlight, and turned the huge room into a kind of submarine cave, paved with moonbeams, full of shimmers, of pools of moonlight. It was as bright as at midday, but the brightness was cold, blue, vaporous, supernatural. The room was completely empty, like a great hay-loft. Only, there hung from the ceiling the ropes which had once supported a chandelier; and in a corner, among stacks of wood and heaps of Indian-corn, whence spread a sickly smell of damp and mildew, there stood a long, thin harpsichord, with spindle-legs, and its cover cracked from end to end.

I felt, all of a sudden, very calm. The one thing that mattered was the phrase that kept moving in my head, the phrase of that unfinished cadence which I had heard but an instant before. I opened the harpsichord, and my fingers came down boldly upon its keys. A jingle-jangle of broken strings, laughable and dreadful, was the only answer.

Then an extraordinary fear overtook me. I clambered out of one of the windows; I rushed up the garden and wandered through the fields, among the canals and the embankments, until the moon had set and the dawn began to shiver, followed, pursued for ever by that jangle of broken strings.

People expressed much satisfaction at my recovery. It seems that one dies of those fevers.

Recovery? But have I recovered? I walk, and eat and drink and talk; I can even sleep. I live the life of other living creatures. But I am wasted by a strange and deadly disease. I can never lay hold of my own inspiration. My head is filled with music which is certainly by me, since I have never heard it before, but which still is not my own, which I despise and abhor: little, tripping flourishes and languishing phrases, and long-drawn, echoing cadences.

O wicked, wicked voice, violin of flesh and blood made by the Evil One's hand, may I not even execrate thee in peace; but is it necessary that, at the moment when I curse, the longing to hear thee again should parch my soul like hell-thirst? And since I have satiated thy lust for revenge, since thou hast withered my life and withered my genius, is it not time for pity? May I not hear one note, only one note of thine, O singer, O wicked and contemptible wretch?

The Judge's House

BRAM STOKER

When the time for his examination drew near Malcolm Malcolmson made up his mind to go somewhere to read by himself. He feared the attractions of the seaside, and also he feared completely rural isolation, for of old he knew its charms, and so he determined to find some unpretentious little town where there would be nothing to distract him. He refrained from asking suggestions from any of his friends, for he argued that each would recommend some place of which he had knowledge, and where he had already acquaintances. As Malcolmson wished to avoid friends he had no wish to encumber himself with the attention of friends' friends, and so he determined to look out for a place for himself. He packed a portmanteau with some clothes and all the books he required, and then took ticket for the first name on the local time-table which he did not know.

When at the end of three hours' journey he alighted at Benchurch, he felt satisfied that he had so far obliterated his tracks as to be sure of having a peaceful opportunity of pursuing his studies. He went straight to the one inn which the sleepy little place contained, and put up for the night. Benchurch was a market town, and once in three weeks was crowded to excess, but for the remainder of the twenty-one days it was as attractive as a desert. Malcolmson looked around the day after his arrival to try to find quarters more isolated than even so quiet an inn as 'The Good Traveller' afforded. There was only one place which took his fancy, and it certainly satisfied his wildest ideas regarding quiet; in fact, quiet was not the proper word to apply to it—desolation was the only term conveying any suitable idea of its isolation. It was an old rambling, heavy-built house of the Jacobean style, with heavy gables and windows, unusually small, and set higher than was customary in such houses, and was surrounded with a high brick wall massively built. Indeed, on examination, it looked more like a fortified house than an ordinary dwelling. But all these things pleased Malcolmson. 'Here,' he thought, 'is the very spot I have been looking for, and if I can only get opportunity of using it I shall be happy.' His joy was increased when he realised beyond doubt that it was not at present inhabited.

From the post-office he got the name of the agent, who was rarely surprised at the application to rent a part of the old house. Mr Carnford, the local lawyer and agent, was a genial old gentleman, and frankly confessed his delight at anyone being willing to live in the house.

'To tell you the truth,' said he, 'I should be only too happy, on behalf of the owners, to let anyone have the house rent free for a term of years if only to accustom the people here to see it inhabited. It has been so long empty that some kind of absurd prejudice has grown up about it, and this can be best put down by its occupation—if only,' he added with a sly glance at Malcolmson, 'by a scholar like yourself, who wants it quiet for a time.'

Malcolmson thought it needless to ask the agent about the 'absurd prejudice'; he knew he would get more information, if he should require it, on that subject from other quarters. He paid his three months' rent, got a receipt, and the name of an old woman who would probably undertake to 'do' for him, and came away with the keys in his pocket. He then went to the landlady of the inn, who was a cheerful and most kindly person, and asked her advice as to such stores and provisions as he would be likely to require. She threw up her hands in amazement when he told her where he was going to settle himself.

'Not in the Judge's House!' she said, and grew pale as she spoke. He explained the locality of the house, saying that he did not know its name. When he had finished she answered:

'Aye, sure enough—sure enough the very place! It is the Judge's House sure enough.' He asked her to tell him about the place, why so called, and what there was against it. She told him that it was so called locally because it had been many years before—how long she could not say, as she was herself from another part of the country, but she thought it must have been a hundred years or more—the abode of a judge who was held in great terror on account of his harsh sentences and his hostility to prisoners at Assizes. As to what there was against the house itself she could not tell. She had often asked, but no one could inform her; but there was a general feeling that there was *something*, and for her own part she would not take all the money in Drinkwater's Bank and stay in the house an hour by herself. Then she apologised to Malcolmson for her disturbing talk.

'It is too bad of me, sir, and you—and a young gentleman, too—if you will pardon me saying it, going to live there all alone. If you were my boy—and you'll excuse me for saying it—you wouldn't sleep there a night, not if I had to go there myself and pull the big alarm bell that's on the roof!' The good creature was so manifestly in earnest, and was so kindly in her intentions, that Malcolmson, although amused, was touched. He told her kindly how much he appreciated her interest in him, and added:

'But, my dear Mrs Witham, indeed you need not be concerned about me! A man who is reading for the Mathematical Tripos has too much to think of to be disturbed by any of these mysterious "somethings", and his work is of too exact and prosaic a kind to allow of his having any corner in his mind for mysteries of any kind. Harmonical Progression, Permutations and Combinations, and Elliptic Functions have sufficient mysteries for me!' Mrs Witham kindly undertook to see after his commissions, and he went himself to look for the old woman who had been recommended to him. When he returned to the Judge's House with her, after an interval of a couple of hours, he found Mrs Witham herself waiting with several men and boys carrying parcels, and an upholsterer's man with a bed in a cart, for she said, though tables and chairs might be all very well, a bed that hadn't been aired for mayhap fifty years was not proper for young bones to lie on. She was evidently curious to see the inside of the house; and though manifestly so afraid of the 'somethings' that at the slightest sound she clutched on to Malcolmson, whom she never left for a moment, went over the whole place.

After his examination of the house, Malcolmson decided to take up his abode in the great dining-room, which was big enough to serve for all his requirements; and Mrs Witham, with the aid of the charwoman, Mrs Dempster, proceeded to arrange matters. When the hampers were brought in and unpacked, Malcolmson saw that with much kind forethought she had sent from her own kitchen sufficient provisions to last for a few days. Before going she expressed all sorts of kind wishes; and at the door turned and said:

'And perhaps, sir, as the room is big and draughty it might be well to have one of those big screens put round your bed at night—though, truth to tell, I would die myself if I were to be so shut in with all kinds of—of "things", that put their heads round the sides, or over the top, and look on me!' The image which she had called up was too much for her nerves, and she fled incontinently.

Mrs Dempster sniffed in a superior manner as the landlady disappeared, and remarked that for her own part she wasn't afraid of all the bogies in the kingdom.

'I'll tell you what it is, sir,' she said; 'bogies is all kinds and sorts of things—except bogies! Rats and mice, and beetles; and creaky doors, and loose slates, and broken panes, and stiff drawer handles, that stay out when you pull them and then fall down in the middle of the night. Look at the wainscot of the room! It is old—hundreds of years old! Do you think there's no rats and beetles there! And do you imagine, sir, that you won't see none of them! Rats is bogies, I tell you, and bogies is rats; and don't you get to think anything else!'

'Mrs Dempster,' said Malcolmson gravely, making her a polite bow, 'you know more than a Senior Wrangler! And let me say, that, as a mark of esteem for your indubitable soundness of head and heart, I shall, when I go, give you possession of this house, and let you stay here by yourself for the last two months of my tenancy, for four weeks will serve my purpose.'

'Thank you kindly, sir!' she answered, 'but I couldn't sleep away from home a night. I am in Greenhow's Charity, and if I slept a night away from my rooms I should lose all I have got to live on. The rules is very strict; and there's too many watching for a vacancy for me to run any risks in the matter. Only for that, sir, I'd gladly come here and attend on you altogether during your stay.'

'My good woman,' said Malcolmson hastily, 'I have come here on purpose to obtain solitude; and believe me that I am grateful to the late Greenhow for having so organised his admirable charity—whatever it is—that I am perforce denied the opportunity of suffering from such a form of temptation! Saint Anthony himself could not be more rigid on the point!'

The old woman laughed harshly. 'Ah, you young gentlemen,' she said, 'you don't fear for naught; and belike you'll get all the solitude you want here.' She set to work with her cleaning; and by nightfall, when Malcolmson returned from his walk—he always had one of his books to study as he walked—he found the room swept and tidied, a fire burning in the old hearth, the lamp lit, and the table spread for supper with Mrs Witham's excellent fare. 'This is comfort, indeed,' he said, as he rubbed his hands.

When he had finished his supper, and lifted the tray to the other end of the great oak dining-table, he got out his books again, put fresh wood on the fire, trimmed his lamp, and set himself down to a spell of real hard work. He went on without pause till about eleven o'clock, when he knocked off for a bit to fix his fire and lamp, and to make himself a cup of tea. He had always been a tea-drinker, and during his college life had sat late at work and had taken tea late. The rest was a great luxury to him, and he enjoyed it with a sense of delicious, voluptuous ease. The renewed fire leaped and sparkled, and threw quaint shadows through the great old room; and as he sipped his hot tea he revelled in the sense of isolation from his kind. Then it was that he began to notice for the first time what a noise the rats were making.

'Surely,' he thought, 'they cannot have been at it all the time I was reading. Had they been, I must have noticed it!' Presently, when the noise increased, he satisfied himself that it was really new. It was evident that at first the rats had been frightened at the presence of a stranger, and the light of fire and lamp; but that as the time went on they had grown bolder and were now disporting themselves as was their wont.

How busy they were! and hark to the strange noises! Up and down behind the old wainscot, over the ceiling and under the floor they raced, and gnawed, and scratched! Malcolmson smiled to himself as he recalled to mind the saying of Mrs Dempster, 'Bogies is rats, and rats is bogies!' The tea began to have its effect of intellectual and nervous stimulus, he saw with joy another long spell of work to be done before the night was past, and in the sense of security which it gave him, he allowed himself the luxury of a good look round the room. He took his lamp in one hand, and went all around, wondering that so quaint and beautiful an old house had been so long neglected. The carving of the oak on the panels of the wainscot was fine, and on and round the doors and windows it was beautiful and of rare merit. There were some old pictures on the walls, but they were coated so thick with dust and dirt that he could not distinguish any detail of them, though he held his lamp as high as he could over his head. Here and there as he went round he saw some crack or hole blocked for a moment by the face of a rat with its bright eyes glittering in the light, but in an instant it was gone, and a squeak and a scamper followed.

The thing that most struck him, however, was the rope of the great alarm bell on the roof, which hung down in a corner of the room on the right-hand side of the fireplace. He pulled up close to the hearth a great high-backed carved oak chair, and sat down to his last cup of tea. When this was done he made up the fire, and went back to his work, sitting at the corner of the table, having the fire to his left. For a while the rats disturbed him somewhat with their perpetual scampering, but he got accustomed to the noise as one does to the ticking of a clock or to the roar of moving water; and he became so immersed in his work that everything in the world, except the problem which he was trying to solve, passed away from him.

He suddenly looked up, his problem was still unsolved, and there was in the air that sense of the hour before the dawn, which is so dread to doubtful life. The noise of the rats had ceased. Indeed it seemed to him that it must have ceased but lately and that it was the sudden cessation which had disturbed him. The fire had fallen low, but still it threw out a deep red glow. As he looked he started in spite of his *sang froid*.

There on the great high-backed carved oak chair by the right side of the fireplace sat an enormous rat, steadily glaring at him with baleful eyes. He made a motion to it as though to hunt it away, but it did not stir. Then he made the motion of throwing something. Still it did not stir, but showed its great white teeth angrily, and its cruel eyes shone in the lamplight with an added vindictiveness.

Malcolmson felt amazed, and seizing the poker from the hearth ran at it to kill it. Before, however, he could strike it, the rat, with a squeak that sounded like the concentration of hate, jumped upon the floor, and, running up the rope of the alarm bell, disappeared in the darkness beyond the range of the green-shaded lamp. Instantly, strange to say, the noisy scampering of the rats in the wainscot began again.

By this time Malcolmson's mind was quite off the problem; and as a shrill cock-crow outside told him of the approach of morning, he went to bed and to sleep.

He slept so sound that he was not even waked by Mrs Dempster coming in to make up his room. It was only when she had tidied up the place and got his breakfast ready and tapped on the screen which closed in his bed that he woke. He was a little tired still after his night's hard work, but a strong cup of tea soon freshened him up, and, taking his book, he went out for his morning walk, bringing with him a few sandwiches lest he should not care to return till dinner time. He found a quiet walk between high elms some way outside the town, and here he spent the greater part of the day studying his Laplace. On his return he looked in to see Mrs Witham and to thank her for her kindness. When she saw him coming through the diamond-paned bay-window of her sanctum she came out to meet him and asked him in. She looked at him searchingly and shook her head as she said:

'You must not overdo it, sir. You are paler this morning than you should be. Too late hours and too hard work on the brain isn't good for any man! But tell me, sir, how did you pass the night? Well, I hope? But, my heart! sir, I was glad when Mrs Dempster told me this morning that you were all right and sleeping sound when she went in.'

'Oh, I was all right,' he answered, smiling, 'the "somethings" didn't worry me, as yet. Only the rats; and they had a circus, I tell you, all over the place. There was one wicked looking old devil that sat up on my own chair by the fire, and wouldn't go till I took the poker to him, and then he ran up the rope of the alarm bell and got to somewhere up the wall or the ceiling—I couldn't see where, it was so dark.'

'Mercy on us,' said Mrs Witham, 'an old devil, and sitting on a chair by the fireside! Take care, sir! take care! There's many a true word spoken in jest.'

'How do you mean? 'Pon my word I don't understand.'

'An old devil! The old devil, perhaps. There! sir, you needn't laugh,' for Malcolmson had broken into a hearty peal. 'You young folks thinks it easy to laugh at things that makes older ones shudder. Never mind, sir!

never mind! Please God, you'll laugh all the time. It's what I wish you myself!' and the good lady beamed all over in sympathy with his enjoyment, her fears gone for a moment.

'Oh, forgive me!' said Malcolmson presently. 'Don't think me rude; but the idea was too much for me—that the old devil himself was on the chair last night!' And at the thought he laughed again. Then he went home to dinner.

This evening the scampering of the rats began earlier; indeed it had been going on before his arrival, and only ceased whilst his presence by its freshness disturbed them. After dinner he sat by the fire for a while and had a smoke; and then, having cleared his table, began to work as before. Tonight the rats disturbed him more than they had done on the previous night. How they scampered up and down and under and over! How they squeaked, and scratched, and gnawed! How they, getting bolder by degrees, came to the mouths of their holes and to the chinks and cracks and crannies in the wainscoting till their eyes shone like tiny lamps as the firelight rose and fell. But to him, now doubtless accustomed to them, their eyes were not wicked; only their playfulness touched him. Sometimes the boldest of them made sallies out on the floor or along the mouldings of the wainscot. Now and again as they disturbed him Malcolmson made a sound to frighten them, smiting the table with his hand or giving a fierce 'Hsh, hsh,' so that they fled straightway to their holes.

And so the early part of the night wore on; and despite the noise Malcolmson got more and more immersed in his work.

All at once he stopped, as on the previous night, being overcome by a sudden sense of silence. There was not the faintest sound of gnaw, or scratch, or squeak. The silence was as of the grave. He remembered the odd occurrence of the previous night, and instinctively he looked at the chair standing close by the fireside. And then a very odd sensation thrilled through him.

There, on the great old high-backed carved oak chair beside the fireplace sat the same enormous rat, steadily glaring at him with baleful eyes.

Instinctively he took the nearest thing to his hand, a book of logarithms, and flung it at it. The book was badly aimed and the rat did not stir, so again the poker performance of the previous night was repeated; and again the rat, being closely pursued, fled up the rope of the alarm bell. Strangely too, the departure of this rat was instantly followed by the renewal of the noise made by the general rat community. On this occasion, as on the previous one, Malcolmson could not see at what part of the room the rat disappeared, for the green shade of his lamp left the upper part of the room in darkness, and the fire had burned low.

On looking at his watch he found it was close on midnight; and, not sorry for the *divertissement*, he made up his fire and made himself his nightly pot of tea. He had got through a good spell of work, and thought himself entitled to a cigarette; and so he sat on the great carved oak chair before the fire and enjoyed it. Whilst smoking he began to think that he would like to know where the rat disappeared to, for he had certain ideas for the morrow not entirely disconnected with a rat-trap. Accordingly he lit another lamp and placed it so that it would shine well into the right-hand corner of the wall by the fireplace. Then he got all the books he had with him, and placed them handy to throw at the vermin. Finally he lifted the rope of the alarm bell and placed the end of it on the table, fixing the extreme end under the lamp. As he handled it he could not help noticing how pliable it was, especially for so strong a rope, and one not in use. 'You could hang a man with it,' he thought to himself. When his preparations were made he looked around, and said complacently:

'There now, my friend, I think we shall learn something of you this time!' He began his work again, and though as before somewhat disturbed at first by the noise of the rats, soon lost himself in his propositions and problems.

Again he was called to his immediate surroundings suddenly. This time it might not have been the sudden silence only which took his attention; there was a slight movement of the rope, and the lamp moved. Without stirring, he looked to see if his pile of books was within range, and then cast his eye along the rope. As he looked he saw the great rat drop from the rope on the oak armchair and sit there glaring at him. He raised a book in his right hand, and taking careful aim, flung it at the rat. The latter, with a quick movement, sprang aside and dodged the missile. He then took another book, and a third, and flung them one after another at the rat, but each time unsuccessfully. At last, as he stood with a book poised in his hand to throw, the rat squeaked and seemed afraid. This made Malcolmson more than ever eager to strike, and the book flew and struck the rat a resounding blow. It gave a terrified squeak, and turning on its pursuer a look of terrible malevolence, ran up the chair-back and made a great jump to the rope of the alarm bell and ran up it like lightning. The lamp rocked under the sudden strain, but it was a heavy one and did not topple over. Malcolmson kept his eyes on the rat, and saw it by the light of the second lamp leap to a moulding of the wainscot and disappear through a hole in one of the great pictures which hung on the wall, obscured and invisible through its coating of dirt and dust.

'I shall look up my friend's habitation in the morning,' said the student, as he went over to collect his books. 'The third picture from the fireplace; I shall not forget.' He picked up the books one by one, commenting on them as he lifted them. '*Conic Sections* he does not mind, nor *Cycloidal Oscillations,* nor the *Principia,* nor *Quaternions,* nor *Thermodynamics.* Now for the book that fetched him!' Malcolmson took it up and looked at it. As he did so he started, and a sudden pallor overspread his face. He looked round uneasily and shivered slightly, as he murmured to himself:

'The Bible my mother gave me! What an odd coincidence.' He sat down to work again, and the rats in the wainscot renewed their gambols. They did not disturb him, however; somehow their presence gave him a sense of companionship. But he could not attend to his work, and after striving to master the subject on which he was engaged gave it up in despair, and went to bed as the first streak of dawn stole in through the eastern window.

He slept heavily but uneasily, and dreamed much; and when Mrs Dempster woke him late in the morning he seemed ill at ease, and for a few minutes did not seem to realise exactly where he was. His first request rather surprised the servant.

'Mrs Dempster, when I am out today I wish you would get the steps and dust or wash those pictures—specially that one the third from the fireplace—I want to see what they are.'

Late in the afternoon Malcolmson worked at his books in the shaded walk, and the cheerfulness of the previous day came back to him as the day wore on, and he found that his reading was progressing well. He had worked out to a satisfactory conclusion all the problems which had as yet baffled him, and it was in a state of jubilation that he paid a visit to Mrs Witham at 'The Good Traveller'. He found a stranger in the cosy sitting-room with the landlady, who was introduced to him as Dr Thornhill. She was not quite at ease, and this, combined with the Doctor's plunging at once into a series of questions, made Malcolmson come to the conclusion that his presence was not an accident, so without preliminary he said:

'Dr Thornhill, I shall with pleasure answer you any question you may choose to ask me if you will answer me one question first.'

The Doctor seemed surprised, but he smiled and answered at once. 'Done! What is it?'

'Did Mrs Witham ask you to come here and see me and advise me?'

Dr Thornhill for a moment was taken aback, and Mrs Witham got fiery red and turned away; but the Doctor was a frank and ready man, and he answered at once and openly:

'She did: but she didn't intend you to know it. I suppose it was my clumsy haste that made you suspect. She told me that she did not like the idea of your being in that house all by yourself, and that she thought you took too much strong tea. In fact, she wants me to advise you if possible to give up the tea and the very late hours. I was a keen student in my time, so I suppose I may take the liberty of a college man, and without offence, advise you not quite as a stranger.'

Malcolmson with a bright smile held out his hand. 'Shake! as they say in America,' he said. 'I must thank you for your kindness and Mrs Witham too, and your kindness deserves a return on my part. I promise to take no more strong tea—no tea at all till you let me—and I shall go to bed tonight at one o'clock at latest. Will that do?'

'Capital,' said the Doctor. 'Now tell us all that you noticed in the old house,' and so Malcolmson then and there told in minute detail all that had happened in the last two nights. He was interrupted every now and then by some exclamation from Mrs Witham, till finally when he told of the episode of the Bible the landlady's pent-up emotions found vent in a shriek; and it was not till a stiff glass of brandy and water had been administered that she grew composed again. Dr Thornhill listened with a face of growing gravity, and when the narrative was complete and Mrs Witham had been restored he asked:

'The rat always went up the rope of the alarm bell?'

'Always.'

'I suppose you know,' said the Doctor after a pause, 'what the rope is?'

'No!'

'It is,' said the Doctor slowly, 'the very rope which the hangman used for all the victims of the Judge's judicial rancour!' Here he was interrupted by another scream from Mrs Witham, and steps had to be taken for her recovery. Malcolmson having looked at his watch, and found that it was close to his dinner hour, had gone home before her complete recovery.

When Mrs Witham was herself again she almost assailed the Doctor with angry questions as to what he meant by putting such horrible ideas into the poor young man's mind. 'He has quite enough there already to upset him,' she added. Dr Thornhill replied:

'My dear madam, I had a distinct purpose in it! I wanted to draw his attention to the bell rope, and to fix it there. It may be that he is in a highly overwrought state, and has been studying too much, although I am bound to say that he seems as sound and healthy a young man, mentally and bodily, as ever I saw—but then the rats—and that suggestion of the devil.' The doctor shook his head and went on. 'I would have offered to go and stay the first night with him but that I felt sure it would have been a cause of offence. He may get in the night some strange fright or hallucination; and if he does I want him to pull that rope. All alone as he is it will give us warning, and we may reach him in time to be of service. I shall be sitting up pretty late tonight and shall keep my ears open. Do not be alarmed if Benchurch gets a surprise before morning.'

'Oh, Doctor, what do you mean? What do you mean?'

'I mean this; that possibly—nay, more probably—we shall hear the great alarm bell from the Judge's House tonight,' and the Doctor made about as effective an exit as could be thought of.

When Malcolmson arrived home he found that it was a little after his usual time, and Mrs Dempster had gone away—the rules of Green-how's Charity were not to be neglected. He was glad to see that the place was bright and tidy with a cheerful fire and a well-trimmed lamp. The evening was colder than might have been expected in April, and a heavy wind was blowing with such rapidly-increasing strength that there was every promise of a storm during the night. For a few minutes after his entrance the noise of the rats ceased; but so soon as they became accustomed to his presence they began again. He was glad to hear them, for he felt once more the feeling of companionship in their noise, and his mind ran back to the strange fact that they only ceased to manifest themselves when that other—the great rat with the baleful eyes—came upon the scene. The reading-lamp only was lit and its green shade kept the ceiling and the upper part of the room in darkness, so that the cheerful light from the hearth spreading over the floor and shining on the white cloth laid over the end of the table was warm and cheery. Malcolmson sat down to his dinner with a good appetite and a buoyant spirit. After his dinner and a cigarette he sat steadily down to work, determined not to let anything disturb him, for he remembered his promise to the doctor, and made up his mind to make the best of the time at his disposal.

For an hour or so he worked all right, and then his thoughts began to wander from his books. The actual circumstances around him, the calls on his physical attention, and his nervous susceptibility were not to be denied. By this time the wind had become a gale, and the gale a storm. The old house, solid though it was, seemed to shake to its foundations, and the storm roared and raged through its many chimneys and its queer old gables, producing strange, unearthly sounds in the empty rooms and corridors. Even the great alarm bell on the roof must have felt the force of the wind, for the rope rose and fell slightly, as though the bell were moved a little from time to time, and the limber rope fell on the oak floor with a hard and hollow sound.

As Malcolmson listened to it he bethought himself of the doctor's words, 'It is the rope which the hangman used for the victims of the Judge's judicial rancour,' and he went over to the corner of the fireplace and took it in his hand to look at it. There seemed a sort of deadly interest in it, and as he stood there he lost himself for a moment in speculation as to who these victims were, and the grim wish of the Judge to have such a ghastly relic ever under his eyes. As he stood there the swaying of the bell on the roof still lifted the rope now and again; but presently there came a new sensation—a sort of tremor in the rope, as though something was moving along it.

Looking up instinctively Malcolmson saw the great rat coming slowly down towards him, glaring at him steadily. He dropped the rope and started back with a muttered curse, and the rat turning ran up the rope again and disappeared, and at the same instant Malcolmson became conscious that the noise of the rats, which had ceased for a while, began again.

All this set him thinking, and it occurred to him that he had not investigated the lair of the rat or looked at the pictures, as he had intended. He lit the other lamp without the shade, and, holding it up, went and stood opposite the third picture from the fireplace on the right-hand side where he had seen the rat disappear on the previous night.

At the first glance he started back so suddenly that he almost dropped the lamp, and a deadly pallor overspread his face. His knees shook, and heavy drops of sweat came on his forehead, and he trembled like an aspen. But he was young and plucky, and pulled himself together, and after the pause of a few seconds stepped forward again, raised the lamp, and examined the picture which had been dusted and washed, and now stood out clearly.

It was of a judge dressed in his robes of scarlet and ermine. His face was strong and merciless, evil, crafty, and vindictive, with a sensual mouth, hooked nose of ruddy colour, and shaped like the beak of a bird of prey. The rest of the face was of a cadaverous colour. The eyes were of peculiar brilliance and with a terribly malignant expression. As he looked at them, Malcolmson grew cold, for he saw there the very counterpart of the eyes of the great rat. The lamp almost fell from his hand, he saw the rat with its baleful eyes peering out through the hole in the corner of the picture, and noted the sudden cessation of the noise of the other rats. However, he pulled himself together, and went on with his examination of the picture.

The Judge was seated in a great high-backed carved oak chair, on the right-hand side of a great stone fireplace where, in the corner, a rope hung down from the ceiling, its end lying coiled on the floor. With a feeling of something like horror, Malcolmson recognised the scene of the room as it stood, and gazed around him in an awe-struck manner as though he expected to find some strange presence behind him. Then he looked over to the corner of the fireplace—and with a loud cry he let the lamp fall from his hand.

There, in the Judge's armchair, with the rope hanging behind, sat the rat with the Judge's baleful eyes, now intensified and with a fiendish leer. Save for the howling of the storm without there was silence.

The fallen lamp recalled Malcolmson to himself. Fortunately it was of metal, and so the oil was not spilt. However, the practical need of attending to it settled at once his nervous apprehensions. When he had turned it out, he wiped his brow and thought for a moment.

'This will not do,' he said to himself. 'If I go on like this I shall become a crazy fool. This must stop! I promised the Doctor I would not take tea. Faith, he was pretty right! My nerves must have been getting into a queer state. Funny I did not notice it. I never felt better in my life. However, it is all right now, and I shall not be such a fool again.'

Then he mixed himself a good stiff glass of brandy and water and resolutely sat down to his work.

It was nearly an hour when he looked up from his book, disturbed by the sudden stillness. Without, the wind howled and roared louder than ever, and the rain drove in sheets against the windows, beating like hail on the glass; but within there was no sound whatever save the echo of the wind as it roared in the great chimney, and now and then a hiss as a few raindrops found their way down the chimney in a lull of the storm. The fire had fallen low and had ceased to flame, though it threw out a red glow. Malcolmson listened attentively, and presently heard a thin, squeaking noise, very faint. It came from the corner of the room where the rope hung down, and he thought it was the creaking of the rope on the floor as the swaying of the bell raised and lowered it. Looking up, however, he saw in the dim light the great rat clinging to the rope and gnawing it. The rope was already nearly gnawed through—he could see the lighter colour where the strands were laid bare. As he looked the job was completed, and the severed end of the rope fell clattering on the oaken floor, whilst for an instant the great rat remained like a knob or tassel at the end of the rope, which now began to sway to and fro. Malcolmson felt for a moment another pang of terror as he thought that now the possibility of calling the outer world to his assistance was cut off, but an intense anger took its place, and seizing the book he was reading he hurled it at the rat. The blow was well aimed, but before the missile could reach it the rat dropped off and struck the floor with a soft thud.

Malcolmson instantly rushed over towards it, but it darted away and disappeared in the darkness of the shadows of the room. Malcolmson felt that his work was over for the night, and determined then and there to vary the monotony of the proceedings by a hunt for the rat, and took off the green shade of the lamp so as to insure a wider spreading light. As he did so the gloom of the upper part of the room was relieved, and in the new flood of light, great by comparison with the previous darkness, the pictures on the wall stood out boldly. From where he stood, Malcolmson saw right opposite to him the third picture on the wall from the right of the fireplace. He rubbed his eyes in surprise, and then a great fear began to come upon him.

In the centre of the picture was a great irregular patch of brown canvas, as fresh as when it was stretched on the frame. The background was as before, with chair and chimney-corner and rope, but the figure of the Judge had disappeared.

Malcolmson, almost in a chill of horror, turned slowly round, and then he began to shake and tremble like a man in a palsy. His strength seemed to have left him, and he was incapable of action or movement, hardly even of thought. He could only see and hear.

There, on the great high-backed carved oak chair sat the Judge in his robes of scarlet and ermine, with his baleful eyes glaring vindictively, and a smile of triumph on the resolute, cruel mouth, as he lifted with his hands a *black cap*. Malcolmson felt as if the blood was running from his heart, as one does in moments of prolonged suspense. There was a singing in his ears. Without, he could hear the roar and howl of the tempest, and through it, swept on the storm, came the striking of midnight by the great chimes in the market place. He stood for a space of time that seemed to him endless, still as a statue and with wide-open, horror-struck eyes, breathless. As the clock struck, so the smile of triumph on the Judge's face intensified, and at the last stroke of midnight he placed the black cap on his head.

Slowly and deliberately the Judge rose from his chair and picked up the piece of rope of the alarm bell which lay on the floor, drew it through his hands as if he enjoyed its touch, and then deliberately began to knot one end of it, fashioning it into a noose. This he tightened and tested with his foot, pulling hard at it till he was satisfied and then making a running noose of it, which he held in his hand. Then he began to move along the table on the opposite side to Malcolmson, keeping his eyes on him until he had passed him, when with a quick movement he stood in front of the door. Malcolmson then began to feel that he was trapped, and tried to think of what he should do. There was some fascination in the Judge's eyes, which he never took off him, and he had, perforce, to look. He saw the Judge approach—still keeping between him and the door—and raise the noose and throw it towards him as if to entangle him. With a great effort he made a quick movement to one side, and saw the rope fall beside him, and heard it strike the oaken floor. Again the Judge raised the noose and tried to ensnare him, ever keeping his baleful eyes fixed on him, and each time by a mighty effort the student just managed to evade it. So this went on for many times, the Judge seeming never discouraged nor discomposed at failure, but playing as a cat does with a mouse. At last in despair, which had reached its climax, Malcolmson cast a quick glance round him. The lamp seemed to have blazed up, and there was a fairly good light in the room. At the many rat-holes and in the chinks and crannies of the wainscot he saw the rats' eyes; and this aspect, that was purely physical, gave him a gleam of comfort. He looked around and saw that the rope of the great alarm bell was laden with rats. Every inch of it was covered with them, and more and more were pouring through the small circular hole in the ceiling whence it emerged, so that with their weight the bell was beginning to sway.

Hark! it had swayed till the clapper had touched the bell. The sound was but a tiny one, but the bell was only beginning to sway, and it would increase.

At the sound the Judge, who had been keeping his eyes fixed on Malcolmson, looked up, and a scowl of diabolical anger overspread his face. His eyes fairly glowed like hot coals, and he stamped his foot with a sound that seemed to make the house shake. A dreadful peal of thunder broke overhead as he raised the rope again, whilst the rats kept running up and down the rope as though working against time. This time, instead of throwing it, he drew close to his victim, and held open the noose as he approached. As he came closer there seemed something paralysing in his very presence, and Malcolmson stood rigid as a corpse. He felt the Judge's icy fingers touch his throat as he adjusted the rope. The noose tightened—tightened. Then the Judge, taking the rigid form of the student in his arms, carried him over and placed him standing in the oak chair, and stepping up beside him, put his hand up and caught the end of the swaying rope of the alarm bell. As he raised his hand the rats fled squeaking, and disappeared through the hole in the ceiling. Taking the end of the noose which was round Malcolmson's neck he tied it to the hanging bell-rope, and then descending pulled away the chair.

When the alarm bell of the Judge's House began to sound a crowd soon assembled. Lights and torches of various kinds appeared, and soon a silent crowd was hurrying to the spot. They knocked loudly at the door, but there was no reply. Then they burst in the door, and poured into the great dining-room, the Doctor at the head.

There at the end of the rope of the great alarm bell hung the body of the student, and on the face of the Judge in the picture was a malignant smile.

Man-Size in Marble

E. NESBIT

Although every word of this story is as true as despair, I do not expect people to believe it. Nowadays a 'rational explanation' is required before belief is possible. Let me then, at once, offer the 'rational explanation' which finds most favour among those who have heard the tale of my life's tragedy. It is held that we were 'under a delusion', Laura and I, on that 31st of October; and that this supposition places the whole matter on a satisfactory and believable basis. The reader can judge, when he, too, has heard my story, how far this is an 'explanation' and in what sense it is 'rational'. There were three who took part in this: Laura and I and another man. The other man still lives, and can speak to the truth of the least credible part of my story.

I never in my life knew what it was to have as much money as I required to supply the most ordinary needs—good colours, books, and cab-fares—and when we were married we knew quite well that we should only be able to live at all by 'strict punctuality and attention to business'. I used to paint in those days, and Laura used to write, and we felt sure we could keep the pot at least simmering. Living in town was out of the question, so we went to look for a cottage in the country, which should be at once sanitary and picturesque. So rarely do these two qualities meet in one cottage that our search was for some time quite fruitless. We tried advertisements, but most of the desirable rural residences which we did look at proved to be lacking in both essentials, and when a cottage chanced to have drains it always had stucco as well and was shaped like a tea-caddy. And if we found a vine or rose-covered porch, corruption invariably lurked within. Our minds got so befogged by the eloquence of house-agents and the rival disadvantages of the fever-traps and outrages to beauty which we had seen and scorned, that I very much doubt whether either of us, on our wedding morning, knew the difference between a house and a haystack. But when we got away from friends and house-agents, on our honeymoon, our wits grew clear again, and we knew a pretty cottage when at last we saw one. It was at Brenzett—a little village set on a hill over against the southern marshes. We had gone there, from the seaside village where we were staying, to see the church, and two fields from the church we found this cottage. It stood quite by itself, about two miles from the village. It was a long, low building, with rooms sticking out in unexpected places. There was a bit of stone-work—ivy-covered and moss-grown, just two old rooms, all that was left of a big house that had once stood there—and round this stone-work the house had grown up. Stripped of its roses and jasmine it would have been hideous. As it stood it was charming, and after a brief examination we took it. It was absurdly cheap. The rest of our honeymoon we spent in grubbing about in secondhand shops in the county town, picking up bits of old oak and Chippendale chairs for our furnishing. We wound up with a run up to town and a visit to Liberty's, and soon the low oak-beamed lattice-windowed rooms began to be home. There was a jolly old-fashioned garden, with grass paths, and no end of hollyhocks and sunflowers, and big lilies. From the window you could see the marsh-pastures, and beyond them the blue, thin line of the sea. We were as happy as the summer was glorious, and settled down into work sooner than we ourselves expected. I was never tired of sketching the view and the wonderful cloud effects from the open lattice, and Laura would sit at the table and write verses about them, in which I mostly played the part of foreground.

We got a tall old peasant woman to do for us. Her face and figure were good, though her cooking was of the homeliest; but she understood all about gardening, and told us all the old names of the coppices and cornfields, and the stories of the smugglers and highwaymen, and, better still, of the 'things that walked', and of the 'sights' which met one in lonely glens of a starlight night. She was a great comfort to us, because Laura hated housekeeping as much as I loved folklore, and we soon came to leave all the domestic business to Mrs Dorman, and to use her legends in little magazine stories which brought in the jingling guinea.

We had three months of married happiness, and did not have a single quarrel. One October evening I had been down to smoke a pipe with the doctor—our only neighbour—a pleasant young Irishman. Laura had stayed at home to finish a comic sketch of a village episode for the *Monthly Marplot*. I left her laughing over her own jokes, and came in to find her a crumpled heap of pale muslin weeping on the window seat.

'Good heavens, my darling, what's the matter?' I cried, taking her in my arms. She leaned her little dark head against my shoulder and went on crying. I had never seen her cry before—we had always been so happy, you see—and I felt sure some frightful misfortune had happened.

'What *is* the matter? Do speak.'

'It's Mrs Dorman,' she sobbed.

'What has she done?' I inquired, immensely relieved.

'She says she must go before the end of the month, and she says her niece is ill; she's gone to see her now, but I don't believe that's the reason, because her niece is always ill. I believe someone has been setting her against us. Her manner was so queer——'

'Never mind, Pussy,' I said; 'whatever you do, don't cry, or I shall have to cry too, to keep you in countenance, and then you'll never respect your man again!'

She dried her eyes obediently on my handkerchief, and even smiled faintly.

'But you see,' she went on, 'it is really serious, because these village people are so sheepy, and if one won't do a thing you may be quite sure none of the others will. And I shall have to cook the dinners, and wash up the hateful greasy plates; and you'll have to carry cans of water about, and clean the boots and knives—and we shall never have any time for work, or earn any money, or anything. We shall have to work all day, and only be able to rest when we are waiting for the kettle to boil!'

I represented to her that even if we had to perform these duties, the day would still present some margin for other toils and recreations. But she refused to see the matter in any but the greyest light. She was very unreasonable, my Laura, but I could not have loved her any more if she had been as reasonable as Whately.

'I'll speak to Mrs Dorman when she comes back, and see if I can't come to terms with her,' I said. 'Perhaps she wants a rise in her screw. It will be all right. Let's walk up to the church.'

The church was a large and lonely one, and we loved to go there, especially upon bright nights. The path skirted a wood, cut through it once, and ran along the crest of the hill through two meadows, and round the churchyard wall, over which the old yews loomed in black masses of shadow. This path, which was partly paved, was called 'the bier-balk', for it had long been the way by which the corpses had been carried to burial. The churchyard was richly treed, and was shaded by great elms which stood just outside and stretched their majestic arms in benediction over the happy dead. A large, low porch let one into the building by a Norman doorway and a heavy oak door studded with iron. Inside, the arches rose into darkness, and between them the reticulated windows, which stood out white in the moonlight. In the chancel, the windows were of rich glass, which showed in faint light their noble colouring, and made the black oak of the choir pews hardly more solid than the shadows. But on each side of the altar lay a grey marble figure of a knight in full plate armour lying upon a low slab, with hands held up in everlasting prayer, and these figures, oddly enough, were always to be seen if there was any glimmer of light in the church. Their names were lost, but the peasants told of them that they had been fierce and wicked men, marauders by land and sea, who had been the scourge of their time, and had been guilty of deeds so foul that the house they had lived in—the big house, by the way, that had stood on the site of our cottage—had been stricken by lightning and the vengeance of Heaven. But for all that, the gold of their heirs had bought them a place in the church. Looking at the bad hard faces reproduced in the marble, this story was easily believed.

The church looked at its best and weirdest on that night, for the shadows of the yew trees fell through the windows upon the floor of the nave and touched the pillars with tattered shade. We sat down together without speaking, and watched the solemn beauty of the old church, with some of that awe which inspired its early builders. We walked to the chancel and looked at the sleeping warriors. Then we rested some time on the stone seat in the porch, looking out over the stretch of quiet moonlit meadows, feeling in every fibre of our being the peace of the night and of our happy love; and came away at last with a sense that even scrubbing and blackleading were but small troubles at their worst.

Mrs Dorman had come back from the village, and I at once invited her to a *tête-à-tête*.

'Now, Mrs Dorman,' I said, when I had got her into my painting room, 'what's all this about your not staying with us?'

'I should be glad to get away, sir, before the end of the month,' she answered, with her usual placid dignity.

'Have you any fault to find, Mrs Dorman?'

'None at all, sir; you and your lady have always been most kind, I'm sure——'

'Well, what is it? Are your wages not high enough?'

'No, sir, I gets quite enough.'

'Then why not stay?'

'I'd rather not'—with some hesitation—'my niece is ill.'

'But your niece has been ill ever since we came.'

No answer. There was a long and awkward silence. I broke it.

'Can't you stay for another month?' I asked.

'No, sir. I'm bound to go by Thursday.'

And this was Monday!

'Well, I must say, I think you might have let us know before. There's no time now to get any one else, and your mistress is not fit to do heavy housework. Can't you stay till next week?'

'I might be able to come back next week.'

I was now convinced that all she wanted was a brief holiday, which we should have been willing enough to let her have, as soon as we could get a substitute.

'But why must you go this week?' I persisted. 'Come, out with it.'

Mrs Dorman drew the little shawl, which she always wore, tightly across her bosom, as though she were cold. Then she said, with a sort of effort——

'They say, sir, as this was a big house in Catholic times, and there was a many deeds done here.'

The nature of the 'deeds' might be vaguely inferred from the inflection of Mrs Dorman's voice—which was enough to make one's blood run cold. I was glad that Laura was not in the room. She was always nervous, as highly-strung natures are, and I felt that these tales about our house, told by this old peasant woman, with her impressive manner and contagious credulity, might have made our home less dear to my wife.

'Tell me all about it, Mrs Dorman,' I said; 'you needn't mind about telling me. I'm not like the young people who make fun of such things.'

Which was partly true.

'Well, sir'—she sank her voice—'you may have seen in the church, beside the altar, two shapes.'

'You mean the effigies of the knights in armour,' I said cheerfully.

'I mean them two bodies, drawed out man-size in marble,' she returned, and I had to admit that her description was a thousand times more graphic than mine, to say nothing of a certain weird force and uncanniness about the phrase 'drawed out man-size in marble'.

'They do say, as on All Saints' Eve them two bodies sits up on their slabs, and gets off of them, and then walks down the aisle, *in their marble*'—(another good phrase, Mrs Dorman)—'and as the church clock strikes eleven they walks out of the church door, and over the graves, and along the bier-balk, and if it's a wet night there's the marks of their feet in the morning.'

'And where do they go?' I asked, rather fascinated.

'They comes back here to their home, sir, and if any one meets them ——'

'Well, what then?' I asked.

But no—not another word could I get from her, save that her niece was ill and she must go. After what I had heard I scorned to discuss the niece, and tried to get from Mrs Dorman more details of the legend. I could get nothing but warnings.

'Whatever you do, sir, lock the door early on All Saints' Eve, and make the cross-sign over the doorstep and on the windows.'

'But has any one ever seen these things?' I persisted.

'That's not for me to say. I know what I know, sir.'

'Well, who was here last year?'

'No one, sir; the lady as owned the house only stayed here in summer, and she always went to London a full month afore *the* night. And I'm sorry to inconvenience you and your lady, but my niece is ill and I must go on Thursday.'

I could have shaken her for her absurd reiteration of that obvious fiction, after she had told me her real reasons.

She was determined to go, nor could our united entreaties move her in the least.

I did not tell Laura the legend of the shapes that 'walked in their marble', partly because a legend concerning our house might perhaps trouble my wife, and partly, I think, from some more occult reason. This was not quite the same to me as any other story, and I did not want to talk about it till the day was over. I had very soon ceased to think of the legend, however. I was painting a portrait of Laura, against the lattice window, and I could not think of much else. I had got a splendid background of yellow and grey sunset, and was working away with enthusiasm at her face. On Thursday Mrs Dorman went. She relented, at parting, so far as to say—

'Don't you put yourself about too much, ma'am, and if there's any little thing I can do next week, I'm sure I shan't mind.'

From which I inferred that she wished to come back to us after Hallowe'en. Up to the last she adhered to the fiction of the niece with touching fidelity.

Thursday passed off pretty well. Laura showed marked ability in the matter of steak and potatoes, and I confess that my knives, and the plates, which I insisted upon washing, were better done than I had dared to expect.

Friday came. It is about what happened on that Friday that this is written. I wonder if I should have believed it, if any one had told it to me. I will write the story of it as quickly and plainly as I can. Everything that happened on that day is burnt into my brain. I shall not forget anything, nor leave anything out.

I got up early, I remember, and lighted the kitchen fire, and had just achieved a smoky success, when my little wife came running down, as sunny and sweet as the clear October morning itself. We prepared breakfast together, and found it very good fun. The housework was soon done, and when brushes and brooms and pails were quiet again, the house was still indeed. It is wonderful what a difference one makes in a house. We really missed Mrs Dorman, quite apart from considerations concerning pots and pans. We spent the day in dusting our books and putting them straight, and dined gaily on cold steak and coffee. Laura was, if possible, brighter and gayer and sweeter than usual, and I began to think that a little domestic toil was really good for her. We had never been so merry since we were married, and the walk we had that afternoon was, I think, the happiest time of all my life. When we had watched the deep scarlet clouds slowly pale into leaden grey against a pale green sky, and saw the white mists curl up along the hedgerows in the distant marsh, we came back to the house, silently, hand in hand.

'You are sad, my darling,' I said, half-jestingly, as we sat down together in our little parlour. I expected a disclaimer, for my own silence had been the silence of complete happiness. To my surprise she said—

'Yes. I think I am sad, or rather I am uneasy. I don't think I'm very well. I have shivered three or four times since we came in and it is not cold, is it?'

'No,' I said, and hoped it was not a chill caught from the treacherous mists that roll up from the marshes in the dying light. No—she said, she did not think so. Then, after a silence, she spoke suddenly—

'Do you ever have presentiments of evil?'

'No,' I said, smiling, 'and I shouldn't believe in them if I had.'

'I do,' she went on; 'the night my father died I knew it, though he was right away in the north of Scotland.' I did not answer in words.

She sat looking at the fire for some time in silence, gently stroking my hand. At last she sprang up, came behind me, and, drawing my head back, kissed me.

'There, it's over now,' she said. 'What a baby I am! Come, light the candles, and we'll have some of these new Rubinstein duets.'

And we spent a happy hour or two at the piano.

At about half-past ten I began to long for the good-night pipe, but Laura looked so white that I felt it would be brutal of me to fill our sitting-room with the fumes of strong cavendish.

'I'll take my pipe outside,' I said.

'Let me come, too.'

'No, sweetheart, not tonight; you're much too tired. I shan't be long. Get to bed, or I shall have an invalid to nurse tomorrow as well as the boots to clean.'

I kissed her and was turning to go, when she flung her arms round my neck, and held me as if she would never let me go again. I stroked her hair.

'Come, Pussy, you're over-tired. The housework has been too much for you.'

She loosened her clasp a little and drew a deep breath.

'No. We've been very happy today, Jack, haven't we? Don't stay out too long.'

'I won't, my dearie.'

I strolled out of the front door, leaving it unlatched. What a night it was! The jagged masses of heavy dark cloud were rolling at intervals from horizon to horizon, and thin white wreaths covered the stars. Through all the rush of the cloud river, the moon swam, breasting the waves and disappearing again in the darkness. When now and again her light reached the woodlands they seemed to be slowly and noiselessly waving in time to the swing of the clouds above them. There was a strange grey light over all the earth; the fields had that shadowy bloom over them which only comes from the marriage of dew and moonshine, or frost and starlight.

I walked up and down, drinking in the beauty of the quiet earth and the changing sky. The night was absolutely silent. Nothing seemed to be abroad. There was no skurrying of rabbits, or twitter of the half-asleep birds. And though the clouds went sailing across the sky, the wind that drove them never came low enough to rustle the dead leaves in the woodland paths. Across the meadows I could see the church tower standing out black and grey against the sky. I walked there thinking over our three months of happiness—and of my wife, her dear eyes, her loving ways. Oh, my little girl! my own little girl; what a vision came then of a long, glad life for you and me together!

I heard a bell-beat from the church. Eleven already! I turned to go in, but the night held me. I could not go back into our little warm rooms yet. I would go up to the church. I felt vaguely that it would be good to carry my love and thankfulness to the sanctuary whither so many loads of sorrow and gladness had been borne by the men and women of the dead years.

I looked in at the low window as I went by. Laura was half lying on her chair in front of the fire. I could not see her face, only her little head showed dark against the pale blue wall. She was quite still. Asleep, no doubt. My heart reached out to her, as I went on. There must be a God, I thought, and a God who was good. How otherwise could anything so sweet and dear as she have ever been imagined?

I walked slowly along the edge of the wood. A sound broke the stillness of the night, it was a rustling in the wood. I stopped and listened. The sound stopped too. I went on, and now distinctly heard another step than mine answer mine like an echo. It was a poacher or a wood-stealer, most likely, for these were not unknown in our Arcadian neighbourhood. But whoever it was, he was a fool not to step more lightly. I turned into the wood, and now the footstep seemed to come from the path I had just left. It must be an echo, I thought. The wood looked perfect in the moonlight. The large dying ferns and the brushwood showed where through thinning foliage the pale light came down. The tree trunks stood up like Gothic columns all around me. They reminded me of the church, and I turned into the bier-balk, and passed through the corpse-gate between the graves to the low porch. I paused for a moment on the stone seat where Laura and I had watched the fading landscape. Then I noticed that the door of the church was open, and I blamed myself for having left it unlatched the other night. We were the only people who ever cared to come to the church except on Sundays, and I was vexed to think that through our carelessness the damp autumn airs had had a chance of getting in and injuring the old fabric. I went in. It will seem strange, perhaps, that I should have gone half-way up the aisle before I remembered—with a sudden chill, followed by as sudden a rush of self-contempt—that this was the very day and hour when, according to tradition, the 'shapes drawed out man-size in marble' began to walk.

Having thus remembered the legend, and remembered it with a shiver, of which I was ashamed, I could not do otherwise than walk up towards the altar, just to look at the figures—as I said to myself; really what I wanted was to assure myself, first, that I did not believe the legend, and, secondly, that it was not true. I was rather glad that I had come. I thought now I could tell Mrs Dorman how vain her fancies were, and how peacefully the marble figures slept on through the ghastly hour. With my hands in my pockets I passed up the aisle. In the grey dim light the eastern end of the church looked larger than usual, and the arches above the two tombs looked larger too. The moon came out and showed me the reason. I stopped short, my heart gave a leap that nearly choked me, and then sank sickeningly.

The 'bodies drawn out man-size' *were gone,* and their marble slabs lay wide and bare in the vague moonlight that slanted through the east window.

Were they really gone? or was I mad? Clenching my nerves, I stooped and passed my hand over the smooth slabs, and felt their flat unbroken surface. Had some one taken the things away? Was it some vile practical joke? I would make sure, anyway. In an instant I had made a torch of a newspaper, which happened to be in my pocket, and lighting it held it high above my head. Its yellow glare illumined the dark arches and those slabs. The figures *were* gone. And I was alone in the church; or was I alone?

And then a horror seized me, a horror indefinable and indescrib-able—an overwhelming certainty of supreme and accomplished calamity. I flung down the torch and tore along the aisle and out through the porch, biting my lips as I ran to keep myself from shrieking aloud. Oh, was I mad—or what was this that possessed me? I leaped the churchyard wall and took the straight cut across the fields, led by the light from our windows. Just as I got over the first stile, a dark figure seemed to spring out of the ground. Mad still with that certainty of misfortune, I made for the thing that stood in my path, shouting, 'Get out of the way, can't you!'

But my push met with a more vigorous resistance than I had expected. My arms were caught just above the elbow and held as in a vice, and the raw-boned Irish doctor actually shook me.

'Would ye?' he cried, in his own unmistakable accents—'would ye, then?'

'Let me go, you fool,' I gasped. 'The marble figures have gone from the church; I tell you they've gone.'

He broke into a ringing laugh. 'I'll have to give ye a draught to-morrow, I see. Ye've bin smoking too much and listening to old wives' tales.'

'I tell you, I've seen the bare slabs.'

'Well, come back with me. I'm going up to old Palmer's—his daughter's ill; we'll look in at the church and let me see the bare slabs.'

'You go, if you like,' I said, a little less frantic for his laughter; 'I'm going home to my wife.'

'Rubbish, man,' said he; 'd'ye think I'll permit of that? Are ye to go saying all yer life that ye've seen solid marble endowed with vitality, and me to go all me life saying ye were a coward? No, sir—ye shan't do it.'

The night air—a human voice—and I think also the physical contact with this six feet of solid common sense, brought me back a little to my ordinary self, and the word 'coward' was a mental shower-bath.

'Come on, then,' I said sullenly; 'perhaps you're right.'

He still held my arm tightly. We got over the stile and back to the church. All was still as death. The place smelt very damp and earthy. We walked up the aisle. I am not ashamed to confess that I shut my eyes: I knew the figures would not be there. I heard Kelly strike a match.

'Here they are, ye see, right enough; ye've been dreaming or drinking, asking yer pardon for the imputation.'

I opened my eyes. By Kelly's expiring vesta I saw two shapes lying 'in their marble' on their slabs. I drew a deep breath, and caught his hand.

'I'm awfully indebted to you,' I said. 'It must have been some trick of light, or I have been working rather hard, perhaps that's it. Do you know, I was quite convinced they were gone.'

'I'm aware of that,' he answered rather grimly; 'ye'll have to be careful of that brain of yours, my friend, I assure ye.'

He was leaning over and looking at the right-hand figure, whose stony face was the most villainous and deadly in expression.

'By Jove,' he said, 'something has been afoot here—this hand is broken.'

And so it was. I was certain that it had been perfect the last time Laura and I had been there.

'Perhaps some one has *tried* to remove them,' said the young doctor.

'That won't account for my impression,' I objected.

'Too much painting and tobacco will account for that, well enough.'

'Come along,' I said, 'or my wife will be getting anxious. You'll come in and have a drop of whisky and drink confusion to ghosts and better sense to me.'

'I ought to go up to Palmer's, but it's so late now I'd best leave it till the morning,' he replied. 'I was kept late at the Union, and I've had to see a lot of people since. All right, I'll come back with ye.'

I think he fancied I needed him more than did Palmer's girl, so, discussing how such an illusion could have been possible, and deducing from this experience large generalities concerning ghostly apparitions, we walked up to our cottage. We saw, as we walked up the garden-path, that bright light streamed out of the front door, and presently saw that the parlour door was open too. Had she gone out?

'Come in,' I said, and Dr Kelly followed me into the parlour. It was all ablaze with candles, not only the wax ones, but at least a dozen guttering, glaring tallow dips, stuck in vases and ornaments in unlikely places. Light, I knew, was Laura's remedy for nervousness. Poor child! Why had I left her? Brute that I was.

We glanced round the room, and at first we did not see her. The window was open, and the draught set all the candles flaring one way. Her chair was empty and her handkerchief and book lay on the floor. I turned to the window. There, in the recess of the window, I saw her. Oh, my child, my love, had she gone to that window to watch for me? And what had come into the room behind her? To what had she turned with that look of frantic fear and horror? Oh, my little one, had she thought that it was I whose step she heard, and turned to meet—what?

She had fallen back across a table in the window, and her body lay half on it and half on the window-seat, and her head hung down over the table, the brown hair loosened and fallen to the carpet. Her lips were drawn back, and her eyes wide, wide open. They saw nothing now. What had they seen last?

The doctor moved towards her, but I pushed him aside and sprang to her; caught her in my arms and cried——

'It's all right, Laura! I've got you safe, wifie.'

She fell into my arms in a heap. I clasped her and kissed her, and called her by all her pet names, but I think I knew all the time that she was dead. Her hands were tightly clenched. In one of them she held something fast. When I was quite sure that she was dead, and that nothing mattered at all any more, I let him open her hand to see what she held.

It was a grey marble finger.

The Roll-Call of the Reef

SIR ARTHUR QUILLER-COUCH

—

'Yes, sir,' said my host the quarryman, reaching down the relics from their hook in the wall over the chimney-piece; 'they've hung there all my time, and most of my father's. The women won't touch 'em; they're afraid of the story. So here they'll dangle, and gather dust and smoke, till another tenant comes and tosses 'em out o' doors for rubbish. Whew! 'tis coarse weather.'

He went to the door, opened it, and stood studying the gale that beat upon his cottage-front, straight from the Manacle Reef. The rain drove past him into the kitchen, aslant like threads of gold silk in the shine of the wreckwood fire. Meanwhile by the same firelight I examined the relics on my knee. The metal of each was tarnished out of knowledge. But the trumpet was evidently an old cavalry trumpet, and the threads of its parti-coloured sling, though frayed and dusty, still hung together. Around the side-drum, beneath its cracked brown varnish, I could hardly trace a royal coat-of-arms, and a legend running—*Per Mare per Terram*—the motto of the Marines. Its parchment, though coloured and scented with wood-smoke, was limp and mildewed; and I began to tighten up the straps—under which the drumsticks had been loosely thrust—with the idle purpose of trying if some music might be got out of the old drum yet.

But as I turned it on my knee, I found the drum attached to the trumpet-sling by a curious barrel-shaped padlock, and paused to examine this. The body of the lock was composed of half a dozen brass rings, set accurately edge to edge; and, rubbing the brass with my thumb, I saw that each of the six had a series of letters engraved around it.

I knew the trick of it, I thought. Here was one of those word padlocks, once so common; only to be opened by getting the rings to spell a certain word, which the dealer confides to you.

My host shut and barred the door, and came back to the hearth.

' 'Twas just such a wind—east by south—that brought in what you've got between your hands. Back in the year 'nine it was; my father has told me the tale a score o' times. You're twisting rounds the rings, I see. But you'll never guess the word. Parson Kendall, he made the word, and locked down a couple o' ghosts in their graves with it; and when his time came, he went to his own grave and took the word with him.'

'Whose ghosts, Matthew?'

'You want the story, I see, sir. My father could tell it better than I can. He was a young man in the year 'nine, unmarried at the time, and living in this very cottage just as I be. That's how he came to get mixed up with the tale.'

He took a chair, lit a short pipe, and unfolded the story in a low musing voice, with his eyes fixed on the dancing violet flames.

'Yes, he'd ha' been about thirty year old in January, of the year 'nine. The storm got up in the night o' the twenty-first o' that month. My father was dressed and out long before daylight; he never was one to 'bide in bed, let be that the gale by this time was pretty near lifting the thatch over his head. Besides which, he'd fenced a small 'taty-patch that winter, down by Lowland Point, and he wanted to see if it stood the night's work. He took the path across Gunner's Meadow—where they buried most of the bodies afterwards. The wind was right in his teeth at the time, and once on the way (he's told me this often) a great strip of ore-weed came flying through the darkness and fetched him a slap on the cheek like a cold hand. But he made shift pretty well till he got to Lowland, and then had to drop upon his hands and knees and crawl, digging his fingers every now and then into the shingle to hold on, for he declared to me that the stones, some of them as big as a man's head, kept rolling and driving past till it seemed the whole foreshore was moving westward under him. The fence was gone, of course; not a stick left to show where it stood; so that, when first he came to the place, he thought he must have missed his bearings. My father, sir, was a very religious man; and if he reckoned the end of the world was at hand—there in the great wind and night, among the moving stones—you may believe he was certain of it when he heard a gun fired, and, with the same, saw a flame shoot up out of the darkness to windward, making a sudden fierce light in all the place about. All he could find to think or say was, "The Second Coming—The Second Coming! The Bridegroom cometh, and the wicked He will toss like a ball into a large country!" and being already upon his knees, he just bowed his head and 'bided, saying this over and over.

'But by'm-by, between two squalls, he made bold to lift his head and look, and then by the light—a bluish colour 'twas—he saw all the coast clear away to Manacle Point, and off the Manacles, in the thick of the weather, a sloop-of-war with top-gallants housed, driving stern foremost towards the reef. It was she, of course, that was burning the flare. My father could see the white streak and the ports of her quite plain as she rose to it, a little outside the breakers, and he guessed easy enough that her captain had just managed to wear ship, and was trying to force her nose to the sea with the help of her small bower anchor and the scrap or two of canvas that hadn't yet been blown out of her. But while he looked, she fell off, giving her broadside to it foot by foot, and drifting back on the breakers around Carn dû and the Varses. The rocks lie so thick thereabouts, that 'twas a toss up which she struck first; at any rate, my father couldn't tell at the time, for just then the flare died down and went out.

'Well, sir, he turned then in the dark and started back for Coverack to cry the dismal tidings—though well knowing ship and crew to be past any hope; and as he turned, the wind lifted him and tossed him forward "like a ball", as he'd been saying, and homeward along the foreshore. As you know, 'tis ugly work, even by daylight, picking your way among the stones there, and my father was prettily knocked about at first in the dark. But by this 'twas nearer seven than six o'clock, and the day spreading. By the time he reached North Corner, a man could see to read print; hows'ever, he looked neither out to sea nor towards Coverack, but headed straight for the first cottage—the same that stands above North Corner today. A man named Billy Ede lived there then, and when my father burst into the kitchen bawling, "Wreck! wreck!" he saw Billy Ede's wife, Ann, standing there in her clogs, with a shawl over her head, and her clothes wringing wet.

' "Save the chap!" says Billy Ede's wife, Ann. "What d' 'ee mean by crying stale fish at that rate?"

' "But 'tis a wreck, I tell 'ee. I've a-zeed 'n!"

' "Why, so 'tis," says she, "and I've a-zeed 'n too; and so has everyone with an eye in his head."

'And with that she pointed straight over my father's shoulder, and he turned; and there, close under Dolor Point, at the end of Coverack town, he saw another wreck washing, and the point black with people, like emmets, running to and fro in the morning light. While we stood staring at her, he heard a trumpet sounded on board, the notes coming in little jerks, like a bird rising against the wind; but faintly, of course, because of the distance and the gale blowing—though this had dropped a little.

' "She's a transport," said Billy Ede's wife, Ann, "and full of horse soldiers, fine long men. When she struck they must ha' pitched the hosses over first to lighten the ship, for a score of dead hosses had washed in afore I left, half an hour back. An' three or four soldiers, too—fine long corpses in white breeches and jackets of blue and gold. I held the lantern to one. Such a straight young man."

'My father asked her about the trumpeting.

' "That's the queerest bit of all. She was burnin' a light when me an' my man joined the crowd down there. All her masts had gone; whether they carried away, or were cut away to ease her, I don't rightly know. Anyway, there she lay 'pon the rocks with her decks bare. Her keelson was broke under her and her bottom sagged and stove, and she had just settled down like a sitting hen—just the leastest list to starboard; but a man could stand there easy. They had rigged up ropes across her from bulwark to bulwark, an' beside these the men were mustered, holding on like grim death whenever the sea made a clean break over them, an' standing up like heroes as soon as it passed. The captain an' the officers were clinging to the rail of the quarter-deck, all in their golden uniforms, waiting for the end as if 'twas King George they expected. There was no way to help, for she lay right beyond cast of line, though our folk tried it fifty times. And beside them clung a trumpeter, a whacking big man, an' between the heavy seas he would lift his trumpet with one hand, and blow a call; and every time he blew, the men gave a cheer. There (she says)—hark 'ee now—there he goes agen! But you won't hear no cheering any more, for few are left to cheer, and their voices weak. Bitter cold the wind is, and I reckon it numbs their grip o' the ropes, for they were dropping off fast with every sea when my man sent me home to get his breakfast. Another wreck, you say? Well, there's no hope for the tender dears, if 'tis the Manacles. You'd better run down and help yonder; though 'tis little help that any man can give. Not one came in alive while I was there. The tide's flowing, an' she won't hold together another hour, they say."

'Well, sure enough, the end was coming fast when my father got down to the point. Six men had been cast up alive, or just breathing—a seaman and five troopers. The seaman was the only one that had breath to speak; and while they were carrying him into the town, the word went round that the ship's name was the *Despatch*, transport, homeward bound from Corunna, with a detachment of the 7th Hussars, that had been fighting out there with Sir John Moore. The seas had rolled her further over by this time, and given her decks a pretty sharp slope; but a dozen men still held on, seven by the ropes near the ship's waist, a couple near the break of the poop, and three on the quarter-deck. Of these three my father made out one to be the skipper; close by him clung an officer in full regimentals—his name, they heard after, was Captain Duncanfield; and last came the tall trumpeter; and if you'll believe me, the fellow was making shift there, at the very last, to blow "*God Save the King*". What's more, he got to "*Send us victorious*" before an extra big sea came bursting across and washed them off the deck—every man but one of the pair beneath the poop—and *he* dropped his hold before the next wave; being stunned, I reckon. The others went out of sight at once, but the trumpeter—being, as I said, a powerful man as well as a tough swimmer—rose like a duck, rode out a couple of breakers, and came in on the crest of the third. The folks looked to see him broke like an egg at their feet; but when the smother cleared, there he was, lying face downward on a ledge below them; and one of the men that happened to have a rope round him—I forget the fellow's name, if I ever heard it—jumped down and grabbed him by the ankle as he began to slip back. Before the next big sea, the pair were hauled high enough to be out of harm, and another heave brought them up to grass. Quick work; but master trumpeter wasn't quite dead; nothing worse than a cracked head and three staved ribs. In twenty minutes or so they had him in bed, with the doctor to tend him.

'Now was the time—nothing being left alive upon the transport—for my father to tell of the sloop he'd seen driving upon the Manacles. And when he got a hearing, though the most were set upon salvage, and believed a wreck in the hand, so to say, to be worth half a dozen they couldn't see, a good few volunteered to start off with him and have a look. They crossed Lowland Point; no ship to be seen on the Manacles, nor anywhere upon the sea. One or two was for calling my father a liar. "Wait till we come to Dean Point," said he. Sure enough, on the far side of Dean Point, they found the sloop's mainmast washing about with half a dozen men lashed to it—men in red jackets—every mother's son drowned and staring; and a little farther on, just under the Dean, three or four bodies cast up on the shore, one of them a small drummer-boy, side-drum and all; and, near by, part of a ship's gig, with "H.M.S. *Primrose*" cut on the stern-board. From this point on, the shore was littered thick with wreckage and dead bodies—the most of them Marines in uniform; and in Godrevy Cove, in particular, a heap of furniture from the captain's cabin, and amongst it a water-tight box, not much damaged, and full of papers, by which, when it came to be examined next day, the wreck was easily made out to be the *Primrose*, of eighteen guns, outward bound from Portsmouth, with a fleet of transports for the Spanish War—thirty sail, I've heard, but I've never heard what became of them. Being handled by merchant skippers, no doubt they rode out the gale and reached the Tagus safe and sound. Not but what the captain of the *Primrose* (Mein was his name) did quite right to try and club-haul his vessel when he found himself under the land: only he never ought to have got there if he took proper soundings. But it's easy talking.

'The *Primrose*, sir, was a handsome vessel—for her size, one of the handsomest in the King's service—and newly fitted out at Plymouth Dock. So the boys had brave pickings from her in the way of brass-work, ship's instruments, and the like, let alone some barrels of stores not much spoiled. They loaded themselves with as much as they could carry, and started for home, meaning to make a second journey before the preventive men got wind of their doings and came to spoil the fun. But as my father was passing back under the Dean, he happened to take a look over his shoulder at the bodies there. "Hullo," says he and dropped his gear, "I do believe there's a leg moving!" And, running fore, he stooped over the small drummer-boy that I told you about. The poor little chap was lying there, with his face a mass of bruises and his eyes closed: but he had shifted one leg an inch or two, and was still breathing. So my father pulled out a knife and cut him free from his drum—that was lashed on to him with a double turn of Manilla rope—and took him up and carried him along here, to this very room that we're sitting in. He lost a good deal by this, for when he went back to fetch his bundle the preventive men had got hold of it, and were thick as thieves along the foreshore; so that 'twas only by paying one or two to look the other way that he picked up anything worth carrying off: which you'll allow to be hard seeing that he was the first man to give news of the wreck.

'Well, the inquiry was held, of course, and my father gave evidence; and for the rest they had to trust to the sloop's papers, for not a soul was saved besides the drummer-boy, and he was raving in a fever, brought on by the cold and the fright. And the seamen and the five troopers gave evidence about the loss of the *Despatch*. The tall trumpeter, too, whose ribs were healing, came forward and kissed the Book; but somehow his head had been hurt in coming ashore, and he talked foolish-like, and 'twas easy seen he would never be a proper man again. The others were taken up to Plymouth, and so went their ways; but the trumpeter stayed on in Coverack; and King George, finding he was fit for nothing, sent him down a trifle of a pension after a while—enough to keep him in board and lodging, with a bit of tobacco over.

'Now the first time that this man—William Tallifer, he called himself—met with the drummer-boy, was about a fortnight after the little chap had bettered enough to be allowed a short walk out of doors, which he took, if you please, in full regimentals. There never was a soldier so proud of his dress. His own suit had shrunk a brave bit with the salt water; but into ordinary frock an' corduroys he declared he would not get—not if he had to go naked the rest of his life; so my father, being a good-natured man and handy with the needle, turned to and repaired damages with a piece or two of scarlet cloth cut from the jacket of one of the drowned Marines. Well, the poor little chap chanced to be standing, in this rigout, down by the gate of Gunner's Meadow, where they had buried two score and over of his comrades. The morning was a fine one, early in March month; and along came the cracked trumpeter, likewise taking a stroll.

' "Hullo!" says he; "good mornin'! And what might you be doin' here?"

' "I was a-wishin'," says the boy, "I had a pair o' drum-sticks. Our lads were buried yonder without so much as a drum tapped or a musket fired; and that's not Christian burial for British soldiers."

' "Phut!" says the trumpeter, and spat on the ground; "a parcel of Marines!"

'The boy eyed him a second or so, and answered up: "If I'd a tab of turf handy, I'd bung it at your mouth, you greasy cavalryman, and learn you to speak respectful of your betters. The Marines are the handiest body of men in the service."

'The trumpeter looked down on him from the height of six foot two, and asked: "Did they die well?"

' "They died very well. There was a lot of running to and fro at first, and some of the men began to cry, and a few to strip off their clothes. But when the ship fell off for the last time, Captain Mein turned and said something to Major Griffiths, the commanding officer on board, and the Major called out to me to beat to quarters. It might have been for a wedding, he sang it out so cheerful. We'd had word already that 'twas to be parade order, and the men fell in as trim and decent as if they were going to church. One or two even tried to shave at the last moment. The Major wore his medals. One of the seamen, seeing I had hard work to keep the drum steady—the sling being a bit loose for me and the wind what you remember—lashed it tight with a piece of rope; and that saved my life afterwards, a drum being as good as a cork until 'tis stove. I kept beating away until every man was on deck; and then the Major formed them up and told them to die like British soldiers, and the chaplain read a prayer or two—the boys standin' all the while like rocks, each man's courage keeping up the other's. The chaplain was in the middle of a prayer when she struck. In ten minutes she was gone. That was how they died, cavalryman."

' "And that was very well done, drummer of the Marines. What's your name?"

' "John Christian."

' "Mine is William George Tallifer, trumpeter, of the 7th Light Dragoons—the Queen's Own. I played *'God Save the King'* while our men were drowning. Captain Duncanfield told me to sound a call or two, to put them in heart; but that matter of *'God Save the King'* was a notion of my own. I won't say anything to hurt the feelings of a Marine, even if he's not much over five-foot tall; but the Queen's Own Hussars is a tearin' fine regiment. As between horse and foot, 'tis a question o' which gets the chance. All the way from Sahagun to Corunna 'twas we that took and gave the knocks—at Mayorga and Rueda, and Benny-venty." (The reason, sir, I can speak the names so pat is that my father learnt 'em by heart afterwards from the trumpeter, who was always talking about Mayorga and Rueda and Bennyventy.) "We made the rear-guard, under General Paget, and drove the French every time; and all the infantry did was to sit about in wine-shops till we whipped 'em out, an' steal an' straggle an' play the tom-fool in general. And when it came to a stand-up fight at Corunna, 'twas the horse, or the best part of it, that had to stay sea-sick aboard the transports, an' watch the infantry in the thick o' the caper. Very well they behaved, too; 'specially the 4th Regiment, an' the 42nd Highlanders an' the Dirty Half-Hundred. Oh, ay; they're decent regiments, all three. But the Queen's Own Hussars is a tearin' fine regiment. So you played on your drum when the ship was goin' down? Drummer John Christian, I'll have to get you a new pair o' drum-sticks for that."

'Well, sir, it appears that the very next day the trumpeter marched into Helston, and got a carpenter there to turn him a pair of box-wood drum-sticks for the boy. And this was the beginning of one of the most curious friendships you ever heard tell of. Nothing delighted the pair more than to borrow a boat off my father and pull out to the rocks where the *Primrose* and the *Despatch* had struck and sunk; and on still days 'twas pretty to hear them out there off the Manacles, the drummer playing his tattoo—for they always took their music with them—and the trumpeter practising calls, and making his trumpet speak like an angel. But if the weather turned roughish, they'd be walking together and talking; leastwise, the youngster listened while the other discoursed about Sir John's campaign in Spain and Portugal, telling how each little skirmish befell; and of Sir John himself and General Baird and General Paget, and Colonel Vivian, his own commanding officer, and what kind of men they were; and of the last bloody stand-up at Corunna, and so forth, as if neither could have enough.

'But all this had to come to an end in the late summer; for the boy, John Christian, being now well and strong again, must go up to Plymouth to report himself. 'Twas his own wish (for I believe King George had forgotten all about him), but his friend wouldn't hold him back. As for the trumpeter, my father had made an arrangement to take him on as a lodger as soon as the boy left; and on the morning fixed for the start, he was up at the door here by five o'clock, with his trumpet slung by his side, and all the rest of his kit in a small valise. A Monday morning it was, and after breakfast he had fixed to walk with the boy some way on the road towards Helston, where the coach started. My father left them at breakfast together, and went out to meat the pig, and do a few odd morning jobs of that sort. When he came back, the boy was still at table and the trumpeter standing here by the chimney-place with the drum and trumpet in his hands hitched together just as they be at this moment.

' "Look at this," he says to my father, showing him the lock; "I picked it up off a starving brass-worker in Lisbon, and it is not one of your common locks that one word of six letters will open at any time. There's *janius* in this lock; for you've only to make the rings spell any six-letter word you please, and snap down the lock upon that, and never a soul can open it—not the maker, even—until somebody comes along that knows the word you snapped it on. Now, Johnny here's goin', and he leaves his drum behind him; for, though he can make pretty music on it, the parchment sags in wet weather, by reason of the sea-water getting at it; an' if he carries it to Plymouth, they'll only condemn it and give him another. And, as for me, I shan't have the heart to put lip to the trumpet any more when Johnny's gone. So we've chosen a word together, and locked 'em together upon that; and, by your leave, I'll hang 'em here together on the hook over your fireplace. Maybe Johnny'll come back; maybe not. Maybe, if he comes, I'll be dead an' gone, an' he'll take 'em apart an' try their music for old sake's sake. But if he never comes, nobody can separate 'em; for nobody beside knows the word. And if you marry and have sons, you can tell 'em that here are tied together the souls of Johnny Christian, drummer of the Marines, and William George Tallifer, once trumpeter of the Queen's Own Hussars. Amen."

'With that he hung the two instruments 'pon the hook here; and the boy stood up and thanked my father and shook hands; and the pair went forth of the door, towards Helston.

'Somewhere on the road they took leave of one another; but nobody saw the parting, nor heard what was said between them. About three in the afternoon the trumpeter came walking back over the hill; and by the time my father came home from the fishing, the cottage was tidied up and the tea ready, and the whole place shining like a new pin. From that time for five years he lodged here with my father, looking after the house and tilling the garden; and all the while he was steadily failing, the hurt in his head spreading, in a manner, to his limbs. My father watched the feebleness growing on him, but said nothing. And from first to last neither spake a word about the drummer, John Christian; nor did any letter reach them, nor word of his doings.

'The rest of the tale you'm free to believe, sir, or not, as you please. It stands upon my father's words, and he always declared he was ready to kiss the Book upon it before judge and jury. He said, too, that he never had the wit to make up such a yarn; and he defied anyone to explain about the lock, in particular, by any other tale. But you shall judge for yourself.

'My father said that about three o'clock in the morning, April fourteenth of the year 'fourteen, he and William Tallifer were sitting here, just as you and I, sir, are sitting now. My father had put on his clothes a few minutes before, and was mending his spiller by the light of the horn lantern, meaning to set off before daylight to haul the trammel. The trumpeter hadn't been to bed at all. Towards the last he mostly spent his nights (and his days, too) dozing in the elbow-chair where you sit at this minute. He was dozing then (my father said), with his chin dropped forward on his chest, when a knock sounded upon the door, and the door opened, and in walked an upright young man in scarlet regimentals.

'He had grown a brave bit, and his face was the colour of wood-ashes; but it was the drummer, John Christian. Only his uniform was different from the one he used to wear, and the figures '38' shone in brass upon his collar.

'The drummer walked past my father as if he never saw him, and stood by the elbow-chair and said:

' "Trumpeter, trumpeter, are you one with me?"

'And the trumpeter just lifted the lids of his eyes, and answered, "How should I not be one with you, drummer Johnny—Johnny boy? The men are patient. 'Till you come, I count; while you march, I mark time; until the discharge comes."

' "The discharge has come tonight," said the drummer, "and the word is Corunna no longer"; and stepping to the chimney-place, he unhooked the drum and trumpet, and began to twist the brass rings of the lock, spelling the word aloud, so—C-O-R-U-N-A. When he had fixed the last letter, the padlock opened in his hand.

' "Did you know, trumpeter, that when I came to Plymouth they put me into a line regiment?"

' "The 38th is a good regiment," answered the old Hussar, still in his dull voice. "I went back with them from Sahagun to Corunna. At Corunna they stood in General Fraser's division, on the right. They behaved well."

' "But I'd fain see the Marines again," says the drummer, handing him the trumpet; "and you—you shall call once more for the Queen's Own. Matthew," he says, suddenly, turning on my father—and when he turned, my father saw for the first time that his scarlet jacket had a round hole by the breastbone, and that the blood was welling there— "Matthew, we shall want your boat."

'Then my father rose on his legs like a man in a dream, while they two slung on, the one his drum, and t'other his trumpet. He took the lantern, and went quaking before them down to the shore, and they breathed heavily behind him; and they stepped into his boat, and my father pushed off.

' "Row you first for Dolor Point," says the drummer. So my father rowed them out past the white houses of Coverack to Dolor Point, and there, at a word, lay on his oars. And the trumpeter, William Tallifer, put his trumpet to his mouth and sounded the *Revelly*. The music of it was like rivers running.

' "They will follow," said the drummer. "Matthew, pull you now for the Manacles."

'So my father pulled for the Manacles, and came to an easy close outside Carn dû. And the drummer took his sticks and beat a tattoo, there by the edge of the reef; and the music of it was like a rolling chariot.

' "That will do," says he, breaking off; "they will follow. Pull now for the shore under Gunner's Meadow."

'Then my father pulled for the shore, and ran his boat in under Gunner's Meadow. And they stepped out, all three, and walked up to the meadow. By the gate the drummer halted and began his tattoo again, looking out towards the darkness over the sea.

'And while the drum beat, and my father held his breath, there came up out of the sea and the darkness a troop of men, horse and foot, and formed up among the graves; and others rose out of the graves and formed up—drowned Marines with bleached faces, and pale Hussars riding their horses, all lean and shadowy. There was no clatter of hoofs or accoutrements, my father said, but a soft sound all the while, like the beating of a bird's wing, and a black shadow lying like a pool about the feet of all. The drummer stood upon a little knoll just inside the gate, and beside him the tall trumpeter, with hand on hip, watching them gather; and behind them both my father, clinging to the gate. When no more came, the drummer stopped playing, and said, "Call the roll."

'Then the trumpeter stepped towards the end man of the rank and called, "Troop-Sergeant-Major Thomas Irons!" and the man in a thin voice answered, "Here!"

' "Troop-Sergeant-Major Thomas Irons, how is it with you?"

'The man answered, "How should it be with me? When I was young, I betrayed a girl; and when I was grown, I betrayed a friend, and for these things I must pay. But I died as a man ought. God save the King!"

'The trumpeter called to the next man "Trooper Henry Buckingham!" and the next man answered, "Here!"

' "Trooper Henry Buckingham, how is it with you?"

' "How should it be with me? I was a drunkard, and I stole, and in Lugo, in a wine-shop, I knifed a man. But I died as a man should. God save the King!"

'So the trumpeter went down the line; and when he had finished, the drummer took it up, hailing the dead Marines in their order. Each man answered to his name, and each man ended with "God save the King!" When all were hailed, the drummer stepped back to his mound, and called:

' "It is well. You are content, and we are content to join you. Wait yet a little while."

'With this he turned and ordered my father to pick up the lantern, and lead the way back. As my father picked it up, he heard the ranks of dead men cheer and call, "God save the King!" all together, and saw them waver and fade back into the dark, like a breath fading off a pane.

'But when they came back here to the kitchen, and my father set the lantern down, it seemed they'd both forgot about him. For the drummer turned in the lantern-light—and my father could see the blood still welling out of the hole in his breast—and took the trumpet-sling from around the other's neck, and locked drum and trumpet together again, choosing the letters on the lock very carefully. While he did this he said:

' "The word is no more Corunna, but Bayonne. As you left out an 'n' in Corunna, so must I leave out an 'n' in Bayonne." And before snapping the padlock, he spelt out the word slowly—"B-A-Y-O-N-E." After that, he used no more speech; but turned and hung the two instruments back on the hook; and then took the trumpeter by the arm; and the pair walked out into the darkness, glancing neither to right nor left.

'My father was on the point of following, when he heard a sort of sigh behind him; and there, sitting in the elbow-chair, was the very trumpeter he had just seen walk out by the door! If my father's heart jumped before, you may believe it jumped quicker now. But after a bit, he went up to the man asleep in the chair, and put a hand upon him. It was the trumpeter in flesh and blood that he touched; but though the flesh was warm, the trumpeter was dead.

'Well, sir, they buried him three days after; and at first my father was minded to say nothing about his dream (as he thought it). But the day after the funeral, he met Parson Kendall coming from Helston market: and the parson called out: "Have 'ee heard the news the coach brought down this mornin'?" "What news?" says my father. "Why, that peace is agreed upon." "None too soon," says my father. "Not soon enough for our poor lads at Bayonne," the parson answered. "Bayonne!" cries my father, with a jump. "Why, yes"; and the parson told him all about a great sally the French had made on the night of April 13th. "Do you happen to know if the 38th Regiment was engaged?" my father asked. "Come, now," said Parson Kendall, "I didn't know you was so well up in the campaign. But, as it happens, I *do* know that the 38th was engaged, for 'twas they that held a cottage and stopped the French advance."

'Still my father held his tongue; and when, a week later, he walked into Helston and bought a *Mercury* off the Sherborne rider, and got the landlord of the "Angel" to spell out the list of killed and wounded, sure enough, there among the killed was Drummer John Christian, of the 38th Foot.

'After this, there was nothing for a religious man but to make a clean breast. So my father went up to Parson Kendall and told the whole story. The parson listened, and put a question or two, and then asked:

' "Have you tried to open the lock since that night?"

' "I han't dared to touch it," says my father.

' "Then come along and try." When the parson came to the cottage here, he took the things off the hook and tried the lock. "Did he say *'Bayonne'*? The word has seven letters."

' "Not if you spell it with one 'n' as *he* did," says my father.

'The parson spelt it out—B-A-Y-O-N-E. "Whew!" says he, for the lock had fallen open in his hand.

'He stood considering it a moment, and then he says, "I tell you what. I shouldn't blab this all round the parish, if I was you. You won't get no credit for truth-telling, and a miracle's wasted on a set of fools. But if you like, I'll shut down the lock again upon a holy word that no one but me shall know, and neither drummer nor trumpeter, dead nor alive, shall frighten the secret out of me."

' "I wish to gracious you would, parson," said my father.

'The parson chose the holy word there and then, and shut the lock back upon it, and hung the drum and trumpet back in their place. He is gone long since, taking the word with him. And till the lock is broken by force, nobody will ever separate those twain.'

The Friends of the Friends

HENRY JAMES

I find, as you prophesied, much that's interesting, but little that helps the delicate question—the possibility of publication. Her diaries are less systematic than I hoped; she only had a blessed habit of noting and narrating. She summarized, she saved; she appears seldom indeed to have let a good story pass without catching it on the wing. I allude of course not so much to things she heard as to things she saw and felt. She writes sometimes of herself, sometimes of others, sometimes of the combination. It's under this last rubric that she's usually most vivid. But it's not, you'll understand, when she's most vivid that she's always most publishable. To tell the truth she's fearfully indiscreet, or has at least all the material for making *me* so. Take as an instance the fragment I send you after dividing it for your convenience into several small chapters. It's the contents of a thin blank-book which I've had copied out and which has the merit of being nearly enough a rounded thing, an intelligible whole. These pages evidently date from years ago. I've read with the liveliest wonder the statement they so circumstantially make and done my best to swallow the prodigy they leave to be inferred. These things would be striking, wouldn't they? to any reader; but can you imagine for a moment my placing such a document before the world, even though, as if she herself had desired the world should have the benefit of it, she has given her friends neither name nor initials? Have you any sort of clue to their identity? I leave her the floor.

I

I know perfectly of course that I brought it upon myself; but that doesn't make it any better. I was the first to speak of her to him—he had never even heard her mentioned. Even if I had happened not to speak some one else would have made up for it: I tried afterwards to find comfort in that reflection. But the comfort of reflections is thin: the only comfort that counts in life is not to have been a fool. That's a beatitude I shall doubtless never enjoy. 'Why you ought to meet her and talk it over' is what I immediately said. 'Birds of a feather flock together.' I told him who she was and that they were birds of a feather because if he had had in youth a strange adventure she had had about the same time just such another. It was well known to her friends—an incident she was constantly called on to describe. She was charming clever pretty unhappy; but it was none the less the thing to which she had originally owed her reputation.

Being at the age of eighteen somewhere abroad with an aunt she had had a vision of one of her parents at the moment of death. The parent was in England hundreds of miles away and so far as she knew neither dying nor dead. It was by day, in the museum of some great foreign town. She had passed alone, in advance of her companions, into a small room containing some famous work of art and occupied at that moment by two other persons. One of these was an old custodian; the second, before observing him, she took for a stranger, a tourist. She was merely conscious that he was bareheaded and seated on a bench. The instant her eyes rested on him, however, she beheld to her amazement her father, who, as if he had long waited for her, looked at her in singular distress and an impatience that was akin to reproach. She rushed to him with a bewildered cry, 'Papa, what *is* it?' but this was followed by an exhibition of still livelier feeling when on her movement he simply vanished, leaving the custodian and her relations, who were by that time at her heels, to gather round her in dismay. These persons, the official, the aunt, the cousins, were therefore in a manner witnesses of the fact—the fact at least of the impression made on her; and there was the further testimony of a doctor who was attending one of the party and to whom it was immediately afterwards communicated. He gave her a remedy for hysterics, but said to the aunt privately: 'Wait and see if something doesn't happen at home.' Something *had* happened—the poor father, suddenly and violently seized, had died that morning. The aunt, the mother's sister, received before the day was out a telegram announcing the event and requesting her to prepare her niece for it. Her niece was already prepared, and the girl's sense of this visitation remained of course indelible. We had all, as her friends, had it conveyed to us and had conveyed it creepily to each other. Twelve years had elapsed, and as a woman who had made an unhappy marriage and lived apart from her husband she had become interesting from other sources; but since the name she now bore was a name frequently borne, and since moreover her judicial separation, as things were going, could hardly count as a distinction, it was usual to qualify her as 'the one, you know, who saw her father's ghost'.

As for him, dear man, he had seen his mother's—so there you are! I had never heard of that till this occasion on which our closer, our pleasanter acquaintance led him, through some turn of the subject of our talk, to mention it and to inspire me in so doing with the impulse to let him know that he had a rival in the field—a person with whom he could compare notes. Later on his story became for him, perhaps because of my unduly repeating it, likewise a convenient worldly label; but it hadn't a year before been the ground on which he was introduced to me. He had other merits, just as she, poor thing, had others. I can honestly say that I was quite aware of them from the first—I discovered them sooner than he discovered mine. I remember how it struck me even at the time that his sense of mine was quickened by my having been able to match, though not indeed straight from my own experience, his curious anecdote. It dated, this anecdote, as hers did, from some dozen years before—a year in which, at Oxford, he had for some reason of his own been staying on into the 'Long'. He had been in the August afternoon on the river. Coming back into his room while it was still distinct daylight he found his mother standing there as if her eyes had been fixed on the door. He had had a letter from her that morning out of Wales, where she was staying with her father. At the sight of him she smiled with extraordinary radiance and extended her arms to him, and then as he sprang forward and joyfully opened his own she vanished from the place. He wrote to her that night, telling her what had happened; the letter had been carefully preserved. The next morning he heard of her death. He was through this chance of our talk extremely struck with the little prodigy I was able to produce for him. He had never encountered another case. Certainly they ought to meet, my friend and he; certainly they would have something in common. I would arrange this, wouldn't I?—if *she* didn't mind; for himself he didn't mind in the least. I had promised to speak to her of the matter as soon as possible, and within the week I was able to do so. She 'minded' as little as he; she was perfectly willing to see him. And yet no meeting was to occur—as meetings are commonly understood.

II

That's just half my tale—the extraordinary way it was hindered. This was the fault of a series of accidents; but the accidents, persisting for years, became, to me and to others, a subject of mirth with either party. They were droll enough at first, then they grew rather a bore. The odd thing was that both parties were amenable; it wasn't a case of their being indifferent, much less of their being indisposed. It was one of the caprices of chance, aided I suppose by some rather settled opposition of their interests and habits. His were centred in his office, his eternal inspectorship, which left him small leisure, constantly calling him away and making him break engagements. He liked society, but he found it everywhere and took it at a run. I never knew at a given moment where he was, and there were times when for months together I never saw him. She was on her side practically suburban: she lived at Richmond and never went 'out'. She was a woman of distinction, but not of fashion, and felt, as people said, her situation. Decidedly proud and rather whimsical, she lived her life as she had planned it. There were things one could do with her, but one couldn't make her come to one's parties. One went indeed a little more than seemed quite convenient to hers, which consisted of her cousin, a cup of tea and the view. The tea was good; but the view was familiar, though perhaps not, like the cousin—a disagreeable old maid who had been of the group at the museum and with whom she now lived—offensively so. This connexion with an inferior relative, which had partly an economic motive—she proclaimed her companion a marvellous manager—was one of the little perversities we had to forgive her. Another was her estimate of the proprieties created by her rupture with her husband. That was extreme—many persons called it even morbid. She made no advances; she cultivated scruples; she suspected, or I should perhaps rather say she remembered, slights: she was one of the few women I've known whom that particular predicament had rendered modest rather than bold. Dear thing, she had some delicacy! Especially marked were the limits she had set to possible attentions from men: it was always her thought that her husband only waited to pounce on her. She discouraged if she didn't forbid the visits of male persons not senile: she said she could never be too careful.

When I first mentioned to her that I had a friend whom fate had distinguished in the same weird way as herself I put her quite at liberty to say 'Oh bring him out to see me!' I should probably have been able to bring him, and a situation perfectly innocent or at any rate comparatively simple would have been created. But she uttered no such word; she only said: 'I must meet him certainly; yes, I shall look out for him!' That caused the first delay, and meanwhile various things happened. One of them was that as time went on she made, charming as she was, more and more friends, and that it regularly befell that these friends were sufficiently also friends of his to bring him up in conversation. It was odd that without belonging, as it were, to the same world, or, according to the horrid term, the same set, my baffled pair should have happened in so many cases to fall in with the same people and make them join in the droll chorus. She had friends who didn't know each other but who inevitably and punctually recommended *him*. She had also the sort of originality, the intrinsic interest, that led her to be kept by each of us as a private resource, cultivated jealously, more or less in secret, as a person whom one didn't meet in society, whom it was not for every one—whom it was not for the vulgar—to approach, and with whom therefore acquaintance was particularly difficult and particularly precious. We saw her separately, with appointments and conditions, and found it made on the whole for harmony not to tell each other. Somebody had always had a note from her still later than somebody else. There was some silly woman who for a long time, among the unprivileged, owed to three simple visits to Richmond a reputation for being intimate with 'lots of awfully clever out-of-the-way people'.

Every one has had friends it has seemed a happy thought to bring together, and every one remembers that his happiest thoughts have not been his greatest successes; but I doubt if there was ever a case in which the failure was in such direct proportion to the quantity of influence set in motion. It's really perhaps here the quantity of influence that was most remarkable. My lady and my gentleman each pronounced it to me and others quite a subject for a roaring farce. The reason first given had with time dropped out of sight and fifty better ones flourished on top of it. They were so awfully alike: they had the same ideas and tricks and tastes, the same prejudices and superstitions and heresies; they said the same things and sometimes did them; they liked and disliked the same persons and places, the same books, authors and styles; there were touches of resemblance even in their looks and features. It established much of a propriety that they were in common parlance equally 'nice' and almost equally handsome. But the great sameness, for wonder and chatter, was their rare perversity in regard to being photographed. They were the only persons ever heard of who had never been 'taken' and who had a passionate objection to it. They just *wouldn't* be—no, not for anything any one could say. I had loudly complained of this; him in particular I had so vainly desired to be able to show on my drawing-room chimney-piece in a Bond Street frame. It was at any rate the very liveliest of all the reasons why they ought to know each other—all the lively reasons reduced to naught by the strange law that had made them bang so many doors in each other's face, made them the buckets in the well, the two ends of the see-saw, the two parties in the State, so that when one was up the other was down, when one was out the other was in; neither by any possibility entering a house till the other had left it or leaving it all unawares till the other was at hand. They only arrived when they had been given up, which was precisely also when they departed. They were in a word alternate and incompatible; they missed each other with an inveteracy that could be explained only by its being pre-concerted. It was however so far from preconcerted that it had ended—literally after several years—by disappointing and annoying them. I don't think their curiosity was lively till it had been proved utterly vain. A great deal was of course done to help them, but it merely laid wires for them to trip. To give examples I should have to have taken notes; but I happen to remember that neither had ever been able to dine on the right occasion. The right occasion for each was the occasion that would be wrong for the other. On the wrong one they were most punctual and there were never any but wrong ones. The very elements conspired and the constitution of man re-enforced them. A cold, a headache, a bereavement, a storm, a fog, an earthquake, a cataclysm, infallibly intervened. The whole business was beyond a joke.

Yet as a joke it had still to be taken, though one couldn't help feeling that the joke had made the situation serious, had produced on the part of each a consciousness, an awkwardness, a positive dread of the last accident of all, the only one with any freshness left, the accident that *would* bring them together. The final effect of its predecessors had been to kindle this instinct. They were quite ashamed—perhaps even a little of each other. So much preparation, so much frustration: what indeed could be good enough for it all to lead up to? A mere meeting would be mere flatness. Did I see them at the end of years, they often asked, just stupidly confronted? If they were bored by the joke they might be worse bored by something else. They made exactly the same reflections and each in some manner was sure to hear of the other's. I really think it was this peculiar diffidence that finally controlled the situation. I mean that if they had failed for the first year or two because they couldn't help it, they kept up the habit because they had—what shall I call it?—grown nervous. It really took some lurking volition to account for anything both so regular and so ridiculous.

III

When to crown our long acquaintance I accepted his renewed offer of marriage it was humorously said, I know, that I had made the gift of his photograph a condition. This was so far true that I had refused to give him mine without it. At any rate I had him at last, in his high distinction, on the chimney-piece, where the day she called to congratulate me she came nearer than she had ever done to seeing him. He had in being taken set her an example that I invited her to follow; he had sacrificed his perversity—wouldn't she sacrifice hers? She too must give me something on my engagement—wouldn't she give me the companion-piece? She laughed and shook her head; she had headshakes whose impulse seemed to come from as far away as the breeze that stirs a flower. The companion-piece to the portrait of my future husband was the portrait of his future wife. She had taken her stand—she could depart from it as little as she could explain it. It was a prejudice, an *entêtement*, a vow—she would live and die unphotographed. Now too she was alone in that state: this was what she liked; it made her so much more original. She rejoiced in the fall of her late associate and looked a long time at his picture, about which she made no memorable remark, though she even turned it over to see the back. About our engagement she was charming—full of cordiality and sympathy. 'You've known him even longer than I've *not*,' she said, 'and that seems a very long time.' She understood how we had jogged together over hill and dale and how inevitable it was that we should now rest together. I'm definite about all this because what followed is so strange that it's a kind of relief to me to mark the point up to which our relations were as natural as ever. It was I myself who in a sudden madness altered and destroyed them. I see now that she gave me no pretext and that I only found one in the way she looked at the fine face in the Bond Street frame. How then would I have had her look at it? What I had wanted from the first was to make her care for him. Well, that was what I still wanted—up to the moment of her having promised me she would on this occasion really aid me to break the silly spell that had kept them asunder. I had arranged with him to do his part if she would as triumphantly do hers. I was on a different footing now—I was on a footing to answer for him. I would positively engage that at five on the following Saturday he should be on that spot. He was out of town on pressing business, but, pledged to keep his promise to the letter, would return on purpose and in abundant time. 'Are you perfectly sure?' I remember she asked, looking grave and considering: I thought she had turned a little pale. She was tired, she was indisposed: it was a pity he was to see her after all at so poor a moment. If he only *could* have seen her five years before! However, I replied that this time I was sure and that success therefore depended simply on herself. At five o'clock on the Saturday she would find him in a particular chair I pointed out, the one in which he usually sat and in which—though this I didn't mention—he had been sitting when, the week before, he put the question of our future to me in the way that had brought me round. She looked at it in silence, just as she had looked at the photograph, while I repeated for the twentieth time that it was too preposterous one shouldn't somehow succeed in introducing to one's dearest friend one's second self. '*Am* I your dearest friend?' she asked with a smile that for a moment brought back her beauty. I replied by pressing her to my bosom; after which she said: 'Well, I'll come. I'm extraordinarily afraid, but you may count on me.'

When she had left me I began to wonder what she was afraid of, for she had spoken as if she fully meant it. The next day, late in the afternoon, I had three lines from her: she had found on getting home the announcement of her husband's death. She hadn't seen him for seven years, but she wished me to know it in this way before I should hear of it in another. It made however in her life, strange and sad to say, so little difference that she would scrupulously keep her appointment. I rejoiced for her—I supposed it would make at least the difference of her having more money; but even in this diversion, far from forgetting she had said she was afraid, I seemed to catch sight of a reason for her being so. Her fear, as the evening went on, became contagious, and the contagion took in my breast the form of a sudden panic. It wasn't jealousy—it just was the dread of jealousy. I called myself a fool for not having been quiet till we were man and wife. After that I should somehow feel secure. It was only a question of waiting another month—a trifle surely for people who had waited so long. It had been plain enough she was nervous, and now she was free her nervousness wouldn't be less. What was it therefore but a sharp foreboding? She had been hitherto the victim of interference, but it was quite possible she would henceforth be the source of it. The victim in that case would be my simple self. What had the interference been but the finger of Providence pointing out a danger? The danger was of course for poor *me*. It had been kept at bay by a series of accidents unexampled in their frequency; but the reign of accident was now visibly at an end. I had an intimate conviction that both parties would keep the tryst. It was more and more impressed on me that they were approaching, converging. They were like the seekers for the hidden object in the game of blindfold; they had one and the other begun to 'burn'. We had talked about breaking the spell; well, it would be effectually broken—unless indeed it should merely take another form and overdo their encounters as it had overdone their escapes. This was something I couldn't sit still for thinking of; it kept me awake—at midnight I was full of unrest. At last I felt there was only one way of laying the ghost. If the reign of accident was over I must just take up the succession. I sat down and wrote a hurried note which would meet him on his return and which, as the servants had gone to bed, I sallied forth bareheaded into the empty gusty street to drop into the nearest pillar-box. It was to tell him that I shouldn't be able to be at home in the afternoon as I had hoped and that he must postpone his visit till dinner-time. This was an implication that he would find me alone.

IV

When accordingly at five she presented herself I naturally felt false and base. My act had been a momentary madness, but I had at least, as they say, to live up to it. She remained an hour: he of course never came; and I could only persist in my perfidy. I had thought it best to let her come; singular as this now seems to me I held it diminished my guilt. Yet as she sat there so visibly white and weary, stricken with a sense of everything her husband's death had opened up, I felt a really piercing pang of pity and remorse. If I didn't tell her on the spot what I had done it was because I was too ashamed. I feigned astonishment—I feigned it to the end; I protested that if ever I had had confidence I had had it that day. I blush as I tell my story—I take it as my penance. There was nothing indignant I didn't say about him; I invented suppositions, attenuations; I admitted in stupefaction, as the hands of the clock travelled, that their luck hadn't turned. She smiled at this vision of their 'luck', but she looked anxious—she looked unusual: the only thing that kept me up was the fact that, oddly enough, she wore mourning—no great depths of crape, but simple and scrupulous black. She had in her bonnet three small black feathers. She carried a little muff of astrakhan. This put me, by the aid of some acute reflection, a little in the right. She had written to me that the sudden event made no difference for her, but apparently it made as much difference as that. If she was inclined to the usual forms why didn't she observe that of not going the first day or two out to tea? There was some one she wanted so much to see that she couldn't wait till her husband was buried. Such a betrayal of eagerness made me hard and cruel enough to practise my odious deceit, though at the same time, as the hour waxed and waned, I suspected in her something deeper still than disappointment and somewhat less successfully concealed. I mean a strange underlying relief, the soft low emission of the breath that comes when a danger is past. What happened as she spent her barren hour with me was that at last she gave him up. She let him go for ever. She made the most graceful joke of it that I've ever seen made of anything; but it was for all that a great date in her life. She spoke with her mild gaiety of all the other vain times, the long game of hide-and-seek, the unprecedented queerness of such a relation. For it *was*, or had been, a relation, wasn't it, hadn't it? That was just the absurd part of it. When she got up to go I said to her that it was more a relation than ever, but that I hadn't the face after what had occurred to propose to her for the present another opportunity. It was plain that the only valid opportunity would be my accomplished marriage. Of course she would be at my wedding? It was even to be hoped that *he* would.

'If *I* am, he won't be!'—I remember the high quaver and the little break of her laugh. I admitted there might be something in that. The thing was therefore to get us safely married first. 'That won't help us. Nothing will help us!' she said as she kissed me farewell.

'I shall never, never see him!' It was with those words she left me.

I could bear her disappointment as I've called it; but when a couple of hours later I received him at dinner I discovered I couldn't bear his. The way my manoeuvre might have affected him hadn't been particularly present to me; but the result of it was the first word of reproach that had ever yet dropped from him. I say 'reproach' because that expression is scarcely too strong for the terms in which he conveyed to me his surprise that under the extraordinary circumstances I shouldn't have found some means not to deprive him of such an occasion. I might really have managed either not to be obliged to go out or to let their meeting take place all the same. They would probably have got on, in my drawing-room, well enough without me. At this I quite broke down—I confessed my iniquity and the miserable reason of it. I hadn't put her off and I hadn't gone out; she had been there and, after waiting for him an hour, had departed in the belief that he had been absent by his own fault.

'She must think me a precious brute!' he exclaimed. 'Did she say of me'—and I remember the just perceptible catch of breath in his pause—'what she had a right to say?'

'I assure you she said nothing that showed the least feeling. She looked at your photograph, she even turned round the back of it, on which your address happens to be inscribed. Yet it provoked her to no demonstration. She doesn't care so much as all that.'

'Then why are you afraid of her?'

'It wasn't of her I was afraid. It was of you.'

'Did you think I'd be so sure to fall in love with her? You never alluded to such a possibility before,' he went on as I remained silent. 'Admirable person as you pronounced her, that wasn't the light in which you showed her to me.'

'Do you mean that if it *had* been you'd have managed by this time to catch a glimpse of her? I didn't fear things then,' I added. 'I hadn't the same reason.'

He kissed me at this, and when I remembered that she had done so an hour or two before I felt for an instant as if he were taking from my lips the very pressure of hers. In spite of kisses the incident had shed a certain chill, and I suffered horribly from the sense that he had seen me guilty of a fraud. He had seen it only through my frank avowal, but I was as unhappy as if I had a stain to efface. I couldn't get over the manner of his looking at me when I spoke of her apparent indifference to his not having come. For the first time since I had known him he seemed to have expressed a doubt of my word. Before we parted I told him that I'd undeceive her—start the first thing in the morning for Richmond and there let her know he had been blameless. At this he kissed me again. I'd expiate my sin, I said; I'd humble myself in the dust: I'd confess and ask to be forgiven. At this he kissed me once more.

V

In the train the next day this struck me as a good deal for him to have consented to; but my purpose was firm enough to carry me on. I mounted the long hill to where the view begins, and then I knocked at her door. I was a trifle mystified by the fact that her blinds were still drawn, reflecting that if in the stress of my compunction I had come early I had certainly yet allowed people time to get up.

'At home, mum? She has left home for ever.'

I was extraordinarily startled by this announcement of the elderly parlour-maid. 'She has gone away?'

'She's dead, mum, please.' Then as I gasped at the horrible word: 'She died last night.'

The loud cry that escaped me sounded even in my own ears like some harsh violation of the hour. I felt for the moment as if I had killed her; I turned faint and saw through a vagueness the woman hold out her arms to me. Of what next happened I've no recollection, nor of anything but my friend's poor stupid cousin, in a darkened room, after an interval that I suppose very brief, sobbing at me in a smothered accusatory way. I can't say how long it took me to understand, to believe and then to press back with an immense effort that pang of responsibility which, superstitiously, insanely, had been at first almost all I was conscious of. The doctor, after the fact, had been superlatively wise and clear: he was satisfied of a long-latent weakness of the heart, determined probably years before by the agitation and terrors to which her marriage had introduced her. She had had in those days cruel scenes with her husband, she had been in fear of her life. All emotion, everything in the nature of anxiety and suspense had been after that to be strongly deprecated, as in her marked cultivation of a quiet life she was evidently well aware; but who could say that any one, especially a 'real lady', might be successfully protected from *every* little rub? She had had one a day or two before in the news of her husband's death—since there were shocks of all kinds, not only those of grief and surprise. For that matter she had never dreamed of so near a release: it had looked uncommonly as if he would live as long as herself. Then in the evening, in town, she had manifestly had some misadventure: something must have happened there that it would be imperative to clear up. She had come back very late—it was past eleven o'clock, and on being met in the hall by her cousin, who was extremely anxious, had allowed she was tired and must rest a moment before mounting the stairs. They had passed together into the dining-room, her companion proposing a glass of wine and bustling to the sideboard to pour it out. This took but a moment, and when my informant turned round our poor friend had not had time to seat herself. Suddenly, with a small moan that was barely audible, she dropped upon the sofa. She was dead. What unknown 'little rub' had dealt her the blow? What concussion, in the name of wonder, *had* awaited her in town? I mentioned immediately the one thinkable ground of disturbance—her having failed to meet at my house, to which by invitation for the purpose she had come at five o'clock, the gentleman I was to be married to, who had been accidentally kept away and with whom she had no acquaintance whatever. This obviously counted for little; but something else might easily have occurred: nothing in the London streets was more possible than an accident, especially an accident in those desperate cabs. What had she done, where had she gone on leaving my house? I had taken for granted she had gone straight home. We both presently remembered that in her excursions to town she sometimes, for convenience, for refreshment, spent an hour or two at the 'Gentlewomen', the quiet little ladies' club, and I promised that it should be my first care to make at that establishment an earnest appeal. Then we entered the dim and dreadful chamber where she lay locked up in death and where, asking after a little to be left alone with her, I remained for half an hour. Death had made her, had kept her beautiful; but I felt above all, as I knelt at her bed, that it had made her, had kept her silent. It had turned the key on something I was concerned to know.

On my return from Richmond and after another duty had been performed I drove to his chambers. It was the first time, but I had often wanted to see them. On the staircase, which, as the house contained twenty sets of rooms, was unrestrictedly public, I met his servant, who went back with me and ushered me in. At the sound of my entrance he appeared in the doorway of a further room, and the instant we were alone I produced my news: 'She's dead!'

'Dead?' He was tremendously struck, and I noticed he had no need to ask whom, in this abruptness, I meant.

'She died last evening—just after leaving me.'

He stared with the strangest expression, his eyes searching mine as for a trap. 'Last evening—after leaving you?' He repeated my words in stupefaction. Then he brought out, so that it was in stupefaction I heard, 'Impossible! I saw her.'

'You "saw" her?'

'On that spot—where you stand.'

This called back to me after an instant, as if to help me to take it in, the great wonder of the warning of his youth. 'In the hour of death—I understand: as you so beautifully saw your mother.'

'Ah *not* as I saw my mother—not that way, not that way!' He was deeply moved by the news—far more moved, it was plain, than he would have been the day before: it gave me a vivid sense that, as I had then said to myself, there was indeed a relation between them and that he had actually been face to face with her. Such an idea, by its reassertion of his extraordinary privilege, would have suddenly presented him as painfully abnormal hadn't he vehemently insisted on the difference. 'I saw her living. I saw her to speak to her. I saw her as I see you now.'

It's remarkable that for a moment, though only for a moment, I found relief in the more personal, as it were, but also the more natural, of the two odd facts. The next, as I embraced this image of her having come to him on leaving me and of just what it accounted for in the disposal of her time, I demanded with a shade of harshness of which I was aware: 'What on earth did she come for?'

He had now a minute to think—to recover himself and judge of effects, so that if it was still with excited eyes he spoke he showed a conscious redness and made an inconsequent attempt to smile away the gravity of his words. 'She came just to see me. She came—after what had passed at your house—so that we *should*, nevertheless, at last meet. The impulse seemed to me exquisite, and that was the way I took it.'

I looked round the room where she had been—where *she* had been and I never had till now. 'And was the way you took it the way she expressed it?'

'She only expressed it by being here and by letting me look at her. That was enough!' he cried with an extraordinary laugh.

I wondered more and more. 'You mean she didn't speak to you?'

'She said nothing. She only looked at me as I looked at her.'

'And you didn't speak either?'

He gave me again his painful smile. 'I thought of *you*. The situation was every way delicate. I used the finest tact. But she saw she had pleased me.' He even repeated his dissonant laugh.

'She evidently "pleased" you!' Then I thought a moment. 'How long did she stay?'

'How can I say? It seemed twenty minutes, but it was probably a good deal less.'

'Twenty minutes of silence!' I began to have my definite view, and now in fact quite to clutch at it. 'Do you know you're telling me a thing positively monstrous?'

He had been standing with his back to the fire; at this, with a pleading look, he came to me. 'I beseech you, dearest, to take it kindly.'

I could take it kindly, and I signified as much, but I couldn't somehow, as he rather awkwardly opened his arms, let him draw me to him. So there fell between us for an appreciable time the discomfort of a great silence.

VI

He broke it by presently saying: 'There's absolutely no doubt of her death?'

'Unfortunately none. I've just risen from my knees by the bed where they've laid her out.'

He fixed his eyes hard on the floor; then he raised them to mine. 'How does she look?'

'She looks—at peace.'

He turned away again while I watched him; but after a moment he began: 'At what hour then——?'

'It must have been near midnight. She dropped as she reached her house—from an affection of the heart which she knew herself and her physician knew her to have, but of which, patiently, bravely, she had never spoken to me.'

He listened intently and for a minute was unable to speak. At last he broke out with an accent of which the almost boyish confidence, the really sublime simplicity, rings in my ears as I write: 'Wasn't she *wonderful*!' Even at the time I was able to do it justice enough to answer that I had always told him so; but the next minute, as if after speaking he had caught a glimpse of what he might have made me feel, he went on quickly: 'You can easily understand that if she didn't get home till midnight——'

I instantly took him up. 'There was plenty of time for you to have seen her? How so,' I asked, 'when you didn't leave my house till late? I don't remember the very moment—I was preoccupied. But you know that though you said you had lots to do you sat for some time after dinner. She, on her side, was all the evening at the "Gentlewomen". I've just come from there—I've ascertained. She had tea there; she remained a long long time.'

'What was she doing all the long long time?'

I saw him eager to challenge at every step my account of the matter; and the more he showed this the more I was moved to emphasize that version, to prefer with apparent perversity an explanation which only deepened the marvel and the mystery, but which, of the two prodigies it had to choose from, my reviving jealousy found easiest to accept. He stood there pleading with a candour that now seems to me beautiful for the privilege of having in spite of supreme defeat known the living woman; while I, with a passion I wonder at today, though it still smoulders in a manner in its ashes, could only reply that, through a strange gift shared by her with his mother and on her own side likewise hereditary, the miracle of his youth had been renewed for him, the miracle of hers for her. She had been to him—yes, and by an impulse as charming as he liked; but oh she hadn't been in the body! It was a simple question of evidence. I had had, I maintained, a definite statement of what she had done—most of the time—at the little club. The place was almost empty, but the servants had noticed her. She had sat motionless in a deep chair by the drawing-room fire; she had leaned back her head, she had closed her eyes, she had seemed softly to sleep.

'I see. But till what o'clock?'

'There,' I was obliged to answer, 'the servants fail me a little. The portress in particular is unfortunately a fool, even though she too is supposed to be a Gentlewoman. She was evidently at that period of the evening, without a substitute and against regulations, absent for some little time from the cage in which it's her business to watch the comings and goings. She's muddled, she palpably prevaricates, so I can't positively, from her observation, give you an hour. But it was remarked towards half-past ten that our poor friend was no longer in the club.'

It suited him down to the ground. She came straight here, and from here she went straight to the train.

'She couldn't have run it so close,' I declared. 'That was a thing she particularly never did.'

'There was no need of running it close, my dear—she had plenty of time. Your memory's at fault about my having left you late: I left you, as it happens, unusually early. I'm sorry my stay with you seemed long, for I was back here by ten.'

'To put yourself into your slippers,' I retorted, 'and fall asleep in your chair. You slept till morning—you saw her in a dream!' He looked at me in silence and with sombre eyes—eyes that showed me he had some irritation to repress. Presently I went on: 'You had a visit, at an extraordinary hour, from a lady—*soit*: nothing in the world's more probable. But there are ladies and ladies. How in the name of goodness, if she was unannounced and dumb and you had into the bargain never seen the least portrait of her—how could you identify the person we're talking of?'

'Haven't I to absolute satiety heard her described? I'll describe her for you in every particular.'

'Don't!' I cried with a promptness that made him laugh once more. I coloured at this, but I continued: 'Did your servant introduce her?'

'He wasn't here—he's always away when he's wanted. One of the features of this big house is that from the street-door the different floors are accessible practically without challenge. My servant makes love to a young person employed in the rooms above these, and he had a long bout of it last evening. When he's out on that job he leaves my outer door, on the staircase, so much ajar as to enable him to slip back without a sound. The door then only requires a push. She pushed it—that simply took a little courage.'

'A little? It took tons! And it took all sorts of impossible calculations.'

'Well, she had them—she made them. Mind you, I don't deny for a moment,' he added, 'that it was very very wonderful!'

Something in his tone kept me a time from trusting myself to speak. At last I said: 'How did she come to know where you live?'

'By remembering the address on the little label the shop-people happily left sticking to the frame I had had made for my photograph.'

'And how was she dressed?'

'In mourning, my own dear. No great depths of crape, but simple and scrupulous black. She had in her bonnet three small black feathers. She carried a little muff of astrakhan. She has near the left eye,' he continued, 'a tiny vertical scar——'

I stopped him short. 'The mark of a caress from her husband.' Then I added: 'How close you must have been to her!' He made no answer to this, and I thought he blushed, observing which I broke straight off. 'Well, goodbye.'

'You won't stay a little?' He came to me again tenderly, and this time I suffered him. 'Her visit had its beauty,' he murmured as he held me, 'but yours has a greater one.'

I let him kiss me, but I remembered, as I had remembered the day before, that the last kiss she had given, as I supposed, in this world had been for the lips he touched. 'I'm life, you see,' I answered. 'What you saw last night was death.'

'It was life—it was life!'

He spoke with a soft stubbornness—I disengaged myself. We stood looking at each other hard. 'You describe the scene—so far as you describe it at all—in terms that are incomprehensible. She was in the room before you knew it?'

'I looked up from my letter-writing—at that table under the lamp I had been wholly absorbed in it—and she stood before me.'

'Then what did you do?'

'I sprang up with an ejaculation, and she, with a smile, laid her finger, ever so warningly, yet with a sort of delicate dignity, to her lips. I knew it meant silence, but the strange thing was that it seemed immediately to explain and to justify her. We at any rate stood for a time that, as I've told you, I can't calculate, face to face. It was just as you and I stand now.'

'Simply staring?'

He shook an impatient head. 'Ah! *we're* not staring!'

'Yes, but we're talking.'

'Well, *we* were—after a fashion.' He lost himself in the memory of it. 'It was as friendly as this.' I had on my tongue's end to ask if that was saying much for it, but I made the point instead that what they had evidently done was to gaze in mutual admiration. Then I asked if his recognition of her had been immediate. 'Not quite,' he replied, 'for of course I didn't expect her; but it came to me long before she went who she was—who only she could be.'

I thought a little. 'And how did she at last go?'

'Just as she arrived. The door was open behind her and she passed out.'

'Was she rapid—slow?'

'Rather quick. But looking behind her,' he smiled to add. 'I let her go, for I perfectly knew I was to take it as she wished.'

I was conscious of exhaling a long vague sigh. 'Well, you must take it now as *I* wish—you must let *me* go.'

At this he drew near me again, detaining and persuading me, declaring with all due gallantry that I was a very different matter. I'd have given anything to have been able to ask him if he had touched her, but the words refused to form themselves: I knew to the last tenth of a tone how horrid and vulgar they'd sound. I said something else—I forget exactly what; it was feebly tortuous and intended, meanly enough, to make him tell me without my putting the question. But he didn't tell me; he only repeated, as from a glimpse of the propriety of soothing and consoling me, the sense of his declaration of some minutes before—the assurance that she was indeed exquisite, as I had always insisted, but that I was his 'real' friend and his very own for ever. This led me to reassert, in the spirit of my previous rejoinder, that I had at least the merit of being alive; which in turn drew from him again the flash of contradiction I dreaded. 'Oh *she* was alive! She was, she was!'

'She was dead, she was dead!' I asseverated with an energy, a determination it should *be* so, which comes back to me now almost as grotesque. But the sound of the word as it rang out filled me suddenly with horror, and all the natural emotion the meaning of it might have evoked in other conditions gathered and broke in a flood. It rolled over me that here was a great affection quenched, and how much I had loved and trusted her. I had a vision at the same time of the lonely beauty of her end. 'She's gone—she's lost to us for ever!' I burst into sobs.

'That's exactly what I feel,' he exclaimed, speaking with extreme kindness and pressing me to him for comfort. 'She's gone; she's lost to us for ever: so what does it matter now?' He bent over me, and when his face had touched mine I scarcely knew if it were wet with my tears or with his own.

VII

It was my theory, my conviction, it became, as I may say, my attitude, that they had still never 'met'; and it was just on this ground I felt it generous to ask him to stand with me at her grave. He did so very modestly and tenderly, and I assumed, though he himself clearly cared nothing for the danger, that the solemnity of the occasion, largely made up of persons who had known them both and had a sense of the long joke, would sufficiently deprive his presence of all light association. On the question of what had happened the evening of her death little more passed between us; I had been taken by a horror of the element of evidence. On either hypothesis it was gross and prying. He on his side lacked producible corroboration—everything, that is, but a statement of his house-porter, on his own admission a most casual and intermittent personage—that between the hours of ten o'clock and midnight no less than three ladies in deep black had flitted in and out of the place. This proved far too much; we had neither of us any use for three. He knew I considered I had accounted for every fragment of her time, and we dropped the matter as settled; we abstained from further discussion. What *I* knew however was that he abstained to please me rather than because he yielded to my reasons. He didn't yield—he was only indulgent; he clung to his interpretation because he liked it better. He liked it better, I held, because it had more to say to his vanity. That, in a similar position, wouldn't have been its effect on me, though I had doubtless quite as much; but these are things of individual humour and as to which no person can judge for another. I should have supposed it more gratifying to be the subject of one of those inexplicable occurrences that are chronicled in thrilling books and disputed about at learned meetings; I could conceive, on the part of a being just engulfed in the infinite and still vibrating with human emotion, of nothing more fine and pure, more high and august, than such an impulse of reparation, of admonition, or even of curiosity. *That* was beautiful, if one would, and I should in his place have thought more of myself for being so distinguished and so selected. It was public that he had already, that he had long figured in that light, and what was such a fact in itself but almost a proof? Each of the strange visitations contributed to establish the other. He had a different feeling; but he had also, I hasten to add, an unmistakable desire not to make a stand or, as they say, a fuss about it. I might believe what I liked—the more so that the whole thing was in a manner a mystery of my producing. It was an event of my history, a puzzle of my consciousness, not of his; therefore he would take about it any tone that struck me as convenient. We had both at all events other business on hand: we were pressed with preparations for our marriage.

Mine were assuredly urgent, but I found as the days went on that to believe what I 'liked' was to believe what I was more and more intimately convinced of. I found also that I didn't like it so much as that came to, or that the pleasure at all events was far from being the cause of my conviction. My obsession, as I may really call it and as I began to perceive, refused to be elbowed away, as I had hoped, by my sense of paramount duties. If I had a great deal to do, I had still more to think of, and the moment came when my occupations were gravely menaced by my thoughts. I see it all now, I feel it, I live it over. It's terribly void of joy, it's full indeed to overflowing of bitterness; and yet I must do myself justice—I couldn't have been other than I was. The same strange impressions, had I to meet them again, would produce the same deep anguish, the same sharp doubts, the same still sharper certainties. Oh it's all easier to remember than to write, but even could I retrace the business hour by hour, could I find terms for the inexpressible, the ugliness and the pain would quickly stay my hand. Let me then note very simply and briefly that a week before our wedding-day, three weeks after her death, I knew in all my fibres that I had something very serious to look in the face and that if I was to make this effort I must make it on the spot and before another hour should elapse. My unextinguished jealousy—that was the Medusa-mask. It hadn't died with her death, it had lividly survived, and it was fed by suspicions unspeakable. They *would* be unspeakable today, that is, if I hadn't felt the sharp need of uttering them at the time. This need took possession of me—to save me, as it seemed, from my fate. When once it had done so I saw—in the urgency of the case, the diminishing hours and shrinking interval—only one issue, that of absolute promptness and frankness. I could at least not do him the wrong of delaying another day; I could at least treat my difficulty as too fine for a subterfuge. Therefore very quietly, but none the less abruptly and hideously, I put it before him on a certain evening that we must reconsider our situation and recognize that it had completely altered.

He stared bravely, 'How in the world altered?'

'Another person has come between us.'

He took but an instant to think. 'I won't pretend not to know whom you mean.' He smiled in pity for my aberration, but he meant to be kind. 'A woman dead and buried!'

'She's buried, but she's not dead. She's dead for the world—she's dead for me. But she's not dead for you.'

'You hark back to the different construction we put on her appearance that evening?'

'No,' I answered, 'I hark back to nothing. I've no need of it. I've more than enough with what's before me.'

'And pray, darling, what may that be?'

'You're completely changed.'

'By that absurdity?' he laughed.

'Not so much by that one as by other absurdities that have followed it.'

'And what may *they* have been?'

We had faced each other fairly, with eyes that didn't flinch; but his had a dim strange light, and my certitude triumphed in his perceptible paleness. 'Do you really pretend,' I asked, 'not to know what they are?'

'My dear child,' he replied, 'you describe them too sketchily!'

I considered a moment. 'One may well be embarrassed to finish the picture! But from that point of view—and from the beginning—what was ever more embarrassing than your idiosyncrasy?'

He invoked his vagueness—a thing he always did beautifully. 'My idiosyncrasy?'

'Your notorious, your peculiar power.'

He gave a great shrug of impatience, a groan of overdone disdain. 'Oh my peculiar power!'

'Your accessibility to forms of life,' I coldly went on, 'your command of impressions, appearances, contacts, closed—for our gain or our loss—to the rest of us. That was originally a part of the deep interest with which you inspired me—one of the reasons I was amused—I was indeed positively proud, to know you. It was a magnificent distinction: it's a magnificent distinction still. But of course I had no prevision then of the way it would operate now; and even had that been the case I should have had none of the extraordinary way in which its action would affect me.'

'To what in the name of goodness,' he pleadingly inquired, 'are you fantastically alluding?' Then as I remained silent, gathering a tone for my charge, 'How in the world *does* it operate?' he went on; 'and how in the world are you affected?'

'She missed you for five years,' I said, 'but she never misses you now. You're making it up!'

'Making it up?' He had begun to turn from white to red.

'You see her—you see her: you see her every night!' He gave a loud sound of derision, but I felt it ring false. 'She comes to you as she came that evening,' I declared; 'having tried it she found she liked it!' I was able, with God's help, to speak without blind passion or vulgar violence; but those were the exact words—and far from 'sketchy' they then appeared to me—that I uttered. He had turned away in his laughter, clapping his hands at my folly, but in an instant he faced me again with a change of expression that struck me. 'Do you dare to deny,' I then asked, 'that you habitually see her?'

He had taken the line of indulgence, of meeting me half-way and kindly humouring me. At all events he to my astonishment suddenly said: 'Well, my dear, what if I do?'

'It's your natural right: it belongs to your constitution and to your wonderful if not perhaps quite enviable fortune. But you'll easily understand that it separates us. I unconditionally release you.'

'Release me?'

'You must choose between me and her.'

He looked at me hard. 'I see.' Then he walked away a little, as if grasping what I had said and thinking how he had best treat it. At last he turned on me afresh. 'How on earth do you know such an awfully private thing?'

'You mean because you've tried so hard to hide it? It *is* awfully private, and you may believe I shall never betray you. You've done your best, you've acted your part, you've behaved, poor dear! loyally and admirably. Therefore I've watched you in silence, playing my part too; I've noted every drop in your voice, every absence in your eyes, every effort in your indifferent hand: I've waited till I was utterly sure and miserably unhappy. How *can* you hide it when you're abjectly in love with her, when you're sick almost to death with the joy of what she gives you?' I checked his quick protest with a quicker gesture. 'You love her as you've *never* loved, and, passion for passion, she gives it straight back! She rules you, she holds you, she has you all! A woman, in such a case as mine, divines and feels and sees; she's not a dull dunce who has to be "credibly informed". You come to me mechanically, compunctiously, with the dregs of your tenderness and the remnant of your life. I can renounce you, but I can't share you: the best of you is hers, I know what it is and freely give you up to her for ever!'

He made a gallant fight, but it couldn't be patched up; he repeated his denial, he retracted his admission, he ridiculed my charge, of which I freely granted him moreover the indefensible extravagance. I didn't pretend for a moment that we were talking of common things, I didn't pretend for a moment that he and she were common people. Pray, if they *had* been, how should I ever have cared for them? They had enjoyed a rare extension of being and they had caught me up in their flight; only I couldn't breathe in such air and I promptly asked to be set down. Everything in the facts was monstrous, and most of all my lucid perception of them; the only thing allied to nature and truth was my having to act on that perception. I felt after I had spoken in this sense that my assurance was complete; nothing had been wanting to it but the sight of my effect on him. He disguised indeed the effect in a cloud of chaff, a diversion that gained him time and covered his retreat. He challenged my sincerity, my sanity, almost my humanity, and that of course widened our breach and confirmed our rupture. He did everything in short but convince me either that I was wrong or that he was unhappy: we separated, and I left him to his inconceivable communion.

He never married, any more than I've done. When six years later, in solitude and silence, I heard of his death I hailed it as a direct contribution to my theory. It was sudden, it was never properly accounted for, it was surrounded by circumstances in which—for oh I took them to pieces—I distinctly read an intention, the mark of his own hidden hand. It was the result of a long necessity, of an unquenchable desire. To say exactly what I mean, it was a response to an irresistible call.

The Red Room

H. G. WELLS

—

'I can assure you,' said I, 'that it will take a very tangible ghost to frighten me.' And I stood up before the fire with my glass in my hand.

'It is your own choosing,' said the man with the withered arm, and glanced at me askance.

'Eight-and-twenty years,' said I, 'I have lived, and never a ghost have I seen as yet.'

The old woman sat staring hard into the fire, her pale eyes wide open. 'Ah,' she broke in: 'and eight-and-twenty years you have lived and never seen the likes of this house, I reckon. There's a many things to see, when one's still but eight-and-twenty.' She swayed her head slowly from side to side. 'A many things to see and sorrow for.'

I half suspected the old people were trying to enhance the spiritual terrors of their house by their droning insistence. I put down my empty glass on the table and looked about the room, and caught a glimpse of myself, abbreviated and broadened to an impossible sturdiness, in the queer old mirror at the end of the room. 'Well,' I said, 'if I see anything tonight, I shall be so much the wiser. For I come to the business with an open mind.'

'It's your own choosing,' said the man with the withered arm once more.

I heard the sound of a stick and a shambling step on the flags in the passage outside, and the door creaked on its hinges as a second old man entered, more bent, more wrinkled, more aged even than the first. He supported himself by a single crutch, his eyes were covered by a shade, and his lower lip, half averted, hung pale and pink from his decaying yellow teeth. He made straight for an armchair on the opposite side of the table, sat down clumsily, and began to cough. The man with the withered arm gave this newcomer a short glance of positive dislike; the old woman took no notice of his arrival, but remained with her eyes fixed steadily on the fire.

'I said—it's your own choosing,' said the man with the withered arm, when the coughing had ceased for a while.

'It's my own choosing,' I answered.

The man with the shade became aware of my presence for the first time, and threw his head back for a moment and sideways, to see me. I caught a momentary glimpse of his eyes, small and bright and inflamed. Then he began to cough and splutter again.

'Why don't you drink?' said the man with the withered arm, pushing the beer towards him. The man with the shade poured out a glassful with a shaky arm that splashed half as much again on the deal table. A monstrous shadow of him crouched upon the wall and mocked his action as he poured and drank. I must confess I had scarce expected these grotesque custodians. There is to my mind something inhuman in senility, something crouching and atavistic; the human qualities seem to drop from old people insensibly day by day. The three of them made me feel uncomfortable, with their gaunt silences, their bent carriage, their evident unfriendliness to me and to one another.

'If,' said I, 'you will show me to this haunted room of yours, I will make myself comfortable there.'

The old man with the cough jerked his head back so suddenly that it startled me, and shot another glance of his red eyes at me from under the shade; but no one answered me. I waited a minute, glancing from one to the other.

'If,' I said a little louder, 'if you will show me to this haunted room of yours, I will relieve you from the task of entertaining me.'

'There's a candle on the slab outside the door,' said the man with the withered arm, looking at my feet as he addressed me. 'But if you go to the red room tonight——'

('This night of all nights!' said the old woman.)

'You go alone.'

'Very well,' I answered. 'And which way do I go?'

'You go along the passage for a bit,' said he, 'until you come to a door, and through that is a spiral staircase, and half-way up that is a landing and another door covered with baize. Go through that and down the long corridor to the end, and the red room is on your left up the steps.'

'Have I got that right?' I said, and repeated his directions. He corrected me in one particular.

'And are you really going?' said the man with the shade, looking at me again for the third time, with that queer, unnatural tilting of the face.

('This night of all nights!' said the old woman.)

'It is what I came for,' I said, and moved towards the door. As I did so, the old man with the shade rose and staggered round the table, so as to be closer to the others and to the fire. At the door I turned and looked at them, and saw they were all close together, dark against the firelight, staring at me over their shoulders, with an intent expression on their ancient faces.

'Good night,' I said, setting the door open.

'It's your own choosing,' said the man with the withered arm.

I left the door wide open until the candle was well alight, and then I shut them in and walked down the chilly, echoing passage.

I must confess that the oddness of these three old pensioners in whose charge her ladyship had left the castle, and the deep-toned, old-fashioned furniture of the housekeeper's room in which they for-gathered, affected me in spite of my efforts to keep myself at a matter of fact phase. They seemed to belong to another age, an older age, an age when things spiritual were different from this of ours, less certain; an age when omens and witches were credible, and ghosts beyond denying. Their very existence was spectral; the cut of their clothing, fashions born in dead brains. The ornaments and conveniences of the room about them were ghostly—the thoughts of vanished men, which still haunted rather than participated in the world of today. But with an effort I sent such thoughts to the right-about. The long, draughty sub-terranean passage was chilly and dusty, and my candle flared and made the shadows cower and quiver. The echoes rang up and down the spiral staircase, and a shadow came sweeping up after me, and one fled before me into the darkness overhead. I came to the landing and stopped there for a moment, listening to a rustling that I fancied I heard; then, satisfied of the absolute silence, I pushed open the baize-covered door and stood in the corridor.

The effect was scarcely what I expected, for the moonlight coming in by the great window on the grand staircase picked out everything in vivid black shadow or silvery illumination. Everything was in its place; the house might have been deserted on the yesterday instead of eighteen months ago. There were candles in the sockets of the sconces, and whatever dust had gathered on the carpets or upon the polished flooring was distributed so evenly as to be invisible in the moonlight. I was about to advance, and stopped abruptly. A bronze group stood upon the landing, hidden from me by the corner of the wall, but its shadow fell with marvellous distinctness upon the white panelling and gave me the impression of some one crouching to waylay me. I stood rigid for half a minute perhaps. Then, with my hand in the pocket that held my revolver, I advanced, only to discover a Ganymede and Eagle glistening in the moonlight. That incident for a time restored my nerve, and a porcelain Chinaman on a buhl table, whose head rocked silently as I passed him, scarcely startled me.

The door to the red room and the steps up to it were in a shadowy corner. I moved my candle from side to side, in order to see clearly the nature of the recess in which I stood before opening the door. Here it was, thought I, that my predecessor was found, and the memory of that story gave me a sudden twinge of apprehension. I glanced over my shoulder at the Ganymede in the moonlight, and opened the door of the red room rather hastily, with my face half-turned to the pallid silence of the landing.

I entered, closed the door behind me at once, turned the key I found in the lock within, and stood with the candle held aloft, surveying the scene of my vigil, the great red room of Lorraine Castle, in which the young duke had died. Or, rather, in which he had begun his dying, for he had opened the door and fallen headlong down the steps I had just ascended. That had been the end of his vigil, of his gallant attempt to conquer the ghostly tradition of the place, and never, I thought, had apoplexy better served the ends of superstition. And there were other and older stories that clung to the room, back to the half-credible beginning of it all, the tale of a timid wife and the tragic end that came to her husband's jest of frightening her. And looking around that large sombre room, with its shadowy window bays, its recesses and alcoves, one could well understand the legends that had sprouted in its black corners, its germinating darkness. My candle was a little tongue of light in its vastness, that failed to pierce the opposite end of the room, and left an ocean of mystery and suggestion beyond its island of light.

I resolved to make a systematic examination of the place at once, and dispel the fanciful suggestions of its obscurity before they obtained a hold upon me. After satisfying myself of the fastening of the door, I began to walk about the room, peering round each article of furniture, tucking up the valances of the bed, and opening its curtains wide. I pulled up the blinds and examined the fastenings of the several windows before closing the shutters, leant forward and looked up the blackness of the wide chimney, and tapped the dark oak panelling for any secret opening. There were two big mirrors in the room, each with a pair of sconces bearing candles, and on the mantelshelf, too, were more candles in china candlesticks. All these I lit one after the other. The fire was laid, an unexpected consideration from the old housekeeper—and I lit it, to keep down any disposition to shiver, and when it was burning well, I stood round with my back to it and regarded the room again. I had pulled up a chintz-covered armchair and a table, to form a kind of barricade before me, and on this lay my revolver ready to hand. My precise examination had done me good, but I still found the remoter darkness of the place, and its perfect stillness, too stimulating for the imagination. The echoing of the stir and crackling of the fire was no sort of comfort to me. The shadow in the alcove at the end in particular had that undefinable quality of a presence, that odd suggestion of a lurking, living thing, that comes so easily in silence and solitude. At last, to reassure myself, I walked with a candle into it, and satisfied myself that there was nothing tangible there. I stood that candle upon the floor of the alcove, and left it in that position.

By this time I was in a state of considerable nervous tension, although to my reason there was no adequate cause for the condition. My mind, however, was perfectly clear. I postulated quite unreservedly that nothing supernatural could happen, and to pass the time I began to string some rhymes together, Ingoldsby fashion, of the original legend of the place. A few I spoke aloud, but the echoes were not pleasant. For the same reason I also abandoned, after a time, a conversation with myself upon the impossibility of ghosts and haunting. My mind reverted to the three old and distorted people downstairs, and I tried to keep it upon that topic. The sombre reds and blacks of the room troubled me; even with seven candles the place was merely dim. The one in the alcove flared in a draught, and the fire's flickering kept the shadows and penumbra perpetually shifting and stirring. Casting about for a remedy, I recalled the candles I had seen in the passage, and, with a slight effort, walked out into the moonlight, carrying a candle and leaving the door open, and presently returned with as many as ten. These I put in various knick-knacks of china with which the room was sparsely adorned, lit and placed where the shadows had lain deepest, some on the floor, some in the window recesses, until at last my seventeen candles were so arranged that not an inch of the room but had the direct light of at least one of them. It occurred to me that when the ghost came, I could warn him not to trip over them. The room was now quite brightly illuminated. There was something very cheery and reassuring in these little streaming flames, and snuffing them gave me an occupation, and afforded a helpful sense of the passage of time.

Even with that, however, the brooding expectation of the vigil weighed heavily upon me. It was after midnight that the candle in the alcove suddenly went out, and the black shadow sprang back to its place there. I did not see the candle go out; I simply turned and saw that the darkness was there, as one might start and see the unexpected presence of a stranger. 'By Jove!' said I aloud; 'that draught's a strong one!' and taking the matches from the table, I walked across the room in a leisurely manner to relight the corner again. My first match would not strike, and as I succeeded with the second, something seemed to blink on the wall before me. I turned my head involuntarily, and saw that the two candles on the little table by the fireplace were extinguished. I rose at once to my feet.

'Odd!' I said. 'Did I do that myself in a flash of absent-mindedness?'

I walked back, relit one, and as I did so, I saw the candle in the right sconce of one of the mirrors wink and go right out, and almost immediately its companion followed it. There was no mistake about it. The flame vanished, as if the wicks had been suddenly nipped between a finger and thumb, leaving the wick neither glowing nor smoking, but black. While I stood gaping, the candle at the foot of the bed went out, and the shadows seemed to take another step towards me.

'This won't do!' said I, and first one and then another candle on the mantelshelf followed.

'What's up?' I cried, with a queer high note getting into my voice somehow. At that the candle on the wardrobe went out, and the one I had relit in the alcove followed.

'Steady on!' I said. 'These candles are wanted,' speaking with a half-hysterical facetiousness, and scratching away at a match the while for the mantel candlesticks. My hands trembled so much that twice I missed the rough paper of the matchbox. As the mantel emerged from darkness again, two candles in the remoter end of the window were eclipsed. But with the same match I also relit the larger mirror candles, and those on the floor near the doorway, so that for the moment I seemed to gain on the extinctions. But then in a volley there vanished four lights at once in different corners of the room, and I struck another match in quivering haste, and stood hesitating whither to take it.

As I stood undecided, an invisible hand seemed to sweep out the two candles on the table. With a cry of terror, I dashed at the alcove, then into the corner, and then into the window, relighting three, as two more vanished by the fireplace; then, perceiving a better way, I dropped the matches on the iron-bound deedbox in the corner, and caught up the bedroom candlestick. With this I avoided the delay of striking matches; but for all that the steady process of extinction went on, and the shadows I feared and fought against returned, and crept in upon me, first a step gained on this side of me and then on that. It was like a ragged storm-cloud sweeping out the stars. Now and then one returned for a minute, and was lost again. I was now almost frantic with the horror of the coming darkness, and my self-possession deserted me. I leaped panting and dishevelled from candle to candle in a vain struggle against that remorseless advance.

I bruised myself on the thigh against the table, I sent a chair headlong, I stumbled and fell and whisked the cloth from the table in my fall. My candle rolled away from me, and I snatched another as I rose. Abruptly this was blown out, as I swung it off the table, by the wind of my sudden movement, and immediately the two remaining candles followed. But there was light still in the room, a red light that staved off the shadows from me. The fire! Of course I could still thrust my candle between the bars and relight it!

I turned to where the flames were still dancing between the glowing coals, and splashing red reflections upon the furniture, made two steps towards the grate, and incontinently the flames dwindled and vanished, the glow vanished, the reflections rushed together and vanished, and as I thrust the candle between the bars darkness closed upon me like the shutting of an eye, wrapped about me in a stifling embrace, sealed my vision, and crushed the last vestiges of reason from my brain. The candle fell from my hand. I flung out my arms in a vain effort to thrust that ponderous blackness away from me, and, lifting up my voice, screamed with all my might—once, twice, thrice. Then I think I must have staggered to my feet. I know I thought suddenly of the moonlit corridor, and, with my head bowed and my arms over my face, made a run for the door.

But I had forgotten the exact position of the door, and struck myself heavily against the corner of the bed. I staggered back, turned, and was either struck or struck myself against some other bulky furniture. I have a vague memory of battering myself thus, to and fro in the darkness, of a cramped struggle, and of my own wild crying as I darted to and fro, of a heavy blow at last upon my forehead, a horrible sensation of falling that lasted an age, of my last frantic effort to keep my footing, and then I remember no more.

I opened my eyes in daylight. My head was roughly bandaged, and the man with the withered arm was watching my face. I looked about me, trying to remember what had happened, and for a space I could not recollect. I rolled my eyes into the corner, and saw the old woman, no longer abstracted, pouring out some drops of medicine from a little blue phial into a glass. 'Where am I?' I asked; 'I seem to remember you, and yet I cannot remember who you are.'

They told me then, and I heard of the haunted red room as one who hears a tale. 'We found you at dawn,' said he, 'and there was blood on your forehead and lips.'

It was very slowly I recovered my memory of my experience. 'You believe now,' said the old man, 'that the room is haunted?' He spoke no longer as one who greets an intruder, but as one who grieves for a broken friend.

'Yes,' said I; 'the room is haunted.'

'And you have seen it. And we, who have lived here all our lives, have never set eyes upon it. Because we have never dared . . . Tell us, is it truly the old earl who——'

'No,' said I; 'it is not.'

'I told you so,' said the old lady, with the glass in her hand. 'It is his poor young countess who was frightened——'

'It is not,' I said. 'There is neither ghost of earl nor ghost of countess in that room, there is no ghost there at all; but worse, far worse——'

'Well?' they said.

'The worst of all the things that haunt poor mortal man,' said I; 'and that is, in all its nakedness—*Fear!* Fear that will not have light nor sound, that will not bear with reason, that deafens and darkens and overwhelms. It followed me through the corridor, it fought against me in the room——'

I stopped abruptly. There was an interval of silence. My hand went up to my bandages.

Then the man with the shade sighed and spoke. 'That is it,' said he. 'I knew that was it. A power of darkness. To put such a curse upon a woman! It lurks there always. You can feel it even in the daytime, even of a bright summer's day, in the hangings, in the curtains, keeping behind you however you face about. In the dusk it creeps along the corridor and follows you, so that you dare not turn. There is Fear in that room of hers—black Fear, and there will be—so long as this house of sin endures.'

The Monkey's Paw

W. W. JACOBS

I

Without, the night was cold and wet, but in the small parlour of Laburnum Villa the blinds were drawn and the fire burned brightly. Father and son were at chess; the former, who possessed ideas about the game involving radical changes, putting his king into such sharp and unnecessary perils that it even provoked comment from the white-haired old lady knitting placidly by the fire.

'Hark at the wind,' said Mr White, who, having seen a fatal mistake after it was too late, was amiably desirous of preventing his son from seeing it.

'I'm listening,' said the latter, grimly surveying the board as he stretched out his hand. 'Check.'

'I should hardly think that he'd come tonight,' said his father, with his hand poised over the board.

'Mate,' replied the son.

'That's the worst of living so far out,' bawled Mr White, with sudden and unlooked-for violence; 'of all the beastly, slushy, out-of-the-way places to live in, this is the worst. Path's a bog, and the road's a torrent. I don't know what people are thinking about. I suppose because only two houses in the road are let, they think it doesn't matter.'

'Never mind, dear,' said his wife soothingly; 'perhaps you'll win the next one.'

Mr White looked up sharply, just in time to intercept a knowing glance between mother and son. The words died away on his lips, and he hid a guilty grin in his thin grey beard.

'There he is,' said Herbert White, as the gate banged to loudly and heavy footsteps came toward the door.

The old man rose with hospitable haste, and opening the door, was heard condoling with the new arrival. The new arrival also condoled with himself, so that Mrs White said, 'Tut, tut!' and coughed gently as her husband entered the room, followed by a tall, burly man, beady of eye and rubicund of visage.

'Sergeant-Major Morris,' he said, introducing him.

The sergeant-major shook hands, and taking the proffered seat by the fire, watched contentedly while his host got out whisky and tumblers and stood a small copper kettle on the fire.

At the third glass his eyes got brighter, and he began to talk, the little family circle regarding with eager interest this visitor from distant parts, as he squared his broad shoulders in the chair and spoke of wild scenes and doughty deeds; of wars and plagues and strange peoples.

'Twenty-one years of it,' said Mr White, nodding at his wife and son. 'When he went away he was a slip of a youth in the warehouse. Now look at him.'

'He don't look to have taken much harm,' said Mrs White politely.

'I'd like to go to India myself,' said the old man, 'just to look round a bit, you know.'

'Better where you are,' said the sergeant-major, shaking his head. He put down the empty glass, and sighing softly, shook it again.

'I should like to see those old temples and fakirs and jugglers,' said the old man. 'What was that you started telling me the other day about a monkey's paw or something, Morris?'

'Nothing,' said the soldier hastily. 'Leastways nothing worth hearing.'

'Monkey's paw?' said Mrs White curiously.

'Well, it's just a bit of what you might call magic, perhaps,' said the sergeant-major offhandedly.

His three listeners leaned forward eagerly. The visitor absent-mindedly put his empty glass to his lips and then set it down again. His host filled it for him.

'To look at,' said the sergeant-major, fumbling in his pocket, 'it's just an ordinary little paw, dried to a mummy.'

He took something out of his pocket and proffered it. Mrs White drew back with a grimace, but her son, taking it, examined it curiously.

'And what is there special about it?' inquired Mr White as he took it from his son, and having examined it, placed it upon the table.

'It had a spell put on it by an old fakir,' said the sergeant-major, 'a very holy man. He wanted to show that fate ruled people's lives, and that those who interfered with it did so to their sorrow. He put a spell on it so that three separate men could each have three wishes from it.'

His manner was so impressive that his hearers were conscious that their light laughter jarred somewhat.

'Well, why don't you have three, sir?' said Herbert White cleverly.

The soldier regarded him in the way that middle age is wont to regard presumptuous youth. 'I have,' he said quietly, and his blotchy face whitened.

'And did you really have the three wishes granted?' asked Mrs White.

'I did,' said the sergeant-major, and his glass tapped against his strong teeth.

'And has anybody else wished?' persisted the old lady.

'The first man had his three wishes. Yes,' was the reply; 'I don't know what the first two were, but the third was for death. That's how I got the paw.'

His tones were so grave that a hush fell upon the group.

'If you've had your three wishes, it's no good to you now, then, Morris,' said the old man at last. 'What do you keep it for?'

The soldier shook his head. 'Fancy, I suppose,' he said slowly. 'I did have some idea of selling it, but I don't think I will. It has caused enough mischief already. Besides, people won't buy. They think it's a fairy tale, some of them; and those who do think anything of it want to try it first and pay me afterward.'

'If you could have another three wishes,' said the old man, eyeing him keenly, 'would you have them?'

'I don't know,' said the other. 'I don't know.'

He took the paw, and dangling it between his forefinger and thumb, suddenly threw it upon the fire. White, with a slight cry, stooped down and snatched it off.

'Better let it burn,' said the soldier solemnly.

'If you don't want it, Morris,' said the other, 'give it to me.'

'I won't,' said his friend doggedly. 'I threw it on the fire. If you keep it, don't blame me for what happens. Pitch it on the fire again like a sensible man.'

The other shook his head and examined his new possession closely. 'How do you do it?' he inquired.

'Hold it up in your right hand and wish aloud,' said the sergeant-major, 'but I warn you of the consequences.'

'Sounds like the *Arabian Nights*,' said Mrs White, as she rose and began to set the supper. 'Don't you think you might wish for four pairs of hands for me?'

Her husband drew the talisman from his pocket, and then all three burst into laughter as the sergeant-major, with a look of alarm on his face, caught him by the arm.

'If you must wish,' he said gruffly, 'wish for something sensible.'

Mr White dropped it back in his pocket, and placing chairs, motioned his friend to the table. In the business of supper the talisman was partly forgotten, and afterward the three sat listening in an enthralled fashion to a second instalment of the soldier's adventures in India.

'If the tale about the monkey's paw is not more truthful than those he has been telling us,' said Herbert, as the door closed behind their guest, just in time to catch the last train, 'we shan't make much out of it.'

'Did you give him anything for it, father?' inquired Mrs White, regarding her husband closely.

'A trifle,' said he, colouring slightly. 'He didn't want it, but I made him take it. And he pressed me again to throw it away.'

'Likely,' said Herbert, with pretended horror. 'Why, we're going to be rich, and famous, and happy. Wish to be an emperor, father, to begin with; then you can't be henpecked.'

He darted round the table, pursued by the maligned Mrs White armed with an antimacassar.

Mr White took the paw from his pocket and eyed it dubiously. 'I don't know what to wish for, and that's a fact,' he said slowly. 'It seems to me I've got all I want.'

'If you only cleared the house, you'd be quite happy, wouldn't you!' said Herbert, with his hand on his shoulder. 'Well, wish for two hundred pounds, then; that'll just do it.'

His father, smiling shamefacedly at his own credulity, held up the talisman, as his son, with a solemn face, somewhat marred by a wink at his mother, sat down at the piano and struck a few impressive chords.

'I wish for two hundred pounds,' said the old man distinctly.

A fine crash from the piano greeted the words, interrupted by a shuddering cry from the old man. His wife and son ran toward him.

'It moved,' he cried, with a glance of disgust at the object as it lay on the floor. 'As I wished, it twisted in my hand like a snake.'

'Well, I don't see the money,' said his son, as he picked it up and placed it on the table, 'and I bet I never shall.'

'It must have been your fancy, father,' said his wife, regarding him anxiously.

He shook his head. 'Never mind, though; there's no harm done, but it gave me a shock all the same.'

They sat down by the fire again while the two men finished their pipes. Outside, the wind was higher than ever, and the old man started nervously at the sound of a door banging upstairs. A silence unusual and depressing settled upon all three, which lasted until the old couple rose to retire for the night.

'I expect you'll find the cash tied up in a big bag in the middle of your bed,' said Herbert, as he bade them good night, 'and something horrible squatting up on top of the wardrobe watching you as you pocket your ill-gotten gains.'

He sat alone in the darkness, gazing at the dying fire, and seeing faces in it. The last face was so horrible and so simian that he gazed at it in amazement. It got so vivid that, with a little uneasy laugh, he felt on the table for a glass containing a little water to throw over it. His hand grasped the monkey's paw, and with a little shiver he wiped his hand on his coat and went up to bed.

II

In the brightness of the wintry sun next morning as it streamed over the breakfast table he laughed at his fears. There was an air of prosaic wholesomeness about the room which it had lacked on the previous night, and the dirty, shrivelled little paw was pitched on the side-board with a carelessness which betokened no great belief in its virtues.

'I suppose all old soldiers are the same,' said Mrs White. 'The idea of our listening to such nonsense! How could wishes be granted in these days? And if they could, how could two hundred pounds hurt you, father?'

'Might drop on his head from the sky,' said the frivolous Herbert.

'Morris said the things happened so naturally,' said his father, 'that you might if you so wished attribute it to coincidence.'

'Well, don't break into the money before I come back,' said Herbert as he rose from the table. 'I'm afraid it'll turn you into a mean, avaricious man, and we shall have to disown you.'

His mother laughed, and following him to the door, watched him down the road; and returning to the breakfast table, was very happy at the expense of her husband's credulity. All of which did not prevent her from scurrying to the door at the postman's knock, nor prevent her from referring somewhat shortly to retired sergeant-majors of bibulous habits when she found that the post brought a tailor's bill.

'Herbert will have some more of his funny remarks, I expect, when he comes home,' she said, as they sat at dinner.

'I dare say,' said Mr White, pouring himself out some beer; 'but for all that, the thing moved in my hand; that I'll swear to.'

'You thought it did,' said the old lady, soothingly.

'I say it did,' replied the other. 'There was no thought about it; I had just—— What's the matter?'

His wife made no reply. She was watching the mysterious movements of a man outside, who, peering in an undecided fashion at the house, appeared to be trying to make up his mind to enter. In mental connexion with the two hundred pounds, she noticed that the stranger was well dressed, and wore a silk hat of glossy newness. Three times he paused at the gate, and then walked on again. The fourth time he stood with his hand upon it, and then with sudden resolution flung it open and walked up the path. Mrs White at the same moment placed her hands behind her, and hurriedly unfastening the strings of her apron, put that useful article of apparel beneath the cushion of her chair.

She brought the stranger, who seemed ill at ease, into the room. He gazed at her furtively, and listened in a preoccupied fashion as the old lady apologized for the appearance of the room, and her husband's coat, a garment which he usually reserved for the garden. She then waited as patiently as her sex would permit, for him to broach his business, but he was at first strangely silent.

'I—was asked to call,' he said at last, and stooped and picked a piece of cotton from his trousers. 'I come from "Maw and Meggins".'

The old lady started. 'Is anything the matter?' she asked breathlessly. 'Has anything happened to Herbert? What is it? What is it?'

Her husband interposed. 'There, there, mother,' he said hastily. 'Sit down, and don't jump to conclusions. You've not brought bad news, I'm sure, sir;' and he eyed the other wistfully.

'I'm sorry——' began the visitor.

'Is he hurt?' demanded the mother wildly.

The visitor bowed in assent. 'Badly hurt,' he said quietly, 'but he is not in any pain.'

'Oh, thank God!' said the old woman, clasping her hands. 'Thank God for that! Thank——'

She broke off suddenly as the sinister meaning of the assurance dawned upon her and she saw the awful confirmation of her fears in the other's averted face. She caught her breath, and turning to her slower-witted husband, laid her trembling old hand upon his. There was a long silence.

'He was caught in the machinery,' said the visitor at length in a low voice.

'Caught in the machinery,' repeated Mr White, in a dazed fashion, 'yes.'

He sat staring blankly out at the window, and taking his wife's hand between his own, pressed it as he had been wont to do in their old courting days nearly forty years before.

'He was the only one left to us,' he said, turning gently to the visitor. 'It is hard.'

The other coughed, and rising, walked slowly to the window. 'The firm wished me to convey their sincere sympathy with you in your great loss,' he said, without looking round. 'I beg that you will understand I am only their servant and merely obeying orders.'

There was no reply; the old woman's face was white, her eyes staring, and her breath inaudible; on the husband's face was a look such as his friend the sergeant might have carried into his first action.

'I was to say that Maw and Meggins disclaim all responsibility,' continued the other. 'They admit no liability at all, but in consideration of your son's services, they wish to present you with a certain sum as compensation.'

Mr White dropped his wife's hand, and rising to his feet, gazed with a look of horror at his visitor. His dry lips shaped the words, 'How much?'

'Two hundred pounds,' was the answer.

Unconscious of his wife's shriek, the old man smiled faintly, put out his hands like a sightless man, and dropped, a senseless heap, to the floor.

III

In the huge new cemetery, some two miles distant, the old people buried their dead, and came back to the house steeped in shadow and silence. It was all over so quickly that at first they could hardly realize it, and remained in a state of expectation as though of something else to happen—something else which was to lighten this load, too heavy for old hearts to bear.

But the days passed, and expectation gave place to resignation—the hopeless resignation of the old, sometimes miscalled apathy. Sometimes they hardly exchanged a word, for now they had nothing to talk about, and their days were long to weariness.

It was about a week after that the old man, waking suddenly in the night, stretched out his hand and found himself alone. The room was in darkness, and the sound of subdued weeping came from the window. He raised himself in bed and listened.

'Come back,' he said tenderly. 'You will be cold.'

'It is colder for my son,' said the old woman, and wept afresh.

The sound of her sobs died away on his ears. The bed was warm, and his eyes heavy with sleep. He dozed fitfully, and then slept until a sudden wild cry from his wife awoke him with a start.

'*The paw!*' she cried wildly. 'The monkey's paw!'

He started up in alarm. 'Where? Where is it? What's the matter?'

She came stumbling across the room toward him. 'I want it,' she said quietly. 'You've not destroyed it?'

'It's in the parlour, on the bracket,' he replied, marvelling. 'Why?'

She cried and laughed together, and bending over, kissed his cheek.

'I only just thought of it,' she said hysterically. 'Why didn't I think of it before? Why didn't *you* think of it?'

'Think of what?' he questioned.

'The other two wishes,' she replied rapidly. 'We've only had one.'

'Was not that enough?' he demanded fiercely.

'No,' she cried triumphantly; 'we'll have one more. Go down and get it quickly, and wish our boy alive again.'

The man sat up in bed and flung the bedclothes from his quaking limbs. 'Good God, you are mad!' he cried, aghast.

'Get it,' she panted; 'get it quickly, and wish—— Oh, my boy, my boy!'

Her husband struck a match and lit the candle. 'Get back to bed,' he said unsteadily. 'You don't know what you are saying.'

'We had the first wish granted,' said the old woman feverishly; 'why not the second?'

'A coincidence,' stammered the old man.

'Go and get it and wish,' cried his wife, quivering with excitement.

The old man turned and regarded her, and his voice shook. 'He has been dead ten days, and besides he—I would not tell you else, but—I could only recognize him by his clothing. If he was too terrible for you to see then, how now?'

'Bring him back,' cried the old woman, and dragged him toward the door. 'Do you think I fear the child I have nursed?'

He went down in the darkness, and felt his way to the parlour, and then to the mantelpiece. The talisman was in its place, and a horrible fear that the unspoken wish might bring his mutilated son before him ere he could escape from the room seized upon him, and he caught his breath as he found that he had lost the direction of the door. His brow cold with sweat, he felt his way round the table, and groped along the wall until he found himself in the small passage with the unwholesome thing in his hand.

Even his wife's face seemed changed as he entered the room. It was white and expectant, and to his fears seemed to have an unnatural look upon it. He was afraid of her.

'*Wish!*' she cried, in a strong voice.

'It is foolish and wicked,' he faltered.

'*Wish!*' repeated his wife.

He raised his hand. 'I wish my son alive again.'

The talisman fell to the floor, and he regarded it fearfully. Then he sank trembling into a chair as the old woman, with burning eyes, walked to the window and raised the blind.

He sat until he was chilled with the cold, glancing occasionally at the figure of the old woman peering through the window. The candle-end, which had burned below the rim of the china candlestick, was throwing pulsating shadows on the ceiling and walls, until, with a flicker larger than the rest, it expired. The old man, with an unspeakable sense of relief at the failure of the talisman, crept back to his bed, and a minute or two afterward the old woman came silently and apathetically beside him.

Neither spoke, but lay silently listening to the ticking of the clock. A stair creaked, and a squeaky mouse scurried noisily through the wall. The darkness was oppressive, and after lying for some time screwing up his courage, he took the box of matches, and striking one, went downstairs for a candle.

At the foot of the stairs the match went out, and he paused to strike another; and at the same moment a knock, so quiet and stealthy as to be scarcely audible, sounded on the front door.

The matches fell from his hand and spilled in the passage. He stood motionless, his breath suspended until the knock was repeated. Then he turned and fled swiftly back to his room, and closed the door behind him. A third knock sounded through the house.

'*What's that?*' cried the old woman, starting up.

'A rat,' said the old man in shaking tones—'a rat. It passed me on the stairs.'

His wife sat up in bed listening. A loud knock resounded through the house.

'It's Herbert!' she screamed. 'It's Herbert!'

She ran to the door, but her husband was before her, and catching her by the arm, held her tightly.

'What are you going to do?' he whispered hoarsely.

'It's my boy; it's Herbert!' she cried, struggling mechanically. 'I forgot it was two miles away. What are you holding me for? Let go. I must open the door.'

'For God's sake don't let it in,' cried the old man, trembling.

'You're afraid of your own son,' she cried, struggling. 'Let me go. I'm coming, Herbert; I'm coming.'

There was another knock, and another. The old woman with a sudden wrench broke free and ran from the room. Her husband followed to the landing, and called after her appealingly as she hurried downstairs. He heard the chain rattle back and the bottom bolt drawn slowly and stiffly from the socket. Then the old woman's voice, strained and panting.

'The bolt,' she cried loudly. 'Come down. I can't reach it.'

But her husband was on his hands and knees groping wildly on the floor in search of the paw. If he could only find it before the thing outside got in. A perfect fusillade of knocks reverberated through the house, and he heard the scraping of a chair as his wife put it down in the passage against the door. He heard the creaking of the bolt as it came slowly back, and at the same moment he found the monkey's paw, and frantically breathed his third and last wish.

The knocking ceased suddenly, although the echoes of it were still in the house. He heard the chair drawn back, and the door opened. A cold wind rushed up the staircase, and a long loud wail of disappointment and misery from his wife gave him courage to run down to her side, and then to the gate beyond. The street lamp flickering opposite shone on a quiet and deserted road.

The Lost Ghost

MARY E. WILKINS

Mrs John Emerson, sitting with her needlework beside the window, looked out and saw Mrs Rhoda Meserve coming down the street, and knew at once by the trend of her steps and the cant of her head that she meditated turning in at her gate. She also knew by a certain something about her general carriage—a thrusting forward of the neck, a bustling hitch of the shoulders—that she had important news. Rhoda Meserve always had the news as soon as the news was in being, and generally Mrs John Emerson was the first to whom she imparted it. The two women had been friends ever since Mrs Meserve had married Simon Meserve and come to the village to live.

Mrs Meserve was a pretty woman, moving with graceful flirts of ruffling skirts; her clearcut, nervous face, as delicately tinted as a shell, looked brightly from the plumy brim of a black hat at Mrs Emerson in the window. Mrs Emerson was glad to see her coming. She returned the greeting with enthusiasm, then rose hurriedly, ran into the cold parlour and brought out one of the best rocking-chairs. She was just in time, after drawing it up beside the opposite window, to greet her friend at the door.

'Good afternoon,' said she. 'I declare, I'm real glad to see you. I've been alone all day. John went to the city this morning. I thought of coming over to your house this afternoon, but I couldn't bring my sewing very well. I am putting the ruffles on my new black dress skirt.'

'Well, I didn't have a thing on hand except my crochet work,' responded Mrs Meserve, 'and I thought I'd just run over a few minutes.'

'I'm real glad you did,' repeated Mrs Emerson. 'Take your things right off. Here, I'll put them on my bed in the bedroom. Take the rocking-chair.'

Mrs Meserve settled herself in the parlour rocking-chair, while Mrs Emerson carried her shawl and hat into the little adjoining bedroom. When she returned Mrs Meserve was rocking peacefully and was already at work hooking blue wool in and out.

'That's real pretty,' said Mrs Emerson.

'Yes, I think it's pretty,' replied Mrs Meserve.

'I suppose it's for the church fair?'

'Yes. I don't suppose it'll bring enough to pay for the worsted, let alone the work, but I suppose I've got to make something.'

'How much did that one you made for the fair last year bring?'

'Twenty-five cents.'

'It's wicked, ain't it?'

'I rather guess it is. It takes me a week every minute I can get to make one. I wish those that bought such things for twenty-five cents had to make them. Guess they'd sing another song. Well, I suppose I oughtn't to complain as long as it is for the Lord, but sometimes it does seem as if the Lord didn't get much out of it.'

'Well, it's pretty work,' said Mrs Emerson, sitting down at the opposite window and taking up her dress skirt.

'Yes, it is real pretty work. I just *love* to crochet.'

The two women rocked and sewed and crocheted in silence for two or three minutes. They were both waiting. Mrs Meserve waited for the other's curiosity to develop in order that her news might have, as it were, a befitting stage entrance. Mrs Emerson waited for the news. Finally she could wait no longer.

'Well, what's the news?' said she.

'Well, I don't know as there's anything very particular,' hedged the other woman, prolonging the situation.

'Yes, there is; you can't cheat me,' replied Mrs Emerson.

'Now, how do you know?'

'By the way you look.'

Mrs Meserve laughed consciously and rather vainly.

'Well, Simon says my face is so expressive I can't hide anything more than five minutes no matter how hard I try,' said she. 'Well, there is some news. Simon came home with it this noon. He heard it in South Dayton. He had some business over there this morning. The old Sargent place is let.'

Mrs Emerson dropped her sewing and stared.

'You don't say so!'

'Yes, it is.'

'Who to?'

'Why, some folks from Boston that moved to South Dayton last year. They haven't been satisfied with the house they had there—it wasn't large enough. The man has got considerable property and can afford to live pretty well. He's got a wife and his unmarried sister in the family. The sister's got money, too. He does business in Boston and it's just as easy to get to Boston from here as from South Dayton, and so they're coming here. You know the old Sargent house is a splendid place.'

'Yes, it's the handsomest house in town, but——'

'Oh, Simon said they told him about that and he just laughed. Said he wasn't afraid and neither was his wife and sister. Said he'd risk ghosts rather than little tucked-up sleeping-rooms without any sun, like they've had in the Dayton house. Said he'd rather risk *seeing* ghosts, than risk being ghosts themselves. Simon said they said he was a great hand to joke.'

'Oh, well,' said Mrs Emerson, 'it is a beautiful house, and maybe there isn't anything in those stories. It never seemed to me they came very straight anyway. I never took much stock in them. All I thought was—if his wife was nervous.'

'Nothing in creation would hire me to go into a house that I'd ever heard a word against of that kind,' declared Mrs Meserve with emphasis. 'I wouldn't go into that house if they would give me the rent. I've seen enough of haunted houses to last me as long as I live.'

Mrs Emerson's face acquired the expression of a hunting hound.

'Have you?' she asked in an intense whisper.

'Yes, I have. I don't want any more of it.'

'Before you came here?'

'Yes; before I was married—when I was quite a girl.'

Mrs Meserve had not married young. Mrs Emerson had mental calculations when she heard that.

'Did you really live in a house that was——' she whispered fearfully.

Mrs Meserve nodded solemnly.

'Did you really ever—see—anything——'

Mrs Meserve nodded.

'You didn't see anything that did you any harm?'

'No, I didn't see anything that did me harm looking at in in one way, but it don't do anybody in this world any good to see things that haven't any business to be seen in it. You never get over it.'

There was a moment's silence. Mrs Emerson's features seemed to sharpen.

'Well, of course I don't want to urge you,' said she, 'if you don't feel like talking about it; but maybe it might do you good to tell it out, if it's on your mind, worrying you.'

'I try to put it out of my mind,' said Mrs Meserve.

'Well, it's just as you feel.'

'I never told anybody but Simon,' said Mrs Meserve. 'I never felt as if it was wise perhaps. I didn't know what folks might think. So many don't believe in anything they can't understand, that they might think my mind wasn't right. Simon advised me not to talk about it. He said he didn't believe it was anything supernatural, but he had to own up that he couldn't give any explanation for it to save his life. He had to own up that he didn't believe anybody could. Then he said he wouldn't talk about it. He said lots of folks would sooner tell folks my head wasn't right than to own up they couldn't see through it.'

'I'm sure I wouldn't say so,' returned Mrs Emerson reproachfully. 'You know better than that, I hope.'

'Yes, I do,' replied Mrs Meserve. 'I know you wouldn't say so.'

'And I wouldn't tell it to a soul if you didn't want me to.'

'Well, I'd rather you wouldn't.'

'I won't speak of it even to Mr Emerson.'

'I'd rather you wouldn't even to him.'

'I won't.'

Mrs Emerson took up her dress skirt again; Mrs Meserve hooked up another loop of blue wool. Then she begun:

'Of course,' said she, 'I ain't going to say positively that I believe or disbelieve in ghosts, but all I tell you is what I saw. I can't explain it. I don't pretend I can, for I can't. If you can, well and good; I shall be glad, for it will stop tormenting me as it has done and always will otherwise. There hasn't been a day nor a night since it happened that I haven't thought of it, and always I have felt the shivers go down my back when I did.'

'That's an awful feeling,' Mrs Emerson said.

'Ain't it? Well, it happened before I was married, when I was a girl and lived in East Wilmington. It was the first year I lived there. You know my family all died five years before that. I told you.'

Mrs Emerson nodded.

'Well, I went there to teach school, and I went to board with a Mrs Amelia Dennison and her sister, Mrs Bird. Abby, her name was—Abby Bird. She was a widow; she had never had any children. She had a little money—Mrs Dennison didn't have any—and she had come to East Wilmington and bought the house they lived in. It was a real pretty house, though it was very old and run down. It had cost Mrs Bird a good deal to put it in order. I guess that was the reason they took me to board. I guess they thought it would help along a little. I guess what I paid for my board about kept us all in victuals. Mrs Bird had enough to live on if they were careful, but she had spent so much fixing up the old house that they must have been a little pinched for awhile.

'Anyhow, they took me to board, and I thought I was pretty lucky to get in there. I had a nice room, big and sunny and furnished pretty, the paper and paint all new, and everything as neat as wax. Mrs Dennison was one of the best cooks I ever saw, and I had a little stove in my room, and there was always a nice fire there when I got home from school. I thought I hadn't been in such a nice place since I lost my own home, until I had been there about three weeks.

'I had been there about three weeks before I found it out, though I guess it had been going on ever since they had been in the house, and that was 'most four months. They hadn't said anything about it, and I didn't wonder, for there they had just bought the house and been to so much expense and trouble fixing it up.

'Well, I went there in September. I begun my school the first Monday. I remember it was a real cold fall, there was a frost the middle of September, and I had to put on my winter coat. I remember when I came home that night (let me see, I began school on a Monday, and that was two weeks from the next Thursday), I took off my coat downstairs and laid it on the table in the front entry. It was a real nice coat—heavy black broadcloth trimmed with fur; I had had it the winter before. Mrs Bird called after me as I went upstairs that I ought not to leave it in the front entry for fear somebody might come in and take it, but I only laughed and called back to her that I wasn't afraid. I never was much afraid of burglars.

'Well, though it was hardly the middle of September, it was a real cold night. I remember my room faced west, and the sun was getting low, and the sky was a pale yellow and purple, just as you see it sometimes in the winter when there is going to be a cold snap. I rather think that was the night the frost came the first time. I know Mrs Dennison covered up some flowers she had in the front yard, anyhow. I remember looking out and seeing an old green plaid shawl of hers over the verbena bed. There was a fire in my little wood-stove. Mrs Bird made it, I know. She was a real motherly sort of woman; she always seemed to be the happiest when she was doing something to make other folks happy and comfortable. Mrs Dennison told me she had always been so. She said she had coddled her husband within an inch of his life. "It's lucky Abby never had any children," she said, "for she would have spoilt them."

'Well, that night I sat down beside my nice little fire and ate an apple. There was a plate of nice apples on my table. Mrs Bird put them there. I was always very fond of apples. Well, I sat down and ate an apple, and was having a beautiful time, and thinking how lucky I was to have got board in such a place with such nice folks, when I heard a queer little sound at my door. It was such a little hesitating sort of sound that it sounded more like a fumble than a knock, as if some one very timid, with very little hands, was feeling along the door, not quite daring to knock. For a minute I thought it was a mouse. But I waited and it came again, and then I made up my mind it was a knock, but a very little scared one, so I said, "Come in."

'But nobody came in, and then presently I heard the knock again. Then I got up and opened the door, thinking it was very queer, and I had a frightened feeling without knowing why.

'Well, I opened the door, and the first thing I noticed was a draught of cold air, as if the front door downstairs was open, but there was a strange close smell about the cold draught. It smelled more like a cellar that had been shut up for years, than out-of-doors. Then I saw something. I saw my coat first. The thing that held it was so small that I couldn't see much of anything else. Then I saw a little white face with eyes so scared and wishful that they seemed as if they might eat a hole in anybody's heart. It was a dreadful little face, with something about it which made it different from any other face on earth, but it was so pitiful that somehow it did away a good deal with the dreadfulness. And there were two little hands spotted purple with the cold, holding up my winter coat, and a strange little far-away voice said: "I can't find my mother."

' "For Heaven's sake," I said, "who are you?"

'Then the little voice said again: "I can't find my mother."

'All the time I could smell the cold and I saw that it was about the child; that cold was clinging to her as if she had come out of some deadly cold place. Well, I took my coat, I did not know what else to do, and the cold was clinging to that. It was as cold as if it had come off ice. When I had the coat I could see the child more plainly. She was dressed in one little white garment made very simply. It was a nightgown, only very long, quite covering her feet, and I could see dimly through it her little thin body mottled purple with the cold. Her face did not look so cold; that was a clear waxen white. Her hair was dark, but it looked as if it might be dark only because it was so damp, almost wet, and might really be light hair. It clung very close to her forehead, which was round and white. She would have been very beautiful if she had not been so dreadful.

' "Who are you?" says I again, looking at her.

'She looked at me with her terrible pleading eyes and did not say anything.

' "What are you?" says I. Then she went away. She did not seem to run or walk like other children. She flitted, like one of those little filmy white butterflies, that don't seem like real ones they are so light, and move as if they had no weight. But she looked back from the head of the stairs. "I can't find my mother," said she, and I never heard such a voice.

' "Who is your mother?" says I, but she was gone.

'Well, I thought for a moment I should faint away. The room got dark and I heard a singing in my ears. Then I flung my coat onto the bed. My hands were as cold as ice from holding it, and I stood in my door, and called first Mrs Bird and then Mrs Dennison. I didn't dare go down over the stairs where that had gone. It seemed to me I should go mad if I didn't see somebody or something like other folks on the face of the earth. I thought I should never make anybody hear, but I could hear them stepping about downstairs, and I could smell biscuits baking for supper. Somehow the smell of those biscuits seemed the only natural thing left to keep me in my right mind. I didn't dare go over those stairs. I just stood there and called, and finally I heard the entry door open and Mrs Bird called back:

' "What is it? Did you call, Miss Arms?"

' "Come up here; come up here as quick as you can, both of you," I screamed out; "quick, quick, quick!"

'I heard Mrs Bird tell Mrs Dennison: "Come quick, Amelia, something is the matter in Miss Arms' room." It struck me even then that she expressed herself rather queerly, and it struck me as very queer, indeed, when they both got upstairs and I saw that they knew what had happened, or that they knew of what nature the happening was.

' "What is it, dear?" asked Mrs Bird, and her pretty, loving voice had a strained sound. I saw her look at Mrs Dennison and I saw Mrs Dennison look back at her.

' "For God's sake," says I, and I never spoke so before—"for God's sake, what was it brought my coat upstairs?"

' "What was it like?" asked Mrs Dennison in a sort of failing voice, and she looked at her sister again and her sister looked back at her.

' "It was a child I have never seen here before. It looked like a child," says I, "but I never saw a child so dreadful, and it had on a nightgown, and said she couldn't find her mother. Who was it? What was it?"

'I thought for a minute Mrs Dennison was going to faint, but Mrs Bird hung onto her and rubbed her hands, and whispered in her ear (she had the cooingest kind of voice), and I ran and got her a glass of cold water. I tell you it took considerable courage to go downstairs alone, but they had set a lamp on the entry table so I could see. I don't believe I could have spunked up enough to have gone downstairs in the dark, thinking every second that child might be close to me. The lamp and the smell of the biscuits baking seemed to sort of keep my courage up, but I tell you I didn't waste much time going down those stairs and out into the kitchen for a glass of water. I pumped as if the house was afire, and I grabbed the first thing I came across in the shape of a tumbler: it was a painted one that Mrs Dennison's Sunday school class gave her, and it was meant for a flower vase.

'Well, I filled it and then ran upstairs. I felt every minute as if something would catch my feet, and I held the glass to Mrs Dennison's lips, while Mrs Bird held her head up, and she took a good long swallow, then she looked hard at the tumbler.

' "Yes," says I, "I know I got this one, but I took the first I came across, and it isn't hurt a mite."

' "Don't get the painted flowers wet," says Mrs Dennison very feebly, "they'll wash off if you do."

' "I'll be real careful," says I. I knew she set a sight by that painted tumbler.

'The water seemed to do Mrs Dennison good, for presently she pushed Mrs Bird away and sat up. She had been laying down on my bed.

' "I'm all over it now," says she, but she was terribly white, and her eyes looked as if they saw something outside things. Mrs Bird wasn't much better, but she always had a sort of settled sweet, good look that nothing could disturb to any great extent. I knew I looked dreadful, for I caught a glimpse of myself in the glass, and I would hardly have known who it was.

'Mrs Dennison, she slid off the bed and walked sort of tottery to a chair. "I was silly to give way so," says she.

' "No, you wasn't silly, sister," says Mrs Bird. "I don't know what this means any more than you do, but whatever it is, no one ought to be called silly for being overcome by anything so different from other things which we have known all our lives."

'Mrs Dennison looked at her sister, then she looked at me, then back at her sister again, and Mrs Bird spoke as if she had been asked a question.

' "Yes," says she, "I do think Miss Arms ought to be told—that is, I think she ought to be told all we know ourselves."

' "That isn't much," said Mrs Dennison with a dying-away sort of sigh. She looked as if she might faint away again any minute. She was a real delicate-looking woman, but it turned out she was a good deal stronger than poor Mrs Bird.

' "No, there isn't much we do know," says Mrs Bird, "but what little there is she ought to know. I felt as if she ought to when she first came here."

' "Well, I didn't feel quite right about it," said Mrs Dennison, "but I kept hoping it might stop, and any way, that it might never trouble her, and you had put so much in the house, and we needed the money, and I didn't know but she might be nervous and think she couldn't come, and I didn't want to take a man boarder."

' "And aside from the money, we were very anxious to have you come, my dear," says Mrs Bird.

' "Yes," says Mrs Dennison, "we wanted the young company in the house; we were lonesome, and we both of us took a great liking to you the minute we set eyes on you."

'And I guess they meant what they said, both of them. They were beautiful women, and nobody could be any kinder to me than they were, and I never blamed them for not telling me before, and, as they said, there wasn't really much to tell.

'They hadn't any sooner fairly bought the house, and moved into it, than they began to see and hear things. Mrs Bird said they were sitting together in the sitting-room one evening when they heard it the first time. She said her sister was knitting lace (Mrs Dennison made beautiful knitted lace) and she was reading the *Missionary Herald* (Mrs Bird was very much interested in mission work), when all of a sudden they heard something. She heard it first and she laid down her *Missionary Herald* and listened, and then Mrs Dennison she saw her listening and she drops her lace. "What is it you are listening to, Abby?" says she. Then it came again and they both heard, and the cold shivers went down their backs to hear it, though they didn't know why. "It's the cat, isn't it?" says Mrs Bird.

' "It isn't any cat," says Mrs Dennison.

' "Oh, I guess it *must* be the cat; maybe she's got a mouse," says Mrs Bird, real cheerful to calm down Mrs Dennison, for she saw she was 'most scared to death, and she was always afraid of her fainting away. Then she opens the door and calls, "Kitty, kitty, kitty!" They had brought their cat with them in a basket when they came to Eas Wilmington to live. It was a real handsome tiger cat, a tommy, and he knew a lot.

'Well, she called "Kitty, kitty, kitty!" and sure enough the kitty came and when he came in the door he gave a big yawl that didn't sound unlik. what they had heard.

' "There, sister, here he is; you see it was the cat," says Mrs Bird. "Poor kitty!"

'But Mrs Dennison she eyed the cat, and she give a great screech.

' "What's that? What's that?" says she.

' "What's what?" says Mrs Bird, pretending to herself that she didn't see what her sister meant.

' "Somethin's got hold of that cat's tail," says Mrs Dennison. "Somethin's got hold of his tail. It's pulled straight out, an' he can't get away. Just hear him yawl!"

' "It isn't anything," says Mrs Bird, but even as she said that she could see a little hand holding fast to that cat's tail, and then the child seemed to sort of clear out of the dimness behind the hand, and the child was sort of laughing then, instead of looking sad, and she said that was a great deal worse. She said that laugh was the most awful and the saddest thing she ever heard.

'Well, she was so dumbfounded that she didn't know what to do, and she couldn't sense at first that it was anything supernatural. She thought it must be one of the neighbour's children who had run away and was making free of their house, and was teasing their cat, and that they must be just nervous to feel so upset by it. So she speaks up sort of sharp.

' "Don't you know that you mustn't pull the kitty's tail?" says she. "Don't you know you hurt the poor kitty, and she'll scratch you if you don't take care. Poor kitty, you mustn't hurt her."

'And with that she said the child stopped pulling that cat's tail and went to stroking her just as soft and pitiful, and the cat put his back up and rubbed and purred as if he liked it. The cat never seemed a mite afraid, and that seemed queer, for I had always heard that animals were dreadfully afraid of ghosts; but then, that was a pretty harmless little sort of ghost.

'Well, Mrs Bird said the child stroked that cat, while she and Mrs Dennison stood watching it, and holding onto each other, for, no matter how hard they tried to think it was all right, it didn't look right. Finally Mrs Dennison she spoke.

' "What's your name, little girl?" says she.

'Then the child looks up and stops stroking the cat, and says she can't find her mother, just the way she said it to me. Then Mrs Dennison she gave such a gasp that Mrs Bird thought she was going to faint away, but she didn't. "Well, who is your mother?" says she. But the child just says again "I can't find my mother—I can't find my mother."

' "Where do you live, dear?" says Mrs Bird.

' "I can't find my mother," says the child.

'Well, that was the way it was. Nothing happened. Those two women stood there hanging onto each other, and the child stood in front of them, and they asked her questions, and everything she would say was: "I can't find my mother."

'Then Mrs Bird tried to catch hold of the child, for she thought in spite of what she saw that perhaps she was nervous and it was a real child, only perhaps not quite right in its head, that had run away in her little nightgown after she had been put to bed.

'She tried to catch the child. She had an idea of putting a shawl around it and going out—she was such a little thing she could have carried her easy enough—and trying to find out to which of the neighbours she belonged. But the minute she moved toward the child there wasn't any child there; there was only that little voice seeming to come from nothing, saying "I can't find my mother," and presently that died away.

'Well, that same thing kept happening, or something very much the same. Once in awhile Mrs Bird would be washing dishes, and all at once the child would be standing beside her with the dish-towel, wiping them. Of course, that was terrible. Mrs Bird would wash the dishes all over. Sometimes she didn't tell Mrs Dennison, it made her so nervous. Sometimes when they were making cake they would find the raisins all picked over, and sometimes little sticks of kindling-wood would be found laying beside the kitchen stove. They never knew when they would come across that child, and always she kept saying over and over that she couldn't find her mother. They never tried talking to her, except once in awhile Mrs Bird would get desperate and ask her something, but the child never seemed to hear it; she always kept right on saying that she couldn't find her mother.

'After they had told me all they had to tell about their experience with the child, they told me about the house and the people that had lived there before they did. It seemed something dreadful had happened in that house. And the land agent had never let on to them. I don't think they would have bought it if he had, no matter how cheap it was, for even if folks aren't really afraid of anything, they don't want to live in houses where such dreadful things have happened that you keep thinking about them. I know after they told me I should never have stayed there another night, if I hadn't thought so much of them, no matter how comfortable I was made; and I never was nervous, either. But I stayed. Of course, it didn't happen in my room. If it had I could not have stayed.'

'What was it?' asked Mrs Emerson in an awed voice.

'It was an awful thing. That child had lived in the house with her father and mother two years before. They had come—or the father had—from a real good family. He had a good situation: he was a drummer for a big leather house in the city, and they lived real pretty, with plenty to do with. But the mother was a real wicked woman. She was as handsome as a picture, and they said she came from good sort of people enough in Boston, but she was bad clean through, though she was real pretty spoken and 'most everybody liked her. She used to dress out and make a great show, and she never seemed to take much interest in the child, and folks began to say she wasn't treated right.

'The woman had a hard time keeping a girl. For some reason one wouldn't stay. They would leave and then talk about her awfully, telling all kinds of things. People didn't believe it at first; then they began to. They said the woman made that little thing, though she wasn't much over five years old, and small and babyish for her age, do most of the work, what there was done; they said the house used to look like a pigsty when she didn't have help. They said the little thing used to stand on a chair and wash dishes, and they'd seen her carrying in sticks of wood 'most as big as she was many a time, and they'd heard her mother scolding her. The woman was a fine singer, and had a voice like a screech-owl when she scolded.

'The father was away most of the time, and when that happened he had been away out West for some weeks. There had been a married man hanging about the mother for some time, and folks had talked some; but they weren't sure there was anything wrong, and he was a man very high up, with money, so they kept pretty still for fear he would hear of it and make trouble for them, and of course nobody was sure, though folks did say afterward that the father of the child had ought to have been told.

'But that was very easy to say; it wouldn't have been so easy to find anybody who would have been willing to tell him such a thing as that, especially when they weren't any too sure. He set his eyes by his wife, too. They said all he seemed to think of was to earn money to buy things to deck her out in. And he about worshipped the child, too. They said he was a real nice man. The men that are treated so bad mostly are real nice men. I've always noticed that.

'Well, one morning that man that there had been whispers about was missing. He had been gone quite a while, though, before they really knew that he was missing, because he had gone away and told his wife that he had to go to New York on business and might be gone a week, and not to worry if he didn't get home, and not to worry if he didn't write, because he should be thinking from day to day that he might take the next train home and there would be no use in writing. So the wife waited, and she tried not to worry until it was two days over the week, then she run into a neighbour's and fainted dead away on the floor; and then they made inquiries and found out that he had skipped—with some money that didn't belong to him, too.

'Then folks began to ask where was that woman, and they found out by comparing notes that nobody had seen her since the man went away; but three or four women remembered that she had told them that she thought of taking the child and going to Boston to visit her folks, so when they hadn't seen her around, and the house shut, they jumped to the conclusion that was where she was. They were the neighbours that lived right around her, but they didn't have much to do with her, and she'd gone out of her way to tell them about her Boston plan, and they didn't make much reply when she did.

'Well, there was this house shut up, and the man and woman missing and the child. Then all of a sudden one of the women that lived the nearest remembered something. She remembered that she had waked up three nights running, thinking she heard a child crying somewhere, and once she waked up her husband, but he said it must be the Bisbees' little girl, and she thought it must be. The child wasn't well and was always crying. It used to have colic spells, especially at night. So she didn't think any more about it until this came up, then all of a sudden she did think of it. She told what she had heard, and finally folks began to think they had better enter that house and see if there was anything wrong.

'Well, they did enter it, and they found that child dead, locked in one of the rooms. (Mrs Dennison and Mrs Bird never used that room; it was a back bedroom on the second floor.)

'Yes, they found that poor child there, starved to death, and frozen, though they weren't sure she had frozen to death, for she was in bed with clothes enough to keep her pretty warm when she was alive. But she had been there a week, and she was nothing but skin and bone. It looked as if the mother had locked her into the house when she went away, and told her not to make any noise for fear the neighbours would hear her and find out that she herself had gone.

'Mrs Dennison said she couldn't really believe that the woman had meant to have her own child starved to death. Probably she thought the little thing would raise somebody, or folks would try to get in the house and find her. Well, whatever she thought, there the child was, dead.

'But that wasn't all. The father came home, right in the midst of it; the child was just buried, and he was beside himself. And—he went on the track of his wife, and he found her, and he shot her dead; it was in all the papers at the time; then he disappeared. Nothing had been seen of him since. Mrs Dennison said that she thought he had either made way with himself or got out of the country, nobody knew, but they did know there was something wrong with the house.

' "I knew folks acted queer when they asked me how I liked it when we first came here," says Mrs Dennison, "but I never dreamed why till we saw the child that night." '

'I never heard anything like it in my life,' said Mrs Emerson, staring at the other woman with awestruck eyes.

'I thought you'd say so,' said Mrs Meserve. 'You don't wonder that I ain't disposed to speak light when I hear there is anything queer about a house, do you?'

'No, I don't, after that,' Mrs Emerson said.

'But that ain't all,' said Mrs Meserve.

'Did you see it again?' Mrs Emerson asked.

'Yes, I saw it a number of times before the last time. It was lucky I wasn't nervous, or I never could have stayed there, much as I liked the place and much as I thought of those two women; they were beautiful women, and no mistake. I loved those women. I hope Mrs Dennison will come and see me sometime.

'Well, I stayed, and I never knew when I'd see that child. I got so I was very careful to bring everything of mine upstairs, and not leave any little thing in my room that needed doing, for fear she would come lugging up my coat or hat or gloves or I'd find things done when there'd been no live being in the room to do them. I can't tell you how I dreaded seeing her; and worse than the seeing her was the hearing her say, "I can't find my mother." It was enough to make your blood run cold. I never heard a living child cry for its mother that was anything so pitiful as that dead one. It was enough to break your heart.

'She used to come and say that to Mrs Bird oftener than to any one else. Once I heard Mrs Bird say she wondered if it was possible that the poor little thing couldn't really find her mother in the other world, she had been such a wicked woman.

'But Mrs Dennison told her she didn't think she ought to speak so nor even think so, and Mrs Bird said she shouldn't wonder if she was right. Mrs Bird was always very easy to put in the wrong. She was a good woman, and one that couldn't do things enough for other folks. It seemed as if that was what she lived on. I don't think she was ever so scared by that poor little ghost, as much as she pitied it, and she was 'most heartbroken because she couldn't do anything for it, as she could have done for a live child.

' "It seems to me sometimes as if I should die if I can't get that awful little white robe off that child and get her in some clothes and feed her and stop her looking for her mother," I heard her say once, and she was in earnest. She cried when she said it. That wasn't long before she died.

'Now I am coming to the strangest part of it all. Mrs Bird died very sudden. One morning—it was Saturday, and there wasn't any school—I went downstairs to breakfast, and Mrs Bird wasn't there; there was nobody but Mrs Dennison. She was pouring out the coffee when I came in. "Why, where's Mrs Bird?" says I.

' "Abby ain't feeling very well this morning ," says she; "there isn't much the matter, I guess, but she didn't sleep very well, and her head aches, and she's sort of chilly, and I told her I thought she'd better stay in bed till the house gets warm." It was a very cold morning.

' "Maybe she's got cold," says I.

' "Yes, I guess she has," says Mrs Dennison. "I guess she's got cold. She'll be up before long. Abby ain't one to stay in bed a minute longer than she can help."

'Well, we went on eating our breakfast, and all at once a shadow flickered across one wall of the room and over the ceiling the way a shadow will sometimes when somebody passes the window outside. Mrs Dennison and I both looked up, then out of the window; then Mrs Dennison she gives a scream.

' "Why, Abby's crazy!" says she. "There she is out this bitter cold morning, and—and——" She didn't finish, but she meant the child. For we were both looking out, and we saw, as plain as we ever saw anything in our lives, Mrs Abby Bird walking off over the white snow-path with that child holding fast to her hand, nestling close to her as if she had found her own mother.

' "She's dead," says Mrs Dennison, clutching hold of me hard. "She's dead; my sister is dead!"

'She was. We hurried upstairs as fast as we could go, and she was dead in her bed, and smiling as if she was dreaming, and one arm and hand was stretched out as if something had hold of it; and it couldn't be straightened even at the last—it lay out over her casket at the funeral.'

'Was the child ever seen again?' asked Mrs Emerson in a shaking voice.

'No,' replied Mrs Meserve; 'that child was never seen again after she went out of the yard with Mrs Bird.'

'Oh, Whistle, and I'll Come to You, My Lad'

M. R. JAMES

—

'I suppose you will be getting away pretty soon, now Full term is over, Professor,' said a person not in the story to the Professor of Ontography, soon after they had sat down next to each other at a feast in the hospitable hall of St James's College.

The Professor was young, neat, and precise in speech.

'Yes,' he said; 'my friends have been making me take up golf this term, and I mean to go to the East Coast—in point of fact to Burnstow—(I dare say you know it) for a week or ten days, to improve my game. I hope to get off tomorrow.'

'Oh, Parkins,' said his neighbour on the other side, 'if you are going to Burnstow, I wish you would look at the site of the Templars' preceptory, and let me know if you think it would be any good to have a dig there in the summer.'

It was, as you might suppose, a person of antiquarian pursuits who said this, but, since he merely appears in this prologue, there is no need to give his entitlements.

'Certainly,' said Parkins, the Professor: 'if you will describe to me whereabouts the site is, I will do my best to give you an idea of the lie of the land when I get back; or I could write to you about it, if you would tell me where you are likely to be.'

'Don't trouble to do that, thanks. It's only that I'm thinking of taking my family in that direction in the Long, and it occurred to me that, as very few of the English preceptories have ever been properly planned, I might have an opportunity of doing something useful on off-days.'

The Professor rather sniffed at the idea that planning out a preceptory could be described as useful. His neighbour continued:

'The site—I doubt if there is anything showing above ground—must be down quite close to the beach now. The sea has encroached tremendously, as you know, all along that bit of coast. I should think, from the map, that it must be about three-quarters of a mile from the Globe Inn, at the north end of the town. Where are you going to stay?'

'Well, *at* the Globe Inn, as a matter of fact,' said Parkins; 'I have engaged a room there. I couldn't get in anywhere else; most of the lodging-houses are shut up in winter, it seems; and, as it is, they tell me that the only room of any size I can have is really a double-bedded one, and that they haven't a corner in which to store the other bed, and so on. But I must have a fairly large room, for I am taking some books down, and mean to do a bit or work; and though I don't quite fancy having an empty bed—not to speak of two—in what I may call for the time being my study, I suppose I can manage to rough it for the short time I shall be there.'

'Do you call having an extra bed in your room roughing it, Parkins?' said a bluff person opposite. 'Look here, I shall come down and occupy it for a bit; it'll be company for you.'

The Professor quivered, but managed to laugh in a courteous manner.

'By all means, Rogers; there's nothing I should like better. But I'm afraid you would find it rather dull; you don't play golf, do you?'

'No, thank Heaven!' said rude Mr Rogers.

'Well, you see, when I'm not writing I shall most likely be out on the links, and that, as I say, would be rather dull for you, I'm afraid.'

'Oh, I don't know! There's certain to be somebody I know in the place; but, of course, if you don't want me, speak the word, Parkins; I shan't be offended. Truth, as you always tell us, is never offensive.'

Parkins was, indeed, scrupulously polite and strictly truthful. It is to be feared that Mr Rogers sometimes practised upon his knowledge of these characteristics. In Parkins's breast there was a conflict now raging, which for a moment or two did not allow him to answer. That interval being over, he said:

'Well, if you want the exact truth, Rogers, I was considering whether the room I speak of would really be large enough to accommodate us both comfortably; and also whether (mind, I shouldn't have said this if you hadn't pressed me) you would not constitute something in the nature of a hindrance to my work.'

Rogers laughed loudly.

'Well done, Parkins!' he said. 'It's all right. I promise not to interrupt your work; don't you disturb yourself about that. No, I won't come if you don't want me; but I thought I should do so nicely to keep the ghosts off.' Here he might have been seen to wink and to nudge his next neighbour. Parkins might also have been seen to become pink. 'I beg pardon, Parkins,' Rogers continued; 'I oughtn't to have said that. I forgot you didn't like levity on these topics.'

'Well,' Parkins said, 'as you have mentioned the matter, I freely own that I do *not* like careless talk about what you call ghosts. A man in my position,' he went on, raising his voice a little, 'cannot, I find, be too careful about appearing to sanction the current beliefs on such subjects.

As you know, Rogers, or as you ought to know; for I think I have never concealed my views——'

'No, you certainly have not, old man,' put in Rogers *sotto voce*.

'—— I hold that any semblance, any appearance of concession to the view that such things might exist is equivalent to a renunciation of all that I hold most sacred. But I'm afraid I have not succeeded in securing your attention.'

'Your *undivided* attention, was what Dr Blimber actually *said*,'[1] Rogers interrupted, with every appearance of an earnest desire for accuracy. 'But I beg your pardon, Parkins: I'm stopping you.'

'No, not at all,' said Parkins. 'I don't remember Blimber; perhaps he was before my time. But I needn't go on. I'm sure you know what I mean.'

'Yes, yes,' said Rogers, rather hastily—'just so. We'll go into it fully at Burnstow, or somewhere.'

In repeating the above dialogue I have tried to give the impression which it made on me, that Parkins was something of an old woman—rather henlike, perhaps, in his little ways; totally destitute, alas! of the sense of humour, but at the same time dauntless and sincere in his convictions, and a man deserving of the greatest respect. Whether or not the reader has gathered so much, that was the character which Parkins had.

On the following day Parkins did, as he had hoped, succeed in getting away from his college, and in arriving at Burnstow. He was made welcome at the Globe Inn, was safely installed in the large double-bedded room of which we have heard, and was able before retiring to rest to arrange his materials for work in apple-pie order upon a commodious table which occupied the outer end of the room, and was surrounded on three sides by windows looking out seaward; that is to say, the central window looked straight out to sea, and those on the left and right commanded prospects along the shore to the north and south respectively. On the south you saw the village of Burnstow. On the north no houses were to be seen, but only the beach and the low cliff backing it. Immediately in front was a strip—not considerable—of rough grass, dotted with old anchors, capstans, and so forth; then a broad path; then the beach. Whatever may have been the original distance between the Globe Inn and the sea, not more than sixty yards now separated them.

The rest of the population of the inn was, of course, a golfing one, and included few elements that call for a special description. The most

---

[1] Mr Rogers was wrong, *vide Dombey and Son*, chapter xii.

conspicuous figure was, perhaps, that of an *ancien militaire*, secretary of a London club, and possessed of a voice of incredible strength, and of views of a pronouncedly Protestant type. These were apt to find utterance after his attendance upon the ministrations of the Vicar, an estimable man with inclinations towards a picturesque ritual, which he gallantly kept down as far as he could out of deference to East Anglian tradition.

Professor Parkins, one of whose principal characteristics was pluck, spent the greater part of the day following his arrival at Burnstow in what he had called improving his game, in company with this Colonel Wilson: and during the afternoon—whether the process of improvement were to blame or not, I am not sure—the Colonel's demeanour assumed a colouring so lurid that even Parkins jibbed at the thought of walking home with him from the links. He determined, after a short and furtive look at that bristling moustache and those incarnadined features, that it would be wiser to allow the influences of tea and tobacco to do what they could with the Colonel before the dinner-hour should render a meeting inevitable.

'I might walk home tonight along the beach,' he reflected—'yes, and take a look—there will be light enough for that—at the ruins of which Disney was talking. I don't exactly know where they are, by the way; but I expect I can hardly help stumbling on them.'

This he accomplished, I may say, in the most literal sense, for in picking his way from the links to the shingle beach his foot caught, partly in a gorse-root and partly in a biggish stone, and over he went. When he got up and surveyed his surroundings, he found himself in a patch of somewhat broken ground covered with small depressions and mounds. These latter, when he came to examine them, proved to be simply masses of flints embedded in mortar and grown over with turf. He must, he quite rightly concluded, be on the site of the preceptory he had promised to look at. It seemed not unlikely to reward the spade of the explorer; enough of the foundations was probably left at no great depth to throw a good deal of light on the general plan. He remembered vaguely that the Templars, to whom this site had belonged, were in the habit of building round churches, and he thought a particular series of the humps or mounds near him did appear to be arranged in something of a circular form. Few people can resist the temptation to try a little amateur research in a department quite outside their own, if only for the satisfaction of showing how successful they would have been had they only taken it up seriously. Our Professor, however, if he felt something of this mean desire, was also truly anxious to oblige Mr Disney. So he paced with care the circular area he had noticed, and wrote down its rough dimensions in his pocket-book. Then he proceeded to examine an oblong eminence which lay east of the centre of the circle, and seemed to his thinking likely to be the base of a platform or altar. At one end of it, the northern, a patch of the turf was gone—removed by some boy or other creature *ferae naturae*. It might, he thought, be as well to probe the soil here for evidences of masonry, and he took out his knife and began scraping away the earth. And now followed another little discovery: a portion of soil fell inward as he scraped, and disclosed a small cavity. He lighted one match after another to help him to see of what nature the hole was, but the wind was too strong for them all. By tapping and scratching the sides with his knife, however, he was able to make out that it must be an artificial hole in masonry. It was rectangular, and the sides, top, and bottom, if not actually plastered, were smooth and regular. Of course it was empty. No! As he withdrew the knife he heard a metallic clink, and when he introduced his hand it met with a cylindrical object lying on the floor of the hole. Naturally enough, he picked it up, and when he brought it into the light, now fast fading, he could see that it, too, was of man's making—a metal tube about four inches long, and evidently of some considerable age.

By the time Parkins had made sure that there was nothing else in this odd receptacle, it was too late and too dark for him to think of undertaking any further search. What he had done had proved so unexpectedly interesting that he determined to sacrifice a little more of the daylight on the morrow to archaeology. The object which he now had safe in his pocket was bound to be of some slight value at least, he felt sure.

Bleak and solemn was the view on which he took a last look before starting homeward. A faint yellow light in the west showed the links, on which a few figures moving towards the club-house were still visible, the squat martello tower, the lights of Aldsey village, the pale ribbon of sands intersected at intervals by black wooden groynes, the dim and murmuring sea. The wind was bitter from the north, but was at his back when he set out for the Globe. He quickly rattled and clashed through the shingle and gained the sand, upon which, but for the groynes which had to be got over every few yards, the going was both good and quiet. One last look behind, to measure the distance he had made since leaving the ruined Templars' church, showed him a prospect of company on his walk, in the shape of a rather indistinct personage, who seemed to be making great efforts to catch up with him, but made little, if any, progress. I mean that there was an appearance of running about his movements, but that the distance between him and Parkins did not seem materially to lessen. So, at least, Parkins thought, and decided that he almost certainly did not know him, and that it would be absurd to wait until he came up. For all that, company, he began to think, would really be very welcome on that lonely shore, if only you could choose your companion. In his unenlightened days he had read of meetings in such places which even now would hardly bear thinking of. He went on thinking of them, however, until he reached home, and particularly of one which catches most people's fancy at some time of their childhood. 'Now I saw in my dream that Christian had gone but a very little way when he saw a foul fiend coming over the field to meet him.' 'What should I do now,' he thought, 'if I looked back and caught sight of a black figure sharply defined against the yellow sky, and saw that it had horns and wings? I wonder whether I should stand or run for it. Luckily, the gentleman behind is not of that kind, and he seems to be about as far off now as when I saw him first. Well, at this rate he won't get his dinner as soon as I shall; and, dear me! it's within a quarter of an hour of the time now. I must run!'

Parkins had, in fact, very little time for dressing. When he met the Colonel at dinner, Peace—or as much of her as that gentleman could manage—reigned once more in the military bosom; nor was she put to flight in the hours of bridge that followed dinner, for Parkins was a more than respectable player. When, therefore, he retired towards twelve o'clock, he felt that he had spent his evening in quite a satisfactory way, and that, even for so long as a fortnight or three weeks, life at the Globe would be supportable under similar conditions—'especially,' thought he, 'if I go on improving my game.'

As he went along the passages he met the boots of the Globe, who stopped and said:

'Beg your pardon, sir, but as I was a-brushing your coat just now there was somethink fell out of the pocket. I put it on your chest of drawers, sir, in your room, sir—a piece of a pipe or somethink of that, sir. Thank you, sir. You'll find it on your chest of drawers, sir—yes, sir. Good night, sir.'

The speech served to remind Parkins of his little discovery of that afternoon. It was with some considerable curiosity that he turned it over by the light of his candles. It was of bronze, he now saw, and was shaped very much after the manner of the modern dog-whistle; in fact it was—yes, certainly it was—actually no more nor less than a whistle. He put it to his lips, but it was quite full of a fine, caked-up sand or earth, which would not yield to knocking, but must be loosened with a knife. Tidy as ever in his habits, Parkins cleared out the earth on to a piece of paper, and took the latter to the window to empty it out. The night was clear and bright, as he saw when he had opened the casement, and he stopped for an instant to look at the sea and note a belated wanderer stationed on the shore in front of the inn. Then he shut the window, a little surprised at the late hours people kept at Burnstow, and took his whistle to the light again. Why, surely there were marks on it, and not merely marks, but letters! A very little rubbing rendered the deeply-cut inscription quite legible, but the Professor had to confess, after some earnest thought, that the meaning of it was as obscure to him as the writing on the wall to Belshazzar. There were legends both on the front and on the back of the whistle. The one read thus:

$$\text{FUR} \quad \substack{\text{FLA} \\ \text{} \\ \text{FLE}} \quad \text{BIS}$$

The other:

✠ QUIS EST ISTE QUI UENIT ✠

'I ought to be able to make it out,' he thought; 'but I suppose I am a little rusty in my Latin. When I come to think of it, I don't believe I even know the word for a whistle. The long one does seem simple enough. It ought to mean, "Who is this who is coming?" Well, the best way to find out is evidently to whistle for him.'

He blew tentatively and stopped suddenly, startled and yet pleased at the note he had elicited. It had a quality of infinite distance in it, and, soft as it was, he somehow felt it must be audible for miles round. It was a sound, too, that seemed to have the power (which many scents possess) of forming pictures in the brain. He saw quite clearly for a moment a vision of a wide, dark expanse at night, with a fresh wind blowing, and in the midst a lonely figure—how employed, he could not tell. Perhaps he would have seen more had not the picture been broken by the sudden surge of a gust of wind against his casement, so sudden that it made him look up, just in time to see the white glint of a sea-bird's wing somewhere outside the dark panes.

The sound of the whistle had so fascinated him that he could not help trying it once more, this time more boldly. The note was little, if at all, louder than before, and repetition broke the illusion—no picture followed, as he had half hoped it might. 'But what is this? Goodness! what force the wind can get up in a few minutes! What a tremendous gust! There! I knew that window-fastening was no use! Ah! I thought so—both candles out. It's enough to tear the room to pieces.'

The first thing was to get the window shut. While you might count twenty Parkins was struggling with the small casement, and felt almost as if he were pushing back a sturdy burglar, so strong was the pressure. It slackened all at once, and the window banged to and latched itself. Now to relight the candles and see what damage, if any, had been done. No, nothing seemed amiss; no glass even was broken in the casement. But the noise had evidently roused at least one member of the household: the Colonel was to be heard stumping in his stockinged feet on the floor above, and growling.

Quickly as it had risen, the wind did not fall at once. On it went, moaning and rushing past the house, at times rising to a cry so desolate that, as Parkins disinterestedly said, it might have made fanciful people feel quite uncomfortable; even the unimaginative, he thought after a quarter of an hour, might be happier without it.

Whether it was the wind, or the excitement of golf, or of the researches in the preceptory that kept Parkins awake, he was not sure. Awake he remained, in any case, long enough to fancy (as I am afraid I often do myself under such conditions) that he was the victim of all manner of fatal disorders: he would lie counting the beats of his heart, convinced that it was going to stop work every moment, and would entertain grave suspicions of his lungs, brain, liver, etc.—suspicions which he was sure would be dispelled by the return of daylight, but which until then refused to be put aside. He found a little vicarious comfort in the idea that someone else was in the same boat. A near neighbour (in the darkness it was not easy to tell his direction) was tossing and rustling in his bed, too.

The next stage was that Parkins shut his eyes and determined to give sleep every chance. Here again over-excitement asserted itself in another form—that of making pictures. *Experto crede*, pictures do come to the closed eyes of one trying to sleep, and are often so little to his taste that he must open his eyes and disperse them.

Parkins's experience on this occasion was a very distressing one. He found that the picture which presented itself to him was continuous. When he opened his eyes, of course, it went; but when he shut them once more it framed itself afresh, and acted itself out again, neither quicker nor slower than before. What he saw was this:

A long stretch of shore—shingle edged by sand, and intersected at short intervals with black groynes running down to the water—a scene, in fact, so like that of his afternoon's walk that, in the absence of any landmark, it could not be distinguished therefrom. The light was obscure, conveying an impression of gathering storm, late winter evening, and slight cold rain. On this bleak stage at first no actor was visible. Then, in the distance, a bobbing black object appeared; a moment more, and it was a man running, jumping, clambering over the groynes, and every few seconds looking eagerly back. The nearer he came the more obvious it was that he was not only anxious, but even terribly frightened, though his face was not to be distinguished. He was, moreover, almost at the end of his strength. On he came; each successive obstacle seemed to cause him more difficulty than the last. 'Will he get over this next one?' thought Parkins; 'it seems a little higher than the others.' Yes; half climbing, half throwing himself, he did get over, and fell all in a heap on the other side (the side nearest to the spectator). There, as if really unable to get up again, he remained crouching under the groyne, looking up in an attitude of painful anxiety.

So far no cause whatever for the fear of the runner had been shown; but now there began to be seen, far up the shore, a little flicker of something light-coloured moving to and fro with great swiftness and irregularity. Rapidly growing larger, it, too, declared itself as a figure in pale, fluttering draperies, ill-defined. There was something about its motion which made Parkins very unwilling to see it at close quarters. It would stop, raise arms, bow itself toward the sand, then run stooping across the beach to the water-edge and back again; and then, rising upright, once more continue its course forward at a speed that was startling and terrifying. The moment came when the pursuer was hovering about from left to right only a few yards beyond the groyne where the runner lay in hiding. After two or three ineffectual castings hither and thither it came to a stop, stood upright, with arms raised high, and then darted straight forward towards the groyne.

It was at this point that Parkins always failed in his resolution to keep his eyes shut. With many misgivings as to incipient failure of eyesight, over-worked brain, excessive smoking, and so on, he finally resigned himself to light his candle, get out a book, and pass the night waking, rather than be tormented by this persistent panorama, which he saw clearly enough could only be a morbid reflection of his walk and his thoughts on that very day.

The scraping of match on box and the glare of light must have startled some creatures of the night—rats or what not—which he heard scurry across the floor from the side of his bed with much rustling. Dear, dear! the match is out! Fool that it is! But the second one burnt better, and a candle and book were duly procured, over which Parkins pored till sleep of a wholesome kind came upon him, and that in no long space. For about the first time in his orderly and prudent life he forgot to blow out the candle, and when he was called next morning at eight there was still a flicker in the socket and a sad mess of guttered grease on the top of the little table.

After breakfast he was in his room, putting the finishing touches to his golfing costume—fortune had again allotted the Colonel to him for a partner—when one of the maids came in.

'Oh, if you please,' she said, 'would you like any extra blankets on your bed, sir?'

'Ah! thank you,' said Parkins. 'Yes, I think I should like one. It seems likely to turn rather colder.'

In a very short time the maid was back with the blanket.

'Which bed should I put it on, sir?' she asked.

'What? Why, that one—the one I slept in last night,' he said, pointing to it.

'Oh yes! I beg your pardon, sir, but you seemed to have tried both of 'em; leastways, we had to make 'em both up this morning.'

'Really? How very absurd!' said Parkins. 'I certainly never touched the other, except to lay some things on it. Did it actually seem to have been slept in?'

'Oh yes, sir!' said the maid. 'Why, all the things was crumpled and throwed about all ways, if you'll excuse me, sir—quite as if anyone 'adn't passed but a very poor night, sir.'

'Dear me,' said Parkins. 'Well, I may have disordered it more than I thought when I unpacked my things. I'm very sorry to have given you the extra trouble, I'm sure. I expect a friend of mine soon, by the way—a gentleman from Cambridge—to come and occupy it for a night or two. That will be all right, I suppose, won't it?'

'Oh yes, to be sure, sir. Thank you, sir. It's no trouble, I'm sure,' said the maid, and departed to giggle with her colleagues.

Parkins set forth, with a stern determination to improve his game.

I am glad to be able to report that he succeeded so far in this enterprise that the Colonel, who had been rather repining at the prospect of a second day's play in his company, became quite chatty as the morning advanced; and his voice boomed out over the flats, as certain also of our own minor poets have said, 'like some great bourdon in a minster tower'.

'Extraordinary wind, that, we had last night,' he said. 'In my old home we should have said someone had been whistling for it.'

'Should you, indeed!' said Parkins. 'Is there a superstition of that kind still current in your part of the country?'

'I don't know about superstition,' said the Colonel. 'They believe in it all over Denmark and Norway, as well as on the Yorkshire coast; and my experience is, mind you, that there's generally something at the bottom of what these country-folk hold to, and have held to for generations. But it's your drive' (or whatever it might have been: the golfing reader will have to imagine appropriate digressions at the proper intervals).

When conversation was resumed, Parkins said, with a slight hesitancy:

'Apropos of what you were saying just now, Colonel, I think I ought to tell you that my own views on such subjects are very strong. I am, in fact, a convinced disbeliever in what is called the "supernatural".'

'What!' said the Colonel, 'do you mean to tell me you don't believe in second-sight, or ghosts, or anything of that kind?'

'In nothing whatever of that kind,' returned Parkins firmly.

'Well,' said the Colonel, 'but it appears to me at that rate, sir, that you must be little better than a Sadducee.'

Parkins was on the point of answering that, in his opinion, the Sadducees were the most sensible persons he had ever read of in the Old Testament; but, feeling some doubt as to whether much mention of them was to be found in that work, he preferred to laugh the accusation off.

'Perhaps I am,' he said; 'but—— Here, give me my cleek, boy!— Excuse me one moment, Colonel.' A short interval. 'Now, as to whistling for the wind, let me give you my theory about it. The laws which govern winds are really not at all perfectly known—to fisher-folk and such, of course, not known at all. A man or woman of eccentric habits, perhaps, or a stranger, is seen repeatedly on the beach at some unusual hour, and is heard whistling. Soon afterwards a violent wind rises; a man who could read the sky perfectly or who possessed a barometer could have foretold that it would. The simple people of a fishing-village have no barometers, and only a few rough rules for prophesying weather. What more natural than that the eccentric per-sonage I postulated should be regarded as having raised the wind, or that he or she should clutch eagerly at the reputation of being able to do so? Now, take last night's wind: as it happens, I myself was whistling. I blew a whistle twice, and the wind seemed to come absolutely in answer to my call. If anyone had seen me——'

The audience had been a little restive under this harangue, and Parkins had, I fear, fallen somewhat into the tone of a lecturer; but at the last sentence the Colonel stopped.

'Whistling, were you?' he said. 'And what sort of whistle did you use? Play this stroke first.' Interval.

'About that whistle you were asking, Colonel. It's rather a curious one. I have it in my—— No; I see I've left it in my room. As a matter of fact, I found it yesterday.'

And then Parkins narrated the manner of his discovery of the whistle, upon hearing which the Colonel grunted, and opined that, in Parkins's place, he should himself be careful about using a thing that had belonged to a set of Papists, of whom, speaking generally, it might be affirmed that you never knew what they might not have been up to. From this topic he diverged to the enormities of the Vicar, who had given notice on the previous Sunday that Friday would be the Feast of St Thomas the Apostle, and that there would be service at eleven o'clock in the church. This and other similar proceedings constituted in the Colonel's view a strong presumption that the Vicar was a concealed Papist, if not a Jesuit; and Parkins, who could not very readily follow the Colonel in this region, did not disagree with him. In fact, they got on so well together in the morning that there was no talk on either side of their separating after lunch.

Both continued to play well during the afternoon, or, at least, well enough to make them forget everything else until the light began to fail them. Not until then did Parkins remember that he had meant to do some more investigating at the preceptory; but it was of no great importance, he reflected. One day was as good as another; he might as well go home with the Colonel.

As they turned the corner of the house, the Colonel was almost knocked down by a boy who rushed into him at the very top of his speed, and then, instead of running away, remained hanging on to him and panting. The first words of the warrior were naturally those of reproof and objurgation, but he very quickly discerned that the boy was almost speechless with fright. Inquiries were useless at first. When the boy got his breath he began to howl, and still clung to the Colonel's legs. He was at last detached, but continued to howl.

'What in the world *is* the matter with you? What have you been up to? What have you seen?' said the two men.

'Ow, I seen it wive at me out of the winder,' wailed the boy, 'and I don't like it.'

'What window?' said the irritated Colonel. 'Come, pull yourself together, my boy.'

'The front winder it was, at the 'otel,' said the boy.

At this point Parkins was in favour of sending the boy home, but the Colonel refused; he wanted to get to the bottom of it, he said; it was most dangerous to give a boy such a fright as this one had had, and if it turned out that people had been playing jokes, they should suffer for it in some way. And by a series of questions he made out this story: The boy had been playing about on the grass in front of the Globe with some others; then they had gone home to their teas, and he was just going, when he happened to look up at the front winder and see it a-wiving at him. *It* seemed to be a figure of some sort, in white as far as he knew—couldn't see its face; but it wived at him, and it warn't a right thing—not to say not a right person. Was there a light in the room? No, he didn't think to look if there was a light. Which was the window? Was it the top one or the second one? The seckind one it was—the big winder what got two little uns at the sides.

'Very well, my boy,' said the Colonel, after a few more questions. 'You run away home now. I expect it was some person trying to give you a start. Another time, like a brave English boy, you just throw a stone— well, no, not that exactly, but you go and speak to the waiter, or to Mr Simpson, the landlord, and—yes—and say that I advised you to do so.'

The boy's face expressed some of the doubt he felt as to the likelihood of Mr Simpson's lending a favourable ear to his complaint, but the Colonel did not appear to perceive this, and went on:

'And here's a sixpence—no, I see it's a shilling—and you be off home, and don't think any more about it.'

The youth hurried off with agitated thanks, and the Colonel and Parkins went round to the front of the Globe and reconnoitred. There was only one window answering to the description they had been hearing.

'Well, that's curious,' said Parkins; 'it's evidently my window the lad was talking about. Will you come up for a moment, Colonel Wilson? We ought to be able to see if anyone has been taking liberties in my room.'

They were soon in the passage, and Parkins made as if to open the door. Then he stopped and felt in his pockets.

'This is more serious than I thought,' was his next remark. 'I remember now that before I started this morning I locked the door. It is locked now, and, what is more, here is the key.' And he held it up. 'Now,' he went on, 'if the servants are in the habit of going into one's room during the day when one is away, I can only say that—well, that I don't approve of it at all.' Conscious of a somewhat weak climax, he busied himself in opening the door (which was indeed locked) and in lighting candles. 'No,' he said, 'nothing seems disturbed.'

'Except your bed,' put in the Colonel.

'Excuse me, that isn't my bed,' said Parkins. 'I don't use that one. But it does look as if someone had been playing tricks with it.'

It certainly did: the clothes were bundled up and twisted together in a most tortuous confusion. Parkins pondered.

'That must be it,' he said at last: 'I disordered the clothes last night in unpacking, and they haven't made it since. Perhaps they came in to make it, and that boy saw them through the window; and then they were called away and locked the door after them. Yes, I think that must be it.'

'Well, ring and ask,' said the Colonel, and this appealed to Parkins as practical.

The maid appeared, and, to make a long story short, deposed that she had made the bed in the morning when the gentleman was in the room, and hadn't been there since. No, she hadn't no other key. Mr Simpson he kep' the keys; he'd be able to tell the gentleman if anyone had been up.

This was a puzzle. Investigation showed that nothing of value had been taken, and Parkins remembered the disposition of the small objects on tables and so forth well enough to be pretty sure that no pranks had been played with them. Mr and Mrs Simpson furthermore agreed that neither of them had given the duplicate key of the room to any person whatever during the day. Nor could Parkins, fair-minded man as he was, detect anything in the demeanour of master, mistress, or maid that indicated guilt. He was much more inclined to think that the boy had been imposing on the Colonel.

The latter was unwontedly silent and pensive at dinner and throughout the evening. When he bade good night to Parkins, he murmured in a gruff undertone:

'You know where I am if you want me during the night.'

'Why, yes, thank you, Colonel Wilson, I think I do; but there isn't much prospect of my disturbing you, I hope. By the way,' he added, 'did I show you that old whistle I spoke of? I think not. Well, here it is.'

The Colonel turned it over gingerly in the light of the candle.

'Can you make anything of the inscription?' asked Parkins, as he took it back.

'No, not in this light. What do you mean to do with it?'

'Oh, well, when I get back to Cambridge I shall submit it to some of the archaeologists there, and see what they think of it; and very likely, if they consider it worth having, I may present it to one of the museums.'

' 'M!' said the Colonel. 'Well, you may be right. All I know is that, if it were mine, I should chuck it straight into the sea. It's no use talking, I'm well aware, but I expect that with you it's a case of live and learn. I hope so, I'm sure, and I wish you a good night.'

He turned away, leaving Parkins in act to speak at the bottom of the stair, and soon each was in his own bedroom.

By some unfortunate accident, there were neither blinds nor curtains to the windows of the Professor's room. The previous night he had thought little of this, but tonight there seemed every prospect of a bright moon rising to shine directly on his bed, and probably wake him later on. When he noticed this he was a good deal annoyed, but, with an ingenuity which I can only envy, he succeeded in rigging up, with the help of a railway-rug, some safety-pins, and a stick and umbrella, a screen which, if it only held together, would completely keep the moonlight off his bed. And shortly afterwards he was comfortably in that bed. When he had read a somewhat solid work long enough to produce a decided wish for sleep, he cast a drowsy glance round the room, blew out the candle, and fell back upon the pillow.

He must have slept soundly for an hour or more, when a sudden clatter shook him up in a most unwelcome manner. In a moment he realized what had happened: his carefully-constructed screen had given way, and a very bright frosty moon was shining directly on his face. This was highly annoying. Could he possibly get up and reconstruct the screen? or could he manage to sleep if he did not?

For some minutes he lay and pondered over the possibilities; then he turned over sharply, and with all his eyes open lay breathlessly listening. There had been a movement, he was sure, in the empty bed on the opposite side of the room. Tomorrow he would have it moved, for there must be rats or something playing about in it. It was quiet now. No! the commotion began again. There was a rustling and shaking: surely more than any rat could cause.

I can figure to myself something of the Professor's bewilderment and horror, for I have in a dream thirty years back seen the same thing happen; but the reader will hardly, perhaps, imagine how dreadful it was to him to see a figure suddenly sit up in what he had known was an empty bed. He was out of his own bed in one bound, and made a dash towards the window, where lay his only weapon, the stick with which he had propped his screen. This was, as it turned out, the worst thing he could have done, because the personage in the empty bed, with a sudden smooth motion, slipped from the bed and took up a position, with outspread arms, between the two beds, and in front of the door. Parkins watched it in a horrid perplexity. Somehow, the idea of getting past it and escaping through the door was intolerable to him; he could not have borne—he didn't know why—to touch it; and as for its touching him, he would sooner dash himself through the window than have that happen. It stood for the moment in a band of dark shadow, and he had not seen what its face was like. Now it began to move, in a stooping posture, and all at once the spectator realized, with some horror and some relief, that it must be blind, for it seemed to feel about it with its muffled arms in a groping and random fashion. Turning half away from him, it became suddenly conscious of the bed he had just left, and darted towards it, and bent over and felt the pillows in a way which made Parkins shudder as he had never in his life thought it possible. In a very few moments it seemed to know that the bed was empty, and then, moving forward into the area of light and facing the window, it showed for the first time what manner of thing it was.

Parkins, who very much dislikes being questioned about it, did once describe something of it in my hearing, and I gathered that what he chiefly remembers about it is a horrible, an intensely horrible, face *of crumpled linen*. What expression he read upon it he could not or would not tell, but that the fear of it went nigh to maddening him is certain.

But he was not at leisure to watch it for long. With formidable quickness it moved into the middle of the room, and, as it groped and waved, one corner of its draperies swept across Parkins's face. He could not—though he knew how perilous a sound was—he could not keep back a cry of disgust, and this gave the searcher an instant clue. It leapt towards him upon the instant, and the next moment he was half-way through the window backwards, uttering cry upon cry at the utmost pitch of his voice, and the linen face was thrust close into his own. At this, almost the last possible second, deliverance came, as you will have guessed: the Colonel burst the door open, and was just in time to see the dreadful group at the window. When he reached the figures only one was left. Parkins sank forward into the room in a faint, and before him on the floor lay a tumbled heap of bedclothes.

Colonel Wilson asked no questions, but busied himself in keeping everyone else out of the room and in getting Parkins back to his bed; and himself, wrapped in a rug, occupied the other bed for the rest of the night. Early on the next day Rogers arrived, more welcome than he would have been a day before, and the three of them held a very long consultation in the Professor's room. At the end of it the Colonel left the hotel door carrying a small object between his finger and thumb, which he cast as far into the sea as a very brawny arm could send it. Later on the smoke of a burning ascended from the back premises of the Globe.

Exactly what explanation was patched up for the staff and visitors at the hotel I must confess I do not recollect. The Professor was somehow cleared of the ready suspicion of delirium tremens, and the hotel of the reputation of a troubled house.

There is not much question as to what would have happened to Parkins if the Colonel had not intervened when he did. He would either have fallen out of the window or else lost his wits. But it is not so evident what more the creature that came in answer to the whistle could have done than frighten. There seemed to be absolutely nothing material about it save the bedclothes of which it had made itself a body. The Colonel, who remembered a not very dissimilar occurrence in India, was of opinion that if Parkins had closed with it it could really have done very little, and that its one power was that of frightening. The whole thing, he said, served to confirm his opinion of the Church of Rome.

There is really nothing more to tell, but, as you may imagine, the Professor's views on certain points are less clear cut than they used to be.

His nerves, too, have suffered: he cannot even now see a surplice hanging on a door quite unmoved, and the spectacle of a scarecrow in a field late on a winter afternoon has cost him more than one sleepless night.

The Empty House

ALGERNON BLACKWOOD

Certain houses, like certain persons, manage somehow to proclaim at once their character for evil. In the case of the latter, no particular feature need betray them; they may boast an open countenance and an ingenuous smile; and yet a little of their company leaves the unalterable conviction that there is something radically amiss with their being: that they are evil. Willy nilly, they seem to communicate an atmosphere of secret and wicked thoughts which makes those in their immediate neighbourhood shrink from them as from a thing diseased.

And, perhaps, with houses the same principle is operative, and it is the aroma of evil deeds committed under a particular roof, long after the actual doers have passed away, that makes the gooseflesh come and the hair rise. Something of the original passion of the evil-doer, and of the horror felt by his victim, enters the heart of the innocent watcher, and he becomes suddenly conscious of tingling nerves, creeping skin, and a chilling of the blood. He is terror-stricken without apparent cause.

There was manifestly nothing in the external appearance of this particular house to bear out the tales of the horror that was said to reign within. It was neither lonely nor unkempt. It stood, crowded into a corner of the square, and looked exactly like the houses on either side of it. It had the same number of windows as its neighbours; the same balcony overlooking the gardens; the same white steps leading up to the heavy black front door; and, in the rear, there was the same narrow strip of green, with neat box borders, running up to the wall that divided it, from the backs of the adjoining houses. Apparently, too, the number of chimney pots on the roof was the same; the breadth and angle of the eaves; and even the height of the dirty area railings.

And yet this house in the square, that seemed precisely similar to its fifty ugly neighbours, was as a matter of fact entirely different—horribly different.

Wherein lay this marked, invisible difference is impossible to say. It cannot be ascribed wholly to the imagination, because persons who had spent some time in the house, knowing nothing of the facts, had declared positively that certain rooms were so disagreeable they would rather die than enter them again, and that the atmosphere of the whole house produced in them symptoms of a genuine terror; while the series of innocent tenants who had tried to live in it and been forced to decamp at the shortest possible notice, was indeed little less than a scandal in the town.

When Shorthouse arrived to pay a 'week-end' visit to his Aunt Julia in her little house on the sea-front at the other end of the town, he found her charged to the brim with mystery and excitement. He had only received her telegram that morning, and he had come anticipating boredom; but the moment he touched her hand and kissed her apple-skin wrinkled cheek, he caught the first wave of her electrical condition. The impression deepened when he learned that there were to be no other visitors, and that he had been telegraphed for with a very special object.

Something was in the wind, and the 'something' would doubtless bear fruit; for this elderly spinster aunt, with a mania for psychical research, had brains as well as willpower, and by hook or by crook she usually managed to accomplish her ends. The revelation was made soon after tea, when she sidled close up to him as they paced slowly along the sea-front in the dusk.

'I've got the keys,' she announced in a delighted, yet half awesome voice. 'Got them till Monday!'

'The keys of the bathing-machine, or——?' he asked innocently, looking from the sea to the town. Nothing brought her so quickly to the point as feigning stupidity.

'Neither,' she whispered. 'I've got the keys of the haunted house in the square—and I'm going there tonight.'

Shorthouse was conscious of the slightest possible tremor down his back. He dropped his teasing tone. Something in her voice and manner thrilled him. She was in earnest.

'But you can't go alone——' he began.

'That's why I wired for you,' she said with decision.

He turned to look at her. The ugly, lined, enigmatical face was alive with excitement. There was the glow of genuine enthusiasm round it like a halo. The eyes shone. He caught another wave of her excitement, and a second tremor, more marked than the first, accompanied it.

'Thanks, Aunt Julia,' he said politely; 'thanks awfully.'

'I should not dare to go quite alone,' she went on, raising her voice; 'but with you I should enjoy it immensely. You're afraid of nothing, I know.'

'Thanks *so* much,' he said again. 'Er—is anything likely to happen?'

'A great deal *has* happened,' she whispered, 'though it's been most cleverly hushed up. Three tenants have come and gone in the last few months, and the house is said to be empty for good now.'

In spite of himself Shorthouse became interested. His aunt was so very much in earnest.

'The house is very old indeed,' she went on, 'and the story—an unpleasant one—dates a long way back. It has to do with a murder committed by a jealous stableman who had some affair with a servant in the house. One night he managed to secrete himself in the cellar, and when everyone was asleep, he crept upstairs to the servants' quarters, chased the girl down to the next landing, and before anyone could come to the rescue threw her bodily over the banisters into the hall below.'

'And the stableman——?'

'Was caught, I believe, and hanged for murder; but it all happened a century ago, and I've not been able to get more details of the story.'

Shorthouse now felt his interest thoroughly aroused; but, though he was not particularly nervous for himself, he hesitated a little on his aunt's account.

'On one condition,' he said at length.

'Nothing will prevent my going,' she said firmly; 'but I may as well hear your condition.'

'That you guarantee your power of self-control if anything really horrible happens. I mean—that you are sure you won't get too frightened.'

'Jim,' she said scornfully, 'I'm not young, I know, nor are my nerves; but *with you* I should be afraid of nothing in the world!'

This, of course, settled it, for Shorthouse had no pretensions to being other than a very ordinary young man, and an appeal to his vanity was irresistible. He agreed to go.

Instinctively, by a sort of sub-conscious preparation, he kept himself and his forces well in hand the whole evening, compelling an accumulative reserve of control by that nameless inward process of gradually putting all the emotions away and turning the key upon them—a process difficult to describe, but wonderfully effective, as all men who have lived through severe trials of the inner man well understand. Later, it stood him in good stead.

But it was not until half-past ten, when they stood in the hall, well in the glare of friendly lamps and still surrounded by comforting human influences, that he had to make the first call upon this store of collected strength. For, once the door was closed, and he saw the deserted silent street stretching away white in the moonlight before them, it came to him clearly that the real test that night would be in dealing with *two fears* instead of one. He would have to carry his aunt's fear as well as his own.

And, as he glanced down at her sphinx-like countenance and realised that it might assume no pleasant aspect in a rush of real terror, he felt satisfied with only one thing in the whole adventure—that he had confidence in his own will and power to stand against any shock that might come.

Slowly they walked along the empty streets of the town; a bright autumn moon silvered the roofs, casting deep shadows; there was no breath of wind; and the trees in the formal gardens by the sea-front watched them silently as they passed along. To his aunt's occasional remarks Shorthouse made no reply, realising that she was simply surrounding herself with mental buffers—saying ordinary things to prevent herself thinking of extraordinary things. Few windows showed lights, and from scarcely a single chimney came smoke or sparks. Shorthouse had already begun to notice everything, even the smallest details. Presently they stopped at the street corner and looked up at the name on the side of the house full in the moonlight, and with one accord, but without remark, turned into the square and crossed over to the side of it that lay in shadow.

'The number of the house is thirteen,' whispered a voice at his side; and neither of them made the obvious reference, but passed across the broad sheet of moonlight and began to march up the pavement in silence.

It was about half-way up the square that Shorthouse felt an arm slipped quietly but significantly into his own, and knew then that their adventure had begun in earnest, and that his companion was already yielding imperceptibly to the influences against them. She needed support.

A few minutes later they stopped before a tall, narrow house that rose before them into the night, ugly in shape and painted a dingy white. Shutterless windows, without blinds, stared down upon them, shining here and there in the moonlight. There were weather streaks in the wall and cracks in the paint, and the balcony bulged out from the first floor a little unnaturally. But, beyond this generally forlorn appearance of an unoccupied house, there was nothing at first sight to single out this particular mansion for the evil character it had most certainly acquired.

Taking a look over their shoulders to make sure they had not been followed, they went boldly up the steps and stood against the huge black door that fronted them forbiddingly. But the first wave of nervousness was now upon them, and Shorthouse fumbled a long time with the key before he could fit it into the lock at all. For a moment, if truth were told, they both hoped it would not open, for they were a prey to various unpleasant emotions as they stood there on the threshold of their ghostly adventure. Shorthouse, shuffling with the key and hampered by the steady weight on his arm, certainly felt the solemnity of the moment. It was as if the whole world—for all experience seemed at that instant concentrated in his own consciouness—were listening to the grating noise of that key. A stray puff of wind wandering down the empty street woke a momentary rustling in the trees behind them, but otherwise this rattling of the key was the only sound audible; and at last it turned in the lock and the heavy door swung open and revealed a yawning gulf of darkness beyond.

With a last glance at the moonlit square, they passed quickly in and the door slammed behind them with a roar that echoed prodigiously through empty halls and passages. But, instantly, with the echoes, another sound made itself heard, and Aunt Julia leaned suddenly so heavily upon him that he had to take a step backwards to save himself from falling.

A man had coughed close beside him—so close that it seemed they must have been actually by his side in the darkness.

With the possibility of practical jokes in his mind, Shorthouse at once swung his heavy stick in the direction of the sound; but it met nothing more solid than air. He heard his aunt give a little gasp beside him.

'There's someone here,' she whispered; 'I heard him.'

'Be quiet!' he said sternly. 'It was nothing but the noise of the front door.'

'Oh! get a light—quick!' she added, as her nephew, fumbling with a box of matches, opened it upside down and let them all fall with a rattle on to the stone floor.

The sound, however, was not repeated; and there was no evidence of retreating footsteps. In another minute they had a candle burning, using an empty end of a cigar case as a holder; and when the first flare had died down he held the impromptu lamp aloft and surveyed the scene. And it was dreary enough in all conscience, for there is nothing more desolate in all the abodes of men than an unfurnished house dimly lit, silent, and forsaken, and yet tenanted by rumour with the memories of evil and violent histories.

They were standing in a wide hall-way; on their left was the open door of a spacious dining-room, and in front the hall ran, ever narrowing, into a long, dark passage that led apparently to the top of the kitchen stairs. The broad uncarpeted staircase rose in a sweep before them, everywhere draped in shadows, except for a single spot about half-way up where the moonlight came in through the window and fell in a bright patch on the boards. This shaft of light shed a faint radiance above and below it, lending to the objects within its reach a misty outline that was infinitely more suggestive and ghostly than complete darkness. Filtered moonlight always seems to paint faces on the surrounding gloom, and as Shorthouse peered up into the well of darkness and thought of the countless empty rooms and passages in the upper part of the old house, he caught himself longing again for the safety of the moonlit square, or the cosy, bright drawing-room they had left an hour before. Then realising that these thoughts were dangerous, he thrust them away again and summoned all his energy for concentration on the present.

'Aunt Julia,' he said aloud, severely, 'we must now go through the house from top to bottom and make a thorough search.'

The echoes of his voice died away slowly all over the building, and in the intense silence that followed he turned to look at her. In the candle-light he saw that her face was already ghastly pale; but she dropped his arm for a moment and said in a whisper, stepping close in front of him—

'I agree. We must be sure there's no one hiding. That's the first thing.'

She spoke with evident effort, and he looked at her with admiration.

'You feel quite sure of yourself? It's not too late——'

'I think so,' she whispered, her eyes shifting nervously towards the shadows behind. 'Quite sure, only one thing——'

'What's that?'

'You must never leave me alone for an instant.'

'As long as you understand that any sound or appearance must be investigated at once, for to hesitate means to admit fear. That is fatal.'

'Agreed,' she said, a little shakily, after a moment's hesitation. 'I'll try——'

Arm in arm, Shorthouse holding the dripping candle and the stick, while his aunt carried the cloak over her shoulders, figures of utter comedy to all but themselves, they began a systematic search.

Stealthily, walking on tip-toe and shading the candle lest it should betray their presence through the shutterless windows, they went first into the big dining-room. There was not a stick of furniture to be seen. Bare walls, ugly mantelpieces and empty grates stared at them. Everything, they felt, resented their intrusion, watching them, as it were, with veiled eyes; whispers followed them; shadows flitted noiselessly to right and left; something seemed ever at their back, watching, waiting an opportunity to do them injury. There was the inevitable sense that operations which went on when the room was empty had been temporarily suspended till they were well out of the way again. The whole dark interior of the old building seemed to become a malignant

Presence that rose up, warning them to desist and mind their own business; every moment the strain on the nerves increased.

Out of the gloomy dining-room they passed through large folding doors into a sort of library or smoking-room, wrapt equally in silence, darkness, and dust; and from this they regained the hall near the top of the back stairs.

Here a pitch black tunnel opened before them into the lower regions, and—it must be confessed—they hesitated. But only for a minute. With the worst of the night still to come it was essential to turn from nothing. Aunt Julia stumbled at the top step of the dark descent, ill lit by the flickering candle, and even Shorthouse felt at least half the decision go out of his legs.

'Come on!' he said peremptorily, and his voice ran on and lost itself in the dark, empty spaces below.

'I'm coming,' she faltered, catching his arm with unnecessary violence.

They went a little unsteadily down the stone steps, a cold, damp air meeting them in the face, close and malodorous. The kitchen, into which the stairs led along a narrow passage, was large, with a lofty ceiling. Several doors opened out of it—some into cupboards with empty jars still standing on the shelves, and others into horrible little ghostly back offices, each colder and less inviting than the last. Black beetles scurried over the floor, and once, when they knocked against a deal table standing in a corner, something about the size of a cat jumped down with a rush and fled, scampering across the stone floor into the darkness. Everywhere there was a sense of recent occupation, an impression of sadness and gloom.

Leaving the main kitchen, they next went towards the scullery. The door was standing ajar, and as they pushed it open to its full extent Aunt Julia uttered a piercing scream, which she instantly tried to stifle by placing her hand over her mouth. For a second Shorthouse stood stock-still, catching his breath. He felt as if his spine had suddenly become hollow and someone had filled it with particles of ice.

Facing them, directly in their way between the doorposts, stood the figure of a woman. She had dishevelled hair and wildly staring eyes, and her face was terrified and white as death.

She stood there motionless for the space of a single second. Then the candle flickered and she was gone—gone utterly—and the door framed nothing but empty darkness.

'Only the beastly jumping candle-light,' he said quickly, in a voice that sounded like someone else's and was only half under control. 'Come on, aunt. There's nothing there.'

He dragged her forward. With a clattering of feet and a great appearance of boldness they went on, but over his body the skin moved as if crawling ants covered it, and he knew by the weight on his arm that he was supplying the force of locomotion for two. The scullery was cold, bare, and empty; more like a large prison cell than anything else. They went round it, tried the door into the yard, and the windows, but found them all fastened securely. His aunt moved beside him like a person in a dream. Her eyes were tightly shut, and she seemed merely to follow the pressure of his arm. Her courage filled him with amazement. At the same time he noticed that a certain odd change had come over her face, which somehow evaded his power of analysis.

'There's nothing here, aunty,' he repeated aloud quickly. 'Let's go upstairs and see the rest of the house. Then we'll choose a room to wait up in.'

She followed him obediently, keeping close to his side, and they locked the kitchen door behind them. It was a relief to get up again. In the hall there was more light than before, for the moon had travelled a little further down the stairs. Cautiously they began to go up into the dark vault of the upper house, the boards creaking under their weight.

On the first floor they found the large double drawing-rooms, a search of which revealed nothing. Here also was no sign of furniture or recent occupancy; nothing but dust and neglect and shadows. They opened the big folding doors between front and back drawing-rooms and then came out again to the landing and went on upstairs.

They had not gone up more than a dozen steps when they both simultaneously stopped to listen, looking into each other's eyes with a new apprehension across the flickering candle flame. From the room they had left hardly ten seconds before came the sound of doors quietly closing. It was beyond all question; they heard the booming noise that accompanies the shutting of heavy doors, followed by the sharp catching of the latch.

'We must go back and see,' said Shorthouse briefly, in a low tone, and turning to go downstairs again.

Somehow she managed to drag after him, her feet catching in her dress, her face livid.

When they entered the front drawing-room it was plain that the folding doors had been closed—half a minute before. Without hesitation Shorthouse opened them. He almost expected to see someone facing him in the back room; but only darkness and cold air met him. They went through both rooms; finding nothing unusual. They tried in every way to make the doors close of themselves, but there was not wind enough even to set the candle flame flickering. The doors would not move without strong pressure. All was silent as the grave. Undeniably the rooms were utterly empty, and the house utterly still.

'It's beginning,' whispered a voice at his elbow which he hardly recognised as his aunt's.

He nodded acquiescence, taking out his watch to note the time. It was fifteen minutes before midnight; he made the entry of exactly what had occurred in his notebook, setting the candle in its case upon the floor in order to do so. It took a moment or two to balance it safely against the wall.

Aunt Julia always declared that at this moment she was not actually watching him, but had turned her head towards the inner room, where she fancied she heard something moving; but, at any rate, both positively agreed that there came a sound of rushing feet, heavy and very swift— and the next instant the candle was out!

But to Shorthouse himself had come more than this, and he has always thanked his fortunate stars that it came to him alone and not to his aunt too. For, as he rose from the stooping position of balancing the candle, and before it was actually extinguished, a face thrust itself forward so close to his own that he could almost have touched it with his lips. It was a face working with passion; a man's face, dark, with thick features, and angry, savage eyes. It belonged to a common man, and it was evil in its ordinary normal expression, no doubt, but as he saw it, alive with intense, aggressive emotion, it was a malignant and terrible human countenance.

There was no movement of the air; nothing but the sound of rushing feet—stockinged or muffled feet; the apparition of the face; and the almost simultaneous extinguishing of the candle.

In spite of himself, Shorthouse uttered a little cry, nearly losing his balance as his aunt clung to him with her whole weight in one moment of real, uncontrollable terror. She made no sound, but simply seized him bodily. Fortunately, however, she had seen nothing, but had only heard the rushing feet, for her control returned almost at once, and he was able to disentangle himself and strike a match.

The shadows ran away on all sides before the glare, and his aunt stooped down and groped for the cigar case with the precious candle. Then they discovered that the candle had not been *blown* out at all; it had been *crushed* out. The wick was pressed down into the wax, which was flattened as if by some smooth, heavy instrument.

How his companion so quickly overcame her terror, Shorthouse never properly understood; but his admiration for her self-control increased tenfold, and at the same time served to feed his own dying flame—for which he was undeniably grateful. Equally inexplicable to him was the evidence of physical force they had just witnessed. He at once suppressed the memory of stories he had heard of 'physical mediums' and their dangerous phenomena; for if these were true, and either his aunt or himself was unwittingly a physical medium, it meant that they were simply aiding to focus the forces of a haunted house already charged to the brim. It was like walking with unprotected lamps among uncovered stores of gunpowder.

So, with as little reflection as possible, he simply relit the candle and went up to the next floor. The arm in his trembled, it is true, and his own tread was often uncertain, but they went on with thoroughness, and after a search revealing nothing they climbed the last flight of stairs to the top floor of all.

Here they found a perfect nest of small servants' rooms, with broken pieces of furniture, dirty cane-bottomed chairs, chests of drawers, cracked mirrors, and decrepit bedsteads. The rooms had low sloping ceilings already hung here and there with cobwebs, small windows, and badly plastered walls—a depressing and dismal region which they were glad to leave behind.

It was on the stroke of midnight when they entered a small room on the third floor, close to the top of the stairs, and arranged to make themselves comfortable for the remainder of their adventure. It was absolutely bare, and was said to be the room—then used as a clothes closet—into which the infuriated groom had chased his victim and finally caught her. Outside, across the narrow landing, began the stairs leading up to the floor above, and the servants' quarters where they had just searched.

In spite of the chilliness of the night there was something in the air of this room that cried for an open window. But there was more than this. Shorthouse could only describe it by saying that he felt less master of himself here than in any other part of the house. There was something that acted directly on the nerves, tiring the resolution, enfeebling the will. He was conscious of this result before he had been in the room five minutes, and it was in the short time they stayed there that he suffered the wholesale depletion of his vital forces, which was, for himself, the chief horror of the whole experience.

They put the candle on the floor of the cupboard, leaving the door a few inches ajar, so that there was no glare to confuse the eyes, and no shadow to shift about on walls and ceiling. Then they spread the cloak on the floor and sat down to wait, with their backs against the wall.

Shorthouse was within two feet of the door on to the landing; his position commanded a good view of the main staircase leading down into the darkness, and also of the beginning of the servants' stairs going to the floor above; the heavy stick lay beside him within easy reach.

The moon was now high above the house. Through the open window they could see the comforting stars like friendly eyes watching in the sky. One by one the clocks of the town struck midnight, and when the sounds died away the deep silence of a windless night fell again over everything. Only the boom of the sea, far away and lugubrious, filled the air with hollow murmurs.

Inside the house the silence became awful; awful, he thought, because any minute now it might be broken by sounds portending terror. The strain of waiting told more and more severely on the nerves; they talked in whispers when they talked at all, for their voices sounded queer and unnatural. A chilliness, not altogether due to the night air, invaded the room, and made them cold. The influences against them, whatever these might be, were slowly robbing them of self-confidence, and the power of decisive action; their forces were on the wane, and the possibility of real fear took on a new and terrible meaning. He began to tremble for the elderly woman by his side, whose pluck could hardly save her beyond a certain extent.

He heard the blood singing in his veins. It sometimes seemed so loud that he fancied it prevented his hearing properly certain other sounds that were beginning very faintly to make themselves audible in the depths of the house. Every time he fastened his attention on these sounds, they instantly ceased. They certainly came no nearer. Yet he could not rid himself of the idea that movement was going on somewhere in the lower regions of the house. The drawing-room floor, where the doors had been so strangely closed, seemed too near; the sounds were further off than that. He thought of the great kitchen, with the scurrying black beetles, and of the dismal little scullery; but, somehow or other, they did not seem to come from there either. Surely they were not *outside* the house!

Then, suddenly, the truth flashed into his mind, and for the space of a minute he felt as if his blood had stopped flowing and turned to ice.

The sounds were not downstairs at all; they were *upstairs*—upstairs, somewhere among those horrid gloomy little servants' rooms with their bits of broken furniture, low ceilings, and cramped windows—upstairs where the victim had first been disturbed and stalked to her death.

And the moment he discovered where the sounds were, he began to hear them more clearly. It was the sound of feet, moving stealthily along the passage overhead, in and out among the rooms, and past the furniture.

He turned quickly to steal a glance at the motionless figure seated beside him, to note whether she had shared his discovery. The faint candle-light coming through the crack in the cupboard door, threw her strongly-marked face into vivid relief against the white of the wall. But it was something else that made him catch his breath and stare again. An extraordinary something had come into her face and seemed to spread over her features like a mask; it smoothed out the deep lines and drew the skin everywhere a little tighter so that the wrinkles disappeared; it brought into the face—with the sole exception of the old eyes—an appearance of youth and almost of childhood.

He stared in speechless amazement—amazement that was dangerously near to horror. It was his aunt's face indeed, but it was her face of forty years ago, the vacant innocent face of a girl. He had heard stories of that strange effect of terror which could wipe a human countenance clean of other emotions, obliterating all previous expressions; but he had never realised that it could be literally true, or could mean anything so simply horrible as what he now saw. For the dreadful signature of overmastering fear was written plainly in that utter vacancy of the girlish face beside him; and when, feeling his intense gaze, she turned to look at him, he instinctively closed his eyes tightly to shut out the sight.

Yet, when he turned a minute later, his feelings well in hand, he saw to his intense relief another expression; his aunt was smiling, and though the face was deathly white, the awful veil had lifted and the normal look was returning.

'Anything wrong?' was all he could think of to say at the moment. And the answer was eloquent, coming from such a woman.

'I feel cold—and a little frightened,' she whispered.

He offered to close the window, but she seized hold of him and begged him not to leave her side even for an instant.

'It's upstairs, I know,' she whispered, with an odd half-laugh; 'but I can't possibly go up.'

But Shorthouse thought otherwise, knowing that in action lay their best hope of self-control.

He took the brandy flask and poured out a glass of neat spirit, stiff enough to help anybody over anything. She swallowed it with a little shiver. His only idea now was to get out of the house before her collapse became inevitable; but this could not safely be done by turning tail and running from the enemy. Inaction was no longer possible; every minute he was growing less master of himself, and desperate, aggressive measures were imperative without further delay. Moreover, the action must be taken *towards* the enemy, not away from it; the climax, if necessary and unavoidable, would have to be faced boldly. He could do it now; but in ten minutes he might not have the force left to act for himself, much less for both!

Upstairs, the sounds were meanwhile becoming louder and closer, accompanied by occasional creaking of the boards. Someone was moving stealthily about, stumbling now and then awkwardly against the furniture.

Waiting a few moments to allow the tremendous dose of spirits to produce its effect, and knowing this would last but a short time under the circumstances, Shorthouse then quietly got on his feet, saying in a determined voice:

'Now Aunt Julia, we'll go upstairs and find out what all this noise is about. You must come too. It's what we agreed.'

He picked up his stick and went to the cupboard for the candle. A limp form rose shakily beside him breathing hard, and he heard a voice say very faintly something about being 'ready to come'. The woman's courage amazed him; it was so much greater than his own; and, as they advanced, holding aloft the dripping candle, some subtle force exhaled from this trembling, white-faced old woman at his side that was the true source of his inspiration. It held something really great that shamed him and gave him the support without which he would have proved far less equal to the occasion.

They crossed the dark landing, avoiding with their eyes the deep black space over the banisters. Then they began to mount the narrow staircase to meet the sounds which, minute by minute, grew louder and nearer. About half-way up the stairs Aunt Julia stumbled and Shorthouse turned to catch her by the arm, and just at that moment there came a terrific crash in the servants' corridor overhead. It was instantly followed by a shrill, agonised scream that was a cry of terror and a cry for help melted into one.

Before they could move aside, or go down a single step, someone came rushing along the passage overhead, blundering horribly, racing madly, at full speed, three steps at a time, down the very staircase where they stood. The steps were light and uncertain; but close behind them sounded the heavier tread of another person, and the staircase seemed to shake.

Shorthouse and his companion just had time to flatten themselves against the wall when the jumble of flying steps was upon them, and two persons, with the slightest possible interval between them, dashed past at full speed. It was a perfect whirlwind of sound breaking in upon the midnight silence of the empty building.

The two runners, pursuer and pursued, had passed clean through them where they stood, and already with a thud the boards below had received first one, then the other. Yet they had seen absolutely nothing—not a hand, or arm, or face, or even a shred of flying clothing.

There came a second's pause. Then the first one, the lighter of the two, obviously the pursued one, ran with uncertain footsteps into the little room which Shorthouse and his aunt had just left. The heavier one followed. There was a sound of scuffling, gasping, and smothered screaming; and then out on to the landing came the step—of a single person *treading weightily*.

A dead silence followed for the space of half a minute, and then was heard a rushing sound through the air. It was followed by a dull, crashing thud in the depths of the house below—on the stone floor of the hall.

Utter silence reigned after. Nothing moved. The flame of the candle was steady. It had been steady the whole time, and the air had been undisturbed by any movement whatsoever. Palsied with terror, Aunt Julia, without waiting for her companion, began fumbling her way downstairs; she was crying gently to herself, and when Shorthouse put his arm round her and half carried her, he felt that she was trembling like a leaf. He went into the little room and picked up the cloak from the floor, and, arm in arm, walking very slowly, without speaking a word or looking once behind them, they marched down the three flights into the hall.

In the hall they saw nothing, but the whole way down the stairs they were conscious that someone followed them; step by step; when they went faster IT was left behind, and when they went more slowly IT caught them up. But never once did they look behind to see; and at each turning of the staircase they lowered their eyes for fear of the following horror they might see upon the stairs above.

With trembling hands Shorthouse opened the front door, and they walked out into the moonlight and drew a deep breath of the cool night air blowing in from the sea.

The Cigarette Case

OLIVER ONIONS

—

'A cigarette, Loder?' I said, offering my case. For the moment Loder was not smoking; for long enough he had not been talking.

'Thanks,' he replied, taking not only the cigarette, but the case also. The others went on talking; Loder became silent again; but I noticed that he kept my cigarette case in his hand, and looked at it from time to time with an interest that neither its design nor its costliness seemed to explain. Presently I caught his eye.

'A pretty case,' he remarked, putting it down on the table. 'I once had one exactly like it.'

I answered that they were in every shop window.

'Oh yes,' he said, putting aside any question of rarity.... 'I lost mine.'

'Oh...?'

He laughed. 'Oh, that's all right—I got it back again—don't be afraid I'm going to claim yours. But the way I lost it—found it—the whole thing—was rather curious. I've never been able to explain it. I wonder if you could?'

I answered that I certainly couldn't till I'd heard it, whereupon Loder, taking up the silver case again and holding it in his hand as he talked, began:

'This happened in Provence, when I was about as old as Marsham there—and every bit as romantic. I was there with Carroll—you remember poor old Carroll and what a blade of a boy he was—as romantic as four Marshams rolled into one. (Excuse me, Marsham, won't you? It's a romantic tale, you see, or at least the setting is.) ... We were in Provence, Carroll and I; twenty-four or thereabouts; romantic, as I say; and—and this happened.

'And it happened on the top of a whole lot of other things, you must understand, the things that do happen when you're twenty-four. If it hadn't been Provence, it would have been somewhere else, I suppose, nearly, if not quite as good; but this was Provence, that smells (as you might say) of twenty-four as it smells of argelasse and wild lavender and broom....

'We'd had the dickens of a walk of it, just with knapsacks—had started somewhere in the Ardèche and I tramped south through the vines and almonds and olives—Montélimar, Orange, Avignon, and a fortnight at that blanched skeleton of a town, Les Baux. We'd nothing to do, and had gone just where we liked, or rather just where Carroll had liked; and Carroll had had the *De Bello Gallico* in his pocket, and had had a notion, I fancy, of taking in the whole ground of the Roman conquest—I remember he lugged me off to some place or other, Pourrières I believe its name was, because—I forget how many thousands—were killed in a river-bed there, and they stove in the water-casks so that if the men wanted water they'd have to go forward and fight for it. And then we'd gone on to Arles, where Carroll had fallen in love with everything that had a bow of black velvet in her hair, and after that Tarascon, Nimes, and so on, the usual round—I won't bother you with that. In a word, we'd had two months of it, eating almonds and apricots from the trees, watching the women at the communal washing-fountains under the dark plane-trees, singing *Magali* and the *Qué Contes*, and Carroll yarning away all the time about Caesar and Vercingetorix and Dante, and trying to learn Provençal so that he could read the stuff in the *Journal des Félibriges* that he'd never have looked at if it had been in English. . . .

'Well, we got to Darbisson. We'd run across some young chap or other—Rangon his name was—who was a vine-planter in those parts, and Rangon had asked us to spend a couple of days with him, with him and his mother, if we happened to be in the neighbourhood. So as we might as well happen to be there as anywhere else, we sent him a postcard and went. This would be in June or early in July. All day we walked across a plain of vines, past hurdles of wattled *cannes* and great wind-screens of velvety cypresses, sixty feet high, all white with dust on the north side of 'em, for the mistral was having its three-days' revel, and it whistled and roared through the *cannes* till scores of yards of 'em at a time were bowed nearly to the earth. A roaring day it was, I remember. . . . But the wind fell a little late in the afternoon, and we were poring over what it had left of our Ordnance Survey—like fools, we'd got the unmounted paper maps instead of the linen ones—when Rangon himself found us, coming out to meet us in a very badly turned-out trap. He drove us back himself through Darbisson, to the house, a mile and a half beyond it, where he lived with his mother.

'He spoke no English, Rangon didn't, though, of course, both French and Provençal; and as he drove us, there was Carroll, using him as a Franco-Provençal dictionary, peppering him with questions about the names of things in the patois—I beg its pardon, the language—though there's a good deal of my eye and Betty Martin about that, and I fancy this Félibrige business will be in a good many places when Frédéric

Mistral is under that Court-of-Love pavilion arrangement he's had put up for himself in the graveyard at Maillanne. If the language has got to go, well, it's got to go, I suppose; and while I personally don't want to give it a kick, I rather sympathise with the Government. Those jaunts of a Sunday out to Les Baux, for instance, with paper lanterns and Bengal fire and a fellow spouting *O blanche Vénus d'Arles*—they're well enough, and compare favourably with our Bank Holidays and Sunday League picnics, but . . . but that's nothing to do with my tale after all. . . . So he drove on, and by the time we got to Rangon's house Carroll had learned the greater part of *Magali*. . . .

'As you, no doubt, know, it's a restricted sort of life in some respects that a young *vigneron* lives in those parts, and it was as we reached the house that Rangon remembered something—or he might have been trying to tell us as we came along for all I know, and not been able to get a word in edgeways for Carroll and his Provençal. It seemed that his mother was away from home for some days—apologies of the most profound, of course; our host was the soul of courtesy, though he did try to get at us a bit later. . . . We expressed our polite regrets, naturally; but I didn't quite see at first what difference it made. I only began to see when Rangon, with more apologies, told us that we should have to go back to Darbisson for dinner. It appeared that when Madame Rangon went away for a few days she dispersed the whole of the female side of her establishment also, and she'd left her son with nobody to look after him except an old man we'd seen in the yard mending one of these double-cylindered sulphur-sprinklers they clap across the horse's back and drive between the rows of vines. . . . Rangon explained all this as we stood in the hall drinking an apéritif—a hall crowded with oak furniture and photographs and a cradle-like bread-crib and doors opening to right and left to the other rooms of the ground floor. He had also, it seemed, to ask us to be so infinitely obliging as to excuse him for one hour after dinner—our postcard had come unexpectedly, he said, and already he had made an appointment with his agent about the *vendange* for the coming autumn. . . . We begged him, of course, not to allow us to interfere with his business in the slightest degree. He thanked us a thousand times.

' "But though we dine in the village, we will take our own wine with us," he said, "a wine *surfin*—one of my wines—you shall see—"

'Then he showed us round his place—I forget how many hundreds of acres of vines, and into the great building with the presses and pumps and casks and the huge barrel they call the thunderbolt—and about seven o'clock we walked back to Darbisson to dinner, carrying our wine with us. I think the restaurant we dined in was the only one in the place, and our gaillard of a host—he was a straight-backed, well-set-up chap, with rather fine eyes—did us on the whole pretty well. His wine certainly was good stuff, and set our tongues going. . . .

'A moment ago I said a fellow like Rangon leads a restricted sort of life in those parts. I saw this more clearly as dinner went on. We dined by an open window, from which we could see the stream with the planks across it where the women washed clothes during the day and assembled in the evening for gossip. There were a dozen or so of them there as we dined, laughing and chatting in low tones—they all seemed pretty— it was quickly falling dusk—all the girls are pretty then, and are quite conscious of it—*you* know, Marsham. Behind them, at the end of the street, one of these great cypress wind-screens showed black against the sky, a ragged edge something like the line the needle draws on a rainfall chart; and you could only tell whether they were men or women under the plantains by their voices rippling and chattering and suddenly a deeper note. . . . Once I heard a muffled scuffle and a sound like a kiss. . . . It was then that Rangon's little trouble came out. . . .

'It seemed that he didn't know any girls—wasn't allowed to know any girls. The girls of the village were pretty enough, but you see how it was—he'd a position to keep up—appearances to maintain—couldn't be familiar during the year with the girls who gathered his grapes for him in the autumn. . . . And as soon as Carroll gave him a chance, *he* began to ask *us* questions, about England, English girls, the liberty they had, and so on.

'Of course, we couldn't tell him much he hadn't heard already, but that made no difference; he could stand any amount of that, our strapping young *vigneron*; and he asked us questions by the dozen, that we both tried to answer at once. And his delight and envy! . . . What! In England did the young men see the young women of their own class without restraint—the sisters of their friends *même*—even at the house? Was it permitted that they drank tea with them in the afternoon, or went without invitations to pass the *soirée*? . . . He had all the later Prévosts in his room, he told us (I don't doubt he had the earlier ones also); Prévost and the Disestablishment between them must be playing the mischief with the convent system of education for young girls; and our young man was—what d'you call it?—"Co-ed" co-educationalist—by Jove, yes! . . . He seemed to marvel that we should have left a country so blessed as England to visit his dusty, wild-lavender-smelling, girl-less Provence. . . . You don't know half your luck, Marsham. . . .

'Well, we talked after this fashion—we'd left the dining-room of the restaurant and had planted ourselves on a bench outside with Rangon between us—when Rangon suddenly looked at his watch and said it

was time he was off to see this agent of his. Would we take a walk, he
asked us, and meet him again there? he said. . . . But as his agent lived
in the direction of his own home, we said we'd meet him at the house in
an hour or so. Off he went, envying every Englishman who stepped, I
don't doubt. . . . I told you how old—how young—we were. . . .
Heigho! . . .

'Well, off goes Rangon, and Carroll and I got up, stretched ourselves,
and took a walk. We walked a mile or so, until it began to get pretty dark,
and then turned; and it was as we came into the blackness of one of these
cypress hedges that the thing I'm telling you of happened. The hedge
took a sharp turn at that point; as we came round the angle we saw a
couple of women's figures hardly more than twenty yards ahead—don't
know how they got there so suddenly, I'm sure; and that same moment I
found my foot on something small and white and glimmering on the
grass.

'I picked it up. It was a handkerchief—a woman's—embroidered—

'The two figures ahead of us were walking in our direction; there was
every probability that the handkerchief belonged to one of them; so we
stepped out. . . .

'At my "Pardon, madame," and lifted hat one of the figures turned
her head; then, to my surprise, she spoke in English—cultivated
English. I held out the handkerchief. It belonged to the elder lady of the
two, the one who had spoken, a very gentle-voiced old lady, older by very
many years than her companion. She took the handkerchief and
thanked me. . . .

'Somebody—Sterne, isn't it?—says that Englishmen don't travel to
see Englishmen. I don't know whether he'd stand to that in the case of
English-women; Carroll and I didn't. . . . We were walking rather
slowly along, four abreast across the road; we asked permission to
introduce ourselves, did so, and received some name in return which,
strangely enough, I've entirely forgotten—I only remember that the
ladies were aunt and niece, and lived at Darbisson. They shook their
heads when I mentioned Mr Rangon's name and said we were visiting
him. They didn't know him. . . .

'I'd never been in Darbisson before, and I haven't been since, so I
don't know the map of the village very well. But the place isn't very big,
and the house at which we stopped in twenty minutes or so is probably
there yet. It had a large double door—a double door in two senses, for it
was a big *porte-cochère* with a smaller door inside it, and an iron grille
shutting in the whole. The gentle-voiced old lady had already taken a
key from her reticule and was thanking us again for the little service of
the handkerchief; then, with the little gesture one makes when one has

found oneself on the point of omitting a courtesy, she gave a little musical laugh.

' "But," she said with a little movement of invitation, "one sees so few compatriots here—if you have the time to come in and smoke a cigarette . . . also the cigarette," she added, with another rippling laugh, "for we have few callers, and live alone—"

'Hastily as I was about to accept, Carroll was before me, professing a nostalgia for the sound of the English tongue that made his recent protestations about Provençal a shameless hypocrisy. Persuasive young rascal, Carroll was—poor chap. . . . So the elder lady opened the grille and the wooden door beyond it, and we entered.

'By the light of the candle which the younger lady took from a bracket just within the door we saw that we were in a handsome hall or vestibule; and my wonder that Rangon had made no mention of what was apparently a considerable establishment was increased by the fact that its tenants must be known to be English and could be seen to be entirely charming. I couldn't understand it, and I'm afraid hypotheses rushed into my head that cast doubts on the Rangons—you know—whether *they* were all right. We knew nothing about our young planter, you see. . . .

'I looked about me. There were tubs here and there against the walls, gaily painted, with glossy-leaved aloes and palms in them—one of the aloes, I remember, was flowering; a little fountain in the middle made a tinkling noise; we put our caps on a carved and gilt console table; and before us rose a broad staircase with shallow steps of spotless stone and a beautiful wrought-iron handrail. At the top of the staircase were more palms and aloes, and double doors painted in a clear grey.

'We followed our hostesses up the staircase. I can hear yet the sharp clean click our boots made on that hard shiny stone—see the lights of the candle gleaming on the handrail. . . . The young girl—she was not much more than a girl—pushed at the doors, and we went in.

'The room we entered was all of a piece with the rest for rather old-fashioned fineness. It was large, lofty, beautifully kept. Carroll went round for Miss . . . whatever her name was . . . lighting candles in sconces; and as the flames crept up they glimmered on a beautifully polished floor, which was bare except for an Eastern rug here and there. The elder lady had sat down in a gilt chair, Louis Fourteenth I should say, with a striped rep of the colour of a petunia; and I really don't know—don't smile, Smith—what induced me to lead her to it by the finger-tips, bending over her hand for a moment as she sat down. There was an old tambour-frame behind her chair, I remember, and a vast oval mirror with clustered candle-brackets filled the greater part of the farther wall, the brightest and clearest glass I've ever seen. . . .'

He paused, looking at my cigarette case, which he had taken into his hand again. He smiled at some recollection or other, and it was a minute or so before he continued.

'I must admit that I found it a little annoying, after what we'd been talking about at dinner an hour before, that Rangon wasn't with us. I still couldn't understand how he could have neighbours so charming without knowing about them, but I didn't care to insist on this to the old lady, who for all I knew might have her own reasons for keeping to herself. And, after all, it was our place to return Rangon's hospitality in London if he ever came there, not, so to speak, on his own doorstep. . . . So presently I forgot all about Rangon, and I'm pretty sure that Carroll, who was talking to his companion of some Félibrige junketing or other and having the air of Gounod's *Mireille* hummed softly over to him, didn't waste a thought on him either. Soon Carroll—you remember what a pretty crooning, humming voice he had—soon Carroll was murmuring what they call "seconds", but so low that the sound hardly came across the room; and I came in with a soft bass note from time to time. No instrument, you know; just an unaccompanied murmur no louder than an Æolian harp; and it sounded infinitely sweet and plaintive and—what shall I say?—weak—attenuated—faint—"pale" you might almost say—in that formal, rather old-fashioned salon, with that great clear oval mirror throwing back the still flames of the candles in the sconces on the walls. Outside the wind had now fallen completely; all was very quiet; and suddenly, in a voice not much louder than a sigh, Carroll's companion was singing *Oft in the Stilly Night*—you know it. . . .'

He broke off again to murmur the beginning of the air. Then, with a little laugh for which we saw no reason, he went on again:

'Well, I'm not going to try to convince you of such a special and delicate thing as the charm of that hour—it wasn't more than an hour— it would be all about an hour we stayed. Things like that just have to be said and left; you destroy them the moment you begin to insist on them; we've already one of us had experiences like that, and don't say much about them. I was as much in love with my old lady as Carroll evidently was with his young one—I can't tell you why—being in love has just to be taken for granted too, I suppose. . . . Marsham understands. . . . We smoked our cigarettes, and sang again, once more filling that clear-painted, quiet apartment with a murmuring no louder than if a light breeze found that the bells of a bed of flowers were really bells and played on 'em. The old lady moved her fingers gently on the round table by the side of her chair . . . oh, infinitely pretty it was. . . . Then Carroll wandered off into the *Qué Contes*—awfully pretty—"It is not for myself I sing, but for my friend who is near to me"—and I can't tell you how like four old friends we were, those two so oddly met ladies and Carroll and myself. . . .

'But for all the sweetness and the glamour of it, we couldn't stay on indefinitely, and I wondered what time it was, but didn't ask—anything to do with clocks and watches would have seemed a cold and mechanical sort of thing just then. . . . And when presently we both got up neither Carroll nor I asked to be allowed to call again in the morning to thank them for a charming hour. . . . And they seemed to feel the same as we did about it. There was no "hoping that we should meet again in London"—neither an au revoir nor a good-bye—just a tacit under-standing that the hour should remain isolated, accepted like a good gift without looking the gift-horse in the mouth, single, unattached to any hours before or after—I don't know whether you see what I mean. . . . Give me a match, somebody. . . .

'And so we left, with no more than looks exchanged and finger-tips resting between the back of our hands and our lips for a moment. We found our way out by ourselves, down that shallow-stepped staircase with the handsome handrail, and let ourselves out of the double door and grille, closing it softly. We made for the village without speaking a word. . . . Heigho . . . !'

Loder had picked up the cigarette case again, but for all the way his eyes rested on it I doubt whether he really saw it. I'm pretty sure he didn't; I knew when he did by the glance he shot at me, as much as to say 'I see you're wondering where the cigarette case comes in.' . . . He resumed with another little laugh.

'Well,' he continued, 'we got back to Rangon's house. I really don't blame Rangon for the way he took it when we told him, you know—he thought we were pulling his leg, of course, and he wasn't having any; not he! There were no English ladies in Darbisson, he said. . . . We told him as nearly as we could just where the house was—we weren't very precise, I'm afraid, for the village had been in darkness as we had come through it, and I had to admit that the cypress hedge I tried to describe where we'd met our friends was a good deal like other cypress hedges—and, as I say, Rangon wasn't taking any. I myself was rather annoyed that he should think we were returning his hospitality by trying to get at him, and it wasn't very easy either to explain in my French and Carroll's Provençal that we were going to let the thing stand as it was and weren't going to call on our charming friends again. . . . The end of it was that Rangon just laughed and yawned. . . .

' "I knew it was good, my wine," he said, "but—" a shrug said the rest. "Not so good as all that," he meant. . . .

'Then he gave us our candles, showed us to our rooms, shook hands, and marched off to his own room and the Prévosts.

'I dreamed of my old lady half the night.

'After coffee the next morning I had put my hand into my pocket for my cigarette case and didn't find it. I went through all my pockets, and then I asked Carroll if he'd got it.

' "No," he replied. . . . "Think you left it behind at that place last night?"

' "Yes; did you?" Rangon popped in with a twinkle.

'I went through all my pockets again. No cigarette case. . . .

'Of course, it was possible that I'd left it behind, and I was annoyed again. I didn't want to go back, you see. . . . But, on the other hand, I didn't want to lose the case—it was a present—and Rangon's smile nettled me a good deal, too. It was both a challenge to our truthfulness and a testimonial to that very good wine of his. . . .

' "Might have done," I grunted. . . . "Well, in that case we'll go and get it."

' "If one tried the restaurant first—?" Rangon suggested, smiling again.

' "By all means," said I stuffily, though I remembered having the case after we'd left the restaurant.

'We were round at the restaurant by half-past nine. The case wasn't there. I'd known jolly well beforehand it wasn't, and I saw Rangon's mouth twitching with amusement.

' "So we now seek the abode of these English ladies, *hein*?" he said.

' "Yes," said I; and we left the restaurant and strode through the village by the way we'd taken the evening before. . . .

'That *vigneron*'s smile became more and more irritating to me. . . "It is then the *next* village?" he said presently, as we left the last house and came out into the open plain.

'We went back. . . .

'I was irritated because we were two to one, you see, and Carroll backed me up. "A double door, with a grille in front of it," he repeated for the fiftieth time. . . . Rangon merely replied that it wasn't our good faith he doubted. He didn't actually use the word "drunk". . . .

' "*Mais tiens*," he said suddenly, trying to conceal his mirth. "*Si c'est possible . . . si c'est possible . . .* a double door with a grille? But perhaps that I know it, the domicile of these so elusive ladies. . . . Come this way."

'He took us back along a plantain-groved street, and suddenly turned up an alley that was little more than two gutters and a crack of sky overhead between two broken-tiled roofs. It was a dilapidated deserted *ruelle,* and I was positively angry when Rangon pointed to a blistered old *porte-cochère* with a half-unhinged railing in front of it.

' "Is it that, your house?" he asked.

' "No," says I, and "No," says Carroll . . . and off we started again. . . .

'But another half-hour brought us back to the same place, and Carroll scratched his head.

' "Who lives there, anyway?" he said, glowering at the *porte-cochère,* chin forward, hands in pockets.

' "Nobody," says Rangon, as much as to say "look at it!" "M'sieu then meditates taking it . . . ?"

'Then I struck in, quite out of temper by this time.

' "How much would the rent be?" I asked, as if I really thought of taking the place just to get back at him.

'He mentioned something ridiculously small in the way of francs.

' "One might at least see the place," says I. "Can the key be got?"

'He bowed. The key was at the baker's, not a hundred yards away, he said. . . .

'We got the key. It was the key of the inner wooden door—that grid of rusty iron didn't need one—it came clean off its single hinge when Carroll touched it. Carroll opened, and we stood for a moment motioning to one another to step in. Then Rangon went in first, and I heard him murmur "Pardon, Mesdames". . . .

'Now this is the odd part. We passed into a sort of vestibule or hall, with a burst lead pipe in the middle of a dry tank in the centre of it. There was a broad staircase rising in front of us to the first floor, and double doors just seen in the half-light at the head of the stairs. Old tubs stood against the walls, but the palms and aloes in them were dead—only a cabbage-stalk or two—and the rusty hoops lay on the ground about them. One tub had come to pieces entirely and was no more than a heap of staves on a pile of spilt earth. And everywhere, everywhere was dust— the floor was an inch deep in dust and old plaster that muffled our footsteps, cobwebs hung like old dusters on the walls, a regular goblin's tatter of cobwebs draped the little bracket inside the door, and the wrought-iron of the handrail was closed up with webs in which not even a spider moved. The whole thing was preposterous. . . .

' "It is possible that for even a less rental—" Rangon murmured, dragging his forefinger across the handrail and leaving an inch-deep furrow.

' "Come upstairs," said I suddenly. . . .

'Up we went. All was in the same state there. A clutter of stuff came down as I pushed at the double doors of the *salon,* and I had to strike a stinking French sulphur match to see into the room at all. Underfoot was like walking on thicknesses of flannel, and except where we put our feet the place was as printless as a snowfield—dust, dust, unbroken grey dust. My match burned down. . . .

' "Wait a minute—I've a *bougie*," said Carroll, and struck the wax match. . . .

'There were the old sconces, with never a candle-end in them. There was the large oval mirror, but hardly reflecting Carroll's match for the dust on it. And the broken chairs were there, all giltless, and the rickety old round table. . . ,

'But suddenly I darted forward. Something new and bright on the table twinkled with the light of Carroll's match. The match went out, and by the time Carroll had lighted another I had stopped. I wanted Rangon to see what was on the table. . . .

' "You'll see by my footprints how far from that table *I've* been," I said. "Will you pick it up?"

'And Rangon, stepping forward, picked up from the middle of the table—my cigarette case.'

Loder had finished. Nobody spoke. For quite a minute nobody spoke, and then Loder himself broke the silence, turning to me.

'Make anything of it?' he said.

I lifted my eyebrows. 'Only your *vigneron*'s expression—' I began, but stopped again, seeing that wouldn't do.

'*Any*body make anything of it?' said Loder, turning from one to another.

I gathered from Smith's face that he thought *one* thing might be made of it—namely, that Loder had invented the whole tale. But even Smith didn't speak.

'Were any English ladies ever found to have lived in the place— murdered, you know—bodies found and all that?' young Marsham asked diffidently, yearning for an obvious completeness.

'Not that we could ever learn,' Loder replied. 'We made inquiries too. . . . So you all give it up? Well, so do I. . . .'

And he rose. As he walked to the door, myself following him to get his hat and stick, I heard him humming softly the lines—they are from *Oft in the Stilly Night*—

'I seem like one who treads alone
Some banquet-hall deserted,
Whose guests are fled, whose garlands dead,
And all but he—departed!'

Rose Rose

BARRY PAIN

Sefton stepped back from his picture. 'Rest now, please,' he said.

Miss Rose Rose, his model, threw the striped blanket around her, stepped down from the throne, and crossed the studio. She seated herself on the floor near the big stove. For a few moments Sefton stood motionless, looking critically at his work. Then he laid down his palette and brushes and began to roll a cigarette. He was a man of forty, thick-set, round-faced, with a reddish moustache turned fiercely upwards. He flung himself down in an easy-chair, and smoked in silence till silence seemed ungracious.

'Well,' he said, 'I've got the place hot enough for you today, Miss Rose.'

'You 'ave indeed,' said Miss Rose.

'I bet it's nearer eighty than seventy.'

The cigarette-smoke made a blue haze in the hot, heavy air. He watched it undulating, curving, melting.

As he watched it Miss Rose continued her observations. The trouble with these studios was the draughts. With a strong east wind, same as yesterday, you might have the stove red-hot, and yet never get the place, so to speak, warm. It is possible to talk commonly without talking like a coster, and Miss Rose achieved it. She did not always neglect the aspirate. She never quite substituted the third vowel for the first. She rather enjoyed long words.

She was beautiful from the crown of her head to the sole of her foot; and few models have good feet. Every pose she took was graceful. She was the daughter of a model, and had been herself a model from childhood. In consequence, she knew her work well and did it well. On one occasion, when sitting for the great Merion, she had kept the same pose, without a rest, for three consecutive hours. She was proud of that. Naturally she stood in the first rank among models, was most in demand, and made the most money. Her fault was that she was slightly capricious; you could not absolutely depend upon her. On a wintry morning when every hour of daylight was precious, she might keep her appointment, she might be an hour or two late, or she might stay away altogether. Merion himself had suffered from her, had sworn never to employ her again, and had gone back to her.

Sefton, as he watched the blue smoke, found that her common accent jarred on him. It even seemed to make it more difficult for him to get the right presentation of the 'Aphrodite' that she was helping him to paint. One seemed to demand a poetical and cultured soul in so beautiful a body. Rose Rose was not poetical nor cultured; she was not even business-like and educated.

Half an hour of silent and strenuous work followed. Then Sefton growled that he could not see any longer.

'We'll stop for today,' he said. Miss Rose Rose retired behind the screen. Sefton opened a window and both ventilators, and rolled another cigarette. The studio became rapidly cooler.

'Tomorrow, at nine?' he called out.

'I've got some way to come,' came the voice of Miss Rose from behind the screen. 'I could be here by a quarter past.'

'Right,' said Sefton, as he slipped on his coat.

When Rose Rose emerged from the screen she was dressed in a blue serge costume, with a picture-hat. As it was her business in life to be beautiful, she never wore corsets, high heels, nor pointed toes. Such abnegation is rare among models.

'I say, Mr Sefton,' said Rose, 'you were to settle at the end of the sittings, but——'

'Oh, you don't want any money, Miss Rose. You're known to be rich.'

'Well, what I've got is in the Post Office, and I don't want to touch it. And I've got some shopping I must do before I go home.'

Sefton pulled out his sovereign-case hesitatingly.

'This is all very well, you know,' he said.

'I know what you are thinking, Mr Sefton. You think I don't mean to come tomorrow. That's all Mr Merion, now, isn't it? He's always saying things about me. I'm not going to stick it. I'm going to 'ave it out with 'im.'

'He recommended you to me. And I'll tell you what he said, if you won't repeat it. He said that I should be lucky if I got you, and that I'd better chain you to the studio.'

'And all because I was once late—with a good reason for it, too. Besides, what's once? I suppose he didn't 'appen to tell you how often he's kept me waiting.'

'Well, here you are, Miss Rose. But you'll really be here in time tomorrow, won't you? Otherwise the thing will have got too tacky to work into.'

'You needn't worry about that,' said Miss Rose, eagerly. 'I'll be here, whatever happens, by a quarter past nine. I'll be here if I die first! There, is that good enough for you? Good afternoon, and thank you, Mr Sefton.'

'Good afternoon, Miss Rose. Let me manage that door for you—the key goes a bit stiffly.'

Sefton came back to his picture. In spite of Miss Rose's vehement assurances he felt by no means sure of her, but it was difficult for him to refuse any woman anything, and impossible for him to refuse to pay her what he really owed. He scrawled in charcoal some directions to the charwoman who would come in the morning. She was, from his point of view, a prize charwoman—one who could, and did, wash brushes properly, one who understood the stove, and would, when required, refrain from sweeping. He picked up his hat and went out. He walked the short distance from his studio to his bachelor flat, looked over an evening paper as he drank his tea, and then changed his clothes and took a cab to the club for dinner. He played one game of billiards after dinner, and then went home. His picture was very much in his mind. He wanted to be up fairly early in the morning, and he went to bed early.

He was at his studio by half-past eight. The stove was lighted, and he piled more coke on it. His 'Aphrodite' seemed to have a somewhat mocking expression. It was a little, technical thing, to be corrected easily. He set his palette and selected his brushes. An attempt to roll a cigarette revealed the fact that his pouch was empty. It still wanted a few minutes to nine. He would have time to go up to the tobacconist at the corner. In case Rose Rose arrived while he was away, he left the studio door open. The tobacconist was also a newsagent, and he bought a morning paper. Rose would probably be twenty minutes late at the least, and this would be something to occupy him.

But on his return he found his model already stepping on to the throne.

'Good morning, Miss Rose. You're a lady of your word.' He hardly heeded the murmur which came to him as a reply. He threw his cigarette into the stove, picked up his palette, and got on excellently. The work was absorbing. For some time he thought of nothing else. There was no relaxing on the part of the model—no sign of fatigue. He had been working for over an hour, when his conscience smote him. 'We'll have a rest now, Miss Rose,' he said cheerily. At the same moment he felt human fingers drawn lightly across the back of his neck, just above the collar. He turned round with a sudden start. There was nobody there. He turned back again to the throne. Rose Rose had vanished.

With the utmost care and deliberation he put down his palette and brushes. He said in a loud voice, 'Where are you, Miss Rose?' For a moment or two silence hung in the hot air of the studio.

He repeated his question and got no answer. Then he stepped behind the screen, and suddenly the most terrible thing in his life happened to him. He knew that his model had never been there at all.

There was only one door out to the back street in which his studio was placed, and that door was now locked. He unlocked it, put on his hat, and went out. For a minute or two he paced the street, but he had got to go back to the studio.

He went back, sat down in the easy-chair, lit a cigarette, and tried for a plausible explanation. Undoubtedly he had been working very hard lately. When he had come back from the tobacconist's to the studio he had been in the state of expectant attention, and he was enough of a psychologist to know that in that state you are especially likely to see what you expect to see. He was not conscious of anything abnormal in himself. He did not feel ill, or even nervous. Nothing of the kind had ever happened to him before. The more he considered the matter, the more definite became his state. He was thoroughly frightened. With a great effort he pulled himself together and picked up the newspaper. It was certain that he could do no more work for that day, anyhow. An ordinary, commonplace newspaper would restore him. Yes, that was it. He had been too much wrapped up in the picture. He had simply supposed the model to be there.

He was quite unconvinced, of course, and merely trying to convince himself. As an artist, he knew that for the last hour or more he had been getting the most delicate modelling right from the living form before him. But he did his best, and read the newspaper assiduously. He read of tariff, protection, and of a new music-hall star. Then his eye fell on a paragraph headed 'Motor Fatalities'.

He read that Miss Rose, an artist's model, had been knocked down by a car in the Fulham Road about seven o'clock on the previous evening; that the owner of the car had stopped and taken her to the hospital, and that she had expired within a few minutes of admission.

He rose from his place and opened a large pocket-knife. There was a strong impulse upon him, and he felt it to be a mad impulse, to slash the canvas to rags. He stopped before the picture. The face smiled at him with a sweetness that was scarcely earthly.

He went back to his chair again. 'I'm not used to this kind of thing,' he said aloud. A board creaked at the far end of the studio. He jumped up with a start of horror. A few minutes later he had left the studio, and locked the door behind him. His common sense was still with him. He ought to go to a specialist. But the picture——

'What's the matter with Sefton?' said Devigne one night at the club after dinner.

'Don't know that anything's the matter with him,' said Merion. 'He hasn't been here lately.'

'I saw him the last time he was here, and he seemed pretty queer. Wanted to let me his studio.'

'It's not a bad studio,' said Merion, dispassionately.

'He's got rid of it now, anyhow. He's got a studio out at Richmond, and the deuce of a lot of time he must waste getting there and back. Besides, what does he do about models?'

'That's a point I've been wondering about myself,' said Merion. 'He'd got Rose Rose for his "Aphrodite," and it looked as if it might be a pretty good thing when I saw it. But, as you know, she died. She was troublesome in some ways, but, taking her all round, I don't know where to find anybody as good today. What's Sefton doing about it?'

'He hasn't got a model at all at present. I know that for a fact, because I asked him.'

'Well,' said Merion, 'he may have got the thing on further than I thought he would in the time. Some chaps can work from memory all right, though I can't do it myself. He's not chucked the picture, I suppose?'

'No; he's not done that. In fact, the picture's his excuse now, if you want him to go anywhere and do anything. But that's not it: the chap's altogether changed. He used to be a genial sort of bounder—bit tyrannical in his manner, perhaps—thought he knew everything. Still, you could talk to him. He was sociable. As a matter of fact, he did know a good deal. Now it's quite different. If you ever do see him—and that's not often—he's got nothing to say to you. He's just going back to his work. That sort of thing.'

'You're too imaginative,' said Merion. 'I never knew a man who varied less than Sefton. Give me his address, will you? I mean his studio. I'll go and look him up one morning. I should like to see how that "Aphrodite's" getting on. I tell you it was promising; no nonsense about it.'

One sunny morning Merion knocked at the door of the studio at Richmond. He heard the sound of footsteps crossing the studio, then Sefton's voice rang out.

'Who's there?'

'Merion. I've travelled miles to see the thing you call a picture.'

'I've got a model.'

'And what does that matter?' asked Merion.

'Well, I'd be awfully glad if you'd come back in an hour. We'd have lunch together somewhere.'

'Right,' said Merion, sardonically. 'I'll come back in about seven million hours. Wait for me.'

He went back to London and his own studio in a state of fury. Sefton had never been a man to pose. He had never put on side about his work. He was always willing to show it to old and intimate friends whose judgment he could trust; and now, when the oldest of his friends had travelled down to Richmond to see him, he was told to come back in an hour, and that they might then lunch together!

'This lets me out,' said Merion, savagely.

But he always speaks well of Sefton nowadays. He maintains that Sefton's 'Aphrodite' would have been a success anyhow. The suicide made a good deal of talk at the time, and a special attendant was necessary to regulate the crowds round it, when, as directed by his will, the picture was exhibited at the Royal Academy. He was found in his studio many hours after his death; and he had scrawled on a blank canvas, much as he left his directions to his charwoman: 'I have finished it, but I can't stand any more.'

The Confession of Charles Linkworth

E. F. BENSON

Dr Teesdale had occasion to attend the condemned man once or twice during the week before his execution, and found him, as is often the case, when his last hope of life has vanished, quiet and perfectly resigned to his fate, and not seeming to look forward with any dread to the morning that each hour that passed brought nearer and nearer. The bitterness of death appeared to be over for him: it was done with when he was told that his appeal was refused. But for those days while hope was not yet quite abandoned, the wretched man had drunk of death daily. In all his experience the doctor had never seen a man so wildly and passionately tenacious of life, nor one so strongly knit to this material world by the sheer animal lust of living. Then the news that hope could no longer be entertained was told him, and his spirit passed out of the grip of that agony of torture and suspense, and accepted the inevitable with indifference. Yet the change was so extraordinary that it seemed to the doctor rather that the news had completely stunned his powers of feeling, and he was below the numbed surface, still knit into material things as strongly as ever. He had fainted when the result was told him, and Dr Teesdale had been called in to attend him. But the fit was but transient, and he came out of it into full consciousness of what had happened.

The murder had been a deed of peculiar horror, and there was nothing of sympathy in the mind of the public towards the perpetrator. Charles Linkworth, who now lay under capital sentence, was the keeper of a small stationery store in Sheffield, and there lived with him his wife and mother. The latter was the victim of his atrocious crime; the motive of it being to get possession of the sum of five hundred pounds, which was this woman's property. Linkworth, as came out at the trial, was in debt to the extent of a hundred pounds at the time, and during his wife's absence from home on a visit to relations, he strangled his mother, and during the night buried the body in the small back-garden of his house. On his wife's return, he had a sufficiently plausible tale to account for the elder Mrs Linkworth's disappearance, for there had been constant jarrings and bickerings between him and his mother for the last year or two, and she had more than once threatened to withdraw herself and the eight shillings a week which she contributed to household expenses, and purchase an annuity with her money. It was true, also, that during the younger Mrs Linkworth's absence from home, mother and son had had a violent quarrel arising originally from some trivial point in household management, and that in consequence of this, she had actually drawn her money out of the bank, intending to leave Sheffield next day and settle in London, where she had friends. That evening she told him this, and during the night he killed her.

His next step, before his wife's return, was logical and sound. He packed up all his mother's possessions and took them to the station, from which he saw them despatched to town by passenger train, and in the evening he asked several friends in to supper, and told them of his mother's departure. He did not (logically also, and in accordance with what they probably already knew) feign regret, but said that he and she had never got on well together, and that the cause of peace and quietness was furthered by her going. He told the same story to his wife on her return, identical in every detail, adding, however, that the quarrel had been a violent one, and that his mother had not even left him her address. This again was wisely thought of: it would prevent his wife from writing to her. She appeared to accept his story completely: indeed there was nothing strange or suspicious about it.

For a while he behaved with the composure and astuteness which most criminals possess up to a certain point, the lack of which, after that, is generally the cause of their detection. He did not, for instance, immediately pay off his debts, but took into his house a young man as lodger, who occupied his mother's room, and he dismissed the assistant in his shop, and did the entire serving himself. This gave the impression of economy, and at the same time he openly spoke of the great improvement in his trade, and not till a month had passed did he cash any of the bank-notes which he had found in a locked drawer in his mother's room. Then he changed two notes of fifty pounds and paid off his creditors.

At that point his astuteness and composure failed him. He opened a deposit account at a local bank with four more fifty-pound notes, instead of being patient, and increasing his balance at the savings bank pound by pound, and he got uneasy about that which he had buried deep enough for security in the back garden. Thinking to render himself safer in this regard, he ordered a cartload of slag and stone fragments, and with the help of his lodger employed the summer evenings when work was over in building a sort of rockery over the spot. Then came the chance circumstance which really set match to this dangerous train. There was a fire in the lost luggage office at King's Cross Station (from which he ought to have claimed his mother's property) and one of the two boxes was partially burned. The company was liable for compensation, and his mother's name on her linen, and a letter with the Sheffield address on it, led to the arrival of a purely official and formal notice, stating that the company were prepared to consider claims. It was directed to Mrs Linkworth, and Charles Linkworth's wife received and read it.

It seemed a sufficiently harmless document, but it was endorsed with his death-warrant. For he could give no explanation at all of the fact of the boxes still lying at King's Cross Station, beyond suggesting that some accident had happened to his mother. Clearly he had to put the matter in the hands of the police, with a view to tracing her movements, and if it proved that she was dead, claiming her property, which she had already drawn out of the bank. Such at least was the course urged on him by his wife and lodger, in whose presence the communication from the railway officials was read out, and it was impossible to refuse to take it. Then the silent, uncreaking machinery of justice, characteristic of England, began to move forward. Quiet men lounged about Smith Street, visited banks, observed the supposed increase in trade, and from a house near by looked into the garden where ferns were already flourishing on the rockery. Then came the arrest and the trial, which did not last very long, and on a certain Saturday night the verdict. Smart women in large hats had made the court bright with colour, and in all the crowd there was not one who felt any sympathy with the young athletic-looking man who was condemned. Many of the audience were elderly and respectable mothers, and the crime had been an outrage on motherhood, and they listened to the unfolding of the flawless evidence with strong approval. They thrilled a little when the judge put on the awful and ludicrous little black cap, and spoke the sentence appointed by God.

Linkworth went to pay the penalty for the atrocious deed, which no one who had heard the evidence could possibly doubt that he had done with the same indifference as had marked his entire demeanour since he knew his appeal had failed. The prison chaplain who had attended him had done his utmost to get him to confess, but his efforts had been quite ineffectual, and to the last he asserted, though without protestation, his innocence. On a bright September morning, when the sun shone warm on the terrible little procession that crossed the prison yard to the shed where was erected the apparatus of death, justice was done, and Dr Teesdale was satisfied that life was immediately extinct. He had been present on the scaffold, had watched the bolt drawn, and the hooded and pinioned figure drop into the pit. He had heard the chunk and creak of the rope as the sudden weight came on to it, and looking down he had seen the queer twitchings of the hanged body. They had lasted but a second or two; the execution had been perfectly satisfactory.

An hour later he made the post-mortem examination, and found that his view had been correct: the vertebrae of the spine had been broken at the neck, and death must have been absolutely instantaneous. It was hardly necessary even to make that little piece of dissection that proved this, but for the sake of form he did so. And at that moment he had a very curious and vivid mental impression that the spirit of the dead man was close beside him, as if it still dwelt in the broken habitation of its body. But there was no question at all that the body was dead: it had been dead an hour. Then followed another little circumstance that at the first seemed insignificant though curious also. One of the warders entered, and asked if the rope which had been used an hour ago, and was the hangman's perquisite, had by mistake been brought into the mortuary with the body. But there was no trace of it, and it seemed to have vanished altogether, though it was a singular thing to be lost: it was not here; it was not on the scaffold. And though the disappearance was of no particular moment it was quite inexplicable.

Dr Teesdale was a bachelor and a man of independent means, and lived in a tall-windowed and commodious house in Bedford Square, where a plain cook of surpassing excellence looked after his food, and her husband his person. There was no need for him to practise a profession at all, and he performed his work at the prison for the sake of the study of the minds of criminals. Most crime—the transgression, that is, of the rule of conduct which the human race has framed for the sake of its own preservation—he held to be either the result of some abnormality of the brain or of starvation. Crimes of theft, for instance, he would by no means refer to one head; often it is true they were the result of actual want, but more often dictated by some obscure disease of the brain. In marked cases it was labelled as kleptomania, but he was convinced there were many others which did not fall directly under dictation of physical need. More especially was this the case where the crime in question involved also some deed of violence, and he mentally placed underneath this heading, as he went home that evening, the criminal at whose last moments he had been present that morning. The crime had been abominable, the need of money not so very pressing, and the very abomination and unnaturalness of the murder inclined him to consider the murderer as lunatic rather than criminal. He had been, as far as was known, a man of quiet and kindly disposition, a good husband, a sociable neighbour. And then he had committed a crime, just one, which put him outside all pales. So monstrous a deed, whether perpetrated by a sane man or a mad one, was intolerable; there was no use for the doer of it on this planet at all. But somehow the doctor felt that he would have been more at one with the execution of justice, if the dead man had confessed. It was morally certain that he was guilty, but he wished that when there was no longer any hope for him he had endorsed the verdict himself.

He dined alone that evening, and after dinner sat in his study which adjoined the dining-room, and feeling disinclined to read, sat in his great red chair opposite the fireplace, and let his mind graze where it would. At once almost, it went back to the curious sensation he had experienced that morning, of feeling that the spirit of Linkworth was present in the mortuary, though life had been extinct for an hour. It was not the first time, especially in cases of sudden death, that he had felt a similar conviction, though perhaps it had never been quite so unmistakable as it had been today. Yet the feeling, to his mind, was quite probably formed on a natural and psychical truth. The spirit—it may be remarked that he was a believer in the doctrine of future life, and the non-extinction of the soul with the death of the body—was very likely unable or unwilling to quit at once and altogether the earthly habitation, very likely it lingered there, earthbound, for a while. In his leisure hours Dr Teesdale was a considerable student of the occult, for like most advanced and proficient physicians, he clearly recognised how narrow was the boundary of separation between soul and body, how tremendous the influence of the intangible was over material things, and it presented no difficulty to his mind that a disembodied spirit should be able to communicate directly with those who still were bounded by the finite and material.

His meditations, which were beginning to group themselves into definite sequence, were interrupted at this moment. On his desk near at hand stood his telephone, and the bell rang, not with its usual metallic insistence, but very faintly, as if the current was weak, or the mechanism impaired. However, it certainly was ringing, and he got up and took the combined ear and mouthpiece off its hook.

'Yes, yes,' he said, 'who is it?'

There was a whisper in reply almost inaudible, and quite unintelligible.

'I can't hear you,' he said.

Again the whisper sounded, but with no greater distinctness. Then it ceased altogether.

He stood there, for some half minute or so, waiting for it to be renewed, but beyond the usual chuckling and croaking, which showed, however, that he was in communication with some other instrument, there was silence. Then he replaced the receiver, rang up the Exchange, and gave his number.

'Can you tell me what number rang me up just now?' he asked.

There was a short pause, then it was given him. It was the number of the prison, where he was doctor

'Put me on to it, please,' he said.

This was done.

'You rang me up just now,' he said down the tube. 'Yes; I am Doctor Teesdale. What is it? I could not hear what you said.'

The voice came back quite clear and intelligible.

'Some mistake, sir,' it said. 'We haven't rang you up.'

'But the Exchange tells me you did, three minutes ago.'

'Mistake at the Exchange, sir,' said the voice.

'Very odd. Well, good night. Warder Draycott, isn't it?'

'Yes, sir; good night, sir.'

Dr Teesdale went back to his big arm-chair, still less inclined to read. He let his thoughts wander on for a while, without giving them definite direction, but ever and again his mind kept coming back to that strange little incident of the telephone. Often and often he had been rung up by some mistake, often and often he had been put on to the wrong number by the Exchange, but there was something in this very subdued ringing of the telephone bell, and the unintelligible whisperings at the other end that suggested a very curious train of reflection to his mind, and soon he found himself pacing up and down his room, with his thoughts eagerly feeding on a most unusual pasture.

'But it's impossible,' he said, aloud.

He went down as usual to the prison next morning, and once again he was strangely beset with the feeling that there was some unseen presence there. He had before now had some odd psychical experiences, and knew that he was a 'sensitive'—one, that is, who is capable, under certain circumstances, of receiving supernormal impressions, and of having glimpses of the unseen world that lies about us. And this morning the presence of which he was conscious was that of the man who had been executed yesterday morning. It was local, and he felt it most strongly in the little prison yard, and as he passed the door of the condemned cell. So strong was it there that he would not have been surprised if the figure of the man had been visible to him, and as he passed through the door at the end of the passage, he turned round, actually expecting to see it. All the time, too, he was aware of a profound horror at his heart; this unseen presence strangely disturbed him. And the poor soul, he felt, wanted something done for it. Not for a moment did he doubt that this impression of his was objective, it was no imaginative phantom of his own invention that made itself so real. The spirit of Linkworth was there.

He passed into the infirmary, and for a couple of hours busied himself with his work. But all the time he was aware that the same invisible presence was near him, though its force was manifestly less here than in those places which had been more intimately associated with the man. Finally, before he left, in order to test his theory he looked into the execution shed. But next moment with a face suddenly stricken pale, he came out again, closing the door hastily. At the top of the steps stood a figure hooded and pinioned, but hazy of outline and only faintly visible. But it was visible, there was no mistake about it.

Dr Teesdale was a man of good nerve, and he recovered himself almost immediately, ashamed of his temporary panic. The terror that had blanched his face was chiefly the effect of startled nerves, not of terrified heart, and yet deeply interested as he was in psychical phenomena, he could not command himself sufficiently to go back there. Or rather he commanded himself, but his muscles refused to act on the message. If this poor earthbound spirit had any communication to make to him, he certainly much preferred that it should be made at a distance. As far as he could understand, its range was circumscribed. It haunted the prison yard, the condemned cell, the execution shed, it was more faintly felt in the infirmary. Then a further point suggested itself to his mind, and he went back to his room and sent for Warder Draycott, who had answered him on the telephone last night.

'You are quite sure,' he asked, 'that nobody rang me up last night, just before I rang you up?'

There was a certain hesitation in the man's manner which the doctor noticed.

'I don't see how it could be possible, sir,' he said. 'I had been sitting close by the telephone for half an hour before, and again before that. I must have seen him, if anyone had been to the instrument.'

'And you *saw* no one?' said the doctor with a slight emphasis.

The man became more markedly ill at ease.

'No, sir, I *saw* no one, ' he said, with the same emphasis.

Dr Teesdale looked away from him.

'But you had perhaps the impression that there was someone there?' he asked, carelessly, as if it was a point of no interest.

Clearly Warder Draycott had something on his mind, which he found it hard to speak of.

'Well, sir, if you put it like that,' he began. 'But you would tell me I was half asleep, or had eaten something that disagreed with me at my supper.'

The doctor dropped his careless manner.

'I should do nothing of the kind,' he said, 'any more than you would tell me that I had dropped asleep last night, when I heard my telephone bell ring. Mind you, Draycott, it did not ring as usual, I could only just hear it ringing, though it was close to me. And I could only hear a whisper when I put my ear to it. But when you spoke I heard you quite distinctly. Now I believe there was something—somebody—at this end of the telephone. You were here, and though you saw no one, you, too, felt there was someone there.

The man nodded.

'I'm not a nervous man, sir,' he said, 'and I don't deal in fancies. But there was something there. It was hovering about the instrument, and it wasn't the wind, because there wasn't a breath of wind stirring, and the night was warm. And I shut the window to make certain. But it went about the room, sir, for an hour or more. It rustled the leaves of the telephone book, and it ruffled my hair when it came close to me. And it was bitter cold, sir.'

The doctor looked him straight in the face.

'Did it remind you of what had been done yesterday morning?' he asked suddenly.

Again the man hesitated.

'Yes, sir,' he said at length. 'Convict Charles Linkworth.'

Dr Teesdale nodded reassuringly.

'That's it,' he said. 'Now, are you on duty tonight?'

'Yes, sir, I wish I wasn't.'

'I know how you feel, I have felt exactly the same myself. Now whatever this is, it seems to want to communicate with me. By the way, did you have any disturbance in the prison last night?'

'Yes, sir, there was half a dozen men who had the nightmare. Yelling and screaming they were, and quiet men, too, usually. It happens sometimes the night after an execution. I've known it before, though nothing like what it was last night.'

'I see. Now, if this—this thing you can't see wants to get at the telephone again tonight, give it every chance. It will probably come about the same time. I can't tell you why, but that usually happens. So unless you must, don't be in this room where the telephone is, just for an hour to give it plenty of time between half-past nine and half-past ten. I will be ready for it at the other end. Supposing I am rung up, I will, when it has finished, ring you up to make sure that I was not being called in—in the usual way.'

'And there is nothing to be afraid of, sir?' asked the man.

Dr Teesdale remembered his own moment of terror this morning, but he spoke quite sincerely.

'I am sure there is nothing to be afraid of,' he said, reassuringly.

Dr Teesdale had a dinner engagement that night, which he broke, and was sitting alone in his study by half past-nine. In the present state of human ignorance as to the law which governs the movements of spirits severed from the body, he could not tell the warder why it was that their visits are so often periodic, timed to punctuality according to our scheme of hours, but in scenes of tabulated instances of the appearance of *revenants*, especially if the soul was in sore need of help, as might be the case here, he found that they came at the same hour of day or night. As a rule, too, their power of making themselves seen or heard or felt grew greater for some little while after death, subsequently growing weaker as they became less earthbound, or often after that ceasing altogether, and he was prepared tonight for a less indistinct impression. The spirit apparently for the early hours of its disembodiment is weak, like a moth newly broken out from its chrysalis—and then suddenly the telephone bell rang, not so faintly as the night before, but still not with its ordinary imperative tone.

Dr Teesdale instantly got up, put the receiver to his ear. And what he heard was heart-broken sobbing, strong spasms that seemed to tear the weeper.

He waited for a little before speaking, himself cold with some nameless fear, and yet profoundly moved to help, if he was able.

'Yes, yes,' he said at length, hearing his own voice tremble. 'I am Dr Teesdale. What can I do for you? And who are you?' he added, though he felt that it was a needless question.

Slowly the sobbing died down, the whispers took its place, still broken by crying.

'I want to tell, sir—I want to tell—I must tell.'

'Yes, tell me, what is it?' said the doctor.

'No, not you—another gentleman, who used to come to see me. Will you speak to him what I say to you?—I can't make him hear me or see me.'

'Who are you?' asked Dr Teesdale suddenly.

'Charles Linkworth. I thought you knew. I am very miserable. I can't leave the prison—and it is cold. Will you send for the other gentleman?'

'Do you mean the chaplain?' asked Dr Teesdale.

'Yes, the chaplain. He read the service when I went across the yard yesterday. I shan't be so miserable when I have told.'

The doctor hesitated a moment. This was a strange story that he would have to tell Mr Dawkins, the prison chaplain, that at the other end of the telephone was the spirit of the man executed yesterday. And yet he soberly believed that it was so, that this unhappy spirit was in misery and wanted to 'tell'. There was no need to ask what he wanted to tell.

'Yes, I will ask him to come here,' he said at length.

'Thank you, sir, a thousand times. You will make him come, won't you?'

The voice was growing fainter.

'It must be tomorrow night,' it said. 'I can't speak longer now. I have to go to see—oh, my God, my God.'

The sobs broke out afresh, sounding fainter and fainter. But it was in a frenzy of terrified interest that Dr Teesdale spoke.

'To see what?' he cried. 'Tell me what you are doing, what is happening to you?'

'I can't tell you; I mayn't tell you,' said the voice very faint. 'That is part——' and it died away altogether.

Dr Teesdale waited a little, but there was no further sound of any kind, except the chuckling and croaking of the instrument. He put the receiver on to its hook again, and then became aware for the first time that his forehead was streaming with some cold dew of horror. His ears sang; his heart beat very quick and faint, and he sat down to recover himself. Once or twice he asked himself if it was possible that some terrible joke was being played on him, but he knew that could not be so; he felt perfectly sure that he had been speaking with a soul in torment of contrition for the terrible and irremediable act it had committed. It was no delusion of his senses, either; here in this comfortable room of his in Bedford Square, with London cheerfully roaring round him, he had spoken with the spirit of Charles Linkworth.

But he had no time (nor indeed inclination, for somehow his soul sat shuddering within him) to indulge in meditation. First of all he rang up the prison.

'Warder Draycott?' he asked.

There was a perceptible tremor in the man's voice as he answered.

'Yes, sir. Is it Dr Teesdale?'

'Yes. Has anything happened here with you?'

Twice it seemed that the man tried to speak and could not. At the third attempt the words came.

'Yes, sir. He has been here. I saw him go into the room where the telephone is.'

'Ah! Did you speak to him?'

'No, sir: I sweated and prayed. And there's half a dozen men as have been screaming in their sleep tonight. But it's quiet again now. I think he has gone into the execution shed.'

'Yes. Well, I think there will be no more disturbance now. By the way, please give me Mr Dawkins's home address.

*			*			*

This was given him, and Dr Teesdale proceeded to write to the chaplain, asking him to dine with him on the following night. But suddenly he found that he could not write at his accustomed desk, with the telephone standing close to him, and he went upstairs to the drawing-room which he seldom used, except when he entertained his friends. There he recaptured the serenity of his nerves, and could control his hand. The note simply asked Mr Dawkins to dine with him next night, when he wished to tell him a very strange history and ask his help. 'Even if you have any other engagement,' he concluded, 'I seriously request you to give it up. Tonight, I did the same. I should bitterly have regretted it if I had not.'

Next night accordingly, the two sat at their dinner in the doctor's dining-room, and when they were left to their cigarettes and coffee the doctor spoke.

'You must not think me mad, my dear Dawkins,' he said, 'when you hear what I have got to tell you.'

Mr Dawkins laughed.

'I will certainly promise not to do that,' he said.

'Good. Last night and the night before, a little later in the evening than this, I spoke through the telephone with the spirit of the man we saw executed two days ago. Charles Linkworth.'

The chaplain did not laugh. He pushed back his chair, looking annoyed.

'Teesdale,' he said, 'is it to tell me this—I don't want to be rude—but this bogey-tale that you have brought me here this evening?'

'Yes. You have not heard half of it. He asked me last night to get hold of you. He wants to tell you something. We can guess, I think, what it is.'

Dawkins got up.

'Please let me hear no more of it,' he said. 'The dead do not return. In what state or under what condition they exist has not been revealed to us. But they have done with all material things.'

'But I must tell you more,' said the doctor. 'Two nights ago I was rung up, but very faintly, and could only hear whispers. I instantly inquired where the call came from and was told it came from the prison. I rang up the prison, and Warder Draycott told me that nobody had rung me up. He, too, was conscious of a presence.'

'I think that man drinks,' said Dawkins, sharply.

The doctor paused a moment.

'My dear fellow, you should not say that sort of thing,' he said. 'He is one of the steadiest men we have got. And if he drinks, why not I also?'

The chaplain sat down again.

'You must forgive me,' he said, 'but I can't go into this. These are dangerous matters to meddle with. Besides, how do you know it is not a hoax?'

'Played by whom?' asked the doctor. 'Hark!'

The telephone bell suddenly rang. It was clearly audible to the doctor.

'Don't you hear it?' he said.

'Hear what?'

'The telephone bell ringing.'

'I hear no bell,' said the chaplain, rather angrily. 'There is no bell ringing.'

The doctor did not answer, but went through into his study, and turned on the lights. Then he took the receiver and mouthpiece off its hook.

'Yes?' he said, in a voice that trembled. 'Who is it? Yes: Mr Dawkins is here. I will try and get him to speak to you.'

He went back into the other room.

'Dawkins,' he said, 'there is a soul in agony. I pray you to listen. For God's sake come and listen.'

The chaplain hesitated a moment.

'As you will,' he said.

He took up the receiver and put it to his ear.

'I am Mr Dawkins,' he said.

He waited.

'I can hear nothing whatever,' he said at length. 'Ah, there was something there. The faintest whisper.'

'Ah, try to hear, try to hear!' said the doctor.

Again the chaplain listened. Suddenly he laid the instrument down, frowning.

'Something—somebody said, "I killed her, I confess it. I want to be forgiven." It's a hoax, my dear Teesdale. Somebody knowing your spiritualistic leanings is playing a very grim joke on you. I *can't* believe it.'

Dr Teesdale took up the receiver.

'I am Dr Teesdale,' he said. 'Can you give Mr Dawkins some sign that it is you?'

Then he laid it down again.

'He says he thinks he can,' he said. 'We must wait.'

The evening was again very warm, and the window into the paved yard at the back of the house was open. For five minutes or so the two men stood in silence, waiting, and nothing happened. Then the chaplain spoke.

'I think that is sufficiently conclusive,' he said.

Even as he spoke a very cold draught of air suddenly blew into the room, making the papers on the desk rustle. Dr Teesdale went to the window and closed it.

'Did you feel that?' he asked.

'Yes, a breath of air. Chilly.'

Once again in the closed room it stirred again.

'And did you feel that?' asked the doctor.

The chaplain nodded. He felt his heart hammering in his throat suddenly.

'Defend us from all peril and danger of this coming night,' he exclaimed.

'Something is coming!' said the doctor.

As he spoke it came. In the centre of the room not three yards away from them stood the figure of a man with his head bent over on to his shoulder, so that the face was not visible. Then he took his head in both his hands and raised it like a weight, and looked them in the face. The eyes and tongue protruded, a livid mark was round the neck. Then there came a sharp rattle on the boards of the floor, and the figure was no longer there. But on the floor there lay a new rope.

For a long while neither spoke. The sweat poured off the doctor's face, and the chaplain's white lips whispered prayers. Then by a huge effort the doctor pulled himself together. He pointed at the rope.

'It has been missing since the execution,' he said.

Then again the telephone bell rang. This time the chaplain needed no prompting. He went to it at once and the ringing ceased. For a while he listened in silence.

'Charles Linkworth,' he said at length, 'in the sight of God, in whose presence you stand, are you truly sorry for your sin?'

Some answer inaudible to the doctor came, and the chaplain closed his eyes. And Dr Teesdale knelt as he heard the words of the Absolution.

At the close there was silence again.

'I can hear nothing more,' said the chaplain, replacing the receiver.

Presently the doctor's man-servant came in with the tray of spirits and syphon. Dr Teesdale pointed without looking to where the apparition had been.

'Take the rope that is there and burn it, Parker,' he said.

There was a moment's silence.

'There is no rope, sir,' said Parker.

On the Brighton Road

RICHARD MIDDLETON

Slowly the sun had climbed up the hard white downs, till it broke with little of the mysterious ritual of dawn upon a sparkling world of snow. There had been a hard frost during the night, and the birds, who hopped about here and there with scant tolerance of life, left no trace of their passage on the silver pavements. In places the sheltered caverns of the hedges broke the monotony of the whiteness that had fallen upon the coloured earth, and overhead the sky melted from orange to deep blue, from deep blue to a blue so pale that it suggested a thin paper screen rather than illimitable space. Across the level fields there came a cold, silent wind which blew fine dust of snow from the trees, but hardly stirred the crested hedges. Once above the sky-line, the sun seemed to climb more quickly, and as it rose higher it began to give out a heat that blended with the keenness of the wind.

It may have been this strange alternation of heat and cold that disturbed the tramp in his dreams, for he struggled for a moment with the snow that covered him, like a man who finds himself twisted uncomfortably in the bed-clothes, and then sat up with staring, questioning eyes. 'Lord! I thought I was in bed,' he said to himself as he took in the vacant landscape, 'and all the while I was out here.' He stretched his limbs, and, rising carefully to his feet, shook the snow off his body. As he did so the wind set him shivering, and he knew that his bed had been warm.

'Come, I feel pretty fit,' he thought. 'I suppose I am lucky to wake at all in this. Or unlucky—it isn't much of a business to come back to.' He looked up and saw the downs shining against the blue like the Alps on a picture-postcard. 'That means another forty miles or so, I suppose,' he continued grimly. 'Lord knows what I did yesterday. Walked till I was done, and now I'm only about twelve miles from Brighton. Damn the snow, damn Brighton, damn everything!' The sun crept up higher and higher, and he started walking patiently along the road with his back turned to the hills.

'Am I glad or sorry that it was only sleep that took me, glad or sorry, glad or sorry?' His thoughts seemed to arrange themselves in a metrical accompaniment to the steady thud of his footsteps, and he hardly sought an answer to his question. It was good enough to walk to.

Presently, when three milestones had loitered past, he overtook a boy who was stooping to light a cigarette. He wore no overcoat, and looked unspeakably fragile against the snow. 'Are you on the road, guv'nor?' asked the boy huskily as he passed.

'I think I am,' the tramp said.

'Oh! then I'll come a bit of the way with you if you don't walk too fast. It's a bit lonesome walking this time of day.' The tramp nodded his head, and the boy started limping along by his side.

'I'm eighteen,' he said casually. 'I bet you thought I was younger.'

'Fifteen, I'd have said.'

'You'd have backed a loser. Eighteen last August, and I've been on the road six years. I ran away from home five times when I was a little 'un, and the police took me back each time. Very good to me, the police was. Now I haven't got a home to run away from.'

'Nor have I,' the tramp said calmly.

'Oh, I can see what you are,' the boy panted; 'you're a gentleman come down. It's harder for you than for me.' The tramp glanced at the limping, feeble figure and lessened his pace.

'I haven't been at it as long as you have,' he admitted.

'No, I could tell that by the way you walk. You haven't got tired yet. Perhaps you expect something the other end?'

The tramp reflected for a moment. 'I don't know,' he said bitterly, 'I'm always expecting things.'

'You'll grow out of that,' the boy commented. 'It's warmer in London, but it's harder to come by grub. There isn't much in it really.'

'Still, there's the chance of meeting somebody there who will understand——'

'Country people are better,' the boy interrupted. 'Last night I took a lease of a barn for nothing and slept with the cows, and this morning the farmer routed me out and gave me tea and toke because I was little. Of course, I score there; but in London, soup on the Embankment at night, and all the rest of the time coppers moving you on.'

'I dropped by the roadside last night and slept where I fell. It's a wonder I didn't die,' the tramp said. The boy looked at him sharply.

'How do you know you didn't?' he said.

'I don't see it,' the tramp said, after a pause.

'I tell you,' the boy said hoarsely, 'people like us can't get away from this sort of thing if we want to. Always hungry and thirsty and dog-tired and walking all the time. And yet if any one offers me a nice home and work my stomach feels sick. Do I look strong? I know I'm little for my age, but I've been knocking about like this for six years, and do you think I'm not dead? I was drowned bathing at Margate, and I was killed by a gipsy with a spike; he knocked my head right in, and twice I was froze like you last night, and a motor cut me down on this very road, and yet I'm walking along here now, walking to London to walk away from it again, because I can't help it. Dead! I tell you we can't get away if we want to.'

The boy broke off in a fit of coughing, and the tramp paused while he recovered.

'You'd better borrow my coat for a bit, Tommy,' he said, 'your cough's pretty bad.'

'You go to hell!' the boy said fiercely, puffing at his cigarette; 'I'm all right. I was telling you about the road. You haven't got down to it yet, but you'll find out presently. We're all dead, all of us who're on it, and we're all tired, yet somehow we can't leave it. There's nice smells in the summer, dust and hay and the wind smack in your face on a hot day; and it's nice waking up in the wet grass on a fine morning. I don't know, I don't know——' he lurched forward suddenly, and the tramp caught him in his arms.

'I'm sick,' the boy whispered—'sick.'

The tramp looked up and down the road, but he could see no houses or any sign of help. Yet even as he supported the boy doubtfully in the middle of the road a motor-car suddenly flashed in the middle distance, and came smoothly through the snow.

'What's the trouble?' said the driver quietly as he pulled up. 'I'm a doctor.' He looked at the boy keenly and listened to his strained breathing.

'Pneumonia,' he commented. 'I'll give him a lift to the infirmary, and you, too, if you like.'

The tramp thought of the workhouse and shook his head. 'I'd rather walk,' he said.

The boy winked faintly as they lifted him into the car.

'I'll meet you beyond Reigate,' he murmured to the tramp. 'You'll see.' And the car vanished along the white road.

All the morning the tramp splashed through the thawing snow, but at midday he begged sone bread at a cottage door and crept into a lonely barn to eat it. It was warm in there, and after his meal he fell asleep among the hay. It was dark when he woke, and started trudging once more through the slushy roads.

Two miles beyond Reigate a figure, a fragile figure, slipped out of the darkness to meet him.

'On the road, guv'nor?' said a husky voice. 'Then I'll come a bit of the way with you if you don't walk too fast. It's a bit lonesome walking this time of day.'

'But the pneumonia!' cried the tramp aghast.

'I died at Crawley this morning,' said the boy.

Bone to His Bone

E. G. SWAIN

William Whitehead, Fellow of Emmanuel College, in the University of Cambridge, became Vicar of Stoneground in the year 1731. The annals of his incumbency were doubtless short and simple: they have not survived. In his day were no newspapers to collect gossip, no Parish Magazines to record the simple events of parochial life. One event, however, of greater moment then than now, is recorded in two places. Vicar Whitehead failed in health after 23 years of work, and journeyed to Bath in what his monument calls 'the vain hope of being restored'. The duration of his visit is unknown; it is reasonable to suppose that he made his journey in the summer, it is certain that by the month of November his physician told him to lay aside all hope of recovery.

Then it was that the thoughts of the patient turned to the comfortable straggling vicarage he had left at Stoneground, in which he had hoped to end his days. He prayed that his successor might be as happy there as he had been himself. Setting his affairs in order, as became one who had but a short time to live, he executed a will, bequeathing to the Vicars of Stoneground, for ever, the close of ground he had recently purchased because it lay next the vicarage garden. And by a codicil, he added to the bequest his library of books. Within a few days, William Whitehead was gathered to his fathers.

A mural tablet in the north aisle of the church, records, in Latin, his services and his bequests, his two marriages, and his fruitless journey to Bath. The house he loved, but never again saw, was taken down 40 years later, and re-built by Vicar James Devie. The garden, with Vicar Whitehead's 'close of ground' and other adjacent lands, was opened out and planted, somewhat before 1850, by Vicar Robert Towerson. The aspect of everything has changed. But in a convenient chamber on the first floor of the present vicarage the library of Vicar Whitehead stands very much as he used it and loved it, and as he bequeathed it to his successors 'for ever'.

The books there are arranged as he arranged and ticketed them. Little slips of paper, sometimes bearing interesting fragments of writing, still mark his places. His marginal comments still give life to pages from which all other interest has faded, and he would have but a dull imagination who could sit in the chamber amidst these books without ever being carried back 180 years into the past, to the time when the newest of them left the printer's hands.

Of those into whose possession the books have come, some have doubtless loved them more, and some less; some, perhaps, have left them severely alone. But neither those who loved them, nor those who loved them not, have lost them, and they passed, some century and a half after William Whitehead's death, into the hands of Mr Batchel, who loved them as a father loves his children. He lived alone, and had few domestic cares to distract his mind. He was able, therefore, to enjoy to the full what Vicar Whitehead had enjoyed so long before him. During many a long summer evening would he sit poring over long-forgotten books; and since the chamber, otherwise called the library, faced the south, he could also spend sunny winter mornings there without discomfort. Writing at a small table, or reading as he stood at a tall desk, he would browse amongst the books like an ox in a pleasant pasture.

There were other times also, at which Mr Batchel would use the books. Not being a sound sleeper (for book-loving men seldom are), he elected to use as a bedroom one of the two chambers which opened at either side into the library. The arrangement enabled him to beguile many a sleepless hour amongst the books, and in view of these nocturnal visits he kept a candle standing in a sconce above the desk, and matches always ready to his hand.

There was one disadvantage in this close proximity of his bed to the library. Owing, apparently, to some defect in the fittings of the room, which, having no mechanical tastes, Mr Batchel had never investigated, there could be heard, in the stillness of the night, exactly such sounds as might arise from a person moving about amongst the books. Visitors using the other adjacent room would often remark at breakfast, that they had heard their host in the library at one or two o'clock in the morning, when, in fact, he had not left his bed. Invariably Mr Batchel allowed them to suppose that he had been where they thought him. He disliked idle controversy, and was unwilling to afford an opening for supernatural talk. Knowing well enough the sounds by which his guests had been deceived, he wanted no other explanation of them than his own, though it was of too vague a character to count as an explanation. He conjectured that the window-sashes, or the doors, or 'something', were defective, and was too phlegmatic and too unpractical to make any investigation. The matter gave him no concern.

Persons whose sleep is uncertain are apt to have their worst nights when they would like their best. The consciousness of a special need for rest seems to bring enough mental disturbance to forbid it. So on

Christmas Eve, in the year 1907, Mr Batchel, who would have liked to
sleep well, in view of the labours of Christmas Day, lay hopelessly wide
awake. He exhausted all the known devices for courting sleep, and, at
the end, found himself wider awake than ever. A brilliant moon shone
into his room, for he hated window-blinds. There was a light wind
blowing, and the sounds in the library were more than usually suggestive
of a person moving about. He almost determined to have the sashes
'seen to', although he could seldom be induced to have anything 'seen
to'. He disliked changes, even for the better, and would submit to great
inconvenience rather than have things altered with which he had
become familiar.

As he revolved these matters in his mind, he heard the clocks strike
the hour of midnight, and having now lost all hope of falling asleep, he
rose from his bed, got into a large dressing gown which hung in
readiness for such occasions, and passed into the library, with the
intention of reading himself sleepy, if he could.

The moon, by this time, had passed out of the south, and the library
seemed all the darker by contrast with the moonlit chamber he had left.
He could see nothing but two blue-grey rectangles formed by the
windows against the sky, the furniture of the room being altogether
invisible. Groping along to where the table stood, Mr Batchel felt over
its surface for the matches which usually lay there; he found, however,
that the table was cleared of everything. He raised his right hand,
therefore, in order to feel his way to a shelf where the matches were
sometimes mislaid, and at that moment, whilst his hand was in mid-air,
the matchbox was gently put into it!

Such an incident could hardly fail to disturb even a phlegmatic
person, and Mr Batchel cried 'Who's this?' somewhat nervously. There
was no answer. He struck a match, looked hastily round the room, and
found it empty, as usual. There was everything, that is to say, that he was
accustomed to see, but no other person than himself.

It is not quite accurate, however, to say that everything was in its usual
state. Upon the tall desk lay a quarto volume that he had certainly not
placed there. It was his quite invariable practice to replace his books
upon the shelves after using them, and what we may call his library
habits were precise and methodical. A book out of place like this, was not
only an offence against good order, but a sign that his privacy had been
intruded upon. With some surprise, therefore, he lit the candle standing
ready in the sconce, and proceeded to examine the book, not sorry, in
the disturbed condition in which he was, to have an occupation found
for him.

The book proved to be one with which he was unfamiliar, and this made it certain that some other hand than his had removed it from its place. Its title was 'The Compleat Gard'ner' of M. de la Quintinye made English by John Evelyn Esquire. It was not a work in which Mr Batchel felt any great interest. It consisted of divers reflections on various parts of husbandry, doubtless entertaining enough, but too deliberate and discursive for practical purposes. He had certainly never used the book, and growing restless now in mind, said to himself that some boy having the freedom of the house, had taken it down from its place in the hope of finding pictures.

But even whilst he made this explanation he felt its weakness. To begin with, the desk was too high for a boy. The improbability that any boy would place a book there was equalled by the improbability that he would leave it there. To discover its uninviting character would be the work only of a moment, and no boy would have brought it so far from its shelf.

Mr Batchel had, however, come to read, and habit was too strong with him to be wholly set aside. Leaving 'The Compleat Gard'ner' on the desk, he turned round to the shelves to find some more congenial reading.

Hardly had he done this when he was startled by a sharp rap upon the desk behind him, followed by a rustling of paper. He turned quickly about and saw the quarto lying open. In obedience to the instinct of the moment, he at once sought a natural cause for what he saw. Only a wind, and that of the strongest, could have opened the book, and laid back its heavy cover; and though he accepted, for a brief moment, that explanation, he was too candid to retain it longer. The wind out of doors was very light. The window sash was closed and latched, and, to decide the matter finally, the book had its back, and not its edges, turned towards the only quarter from which a wind could strike.

Mr Batchel approached the desk again and stood over the book. With increasing perturbation of mind (for he still thought of the matchbox) he looked upon the open page. Without much reason beyond that he felt constrained to do something, he read the words of the half completed sentence at the turn of the page—

'at dead of night he left the house and passed into the solitude of the garden.'

But he read no more, nor did he give himself the trouble of discovering whose midnight wandering was being described, although the habit was singularly like one of his own. He was in no condition for reading, and turning his back upon the volume he slowly paced the length of the chamber, 'wondering at that which had come to pass.'

He reached the opposite end of the chamber and was in the act of turning, when again he heard the rustling of paper, and by the time he had faced round, saw the leaves of the book again turning over. In a moment the volume lay at rest, open in another place, and there was no further movement as he approached it. To make sure that he had not been deceived, he read again the words as they entered the page. The author was following a not uncommon practice of the time, and throwing common speech into forms suggested by Holy Writ: 'So dig,' it said, 'that ye may obtain.'

This passage, which to Mr Batchel seemed reprehensible in its levity, excited at once his interest and his disapproval. He was prepared to read more, but this time was not allowed. Before his eye could pass beyond the passage already cited, the leaves of the book slowly turned again, and presented but a termination of five words and a colophon.

The words were, 'to the North, an Ilex.' These three passages, in which he saw no meaning and no connection, began to entangle themselves together in Mr Batchel's mind. He found himself repeating them in different orders, now beginning with one, and now with another. Any further attempt at reading he felt to be impossible, and he was in no mind for any more experiences of the unaccountable. Sleep was, of course, further from him than ever, if that were conceivable. What he did, therefore, was to blow out the candle, to return to his moonlit bedroom, and put on more clothing, and then to pass downstairs with the object of going out of doors.

It was not unusual with Mr Batchel to walk about his garden at night-time. This form of exercise had often, after a wakeful hour, sent him back to his bed refreshed and ready for sleep. The convenient access to the garden at such times lay through his study, whose French windows opened on to a short flight of steps, and upon these he now paused for a moment to admire the snow-like appearance of the lawns, bathed as they were in the moonlight. As he paused, he heard the city clocks strike the half-hour after midnight, and he could not forbear repeating aloud

'At dead of night he left the house, and passed into the solitude of the garden.'

It was solitary enough. At intervals the screech of an owl, and now and then the noise of a train, seemed to emphasise the solitude by drawing attention to it and then leaving it in possession of the night. Mr Batchel found himself wondering and conjecturing what Vicar Whitehead, who had acquired the close of land to secure quiet and privacy for a garden, would have thought of the railways to the west and north. He turned his face northwards, whence a whistle had just sounded, and saw a tree beautifully outlined against the sky. His breath caught at the sight. Not because the tree was unfamiliar. Mr Batchel knew all his trees. But what he had seen was 'to the north, an Ilex.'

Mr Batchel knew not what to make of it all. He had walked into the garden hundreds of times and as often seen the Ilex, but the words out of 'The Compleat Gard'ner' seemed to be pursuing him in a way that made him almost afraid. His temperament, however, as has been said already, was phlegmatic. It was commonly said, and Mr Batchel approved the verdict, whilst he condemned its inexactness, that 'his nerves were made of fiddle-string', so he braced himself afresh and set upon his walk round the silent garden, which he was accustomed to begin in a northerly direction, and was now too proud to change. He usually passed the Ilex at the beginning of his perambulation, and so would pass it now.

He did not pass it. A small discovery, as he reached it, annoyed and disturbed him. His gardener, as careful and punctilious as himself, never failed to house all his tools at the end of a day's work. Yet there, under the Ilex, standing upright in moonlight brilliant enough to cast a shadow of it, was a spade.

Mr Batchel's second thought was one of relief. After his extraordinary experiences in the library (he hardly knew now whether they had been real or not) something quite commonplace would act sedatively, and he determined to carry the spade to the tool-house.

The soil was quite dry, and the surface even a little frozen, so Mr Batchel left the path, walked up to the spade, and would have drawn it towards him. But it was as if he had made the attempt upon the trunk of the Ilex itself. The spade would not be moved. Then, first with one hand, and then with both, he tried to raise it, and still it stood firm. Mr Batchel, of course, attributed this to the frost, slight as it was. Wondering at the spade's being there, and annoyed at its being frozen, he was about to leave it and continue his walk, when the remaining works of 'The Compleat Gard'ner' seemed rather to utter themselves, than to await his will—

'So dig, that ye may obtain.'

Mr Batchel's power of independent action now deserted him. He took the spade, which no longer resisted, and began to dig. 'Five spadefuls and no more,' he said aloud. 'This is all foolishness.'

Four spadefuls of earth he then raised and spread out before him in the moonlight. There was nothing unusual to be seen. Nor did Mr Batchel decide what he would look for, whether coins, jewels, documents in canisters, or weapons. In point of fact, he dug against what he deemed his better judgement, and expected nothing. He spread before him the fifth and last spadeful of earth, not quite without result, but with no result that was at all sensational. The earth contained a bone. Mr Batchel's knowledge of anatomy was sufficient to show him that it was a human bone. He identified it, even by moonlight, as the *radius*, a bone of the forearm, as he removed the earth from it, with his thumb.

Such a discovery might be thought worthy of more than the very ordinary interest Mr Batchel showed. As a matter of fact, the presence of a human bone was easily to be accounted for. Recent excavations within the church had caused the upturning of numberless bones, which had been collected and reverently buried. But an earth-stained bone is also easily overlooked, and this *radius* had obviously found its way into the garden with some of the earth brought out of the church.

Mr Batchel was glad, rather than regretful at this termination to his adventure. He was once more provided with something to do. The re-interment of such bones as this had been his constant care, and he decided at once to restore the bone to consecrated earth. The time seemed opportune. The eyes of the curious were closed in sleep, he himself was still alert and wakeful. The spade remained by his side and the bone in his hand. So he betook himself, there and then, to the churchyard. By the still generous light of the moon, he found a place where the earth yielded to his spade, and within a few minutes the bone was laid decently to earth, some 18 inches deep.

The city clocks struck one as he finished. The whole world seemed asleep, and Mr Batchel slowly returned to the garden with his spade. As he hung it in its accustomed place he felt stealing over him the welcome desire to sleep. He walked quietly on to the house and ascended to his room. It was now dark: the moon had passed on and left the room in shadow. He lit a candle, and before undressing passed into the library. He had an irresistible curiosity to see the passages in John Evelyn's book which had so strangely adapted themselves to the events of the past hour.

In the library a last surprise awaited him. The desk upon which the book had lain was empty. 'The Compleat Gard'ner' stood in its place on the shelf. And then Mr Batchel knew that he had handled a bone of William Whitehead, and that in response to his own entreaty.

The True History of Anthony Ffryar

ARTHUR GRAY

The world, it is said, knows nothing of its greatest men. In our Cambridge microcosm it may be doubted whether we are better informed concerning some of the departed great ones who once walked the confines of our Colleges. Which of us has heard of Anthony Ffryar of Jesus? History is dumb respecting him. Yet but for the unhappy event recorded in this unadorned chronicle his fame might have stood with that of Bacon of Trinity, or Harvey of Caius. *They* lived to be old men : Ffryar died before he was thirty—his work unfinished, his fame unknown even to his contemporaries.

So meagre is the record of his life's work that it is contained in a few bare notices in the College Bursar's Books, in the Grace Books which date his matriculation and degrees, and in the entry of his burial in the register of All Saints' Parish. These simple annals I have ventured to supplement with details of a more or less hypothetical character which will serve to show what humanity lost by his early death. Readers will be able to judge for themselves the degree of care which I have taken not to import into the story anything which may savour of the improbable or romantic.

Anthony Ffryar matriculated in the year 1541–2, his age being then probably fifteen or sixteen. He took his BA degree in 1545, his MA in 1548. He became a Fellow about the end of 1547, and died in the summer of 1551. Such are the documentary facts relating to him. Dr Reston was Master of the College during the whole of his tenure of a Fellowship and died in the same year as Ffryar. The chamber which Ffryar occupied as a Fellow was on the first floor of the staircase at the west end of the Chapel. The staircase has since been absorbed in the Master's Lodge, but the doorway through which it was approached from the cloister may still be seen. At the time when Ffryar lived there the nave of the Chapel was used as a parish church, and his windows overlooked the graveyard, then called 'Jesus churchyard', which is now a part of the Master's garden.

Ffryar was of course a priest, as were nearly all the Fellows in his day. But I do not gather that he was a theologian, or complied more than formally with the obligation of his orders. He came to Cambridge when the Six Articles and the suppression of the monasteries were of fresh and burning import: he became a Fellow in the harsh Protestant days of Protector Somerset: and in all his time the Master and the Fellows were in scarcely disavowed sympathy with the rites and beliefs of the Old Religion. Yet in the battle of creeds I imagine that he took no part and no interest. I should suppose that he was a somewhat solitary man, an insatiable student of Nature, and that his sympathies with humanity were starved by his absorption in the New Science which dawned on Cambridge at the Reformation.

When I say that he was an alchemist do not suppose that in the middle of the sixteenth century the name of alchemy carried with it any associations with credulity or imposture. It was a real science and a subject of University study then, as its god-children, Physics and Chemistry, are now. If the aims of its professors were transcendental its methods were genuinely based on research. Ffryar was no visionary, but a man of sense, hard and practical. To the study of alchemy he was drawn by no hopes of gain, not even of fame, and still less by any desire to benefit mankind. He was actuated solely by an unquenchable passion for enquiry, a passion sterilizing to all other feeling. To the somnambulisms of the less scientific disciples of his school, such as the philosopher's stone and the elixir of life, he showed himself a chill agnostic. All his thought and energies were concentrated on the discovery of the *magisterium*, the master-cure of all human ailments.

For four years in his laboratory in the cloister he had toiled at this pursuit. More than once, when it had seemed most near, it had eluded his grasp; more than once he had been tempted to abandon it as a mystery insoluble. In the summer of 1551 the discovery waited at his door. He was sure, certain of success, which only experiment could prove. And with the certainty arose a new passion in his heart—to make the name of Ffryar glorious in the healing profession as that of Galen or Hippocrates. In a few days, even within a few hours, the fame of his discovery would go out into all the world.

The summer of 1551 was a sad time in Cambridge. It was marked by a more than usually fatal outbreak of the epidemic called 'the sweat', when, as Fuller says, 'patients ended or mended in twenty-four hours.' It had smouldered some time in the town before it appeared with sudden and dreadful violence in Jesus College. The first to go was little Gregory Graunge, schoolboy and chorister, who was lodged in the College school in the outer court. He was barely thirteen years old, and known by sight to Anthony Ffryar. He died on July 31, and was buried the same day in Jesus churchyard. The service for his burial was held in the

Chapel and at night, as was customary in those days. Funerals in College were no uncommon events in the sixteenth century. But in the death of the poor child, among strangers, there was something to move even the cold heart of Ffryar. And not the pity of it only impressed him. The dim Chapel, the Master and Fellows obscurely ranged in their stalls and shrouded in their hoods, the long-drawn miserable chanting and the childish trebles of the boys who had been Gregory's fellows struck a chill into him which was not to be shaken off.

Three days passed and another chorister died. The College gates were barred and guarded, and, except by a selected messenger, communication with the town was cut off. The precaution was unavailing, and the boys' usher, Mr Stevenson, died on August 5. One of the junior Fellows, sir Stayner—'sir' being the equivalent of BA—followed on August 7. The Master, Dr Reston, died the next day. A gaunt, severe man was Dr Reston, whom his Fellows feared. The death of a Master of Arts on August 9 for a time completed the melancholy list.

Before this the frightened Fellows had taken action. The scholars were dismissed to their homes on August 6. Some of the Fellows abandoned the College at the same time. The rest—a terrified conclave—met on August 8 and decreed that the College should be closed until the pestilence should have abated. Until that time it was to be occupied by a certain Robert Laycock, who was a College servant, and his only communication with the outside world was to be through his son, who lived in Jesus Lane. The decree was perhaps the result of the Master's death, for he was not present at the meeting.

Goodman Laycock, as he was commonly called, might have been the sole tenant of the College but for the unalterable decision of Ffryar to remain there. At all hazards his research, now on the eve of realisation, must proceed; without the aid of his laboratory in College it would miserably hang fire. Besides, he had an absolute assurance of his own immunity if the experiment answered his confident expectations, and his fancy was elated with the thought of standing, like another Aaron, between the living and the dead, and staying the pestilence with the potent *magisterium*. Until then he would bar his door even against Laycock, and his supplies of food should be left on the staircase landing. Solitude for him was neither unfamiliar nor terrible.

So for three days Ffryar and Laycock inhabited the cloister, solitary and separate. For three days, in the absorption of his research, Ffryar forgot fear, forgot the pestilence-stricken world beyond the gate, almost forgot to consume the daily dole of food laid outside his door. August 12 was the day, so fateful to humanity, when his labours were to be crowned with victory: before midnight the secret of the *magisterium* would be solved.

Evening began to close in before he could begin the experiment which was to be his last. It must of necessity be a labour of some hours, and, before it began, he bethought him that he had not tasted food since early morning. He unbarred his door and looked for the expected portion. It was not there. Vexed at the remissness of Laycock he waited for a while and listened for his approaching footsteps. At last he took courage and descended to the cloister. He called for Laycock, but heard no response. He resolved to go as far as the Buttery door and knock. Laycock lived and slept in the Buttery.

At the Buttery door he beat and cried on Laycock; but in answer he heard only the sound of scurrying rats. He went to the window, by the hatch, where he knew that the old man's bed lay, and called to him again. Still there was silence. At last he resolved to force himself through the unglazed window and take what food he could find. In the deep gloom within he stumbled and almost fell over a low object, which he made out to be a truckle-bed. There was light enough from the window to distinguish, stretched upon it, the form of Goodman Laycock, stark and dead.

Sickened and alarmed Ffryar hurried back to his chamber. More than ever he must hasten the great experiment. When it was ended his danger would be past, and he could go out into the town to call the buryers for the old man. With trembling hands he lit the brazier which he used for his experiments, laid it on his hearth and placed thereon the alembic which was to distil the *magisterium*.

Then he sat down to wait. Gradually the darkness thickened and the sole illuminant of the chamber was the wavering flame of the brazier. He felt feverish and possessed with a nameless uneasiness which, for all his assurance, he was glad to construe as fear: better that than sickness. In the College and the town without was a deathly silence, stirred only by the sweltering of the distilment, and, as the hours struck, by the beating of the Chapel clock, last wound by Laycock. It was as though the dead man spoke. But the repetition of the hours told him that the time of his emancipation was drawing close.

Whether he slept I do not know. He was aroused to vivid consciousness by the clock sounding *one*. The time when his experiment should have ended was ten, and he started up with a horrible fear that it had been ruined by his neglect. But it was not so. The fire burnt, the liquid simmered quietly, and so far all was well.

Again the College bell boomed a solitary stroke: then a pause and another. He opened, or seemed to open, his door and listened. Again the knell was repeated. His mind went back to the night when he had attended the obsequies of the boy-chorister. This must be a funeral tolling. For whom? He thought with a shudder of the dead man in the Buttery.

He groped his way cautiously down the stairs. It was a still, windless night, and the cloister was dark as death. Arrived at the further side of the court he turned towards the Chapel. Its panes were faintly lighted from within. The door stood open and he entered.

In the place familiar to him at the chancel door one candle flickered on a bracket. Close to it—his face cast in deep shade by the light from behind—stood the ringer, in a gown of black, silent and absorbed in his melancholy task. Fear had almost given way to wonder in the heart of Ffryar, and, as he passed the sombre figure on his way to the chancel door, he looked him resolutely in the face. The ringer was Goodman Laycock.

Ffryar passed into the choir and quietly made his way to his accustomed stall. Four candles burnt in the central walk about a figure laid on trestles and draped in a pall of black. Two choristers—one on either side—stood by it. In the dimness he could distinguish four figures, erect in the stalls on either side of the Chapel. Their faces were concealed by their hoods, but in the tall form which occupied the Master's seat it was not difficult to recognise Dr Reston.

The bell ceased and the service began. With some faint wonder Ffryar noted that it was the proscribed Roman Mass for the Dead. The solemn introit was uttered in the tones of Reston, and in the deep responses of the nearest cowled figure he recognised the voice of Stevenson, the usher. None of the mourners seemed to notice Ffryar's presence.

The dreary ceremony drew to a close. The four occupants of the stalls descended and gathered round the palled figure in the aisle. With a mechanical impulse, devoid of fear or curiosity, and with a half-prescience of what he should see, Anthony Ffryar drew near and uncovered the dead man's face. He saw—himself.

At the same moment the last wailing notes of the office for the dead broke from the band of mourners, and, one by one, the choristers extinguished the four tapers.

'Requiem aeternam dona ei, Domine,' chanted the hooded four: and one candle went out.

'Et lux perpetua luceat ei,' was the shrill response of the two choristers: and a second was extinguished.

'Cum sanctis tuis in aeternum,' answered the four: and one taper only remained.

The Master threw back his hood, and turned his dreadful eyes straight upon the living Anthony Ffryar: he threw his hand across the bier and held him tight. 'Cras tu eris mecum,'[1] he muttered, as if in antiphonal reply to the dirge-chanters.

With a hiss and a sputter the last candle expired.

The hiss and the sputter and a sudden sense of gloom recalled Ffryar to the waking world. Alas for labouring science, alas for the fame of Ffryar, alas for humanity, dying and doomed to die! The vessel containing the wonderful brew which should have redeemd the world had fallen over and dislodged its contents on the fire below. An accident reparable, surely, within a few hours; but not by Anthony Ffryar. How the night passed with him no mortal can tell. All that is known further of him is written in the register of All Saints' Parish. If you can discover the ancient volume containing the records of the year 1551—and I am not positive that it now exists—you will find it written:

> Die Augusti xiii
>   Buryalls in Jhesus churchyarde
>   Goodman Laycock ⎱
>   Anthony Ffryar   ⎰   of ye sicknesse

Whether he really died of 'the sweat' I cannot say. But that the living man was sung to his grave by the dead, who were his sole companions in Jesus College, on the night of August 12, 1551, is as certain and indisputable as any other of the facts which are here set forth in the history of Anthony Ffryar.

[1] Samuel xxvii. 19.

The Taipan

W. SOMERSET MAUGHAM

No one knew better than he that he was an important person. He was
number one in not the least important branch of the most important
English firm in China. He had worked his way up through solid ability
and he looked back with a faint smile at the callow clerk who had come
out to China thirty years before. When he remembered the modest
home he had come from, a little red house in a long row of little red
houses, in Barnes, a suburb which, aiming desperately at the genteel,
achieves only a sordid melancholy, and compared it with the magnificent stone mansion, with its wide verandahs and spacious rooms, which
was at once the office of the company and his own residence, he
chuckled with satisfaction. He had come a long way since then. He
thought of the high tea to which he sat down when he came home from
school (he was at St Paul's), with his father and mother and his two
sisters, a slice of cold meat, a great deal of bread and butter and plenty of
milk in his tea, everybody helping himself, and then he thought of the
state in which now he ate his evening meal. He always dressed and
whether he was alone or not he expected the three boys to wait at table.
His number one boy knew exactly what he liked and he never had to
bother himself with the details of housekeeping; but he always had a set
dinner with soup and fish, entrée, roast, sweet and savoury, so that if he
wanted to ask anyone in at the last moment he could. He liked his food
and he did not see why when he was alone he should have less good a
dinner than when he had a guest.

He had indeed gone far. That was why he did not care to go home
now, he had not been to England for ten years, and he took his leave in
Japan or Vancouver, where he was sure of meeting old friends from the
China coast. He knew no one at home. His sisters had married in their
own station, their husbands were clerks and their sons were clerks; there
was nothing between him and them; they bored him. He satisfied the
claims of relationship by sending them every Christmas a piece of fine
silk, some elaborate embroidery, or a case of tea. He was not a mean man
and as long as his mother lived he had made her an allowance. But when
the time came for him to retire he had no intention of going back to
England, he had seen too many men do that and he knew how often it

was a failure; he meant to take a house near the racecourse in Shanghai: what with bridge and his ponies and golf he expected to get through the rest of his life very comfortably. But he had a good many years before he need think of retiring. In another five or six Higgins would be going home and then he would take charge of the head office in Shanghai. Meanwhile he was very happy where he was, he could save money, which you couldn't do in Shanghai, and have a good time into the bargain. This place had another advantage over Shanghai: he was the most prominent man in the community and what he said went. Even the consul took care to keep on the right side of him. Once a consul and he had been at loggerheads and it was not he who had gone to the wall. The taipan thrust out his jaw pugnaciously as he thought of the incident.

But he smiled, for he felt in an excellent humour. He was walking back to his office from a capital luncheon at the Hong-Kong and Shanghai Bank. They did you very well there. The food was first-rate and there was plenty of liquor. He had started with a couple of cocktails, then he had some excellent sauterne and he had finished up with two glasses of port and some fine old brandy. He felt good. And when he left he did a thing that was rare with him; he walked. His bearers with his chair kept a few paces behind him in case he felt inclined to slip into it, but he enjoyed stretching his legs. He did not get enough exercise these days. Now that he was too heavy to ride it was difficult to get exercise. But if he was too heavy to ride he could still keep ponies, and as he strolled along in the balmy air he thought of the spring meeting. He had a couple of griffins that he had hopes of and one of the lads in his office had turned out a fine jockey (he must see they didn't sneak him away, old Higgins in Shanghai would give a pot of money to get him over there) and he ought to pull off two or three races. He flattered himself that he had the finest stable in the city. He pouted his broad chest like a pigeon. It was a beautiful day, and it was good to be alive.

He paused as he came to the cemetery. It stood there, neat and orderly, as an evident sign of the community's opulence. He never passed the cemetery without a little glow of pride. He was pleased to be an Englishman. For the cemetery stood in a place, valueless when it was chosen, which with the increase of the city's affluence was now worth a great deal of money. It had been suggested that the graves should be moved to another spot and the land sold for building, but the feeling of the community was against it. It gave the taipan a sense of satisfaction to think that their dead rested on the most valuable site on the island. It showed that there were things they cared for more than money. Money be blowed! When it came to 'the things that mattered' (this was a favourite phrase with the taipan), well, one remembered that money wasn't everything.

And now he thought he would take a stroll through. He looked at the graves. They were neatly kept and the pathways were free from weeds. There was a look of prosperity. And as he sauntered along he read the names on the tombstones. Here were three side by side; the captain, the first mate, and the second mate of the barque *Mary Baxter*, who had all perished together in the typhoon of 1908. He remembered it well. There was a little group of two missionaries, their wives and children, who had been massacred during the Boxer troubles. Shocking thing that had been! Not that he took much stock in missionaries; but, hang it all, one couldn't have these damned Chinese massacring them. Then he came to a cross with a name on it he knew. Good chap, Edward Mulock, but he couldn't stand his liquor, drank himself to death, poor devil, at twenty-five; the taipan had known a lot of them do that; there were several more neat crosses with a man's name on them and the age, twenty-five, twenty-six, or twenty-seven; it was always the same story: they had come out to China; they had never seen so much money before, they were good fellows and they wanted to drink with the rest: they couldn't stand it, and there they were in the cemetery. You had to have a strong head and a fine constitution to drink drink for drink on the China coast. Of course it was very sad, but the taipan could hardly help a smile when he thought how many of those young fellows he had drunk underground. And there was a death that had been useful, a fellow in his own firm, senior to him and a clever chap too: if that fellow had lived he might not have been taipan now. Truly the ways of fate were inscrutable. Ah, and here was little Mrs Turner, Violet Turner, she had been a pretty little thing, he had had quite an affair with her; he had been devilish cut up when she died. He looked at her age on the tombstone. She'd be no chicken if she were alive now. And as he thought of all those dead people a sense of satisfaction spread through him. He had beaten them all. They were dead and he was alive, and by George he'd scored them off. His eyes collected in one picture all those crowded graves and he smiled scornfully. He very nearly rubbed his hands.

'No one ever thought I was a fool,' he muttered.

He had a feeling of good-natured contempt for the gibbering dead. Then, as he strolled along, he came suddenly upon two coolies digging a grave. He was astonished, for he had not heard that anyone in the community was dead.

'Who the devil's that for?' he said aloud.

The coolies did not even look at him, they went on with their work, standing in the grave, deep down, and they shovelled up heavy clods of earth. Though he had been so long in China he knew no Chinese, in his day it was not thought necessary to learn the damned language, and he asked the coolies in English whose grave they were digging. They did not understand. They answered him in Chinese and he cursed them for ignorant fools. He knew that Mrs Broome's child was ailing and it might have died, but he would certainly have heard of it, and besides, that wasn't a child's grave, it was a man's and a big man's too. It was uncanny. He wished he hadn't gone into that cemetery; he hurried out and stepped into his chair. His good-humour had all gone and there was an uneasy frown on his face. The moment he got back to his office he called to his number two:

'I say, Peters, who's dead, d'you know?'

But Peters knew nothing. The taipan was puzzled. He called one of the native clerks and sent him to the cemetery to ask the coolies. He began to sign his letters. The clerk came back and said the coolies had gone and there was no one to ask. The taipan began to feel vaguely annoyed: he did not like things to happen of which he knew nothing. His own boy would know, his boy always knew everything, and he sent for him; but the boy had heard of no death in the community.

'I knew no one was dead,' said the taipan irritably. 'But what's the grave for?'

He told the boy to go to the overseer of the cemetery and find out what the devil he had dug a grave for when no one was dead.

'Let me have a whisky and soda before you go,' he added, as the boy was leaving the room.

He did not know why the sight of the grave had made him uncomfortable. But he tried to put it out of his mind. He felt better when he had drunk the whisky, and he finished his work. He went upstairs and turned over the pages of *Punch*. In a few minutes he would go to the club and play a rubber or two of bridge before dinner. But it would ease his mind to hear what his boy had to say and he waited for his return. In a little while the boy came back and he brought the overseer with him.

'What are you having a grave dug for?' he asked the overseer point-blank. 'Nobody's dead.'

'I no dig glave,' said the man.

'What the devil do you mean by that? There were two coolies digging a grave this afternoon.'

The two Chinese looked at one another. Then the boy said they had been to the cemetery together. There was no new grave there.

The taipan only just stopped himself from speaking.

'But damn it all, I saw it myself,' were the words on the tip of his tongue.

But he did not say them. He grew very red as he choked them down. The two Chinese looked at him with their steady eyes. For a moment his breath failed him.

'All right. Get out,' he gasped.

But as soon as they were gone he shouted for the boy again, and when he came, maddeningly impassive, he told him to bring some whisky. He rubbed his sweating face with a handkerchief. His hand trembled when he lifted the glass to his lips. They could say what they liked, but he had seen the grave. Why, he could hear still the dull thud as the coolies threw the spadefuls of earth on the ground above them. What did it mean? He could feel his heart beating. He felt strangely ill at ease. But he pulled himself together. It was all nonsense. If there was no grave there it must have been an hallucination. The best thing he could do was to go to the club, and if he ran across the doctor he would ask him to give him a look over.

Everyone in the club looked just the same as ever. He did not know why he should have expected them to look different. It was a comfort. These men, living for many years with one another lives that were methodically regulated, had acquired a number of little idiosyncrasies— one of them hummed incessantly while he played bridge, another insisted on drinking beer through a straw—and these tricks which had so often irritated the taipan now gave him a sense of security. He needed it, for he could not get out of his head that strange sight he had seen; he played bridge very badly; his partner was censorious, and the taipan lost his temper. He thought the men were looking at him oddly. He wondered what they saw in him that was unaccustomed.

Suddenly he felt he could not bear to stay in the club any longer. As he went out he saw the doctor reading *The Times* in the reading-room, but he could not bring himself to speak to him. He wanted to see for himself whether that grave was really there and stepping into his chair he told his bearers to take him to the cemetery. You couldn't have an hallucination twice, could you? And besides, he would take the overseer in with him and if the grave was not there he wouldn't see it, and if it was he'd give the overseer the soundest thrashing he'd ever had. But the overseer was nowhere to be found. He had gone out and taken the keys with him. When the taipan found he could not get into the cemetery he felt suddenly exhausted. He got back into his chair and told his bearers to take him home. He would lie down for half an hour before dinner. He was tired out. That was it. He had heard that people had hallucinations when they were tired. When his boy came in to put out his clothes for dinner it was only by an effort of will that he got up. He had a strong inclination not to dress that evening, but he resisted it: he made it a rule to dress, he had dressed every evening for twenty years and it would never do to break his rule. But he ordered a bottle of champagne with his dinner and that made him feel more comfortable. Afterwards he told the boy to bring him the best brandy. When he had drunk a couple of glasses of this he felt himself again. Hallucinations be damned! He went to the billiard-room and practised a few difficult shots. There could not be much the matter with him when his eye was so sure. When he went to bed he sank immediately into a sound sleep.

But suddenly he awoke. He had dreamed of that open grave and the coolies digging leisurely. He was sure he had seen them. It was absurd to say it was an hallucination when he had seen them with his own eyes. Then he heard the rattle of the night-watchman going his rounds. It broke upon the stillness of the night so harshly that it made him jump out of his skin. And then terror seized him. He felt a horror of the winding multitudinous streets of the Chinese city, and there was something ghastly and terrible in the convoluted roofs of the temples with their devils grimacing and tortured. He loathed the smells that assaulted his nostrils. And the people. Those myriads of blue-clad coolies, and the beggars in their filthy rags, and the merchants and the magistrates, sleek, smiling, and inscrutable, in their long black gowns. They seemed to press upon him with menace. He hated the country. China. Why had he ever come? He was panic-stricken now. He must get out. He would not stay another year, another month. What did he care about Shanghai?

'Oh, my God,' he cried, 'if I were only safely back in England.'

He wanted to go home. If he had to die he wanted to die in England. He could not bear to be buried among all these yellow men, with their slanting eyes and their grinning faces. He wanted to be buried at home, not in that grave he had seen that day. He could never rest there. Never. What did it matter what people thought? Let them think what they liked. The only thing that mattered was to get away while he had the chance.

He got out of bed and wrote to the head of the firm and said he had discovered he was dangerously ill. He must be replaced. He could not stay longer than was absolutely necessary. He must go home at once.

They found the letter in the morning clenched in the taipan's hand. He had slipped down between the desk and the chair. He was stone dead.

The Victim

MAY SINCLAIR

~

I

Steven Acroyd, Mr Greathead's chauffeur, was sulking in the garage.

Everybody was afraid of him. Everybody hated him except Mr Greathead, his master, and Dorsy, his sweetheart.

And even Dorsy now, after yesterday!

Night had come. On one side the yard gates stood open to the black tunnel of the drive. On the other the high moor rose above the wall, immense, darker than the darkness. Steven's lantern in the open doorway of the garage and Dorsy's lamp in the kitchen window threw a blond twilight into the yard between. From where he sat, slantways on the step of the car, he could see, through the lighted window, the table with the lamp and Dorsy's sewing huddled up in a white heap as she left it just now, when she had jumped up and gone away. Because she was afraid of him.

She had gone straight to Mr Greathead in his study, and Steven, sulking, had flung himself out into the yard.

He stared into the window, thinking, thinking. Everybody hated him. He could tell by the damned spiteful way they looked at him in the bar of the King's Arms; kind of sideways and slink-eyed, turning their dirty tails and shuffling out of his way.

He had said to Dorsy he'd like to know what he'd done. He'd just dropped in for his glass as usual; he'd looked round and said 'Good evening', civil, and the dirty tykes took no more notice of him than if he'd been a toad. Mrs Oldishaw, Dorsy's aunt, *she* hated him, boiled-ham-face, swelling with spite, shoving his glass at the end of her arm, without speaking, as if he'd been a bloody cockroach.

All because of the thrashing he'd given young Ned Oldishaw. If she didn't want the cub's neck broken she'd better keep him out of mischief. Young Ned knew what he'd get if he came meddling with *his* sweetheart.

It had happened yesterday afternoon, Sunday, when he had gone down with Dorsy to the King's Arms to see her aunt. They were sitting out on the wooden bench against the inn wall when young Ned began it. He could see him now with his arm round Dorsy's neck and his mouth gaping. And Dorsy laughing like a silly fool and the old woman snorting and shaking.

He could hear him. 'She's my cousin if she *is* your sweetheart. You can't stop me kissing her.' *Couldn't* he!

Why, what did they think? When he'd given up his good job at the Darlington Motor Works to come to Eastthwaite and black Mr Greathead's boots, chop wood, carry coal and water for him, and drive his shabby secondhand car. Not that he cared what he did so long as he could live in the same house with Dorsy Oldishaw. It wasn't likely he'd sit like a bloody Moses, looking on, while Ned——

To be sure, he had half killed him. He could feel Ned's neck swelling and rising up under the pressure of his hands, his fingers. He had struck him first, flinging him back against the inn wall, then he had pinned him—till the men ran up and dragged him off.

And now they were all against him. Dorsy was against him. She had said she was afraid of him.

'Steven,' she had said, 'tha med 'a killed him.'

'Well—p'r'aps next time he'll knaw better than to coom meddlin' with *my* lass.'

'I'm not thy lass, ef tha canna keep thy hands off folks. I should be feared for my life of thee. Ned wurn't doing naw 'arm.'

'Ef he doos it again, ef he cooms between thee and me, Dorsy, I shall do 'im in.'

'Naw, tha maunna talk that road.'

'It's Gawd's truth. Anybody that cooms between thee and me, loove, I shall do 'im in. Ef 'twas thy aunt, I should wring 'er neck, same as I wroong Ned's.'

'And ef it was me, Steven?'

'Ef it wur thee, ef tha left me—— Aw, doan't tha assk me, Dorsy.'

'There—that's 'ow tha scares me.'

'But tha' 'astna left me—'tes thy wedding claithes tha'rt making.'

'Aye, 'tes my wedding claithes.'

She had started fingering the white stuff, looking at it with her head on one side, smiling prettily. Then all of a sudden she had flung it down in a heap and burst out crying. When he tried to comfort her she pushed him off and ran out of the room, to Mr Greathead.

It must have been half an hour ago and she had not come back yet.

He got up and went through the yard gates into the dark drive. Turning there, he came to the house front and the lighted window of the study. Hidden behind a clump of yew he looked in.

Mr Greathead had risen from his chair. He was a little old man, shrunk and pinched, with a bowed narrow back and slender neck under his grey hanks of hair.

Dorsy stood before him, facing Steven. The lamplight fell full on her. Her sweet flower-face was flushed. She had been crying.

Mr Greathead spoke.

'Well, that's my advice,' he said. 'Think it over, Dorsy, before you do anything.'

That night Dorsy packed her boxes, and the next day at noon, when Steven came in for his dinner, she had left the Lodge. She had gone back to her father's house in Garthdale.

She wrote to Steven saying that she had thought it over and found she daren't marry him. She was afraid of him. She would be too unhappy.

II

That was the old man, the old man. He had made her give him up. But for that, Dorsy would never have left him. She would never have thought of it herself. And she would never have got away if he had been there to stop her. It wasn't Ned. Ned was going to marry Nancy Peacock down at Morfe. Ned hadn't done any harm.

It was Mr Greathead who had come between them. He hated Mr Greathead.

His hate became a nausea of physical loathing that never ceased. Indoors he served Mr Greathead as footman and valet, waiting on him at meals, bringing the hot water for his bath, helping him to dress and undress. So that he could never get away from him. When he came to call him in the morning, Steven's stomach heaved at the sight of the shrunken body under the bedclothes, the flushed, pinched face with its peaked, finicking nose upturned, the thin silver tuft of hair pricked up above the pillow's edge. Steven shivered with hate at the sound of the rattling, old-man's cough, and the 'shoob-shoob' of the feet shuffling along the flagged passages.

He had once had a feeling of tenderness for Mr Greathead as the tie that bound him to Dorsy. He even brushed his coat and hat tenderly, as if he loved them. Once Mr Greathead's small, close smile—the greyish bud of the lower lip pushed out, the upper lip lifted at the corners—and his kind, thin 'Thank you, my lad,' had made Steven smile back, glad to serve Dorsy's master. And Mr Greathead would smile again and say, 'It does me good to see your bright face, Steven.' Now Steven's face writhed in a tight contortion to meet Mr Greathead's kindliness, while his throat ran dry and his heart shook with hate.

At meal-times from his place by the sideboard he would look on at Mr

Greathead eating, in a long contemplative disgust. He could have snatched the plate away from under the slow, fumbling hands that hovered and hesitated. He would catch words coming into his mind: 'He ought to be dead. He ought to be dead.' To think that this thing that ought to be dead, this old, shrivelled skin-bag of creaking bones should come between him and Dorsy, should have power to drive Dorsy from him.

One day when he was brushing Mr Greathead's soft felt hat a paroxysm of hatred gripped him. He hated Mr Greathead's hat. He took a stick and struck at it again and again; he threw it on the flags and stamped on it, clenching his teeth and drawing in his breath with a sharp hiss. He picked up the hat, looking round furtively, for fear lest Mr Greathead or Dorsy's successor, Mrs Blenkiron, should have seen him. He pinched and pulled it back into shape and brushed it carefully and hung it on the stand. He was ashamed, not of his violence, but of its futility.

Nobody but a damned fool, he said to himself, would have done that. He must have been mad.

It wasn't as if he didn't know what he was going to do. He had known ever since the day when Dorsy left him.

'I shan't be myself again till I've done him in,' he thought.

He was only waiting till he had planned it out; till he was sure of every detail; till he was fit and cool. There must be no hesitation, no uncertainty at the last minute, above all, no blind, headlong violence. Nobody but a fool would kill in mad rage, and forget things, and be caught and swing for it. Yet that was what they all did. There was always something they hadn't thought of that gave them away.

Steven had thought of everything, even the date, even the weather.

Mr Greathead was in the habit of going up to London to attend the debates of a learned Society he belonged to that held its meetings in May and November. He always travelled up by the five o'clock train, so that he might go to bed and rest as soon as he arrived. He always stayed for a week and gave his housekeeper a week's holiday. Steven chose a dark, threatening day in November, when Mr Greathead was going up to his meeting and Mrs Blenkiron had left Eastthwaite for Morfe by the early morning bus. So that there was nobody in the house but Mr Greathead and Steven.

Eastthwaite Lodge stands alone, grey, hidden between the shoulder of the moor and the ash-trees of its drive. It is approached by a bridle-path across the moor, a turning off the road that runs from Eastthwaite in Rathdale to Shawe in Westleydale, about a mile from the village and a mile from Hardraw Pass. No tradesmen visited it. Mr Greathead's letters and his newspaper were shot into a post-box that hung on the ash-tree at the turn.

The hot water laid on in the house was not hot enough for Mr Greathead's bath, so that every morning, while Mr Greathead shaved, Steven came to him with a can of boiling water.

Mr Greathead, dressed in a mauve and grey striped sleeping-suit, stood shaving himself before the looking-glass that hung on the wall beside the great white bath. Steven waited with his hand on the cold tap, watching the bright curved rod of water falling with a thud and a splash.

In the white, stagnant light from the muffed window-pane the knife-blade flame of a small oil-stove flickered queerly. The oil sputtered and stank.

Suddenly the wind hissed in the water-pipes and cut off the glittering rod. To Steven it seemed the suspension of all movement. He would have to wait there till the water flowed again before he could begin. He tried not to look at Mr Greathead and the lean wattles of his lifted throat. He fixed his eyes on the long crack in the soiled green distemper of the wall. His nerves were on edge with waiting for the water to flow again. The fumes of the oil-stove worked on them like a rank intoxicant. The soiled green wall gave him a sensation of physical sickness.

He picked up a towel and hung it over the back of a chair. Thus he caught sight of his own face in the glass above Mr Greathead's; it was livid against the soiled green wall. Steven stepped aside to avoid it.

'Don't you feel well, Steven?'

'No, sir.' Steven picked up a small sponge and looked at it.

Mr Greathead had laid down his razor and was wiping the lather from his chin. At that instant, with a gurgling, spluttering haste, the water leaped from the tap.

It was then that Steven made his sudden, quiet rush. He first gagged Mr Greathead with the sponge, then pushed him back and back against the wall and pinned him there with both hands round his neck, as he had pinned Ned Oldishaw. He pressed in on Mr Greathead's throat, strangling him.

Mr Greathead's hands flapped in the air, trying feebly to beat Steven off; then his arms, pushed back by the heave and thrust of Steven's shoulders, dropped. Then Mr Greathead's body sank, sliding along the wall, and fell to the floor, Steven still keeping his hold, mounting it, gripping it with his knees. His fingers tightened, pressing back the blood. Mr Greathead's face swelled up; it changed horribly. There was a groaning and rattling sound in his throat. Steven pressed in till it had ceased.

Then he stripped himself to the waist. He stripped Mr Greathead of his sleeping-suit and hung his naked body face downwards in the bath. He took the razor and cut the great arteries and veins in the neck. He pulled up the plug of the waste-pipe, and left the body to drain in the running water.

He left it all day and all night.

He had noticed that murderers swung just for want of attention to little things like that; messing up themselves and the whole place with blood; always forgetting something essential. He had no time to think of horrors. From the moment he had murdered Mr Greathead his own neck was in danger; he was simply using all his brain and nerve to save his neck. He worked with the stern, cool hardness of a man going through with an unpleasant, necessary job. He had thought of everything.

He had even thought of the dairy.

It was built on to the back of the house under the shelter of the high moor. You entered it through the scullery, which cut it off from the yard. The window-panes had been removed and replaced by sheets of perforated zinc. A large corrugated glass sky-light lit it from the roof. Impossible either to see in or to approach it from the outside. It was fitted up with a long, black slate shelf, placed, for the convenience of butter-makers, at the height of an ordinary work-bench. Steven had his tools, a razor, a carving-knife, a chopper and a meat-saw, laid there ready, beside a great pile of cotton waste.

Early the next day he took Mr Greathead's body out of the bath, wrapped a thick towel round the neck and head, carried it down to the dairy and stretched it out on the slab. And there he cut it up into seventeen pieces.

These he wrapped in several layers of newspaper, covering the face and the hands first, because, at the last moment, they frightened him. He sewed them up in two sacks and hid them in the cellar.

He burnt the towel and the cotton waste in the kitchen fire; he cleaned his tools thoroughly and put them back in their places; and he washed down the marble slab. There wasn't a spot on the floor except for one flagstone where the pink rinsing of the slab had splashed over. He scrubbed it for half an hour, still seeing the rusty edges of the splash long after he had scoured it out.

He then washed and dressed himself with care.

As it was war-time Steven could only work by day, for the light in the dairy roof would have attracted the attention of the police. He had murdered Mr Greathead on a Tuesday; it was now three o'clock on Thursday afternoon. Exactly at ten minutes past four he had brought out the car, shut in close with its black hood and side curtains. He had packed Mr Greathead's suit-case and placed it in the car with his umbrella, railway rug, and travelling cap. Also, in a bundle, the clothes that his victim would have gone to London in.

He stowed the body in the two sacks beside him on the front.

By Hardraw Pass, half-way between Eastthwaite and Shawe, there are three round pits, known as the Churns, hollowed out of the grey rock and said to be bottomless. Steven had thrown stones, big as a man's chest, down the largest pit, to see whether they would be caught on any ledge or boulder. They had dropped clean, without a sound.

It poured with rain, the rain that Steven had reckoned on. The Pass was dark under the clouds and deserted. Steven turned his car so that the headlights glared on the pit's mouth. Then he ripped open the sacks and threw down, one by one, the seventeen pieces of Mr Greathead's body, and the sacks after them, and the clothes.

It was not enough to dispose of Mr Greathead's dead body; he had to behave as though Mr Greathead were alive. Mr Greathead had disappeared and he had to account for his disappearance. He drove on to Shawe station to the five o'clock train, taking care to arrive close on its starting. A troop-train was due to depart a minute earlier. Steven, who had reckoned on the darkness and the rain, reckoned also on the hurry and confusion on the platform.

As he had foreseen, there were no porters in the station entry; nobody to notice whether Mr Greathead was or was not in the car. He carried his things through on to the platform and gave the suit-case to an old man to label. He dashed into the booking-office and took Mr Greathead's ticket, and then rushed along the platform as if he were following his master. He heard himself shouting to the guard, 'Have you see Mr Greathead?' And the guard's answer, 'Naw!' And his own inspired statement, 'He must have taken his seat in the front, then.' He ran to the front of the train, shouldering his way among the troops. The drawn blinds of the carriages favoured him.

Steven thrust the umbrella, the rug, and the travelling cap into an empty compartment, and slammed the door to. He tried to shout something through the open window; but his tongue was harsh and dry against the roof of his mouth, and no sound came. He stood, blocking the window, till the guard whistled. When the train moved he ran alongside with his hand on the window ledge, as though he were taking the last instructions of his master. A porter pulled him back.

'Quick work, that,' said Steven.

Before he left the station he wired to Mr Greathead's London hotel, announcing the time of his arrival.

He felt nothing, nothing but the intense relief of a man who has saved himself by his own wits from a most horrible death. There were even moments, in the week that followed, when, so powerful was the illusion of his innocence, he could have believed that he had really seen Mr Greathead off by the five o'clock train. Moments when he literally stood still in amazement before his own incredible impunity. Other moments when a sort of vanity uplifted him. He had committed a murder that for sheer audacity and cool brain work surpassed all murders celebrated in the history of crime. Unfortunately the very perfection of his achievement doomed it to oblivion. He had left not a trace.

Not a trace.

Only when he woke in the night a doubt sickened him. There was the rusted ring of that splash on the dairy floor. He wondered, had he really washed it out clean. And he would get up and light a candle and go down to the dairy to make sure. He knew the exact place; bending over it with the candle, he could imagine that he still saw a faint outline.

Daylight reassured him. *He* knew the exact place, but nobody else knew. There was nothing to distinguish it from the natural stains in the flagstone. Nobody would guess. But he was glad when Mrs Blenkiron came back again.

On the day that Mr Greathead was to have come home by the four o'clock train Steven drove into Shawe and bought a chicken for the master's dinner. He met the four o'clock train and expressed surprise that Mr Greathead had not come by it. He said he would be sure to come by the seven. He ordered dinner for eight; Mrs Blenkiron roasted the chicken, and Steven met the seven o'clock train. This time he showed uneasiness.

The next day he met all the trains and wired to Mr Greathead's hotel for information. When the manager wired back that Mr Greathead had not arrived, he wrote to his relatives and gave notice to the police.

Three weeks passed. The police and Mr Greathead's relatives accepted Steven's statements, backed as they were by the evidence of the booking office clerk, the telegraph clerk, the guard, the porter who had labelled Mr Greathead's luggage and the hotel manager who had received his telegram. Mr Greathead's portrait was published in the illustrated papers with requests for any information which might lead to his discovery. Nothing happened, and presently he and his disappearance were forgotten. The nephew who came down to Eastthwaite to look into his affairs was satisfied. His balance at his bank was low owing to the non-payment of various dividends, but the accounts and the contents of Mr Greathead's cash-box and bureau were in order and Steven had put down every penny he had spent. The nephew paid Mrs Blenkiron's wages and dismissed her and arranged with the chauffeur to stay on and take care of the house. And as Steven saw that this was the best way to escape suspicion, he stayed on.

Only in Westleydale and Rathdale excitement lingered. People wondered and speculated. Mr Greathead had been robbed and murdered in the train (Steven said he had had money on him). He had lost his memory and wandered goodness knew where. He had thrown himself out of the railway carriage. Steven said Mr Greathead wouldn't do *that*, but he shouldn't be surprised if he had lost his memory. He knew a man who forgot who he was and where he lived. Didn't know his own wife and children. Shell-shock. And lately Mr Greathead's memory hadn't been what it was. Soon as he got it back he'd turn up again. Steven wouldn't be surprised to see him walking in any day.

But on the whole people noticed that he didn't care to talk much about Mr Greathead. They thought this showed very proper feeling. They were sorry for Steven. He had lost his master and he had lost Dorsy Oldishaw. And if he *did* half kill Ned Oldishaw, well, young Ned had no business to go meddling with his sweetheart. Even Mrs Oldishaw was sorry for him. And when Steven came into the bar of the King's Arms everybody said 'Good evening, Steve,' and made room for him by the fire.

III

Steven came and went now as if nothing had happened. He made a point of keeping the house as it would be kept if Mr Greathead were alive. Mrs Blenkiron, coming in once a fortnight to wash and clean, found the fire lit in Mr Greathead's study and his slippers standing on end in the fender. Upstairs his bed was made, the clothes folded back, ready. This ritual guarded Steven not only from the suspicions of outsiders, but from his own knowledge. By behaving as though he believed that Mr Greathead was still living he almost made himself believe it. By refusing to let his mind dwell on the murder he came to forget it. His imagination saved him, playing the play that kept him sane, till the murder became vague to him and fantastic like a thing done in a dream. He had waked up and this was the reality; this round of caretaking, this look the house had of waiting for Mr Greathead to come back to it. He had left off getting up in the night to examine the place on the dairy floor. He was no longer amazed at his impunity.

Then suddenly, when he really had forgotten, it ended. It was on a Saturday in January, about five o'clock. Steven had heard that Dorsy Oldishaw was back again, living at the King's Arms with her aunt. He had a mad, uncontrollable longing to see her again.

But it was not Dorsy that he saw.

His way from the Lodge kitchen into the drive was through the yard gates and along the flagged path under the study window. When he turned on to the flags he saw it shuffling along before him. The lamplight from the window lit it up. He could see distinctly the little old man in the long, shabby black overcoat, with the grey woollen muffler round his neck hunched up above his collar, lifting the thin grey hair that stuck out under the slouch of the black hat.

In the first moment that he saw it Steven had no fear. He simply felt that the murder had not happened, that he really *had* dreamed it, and that this was Mr Greathead come back, alive among the living. The phantasm was now standing at the door of the house, its hand on the door-knob as if about to enter.

But when Steven came up to the door it was not there.

He stood, fixed, staring at the space which had emptied itself so horribly. His heart heaved and staggered, snatching at his breath. And suddenly the memory of the murder rushed at him. He saw himself in the bathroom, shut in with his victim by the soiled green walls. He smelt the reek of the oil-stove; he heard the water running from the tap. He felt his feet springing forward, and his fingers pressing, tighter and tighter, on Mr Greathead's throat. He saw Mr Greathead's hands flapping helplessly, his terrified eyes, his face swelling and discoloured, changing horribly, and his body sinking to the floor.

He saw himself in the dairy, afterwards; he could hear the thudding, grinding, scraping noises of his tools. He saw himself on Hardraw Pass and the headlights glaring on the pit's mouth. And the fear and the horror he had not felt then came on him now.

He turned back; he bolted the yard gates and all the doors of the house, and shut himself up in the lighted kitchen. He took up his magazine, *The Autocar*, and forced himself to read it. Presently his terror left him. He said to himself it was nothing. Nothing but his fancy. He didn't suppose he'd ever see anything again.

Three days passed. On the third evening, Steven had lit the study lamp and was bolting the window when he saw it again.

It stood on the path outside, close against the window, looking in. He saw its face distinctly, the greyish, stuck-out bud of the under-lip, and the droop of the pinched nose. The small eyes peered at him, glittering. The whole figure had a glassy look between the darkness behind it and the pane. One moment it stood outside, looking in; and the next it was mixed up with the shimmering picture of the lighted room that hung there on the blackness of the trees. Mr Greathead then showed as if reflected, standing with Steven in the room.

And now he was outside again, looking at him, looking at him through the pane.

Steven's stomach sank and dragged, making him feel sick. He pulled down the blind between him and Mr Greathead, clamped the shutters to and drew the curtains over them. He locked and double-bolted the front door, all the doors, to keep Mr Greathead out. But, once that night, as he lay in bed, he heard the 'shoob-shoob' of feet shuffling along the flagged passages, up the stairs, and across the landing outside his door. The door handle rattled; but nothing came. He lay awake till morning, the sweat running off his skin, his heart plunging and quivering with terror.

When he got up he saw a white, scared face in the looking-glass. A face with a half-open mouth, ready to blab, to blurt out his secret; the face of an idiot. He was afraid to take that face into Eastthwaite or into Shawe. So he shut himself up in the house, half starved on his small stock of bread, bacon and groceries.

Two weeks passed; and then it came again in broad daylight.

It was Mrs Blenkiron's morning. He had lit the fire in the study at noon and set up Mr Greathead's slippers in the fender. When he rose from his stooping and turned round he saw Mr Greathead's phantasm standing on the hearthrug close in front of him. It was looking at him and smiling in a sort of mockery, as if amused at what Steven had been doing. It was solid and completely lifelike at first. Then, as Steven in his terror backed and backed away from it (he was afraid to turn and feel it there behind him), its feet became insubstantial. As if undermined, the whole structure sank and fell together on the floor, where it made a pool of some whitish glistening substance that mixed with the pattern of the carpet and sank through.

That was the most horrible thing it had done yet, and Steven's nerve broke under it. He went to Mrs Blenkiron, whom he found scrubbing out the dairy.

She sighed as she wrung out the floor-cloth.

'Eh, these owd yeller stawnes, scroob as you will they'll navver look clean.'

'Naw,' he said. 'Scroob and scroob, you'll navver get them clean.'

She looked up at him.

'Eh, lad, what ails 'ee? Ye've got a faace like a wroong dishclout hanging ower t' sink.'

'I've got the colic.'

'Aye, an' naw woonder wi' the damp, and they misties, an' your awn bad cooking. Let me roon down t' King's Arms and get you a drop of whisky.'

'Naw, I'll gaw down mysen.'

He knew now he was afraid to be left alone in the house. Down at the King's Arms Dorsy and Mrs Oldishaw were sorry for him. By this time he was really ill with fright. Dorsy and Mrs Oldishaw said it was a chill. They made him lie down on the settle by the kitchen fire and put a rug over him, and gave him stiff hot grog to drink. He slept. And when he woke he found Dorsy sitting beside him with her sewing.

He sat up and her hand was on his shoulder.

'Lay still, lad.'

'I maun get oop and gaw.'

'Nay, there's naw call for 'ee to gaw. Lay still and I'll make thee a coop o' tea.'

He lay still.

Mrs Oldishaw had made up a bed for him in her son's room, and they kept him there that night and till four o'clock the next day.

When he got up to go Dorsy put on her coat and hat.

'Is tha gawing out, Dorsy?'

'Aye. I canna let thee gaw and set there by thysen. I'm cooming oop to set with 'ee till night time.'

She came up and they sat side by side in the Lodge kitchen by the fire as they used to sit when they were together there, holding each other's hands and not talking.

'Dorsy,' he said at last, 'what astha coom for? Astha coom to tell me tha'll navver speak to me again?'

'Nay. Tha knaws what I've coom for.'

'To saay tha'll marry me?'

'Aye.'

'I maunna marry thee, Dorsy. 'Twouldn' be right.'

'Right? What dostha mean? 'Twouldn't be right for me to coom and set wi' thee this road ef I doan't marry thee.'

'Nay. I darena'. Tha said tha was afraid of me, Dorsy. I doan't want 'ee to be afraid. Tha said tha'd be unhappy. I doan't want 'ee to be unhappy.'

'That was lasst year. I'm not afraid of 'ee, now, Steve.'

'Tha doan't knaw me, lass.'

'Aye, I knaw thee. I knaw tha's sick and starved for want of me. Tha canna live wi'out thy awn lass to take care of 'ee.'

She rose.

'I maun gaw now. But I'll be oop tomorrow and the next day.'

And tomorrow and the next day and the next, at dusk, the hour that Steven most dreaded, Dorsy came. She sat with him till long after the night had fallen.

Steven would have felt safe so long as she was with him, but for his fear that Mr Greathead would appear to him while she was there and that she would see him. If Dorsy knew he was being haunted she might guess why. Or Mr Greathead might take some horrible blood-dripping and dismembered shape that would show her how he had been murdered. It would be like him, dead, to come between them as he had come when he was living.

They were sitting at the round table by the fireside. The lamp was lit and Dorsy was bending over her sewing. Suddenly she looked up, her head on one side, listening. Far away inside the house, on the flagged passage from the front door, he could hear the 'shoob-shoob' of the footsteps. He could almost believe that Dorsy shivered. And somehow, for some reason, this time he was not afraid.

'Steven,' she said, 'didsta 'ear anything?'

'Naw. Nobbut t' wind oonder t' roogs.'

She looked at him; a long wondering look. Apparently it satisfied her, for she answered: 'Aye. Mebbe 'tes nobbut wind,' and went on with her sewing.

He drew his chair nearer to her to protect her if it came. He could almost touch her where she sat.

The latch lifted. The door opened, and, his entrance and his passage unseen, Mr Greathead stood before them.

The table hid the lower half of his form; but above it he was steady and solid in his terrible semblance of flesh and blood.

Steven looked at Dorsy. She was staring at the phantasm with an innocent, wondering stare that had no fear in it at all. Then she looked at Steven. An uneasy, frightened, searching look, as though to make sure whether he had seen it.

That was her fear—that *he* should see it, that *he* should be frightened, that *he* should be haunted.

He moved closer and put his hand on her shoulder. He thought, perhaps, she might shrink from him because she knew that it *was* he who was haunted. But no, she put up her hand and held his, gazing up into his face and smiling.

Then, to his amazement, the phantasm smiled back at them; not with mockery, but with a strange and terrible sweetness. Its face lit up for one instant with a sudden, beautiful, shining light; then it was gone.

'Did tha see 'im, Steve?'

'Aye.'

'Astha seen annything afore?'

'Aye, three times I've seen 'im.'

'Is it that 'as scared thee?'

''Oo tawled 'ee I was scared?'

'I knawed. Because nowt can 'appen to thee but I maun knaw it.'

'What dostha think, Dorsy?'

'I think tha needna be scared, Steve. 'E's a kind ghawst. Whatever 'e is 'e doan't mean thee no 'arm. T' owd gentleman navver did when he was alive.'

'Didn' 'e? Didn' 'e? 'E served me the woorst turn 'e could when 'e coomed between thee and me.'

'Whatever makes 'ee think that, lad?'

'I doan' think it. I *knaw*.'

'Nay, loove, tha dostna.'

''E did. 'E did, I tell thee.'

'Doan' tha say that,' she cried. 'Doan' tha say it, Stevey.'

'Why shouldn't I?'

'Tha'll set folk talking that road.'

'What do they knaw to talk about?'

'Ef they was to remember what tha said.'

'And what did I say?'

'Why, that ef annybody was to coom between thee and me, tha'd do them in.'

'I wasna thinking of '*im*. Gawd knaws I wasna.'

'*They* doan't,' she said.

'*Tha* knaws? Tha knaws I didna mean 'im?'

'Aye, *I* knaw, Steve.'

'An', Dorsy, tha 'rn't afraid of me? Tha 'rn't afraid of me anny more?'

'Nay, lad. I loove thee too mooch. I shall navver be afraid of 'ee again. Would I coom to thee this road ef I was afraid?'

'Tha'll be afraid now.'

'And what should I be afraid of?'

'Why—'*im*.'

''*Im?* I should be a deal more afraid to think of 'ee setting with 'im oop 'ere, by thysen. Wuntha coom down and sleep at aunt's?'

'That I wunna. But I shall set 'ee on t' road passt t' moor.'

He went with her down the bridle-path and across the moor and along the main road that led through Eastthwaite. They parted at the turn where the lights of the village came in sight.

The moon had risen as Steven went back across the moor. The ash-tree at the bridle-path stood out clear, its hooked, bending branches black against the grey moor-grass. The shadows in the ruts laid stripes along the bridle-path, black on grey. The house was black-grey in the darkness of the drive. Only the lighted study window made a golden square in its long wall.

Before he could go up to bed he would have to put out the study lamp. He was nervous; but he no longer felt the sickening and sweating terror of the first hauntings. Either he was getting used to it, or—something had happened to him.

He had closed the shutters and put out the lamp. His candle made a ring of light round the table in the middle of the room. He was about to take it up and go when he heard a thin voice calling his name: 'Steven.' He raised his head to listen. The thin thread of sound seemed to come from outside, a long way off, at the end of the bridle-path.

'Steven, Steven——'

This time he could have sworn the sound came from inside his head, like the hiss of air in his ears.

'Steven——'

He knew the voice now. It was behind him in the room. He turned, and saw the phantasm of Mr Greathead sitting, as he used to sit, in the arm-chair by the fire. The form was dim in the dusk of the room outside the ring of candlelight. Steven's first movement was to snatch up the candlestick and hold it between him and the phantasm, hoping that the light would cause it to disappear. Instead of disappearing the figure became clear and solid, indistinguishable from a figure of flesh and blood dressed in black broadcloth and white linen. Its eyes had the shining transparency of blue crystal; they were fixed on Steven with a look of quiet, benevolent attention. Its small, narrow mouth was lifted at the corners, smiling.

It spoke.

'You needn't be afraid,' it said.

The voice was natural now, quiet, measured, slightly quavering. Instead of frightening Steven it soothed and steadied him.

He put the candle on the table behind him and stood up before the phantasm, fascinated.

'*Why* are you afraid?' it asked.

Steven couldn't answer. He could only stare, held there by the shining, hypnotizing eyes.

'You are afraid,' it said, 'because you think I'm what you call a ghost, a supernatural thing. You think I'm dead and that you killed me. You think you took a horrible revenge for a wrong you thought I did you. You think I've come back to frighten you, to revenge myself in my turn.

'And every one of those thoughts of yours, Steven, is wrong. I'm real, and my appearance is as natural and real as anything in this room—*more* natural and more real if you did but know. You didn't kill me, as you see; for here I am, as alive, more alive than you are. Your revenge consisted in removing me from a state which had become unbearable to a state more delightful than you can imagine. I don't mind telling you, Steven, that I was in serious financial difficulties (which, by the way, is a good thing for you, as it provides a plausible motive for my disappearance). So that, as far as revenge goes, the thing was a complete frost. You were my benefactor. Your methods were somewhat violent, and I admit you gave me some disagreeable moments before my actual deliverance; but as I was already developing rheumatoid arthritis there can be no doubt that in your hands my death was more merciful than if it had been left to Nature. As for the subsequent arrangements, I congratulate you, Steven, on your coolness and resource. I always said you were equal to any emergency, and that your brains would pull you safe through any scrape. You committed an appalling and dangerous crime, a crime of all things the most difficult to conceal, and you contrived so that it was not discovered and never will be discovered. And no doubt the details of this crime seemed to you horrible and revolting to the last degree; and the more horrible and the more revolting they were, the more you piqued yourself on your nerve in carrying the thing through without a hitch.

'I don't want to put you entirely out of conceit with your performance. It was very creditable for a beginner, very creditable indeed. But let me tell you, this idea of things being horrible and revolting is all illusion. The terms are purely relative to your limited perceptions.

'I'm speaking now to your intelligence—I don't mean that practical ingenuity which enabled you to dispose of me so neatly. When I say intelligence I mean intelligence. All you did, then, was to redistribute matter. To our incorruptible sense matter never takes any of those offensive forms in which it so often appears to you. Nature has evolved all this horror and repulsion just to prevent people from making too many little experiments like yours. You mustn't imagine that these things have any eternal importance. Don't flatter yourself you've electrified the universe. For minds no longer attached to flesh and blood, that horrible butchery you were so proud of, Steven, is simply silly. No more terrifying than the spilling of red ink or the rearrangement of a jig-saw puzzle. I saw the whole business, and I can assure you I felt nothing but intense amusement. Your face, Steven, was so absurdly serious. You've no idea what you looked like with that chopper. I'd have appeared to you then and told you so, only I knew I should frighten you into fits.

'And there's another grand mistake, my lad—your thinking that I'm haunting you out of revenge, that I'm trying to frighten you. . . . My dear Steven, if I'd wanted to frighten you I'd have appeared in a very different shape. I needn't remind you what shape I *might* have appeared in. . . . What do you suppose I've come for?'

'I don't know,' said Steven in a husky whisper. 'Tell me.'

'I've come to forgive you. And to save you from the horror you *would* have felt sooner or later. And to stop your going on with your crime.'

'You needn't,' Steven said. 'I'm not going on with it. I shall do no more murders.'

'There you are again. Can't you understand that I'm not talking about your silly butcher's work? I'm talking about your *real* crime. Your real crime was hating me.

'And your very hate was a blunder, Steven. You hated me for something I hadn't done.'

'Aye, what did you do? Tell me that.'

'You thought I came between you and your sweetheart. That night when Dorsy spoke to me, you thought I told her to throw you over, didn't you?'

'Aye. And what did you tell her?'

'I told her to stick to you. It was you, Steven, who drove her away. You frightened the child. She said she was afraid for her life of you. Not because you half killed that poor boy, but because of the look on your face before you did it. The look of hate, Steven.

'I told her not to be afraid of you. I told her that if she threw you over you might go altogether to the devil; that she might even be responsible for some crime. I told her that if she married you and was faithful—*if she loved you*—I'd answer for it you'd never go wrong.

'She was too frightened to listen to me. Then I told her to think over what I'd said before she did anything. You heard me say that.'

'Aye. That's what I heard you say. I didn't knaw. I didn't knaw. I thought you'd set her agen me.'

'If you don't believe me, you can ask her, Steven.'

'That's what she said t'other night. That you navver coom between her and me. Navver.'

'Never,' the phantasm said. 'And you don't hate me now.'

'Naw. Naw. I should navver 'a hated 'ee. I should navver 'a laid a finger on thee, ef I'd knawn.'

'It's not your laying fingers on me, it's your hatred that matters. If that's done with, the whole thing's done with.'

'Is it? Is it? Ef it was knawn, I should have to hang for it. Maunna I gie mysen oop? Tell me, maun I gie mysen oop?'

'You want me to decide that for you?'

'Aye. Doan't gaw,' he said. 'Doan't gaw.'

It seemed to him that Mr Greathead's phastasm was getting a little thin, as if it couldn't last more than an instant. He had never so longed for it to go, as he longed now for it to stay and help him.

'Well, Steven, any flesh-and-blood man would tell you to go and get hanged tomorrow; that it was no more than your plain duty. And I daresay there are some mean, vindictive spirits even in my world who would say the same, not because *they* think death important but because they know *you* do, and want to get even with you that way.

'It isn't *my* way. I consider this little affair is strictly between ourselves. There isn't a jury of flesh-and-blood men who would understand it. They all think death so important.'

'What do you want me to do, then? Tell me and I'll do it! Tell me!'

He cried it out loud; for Mr Greathead's phantasm was getting thinner and thinner; it dwindled and fluttered, like a light going down. Its voice came from somewhere away outside, from the other end of the bridle-path.

'Go on living,' it said. 'Marry Dorsy.'

'I darena. She doan' knaw I killed 'ee.'

'Oh, yes'—the eyes flickered up, gentle and ironic—'she does. She knew all the time.'

And with that the phantasm went out.

A Visitor From Down Under

L. P. HARTLEY

And who will you send to fetch him away?

After a promising start, the March day had ended in a wet evening. It was hard to tell whether rain or fog predominated. The loquacious 'bus-conductor said 'A foggy evening' to those who rode inside, and 'A wet evening' to such as were obliged to ride outside. But in or on the 'buses, cheerfulness held the field, for their patrons, inured to discomfort, made light of climatic inclemency. All the same, the weather was worth remarking on: the most scrupulous conversationalist could refer to it without feeling self-convicted of banality. How much more the conductor, who, in common with most of his kind, had a considerable conversational gift.

The 'bus was making its last journey through the heart of London before turning in for the night. Inside it was only half full. Outside, as the conductor was aware by virtue of his sixth sense, there still remained a passenger too hardy or too lazy to seek shelter. And now, as the 'bus rattled rapidly down the Strand, the footsteps of this person could be heard shuffling and creaking upon the metal-shod stairs.

'Anyone on top?' asked the conductor, addressing an errant umbrella-point and the hem of a mackintosh.

'I didn't notice anyone,' the man replied.

'It's not that I don't trust you,' remarked the conductor, pleasantly giving a hand to his alighting fare; 'but I think I'll go up and make sure.'

Moments like these, moments of mistrust in the infallibility of his observation, occasionally visited the conductor. They came at the end of a tiring day, and if he could he withstood them. They were signs of weakness, he thought; and to give away to them matter for self-reproach. 'Going barmy, that's what you are,' he told himself, and he casually took a fare inside to prevent his mind dwelling on the unvisited outside. But his unreasoning disquietude survived this distraction, and murmuring against himself he started to climb the stairs.

To his surprise, almost stupefaction, he found that his misgivings were justified. Breasting the ascent, he saw a passenger sitting on the right-hand front seat; and the passenger, in spite of his hat turned down, his collar turned up and the creased white muffler that showed between the two, must have heard him coming; for though the man was looking straight ahead, in his outstretched left hand, wedged between the first and second fingers, he held a coin.

'Jolly evening, don't you think?' asked the conductor, who wanted to say something. The passenger made no reply, but the penny, for such it was, slipped the fraction of an inch lower in the groove between the pale freckled fingers.

'I said it was a damn wet night,' the conductor persisted irritably, annoyed by the man's reserve. Still no reply.

'Where you for?' asked the conductor, in a tone suggesting that, wherever it was, it must be a discreditable destination.

'Carrick Street.'

'Where?' the conductor demanded. He had heard all right, but a slight peculiarity in the passenger's pronunciation made it appear reasonable to him, and possibly humiliating to the passenger, that he should not have heard.

'Carrick Street.'

'Then why don't you say Carrick Street?' the conductor grumbled as he punched the ticket.

There was a moment's pause, then 'Carrick Street,' the passenger repeated.

'Yes, I know, I know; you needn't go on telling me,' fumed the conductor, fumbling with the passenger's penny. He couldn't get hold of it from above, it had slipped too far, so he passed his hand underneath the other's and drew the coin from between his fingers.

It was cold, even where it had been held.

'Know?' said the stranger suddenly, 'what do you know?'

The conductor was trying to draw his fare's attention to the ticket, but could not make him look round. 'I suppose I know you are a clever chap,' he remarked. 'Look here now. Where do you want this ticket? In your button-hole?'

'Put it here,' said the passenger.

'Where?' asked the conductor. 'You aren't a blooming letter-rack.'

'Where the penny was,' replied the passenger. 'Between my fingers.'

The conductor felt reluctant, he did not know why, to oblige the passenger in this. The rigidity of the hand disconcerted him: it was stiff, he supposed, or perhaps paralysed. And since he had been standing on the top his own hands were none too warm. The ticket doubled up and grew limp under his repeated efforts to push it in. He bent lower, for he was a good-hearted fellow, and using both hands, one above and one below, he slid the ticket into its bony slot.

'Right you are, Kaiser Bill.'

Perhaps the passenger resented this jocular allusion to his physical infirmity; perhaps he merely wanted to be quiet. All he said was:

'Don't speak to me again.'

'Speak to you!' shouted the conductor, losing all self-control. 'Catch me speaking to a stuffed dummy!'

Muttering to himself, he withdrew into the bowels of the 'bus.

At the corner of Carrick Street quite a number of people got on board. All wanted to be first, but pride of place was shared by three women, who all tried to enter simultaneously.

The conductor's voice made itself audible above the din: 'Now then, now then, look where you're shoving! This isn't a bargain-sale. Gently *please*, lady; he's only a pore old man.' In a moment or two the confusion abated, and the conductor, his hand on the cord of the bell, bethought himself of the passenger on top whose destination Carrick Street was. He had forgotten to get down. Yielding to his good nature, for the conductor was adverse to further conversation with his uncommunicative fare, he mounted the stairs, put his head over the top and shouted, 'Carrick Street! Carrick Street!' That was the utmost he could bring himself to do. But his admonition was without effect; his summons remained unanswered; nobody came. 'Well, if he wants to stay up there he can,' muttered the condutor, still aggrieved. 'I won't fetch him down, cripple or no cripple.' The 'bus moved on. He slipped by me, thought the conductor, while all that Cup-tie crowd was getting in.

The same evening, some five hours earlier, a taxi turned into Carrick Street and pulled up at the door of a small hotel. The street was empty. It looked like a cul-de-sac, but in reality it was pierced at the far end by an alley, like a thin sleeve, which wound its way into Soho.

'That the last, sir?' enquired the driver, after several transits between the cab and the hotel.

'How many does that make?'

'Nine packages in all, sir.'

'Could you get all your worldly goods into nine packages, driver?'

'That I could; into two.'

'Well, have a look inside and see if I have left anything.'

The cabman felt about among the cushions. 'Can't find nothing, sir.'

'What do you do with anything you find?' asked the stranger.

'Take it to New Scotland Yard, sir,' the driver promptly replied.

'Scotland Yard?' said the stranger. 'Strike a match, will you, and let me have a look.'

But he, too, found nothing, and, reassured, followed his luggage into the hotel.

A chorus of welcome and congratulation greeted him. The manager, the manager's wife, the ministers without portfolio of which all hotels are full, the porters, the lift-man, all clustered around him.

'Well, Mr Rumbold, after all these years! We thought you'd forgotten us! And wasn't it odd, the very night your telegram came from Australia we'd been talking about you! And my husband said, "Don't you worry about Mr Rumbold. He'll fall on his feet all right. Some fine day he'll walk in here a rich man." Not that you weren't always well-off, but my husband meant a millionaire.'

'He was quite right,' said Mr Rumbold slowly savouring his words; 'I am.'

'There, what did I tell you?' the manager exclaimed, as though one recital of his prophecy was not enough. 'But I wonder you're not too grand to come to Rossall's Hotel.'

'I've nowhere else to go,' said the millionaire shortly. 'And if I had, I wouldn't. This place is like home to me.'

His eyes softened as they scanned the familiar surroundings. They were light-grey eyes, very pale, and seeming paler from their setting in his tanned face. His cheeks were slightly sunken and very deeply lined; his blunt-ended nose was straight. He had a thin straggling moustache, straw-coloured, which made his age difficult to guess. Perhaps he was nearly fifty, so wasted was the skin on his neck, but his movements, unexpectedly agile and decided, were those of a younger man.

'I won't go up to my room now,' he said, in response to the manageress's question. 'Ask Clutsam—he's still with you?—good—to unpack my things. He'll find all I want for the night in the green suit-case. I'll take my despatch-box with me. And tell them to bring me a sherry-and-bitters in the lounge.'

As the crow flies, it was not far to the lounge. But by way of the tortuous, ill-lit passages, doubling on themselves, yawning with dark entries, plunging into kitchen stairs—the catacombs so dear to habitués of Rossall's Hotel—it was a considerable distance. Anyone posted in the shadow of these alcoves, or arriving at the head of the basement staircase, could not have failed to notice the air of utter content which marked Mr Rumbold's leisurely progress: the droop of his shoulders, acquiescing in weariness; the hands turned inwards and swaying slightly, but quite forgotten by their owner; the chin, always prominent, now pushed forward so far that it looked relaxed and helpless, not at all defiant. The unseen witness would have envied Mr Rumbold, perhaps even grudged him his holiday airs, his untroubled acceptance of the present and the future.

A waiter whose face he did not remember brought him the *apéritif*, which he drank slowly, his feet propped unconventionally upon a ledge of the chimney-piece; a pardonable relaxation, for the room was empty. Judge therefore his surprise when, out of a fire-engendered drowsiness, he heard a voice which seemed to come from the wall above his head. A cultivated voice, perhaps too cultivated, slightly husky, yet careful and precise in its enunciation. Even while his eyes searched the room to make sure that no one had come in, he could not help hearing everything the voice said. It seemed to be talking to him, and yet the rather oracular utterance implied a less restricted audience. The utterance of a man who was aware that, though it was a duty for him to speak, for Mr Rumbold to listen would be both a pleasure and a profit.

'—A Children's Party,' the voice announced in an even, neutral tone, nicely balanced between approval and distaste, between enthusiasm and boredom; 'six little girls and six little' (a faint lift in the voice, expressive of tolerant surprise) 'boys. The Broadcasting Company has invited them to tea, and they are anxious that you should share some of their fun.' (At the last word the voice became almost positively colourless.) 'I must tell you that they have had tea, and enjoyed it, didn't you, children?' (A cry of 'Yes,' muffled and timid, greeted this leading question.) 'We should have liked you to hear our table-talk, but there wasn't much of it, we were so busy eating.' For a moment the voice identified itself with the children. 'But we can tell you what we ate. Now, Percy, tell us what you had.'

A piping little voice recited a long list of comestibles; like the children in the treacle-well, thought Rumbold, Percy must have been, or soon would be, very ill. A few others volunteered the items of their repast. 'So you see,' said the voice, 'we have not done so badly. And now we are going to have crackers, and afterwards' (the voice hesitated and seemed to dissociate itself from the words) 'children's games.' There was an impressive pause, broken by the muttered exhortation of a little girl: 'Don't cry, Philip, it won't hurt you.' Fugitive sparks and snaps of sound followed; more like a fire being mended, thought Rumbold, than crackers. A murmur of voices pierced the fusillade. 'What have you got, Alec, what have you *got*?' 'I've got a cannon.' 'Give it to me.' 'No.' 'Well, lend it to me.' 'What do you want it for?' 'I want to shoot Jimmy.'

Mr Rumbold started. Something had disturbed him. Was it imagination, or did he hear, above the confused medley of sound, a tiny click? The voice was speaking again. 'And now we're going to begin the games.' As though to make amends for past luke-warmness a faint flush of anticipation gave colour to the decorous voice. 'We will commence with that old favourite, Ring-a-ring-of-Roses.'

The children were clearly shy, and left each other to do the singing.

Their courage lasted for a line or two, and then gave out. But fortified by the Speaker's baritone, powerful though subdued, they took heart, and soon were singing without assistance or direction. Their light wavering voices had a charming effect. Tears stood in Mr Rumbold's eyes. 'Oranges and Lemons' came next. A more difficult game, it yielded several unrehearsed effects before it finally got under way. One could almost see the children being marshalled into their places, as though for a figure in the Lancers. Some of them no doubt had wanted to play another game; children are contrary, and the dramatic side of 'Oranges and Lemons', though it appeals to many, always affrights a few. The disinclination of these last would account for the pauses and hesitations which irritated Mr Rumbold, who, as a child, had always had a strong fancy for this particular game. When, to the tramping and stamping of many small feet, the droning chant began, he leaned back and closed his eyes in ecstasy. He listened intently for the final accelerando which leads up to the catastrophe. Still the prologue maundered on, as though the children were anxious to extend the period of security, the joyous care-free promenade which the great Bell of Bow by his inconsiderate profession of ignorance, was so rudely to curtail. The Bells of Old Bailey pressed their usurers' question; the Bells of Shoreditch answered with becoming flippancy; the Bells of Stepney posed their ironical query, when suddenly before the great Bell of Bow had time to get his word in, Mr Rumbold's feelings underwent a strange revolution. Why couldn't the game continue, all sweetness and sunshine? Why drag in the fatal issue? Let payment be deferred; let the bells go on chiming and never strike the hour. But heedless of Mr Rumbold's squeamishness, the game went its way. After the eating comes the reckoning.

> 'Here is a candle to light you to bed,
> And here comes a chopper to chop off your head!
> Chop, chop, chop . . .'

A child screamed, and there was silence.

Mr Rumbold felt quite upset, and great was his relief when, after a few more half-hearted rounds of 'Oranges and Lemons', the voice announced, 'Here we come gathering Nuts and May'. At least there was nothing sinister in that. Delicious sylvan scene, comprising in one splendid botanical inexactitude all the charms of winter, spring, and autumn.

What superiority to circumstance was implied in the conjunction of nuts and may! What defiance of cause and effect! What a testimony to coincidence! For cause and effect are against us, as witness the fate of Old Bailey's Debtor; but coincidence is always on our side, always teaching us how to eat our cake and have it! The long arm of coincidence; Mr Rumbold would have liked to clasp it by the hand.

Meanwhile his own hand conducted the music of the revels and his foot kept time. Their pulses quickened by enjoyment, the children put more heart into the singing; the game went with a swing; the ardour and rhythm of it invaded the little room where Mr Rumbold sat. Like heavy fumes the waves of sound poured in, so penetrating, they ravished the sense, so sweet they intoxicated it, so light they fanned it to a flame. Mr Rumbold was transported. His hearing, sharpened by the subjugation and quiescence of his other faculties, began to take in new sounds; the names, for instance, of the players who were 'wanted' to make up each side and of the champions who were to pull them over. For the listeners-in, the issues of the struggles remained in doubt. Did Nancy Price succeed in detracting Percy Kingham from his allegiance? Probably. Did Alec Wharton prevail against Maisie Drew? It was certainly an easy win for someone: the contest lasted only a second, and a ripple of laughter greeted it. Did Violet Kingham make good against Horace Gold? This was a dire encounter, punctuated by deep irregular panting. Mr Rumbold could see, in his mind's eye, the two champions straining backwards and forwards across the white motionless handkerchief, their faces red and puckered with exertion. Violet or Horace, one of them had to go: Violet might be bigger than Horace, but then Horace was a boy: they were evenly matched: they had their pride to maintain. The moment when the will was broken and the body went limp in surrender would be like a moment of dissolution. Yes, even this game had its stark, uncomfortable side. Violet or Horace, one of them was smarting now; crying perhaps under the humiliation of being fetched away.

The game began afresh. This time there was an eager ring in the children's voices: two tried antagonists were going to meet: it would be a battle of giants. The chant throbbed into a war-cry.

> 'Who will you have for your Nuts and May,
>   Nuts and May, Nuts and May:
> Who will you have for your Nuts and May
>   On a cold and frosty morning?'

They would have Victor Rumbold for Nuts and May, Victor Rumbold, Victor Rumbold; and from the vindictiveness in their voices they might have meant to have his blood too.

> 'And who will you send to fetch him away
>   Fetch him away, fetch him away:
> Who will you send to fetch him away
>   On a cold and frosty morning?'

Like a clarion call, a shout of defiance, came the reply:

> 'We'll send Jimmy Hagberd to fetch him away,
>   Fetch him away, fetch him away;
> We'll send Jimmy Hagberd to fetch him away,
>   On a wet and foggy evening.'

This variation, it might be supposed, was intended to promote the contest from the realms of pretence into the world of reality. But Mr Rumbold probably did not hear that his abduction had been antedated. He had turned quite green and his head was lolling against the back of the chair.

'Any wine, sir?'

'Yes, Clutsam, a bottle of champagne.'

'Very good, sir.'

Mr Rumbold drained the first glass at one go.

'Anyone coming in to dinner besides me, Clutsam?' he presently enquired.

'Not now, sir, it's nine o'clock,' replied the waiter, his voice edged with reproach.

'Sorry, Clutsam, I didn't feel up to the mark before dinner, so I went and lay down.'

The waiter was mollified.

'Thought you weren't looking quite yourself, sir. No bad news, I hope?'

'No, nothing. Just a bit tired after the journey.'

'And how did you leave Australia, sir?' enquired the waiter, to accommodate Mr Rumbold, who seemed anxious to talk.

'In better weather than you have here,' Mr Rumbold replied, finishing his second glass, and measuring with his eye the depleted contents of the bottle.

The rain kept up a steady patter on the glass roof of the coffee room.

'Still, a good climate isn't everything; it isn't like home, for instance,' the waiter remarked.

'No, indeed.'

'There's many parts of the world as would be glad of a good day's rain,' affirmed the waiter.

'There certainly are,' said Mr Rumbold, who found the conversation sedative.

'Did you do much fishing when you were abroad, sir?' the waiter pursued.

'A little.'

'Well, you want rain for that,' declared the waiter, as one who scores a point. 'The fishing isn't preserved in Australia, like what it is here?'

'No.'

'Then there ain't no poaching,' concluded the waiter philosophically. 'It's every man for himself.'

'Yes, that's the rule in Australia.'

'Not much of a rule, is it?' the waiter took him up. 'Not much like law, I mean.'

'It depends what you mean by law.'

'Oh, Mr Rumbold, sir, you know very well what I mean. I mean the police. Now, if you was to have done a man in out in Australia— murdered him, I mean—they'd hang you for it if they caught you, wouldn't they?'

Mr Rumbold teased the champagne with the butt-end of his fork and drank again.

'Probably they would, unless there were special circumstances.'

'In which case you might get off?'

'I might.'

'That's what I mean by law,' pronounced the waiter. 'You know what the law is: you go against it, and you're punished. Of course I don't mean you, sir; I only say "you" as—as an illustration to make my meaning clear.'

'Quite, quite.'

'Whereas if there was only what you call a rule,' the waiter pursued, deftly removing the remains of Mr Rumbold's chicken, 'it might fall to the lot of any man to round you up. Might be anybody; might be me.'

'Why should you or they,' asked Mr Rumbold, 'want to round me up? I haven't done you any harm, or them.'

'Oh, but we should have to, sir.'

'Why?'

'We couldn't rest in our beds, sir, knowing you was at large. You might do it again. Somebody'd have to see to it.'

'But supposing there was nobody?'

'Sir?'

'Supposing the murdered man hadn't any relatives or friends; supposing he just disappeared, and no one ever knew that he was dead?'

'Well, sir,' said the waiter, winking portentously, 'in that case he'd have to get on your track himself. He wouldn't rest in his grave, sir, no, not he, and knowing what he did.'

'Clutsam,' said Mr Rumbold suddenly, 'bring me another bottle of wine and don't trouble to ice it.'

The waiter took the bottle from the table and held it up to the light. 'Yes, it's dead, sir.'

'Dead?'

'Yes, sir, finished—empty—dead.'

'You're right,' Mr Rumbold agreed. 'It's quite dead.'

It was nearly eleven o'clock. Mr Rumbold again had the lounge to himself. Clutsam would be bringing his coffee presently. Too bad of Fate to have him haunted by these casual reminders; too bad, his first day at home. 'Too bad, too bad,' he muttered, while the fire warmed the soles of his slippers. But it was excellent champagne, he would take no harm from it: the brandy Clutsam was bringing him would do the rest. Clutsam was a good sort, nice, old-fashioned servant . . . nice, old-fashioned house . . . . Warmed by the wine, his thoughts began to pass out of his control.

'Your coffee, sir,' said a voice at his elbow.

'Thank you, Clutsam, I'm very much obliged to you,' said Mr Rumbold, with the exaggerated civility of slight intoxication. 'You're an excellent fellow. I wish there were more like you.'

'I hope so, too, I'm sure,' said Clutsam, trying in his muddle-hearted way to deal with both observations at once.

'Don't seem many people about,' Mr Rumbold remarked. 'Hotel pretty full?'

'Oh yes, sir, all the suites are let, and the other rooms too. We're turning people away every day. Why, only tonight a gentleman rang up. Said he would come round late, on the off-chance. But, bless me, he'll find the birds have flown.'

'Birds?' echoed Mr Rumbold.

'I mean, there ain't any more rooms, not for love nor money.'

'Well, I'm sorry for him,' said Mr Rumbold, with ponderous sincerity. 'I'm sorry for any man, friend or foe, who has to go tramping about London on a night like this. If I had an extra bed in my room, I'd put it at his disposal.'

'You have, sir,' the waiter said.

'Why, of course I have. How stupid! Well, well. I'm sorry for the poor chap. I'm sorry for all homeless ones, Clutsam, wandering on the face of the earth.'

'Amen to that,' said the waiter devoutly.

'And doctors and such, pulled out of their bed at midnight. It's a hard life. Ever thought about a doctor's life, Clutsam?'

'Can't say I have, sir.'

'Well, well, but it's hard; you can take that from me.'

'What time shall I call you in the morning, sir?' the waiter asked, seeing no reason why the conversation should ever stop.

'You needn't call me Clutsam,' replied Mr Rumbold in a sing-song voice, and running the words together as though he were excusing the waiter from addressing him by the waiter's own name. 'I'll get up when I'm ready. And that may be pretty late, pretty late.' He smacked his lips over the words. 'Nothing like a good lie, eh, Clutsam?'

'That's right, sir. You have your sleep out,' the waiter encouraged him. 'You won't be disturbed.'

'Good night, Clutsam, you're an excellent fellow, and I don't care who hears me say so.'

'Good night, sir.'

Mr Rumbold returned to his chair. It lapped him round, it ministered to his comfort; he felt at one with it. At one with the fire, the clock, the tables, all the furniture. Their usefulness, their goodness, went out to meet his usefulness, his goodness, met and were friends. Who could bind their sweet influences or restrain them in the exercise of their kind offices? No one. No one; certainly not a shadow from the past. The room was perfectly quiet. Street sounds reached it only as a low continuous hum, infinitely reassuring. Mr Rumbold fell asleep.

He dreamed that he was a boy again, living in his old home in the country. He was possessed, in the dream, by a master-passion; he must collect firewood whenever and wherever he saw it. He found himself one autumn afternoon in the woodhouse; that was how the dream began. The door was partly open, admitting a little light, but he could not recall how he got in. The floor of the shed was littered with bits of bark and thin twigs; but, with the exception of the chopping block which he knew could not be used, there was nowhere a log of sufficient size to make a fire. Though he did not like being in the woodhouse alone he stayed long enough to make a thorough search. But he could find nothing. The compulsion he knew so well descended on him, and he left the woodhouse and went into the garden. His steps took him to the foot of a high tree, standing by itself in a tangle of long grass at some distance from the house. The tree had been lopped; for half its height it had no branches, only leafy tufts, sticking out at irregular intervals. He knew what he would see when he looked up into the dark foliage. And there, sure enough it was; a long dead bough, bare in patches where the bark had peeled off, and crooked in the middle like an elbow.

He began to climb the tree. The ascent proved easier than he expected, his body seemed no weight at all. But he was visited by a terrible oppression, which increased as he mounted. The bough did not want him; it was projecting its hostility down the trunk of the tree. And every second brought him nearer to an object which he had always dreaded: a growth, people called it. It stuck out from the trunk of the tree, a huge circular swelling thickly matted with twigs. Victor would have rather died than hit his head against it.

By the time he reached the bough twilight had deepened into night. He knew what he had to do: sit astride the bough, since there was none near by from which he could reach it, and press with his hands until it broke. Using his legs to get what purchase he could, he set his back against the tree, and pushed with all his might downwards. To do this he was obliged to look beneath him, and he saw, far below him on the ground, a white sheet spread out as though to catch him; and he knew at once that it was a shroud.

Frantically he pulled and pushed at the stiff brittle bough; a lust to break it took hold of him; leaning forward his whole length, he seized the bough at the elbow joint and strained it away from him. As it cracked he toppled over and the shroud came rushing upwards. . . .

Mr Rumbold waked in a cold sweat to find himself clutching the curved arm of the chair on which the waiter had set his brandy. The glass had fallen over, and the spirit lay in a little pool on the leather seat. 'I can't let it go like that,' he thought, 'I must get some more.' A man he did not know answered the bell. 'Waiter,' he said, 'bring me a brandy and soda in my room in a quarter of an hour's time. Rumbold, the name is.' He followed the waiter out of the room The passage was completely dark except for a small blue gas-jet, beneath which was huddled a cluster of candlesticks. The hotel, he remembered, maintained an old-time habit of deference towards darkness. As he held the wick to the gas-jet, he heard himself mutter, 'Here is a candle to light you to bed.' But he recollected the ominous conclusion of the distich, and, fuddled as he was, he left it unspoken.

Shortly after Mr Rumbold's retirement the door-bell of the hotel rang. Three sharp peals, and no pause between them. 'Someone in a hurry to get in,' the night porter grumbled to Clutsam, who was on duty till midnight. 'Expect he's forgotten his key.' He made no haste to answer the summons, it would do the forgetful fellow good to wait: teach him a lesson. So dilatory was he that by the time he reached the hall-door the bell was tinkling again. Irritated by such importunity, he deliberately went back to set straight a pile of newspapers before letting this impatient devil in. To mark his indifference he even kept behind the door while he opened it; so that his first sight of the visitor only took in his back. But this limited inspection sufficed to show that the man was a stranger and not a guest at the hotel.

In the long black cape which fell almost sheer one side and on the other stuck out as though he had a basket under his arm, he looked like a crow with a broken wing. A bald-headed crow, thought the porter, for there's a patch of bare skin between that white linen thing and his hat.

'Good evening, sir,' he said, 'what can I do for you?'

The stranger made no answer, but glided to a side table and began turning over some letters with his right hand.

'Are you expecting a message?' asked the porter.

'No,' the stranger replied. 'I want a room for the night.'

'Was you the gentleman who telephoned for a room this evening?' 'Yes.'

'In that case I was to tell you we're afraid you can't have one, the hotel's booked right up.'

'Are you quite sure?' asked the stranger. 'Think again.'

'Them's my orders, sir. It don't do me no good to think.' At this moment the porter had a curious sensation as though some important part of him, his life maybe, had gone adrift inside him and was spinning round and round. The sensation ceased when he began to speak.

'I'll call the waiter, sir,' he said.

But before he called the waiter appeared, intent on an errand of his own.

'I say, Bill,' he began, 'what's the number of Mr Rumbold's room? He wants a drink taken up, and I forgot to ask him.'

'It's thirty-three,' said the porter unsteadily. 'The double room.'

'Why, Bill, what's up?' the waiter exclaimed. 'You look as if you'd seen a ghost.'

Both men stared round the hall, and then back at each other. The room was empty.

'God,' said the porter. 'I must have had the horrors. But he was here a moment ago. Look at this.'

On the stone flags lay an icicle, an inch or two long, around which a little pool was fast collecting.

'Why, Bill,' cried the waiter, 'how did that get here? It's not freezing.'

'*He* must have brought it,' the porter said.

They looked at each other in consternation, which changed into terror as the sound of a bell made itself heard, coming from the depths of the hotel.

'Clutsam's there,' whispered the porter. 'He'll have to answer it, whoever it is.'

Clutsam had taken off his tie, and was getting ready for bed. What on earth could anyone want in the lounge at this hour? He pulled on his coat and went upstairs.

Standing by the fire he saw the same figure whose appearance and disappearance had so disturbed the porter. 'Yes, sir,' he said.

'I want you to go to Mr Rumbold,' said the stranger, 'and ask him if he is prepared to put the other bed in his room at the disposal of a friend.'

In a few moments Clutsam returned.

'Mr Rumbold's compliments, sir, and he wants to know who it is.' The stranger went to the table in the centre of the room. An Australian newspaper was lying on it, which Clutsam had not noticed before. The aspirant to Mr Rumbold's hospitality turned over the pages. Then with his finger, which appeared, even to Clutsam standing by the door, unusually pointed, he cut out a rectangular slip, about the size of a visiting card, and, moving away, motioned the waiter to take it.

By the light of the gas-jet in the passage Clutsam read the excerpt. It seemed to be a kind of obituary notice; but of what possible interest could it be to Mr Rumbold, to know that the body of Mr James Hagberd had been discovered in circumstances which suggested that he had met his death by violence?

After a long interval Clutsam returned, looking puzzled and a little frightened.

'Mr Rumbold's compliments, sir, but he knows no one of that name.'

'Then take this message to Mr Rumbold,' said the stranger. 'Say "would he rather that I went up to him, or that he came down to me?" '

For the third time Clutsam went to do the stranger's bidding. He did not, however, upon his return open the door of the smoking-room, but shouted through it:

'Mr Rumbold wishes you to Hell, sir, where you belong, and says "Come up if you dare." '

Then he bolted.

A minute later, from his retreat in an underground coal-cellar, he heard a shot fired. Some old instinct, danger-loving or danger-disregarding, stirred in him, and he ran up the stairs quicker than he had ever run up them in his life. In the passage he stumbled over Mr Rumbold's boots. The bedroom door was ajar. Putting his head down he rushed in. The brightly lit room was empty. But almost all the movables in it were overturned, and the bed was in a frightful mess. The pillow with its fivefold perforation was the first object on which Clutsam noticed blood-stains. Thenceforward he seemed to see them every-where. But what sickened him and kept him so long from going down to rouse the others was the sight of an icicle on the window-sill, a thin claw of ice curved like a Chinaman's nail, with a bit of flesh sticking to it.

That was the last he saw of Mr Rumbold. But a policeman patrolling

Carrick Street noticed a man in a long black cape who seemed, from the position of his arm, to be carrying something heavy. He called out to the man and ran after him; but though he did not seem to be moving very fast the policeman could not overtake him.

Fullcircle

JOHN BUCHAN

▬

Peckwether, the historian, whose turn for story-telling came at our last dinner before the summer interregnum, apologized for reading his narrative. He was not good, he said, at impromptu composition. He also congratulated himself on Leithen's absence. 'He comes into the story, and I should feel rather embarrassed talking about him to his face. But he has read my manuscript and approved it, so you have two reliable witnesses to a queerish tale.'

In his precise academic voice he read what follows.

The October day was brightening towards late afternoon when Leithen and I climbed the hill above the stream and came in sight of the house. All morning a haze with a sheen of pearl in it had lain on the folds of downland, and the vision of far horizons, which is the glory of Cotswold, had been veiled, so that every valley seemed a place enclosed and set apart. But now a glow had come into the air, and for a little the autumn lawns had the tints of summer. The gold of sunshine was warm on the grasses, and only the riot of colour in the berry-laden edges of the fields and the slender woodlands told of the failing year.

We were looking into a green cup of the hills, and it was all a garden. A little place, bounded by slopes that defined its graciousness with no hint of barrier, so that a dweller there, though his view was but half a mile on any side, would yet have the sense of dwelling on uplands and commanding the world. Round the top edge ran an old wall of stones, beyond which the October bracken flamed to the skyline. Inside were folds of ancient pasture with here and there a thorn-bush, falling to rose gardens, and, on one side, to the smooth sward of a terrace above a tiny lake. At the heart of it stood the house, like a jewel well set. It was a miniature, but by the hand of a master. The style was late seventeenth century, when an agreeable classic convention had opened up to sunlight and comfort the dark magnificence of the Tudor fashion. The place had the spacious air of a great mansion, and was finished in every detail with a fine scrupulousness. Only when the eye measured its proportions with the woods and the hillside did the mind perceive that it was a small dwelling. The stone of Cotswold takes curiously the colour of the weather. Under thunder-clouds it will be as dark as basalt; on a grey day it is grey like lava; but in sunshine it absorbs the sun. At the moment the little house was pale gold, like honey.

Leithen swung a long leg across the stile.

'Pretty good, isn't it?' he said. 'It's pure authentic Sir Christopher Wren. The name is worthy of it, too. It is called Fullcircle.'

He told me its story. It had been built after the Restoration by the Carteron family, whose wide domains ran into these hills. The Lord Carteron of the day was a friend of the Merry Monarch, but it was not as a sanctuary for orgies that he built the house. Perhaps he was tired of the gloomy splendour of Minster Carteron, and wanted a home of his own and not of his ancestors' choosing. He had an elegant taste in letters, as we can learn from his neat imitations of Martial, his pretty *Bucolics*, and the more than respectable Latin hexameters of his *Ars Vivendi*. Being a great nobleman, he had the best skill of the day to construct his hermitage, and here he would retire for months at a time with like-minded friends to a world of books and gardens. He seems to have had no ill-wishers; contemporary memoirs speak of him charitably, and Dryden spared him four lines of encomium. 'A selfish old dog,' Leithen called him. 'He had the good sense to eschew politics and enjoy life. His soul is in that little house. He only did one rash thing in his career—he anticipated the King, his master, by some years in turning Papist.'

I asked about its later history.

'After his death it passed to a younger branch of the Carterons. It left them in the eighteenth century, and the Applebys got it. They were a jovial lot of hunting squires, and let the library go to the dogs. Old Colonel Appleby was still alive when I came to Borrowby. Something went wrong in his inside when he was nearly seventy, and the doctors knocked him off liquor. Not that he drank too much, though he did himself well. That finished the poor old boy. He told me that it revealed to him the amazing truth that during a long and, as he hoped, publicly useful life he had never been quite sober. He was a good fellow, and I missed him when he died. . . . The place went to a remote cousin called Giffen.'

Leithen's eyes, as they scanned the prospect, seemed amused.

'Julian and Ursula Giffen. . . . I daresay you know the names. They always hunt in couples, and write books about sociology and advanced ethics and psychics—books called either "The New This or That" or "Towards Something or Other". You know the sort of thing. They're deep in all the pseudo-sciences. . . . Decent souls, but you can guess the type. I came across them in a case I had at the Old Bailey—defending a ruffian who was charged with murder. I hadn't a doubt he deserved hanging on twenty counts, but there wasn't enough evidence to convict him on this one. Dodderidge was at his worst—it was just before they induced him to retire—and his handling of the jury was a masterpiece of misdirection. Of course there was a shindy. The thing was a scandal, and it stirred up all the humanitarians, till the murderer was almost forgotten in the iniquities of old Dodderidge. You must remember the case. It filled the papers for weeks. Well, it was in that connection that I fell in with the Giffens. I got rather to like them, and I've been to see them at their house in Hampstead. Golly, what a place! Not a chair fit to sit down on, and colours that made you want to weep. I never met people with heads so full of feathers.'

I said something about that being an odd *milieu* for him.

'Oh, I like human beings—all kinds. It's my profession to study them, for without that the practice of the law would be a lean affair. There are hordes of people like the Giffens—only not so good, for they really have hearts of gold. They are the rootless stuff in the world today—in revolt against everything and everybody with any ancestry. A kind of innocent self-righteousness—wanting to be the people with whom wisdom begins and ends. They are mostly sensitive and tender-hearted, but they wear themselves out in an eternal dissidence. Can't build, you know, for they object to all tools, but very ready to crab. They scorn any form of Christianity, but they'll walk miles to patronize some wretched sect that has the merit of being brand-new. "Pioneers" they call themselves—funny little unclad people adventuring into the cold desert with no maps. Giffen once described himself and his friends to me as "forward-looking", but that, of course, is just what they are not. To tackle the future you must have a firm grip of the past, and for them the past is only a pathological curiosity. They're up to their necks in the mud of the present. . . . But good, after a fashion; and innocent—sordidly innocent. Fate was in an ironical mood when she saddled them with that wicked little house.'

'Wicked' did not seem to me to be a fair word. It sat honey-coloured among its gardens with the meekness of a dove. The sound of a bicycle on the road behind made us turn round, and Leithen advanced to meet a dismounting rider.

He was a tallish fellow, some forty years old perhaps, with one of those fluffy blond beards that have never been shaved. Short-sighted, of course, and wore glasses. Biscuit-coloured knickerbockers and stockings clad his lean limbs.

Leithen introduced me. 'We are walking to Borrowby, and stopped to admire your house. Could we have just a glimpse inside? I want Peckwether to see the staircase.'

Mr Giffen was very willing. 'I've been over to Clyston to send a telegram. We have some friends for the week-end who might interest you. Won't you stay to tea?'

There was a gentle formal courtesy about him, and his voice had the facile intonations of one who loves to talk. He led us through a little gate, and along a shorn green walk among the bracken to a postern which gave entrance to the garden. Here, though it was October, there was still a bright show of roses, and the jet of water from the leaden Cupid dripped noiselessly among fallen petals. And then we stood before the doorway, above which the old Carteron had inscribed a line of Horace.

I have never seen anything quite like the little hall. There were two, indeed, separated by a staircase of a wood that looked like olive. Both were paved with black and white marble, and the inner was oval in shape, with a gallery supported on slender walnut pillars. It was all in miniature, but it had a spaciousness which no mere size could give. Also it seemed to be permeated by the quintessence of sunlight. Its air was of long-descended, confident, equable happiness.

There were voices on the terrace beyond the hall. Giffen led us into a room on the left. 'You remember the house in Colonel Appleby's time, Leithen. This was the chapel. It had always been the chapel. You see the change we have made. . . . I beg your pardon, Mr Peckwether. You're not by any chance a Roman Catholic?'

The room had a white panelling, and on two sides deep windows. At one end was a fine Italian shrine of marble, and the floor was mosaic, blue and white, in a quaint Byzantine pattern. There was the same air of sunny cheerfulness as in the rest of the house. No mystery could find a lodgment here. It might have been a chapel for three centuries, but the place was pagan. The Giffens' changes were no sort of desecration. A green-baize table filled most of the floor, surrounded by chairs like a committee room. On new raw-wood shelves were files of papers and stacks of blue-books and those desiccated works into which reformers of society torture the English tongue. Two typewriters stood on a side-table.

'It is our workroom,' Giffen explained, 'where we hold our Sunday moots. Ursula thinks that a week-end is wasted unless it produces some piece of real work. Often a quite valuable committee has its beginning here. We try to make our home a refuge for busy workers, where they need not idle, but can work under happy conditions.'

' "A college situate in a clearer air," ' Leithen quoted. But Giffen did not respond except with a smile; he had probably never heard of Lord Falkland.

A woman entered the room, a woman who might have been pretty if she had taken a little pains. Her reddish hair was drawn tightly back and dressed in a hard knot, and her clothes were horribly incongruous in a remote manor-house. She had bright eager eyes, like a bird, and hands that fluttered nervously. She greeted Leithen with warmth.

'We have settled down marvellously,' she told him. 'Julian and I feel as if we had always lived here, and our life has arranged itself so perfectly. My Mothers' Cottages in the village will soon be ready, and the Club is to be opened next week. Julian and I will carry on the classes ourselves for the first winter. Next year we hope to have a really fine programme. . . . And then it is so pleasant to be able to entertain one's friends. . . . Won't you stay to tea? Dr Swope is here, and Mary Elliston, and Mr Percy Blaker—you know, the Member of Parliament. Must you hurry off? I'm so sorry. . . . What do you think of our workroom? It was utterly terrible when we first came here—a sort of decayed chapel, like a withered tuberose. We have let the air of heaven into it.'

I observed that I had never seen a house so full of space and light.

'Ah, you notice that? It is a curiously happy place to live in. Sometimes I'm almost afraid to feel so light-hearted. But we look on ourselves as only trustees. It is a trust we have to administer for the common good. You know, it's a house on which you can lay your own impress. I can imagine places which dominate the dwellers, but Fullcircle is plastic, and we can make it our own just as much as if we had planned and built it. That's our chief piece of good fortune.'

We took our leave, for we had no desire for the company of Dr Swope and Mr Percy Blaker. When we reached the highway we halted and looked back on the little jewel. Shafts of the westering sun now caught the stone and turned the honey to ripe gold. Thin spires of amethyst smoke rose into the still air. I thought of the well-meaning restless couple inside its walls, and somehow they seemed out of the picture. They simply did not matter. The house was the thing, for I had never met in inanimate stone such an air of gentle masterfulness. It had a personality of its own, clean-cut and secure, like a high-born old dame among the females of profiteers. And Mrs Giffen claimed to have given it her impress!

That night in the library at Borrowby, Leithen discoursed of the Restoration. Borrowby, of which, by the expenditure of much care and a good deal of money, he has made a civilized dwelling, is a Tudor manor of the Cotswold type, with high pitched narrow roofs and tall stone chimneys, rising sheer from the meadows with something of the massiveness of a Border keep. He nodded towards the linen-fold panelling and the great carven chimney-piece.

'In this kind of house you have the mystery of the elder England. What was Raleigh's phrase? "High thoughts, and divine contemplations." The people who built this sort of thing lived close to another world, and they thought bravely of death. It doesn't matter who they were— Crusaders or Elizabethans or Puritans—they had all poetry in them, and the heroic, and a great unworldliness. They had marvellous spirits, and plenty of joys and triumphs; but they had also their hours of black gloom. Their lives were like our weather—storm and sun. One thing they never feared—death. He walked too near them all their days to be a bogy.

'But the Restoration was a sharp break. It brought paganism into England—paganism and the art of life. No people have ever known better the secret of a bland happiness. Look at Fullcircle. There are no dark corners there. The man that built it knew all there was to be known about how to live. . . . The trouble was that they did not know how to die. That was the one shadow on the glass. So they provided for it in the pagan way. They tried magic. They never became true Catholics—they were always pagan to the end, but they smuggled a priest into their lives. He was a kind of insurance premium against unwelcome mystery.'

It was not till nearly two years later that I saw the Giffens again. The May-fly season was near its close, and I had snatched a day on a certain limpid Cotswold river. There was another man on the same beat, fishing from the opposite bank, and I watched him with some anxiety, for a duffer would have spoilt my day. To my relief I recognized Giffen. With him it was easy to come to terms, and presently the water was parcelled out between us.

We forgathered for luncheon, and I stood watching while he neatly stalked, rose, and landed a trout. I confessed to some surprise—first, that Giffen should be a fisherman at all, for it was not in keeping with my old notion of him; and second, that he should cast such a workmanlike line. As we lunched together, I observed several changes. He had shaved his fluffy beard, and his face was notably less lean, and had the clear even sunburn of the countryman. His clothes, too, were different. They also were workmanlike, and looked as if they belonged to him—no more the uneasy knickerbockers of the Sunday golfer.

'I'm desperately keen,' he told me. 'You see it's only my second May-fly season, and last year I was no better than a beginner. I wish I had known long ago what good fun fishing was. Isn't this a blessed place?' And he looked up through the canopy of flowering chestnuts to the June sky.

'I'm glad you've taken to sport,' I said. 'Even if you only come here for the week-ends, sport lets you into the secrets of the countryside.'

'Oh, we don't go much to London now,' was his answer. 'We sold our

Hampstead house a year ago. I can't think how I ever could stick that place. Ursula takes the same view. . . . I wouldn't leave Oxfordshire just now for a thousand pounds. Do you smell the hawthorn? Last week this meadow was scented like Paradise. D'you know, Leithen's a queer fellow?'

I asked why.

'He once told me that this countryside in June made him sad. He said it was too perfect a thing for fallen humanity. I call that morbid. Do you see any sense in it?'

I knew what Leithen meant, but it would have taken too long to explain.

'I feel warm and good and happy here,' he went on. 'I used to talk about living close to Nature. Rot! I didn't know what Nature meant. Now——' He broke off. 'By Jove, there's a kingfisher. That is only the second I've seen this year. They're getting uncommon with us.

'With us'—I liked the phrase. He was becoming a true countryman.

We had a good day—not extravagantly successful, but satisfactory, and he persuaded me to come home with him to Fullcircle for the night, explaining that I could catch an early train next morning at the junction. So we extricated a little two seater from a thicket of lilacs, and he drove me through four miles of sweet-scented dusk, with nightingales shouting in every thicket. I changed into a suit of his flannels in a bedroom looking out on the little lake where trout were rising, and I remember that I whistled from pure lightheartedness. In that adorable house one seemed to be still breathing the air of the spring meadows.

Dinner was my first big surprise. It was admirable—plain but perfectly cooked, and with that excellence of basic material which is the glory of a well-appointed country house. There was wine too, which, I am certain, was a new thing. Giffen gave me a bottle of sound claret, and afterwards some more than decent port. My second surprise was my hostess. Her clothes, like her husband's, must have changed, for I did not notice what she was wearing, and I had noticed it only too clearly the last time we met. More remarkable still was the difference in her face. For the first time I realized that she was a pretty woman. The contours had softened and rounded, and there was a charming well-being in her eyes, very different from the old restlessness. She looked content—infinitely content.

I asked about her Mothers' Cottages. She laughed cheerfully.

'I gave them up after the first year. They didn't mix well with the village people. I'm quite ready to admit my mistake, and it was the wrong kind of charity. The Londoners didn't like it—felt lonesome and sighed for the fried-fish shop; and the village women were shy of them—afraid of infectious complaints, you know. Julian and I have decided that our business is to look after our own people.'

It may have been malicious, but I said something about the wonderful scheme of village education.

'Another relic of Cockneyism,' laughed the lady; but Giffen looked a trifle shy.

'I gave it up because it didn't seem worth while. What is the use of spoiling a perfectly wholesome scheme of life by introducing unnecessary complications? Medicine is no good unless a man is sick, and these people are not sick. Education is the only cure for certain diseases the modern world has engendered, but if you don't find the disease the remedy is superfluous. The fact is, I hadn't the face to go on with the thing. I wanted to be taught rather than to teach. There's a whole world round me of which I know very little, and my first business is to get to understand it. Any village poacher can teach me more of the things that matter than I have to tell him.'

'Besides, we have so much to do,' his wife added. 'There's the house and the garden, and the home-farm and the property. It isn't large, but it takes a lot of looking after.'

The dining-room was long and low-ceilinged, and had a white panelling in bold relief. Through the windows came odours of the garden and a faint tinkle of water. The dusk was deepening, and the engravings in their rosewood frames were dim, but sufficient light remained to reveal the picture above the fireplace. It showed a middle-aged man in the clothes of the later Carolines. The plump tapering fingers of one hand held a book, the other was hidden in the folds of a flowered waistcoat. The long, curled wig framed a delicate face, with something of the grace of youth left to it. There were quizzical lines about the mouth, and the eyes smiled pleasantly yet very wisely. It was the face of a man I should have liked to dine with. He must have been the best of company.

Giffen answered my question.

'That's the Lord Carteron who built the house. No. No relation. Our people were the Applebys, who came in 1753. We've both fallen so deep in love with Fullcircle that we wanted to see the man who conceived it. I had some trouble getting it. It came out of the Minster Carteron sale, and I had to give a Jew dealer twice what he paid for it. It's a jolly thing to live with.'

It was indeed a curiously charming picture. I found my eyes straying to it till the dusk obscured the features. It was the face of one wholly at home in a suave world, learned in all the urbanities. A good friend, I thought, the old lord must have been, and a superlative companion. I could imagine neat Horatian tags coming ripely from his lips. Not a strong face, but somehow a dominating one. The portrait of the long-dead gentleman had still the atmosphere of life. Giffen raised his glass of port to him as we rose from the table, as if to salute a comrade.

We moved to the room across the hall, which had once been the Giffens' workroom, the cradle of earnest committees and weighty memoranda. This was my third surprise. Baize-covered table and raw-wood shelves had disappeared. The place was now half smoking-room, half library. On the walls hung a fine collection of coloured sporting prints, and below them were ranged low Hepplewhite bookcases. The lamplight glowed on the ivory walls, and the room, like everything else in the house, was radiant. Above the mantelpiece was a stag's head—a fair eleven-pointer.

Giffen nodded proudly towards it. 'I got that last year at Machray. My first stag.'

There was a little table with an array of magazines and weekly papers. Some amusement must have been visible in my face as I caught sight of various light-hearted sporting journals, for he laughed apologetically. 'You mustn't think that Ursula and I take in that stuff for ourselves. It amuses our guests, you know.'

I dared say it did, but I was convinced that the guests were no longer Dr Swope and Mr Percy Blaker.

One of my many failings is that I can never enter a room containing books without scanning the titles. Giffen's collection won my hearty approval. There were the very few novelists I can read myself—Miss Austen and Sir Walter and the admirable Marryat; there was a shelf full of memoirs, and a good deal of seventeenth- and eighteenth-century poetry; there was a set of the classics in fine editions, Bodonis and Baskervilles and suchlike; there was much county history, and one or two valuable old herbals and itineraries. I was certain that two years before Giffen would have had no use for literature except some muddy Russian oddments, and I am positive that he would not have known the name of Surtees. Yet there stood the tall octavos recording the unedifying careers of Mr Jorrocks, Mr Facey Romford, and Mr Soapy Sponge.

I was a little bewildered as I stretched my legs in a very deep armchair. Suddenly I had a strong impression of looking on at a play. My hosts seemed to be automata, moving docilely at the orders of a masterful stage-manager, and yet with no sense of bondage. And as I looked on they faded off the scene, and there was only one personality—that house so serene and secure, smiling at our modern antics, but weaving all the while an iron spell round its lovers. For a second I felt an oppression as of something to be resisted. But no. There was no oppression. The house was too well-bred and disdainful to seek to captivate. Only those who fell in love with it could know its mastery, for all love exacts a price. It was far more than a thing of stone and lime; it was a creed, an art, a scheme of life—older than any Carteron, older than England. Somewhere far back in time—in Rome, in Attica, or in an Ægean island—there must have been such places; but then they called them temples, and gods dwelt in them.

I was roused by Giffen's voice discoursing of his books. 'I've been rubbing up my classics again,' he was saying. 'Queer thing, but ever since I left Cambridge I have been out of the mood for them. And I'm shockingly ill-read in English literature. I wish I had more time for reading, for it means a lot to me.'

'There is such an embarrassment of riches here,' said his wife. 'The days are far too short for all there is to do. Even when there is nobody staying in the house I find every hour occupied. It's delicious to be busy over things one really cares for.'

'All the same I wish I could do more reading,' said Giffen. 'I've never wanted to so much before.'

'But you come in tired from shooting and sleep sound till dinner,' said the lady, laying an affectionate hand on his shoulder.

They were happy people, and I like happiness. Self-absorbed perhaps, but I prefer selfishness in the ordinary way of things. We are most of us selfish dogs, and altruism makes us uncomfortable. But I had somewhere in my mind a shade of uneasiness, for I was the witness of a transformation too swift and violent to be wholly natural. Years, no doubt, turn our eyes inward and abate our heroics, but not a trifle of two or three. Some agency had been at work here, some agency other and more potent than the process of time. The thing fascinated and partly frightened me. For the Giffens—though I scarcely dared to admit it— had deteriorated. They were far pleasanter people. I liked them infinitely better. I hoped to see them often again. I detested the type they used to represent, and shunned it like the plague. They were wise now, and mellow, and most agreeable human beings. But some virtue had gone out of them. An uncomfortable virtue, no doubt, but a virtue, something generous and adventurous. Before, their faces had had a sort of wistful kindness. Now they had geniality—which is not the same thing.

What was the agency of this miracle? It was all around me: the ivory panelling, the olive-wood staircase, the lovely pillared hall. I got up to go to bed with a kind of awe on me. As Mrs Giffen lit my candle, she saw my eyes wandering among the gracious shadows.

'Isn't it wonderful,' she said, 'to have found a house which fits us like a glove? No! Closer. Fits us as a bearskin fits the bear. It has taken our impress like wax.'

Somehow I didn't think that the impress had come from the Giffens' side.

A November afternoon found Leithen and myself jogging homewards from a run with the Heythrop. It had been a wretched day. Twice we had found and lost, and then a deluge had set in which scattered the field. I had taken a hearty toss into a swamp, and got as wet as a man may be, but the steady downpour soon reduced every one to a like condition. When we turned towards Borrowby the rain ceased, and an icy wind blew out of the east which partially dried our sopping clothes. All the grace had faded from the Cotswold valleys. The streams were brown torrents, the meadows lagoons, the ridges bleak and grey, and a sky of scurrying clouds cast leaden shadows. It was a matter of ten miles to Borrowby: we had long ago emptied our flasks, and I longed for something hot to take the chill out of my bones.

'Let's look in at Fullcircle,' said Leithen, as we emerged on the highroad from a muddy lane. 'We'll make the Giffens give us tea. You'll find changes there.' I asked what changes, but he only smiled and told me to wait and see.

My mind was busy with surmises as we rode up the avenue. I thought of drink or drugs, and promply discarded the notion. Fullcircle was above all things decorous and wholesome. Leithen could not mean the change in the Giffens' ways which had so impressed me a year before, for he and I had long ago discussed that. I was still puzzling over his words when we found ourselves in the inner hall, with the Giffens making a hospitable fuss over us.

The place was more delectable than ever. Outside was a dark November day, yet the little house seemed to be transfused with sunshine. I do not know by what art the old builders had planned it, but the airy pilasters, the perfect lines of the ceiling, the soft colouring of the wood seemed to lay open the house to a clear sky. Logs burned brightly on the massive steel andirons, and the scent and the fine blue smoke of them strengthened the illusion of summer.

Mrs Giffen would have had us change into dry things, but Leithen pleaded a waiting dinner at Borrowby. The two of us stood by the fireplace drinking tea, the warmth drawing out a cloud of vapour from our clothes to mingle with the wood-smoke. Giffen lounged in an armchair, and his wife sat by the tea-table. I was looking for the changes of which Leithen had spoken.

I did not find them in Giffen. He was much as I remembered him on the June night when I had slept here, a trifle fuller in the face perhaps, a little more placid about the mouth and eyes. He looked a man completely content with life. His smile came readily and his easy laugh. Was it my fancy or had he acquired a look of the picture in the dining-room? I nearly made an errand to go and see it. It seemed to me that his mouth had now something of the portrait's delicate complacence. Lely would have found him a fit subject, though he might have boggled at his lean hands.

But his wife! Ah, there the changes were unmistakable. She was comely now rather than pretty, and the contours of her face had grown heavier. The eagerness had gone from her eyes and left only comfort and good-humour. There was a suspicion, ever so slight, of rouge and powder. She had a string of good pearls—the first time I had seen her wear jewels. The hand that poured out the tea was plump, shapely, and well cared for. I was looking at a most satisfactory mistress of a country house, who would see that nothing was lacking to the part.

She talked more and laughed oftener. Her voice had an airy lightness which would have made the silliest prattle charming.

'We are going to fill the house with young people and give a ball at Christmas,' she announced. 'This hall is simply clamouring to be danced in. You must come both of you. Promise me. And, Mr Leithen, it would be very kind if you brought a party from Borrowby. Young men, please. We are overstocked with girls in these parts. . . . We must do something to make the country cheerful in winter-time.'

I observed that no season could make Fullcircle other than cheerful.

'How nice of you!' she cried. 'To praise a house is to praise the householders, for a dwelling is just what its inmates make it. Borrowby is you, Mr Leithen, and Fullcircle us.'

'Shall we exchange?' Leithen asked.

She made a mouth. 'Borrowby would crush me, but it suits a Gothic survival like you. Do you think you would be happy here?'

'Happy?' said Leithen thoughtfully. 'Happy? Yes, undoubtedly. But it might be bad for my soul. . . . There's just time for a pipe, Giffen, and then we must be off.'

I was filling my pipe as we crossed the outer hall, and was about to enter the smoking-room I so well remembered when Giffen laid a hand on my arm.

'We don't smoke there now,' he said hastily.

He opened the door and I looked in. . . . The place had suffered its third metamorphosis. The marble shrine which I had noticed on my first visit had been brought back, and the blue mosaic pavement and the ivory walls were bare. At the eastern end stood a little altar with above it a copy of a Correggio Madonna.

A faint smell of incense hung in the air and the fragrance of hothouse flowers. It was a chapel, but, I swear, a more pagan place than when it had been workroom or smoking-room.

Giffen gently shut the door. 'Perhaps you didn't know, but some months ago my wife became a Catholic. It is a good thing for women, I think. It gives them a regular ritual for their lives. So we restored the chapel. It had always been there in the days of the Carterons and the Applebys.'

'And you?' I asked.

He shrugged his shoulders. 'I don't bother much about these things. But I propose to follow suit. It will please Ursula and do no harm to anybody.'

We halted on the brow of the hill and looked back on the garden valley. Leithen's laugh, as he gazed, had more awe than mirth in it.

'That little wicked house! I'm going to hunt up every scrap I can find about old Tom Carteron. He must have been an uncommon clever fellow. He's still alive down there and making people do as he did. . . . In that kind of place you may expel the priest and sweep it and garnish it. But he always returns.'

The wrack was lifting before the wind and a shaft of late watery sun fell on the grey walls. It seemed to me that the little house wore an air of gentle triumph.

The Clock

W. F. HARVEY

—

I liked your description of the people at the *pension*. I can just picture that rather sinister Miss Cornelius, with her toupee and clinking bangles. I don't wonder you felt frightened that night when you found her sleep-walking in the corridor. But after all, why shouldn't she sleep-walk? As to the movements of the furniture in the lounge on the Sunday, you are, I suppose, in an earthquake zone, though an earthquake seems too big an explanation for the ringing of that little handbell on the mantelpiece. It's rather as if our parlourmaid—another new one!—were to call a stray elephant to account for the teapot we found broken yesterday. You have at least escaped the eternal problem of maids in Italy.

Yes, my dear, I most certainly believe you. I have never had experiences quite like yours, but your mention of Miss Cornelius has reminded me of something rather similar that happened nearly twenty years ago, soon after I left school. I was staying with my aunt in Hampstead. You remember her, I expect; or, if not her, the poodle, Monsieur, that she used to make perform such pathetic tricks. There was another guest, whom I had never met before, a Mrs Caleb. She lived in Lewes and had been staying with my aunt for about a fortnight, recuperating after a series of domestic upheavals, which had culminated in her two servants leaving her at an hour's notice, without any reason, according to Mrs Caleb; but I wondered. I had never seen the maids; I had seen Mrs Caleb and, frankly, I disliked her. She left the same sort of impression on me as I gather your Miss Cornelius leaves on you—something queer and secretive; underground, if you can use the expression, rather than underhand. And I could feel in my body that she did not like me.

It was summer. Joan Denton—you remember her; her husband was killed in Gallipoli—had suggested that I should go down to spend the day with her. Her people had rented a little cottage some three miles out of Lewes. We arranged a day. It was gloriously fine for a wonder, and I had planned to leave that stuffy old Hampstead house before the old ladies were astir. But Mrs Caleb waylaid me in the hall, just as I was going out.

'I wonder,' she said, 'I wonder if you could do me a small favour. If you *do* have any time to spare in Lewes—only if you do—would you be so kind as to call at my house? I left a little travelling-clock there in the hurry of parting. If it's not in the drawing-room, it will be in my bedroom or in one of the maids' bedrooms. I know I lent it to the cook, who was a poor riser, but I can't remember if she returned it. Would it be too much to ask? The house has been locked up for twelve days, but everything is in order. I have the keys here; the large one is for the garden gate, the small one for the front door.'

I could only accept, and she proceeded to tell me how I could find Ash Grove House.

'You will feel quite like a burglar,' she said. 'But mind, it's only if you have time to spare.'

As a matter of fact I found myself glad of any excuse to kill time. Poor old Joan had been taken suddenly ill in the night—they feared appendicitis—and though her people were very kind and asked me to stay to lunch, I could see that I should only be in the way, and made Mrs Caleb's commission an excuse for an early departure.

I found Ash Grove without difficulty. It was a medium-sized red-brick house, standing by itself in a high walled garden that bounded a narrow lane. A flagged path led from the gate to the front door, in front of which grew, not an ash, but a monkey-puzzle, that must have made the rooms unnecessarily gloomy. The side door, as I expected, was locked. The dining-room and drawing-room lay on either side of the hall and, as the windows of both were shuttered, I left the hall door open, and in the dim light looked round hurriedly for the clock, which, from what Mrs Caleb had said, I hardly expected to find in either of the downstairs rooms. It was neither on table nor mantelpiece. The rest of the furniture was carefully covered over with white dust-sheets. Then I went upstairs. But, before doing so, I closed the front door. I did in fact feel rather like a burglar, and I thought that if anyone did happen to see the front door open, I might have difficulty in explaining things. Happily the upstairs windows were not shuttered. I made a hurried search of the principal bedrooms. They had been left in apple-pie order; nothing was out of place; but there was no sign of Mrs Caleb's clock. The impression that the house gave me—you know the sense of personality that a house conveys—was neither pleasing nor displeasing, but it was stuffy, stuffy from the absence of fresh air, with an additional stuffiness added, that seemed to come out from the hangings and quilts and antimacassars. The corridor, on to which the bedrooms I had examined opened, communicated with a smaller wing, an older part of the house, I imagined, which contained a box-room and the maids' sleeping-quarters. The last door that I unlocked—(I should say that the doors of all the rooms were locked, and relocked by me after I had glanced inside them)—contained the object of my search. Mrs Caleb's travelling-clock was on the mantelpiece, ticking away merrily.

That was how I thought of it at first. And then for the first time I realised that there was something wrong. The clock had no business to be ticking. The house had been shut up for twelve days. No one had come in to air it or to light fires. I remember how Mrs Caleb had told my aunt that if she left the keys with a neighbour, she was never sure who might get hold of them. And yet the clock was going. I wondered if some vibration had set the mechanism in motion, and pulled out my watch to see the time. It was five minutes to one. The clock on the mantelpiece said four minutes to the hour. Then, without quite knowing why, I shut the door on to the landing, locked myself in, and again looked round the room. Nothing was out of place. The only thing that might have called for remark was that there appeared to be a slight indentation on the pillow and the bed; but the mattress was a feather mattress, and you know how difficult it is to make them perfectly smooth. You won't need to be told that I gave a hurried glance under the bed—do you remember your supposed burglar in Number Six at St Ursula's?—and then, and much more reluctantly, opened the doors of two horribly capacious cupboards, both happily empty, except for a framed text with its face to the wall. By this time I really was frightened. The clock went ticking on. I had a horrible feeling that an alarm might go off at any moment, and the thought of being in that empty house was almost too much for me. However, I made an attempt to pull myself together. It might after all be a fourteen-day clock. If it were, then it would be almost run down. I could roughly find out how long the clock had been going by winding it up. I hesitated to put the matter to the test; but the uncertainty was too much for me. I took it out of its case and began to wind. I had scarcely turned the winding-screw twice when it stopped. The clock clearly was not running down; the hands had been set in motion probably only an hour or two before. I felt cold and faint and, going to the window, threw up the sash, letting in the sweet, live air of the garden. I knew now that the house was queer, horribly queer. Could someone be living in the house? Was someone else in the house now? I thought that I had been in all the rooms, but had I? I had only just opened the bathroom door, and I had certainly not opened any cupboards, except those in the room in which I was. Then, as I stood by the open window, wondering what I should do next and feeling that I just couldn't go down that corridor into the darkened hall to fumble at the latch of the front door with I don't know what behind me, I heard a noise. It was very faint at first, and seemed to be coming from the stairs. It was a curious noise—not the noise of anyone climbing up the stairs, but—you will laugh if this letter reaches you by a morning post—of something hopping up the stairs, like a very big bird would hop. I heard it on the landing; it stopped. Then there was a curious scratching noise against one of the bedroom doors, the sort of noise you can make with the nail of your little finger scratching polished wood. Whatever it was, was coming slowly down the corridor, scratching at the doors as it went. I could stand it no longer. Nightmare pictures of locked doors opening filled my brain. I took up the clock wrapped it in my macintosh and dropped it out of the window on to a flower-bed. Then I managed to crawl out of the window and, getting a grip of the sill, 'successfully negotiated', as the journalists would say, 'a twelve-foot drop.' So much for our much abused Gym at St Ursula's. Picking up the mackintosh, I ran round to the front door and locked it. Then I felt I could breathe, but not until I was on the far side of the gate in the garden wall did I feel safe.

Then I remembered that the bedroom window was open. What was I to do? Wild horses wouldn't have dragged me into that house again unaccompanied. I made up my mind to go to the police-station and tell them everything. I should be laughed at, of course, and they might easily refuse to believe my story of Mrs Caleb's commission. I had actually begun to walk down the lane in the direction of the town, when I chanced to look back at the house. The window that I had left open was shut.

No, my dear, I didn't see any face or anything dreadful like that . . . and, of course, it may have shut by itself. It was an ordinary sash-window, and you know they are often difficult to keep open.

And the rest? Why, there's really nothing more to tell. I didn't even see Mrs Caleb again. She had had some sort of fainting fit just before lunch-time, my aunt informed me on my return, and had had to go to bed. Next morning I travelled down to Cornwall to join mother and the children. I thought I had forgotten all about it, but when three years later Uncle Charles suggested giving me a travelling-clock for a twenty-first birthday present, I was foolish enough to prefer the alternative that he offered, a collected edition of the works of Thomas Carlyle.

Old Man's Beard

H. RUSSELL WAKEFIELD

Mr Bickley almost precisely satisfies our American friends' definition of a 'regular fellar'. That is to say, he makes an article of commerce, and by selling it at seven times its cost of production has prospered greatly. Mr Bickley has merely supertax worries. He is a good 'mixer'—he knows sixty-three persons by their Christian names: he is always ready to talk golf shop, with particular reference to a gross eighty-seven he once 'shot' on a short course burnt to a cinder. He makes almost exactly the same slice off the first tee twice on Saturday and twice on Sunday, and can stow away several rounds of drinks without becoming unduly pugnacious, verbose or pleased with himself. He goes to and from the city in a big car and smokes a big cigar during the process. And so on and so on. But he slightly diverges from type in two respects; he quite frequently reads a book that has neither been written by Mr Edgar Wallace nor recommended to him for its candid treatment of the sex question, and he hasn't got quite the orthodox regular fellar's life partner. Mrs Bickley is a bit of an enigma to the other RF's. Sometimes they are reassured that she is just what she ought to be—a 'lovely little woman', again in our American friends' idiom—the adjective being a tribute to her character rather than her physical charms, though these are still considerable. But at other times the RF's have an unpalatable impression that she would like to take them by the shoulders and drown them in deep water. And then they are rather afraid of her and very sorry for Mr Bickley. As a matter of fact, her mother was an Hungarian and temperamental, one who found even the Buda-Pesth variety of RF so desperately, irredeemably deadly that none such ventured for long into her presence. She had been the perfect mistress in her youth, a perfect wife to an Englishman of high intelligence in her middle age, and a formidable and indomitable old woman. In her daughter these characteristics were strongly diluted by Anglo-Saxon tolerance and phlegm; though sufficient of the fiery spirit remained to save her from becoming just a British female yawn. She was an avid but virtuous flirt in her youth, she is at present a perfect wife for an Englishman of no particular intelligence, and in her old age she will probably be a bit of an autocrat and a nuisance. And there are still to be found traces of that scarifying old mother of hers; sudden, sharp explosions caused by boredom; quick, short-lived ardours for good-looking men with brains—though she meets very few—and apparently causeless fits of temper, so uncontrollable and uncompromising that poor Mr Bickley—that nice little man—has always urgently watched the temperamental development of his daughter and only child, Mariella, for symptoms of that dangerous and irregular Mittel-European strain. And, though they are still further diluted, they are there. She is all right in many respects. She is physically flawless and saved from being merely the ordinary, full-blooded, smooth-skinned, regular-featured *Daily Mirror* bathing belle by a delicate upward slant of her eyelids, and a certain indefinable but captivating 'chic', by an air of slightly exotic breeding and an absolute incapacity for giggling at little odd, erotic moments. Again, though she is as intellectually incurious as a portable wireless set she is as sexually inquisitive as a curate, and in Mr Bickley's opinion she knew What Every Young Girl Ought To Know much sooner than any young girl ought to know it. At the age of fifteen she had driven the chauffeur—a most high-minded young man—almost out of his mind by the warmth of her feelings towards him, and when they were discovered together by Mrs Bickley he had spilled indignant protests all over the garage where Mariella had neatly cornered him. After this infatuation faded, she had experienced a succession of hurried, hot passions for a number of hopelessly ineligible youths, so that Mr Bickley, with a meanness only excused by his desperation, once upbraided her mother for introducing this culpable and devilish strain into the staid and seemly Bickley stock. Whereupon, the old lady being in the ascendant, he got about five times as good as he gave and spent a restless night composing a dignified letter to *The Times* on the dangers of mixed marriages.

And then came that most desired return to Bickleyism, for Mariella accepted the hand—the in every way desirable hand—of young Arthur Randall. Six weeks before it hadn't been desirable at all, for then he had been extremely impecunious, and merely—or so at least it appeared—a superlative player of games. Mariella had seen him make eighty-four runs against Larwood, Barratt and Staples when the dust was flying, and beat three men in succession to score the winning try against Wales, and as the applause rose and towered she had made up her mind, and prepared herself for a long and fiercely contested battle with her father. And then Arthur's uncle suddenly slipped his anchor, leaving his nephew £80,000! This timely and unexpected event eased the situation completely, and Mariella was soon flourishing a solitaire diamond ring and the wedding was fixed for the end of October. The beginning of August found them all installed in a well-appointed furnished house at that aristocratic resort, Brinton-on-Sea, which Mr Bickley had rented for seven weeks.

This confinement within four walls gave Mr Bickley a not too earnestly desired opportunity of scrutinising the character of his prospective son-in-law, so far as that young gentleman permitted him to do so. Physically he was beyond criticism. Tall, lithe and dark he had exceptional vitality and perfect health. He was a joy to look upon, and the fact that he had stood up to the Notts' fast bowlers for two hours, and had picked their short ones off his nose and plunked them up against the square-leg boundary was sufficient evidence of his courage and pugnacity, as was that vicious 'hand-off' which had turned the Welsh full-back turtle and given him a very sore jaw-bone for a week. It would have been very soothing to have been able to couple these moral qualities and physical attributes with £80,000 and find nothing more to scutinise. But Mr Bickley reluctantly and irritably nosed up something else; something enigmatic, elusive, buried so deep, as it were, that Mr Bickley felt his nose was only long enough to unearth its fringes and vague outline. What was it? Well, it sometimes revealed itself in sudden and most unexpected flashes of brutal, ruthless insight, almost a devilish sort of flourished egoism, most singular in so usually commonplace a master of moving spheres and ovals. Yet was he ever quite commonplace? Wasn't that orthodox exterior possibly a very cunningly adjusted mask? Unpleasant questions which Mr Bickley reprimanded his mind for asking about his prospective son-in-law. Yet they had some justification. For example, on one occasion they had all been sitting on the beach and he had been reading out from the *Daily Express* an account of the lamentable defalcations of a former business acquaintance, with appropriate comments. And then young Randall had suddenly stared into his face with a most ironical and piercing expression and said, 'There, but for a spot of caution and the grace of Old Nick, went Horace Bickley.' Which was exceedingly rude and he hoped unjustified. It had taken him very much aback, though both Mariella and her mother had seemed amused. And then again, when they had been discussing a peculiarly unpleasant murder of a young woman by a solicitor's clerk, and marvelling how he could have brought himself to commit such an atrocity, young Randall had remarked with frigid detachment, 'She probably bored him, and if by slitting her gullet he prevented her from boring anyone else, I consider he did a service to Society.' He said something unexpected and in bad taste like that quite often. Did he mean such things? He certain appeared to. So he couldn't be quite ordinary. Was that a good or a bad thing? Well, Mariella wasn't quite ordinary either. All those difficult, adolescent tendencies, now so pleasantly dormant, that her foreign blood explained but didn't eliminate, and other little signs here and there showed she had a slight streak of some kind. Perhaps their prospects of marital happiness would be increased by the fact that each was slightly peculiar, and certainly it was most reassuring that young Randall seemed so utterly devoted to Mariella, fiercely and fanatically so, and she seemed to have concentrated at last in a sort of smouldering and unvarying way.

Mr Bickley had waded his way through the evidence to a fairly favourable summing-up when something else came to worry him. Mariella didn't seem very flourishing. The family GP had described her as the most flawless physical specimen he had ever examined, and the sun and sea and air of Brinton should have put the keenest edge on this brilliant Toledo blade, and the close presence of her lover should have made her spirit leap within her. But the actual result was depressingly different. After the first few days she seemed limp and lethargic and 'snappy' in the mornings. She shook this off during the day, but began to droop again at sundown and showed a marked distaste for going to bed; not a distaste born of overmastering vitality, but something less reassuring than that, something less readily explicable. Her mother had noticed it, of course, and was rather worried, had questioned her gently and been testily repulsed.

Look at her now, for example, just come in from bathing on such a glorious day, and young Randall gazing at her with such undisguised adoration. What more could she want? Yet she seemed shadowed, brooding over something. She really almost looked ill and yet, in a purely physical sense, radiantly healthy. It must be some mental trouble; but what conceivable reason could there be for it? Yes, she was looking in that way worse than he'd ever seen her look, worse even than when he'd kicked that ghastly young dancing partner creature down the steps at home. It then occurred to Mr Bickley that his old friend, Sir Perseus Farrar, had just arrived at the Royal Hotel, and that he was the greatest authority in Europe on that awful and occult business, the female nervous system. How Mr Bickley admired a man who had the audacity to make a living out of delving into that monstrous region, that scarifying inferno! He knew it was the unforgivable sin to consult members of the medical profession out of office hours, and specially while on holiday, but Sir Perseus was such an old friend and kindly person and so fond of Mariella that he'd risk it, if she didn't get better. So far from getting better she burst into hysterical tears in the middle of breakfast the very next morning, ran up to her bedroom, locked the door and refused to see anyone. So Mr Bickley trotted round to the Royal. He found Sir Perseus smoking in the lounge, and forthwith burst into a halting recital concerning Mariella, liberally studded with apologies. These Sir Perseus cut short. 'My dear Horace,' he said, 'I was just thinking when you came in how glad I should be to have a little work to do. I'm always like that after a week's idling, and though I am very sorry that that which will rescue me from my sloth is some trouble with my dear and exquisite Mariella, I don't suppose there's much wrong, and if I can set it right, I shall feel doubly grateful to you for allowing me to don my harness for an hour or two. I'll drop in casually after lunch.' Which he did, and Mariella came out of her seclusion to greet him. By arrangement Mrs Bickley and young Randall had gone out before his arrival, and very soon Mr Bickley found an excuse to absent himself. Sir Perseus was not a famous authority on the female nervous system for nothing, and within a quarter of an hour Mariella was telling him something to which he was listening with an absorbed and authoritative attention. At the end of half an hour he began to ask questions, and at the end of an hour he patted her hand and told her there was nothing seriously to fuss about, but that unless she objected he would like her to put herself in his hands, by which he meant that she should tell him at once anything else which happened, and confide absolutely in him. She agreed thankfully. And then he left her with a very puzzled and thoughtful expression on his face and, as arranged, met Mr Bickley on the front.

They sat down on a seat overlooking the sea, on which Sir Perseus stared for a time, while Mr Bickley waited rather anxiously for him to speak.

'I don't think it's anything at all serious,' said Sir Perseus at length, 'but very unpleasant for her, poor child. It's a nightmare she's been having. I asked her if she were accustomed to dream, and she replied with great candour that ever since she could remember she had dreamed frequently and vividly of young men.'

Mr Bickley shuffled on his seat, his thoughts winging back. 'I suppose,' he said, 'that's quite usual, quite natural? I mean, most young girls dream of young men.'

'Oh, quite, quite,' replied Sir Perseus; 'but I gather that her dreams have been exceptionally, well—vivid. I was relieved to hear it, for it makes the deep etching of this nightmare less hard to explain. Apparently she experienced it for the first time ten days ago—on the second evening she was here. She has had it twice since. It takes this form. As she relates it, her room appears to be divided into two parts; that in which she herself is in is in darkness, the rest of the room is highly lighted. In it there is a bed, rather a big bed, and on it is an old man with a longish, grey beard, wearing a nightshirt. He is apparently writhing in great agony. He is twisting over and over, his hands to his heart, his head flung back. And then he suddenly rolls over and drops from the bed to the floor and is hidden from her. Then the light seems to spread towards her across the carpet, and she sees between the bed and where she is placed a coffin on the ground. And it seems to her as though there must be many cracks in this coffin, for long grey hair is streaming through it, some coiled over the lid and some streaming upwards. And presently the lid starts slowly to rise, and then the whole room is in darkness, and she has the impression that something is moving towards her and then bending over her, and she feels something spreading over her face—hair, she thinks; she has a sensation of suffocation, and awakes.'

'My God!' cried Mr Bickley. 'That is foul, dreadful! Poor little girl, what a bestial, terrifying experience!'

'Yes,' replied Sir Perseus, 'it is one of the most disgusting and unnerving dreams of the kind I have ever had described to me. There must be some explanation of it. Recurrent nightmares of this type are invariably the echo—stored in the subconscious—of some sharp experience once upon a time recorded. That sounds obscure, and it is so, but I have known very many such cases. Can you recall anything in Mariella's short existence which, when regurgitated, as it were, might cause this beastly dream; anything to do with a grey-bearded man, for example?'

'Nothing whatever,' said Mr Bickley, emphatically. 'I have certainly come across grey-bearded men in the course of business and so on, but I cannot remember that Mariella ever met one.' ('But what a lot of men Mariella has taken to,' he thought to himself. 'It is conceivable there *was* one with a grey beard, but it is excessively improbable.')

'I stress the detail of the beard,' continued Sir Perseus, 'because it seems to be the *hair* which sharply dominates this dream, and chiefly disturbs Mariella's mind; for example, when she broke down at breakfast it was because, so she told me, she saw someone with a grey beard pass by the window, which shows how sensitive she is to, and preoccupied by, the hair element. And I am convinced that she must have had some shock—long ago quite possibly—connected with a person so adorned, and that this vile dream is a throwback to this experience. I have told her to sift her memory for something of the kind. I am interested in her case, not only for professional reasons—I am very fond of her—and I feel it is up to me to exorcise this horror. She is too young and too innocent to be made a victim of such devilry. She has agreed to put herself in my hands and consult me at once if there are any developments. I will send her a sleeping draught, and I suggest she should not sleep alone. She had better have her mother with her in the same room, also a night-light, and try to give her as amusing and *tiring* a day as possible.'

'I certainly will,' said Mr Bickley, 'and I'm deeply grateful to you for taking up the case—if that isn't too alarming a way of putting it. She shall sleep in our room and I'll move into hers. But, good heavens, if I thought as I got into bed I was doomed to have that dream, I should never dare to close my eyes!'

'Remember this,' said Sir Perseus; 'if you actually had such a dream it would not seem quite as dreadful as you expected it to be; that is an axiom of human experience. It is not quite as shocking to Mariella as you think it must be. Nevertheless, it is loathsome enough, and therefore we've got to be very gentle and swift-witted with her. Oh, these dreams—how often I've puzzled over them! I've always firmly maintained they were distorted echoes of reality, though I know there is a school which regards them as nothing of the sort, but as reflections from another mode of consciousness, so that they can be prophetic—more than that—definitely another existence as it were, so much so that if the dreaming faculty was fostered to its highest voltage, waking up might be equivalent to slipping into dreamland, and sinking into dreamland really waking up; but that is too hard a saying for my old cranium to digest. But the land of dreams is largely an unexplored terrain, or anyway unsuccessfully mapped and surveyed, and Mariella's case sharply reminds me of it. And now I must be off, my dear Horace. Don't worry; we will make her once more as sweetly light-hearted and fancy-free as she deserves to be.'

When Mr Bickley got back to the house Mariella had gone to lie down, but her mother and young Randall were awaiting him. He retailed to them a brief résumé of what Sir Perseus had told him. Mrs Bickley had one admirable trait; in moments of crisis she acted first and talked afterwards, though most certainly she talked afterwards! So with hardly a word she bustled off to see about the change of rooms and the purchase of night-lights. Compared with young Randall's reception of the news hers seemed almost callous and unfeeling. For he became highly agitated and upset to an extent that slightly surprised Mr Bickley, for surely it wasn't as bad as all that! Young Randall went very white, and cross-examined him closely and urgently concerning the details of Mariella's nightmare, and seemed more and more distressed at every additional detail of it. As if such minutiæ made any great difference, wondered Mr Bickley. How very much in love with her he must be! He felt compelled to impress on him that they must all do as Sir Perseus had decreed and keep Mariella's spirits up and her mind off her trouble as much as possible, and so on; but young Randall hardly seemed to be listening to these excellent platitudes, and if he hadn't been drinking a good deal when he came down to dinner, Mr Bickley was no judge of the earlier stages of intoxication. Mariella, on the other hand, seemed better, and the doctor's visit had restored her confidence. And this was justified, for under the influence of the sleeping-draught she enjoyed ten hours of dreamless slumber and was very glad to have her mother by her side and a tiny light shining between them. The next morning she was in excellent spirits and once more keenly appreciative of those glances of masculine admiration and feminine envy which she always evoked as she slipped her wrap from her shoulders and stepped slowly down the beach to the sea. She was—and still is for that matter—five feet nine inches and a half in height, magnificently 'marshalled'. The peculiar beauty of her figure is due to the fact that while she seems very long from hip to knee, she is one inch longer from knee to foot, and her torso, rippling, taut and beautifully developed, is just exactly proportionately right. When the critical eye of the Brinton visitor turned from her perfection to the many other 'very good figures' on the beach, their slight but recognisable flaws seemed brutally intensified. And then those tantalisingly lifted eyelids! Well, young Randall was deemed a damned lucky dog so soon to have all those rare felicities to sample. Yet on that occasion he didn't look as if he sufficiently appreciated the fact. He looked morose and hardly said a word. 'A thick night or a tiff,' surmised the knowing onlookers.

Sir Perseus looked in during the afternoon and professed himself quite satisfied with the patient. And for forty-eight hours he had every reason to be. But three nights later Mrs Bickley woke up suddenly and looked across to Mariella. She was lying on her back and moving about with a slight incessant restlessness. 'Shall I wake her?' thought her mother. 'No, I'll wait a little while, it may be nothing.' Presently Mariella's motions became more rapid, pronounced and urgent. And then she sat up in bed and began thrusting with her hands, and then brushing her face as if to free it from something which was spreading over it. This impressed her mother very horribly, and she jumped out of bed and went over to her, spoke her name, and touched her gently. And presently she awoke, her eyes staring, her body trembling. And then she burst into tears. Her mother gave her a sleeping-draught, stroked her hair and comforted her, and took her to her own bed. Soon her sobbing became less violent and, as the drug allied itself with her exhaustion, she fell into a deep sleep. Mrs Bickley, however, didn't close her eyes again that night. Early next morning she rang up Sir Perseus, who was vaguely reassuring. 'Whatever the cause,' he said, 'it cannot be expected that complete recovery can be immediate.' For the present he ordered a sleeping-draught every night.

Mariella seemed listless but fairly cheerful and, after her bathe, almost her usual self. Mr Bickley was worried, but succeeded in disguising the fact. Young Randall was told nothing about it. And then there was another three days' pause and everyone's spirits rose again.

Mariella's temperament demanded a certain amount of solitude. She had found a very secluded spot wherein to rest and read in the afternoons, and she liked to go there alone after tea for a while. It was beside a groyne about half a mile from the house. She used to go there in her bathing dress and have a dip just before going back to change for dinner.

On the fourth day after her bad night she strolled down there about five o'clock. Randall and her father were playing golf, and Mrs Bickley was busy with the laundry. Mariella usually returned about half-past six, but on this occasion a quarter-past seven struck and still she had not appeared.

'We'd better go and fetch her,' said Mr Bickley to young Randall. 'She may have gone to sleep.' He tried to keep all trace of uneasiness out of his voice, but each knew the other was anxious as they walked at top speed towards that cosy little spot under the shelter of the groin. What they saw when they reached it made young Randall leap recklessly down the fifteen feet from the sea-wall to the beach, while Mr Bickley ran for the steps. For Mariella lay sprawled down the shingle. Her beach cloak had draped itself over her head so that only her legs were visible. Her book lay where she had flung it, almost at the water's edge. Young Randall pulled back the cloak. Her face was dead white and she was unconscious. He dashed down to the sea, soaked his handkerchief and squeezed the water over Mariella's face, but she showed no sign of recovery. 'We must carry her back,' said Mr Bickley. By good fortune a taxi was passing just as they got her to the top of the steps, and three minutes later she was lying on her bed and Mr Bickley was telephoning to Sir Perseus. He was in, and the taxi was sent to fetch him. Meanwhile Mrs Bickley and young Randall were busy with restoratives and hot-water bottles.

Mariella was just conscious but quite dazed when Sir Perseus arrived. After a few hurried words with Mr Bickley he went upstairs and asked to be left alone with his patient. Half an hour later he left her in charge of her mother and came downstairs. He was looking grave as he joined the two men in the study. Though he had something else almost monopolising his mind, the attention of his expert eye was fleetingly seized by the appearance of young Randall, who was looking almost as ill as his young woman, he thought.

'Well,' he said, 'the bare facts are these. Mariella was resting against the breakwater and reading, when she felt something tickling her neck.

She paid no heed for a while, and then the irritation became more insistent. She looked round casually and, according to her account, streamers of grey hair were flowing through the cracks in the woodwork and coiling round her neck. She remembers nothing more.' Young Randall poured himself out half a tumbler of neat whisky and drained it.

'What is it? What is it?' cried Mr Bickley desperately.

'It is, to put it crudely, an hallucination,' replied Sir Perseus, 'and I will not disguise from you the fact that it is a serious matter. A nightmare is one thing, a violent waking illusion of this kind quite another. I must tell you one thing. She says she occasionally has the impression that someone is whispering in her ear.'

'But, good God!' said Mr Bickley miserably, 'that sounds like madness!'

'It sounds like nothing of the sort,' replied Sir Perseus sharply; 'get any such idea out of your head. Mariella is ill, but she's absolutely sane.'

'Of course she's sane,' said young Randall violently.

Sir Perseus looked across at him, and once more his expert eye was steeply challenged by that look about him.

'What does she hear whispered?' asked Mr Bickley.

'She is uncertain about that. She thinks she has heard the words "September the tenth," but usually it sounds more like vague chatter. She likened it rather vividly to those soft, husky mutterings one often hears between items on the radio. And once or twice she fancies she hears a sort of sniggering chuckle. She believes she heard such a sound first before she felt that tickling sensation. However, I don't think such details have much significance. The point is, she is ill, she has some disturbing, I may say dangerous, symptoms. She must not be left alone; she must have the reinforcement and comfort of you all, and especially of you, Mr Randall. You are to be her future husband, and she naturally already regards you as the person who will guard and cherish her in the coming time. All this is inevitably a very horrible business for you, but you must do your utmost to conceal the fact in front of her.'

'Have you really ever known a case like this?' asked young Randall, leaning forward and regarding the specialist with a haggard and earnest gaze. 'I mean, I mean, do people have such hallucinations without any real cause for them?'

Sir Perseus paused before replying, 'That depends on what you mean by a "*real cause*". I *have* known similar cases, but only when, as I have told Mr Bickley, some deep indentation has been made on the patient's mind from severe shock—psychic shock, I mean. I have read, of course, of some alleged phenomena, reported from Eastern lands, which have always seemed to be hopelessly unsubstantiated—witchery, hocus-pocus, mumbo-jumbo. If such phenomena have any basis in fact they can, in my opinion, be satisfactorily explained by the potent influence of auto-suggestion on the primitive mind. It is significant that they seem to lose their force with the donning of trousers. But we are wandering from the point, the subject on hand, and I must go and get something to eat. Mariella,' he concluded impressively, 'is a healthy-minded Western girl, she isn't a Zulu or a South-Sea Islander, and she is in great trouble; I do not wish to minimise the extent of that trouble, but she can and must be cured, and you two, and of course her mother, but you especially, Mr Randall, can greatly assist the process of recovery by your tact, your love, your intelligent determination.'

Mr Bickley saw him out, and while he was doing so young Randall drank another half-tumbler of neat whisky.

Mariella recovered slowly. The next day she had several attacks of semi-hysteria, and she insisted that everything grey should be taken from her room. And she had a strong but diminishing antipathy for hair, so much so that she asked her mother to wear a shawl over her head. And the latter cut away the ribboned streamers from the electric fan, because she noticed Mariella staring at them in a rather strange way as they fluttered in the draught.

Young Randall spent several hours a day with her and appeared to be attempting—without complete success—to be obeying Sir Perseus's instructions. The latter came every afternoon and was breezily chatty and reassuring, but it was a full week before his patient was well enough to come downstairs, though she had no relapse in the meantime; but Sir Perseus was less reassured by this than he allowed himself to appear. She never referred to her condition or trouble, and seemed indeed rather disinterested in her progress, and yet, so it seemed to Sir Perseus, she was psychically abnormal, subtly so, almost as though she were 'entranced'; hypnotised, though in a very sly, unobtrusive way. He attributed this vague spiritual eccentricity to shock, and he told himself that she would either make a slow but sure recovery or relapse suddenly and violently and become past his aid. She talked very little and paid the very slightest heed to anything anyone else said, and spent most of the day sitting in a chair on the beach and staring out to sea. 'Somehow she doesn't seem quite a free agent,' thought Sir Perseus. Her mother, who hid a very deep distress with heroic success and had become just the mother of a sick child, had formed the habit of waking up frequently during the night, but only once found anything to report to Sir Perseus, when Mariella suddenly sat up in bed and said, 'Who's that whispering?' and then sank back again and went to sleep, though she muttered at intervals, as if discussing something almost under her breath with someone who was visiting her in her dreams. That happened during the early hours of September 9th. On the next morning there was a remarkable change in her. She came down to breakfast in her bathing costume and seemed her old care-free self. She talked away fluently and flippantly and, one would have judged, she kept no remembrance whatsoever of any displeasing experiences. Young Randall, who had been a wretched, withered shadow of himself ever since that evening when he had seen Mariella sprawled down the shingle, and drinking far too much in Mr Bickley's opinion, responded instantly to his fiancée's changed state, and it was a very thankful and delighted trio which went down with Mariella to the beach about eleven o'clock. It was a blithe day, cloudless and breezy, and the small waves chased in hard on each other's heels.

Mariella and young Randall stretched themselves out and let the searching rays of the sun pour through them, and then, just before twelve o'clock, they got up lazily and dawdled down to the water's edge. The beach was crowded, and Mariella seemed quite content that everyone should have a generous opportunity of scrutinising once more her exquisite workmanship and finish.

'I heard a rumour,' said one envious damsel to another, 'that she's really not quite "all there"; gets fits about once a week.'

'She certainly has got something rather odd about her,' said her girl friend. 'I expect that's why that Mr Randall has been looking so worried lately. What a figure he's got and how good-looking! I'd give ten years of my life for a month with him. What a shame he should be tied up to someone who isn't quite sane!'

These charitable and erotic observations had just been exchanged when Mariella began to step delicately into the sea. Young Randall was already swimming about and waiting for her to join him in a cruise to the raft. She forced her way slowly in, rubbing her hands and uttering the conventional light cries evoked by the tart embraces of the North Sea. She paused for a moment as it splashed up over her waist, waved her hands to her parents, and then strode forward again. The water had just reached her neck when she suddenly screamed, flung up her arms and disappeared. In an instant the beach was in an uproar. Those in the sea swam furiously towards the spot where she had last been seen, a dozen sun-bathers dashed down into the sea, the boatman struggled at his oars, but young Randall was there first, and he dived for her. To Mr and Mrs Bickley, who had dashed down to the sea, it seemed a thousand years till he appeared holding Mariella round her armpits and brought her ashore. A doctor had run up and he got busy with artificial respiration, but Mariella, though she had swallowed more sea-water than was good for her, was in no danger of death from drowning, and though she showed no sign of coming-to she was very soon in a condition to be carried back to the house. A quarter of an hour later Sir Perseus was at her bedside. And then for a moment she recovered consciousness, and after staring fixedly at Sir Perseus for a full ten seconds, she said in a cold, toneless voice: 'I put my foot on a face. I could feel it. And then I felt the hair, and it began to come up my legs and pull me down.' And then she began to scream and scream and scream, and it took all the strength of Sir Perseus and young Randall to hold her down in bed. Presently her struggles became less violent and Sir Perseus put a hypodermic syringe to her arm.

Five hours later she was on her way to a London nursing home in an ambulance which paid no heed to speed limits, her mother and Sir Perseus with her. His last words to her father and young Randall were: 'I will save her reason if I can, but you must be prepared for the worst.' And then with the light of battle in his eye he leaped into the ambulance. Mr Bickley and young Randall stayed behind by his orders; they would only be in the way for the present. He would ring up early the next morning and tell them what to do.

Mr Bickley, who spent the evening in deep and melancholy reverie, hardly noticed the absence of young Randall. He in no way wished for company, and no doubt Randall felt the same way. Could Mariella have had some affair with a Grey Beard? She might have had. Certain horrible conjectures tapped for entrance to his brain. Utterly worn out, he lay down on the sofa in the drawing-room, but he could not sleep. At seven o'clock a maid came in and handed him a letter. To his surprise he recognised young Randall's writing on the envelope. He opened it and found it contained two separate enclosures. The first he took up was headed 'Letter 2. Letter 1 to be read first.' So he unfolded number 1 and read as follows:

'DEAR MR BICKLEY,

'When you get this I shall be lying in the gorse patch below the eighth tee, and I shall have even less brains in my head than I was born with. Incidentally it will be the first time I was ever on the left-hand side of that fairway. No doubt that sounds very flippant, but once I had finally made up my mind to shoot myself and knew I should have the guts to do it—four hours ago—I became almost light-hearted in a way exalted, scrubbed and robed for death. This mood would not have lasted, but it will remain with me at least long enough. The fact is, I poisoned my uncle, which was not nearly so difficult a feat as it sounds, for his doctor was half-witted and I made a careful study of his habits and his medicine chest. He was a vile, disgusting old Sadist and I feel no remorse whatsoever. Killing him seemed as natural a performance as beating down a wasp, and by killing him I did many people a service, for everyone who served him and was in his employ breathed a sigh of relief when they heard of his death. However, I am no altruist, and I should never have taken the serious risk entailed by experimenting with his sleeping draught but for one thing. It came to my knowledge that he was about to make a new will, and cutting me right out of it. Consequently I should have to give up Mariella. Now I am not going to dwell on what that knowledge meant to me, for I know you realise how I feel about her. Life without her is unthinkable. Well, why am I going to kill myself? For this reason—my uncle had a rather *long grey beard*. That is why. The moment I heard of Mariella's nightmares I had a dreadful suspicion that my plans had failed. When I heard why she had that seizure on the beach I almost believed it was hopeless. What happened this morning convinced me that the rest was up to me. Now I have no belief in a future life. My uncle was one of the few people I have met who deserved to go to the conventional hell, and I have never met any one bad enough to merit the conventional heaven. Nevertheless, by some agency Mariella is being attacked, and I have a curious feeling of certainty that those attacks will cease when I am dead. Her sanity, I am convinced, depends on what I am about to do. Now I have worked out what I believe to be a consistent and plausible explanation of this, but I shall not go into it, for I must hurry, and very probably it would sound like lunacy to anyone but me. If, however, I am wrong and I meet Uncle Walter hereafter and find out something, then he'll really know what hell can be! But I'm afraid that is too optimistic a prospect. Now I want you to do something for me. I want you to tear up this letter as soon as you've read it and send the other to the coroner—or whatever the procedure is. I can't bear to think that people might point at Mariella as someone who almost married a murderer, and I don't want her to know I was one. She won't—and I am reconciled to the fact—sorrow for me for long. When she is well again I shall just seem part of a horrible memory, and as she forgets that she will forget me. And I'd rather it was so. Good-bye. I was once so happy with you all.

                                                                    A. R.'

When he had finished reading it Mr Bickley tore the letter to small pieces and burnt it in the grate. And then he took up the other and read:

'DEAR MR BICKLEY,

 'I am about to shoot myself, in the gorse below the eighth tee, because I have discovered a horrible secret about myself. There is no need to tell you what this is, and I'd rather no one knew it, but it makes it impossible for me to marry your daughter, and life without her is unthinkable, so I am doing this.

                                                                    A. R.'

Mr Bickley put this epistle back into its envelope and went to the telephone.

The following April Mariella returned from a long sea voyage perfectly restored to health. The following August she became affianced to a certain Mr Peter Raines, whose past is as bland and innocent as an infant's posterior, but concerning whose future stupendous prophecies are made. He has just left Oxford, where he was President of the Union, and only the fact that he has been adopted as Conservative candidate for a midland constituency has prevented him from completing a really 'brilliant and daring' novel. As it is, he is about to publish a slim volume of essays entitled *Constructive Toryism.* Mariella is blissfully happy, and if she dreams at all it is of this formidable young thinker. Except just once when she had a very sharp dream vision of someone dark and lithe, beautifully poised, and flicking Larwood's cannon-balls from his nose to the rails. She has just one idiosyncrasy—she cannot remain in the same room with a grey-bearded male person. But the owners of such are fortunately uncommon and, even in Scotland, becoming rarer every day.

Mr and Mrs Bickley are very well indeed.

Mr Jones

EDITH WHARTON

‿

I

Lady Jane Lynke·was unlike other people: when she heard that she had inherited Bells, the beautiful old place which had belonged to the Lynkes of Thudeney for something like six hundred years, the fancy took her to go and see it unannounced. She was staying at a friend's nearby, in Kent, and the next morning she borrowed a motor and slipped away alone to Thudeney-Blazes, the adjacent village.

It was a lustrous motionless day. Autumn bloom lay on the Sussex downs, on the heavy trees of the weald, on streams moving indolently, far off across the marshes. Farther still, Dungeness, a fitful streak, floated on an immaterial sea which was perhaps, after all, only sky.

In the softness Thudeney-Blazes slept: a few aged houses bowed about a duck pond, a silvery spire, orchards thick with dew. Did Thudeney-Blazes ever wake?

Lady Jane left the motor to the care of the geese on a miniature common, pushed open a white gate into a field (the griffoned portals being padlocked), and struck across the park toward a group of carved chimney stacks. No one seemed aware of her.

In a dip of the land, the long low house, its ripe brick masonry overhanging a moat deeply sunk about its roots, resembled an aged cedar spreading immemorial red branches. Lady Jane held her breath and gazed.

A silence distilled from years of solitude lay on lawns and gardens. No one had lived at Bells since the last Lord Thudeney, then a penniless younger son, had forsaken it sixty years before to seek his fortune in Canada. And before that, he and his widowed mother, distant poor relations, were housed in one of the lodges, and the great place, even in their day, had been as mute and solitary as the family vault.

Lady Jane, daughter of another branch, to which an earldom and considerable possessions had accrued, had never seen Bells, hardly heard its name. A succession of deaths, and the whim of an old man she had never known, now made her heir to all this beauty; and as she stood and looked she was glad she had come to it from so far, from impressions so remote and different. 'It would be dreadful to be used to it—to be thinking already about the state of the roof, or the cost of a heating system.'

Till this, her thirty-fifth year, Lady Jane had led an active, independent and decided life. One of several daughters, moderately but sufficiently provided for, she had gone early from home, lived in London lodgings, travelled in tropic lands, spent studious summers in Spain and Italy, and written two or three brisk business-like little books about cities usually dealt with sentimentally. And now, just back from a summer in the south of France, she stood ankle-deep in wet bracken, and gazed at Bells lying there under a September sun that looked like moonlight.

'I shall never leave it!' she ejaculated, her heart swelling as if she had taken the vow to a lover.

She ran down the last slope of the park and entered the faded formality of gardens with clipped yews as ornate as architecture, and holly hedges as solid as walls. Adjoining the house rose a low deep-buttressed chapel. Its door was ajar, and she thought this of good augury: her forebears were waiting for her. In the porch she remarked fly-blown notices of services, an umbrella stand, a dishevelled door mat: no doubt the chapel served as the village church. The thought gave her a sense of warmth and neighbourliness. Across the damp flags of the chancel, monuments and brasses showed through a traceried screen. She examined them curiously. Some hailed her with vocal memories, others whispered out of the remote and the unknown: it was a shame to know so little about her own family. But neither Crofts nor Lynkes had ever greatly distinguished themselves; they had gathered substance simply by holding on to what they had, and slowly accumulating privileges and acres. 'Mostly by clever marriages,' Lady Jane thought with a faint contempt.

At that moment her eyes lit on one of the less ornate monuments: a plain sarcophagus of gray marble niched in the wall and surmounted by the bust of a young man with a fine arrogant head, a Byronic throat and tossed-back curls.

'Peregrine Vincent Theobald Lynke, Baron Clouds, fifteenth Viscount Thudeney of Bells, Lord of the Manors of Thudeney, Thudeney-Blazes, Upper Lynke, Lynke-Linnet——' so it ran, with the usual tedious enumeration of honours, titles, court and county offices, ending with: 'Born on May 1st, 1790, perished of the plague at Aleppo in 1828.' And underneath, in small cramped characters, as if crowded as an afterthought into an insufficient space: 'Also His Wife.'

That was all. No names, dates, honors, epithets, for the Viscountess Thudeney. Did she too die of the plague at Aleppo? Or did the 'also' imply her actual presence in the sarcophagus which her husband's pride had no doubt prepared for his own last sleep, little guessing that some Syrian drain was to receive him? Lady Jane racked her memory in vain. All she knew was that the death without issue of this Lord Thudeney had caused the property to revert to the Croft-Lynkes, and so, in the end, brought her to the chancel step where, shyly, she knelt a moment, vowing to the dead to carry on their trust.

She passed on to the entrance court, and stood at last at the door of her new home, a blunt tweed figure in heavy mud-stained shoes. She felt as intrusive as a tripper, and her hand hesitated on the doorbell. 'I ought to have brought someone with me,' she thought; an odd admission on the part of a young woman who, when she was doing her books of travel, had prided herself on forcing single-handed the most closely guarded doors. But those other places, as she looked back, seemed easy and accessible compared to Bells.

She rang, and a tinkle answered, carried on by a flurried echo which seemed to ask what in the world was happening. Lady Jane, through the nearest window, caught the spectral vista of a long room with shrouded furniture. She could not see its farther end, but she had the feeling that someone stationed there might very well be seeing her.

'Just at first,' she thought, 'I shall have to invite people here—to take the chill off.'

She rang again, and the tinkle again prolonged itself; but no one came.

At last she reflected that the caretakers probably lived at the back of the house, and pushing open a door in the courtyard wall she worked her way around to what seemed a stable yard. Against the purple brick sprawled a neglected magnolia, bearing one late flower as big as a planet. Lady Jane rang at a door marked 'Service'. This bell, though also languid, had a wakefuller sound, as if it were more used to being rung, and still knew what was likely to follow; and after a delay during which Lady Jane again had the sense of being peered at—from above, through a lowered blind—a bolt shot, and a woman looked out. She was youngish, unhealthy, respectable and frightened; and she blinked at Lady Jane like someone waking out of sleep.

'Oh,' said Lady Jane—'do you think I might visit the house?'

'The house?'

'I'm staying near here—I'm interested in old houses. Mightn't I take a look?'

The young woman drew back. 'The house isn't shown.'

'Oh, but not to—not to—' Jane weighed the case. 'You see,' she explained, 'I know some of the family: the Northumberland branch.'

'You're related, madam?'

'Well—distantly, yes.' It was exactly what she had not meant to say; but there seemed no other way.

The woman twisted her apron strings in perplexity.

'Come, you know,' Lady Jane urged, producing half-a-crown. The woman turned pale.

'I couldn't, madam; not without asking.' It was clear that she was sorely tempted.

'Well, ask, won't you?' Lady Jane pressed the tip into a hesitating hand. The young woman shut the door and vanished. She was away so long that the visitor concluded her half-crown had been pocketed, and there was an end; and she began to be angry with herself, which was more often her habit than to be so with others.

'Well, for a fool, Jane, you're a complete one,' she grumbled.

A returning footstep, listless, reluctant—the tread of one who was not going to let her in. It began to be rather comic.

The door opened, and the young woman said in her dull singsong: 'Mr Jones says that no one is allowed to visit the house.'

She and Lady Jane looked at each other for a moment, and Lady Jane read the apprehension in the other's eyes.

'Mr Jones? Oh?—Yes; of course, keep it. . . . ' She waved away the woman's hand.

'Thank you, madam.' The door closed again, and Lady Jane stood and gazed up at the inexorable face of her own home.

II

'But you didn't get in? You actually came back without so much as a peep?'

Her story was received, that evening at dinner, with mingled mirth and incredulity.

'But, my dear! You mean to say you asked to see the house, and they wouldn't let you? *Who* wouldn't?' Lady Jane's hostess insisted.

'Mr Jones.'

'Mr Jones?'

'He said no one was allowed to visit it.'

'Who on earth is Mr Jones?'

'The caretaker, I suppose. I didn't see him.'

'Didn't see him either? But I never heard such nonsense! Why in the world didn't you insist?'

'Yes; why didn't you?' they all chorused; and she could only answer, a little lamely: 'I think I was afraid.'

'Afraid? *You*, darling?' There was fresh hilarity. 'Of Mr Jones?'

'I suppose so.' She joined in the laugh, yet she knew it was true: she had been afraid.

Edward Stramer, the novelist, an old friend of her family, had been listening with an air of abstraction, his eyes on his empty coffee cup. Suddenly, as the mistress of the house pushed back her chair, he looked across the table at Lady Jane. 'It's odd: I've just remembered something. Once, when I was a youngster, I tried to see Bells; over thirty years ago it must have been.' He glanced at his host. 'Your mother drove me over. And we were not let in.'

There was a certain flatness in this conclusion, and someone remarked that Bells had always been known as harder to get into than any other house thereabouts.

'Yes,' said Stramer; 'but the point is that we were refused in exactly the same words. Mr Jones said no one was allowed to visit the house.'

'Ah—he was in possession already? Thirty years ago? Unsociable fellow, Jones. Well, Jane, you've got a good watchdog.'

They moved to the drawing room, and the talk drifted to other topics. But Stramer came and sat down beside Lady Jane. 'It is queer, though, that at such a distance of time we should have been given exactly the same answer.'

She glanced up at him curiously. 'Yes; and you didn't try to force your way in either?'

'Oh, no: it was not possible.'

'So I felt,' she agreed.

'Well, next week, my dear, I hope we shall see it all, in spite of Mr Jones,' their hostess intervened, catching their last words as she moved toward the piano.

'I wonder if we shall see Mr Jones,' said Stramer.

III

Bells was not nearly as large as it looked; like many old houses it was very narrow, and but one story high, with servants' rooms in the low attics, and much space wasted in crooked passages and superfluous stairs. If she closed the great salon, Jane thought, she might live there comfortably with the small staff which was the most she could afford. It was a relief to find the place less important than she had feared.

For already, in that first hour of arrival, she had decided to give up everything else for Bells. Her previous plans and ambitions—except such as might fit in with living there—had fallen from her like a discarded garment, and things she had hardly thought about, or had shrugged away with the hasty subversiveness of youth, were already laying quiet hands on her; all the lives from which her life had issued, with what they bore of example or admonishment. The very shabbiness of the house moved her more than splendours, made it, after its long abandonment, seem full of the careless daily coming and going of people long dead, people to whom it had not been a museum, or a page of history, but cradle, nursery, home, and sometimes, no doubt, a prison. If those marble lips in the chapel could speak! If she could hear some of their comments on the old house which had spread its silent shelter over their sins and sorrows, their follies and submissions! A long tale, to which she was about to add another chapter, subdued and humdrum beside some of those earlier annals, yet probably freer and more varied than the unchronicled lives of the great-aunts and great-grandmothers buried there so completely that they must hardly have known when they passed from their beds to their graves. 'Piled up like dead leaves,' Jane thought, 'layers and layers of them, to preserve something forever budding underneath.'

Well, all these piled-up lives had at least preserved the old house in its integrity; and that was worth-while. She was satisfied to carry on such a trust.

She sat in the garden looking up at those rosy walls, iridescent with damp and age. She decided which windows should be hers, which rooms given to the friends from Kent who were motoring over, Stramer among them, for a modest housewarming; then she got up and went in.

The hour had come for domestic questions; for she had arrived alone, unsupported even by the old family housemaid her mother had offered her. She preferred to start afresh, convinced that her small household could be staffed from the neighbourhood. Mrs Clemm, the rosy-cheeked old person who had curtsied her across the threshold, would doubtless know.

Mrs Clemm, summoned to the library, curtsied again. She wore black silk, gathered and spreading as to skirt, flat and perpendicular as to bodice. On her glossy false front was a black lace cap with ribbons which had faded from violet to ash-colour, and a heavy watch chain descended from the lava brooch under her crochet collar. Her small round face rested on the collar like a red apple on a white plate: neat, smooth, circular, with a pursed-up mouth, eyes like black seeds, and round ruddy cheeks with the skin so taut that one had to look close to see that it was as wrinkled as a piece of old crackly.

Mrs Clemm was sure there would be no trouble about servants. She herself could do a little cooking: though her hand might be a bit out. But there was her niece to help; and she was quite of her ladyship's opinion, that there was no need to get in strangers. They were mostly a poor lot; and besides, they might not take to Bells. There were persons who didn't. Mrs Clemm smiled a sharp little smile, like the scratch of a pin, as she added that she hoped her ladyship wouldn't be one of them.

As for under-servants . . . well, a boy, perhaps? She had a great-nephew she might send for. But about women—under-housemaids—if her ladyship thought they couldn't manage as they were; well, she really didn't know. Thudeney-Blazes? Oh, she didn't think so. . . . There was more dead than living at Thudeney-Blazes . . . everyone was leaving there . . . or in the church yard . . . one house after another being shut . . . death was everywhere, wasn't it, my lady? Mrs Clemm said it with another of her short sharp smiles, which provoked the appearance of a frosty dimple.

'But my niece Georgiana is a hard worker, my lady; her that let you in the other day. . . . '

'That didn't,' Lady Jane corrected.

'Oh, my lady, it was too unfortunate. If only your ladyship had have said . . . poor Georgiana had ought to have seen, but she never *did* have her wits about her, not for answering the door.'

'But she was only obeying orders. She went to ask Mr Jones.'

Mrs Clemm was silent. Her small hands, wrinkled and resolute, fumbled with the folds in her apron, and her quick eyes made the circuit of the room and then came back to Lady Jane's.

'Just so, my lady; but, as I told her, she'd ought to have known—'

'And who is Mr Jones?'

Mrs Clemm's smile snapped out again, deprecating, respectful. 'Well, my lady, he's more dead than living, too . . . if I may say so,' was her surprising answer.

'Is he? I'm sorry to hear that; but who is he?'

'Well, my lady, he's . . . he's my great-uncle, as it were . . . my grandmother's own brother, as you might say.'

'Ah; I see.' Lady Jane considered her with growing curiosity. 'He must have reached a great age, then.'

'Yes, my lady; he has that. Though I'm not,' Mrs Clemm added, the dimple showing, 'as old myself as your ladyship might suppose. Living at Bells all these years has been ageing to me; it would be to anybody.'

'I suppose so. And yet,' Lady Jane continued, 'Mr Jones has survived; has stood it well—as you certainly have?'

'Oh, not as well as I have,' Mrs Clemm interjected, as if resentful of the comparison.

'At any rate, he still mounts guard; mounts it as well as he did thirty years ago.'

'Thirty years ago?' Mrs Clemm echoed, her hands dropping from her apron to her sides.

'Wasn't he here thirty years ago?'

'Oh, yes, my lady, certainly; he's never once been away that I know of.'

'What a wonderful record! And what exactly are his duties?'

Mrs Clemm paused again, her hands still motionless in the folds of her skirt. Lady Jane noticed that the fingers were tightly clenched, as if to check an involuntary gesture.

'He began as pantry boy; then footman, then butler, my lady; but it's hard to say, isn't it, what an old servant's duties are, when he's stayed on in the same house so many years?'

'Yes; and that house always empty.'

'Just so, my lady. Everything came to depend on him; one thing after another. His late lordship thought the world of him.'

'His late lordship? But he was never here! He spent all his life in Canada.'

Mrs Clemm seemed slightly disconcerted. 'Certainly, my lady.' (Her voice said: 'Who are you, to set me right as to the chronicles of Bells?') 'But by letter, my lady; I can show you the letters. And there was his lordship before, the sixteenth Viscount. He *did* come here once.'

'Ah, did he?' Lady Jane was embarrassed to find how little she knew of them all. She rose from her seat. 'They were lucky, all these absentees, to have some one to watch over their interests so faithfully. I should like to see Mr Jones—to thank him. Will you take me to him now?'

'Now?' Mrs Clemm moved back a step or two; Lady Jane fancied her cheeks paled a little under their ruddy varnish. 'Oh, not today, my lady.'

'Why? Isn't he well enough?'

'Not nearly. He's between life and death, as it were,' Mrs Clemm repeated, as if the phrase were the nearest approach she could find to a definition of Mr Jones's state.

'He wouldn't even know who I was?'

Mrs Clemm considered a moment. 'I don't say *that*, my lady'; her tone implied that to do so might appear disrespectful. 'He'd know you, my lady; but you wouldn't know *him*.' She broke off and added hastily: 'I mean, for what he is; he's in no state for you to see him.'

'He's so very ill? Poor man! And is everything possible being done?'

'Oh, everything; and more too, my lady. But perhaps,' Mrs Clemm suggested, with a clink of keys, 'this would be a good time for your ladyship to take a look about the house. If your ladyship has no objection, I should like to begin with the linen.'

IV

'And Mr Jones?' Stramer queried, a few days later, as they sat, Lady Jane and the party from Kent, about an improvised tea table in a recess of one of the great holly hedges.

The day was as hushed and warm as that on which she had first come to Bells, and Lady Jane looked up with a smile of ownership at the old walls which seemed to smile back, the windows which now looked at her with friendly eyes.

'Mr Jones? Who's Mr Jones?' the others asked; only Stramer recalled their former talk.

Lady Jane hesitated. 'Mr Jones is my invisible guardian; or rather, the guardian of Bells.'

They remembered then. 'Invisible? You don't mean to say you haven't seen him yet?'

'Not yet; perhaps I never shall. He's very old—and very ill, I'm afraid.'

'And he still rules here?'

'Oh, absolutely. The fact is,' Lady Jane added, 'I believe he's the only person left who really knows all about Bells.'

'Jane, my *dear*! That big shrub over there against the wall! I verily believe it's *Templetonia retusa*. It *is*! Did any one ever hear of its standing an English winter?' Gardeners all, they dashed off toward the shrub in its sheltered angle. 'I shall certainly try it on a south wall at Dipway,' cried the hostess from Kent.

Tea over, they moved on to inspect the house. The short autumn day was drawing to a close; but the party had been able to come only for an afternoon, instead of staying over the weekend, and having lingered so long in the gardens they had only time, indoors, to puzzle out what they could through the shadows. Perhaps, Lady Jane thought, it was the best hour to see a house like Bells, so long abandoned, and not yet warmed into new life.

The fire she had had lit in the salon sent its radiance to meet them, giving the great room an air of expectancy and welcome. The portraits, the Italian cabinets, the shabby armchairs and rugs, all looked as if life had but lately left them; and Lady Jane said to herself: 'Perhaps Mrs Clemm is right in advising me to live here and close the blue parlour.'

'My dear, what a fine room! Pity it faces north. Of course you'll have to shut it in winter. It would cost a fortune to heat.'

Lady Jane hesitated. 'I don't know: I *had* meant to. But there seems to be no other. . . .'

'No other? In all this house?' They laughed; and one of the visitors, going ahead and crossing a panelled anteroom, cried out: 'But here! A delicious room; windows south—yes, and west. The warmest of the house. This is perfect.'

They followed, and the blue room echoed with exclamations. 'Those charming curtains with the parrots . . . and the blue of that petit point fire screen! But, Jane, of course you must live here. Look at this citron wood desk!'

Lady Jane stood on the threshold. 'It seems that the chimney smokes hopelessly.'

'Hopelessly? Nonsense! Have you consulted anybody? I'll send you a wonderful man. . . . '

'Besides, if you put in one of those one-pipe heaters. . . . At Dipway. . . . '

Stramer was looking over Lady Jane's shoulder. 'What does Mr Jones say about it?'

'He says no one has ever been able to use this room; not for ages. It was the housekeeper who told me. She's his great-niece, and seems simply to transmit his oracles.'

Stramer shrugged. 'Well, he's lived at Bells longer than you have. Perhaps he's right.'

'How absurd!' one of the ladies cried. 'The housekeeper and Mr Jones probably spend their evenings here, and don't want to be disturbed. Look—ashes on the hearth! What did I tell you?'

Lady Jane echoed the laugh as they turned away. They had still to see the library, damp and dilapidated, the panelled dining room, the breakfast parlour, and such bedroooms as had any old furniture left; not many, for the late lords of Bells, at one time or another, had evidently sold most of its removable treasures.

When the visitors came down their motors were waiting. A lamp had been placed in the hall, but the rooms beyond were lit only by the broad clear band of western sky showing through uncurtained casements. On the doorstep one of the ladies exclaimed that she had lost her handbag—no, she remembered; she had laid it on the desk in the blue room. Which way was the blue room?

'I'll get it,' Jane said, turning back. She heard Stramer following. He asked if he should bring the lamp.

'Oh, no; I can see.'

She crossed the threshold of the blue room, guided by the light from its western window; then she stopped. Some one was in the room already; she felt rather than saw another presence. Stramer, behind her, paused also; he did not speak or move. What she saw, or thought she saw, was simply an old man with bent shoulders turning away from the citron wood desk. Almost before she had received the impression there was no one there; only the slightest stir of the needlework curtain over the farther door. She heard no step or other sound.

'There's the bag,' she said, as if the act of speaking, and saying something obvious, were a relief.

In the hall her glance crossed Stramer's, but failed to find there the reflection of what her own had registered.

He shook hands, smiling. 'Well, good-bye. I commit you to Mr Jones's care; only don't let him say that *you're* not shown to visitors.'

She smiled: 'Come back and try,' and then shivered a little as the lights of the last motor vanished beyond the great black hedges.

V

Lady Jane had exulted in her resolve to keep Bells to herself till she and the old house should have had time to make friends. But after a few days she recalled the uneasy feeling which had come over her as she stood on the threshold after her first tentative ring. Yes; she had been right in thinking she would have to have people about her to take the chill off. The house was too old, too mysterious, too much withdrawn into its own secret past, for her poor little present to fit into it without uneasiness.

But it was not a time of year when, among Lady Jane's friends, it was easy to find people free. Her own family were all in the north, and impossible to dislodge. One of her sisters, when invited, simply sent her back a list of shooting dates; and her mother wrote: 'Why not come to us? What can you have to do all alone in that empty house at this time of year? Next summer we're all coming.'

Having tried one or two friends with the same result, Lady Jane bethought her of Stramer. He was finishing a novel, she knew, and at such times he liked to settle down somewhere in the country where he could be sure of not being disturbed. Bells was a perfect asylum, and though it was probable that some other friend had anticipated her, and provided the requisite seclusion, Lady Jane decided to invite him. 'Do bring your work and stay till it's finished—and don't be in a hurry to finish. I promise that no one shall bother you—' and she added, half-nervously: 'Not even Mr Jones.' As she wrote she felt an absurd impulse to blot the words out. 'He might not like it,' she thought; and the 'he' did not refer to Stramer.

Was the solitude already making her superstitious? She thrust the letter into an envelope, and carried it herself to the post office at Thudeney-Blazes. Two days later a wire from Stramer announced his arrival.

*　　*　　*

He came on a cold stormy afternoon, just before dinner, and as they went up to dress Lady Jane called after him: 'We shall sit in the blue parlour this evening.' The housemaid Georgiana was crossing the passage with hot water for the visitor. She stopped and cast a vacant glance at Lady Jane. The latter met it, and said carelessly: 'You hear, Georgiana? The fire in the blue parlour.'

While Lady Jane was dressing she heard a knock, and saw Mrs Clemm's round face just inside the door, like a red apple on a garden wall.

'Is there anything wrong about the salon, my lady? Georgiana understood—'

'That I want the fire in the blue parlour. Yes. What's wrong with the salon is that one freezes there.'

'But the chimney smokes in the blue parlour.'

'Well, we'll give it a trial, and if it does I'll send for someone to arrange it.'

'Nothing can be done, my lady. Everything has been tried, and—'

Lady Jane swung about suddenly. She had heard Stramer singing a cheerful hunting song in a cracked voice, in his dressing room at the other end of the corridor.

'That will do, Mrs Clemm. I want the fire in the blue parlour.'

'Yes, my lady.' The door closed on the housekeeper.

'So you decided on the salon after all?' Stramer said, as Lady Jane led the way there after their brief repast.

'Yes: I hope you won't be frozen. Mr Jones swears that the chimney in the blue parlour isn't safe; so, until I can fetch the mason over from Strawbridge—'

'Oh, I see.' Stramer drew up to the blaze in the great fireplace. 'We're very well off here; though heating this room is going to be ruinous. Meanwhile, I note that Mr Jones still rules.'

Lady Jane gave a slight laugh.

'Tell me,' Stramer continued, as she bent over the mixing of the Turkish coffee, 'what is there about him? I'm getting curious.'

Lady Jane laughed again, and heard the embarrassment in her laugh. 'So am I.'

'Why—you don't mean to say you haven't seen him yet?'

'No. He's still too ill.'

'What's the matter with him? What does the doctor say?'

'He won't see the doctor.'

'But look here—if things take a worse turn—I don't know; but mightn't you be held to have been negligent?'

'What can I do? Mrs Clemm says he has a doctor who treats him by correspondence. I don't see that I can interfere.'

'Isn't there someone beside Mrs Clemm whom you can consult?'

She considered: certainly, as yet, she had not made much effort to get into relations with her neighbours. 'I expected the vicar to call. But I've inquired: there's no vicar any longer at Thudeney-Blazes. A curate comes from Strawbridge every other Sunday. And the one who comes now is new: nobody about the place seems to know him.'

'But I thought the chapel here was in use? It looked so when you showed it to us the other day.'

'I thought so too. It used to be the parish church of Lynke-Linnet and Lower-Lynke; but it seems that was years ago. The parishioners objected to coming so far; and there weren't enough of them. Mrs Clemm says that nearly everybody has died off or left. It's the same at Thudeney-Blazes.'

Stramer glanced about the great room, with its circle of warmth and light by the hearth, and the sullen shadows huddled at its farther end, as if hungrily listening. 'With this emptiness at the centre, life was bound to cease gradually on the outskirts.'

Lady Jane followed his glance. 'Yes; it's all wrong. I must try to wake the place up.'

'Why not open it to the public? Have a visitors' day?'

She thought a moment. In itself the suggestion was distasteful; she could imagine few things that would bore her more. Yet to do so might be a duty, a first step toward re-establishing relations between the lifeless house and its neighbourhood. Secretly, she felt that even the coming and going of indifferent unknown people would help to take the chill from those rooms, to brush from their walls the dust of too-heavy memories.

'Who's that?' asked Stramer. Lady Jane started in spite of herself, and glanced over her shoulder; but he was only looking past her at a portrait which a dart of flame from the hearth had momentarily called from its obscurity.

'That's a Lady Thudeney.' She got up and went toward the picture with a lamp. 'Might be an Opie, don't you think? It's a strange face, under the smirk of the period.'

Stramer took the lamp and held it up. The portrait was that of a young woman in a short-waisted muslin gown caught beneath the breast by a cameo. Between clusters of beribboned curls a long fair oval looked out dumbly, inexpressively, in a stare of frozen beauty. 'It's as if the house had been too empty even then,' Lady Jane murmured. 'I wonder which she was? Oh, I know: it must be "*Also His Wife.*" '

Stramer stared.

'It's the only name on her monument. The wife of Peregrine Vincent Theobald, who perished of the plague at Aleppo in 1828. Perhaps she was very fond of him, and this was painted when she was an inconsolable widow.'

'They didn't dress like that as late as 1828.' Stramer, holding the lamp closer, deciphered the inscription on the border of the lady's India scarf; *Juliana, Viscountess Thudeney, 1818.* 'She must have been inconsolable before his death, then.'

Lady Jane smiled. 'Let's hope she grew less so after it.'

Stramer passed the lamp across the canvas. 'Do you see where she was painted? In the blue parlour. Look: the old panelling; and she's leaning on the citron wood desk. They evidently used the room in winter then.' The lamp paused on the background of the picture: a window framing snow-laden paths and hedges in icy perspective.

'Curious,' Stramer said—'and rather melancholy: to be painted against that wintry desolation. I wish you could find out more about her. Have you dipped into your archives?'

'No. Mr Jones—'

'He won't allow that either?'

'Yes; but he's lost the key of the muniment room. Mrs Clemm has been trying to get a locksmith.'

'Surely the neighbourhood can still produce one?'

'There *was* one at Thudeney-Blazes; but he died the week before I came.'

'Of course!'

'Of course?'

'Well, in Mrs Clemm's hands keys get lost, chimneys smoke, locksmiths die. . . .' Stramer stood, light in hand, looking down the shadowy length of the salon. 'I say, let's go and see what's happening now in the blue parlour.'

Lady Jane laughed: a laugh seemed easy with another voice near by to echo it. 'Let's—'

She followed him out of the salon, across the hall in which a single candle burned on a far-off table, and past the stairway yawning like a black funnel above them. In the doorway of the blue parlour Stramer paused. 'Now, then, Mr Jones!'

It was stupid, but Lady Jane's heart gave a jerk: she hoped the challenge would not evoke the shadowy figure she had half seen that other day.

'Lord, it's cold!' Stramer stood looking about him. 'Those ashes are still on the hearth. Well, it's all very queer.' He crossed over to the citron wood desk. 'There's where she sat for her picture—and in this very armchair—look!'

'Oh, don't!' Lady Jane exclaimed. The words slipped out unawares.

'Don't—what?'

'Try those drawers—' she wanted to reply; for his hand was stretched toward the desk.

'I'm frozen; I think I'm starting a cold. Do come away,' she grumbled, backing toward the door.

Stramer lighted her out without comment. As the lamplight slid along the walls Lady Jane fancied that the needlework curtain over the farther door stirred as it had that other day. But it may have been the wind rising outside. . . .

The salon seemed like home when they got back to it.

'There *is* no Mr Jones!'

Stramer proclaimed it triumphantly when they met the next morning. Lady Jane had motored off early to Strawbridge in quest of a mason and a locksmith. The quest had taken longer than she had expected, for everybody in Strawbridge was busy on jobs nearer by, and unaccustomed to the idea of going to Bells, with which the town seemed to have had no communication within living memory. The younger workmen did not even know where the place was, and the best Lady Jane could do was to coax a locksmith's apprentice to come with her, on the understanding that he would be driven back to the nearest station as soon as his job was over. As for the mason, he had merely taken note of her request, and promised half-heartedly to send somebody when he could. 'Rather off our beat, though.'

She returned, discouraged and somewhat weary, as Stramer was coming downstairs after his morning's work.

'No Mr Jones?' she echoed.

'Not a trace! I've been trying the old Glamis experiment—situating his room by its window. Luckily the house is smaller. . . . '

Lady Jane smiled. 'Is this what you call locking yourself up with your work?'

'I can't work: that's the trouble. Not till this is settled. Bells is a fidgety place.'

'Yes,' she agreed.

'Well, I wasn't going to be beaten; so I went to try to find the head gardener.'

'But there isn't—'

'No. Mrs Clemm told me. The head gardener died last year. That woman positively glows with life whenever she announces a death. Have you noticed?'

Yes: Lady Jane had.

'Well—I said to myself that if there wasn't a head gardener there must be an underling; at least one. I'd seen somebody in the distance, raking leaves, and I ran him down. Of course he'd never seen Mr Jones.'

'You mean that poor old half-blind Jacob? He couldn't see anybody.'

'Perhaps not. At any rate, he told me that Mr Jones wouldn't let the leaves be buried for leaf mould—I forget why. Mr Jones's authority extends even to the gardens.'

'Yet you say he doesn't exist!'

'Wait. Jacob is half blind, but he's been here for years, and knows more about the place than you'd think. I got him talking about the house, and I pointed to one window after another, and he told me each time whose the room was, or had been. But he couldn't situate Mr—Jones.'

'I beg your ladyship's pardon—' Mrs Clemm was on the threshold, cheeks shining, skirt rustling, her eyes like drills. 'The locksmith your ladyship brought back; I understand it was for the lock of the muniment room—'

'Well?'

'He's lost one of his tools, and can't do anything without it. So he's gone. The butcher's boy gave him a lift back.'

Lady Jane caught Stramer's faint chuckle. She stood and stared at Mrs Clemm, and Mrs Clemm stared back, deferential but unflinching.

'Gone? Very well; I'll motor after him.'

'Oh, my lady, it's too late. The butcher's boy had his motorcycle. . . . Besides, what could he do?'

'Break the lock,' exclaimed Lady Jane, exasperated.

'Oh, my lady—' Mrs Clemm's intonation marked the most respectful incredulity. She waited another moment, and then withdrew, while Lady Jane and Stramer considered each other.

'But this is absurd,' Lady Jane declared when they had lunched, waited on, as usual, by the flustered Georgiana. 'I'll break in that door myself, if I have to.—Be careful please, Georgiana,' she added; 'I was speaking of doors, not dishes.' For Georgiana had let fall with a crash the dish she was removing from the table. She gathered up the pieces in her tremulous fingers, and vanished. Jane and Stramer returned to the salon.

'Queer!' the novelist commented.

'Yes.' Lady Jane, facing the door, started slightly. Mrs Clemm was there again; but this time subdued, unrustling, bathed in that odd pallor which enclosed but seemed unable to penetrate the solid crimson of her cheeks.

'I beg pardon, my lady. The key is found.' Her hand, as she held it out, trembled like Georgiana's.

VI

'It's not here,' Stramer announced, a couple of hours later.

'What isn't?' Lady Jane queried, looking up from a heap of disordered papers. Her eyes blinked at him through the fog of yellow dust raised by her manipulations.

'The clue.—I've got all the 1800 to 1840 papers here; and there's a gap.'

She moved over to the table above which he was bending. 'A gap?'

'A big one. Nothing between 1815 and 1835. No mention of Peregrine or of Juliana.'

They looked at each other across the tossed papers, and suddenly Stramer exclaimed: 'Someone has been here before us—just lately.'

Lady Jane stared, incredulous, and then followed the direction of his downward pointing hand.

'Do you wear flat heelless shoes?' he questioned. 'And of that size? Even my feet are too small to fit into those footprints. Luckily there wasn't time to sweep the floor!'

Lady Jane felt a slight chill, a chill of a different and more inward quality than the shock of stuffy coldness which had met them as they entered the unaired attic set apart for the storing of the Thudeney archives.

'But how absurd! Of course when Mrs Clemm found we were coming up she came—or sent someone—to open the shutters.'

'That's not Mrs Clemm's foot, or the other woman's. She must have sent a man—an old man with a shaky uncertain step. Look how it wanders.'

'Mr Jones, then!' said Lady Jane, half impatiently.

'Mr Jones. And he got what he wanted, and put it—where?'

'Ah, *that*—! I'm freezing, you know; let's give this up for the present.' She rose, and Stramer followed her without protest; the muniment room was really untenable.

'I must catalogue all this stuff someday, I suppose,' Lady Jane continued, as they went down the stairs. 'But meanwhile, what do you say to a good tramp, to get the dust out of our lungs?'

He agreed, and turned back to his room to get some letters he wanted to post at Thudeney-Blazes.

Lady Jane went down alone. It was a fine afternoon, and the sun, which had made the dust clouds of the muniment room so dazzling, sent a long shaft through the west window of the blue parlour, and across the floor of the hall.

Certainly Georgiana kept the oak floors remarkably well; considering how much else she had to do, it was surp—

Lady Jane stopped as if an unseen hand had jerked her violently back. On the smooth parquet before her she had caught the trace of dusty footprints—the prints of broad-soled heelless shoes—making for the blue parlour and crossing its threshold. She stood still with the same inward shiver that she had felt upstairs; then, avoiding the footprints, she too stole very softly toward the blue parlour, pushed the door wider, and saw, in the long dazzle of autumn light, as if translucid, edged with the glitter, an old man at the desk.

'Mr Jones!'

A step came up behind her: Mrs Clemm with the post bag. 'You called, my lady?'

'I . . . yes. . . . '

When she turned back to the desk there was no one there.

She faced about on the housekeeper. 'Who was that?'

'Where, my lady?'

Lady Jane, without answering, moved toward the needlework curtain, in which she had detected the same faint tremor as before. 'Where does that door go to—behind the curtain?'

'Nowhere, my lady. I mean; there is no door.'

Mrs Clemm had followed; her step sounded quick and assured. She lifted up the curtain with a firm hand. Behind it was a rectangle of roughly plastered wall, where an opening had visibly been bricked up.

'When was that done?'

'The wall built up? I couldn't say. I've never known it otherwise,' replied the housekeeper.

The two women stood for an instant measuring each other with level eyes; then the housekeeper's were slowly lowered, and she let the curtain fall from her hand. 'There are a great many things in old houses that nobody knows about,' she said.

'There shall be as few as possible in mine,' said Lady Jane.

'My lady!' The housekeeper stepped quickly in front of her. 'My lady, what are you doing?' she gasped.

Lady Jane had turned back to the desk at which she had just seen—or fancied she had seen—the bending figure of Mr Jones.

'I am going to look through these drawers,' she said.

The housekeeper still stood in pale immobility between her and the desk. 'No, my lady—no. You won't do that.'

'Because—?'

Mrs Clemm crumpled up her black silk apron with a despairing gesture. 'Because—if you *will* have it—that's where Mr Jones keeps his private papers. I know he'd oughtn't to . . . . '

'Ah—then it was Mr Jones I saw here?'

The housekeeper's arms sank to her sides and her mouth hung open on an unspoken word. 'You *saw* him?' The question came out in a confused whisper; and before Lady Jane could answer, Mrs Clemm's arms rose again, stretched before her face as if to fend off a blaze of intolerable light, or some forbidden sight she had long since disciplined herself not to see. Thus screening her eyes she hurried across the hall to the door of the servants' wing.

Lady Jane stood for a moment looking after her; then, with a slightly shaking hand, she opened the desk and hurriedly took out from it all the papers—a small bundle—that it contained. With them she passed back into the salon.

As she entered it her eye was caught by the portrait of the melancholy lady in the short-waisted gown whom she and Stramer had christened 'Also His Wife'. The lady's eyes, usually so empty of all awareness save of her own frozen beauty, seemed suddenly waking to an anguished participation in the scene.

'Fudge!' muttered Lady Jane, shaking off the spectral suggestion as she turned to meet Stramer on the threshold.

VII

The missing papers were all there. Stramer and she spread them out hurriedly on a table and at once proceeded to gloat over their find. Not a particularly important one, indeed; in the long history of the Lynkes and Crofts it took up hardly more space than the little handful of documents did, in actual bulk, among the stacks of the muniment room. But the fact that these papers filled a gap in the chronicles of the house, and situated the sad-faced beauty as veritably the wife of the Peregrine Vincent Theobald Lynke who had 'perished of the plague at Aleppo in 1828'— this was a discovery sufficiently exciting to whet amateur appetites, and to put out of Lady Jane's mind the strange incident which had attended the opening of the cabinet.

For a while she and Stramer sat silently and methodically going through their respective piles of correspondence; but presently Lady

Jane, after glancing over one of the yellowing pages, uttered a startled exclamation.

'How strange! Mr Jones again—always Mr Jones!'

Stramer looked up from the papers he was sorting. 'You too? I've got a lot of letters here addressed to a Mr Jones by Peregrine Vincent, who seems to have been always disporting himself abroad, and chronically in want of money. Gambling debts, apparently . . . ah and women . . . a dirty record altogether. . . . '

'Yes? My letter is not written to a Mr Jones; but it's about one. Listen.' Lady Jane began to read. ' "Bells, February 20th, 1826. . . . " (It's from poor "Also His Wife" to her husband.) "My dear Lord, Acknowledging as I ever do the burden of the sad impediment which denies me the happiness of being more frequently in your company, I yet fail to conceive how anything in my state obliges that close seclusion in which Mr Jones persists—and by your express orders, so he declares—in confining me. Surely, my lord, had you found it possible to spend more time with me since the day of our marriage, you would yourself have seen it to be unnecessary to put this restraint upon me. It is true, alas, that my unhappy infirmity denies me the happiness to speak with you, or to hear the accents of the voice I should love above all others could it but reach me; but, my dear husband, I would have you consider that my mind is in no way affected by this obstacle, but goes out to you, as my heart does, in a perpetual eagerness of attention, and that to sit in this great house alone, day after day, month after month, deprived of your company, and debarred also from any intercourse but that of the servants you have chosen to put about me, is a fate more cruel than I deserve and more painful than I can bear. I have entreated Mr Jones, since he seems all-powerful with you, to represent this to you, and to transmit this my last request—for should I fail I am resolved to make no other—that you should consent to my making the acquaintance of a few of your friends and neighbours, among whom I cannot but think there must be some kind hearts that would take pity on my unhappy situation, and afford me such companionship as would give me more courage to bear your continual absence . . . . " ' '

Lady Jane folded up the letter. 'Deaf and dumb—ah, poor creature! That explains the look—'

'And this explains the marriage,' Stramer continued, unfolding a stiff parchment document. 'Here are the Viscountess Thudeney's marriage settlements. She appears to have been a Miss Portallo, daughter of Obadiah Portallo Esqre, of Purflew Castle, Caermarthenshire, and Bombay House, Twickenham, East India merchant, senior member of the banking house of Portallo and Prest—and so on and so on. And the figures run up into hundreds of thousands.'

'It's rather ghastly—putting the two things together. All the millions and—imprisonment in the blue parlour. I suppose her Viscount had to have the money, and was ashamed to have it known how he had got it . . . . ' Lady Jane shivered. 'Think of it—day after day, winter after winter, year after year . . . speechless, soundless, alone . . . under Mr Jones's guardianship. Let me see: what year were they married?'

'In 1817.'

'And only a year later that portrait was painted. And she had the frozen look already.'

Stramer mused: 'Yes, it's grim enough. But the strangest figure in the whole case is still—Mr Jones.'

'Mr Jones—yes. Her keeper,' Lady Jane mused. 'I suppose he must have been this one's ancestor. The office seems to have been hereditary at Bells.'

'Well—I don't know.'

Stramer's voice was so odd that Lady Jane looked up at him with a stare of surprise. 'What if it were the same one?' suggested Stramer with a queer smile.

'The same?' Lady Jane laughed. 'You're not good at figures are you? If poor Lady Thudeney's Mr Jones were alive now he'd be—'

'I didn't say ours was alive now,' said Stramer.

'Oh—why, what . . . ?' she faltered.

But Stramer did not answer; his eyes had been arrested by the precipitate opening of the door behind his hostess, and the entry of Georgiana, a livid, dishevelled Georgiana, more than usually bereft of her faculties, and gasping out something inarticulate.

'Oh, my lady—it's my aunt—she won't answer me,' Georgiana stammered in a voice of terror.

Lady Jane uttered an impatient exclamation. 'Answer you? Why—what do you want her to answer?'

'Only whether she's alive, my lady,' said Georgiana with streaming eyes.

Lady Jane continued to look at her severely. 'Alive? Alive? Why on earth shouldn't she be?'

'She might as well be dead—by the way she just lies there.'

'Your aunt dead? I saw her alive enough in the blue parlour half an hour ago,' Lady Jane returned. She was growing rather blasé with regard to Georgiana's panics; but suddenly she felt this to be of a different nature from any of the others. 'Where is it your aunt's lying?'

'In her own bedroom, on her bed,' the other wailed, 'and won't say why.'

Lady Jane got to her feet, pushing aside the heaped-up papers, and hastening to the door with Stramer in her wake.

As they went up the stairs she realized that she had seen the housekeeper's bedroom only once, on the day of her first obligatory round of inspection, when she had taken possession of Bells. She did not even remember very clearly where it was, but followed Georgiana down the passage and through a door which communicated, rather surprisingly, with a narrow walled-in staircase that was unfamiliar to her. At its top she and Stramer found themselves on a small landing upon which two doors opened. Through the confusion of her mind Lady Jane noticed that these rooms, with their special staircase leading down to what had always been called his lordship's suite, must obviously have been occupied by his lordship's confidential servants. In one of them, presumably, had been lodged the original Mr Jones, the Mr Jones of the yellow letters, the letters purloined by Lady Jane. As she crossed the threshold, Lady Jane remembered the housekeeper's attempt to prevent her touching the contents of the desk.

Mrs Clemm's room, like herself, was neat, glossy and extremely cold. Only Mrs Clemm herself was no longer like Mrs Clemm. The red-apple glaze had barely faded from her cheeks, and not a lock was disarranged in the unnatural lustre of her false front; even her cap ribbons hung symmetrically along either cheek. But death had happened to her, and had made her into someone else. At first glance it was impossible to say if the unspeakable horror in her wide open eyes were only the reflection of that change, or of the agent by whom it had come. Lady Jane, shuddering, paused a moment while Stramer went up to the bed.

'Her hand is warm still—but no pulse.' He glanced about the room. 'A glass anywhere?' The cowering Georgiana took a hand glass from the neat chest of drawers, and Stramer held it over the housekeeper's drawn-back lip. . . .

'She's dead,' he pronounced.

'Oh, poor thing! But how—?' Lady Jane drew near, and was kneeling down, taking the inanimate hand in hers, when Stramer touched her on the arm, and then silently raised a finger of warning. Georgiana was crouching in the farther corner of the room, her face buried in her lifted arms.

'Look here,' Stramer whispered. He pointed to Mrs Clemm's throat, and Lady Jane, bending over, distinctly saw a circle of red marks on it—the marks of recent bruises. She looked again into the awful eyes.

'She's been strangled,' Stramer whispered.

Lady Jane, with a shiver of fear, drew down the housekeeper's lids. Georgiana, her face hidden, was still sobbing convulsively in the corner. There seemed, in the air of the cold orderly room, something that forbade wonderment and silenced conjecture. Lady Jane and Stramer stood and looked at each other without speaking. At length Stramer crossed over to Georgiana, and touched her on the shoulder. She appeared unaware of the touch, and he grasped her shoulder and shook it. 'Where is Mr Jones?' he asked.

The girl looked up, her face blurred and distorted with weeping, her eyes dilated as if with the vision of some latent terror. 'Oh, sir, she's not really dead, is she?'

Stramer repeated his question in a loud authoritative tone; and slowly she echoed it in a scarce-heard whisper. 'Mr Jones—?'

'Get up, my girl, and send him here to us at once, or tell us where to find him.'

Georgiana, moved by the old habit of obedience, struggled to her feet and stood unsteadily, her heaving shoulders braced against the wall. Stramer asked her sharply if she had not heard what he had said.

'Oh, poor thing, she's so upset—' Lady Jane intervened compassionately. 'Tell me, Georgiana: where shall we find Mr Jones?'

The girl turned to her with eyes as fixed as the dead woman's. 'You won't find him anywhere,' she slowly said.

'Why not?'

'Because he's not here.'

'Not here? Where is he, then?' Stramer broke in.

Georgiana did not seem to notice the interruption. She continued to stare at Lady Jane with Mrs Clemm's awful eyes. 'He's in his grave in the churchyard—these years and years he is. Long before ever I was born . . . my aunt hadn't ever seen him herself, not since she was a tiny child. . . . That's the terror of it . . . that's why she always had to do what he told her to . . . because you couldn't ever answer him back. . . . ' Her horrified gaze turned from Lady Jane to the stony face and fast-glazing pupils of the dead woman. 'You hadn't ought to have meddled with his papers, my lady. . . . That's what he's punished her for. . . . When it came to those papers he wouldn't ever listen to human reason . . . he wouldn't. . . . ' Then, flinging her arms above her head, Georgiana straightened herself to her full height before falling in a swoon at Stramer's feet.

Smee

A. M. BURRAGE

~

'No,' said Jackson, with a deprecatory smile, 'I'm sorry. I don't want to
upset your game. I shan't be doing that because you'll have plenty
without me. But I'm not playing any games of hide-and-seek.'

It was Christmas Eve, and we were a party of fourteen with just the
proper leavening of youth. We had dined well; it was the season for
childish games, and we were all in the mood for playing them—all, that
is, except Jackson. When somebody suggested hide-and-seek there was
rapturous and almost unanimous approval. His was the one dissentient
voice.

It was not like Jackson to spoil sport or refuse to do as others wanted.
Somebody asked him if he were feeling seedy.

'No,' he answered, 'I feel perfectly fit, thanks. But,' he added with a
smile which softened without retracting the flat refusal, 'I'm not playing
hide-and-seek.'

One of us asked him why not. He hesitated for some seconds before
replying.

'I sometimes go and stay at a house where a girl was killed through
playing hide-and-seek in the dark. She didn't know the house very well.
There was a servants' staircase with a door to it. When she was pursued
she opened the door and jumped into what she must have thought was
one of the bedrooms—and she broke her neck at the bottom of the
stairs.'

We all looked concerned, and Mrs Fernley said:

'How awful! And you were there when it happened?'

Jackson shook his head very gravely. 'No,' he said, 'but I was there
when something else happened. Something worse.'

'I shouldn't have thought anything could be worse.'

'This was,' said Jackson, and shuddered visibly. 'Or so it seemed to
me.'

I think he wanted to tell the story and was angling for encouragement.
A few requests which may have seemed to him to lack urgency, he
affected to ignore and went off at a tangent.

'I wonder if any of you have played a game called "Smee". It's a great
improvement on the ordinary game of hide-and-seek. The name

derives from the ungrammatical colloquialism, "It's me." You might care to play if you're going to play a game of that sort. Let me tell you the rules.

'Every player is presented with a sheet of paper. All the sheets are blank except one, on which is written "Smee". Nobody knows who is "Smee" except "Smee" himself—or herself, as the case may be. The lights are then turned out and "Smee" slips from the room and goes off to hide, and after an interval the other players go off in search, without knowing whom they are actually in search of. One player meeting another challenges with the word "Smee" and the other player, if not the one concerned, answers "Smee".

'The real "Smee" makes no answer when challenged, and the second player remains quietly by him. Presently they will be discovered by a third player, who, having challenged and received no answer, will link up with the first two. This goes on until all the players have formed a chain, and the last to join is marked down for a forfeit. It's a good noisy, romping game, and in a big house it often takes a long time to complete the chain. You might care to try it; and I'll pay my forfeit and smoke one of Tim's excellent cigars here by the fire until you get tired of it.'

I remarked that it sounded a good game and asked Jackson if he had played it himself.

'Yes,' he answered; 'I played it in the house I was telling you about.'

'And *she* was there? The girl who broke—'

'No, no,' Mrs Fernley interrupted. 'He told us he wasn't there when it happened.'

Jackson considered. 'I don't know if she was there or not. I'm afraid she was. I know that there were thirteen of us and there ought only to have been twelve. And I'll swear that I didn't know her name, or I think I should have gone clean off my head when I heard that whisper in the dark. No, you don't catch me playing that game, or any other like it, any more. It spoiled my nerve quite a while, and I can't afford to take long holidays. Besides, it saves a lot of trouble and inconvenience to own up at once to being a coward.'

Tim Vouce, the best of hosts, smiled around at us, and in that smile there was a meaning which is sometimes vulgarly expressed by the slow closing of an eye. 'There's a story coming,' he announced.

'There's certainly a story of sorts,' said Jackson, 'but whether it's coming or not—' He paused and shrugged his shoulders.

'Well, you're going to pay a forfeit instead of playing?'

'Please. But have a heart and let me down lightly. It's not just a sheer cussedness on my part.'

'Payment in advance,' said Tim, 'insures honesty and promotes good feeling. You are therefore sentenced to tell the story here and now.'

And here follows Jackson's story, unrevised by me and passed on without comment to a wider public:

Some of you, I know, have run across the Sangstons. Christopher Sangston and his wife, I mean. They're distant connections of mine—at least, Violet Sangston is. About eight years ago they bought a house between the North and South Downs on the Surrey and Sussex border, and five years ago they invited me to come and spend Christmas with them.

It was a fairly old house—I couldn't say exactly of what period—and it certainly deserved the epithet 'rambling'. It wasn't a particularly big house, but the original architect, whoever he may have been, had not concerned himself with economising in space, and at first you could get lost in it quite easily.

Well, I went down for that Christmas, assured by Violet's letter that I knew most of my fellow-guests and that the two or three who might be strangers to me were all 'lambs'. Unfortunately, I'm one of the world's workers, and I couldn't get away until Christmas Eve, although the other members of the party had assembled on the preceding day. Even then I had to cut it rather fine to be there for dinner on my first night. They were all dressing when I arrived and I had to go straight to my room and waste no time. I may even have kept dinner waiting a bit, for I was last down, and it was announced within a minute of my entering the drawing-room. There was just time to say 'hullo' to everybody I knew, to be briefly introduced to the two or three I didn't know, and then I had to give my arm to Mrs Gorman.

I mention this as the reason why I didn't catch the name of a tall, dark, handsome girl I hadn't met before. Everything was rather hurried and I am always bad at catching people's names. She looked cold and clever and rather forbidding, the sort of girl who gives the impression of knowing all about men and the more she knows of them the less she likes them. I felt that I wasn't going to hit it off with this particular 'lamb' of Violet's, but she looked interesting all the same, and I wondered who she was. I didn't ask, because I was pretty sure of hearing somebody address her by name before very long.

Unluckily, though, I was a long way off her at table, and as Mrs Gorman was at the top of her form that night I soon forgot to worry about who she might be. Mrs Gorman is one of the most amusing women I know, an outrageous but quite innocent flirt, with a very sprightly wit which isn't always unkind. She can think half a dozen moves ahead in conversation just as an expert can in a game of chess. We were soon sparring, or, rather, I was 'covering' against the ropes, and I quite forgot to ask her in an undertone the name of the cold, proud beauty. The lady on the other side of me was a stranger, or had been until a few minutes since, and I didn't think of seeking information in that quarter.

There was a round dozen of us, including the Sangstons themselves, and we were all young or trying to be. The Sangstons themselves were the oldest members of the party and their son Reggie, in his last year at Marlborough, must have been the youngest. When there was talk of playing games after dinner it was he who suggested 'Smee'. He told us how to play it just as I've described it to you.

His father chipped in as soon as we all understood what was going to be required of us. 'If there are any games of that sort going on in the house,' he said, 'for goodness' sake be careful of the back stairs on the first-floor landing. There's a door to them and I've often meant to take it down. In the dark anybody who doesn't know the house very well might think they were walking into a room. A girl actually did break her neck on those stairs about ten years ago when the Ainsties lived here.'

I asked how it happened.

'Oh,' said Sangston, 'there was a party here one Christmas time and they were playing hide-and-seek as you propose doing. This girl was one of the hiders. She heard somebody coming, ran along the passage to get away, and opened the door of what she thought was a bedroom, evidently with the intention of hiding behind it while her pursuer went past. Unfortunately it was the door leading to the back stairs, and that staircase is as straight and almost as steep as the shaft of a pit. She was dead when they picked her up.'

We all promised for our own sakes to be careful. Mrs Gorman said that she was sure nothing could happen to her, since she was insured by three different firms, and her next-of-kin was a brother whose consistent ill-luck was a byword in the family. You see, none of us had known the unfortunate girl, and as the tragedy was ten years old there was no need to pull long faces about it.

Well, we started the game almost immediately after dinner. The men allowed themselves only five minutes before joining the ladies, and then young Reggie Sangston went round and assured himself that the lights were out all over the house except in the servants' quarters and in the drawing-room where we were assembled. We then got busy with twelve sheets of paper which he twisted into pellets and shook up between his hands before passing them round. Eleven of them were blank, and 'Smee' was written on the twelfth. The person drawing the latter was the one who had to hide. I looked and saw that mine was a blank. A moment later out went the electric lights, and in the darkness I heard somebody get up and creep to the door.

After a minute or so somebody gave a signal and we made a rush for the door. I for one hadn't the least idea which of the party was 'Smee'. For five or ten minutes we were all rushing up and down passages and in and out rooms challenging one another and answering, '*Smee?—Smee!*'

After a bit the alarums and excursions died down, and I guessed that 'Smee' was found. Eventually I found a chain of people all sitting still and holding their breath on some narrow stairs leading up to a row of attics. I hastily joined it, having challenged and been answered with silence, and presently two more stragglers arrived, each racing the other to avoid being last. Sangston was one of them, indeed it was he who was marked down for a forfeit, and after a little while he remarked in an undertone, 'I think we're all here now, aren't we?'

He struck a match, looked up the shaft of the staircase, and began to count. It wasn't hard, although we just about filled the staircase, for we were sitting each a step or two above the next, and all our heads were visible.

' . . . nine, ten, eleven, twelve—*thirteen,*' he concluded, and then laughed. 'Dash it all, that's one too many!'

The match had burned out and he struck another and began to count. He got as far as twelve, and then uttered an exclamation.

'There are thirteen people here!' he exclaimed. 'I haven't counted myself yet.'

'Oh, nonsense!' I laughed. 'You probably began with yourself, and now you want to count yourself twice.'

Out came his son's electric torch, giving a brighter and steadier light and we all began to count. Of course we numbered twelve.

Sangston laughed.

'Well,' he said, 'I could have sworn I counted thirteen twice.'

From halfway up the stairs came Violet Sangston's voice with a little nervous trill in it. 'I thought there was somebody sitting two steps above me. Have you moved up, Captain Ransome?'

Ransome said that he hadn't: he also said that he thought there was somebody sitting between Violet and himself. Just for a moment there was an uncomfortable Something in the air, a little cold ripple which touched us all. For that little moment it seemed to all of us, I think, that something odd and unpleasant had happened and was liable to happen again. Then we laughed at ourselves and at one another and were comfortable once more. There *were* only twelve of us, and there *could* only have been twelve of us, and there was no argument about it. Still laughing we trooped back to the drawing-room to begin again.

This time I was 'Smee', and Violet Sangston ran me to earth while I was still looking for a hiding-place. That round didn't last long, and we were a chain of twelve within two or three minutes. Afterwards there was a short interval. Violet wanted a wrap fetched for her, and her husband went up to get it from her room. He was no sooner gone than Reggie pulled me by the sleeve. I saw that he was looking pale and sick.

'Quick!' he whispered, 'while father's out of the way. Take me into the smoke room and give me a brandy or a whisky or something.'

Outside the room I asked him what was the matter, but he didn't answer at first, and I thought it better to dose him first and question him afterward. So I mixed him a pretty dark-complexioned brandy and soda which he drank at a gulp and then began to puff as if he had been running.

'I've had rather a turn,' he said to me with a sheepish grin.

'What's the matter?'

'I don't know. You were "Smee" just now, weren't you? Well, of course I didn't know who "Smee" was, and while mother and the others ran into the west wing and found you, I turned east. There's a deep clothes cupboard in my bedroom—I'd marked it down as a good place to hide when it was my turn, and I had an idea that "Smee" might be there. I opened the door in the dark, felt round, and touched somebody's hand. "Smee?" I whispered, and not getting any answer I though I had found "Smee".'

'Well, I don't know how it was, but an odd creepy feeling came over me, I can't describe it, but I felt that something was wrong. So I turned on my electric torch and there was nobody there. Now, I swear I touched a hand, and I was filling up the doorway of the cupboard at the time, so nobody could get out and past me.' He puffed again. 'What do you make of it?' he asked.

'You imagined that you had touched a hand,' I answered, naturally enough.

He uttered a short laugh. 'Of course I knew you were going to say that,' he said. 'I must have imagined it, mustn't I?' He paused and swallowed. 'I mean, it couldn't have been anything else *but* imagination, could it?'

I assured him that it couldn't, meaning what I said, and he accepted this, but rather with the philosophy of one who knows he is right but doesn't expect to be believed. We returned together to the drawing-room where, by that time, they were all waiting for us and ready to start again.

It may have been my imagination—although I'm almost sure it wasn't—but it seemed to me that all enthusiasm for the game had suddenly melted like a white frost in strong sunlight. If anybody had suggested another game I'm sure we should all have been grateful and abandoned 'Smee'. Only nobody did. Nobody seemed to like to. I for one, and I can speak for some of the others too, was oppressed with the feeling that there was something wrong. I couldn't have said what I thought was wrong, indeed I didn't think about it at all, but somehow all the sparkle had gone out of the fun, and hovering over my mind like a shadow was the warning of some sixth sense which told me that there was an influence in the house which was neither sane, sound nor healthy. Why did I feel like that? Because Sangston had counted thirteen of us instead of twelve, and his son had thought he had touched somebody in an empty cupboard. No, there was more in it than just that. One would have laughed at such things in the ordinary way, and it was just that feeling of something being wrong which stopped me from laughing.

Well, we started again, and when we went in pursuit of the unknown 'Smee', we were as noisy as ever, but it seemed to me that most of us were acting. Frankly, for no reason other than the one I've given you, we'd stopped enjoying the game. I had an instinct to hunt with the main pack, but after a few minutes, during which no 'Smee' had been found, my instinct to play winning games and be first if possible, set me searching on my own account. And on the first floor of the west wing following the wall which was actually the shell of the house, I blundered against a pair of human knees.

I put out my hand and touched a soft, heavy curtain. Then I knew where I was. There were tall, deeply-recessed windows with seats along the landing, and curtains over the recesses to the ground. Somebody was sitting in a corner of this window-seat behind the curtain. Aha, I had caught 'Smee'! So I drew the curtain aside, stepped in, and touched the bare arm of a woman.

It was a dark night outside, and, moreover, the window was not only curtained but a blind hung down to where the bottom panes joined up with the frame. Between the curtain and the window it was as dark as the plague of Egypt. I could not have seen my hand held six inches before my face, much less the woman sitting in the corner.

'Smee?' I whispered.

I had no answer. 'Smee' when challenged does not answer. So I sat down beside her, first in the field, to await the others. Then, having settled myself I leaned over to her and whispered:

'Who is it? What's your name, "Smee"?'

And out of the darkness beside me the whisper came back: 'Brenda Ford.'

I didn't know the name, but because I didn't know it I guessed at once who she was. The tall, pale, dark girl was the only person in the house I didn't know by name. Ergo my companion was the tall, pale, dark girl. It seemed rather intriguing to be there with her, shut in between a heavy curtain and a window, and I rather wondered whether she was enjoying the game we were all playing. Somehow she hadn't seemed to me to be one of the romping sort. I muttered one or two commonplace questions to her and had no answer.

'Smee' is a game of silence. 'Smee' and the person or persons who have found 'Smee' are supposed to keep quiet to make it hard for the others. But there was nobody else about, and it occurred to me that she was playing the game a little too much to the letter. I spoke again and got no answer, and then I began to be annoyed. She was of that cold, 'superior' type which affects to despise men; she didn't like me; and she was sheltering behind the rules of a game for children to be discourteous. Well, if she didn't like sitting there with me, I certainly didn't want to be sitting there with her! I half turned from her and began to hope that we should both be discovered without much more delay.

Having discovered that I didn't like being there alone with her, it was queer how soon I found myself hating it, and that for a reason very different from the one which had at first whetted my annoyance. The girl I had met for the first time before dinner, and seen diagonally across the table, had a sort of cold charm about her which had attracted while it had half angered me. For the girl who was with me, imprisoned in the opaque darkness between the curtain and the window, I felt no attraction at all. It was so very much the reverse that I should have wondered at myself if, after the first shock of the discovery that she had suddenly become repellent to me, I had had room in my mind for anything besides the consciousness that her close presence was an increasing horror to me.

It came upon me just as quickly as I've uttered the words. My flesh suddenly shrank from her as you see a strip of gelatine shrink and wither before the heat of a fire. That feeling of something being wrong had come back to me, but multiplied to an extent which turned foreboding into actual terror. I firmly believe that I should have got up and run if I had not felt that at my first movement she would have divined my intention and compelled me to stay, by some means of which I could not bear to think. The memory of having touched her bare arm made me wince and draw in my lips. I prayed that somebody else would come along soon.

My prayer was answered. Light footfalls sounded on the landing. Somebody on the other side of the curtain brushed again my knees. The curtain was drawn aside and a woman's hand, fumbling in the darkness, presently rested on my shoulder. 'Smee?' whispered a voice which I instantly recognised as Mrs Gorman's

Of course she received no answer. She came and settled down beside me with a rustle, and I can't describe the sense of relief she brought me.

'It's Tony, isn't it?' she whispered.

'Yes,' I whispered back.

'You're not "Smee" are you?'

'No, she's on my other side.'

She reached a hand across me, and I heard one of her nails scratch the surface of a woman's silk gown.

'Hullo, "Smee"! How are you? *Who* are you? Oh, is it against the rules to talk? Never mind, Tony, we'll break the rules. Do you know, Tony, this game is beginning to irk me a little. I hope they're not going to run it to death by playing it all the evening. I'd like to play some game where we can all be together in the same room with a nice bright fire.'

'Same here,' I agreed fervently.

'Can't you suggest something when we go down? There's something rather uncanny in this particular amusement. I can't quite shed the delusion that there's somebody in this game who oughtn't to be in at all.'

That was just how I had been feeling, but I didn't say so. But for my part the worst of my qualms were now gone; the arrival of Mrs Gorman had dissipated them. We sat on talking, wondering from time to time when the rest of the party would arrive.

I don't know how long elapsed before we heard a clatter of feet on the landing and young Reggie's voice shouting, 'Hullo! Hullo, there! Anybody there?'

'Yes,' I answered.

'Mrs Gorman with you?'

'Yes.'

'Well, you're a nice pair! You've both forfeited. We've all been waiting for you for hours.'

'Why, you haven't found "Smee" yet,' I objected.

'*You* haven't, you mean. I happen to have been "Smee" myself.'

'But "Smee's" here with us,' I cried.

'Yes,' agreed Mrs Gorman.

The curtain was stripped aside and in a moment we were blinking into the eye of Reggie's electric torch. I looked at Mrs Gorman and then on my other side. Between me and the wall there was an empty space on the window seat. I stood up at once and wished I hadn't, for I found myself sick and dizzy.

'There *was* somebody there,' I maintained, 'because I touched her.'

'So did I,' said Mrs Gorman in a voice which had lost its steadiness. 'And I don't see how she could have got up and gone without our knowing it.'

Reggie uttered a queer, shaken laugh. He, too, had had an unpleasant experience that evening. 'Somebody's been playing the goat,' he remarked. 'Coming down?'

We were not very popular when we arrived in the drawing-room. Reggie rather tactlessly gave it out that he had found us sitting on a window-seat behind the curtain. I taxed the tall, dark girl with having pretended to be 'Smee' and afterwards slipping away. She denied it. After which we settled down and played other games. 'Smee' was done with for the evening, and I for one was glad of it.

Some long while later, during an interval, Sangston told me, if I wanted a drink, to go into the smoke room and help myself. I went, and he presently followed me. I could see that he was rather peeved with me, and the reason came out during the following minute or two. It seemed that, in his opinion, if I must sit out and flirt with Mrs Gorman—in circumstances which would have been considered highly compromising in his young days—I needn't do it during a round game and keep everybody waiting for us.

'But there was somebody else there,' I protested, 'somebody pretending to be "Smee". I believe it was that tall, dark girl, Miss Ford, although she denied it. She even whispered her name to me.'

Sangston stared at me and nearly dropped his glass.

'Miss *Who*?' he shouted.

'Brenda Ford—she told me her name was.'

Sangston put down his glass and laid a hand on my shoulder.

'Look here, old man,' he said, 'I don't mind a joke, but don't let it go too far. We don't want all the women in the house getting hysterical. Brenda Ford is the name of the girl who broke her neck on the stairs playing hide-and-seek here ten years ago.'

The Little Ghost

HUGH WALPOLE

I

Ghosts? I looked across the table at Truscott and had a sudden desire to impress him. Truscott has, before now, invited confidences in just that same way, with his flat impassivity, his air of not caring whether you say anything to him or no, his determined indifference to your drama and your pathos. On this particular evening he had been less impassive. He had himself turned the conversation towards Spiritualism, séances, and all that world of humbug, as he believed it to be, and suddenly I saw, or fancied that I saw, a real invitation in his eyes, something that made me say to myself: 'Well, hang it all, I've known Truscott for nearly twenty years; I've never shown him the least little bit of my real self; he thinks me a writing money-machine, with no thought in the world besides my brazen serial stories and the yacht that I purchased out of them.'

So I told him this story, and I will do him the justice to say that he listened to every word of it most attentively, although it was far into the evening before I had finished. He didn't seem impatient with all the little details that I gave. Of course, in a ghost story, details are more important than anything else. But was it a ghost story? Was it a story at all? Was it true even in its material background? Now, as I try to tell it again, I can't be sure. Truscott is the only other person who has ever heard it, and at the end of it he made no comment whatever.

It happened long ago, long before the war, when I had been married for about five years, and was an exceedingly prosperous journalist, with a nice little house and two children, in Wimbledon.

I lost suddenly my greatest friend. That may mean little or much as friendship is commonly held, but I believe that most Britishers, most Americans, most Scandinavians, know before they die one friendship at least that changes their whole life experience by its depth and colour. Very few Frenchmen, Italians or Spaniards, very few Southern people at all, understand these things.

The curious part of it in my particular case was that I had known this friend only four or five years before his death, that I had made many friendships both before and since that have endured over much longer periods, and yet this particular friendship had a quality of intensity and happiness that I have never found elsewhere.

Another curious thing was that I met Bond only a few months before my marriage, when I was deeply in love with my wife, and so intensely preoccupied with my engagement that I could think of nothing else. I met Bond quite casually at someone's house. He was a large-boned, broad-shouldered, slow-smiling man with close-cropped hair turning slightly grey, and our meeting was casual; the ripening of our friendship was casual; indeed, the whole affair may be said to have been casual to the very last. It was, in fact, my wife who said to me one day, when we had been married about a year or so: 'Why, I believe you care more for Charlie Bond than for anyone else in the world.' She said it in that sudden, disconcerting, perceptive way that some women have. I was entirely astonished. Of course I laughed at the idea. I saw Bond frequently. He came often to the house. My wife, wiser than many wives, encouraged all my friendships, and she herself liked Charlie immensely. I don't suppose that anyone disliked him. Some men were jealous of him; some men, the merest acquaintances, called him conceited; women were sometimes irritated by him because so clearly he could get on very easily without them; but he had, I think, no real enemy.

How could he have had? His good-nature, his freedom from all jealousy, his naturalness, his sense of fun, the absence of all pettiness, his common sense, his manliness, and at the same time his broad-minded intelligence, all these things made him a most charming personality. I don't know that he shone very much in ordinary society. He was very quiet and his wit and humour came out best with his intimates.

I was the showy one, and he always played up to me, and I think I patronised him a little and thought deep down in my subconscious self that it was lucky for him to have such a brilliant friend, but he never gave a sign of resentment. I believe now that he knew me, with all my faults and vanities and absurdities, far better than anyone else, even my wife, did, and that is one of the reasons, to the day of my death, why I shall always miss him so desperately.

However, it was not until his death that I realised how close we had been. One November day he came back to his flat, wet and chilled, didn't change his clothes, caught a cold, which developed into pneumonia, and after three days was dead. It happened that that week I was in Paris, and I returned to be told on my doorstep by my wife of what had occurred. At first I refused to believe it. When I had seen him a week before he had been in splendid health; with his tanned, rather rough and clumsy face, his clear eyes, no fat about him anywhere, he had looked as though he would live to a thousand, and then when I realised that it was indeed true I did not during the first week or two grasp my loss.

I missed him, of course; was vaguely unhappy and discontented; railed against life, wondering why it was always the best people who were taken and the others left; but I was not actually aware that for the rest of my days things would be different, and that that day of my return from Paris was a crisis in my human experience. Suddenly one morning, walking down Fleet Street, I had a flashing, almost blinding, need of Bond that was like a revelation. From that moment I knew no peace. Everyone seemed to me dull, profitless and empty. Even my wife was a long way away from me, and my children, whom I dearly loved, counted nothing to me at all. I didn't, after that, know what was the matter with me. I lost my appetite, I couldn't sleep, I was grumpy and nervous. I didn't myself connect it with Bond at all. I thought that I was over-worked, and when my wife suggested a holiday, I agreed, got a fortnight's leave from my newspaper, and went down to Glebeshire.

Early December is not a bad time for Glebeshire. It is just then the best spot in the British Isles. I knew a little village beyond St Mary's Moor, that I had not seen for ten years, but always remembered with romantic gratitude, and I felt that that was the place for me now.

I changed trains at Polchester and found myself at last in a little jingle driving out to the sea. The air, the wide open moor, the smell of the sea delighted me, and when I reached my village, with its sandy cove and the boats drawn up in two rows in front of a high rocky cave, and when I ate my eggs and bacon in the parlour of the inn overlooking the sea, I felt happier than I had done for weeks past; but my happiness did not last long. Night after night I could not sleep. I began to feel acute loneliness and knew at last in full truth that it was my friend whom I was missing, and that it was not solitude I needed, but his company. Easy enough to talk about having his company, but I only truly knew, down here in this little village, sitting on the edge of the green cliff, looking over into limitless sea, that I was indeed never to have his company again. There followed after that a wild, impatient regret that I had not made more of my time with him. I saw myself, in a sudden vision, as I had really been with him, patronising, indulgent, a little contemptuous of his good-natured ideas. Had I only a week with him now, how eagerly I would show him that I was the fool and not he, that I was the lucky one every time!

One connects with one's own grief the place where one feels it, and before many days had passed I had grown to loathe the little village, to dread, beyond words, the long, soughing groan of the sea as it drew back down the slanting beach, the melancholy wail of the seagulls, the chattering women under my little window. I couldn't stand it. I ought to go back to London, and yet from that, too, I shrank. Memories of Bond lingered there as they did in no other place, and it was hardly fair to my wife and family to give them the company of the dreary, discontented man that I just then was.

And then, just in the way that such things always happen, I found on my breakfast-table one fine morning a forwarded letter. It was from a certain Mrs Baldwin, and, to my surprise, I saw that it came from Glebeshire, but from the top of the county and not its southern end.

John Baldwin was a Stock Exchange friend of my brother's, a rough diamond, but kindly and generous, and not, I believed, very well off. Mrs Baldwin I had always liked, and I think she always liked me. We had not met for some little time and I had no idea what had happened to them. Now in her letter she told me that they had taken an old eighteenth-century house on the north coast of Glebeshire, not very far from Drymouth, that they were enjoying it very much indeed, that Jack was fitter than he had been for years, and that they would be delighted, were I ever in that part of the country, to have me as their guest. This suddenly seemed to me the very thing. The Baldwins had never known Charlie Bond, and they would have, therefore, for me no association with his memory. They were jolly, noisy people, with a jolly, noisy family, and Jack Baldwin's personality was so robust that it would surely shake me out of my gloomy mood. I sent a telegram at once to Mrs Baldwin, asking her whether she could have me for a week, and before the day was over I received the warmest of invitations.

Next day I left my fishing village and experienced one of those strange, crooked, in-and-out little journeys that you must undergo if you are to find your way from one obscure Glebeshire village to another.

About midday, a lovely, cold, blue December midday, I discovered myself in Polchester with an hour to wait for my next train. I went down into the town, climbed the High Street to the magnificent cathedral, stood beneath the famous Arden Gate, looked at the still more famous tomb of the Black Bishop, and it was there, as the sunlight, slanting through the great east window, danced and sparkled about the wonderful blue stone of which that tomb is made, that I had a sudden sense of having been through all this before, of having stood just there in some earlier time, weighed down by some earlier grief, and that nothing that I was experiencing was unexpected. I had a curious sense, too, of comfort and condolence, that horrible grey loneliness that I had felt in the fishing village suddenly fell from me, and for the first time since Bond's death, I was happy. I walked away from the cathedral, down the busy street, and through the dear old market-place, expecting I know not what. All that I knew was that I was intending to go to the Baldwins' and that I would be happy there.

The December afternoon fell quickly, and during the last part of my journey I was travelling in a ridiculous little train, through dusk, and the little train went so slowly and so casually that one was always hearing the murmurs of streams beyond one's window, and lakes of grey water suddenly stretched like plates of glass to thick woods, black as ink, against a faint sky. I got out at my little wayside station, shaped like a rabbit-hutch, and found a motor waiting for me. The drive was not long, and suddenly I was outside the old eighteenth-century house and Baldwin's stout butler was conveying me into the hall with that careful, kindly patronage, rather as though I were a box of eggs that might very easily be broken.

It was a spacious hall, with a large open fireplace, in front of which they were all having tea. I say 'all' advisedly, because the place seemed to be full of people, grown-ups and children, but mostly children. There were so many of these last that I was not, to the end of my stay, to be able to name most of them individually.

Mrs Baldwin came forward to greet me, introduced me to one or two people, sat me down and gave me my tea, told me that I wasn't looking at all well, and needed feeding up, and explained that Jack was out shooting something, but would soon be back.

My entrance had made a brief lull, but immediately everyone recovered and the noise was terrific. There is a lot to be said for the freedom of the modern child. There is a lot to be said against it, too. I soon found that in this party, at any rate, the elders were completely disregarded and of no account. Children rushed about the hall, knocked one another down, shouted and screamed, fell over grown-ups as though they were pieces of furniture, and paid no attention at all to the mild 'Now, children' of a plain, elderly lady who was, I supposed, a governess. I fancy that I was tired with my criss-cross journey, and I soon found a chance to ask Mrs Baldwin if I could go up to my room. She said: 'I expect you find these children noisy. Poor little things. They must have their fun. Jack always says that one can only be young once, and I do so agree with him.'

I wasn't myself feeling very young that evening (I was really about nine hundred years old), so that I agreed with her and eagerly left youth to its own appropriate pleasures. Mrs Baldwin took me up the fine broad staircase. She was a stout, short woman, dressed in bright colours, with what is known, I believe, as an infectious laugh. Tonight, although I was fond of her, and knew very well her good, generous heart, she irritated me, and for some reason that I could not quite define. Perhaps I felt at once that she was out of place there and that the house resented her, but in all this account I am puzzled by the question as to whether I imagine now, on looking back, all sorts of feelings that were not really there at all, but come to me now because I know of what happened afterwards. But I am so anxious to tell the truth, the whole truth, and nothing but the truth, and there is nothing in the world so difficult to do as that.

We went through a number of dark passages, up and down little pieces of staircase that seemed to have no beginning, no end, and no reason for their existence, and she left me at last in my bedroom, said that she hoped I would be comfortable, and that Jack would come and see me when he came in, and then paused for a moment, looking at me. 'You really don't look well,' she said. 'You've been overdoing it. You're too conscientious. I always said so. You shall have a real rest here. And the children will see that you're not dull.'

Her last two sentences seemed scarcely to go together. I could not tell her about my loss. I realised suddenly, as I had never realised in our older acquaintance, that I should never be able to speak to her about anything that really mattered.

She smiled, laughed and left me. I looked at my room and loved it at once. Broad and low-ceilinged, it contained very little furniture, an old four-poster, charming hangings of some old rose-coloured damask, an old gold mirror, an oak cabinet, some high-backed chairs, and then, for comfort, a large armchair with high elbows, a little quaintly shaped sofa dressed in the same rose colour as the bed, a bright crackling fire and a grandfather clock. The walls, faded primrose, had no pictures, but on one of them, opposite my bed, was a gay sampler worked in bright colours of crimson and yellow and framed in oak.

I liked it, I loved it, and drew the armchair in front of the fire, nestled down into it, and before I knew, I was fast asleep. How long I slept I don't know, but I suddenly woke with a sense of comfort and well-being which was nothing less than exquisite. I belonged to it, that room, as though I had been in it all my days. I had a curious sense of companionship that was exactly what I had been needing during these last weeks. The house was very still, no voices of children came to me, no sound anywhere, save the sharp crackle of the fire and the friendly ticking of the old clock. Suddenly I thought that there was someone in the room with me, a rustle of something that might have been the fire and yet was not.

I got up and looked about me, half smiling, as though I expected to see a familiar face. There was no one there, of course, and yet I had just that consciousness of companionship that one has when someone whom one loves very dearly and knows very intimately is sitting with one in the same room. I even went to the other side of the four-poster and looked around me, pulled for a moment at the rose-coloured curtains, and of course saw no one. Then the door suddenly opened and Jack Baldwin came in, and I remember having a curious feeling of irritation as though I had been interrupted. His large, breezy, knickerbockered figure filled the room. 'Hullo!' he said, 'delighted to see you. Bit of luck your being down this way. Have you got everything you want?'

II

That was a wonderful old house. I am not going to attempt to describe it, although I have stayed there quite recently. Yes, I stayed there on many occasions since that first of which I am now speaking. It has never been quite the same to me since that first time. You may say, if you like, that the Baldwins fought a battle with it and defeated it. It is certainly now more Baldwin than—well, whatever it was before they rented it. They are not the kind of people to be defeated by atmosphere. Their chief duty in this world, I gather, is to make things Baldwin, and very good for the world too; but when I first went down to them the house was still challenging them. 'A wee bit creepy,' Mrs Baldwin confided to me on the second day of my visit. 'What exactly do you mean by that?' I asked her. 'Ghosts?'

'Oh, there are those, of course,' she answered. 'There's an underground passage, you know, that runs from here to the sea, and one of the wickedest of the smugglers was killed in it, and his ghost still haunts the cellar. At least that's what we were told by our first butler, here; and then, of course, we found that it was the butler, not the smuggler, who was haunting the cellar, and since his departure the smuggler hasn't been visible.' She laughed. 'All the same, it isn't a comfortable place. I'm going to wake up some of those old rooms. We're going to put in some more windows. And then there are the children,' she added.

Yes, there were the children. Surely the noisiest in all the world. They had reverence for nothing. They were the wildest savages, and especially those from nine to thirteen, the cruellest and most uncivilised age for children. There were two little boys, twins I should think, who were nothing less than devils, and regarded their elders with cold, watching eyes, said nothing in protest when scolded, but evolved plots afterwards that fitted precisely the chastiser. To do my host and hostess justice, all the children were not Baldwins, and I fancy that the Baldwin contingent was the quietest.

Nevertheless, from early morning until ten at night, the noise was terrific and you were never sure how early in the morning it would recommence. I don't know that I personally minded the noise very greatly. It took me out of myself and gave me something better to think of, but, in some obscure and unanalysed way, I felt that the house minded it. One knows how the poets have written about old walls and rafters rejoicing in the happy, careless laughter of children. I do not think this house rejoiced at all, and it was queer how consistently I, who am not supposed to be an imaginative person, thought about the house.

But it was not until my third evening that something really happened. I say 'happened', but did anything really happen? You shall judge for yourself.

I was sitting in my comfortable armchair in my bedroom, enjoying that delightful half-hour before one dresses for dinner. There was a terrible racket up and down the passages, the children being persuaded, I gathered, to go into the schoolroom and have their supper, when the noise died down and there was nothing but the feathery whisper of the snow—snow had been falling all day—against my window-pane. My thoughts suddenly turned to Bond, directed to him as actually and precipitately as though he had suddenly sprung before me. I did not want to think of him. I had been fighting his memory these last days, because I had thought that the wisest thing to do, but now he was too much for me.

I luxuriated in my memories of him, turning over and over all sorts of times that we had had together, seeing his smile, watching his mouth that turned up at the corners when he was amused, and wondering finally why he should obsess me the way that he did, when I had lost so many other friends for whom I had thought I cared much more, who, nevertheless, never bothered my memory at all. I sighed, and it seemed to me that my sigh was very gently repeated behind me. I turned sharply round. The curtains had not been drawn. You know the strange, milky pallor that reflected snow throws over objects, and although three lighted candles shone in the room, moon-white shadows seemed to hang over the bed and across the floor. Of course there was no one there, and yet I stared and stared about me as though I were convinced that I was not alone. And then I looked especially at one part of the room, a distant corner beyond the four-poster, and it seemed to me that someone was there. And yet no one was there. But whether it was that my mind had been distracted, or that the beauty of the old snow-lit room enchanted me, I don't know, but my thoughts of my friend were happy and reassured. I had not lost him, I seemed to say to myself. Indeed, at that special moment he seemed to be closer to me than he had been while he was alive.

From that evening a curious thing occurred. I only seemed to be close to my friend when I was in my own room—and I felt more than that. When my door was closed and I was sitting in my armchair, I fancied that our new companionship was not only Bond's, but was something more as well. I would wake in the middle of the night or in the early morning and feel quite sure that I was not alone; so sure that I did not even want to investigate it further, but just took the companionship for granted and was happy.

Outside that room, however, I felt increasing discomfort. I hated the way in which the house was treated. A quite unreasonable anger rose within me as I heard the Baldwins discussing the improvements that they were going to make, and yet they were so kind to me, and so patently unaware of doing anything that would not generally be commended, it was quite impossible for me to show my anger. Nevertheless, Mrs Baldwin noticed something. 'I am afraid the children are worrying you,' she said one morning, half interrogatively. 'In a way it will be a rest when they go back to school, but the Christmas holidays is their time, isn't it? I do like to see them happy. Poor little dears.'

The poor little dears were at that moment being Red Indians all over the hall.

'No, of course, I like children,' I answered her. 'The only thing is that they don't—I hope you won't think me foolish—somehow quite fit in with the house.'

'Oh, I think it's so good for old places like this,' said Mrs Baldwin briskly, 'to be woken up a little. I'm sure if the old people who used to live here came back they'd love to hear all the noise and laughter.'

I wasn't so sure myself, but I wouldn't disturb Mrs Baldwin's contentment for anything.

That evening in my room I was so convinced of companionship that I spoke.

'If there's anyone here,' I said aloud, 'I'd like them to know that I'm aware of it and am glad of it.'

Then, when I caught myself speaking aloud, I was suddenly terrified. Was I really going crazy? Wasn't that the first step towards insanity when you talked to yourself? Nevertheless, a moment later I was reassured. There *was* someone there.

That night I woke, looked at my luminous watch and saw that it was a quarter past three. The room was so dark that I could not even distinguish the posts of my bed, but there was a very faint glow from the fire, now nearly dead. Opposite my bed there seemed to me to be something white. Not white in the accepted sense of a tall, ghostly figure; but, sitting up and staring, it seemed to me that the shadow was very small, hardly reaching above the edge of the bed.

'Is there anyone there?' I asked. 'Because, if there is, do speak to me. I'm not frightened. I know that someone has been here all this last week, and I am glad of it.'

Very faintly then, and so faintly that I cannot to this day be sure that I saw anything at all, the figure of a child seemed to me to be visible.

We all know how we have at one time and another fancied that we have seen visions and figures, and then have discovered that it was something in the room, the chance hanging of a coat, the reflection of a glass, a trick of moonlight that has fired our imagination. I was quite prepared for that in this case, but it seemed to me then that as I watched the shadow moved directly in front of the dying fire, and delicate as the leaf of a silver birch, like the trailing rim of some evening cloud, the figure of a child hovered in front of me.

Curiously enough the dress, which seemed to be of some silver tissue, was clearer than anything else. I did not, in fact, see the face at all, and yet I could swear in the morning that I had seen it, that I knew large, black, wide-open eyes, a little mouth very faintly parted in a timid smile, and that, beyond anything else, I had realised in the expression of that face fear and bewilderment and a longing for some comfort.

III

After that night the affair moved very quickly to its little climax.

I am not a very imaginative man, nor have I any sympathy with the modern craze for spooks and spectres. I have never seen, nor fancied that I had seen, anything of a supernatural kind since that visit, but then I have never known since that time such a desperate need of companionship and comfort, and is it not perhaps because we do not want things badly enough in this life that we do not get more of them? However that may be, I was sure on this occasion that I had some companionship that was born of a need greater than mine. I suddenly took the most frantic and unreasonable dislike to the children in that house. It was exactly as though I had discovered somewhere in a deserted part of the building some child who had been left behind by mistake by the last occupants and was terrified by the noisy exuberance and ruthless selfishness of the new family.

For a week I had no more definite manifestation of my little friend, but I was as sure of her presence there in my room as I was of my own clothes and the armchair in which I used to sit.

It was time for me to go back to London, but I could not go. I asked everyone I met as to legends and stories connected with the old house, but I never found anything to do with a little child. I looked forward all day to my hour in my room before dinner, the time when I felt the companionship closest. I sometimes woke in the night and was conscious of its presence, but, as I have said, I never saw anything.

One evening the older children obtained leave to stay up later. It was somebody's birthday. The house seemed to be full of people, and the presence of the children led after dinner to a perfect riot of noise and confusion. We were to play hide-and-seek all over the house. Everybody was to dress up. There was, for that night at least, to be no privacy anywhere. We were all, as Mrs Baldwin said, to be ten years old again. I hadn't the least desire to be ten years old, but I found myself caught into the game, and had, in sheer self-defence, to run up and down the passages and hide behind doors. The noise was terrific. It grew and grew in volume. People got hysterical. The smaller children jumped out of bed and ran about the passages. Somebody kept blowing a motor-horn. Somebody else turned on the gramophone.

Suddenly I was sick of the whole thing, retreated into my room, lit one candle and locked the door. I had scarcely sat down in my chair when I was aware that my little friend had come. She was standing near to the bed, staring at me, terror in her eyes. I have never seen anyone so frightened. Her little breasts panting beneath her silver gown, her very fair hair falling about her shoulders, her little hands clenched. Just as I saw her, there were loud knocks on the door, many voices shouting to be admitted, a perfect babel of noise and laughter. The little figure moved, and then—how can I give any idea of it?—I was conscious of having something to protect and comfort. I saw nothing, physically I felt nothing, and yet I was murmuring, 'There, there, don't mind. They shan't come in. I'll see that no one touches you. I understand. I understand.' For how long I sat like that I don't know. The noises died away, voices murmured at intervals, and then were silent. The house slept. All night I think I stayed there comforting and being comforted.

I fancy now—but how much of it may not be fancy?—that I knew that the child loved the house, had stayed so long as was possible, at last was driven away, and that that was her farewell, not only to me, but all that she most loved in this world and the next.

I do not know—I could swear to nothing. What I am sure of is that my sense of loss in my friend was removed from that night and never returned. Did I argue with myself that that child companionship included also my friend? Again, I do not know. But of one thing I am now sure, that if love is strong enough, physical death cannot destroy it, and however platitudinous that may sound to others, it is platitudinous no longer when you have discovered it by actual experience for yourself.

That moment in that fire-lit room, when I felt that spiritual heart beating with mine, is and always will be enough for me.

One thing more. Next day I left for London, and my wife was delighted to find me so completely recovered—happier, she said, than I had ever been before.

Two days afterwards, I received a parcel from Mrs Baldwin. In the note that accompanied it, she said:

I think that you must have left this by mistake behind you. It was found in the small drawer in your dressing-table.

I opened the parcel and discovered an old blue silk handkerchief, wrapped round a long, thin wooden box. The cover of the box lifted very easily, and I saw inside it an old, painted wooden doll, dressed in the period, I should think, of Queen Anne. The dress was very complete, even down to the little shoes, and the little grey mittens on the hands. Inside the silk skirt there was sewn a little tape, and on the tape, in very faded letters, 'Ann Trelawney, 1710.'

Ahoy, Sailor Boy!

A. E. COPPARD

Archie Malin, a young sailor just off the sea, rambled into a tavern one summer evening with a bundle under his arm. There was hearty company, and sawdust on the floor, but he was looking for a night's lodging and they could not do with him there, so they sent him along to the widow Silvertough who keeps a button-and-bullseye shop down by the shore. (You would know her again: she's a mulatto, with a restive eye.) And could she give him a night's lodging? He would be off by the first train in the morning—would a gone tonight only the last train had beat it—just a bed? She could; so he threw down his bundle, bought a packet of butterscotch, and went off back to the tavern, *The Cherry Tree*. Outside it was a swing-sign showing about forty painted cherries as fat as tomatoes on a few twigs with no more than a leaf apiece. Inside there was singing, and hearty company, and sawdust on the floor.

'Happy days!' said the sailor, drinking and doing as others do.

Well, this fair young stranger, you must know, was not just a common seaman; he wore a dressy uniform with badges on his arm, and looked a dandy. He could swop tales with any of them there, and he sang a song in a pleasant country voice, but at times his face was sad and his eyes mournful. Been to Sitka, so he said, but said in such a way that nobody liked to ask him where that was, or where he was bound for now. They thought, indeed, that maybe some of his family had grief or misfortune come upon them, and no one wanted to go blundering into the sort of private matters that put a man down; but when someone spoke about the numbers of people dying in the neighbourhood just then, the sailor became rather contentious.

'Baw! Plenty of people die every hour, but you don't know any of them. There's thousands die every day, but devil a one of them all is known to you or to me. I don't know them, and you do not know them, and if you don't know them it's all the same, death or life. Of course, when a big one falls—like President Roosevelt, it might be, or old Charley the linendraper over at Crofters—you hear about that; but else you don't know them, so what does it matter to you—if you ain't acquainted with them? I tell you what, it is very curious how few of the people you *do* know ever seem to die; but it's true—they don't. I knew my own father, of course, as died; and a friend or two that died was well known to me; but I don't know any of these other corpses, nor what becomes of them I do not care. And that's as true as the dust on the road.'

'Young feller,' an oldish man, drinking rum, said, 'you are young yet. When you get to my age you will find your friends a tumbling off like tiles from a roof.'

'And what becomes of them?'

'They'll get their true sleep.'

'That all there is to it then?'

'O, there's goodly mercy everywhere. Accorden to your goings-on before, so it is. Whatsoever you does here must be paid for there.'

'Aye,' said the sailor, with a general wink, 'even up yonder money talks, I suppose?'

'God help you! To be thinking of that!' the old man cried. 'Money talks, 'tis true; but there's only two ways it gives you any satisfaction: one is earning it, the other spending it.'

'There's many though,' the sailor said, 'as spends a lot they don't earn.'

'Ah, that's their own look-out,' said the other, with his glass of rum in his hand. 'And you can take your mighty oath it's the sacramental truth. You can't thread a camel through a needle's eye. Dust to dust, you know; ashes to ashes.'

'Here!' growled the landlord. 'Tip us a lively song, someone. I feels like I was going to be haunted.'

So they persuaded the young sailor to sing his song.

'What's become of all the lassies used to smile up on a hearty?
  Luck my lay, luck my laddie, heave and ho!'

'What's the news of Jane and Katey with their mi-ra-fah-so-lah-ty?
  I dunno, Archy Malin, I dunno.'

'Where's the lass as swore she'd wed me when I shipped again this way?
  Luck my lay, luck my laddie, heave and ho!'

'Was it booze, or was it blarney? Was it just my bit of pay?
  I dunno, Archy Malin, I dunno.'

'O, young men are fond of pleasure, but the girls are full of vice.
  Luck my lay, luck my laddie, heave and ho!'

'Is there ne'er a pretty creature who's as simple as she's nice?
  I dunno, Archy Malin, I dunno.'

They gave him a hearty clap for singing it, though it wasn't very lively. 'I never heard that ballad before,' the old rum man said.

'You wouldn't,' replied the sailor.

'And I thought I knew most every song as ever was, most of 'em!'

'You wouldn't know that one,' the sailor said, 'because I made it myself.'

'Ah!' the other gleefully cried, 'I knew; I knew there was some craft about it.'

'And it's true,' added the singer, 'true as the dust in the road.'

With that he got up, pushed his drink back on the table, and away he went.

With a bit of a lurch now and then he strode moodily along the sea wall of the little harbour. Most of the shops were closed, and a calm midsummer dusk was nestling on street and sea. At the end of a rocky mole protruding seawards he was quite alone and leaned on a parapet. The moon rose drowsily over the bay, whose silent waters only moved when near the shore; the waves frilled pettishly on grey rocks veined with silica. A ship passed over the sad evening sea, its lamps faintly glowing, and a few houses on shore beamed with lights as well. The mountains around were black already, though the sky behind them was pearly. Somewhere a bell was ringing.

He wished himself gone out of the dull little town, but he was bound to stay until morning, and so after sighing away a half hour or more he turned at ten o'clock to ramble back to his lodging, but on the border of the town he took a turn up on to a little rampart of the hills, a place newly laid out on its banks in municipal fashion with shrubs and young birch trees and seats on winding paths. Up there he lounged down on one of the seats under the slim birches, between whose branches he saw the now risen moon over a darker bay, the harbour with its red and green lights, one or two funnels, a few masts and spars. And he could hear, though he could not see, a motor passing below and the clatter of a trolley. Half full of beer and melancholy he began to drowse, until someone passed quietly by him like a shadow. The night was come, and despite the moon's rays he only took in the impression of a lady, richly dressed and walking with a grand air. There was a waft of curious perfume.

Now the handsome sailor had a romantic nature, he was inclined to gallantry, but the lady was gone before he could collect his hazy senses. He had not seen her face, but she seemed to be wearing a dark cloak that might have been of velvet. He stared until he could no longer see her. 'Smells like an actress,' he mused, and yawned. Leaning back on the seat again he soon fell into a light slumber, until roused once more by a feeling that some one had just gone past. The path was empty, up and down, but though he could see no one, or hear anything, that strange perfume hung in the air. Then he caught sight of a little thing on the seat beside him. In the chequered moonlight it looked white, but it was not white. The stranger knew it was unlucky to pick up a strange handkerchief, but he did pick it up. He found it was charged with that elegant smell he had imputed to actresses.

The moon glittered on his buttons, the patterns of slim boughs and leaves lay across him. *I dunno, Archy Malin, I dunno!* he hummed, and stuffing the scented handkerchief into his breast-pocket he sat blinking in the direction he had seen the mysterious lady take. It was late, she had gone *up* the hill; she ought to be coming *down* again, soon.

'That's a nice smell, so help me,' he observed; and pulled the handkerchief from his pocket again, 'I bet it's hers.' While twiddling it musingly in his fingers he maintained an expectant gaze along the upward path. 'Couldn't have been any handkerchief there when I sat down, or I'd have seen it.' As he replaced it in his pocket he concluded: 'I bet a crown she dropped it here on purpose. Well, you done it, Jane; *you* done it.' Leaning with his arm along the back of the seat he sat so that he would be facing her when she came down the hill again. And he waited for her.

It was in his mind that he ought to have followed her—she might be waiting for him somewhere up there. But she would be coming back— they always did!—and he felt a little unwilling to move now. Time passed very slowly. In the gloss of the moon his brass buttons shone like tiny stars; the patterns of leaves and branches were draped solemnly across his body and seemed to cling to his knees. He held his breath and strained his ears to catch a sound of her returning footsteps. As still as death it was. And then the shock came; the sudden feeling that there, round about him, just behind him, some malignant thing was watching, was about to pounce and rend him, and he shrank at once like a touched nerve, waiting for some certainty of horror—or relief. And it gave him a breathless tremble when his eyes swivelled round and he *did* see something there, sitting on the seat behind him. But it was all right—it was her!

Calmly he said: 'Hello! How did you get here?' (God Almighty, his brain had been on the point of bursting!)

She did not reply. She sat gracefully, but still and silent, in a black velvet cloak, one knee linked over the other. Whether she had a hat or not he could not tell, there was a dark veil covering her head and face. But none the less he could tell she was a handsome woman all right. Her arms were folded under the cloak, where her fingers must have been clinging to hold it tight around her.

'I saw you go by,' began the young sailor, 'but I didn't hear you come back.'

Well, she did not answer him then, she did not utter a word, but she certainly did pay a lot of attention to what he said to her, and her eyes gleamed quite friendly under her veil. So Archy kept on chaffing her, because he was sure she had not dumped herself down there beside him in that lonely spot, at that time of night, for nothing; and of course he felt quite gay. She nodded a lot at the things he said to her, but it was quite some time before she opened her mouth to him, and then he was rather surprised. Because she was a fine well-built girl, with a lovely bosom and all that, but her voice really did surprise him.

'I have never been here before,' was what she said, but her voice was thin and reedy, as if she had asthma or something. 'I happened to see you—so I came along.'

'O, that's dandy,' said Archy, and he hauled up to her and was for putting his arm around her straight away.

'No . . . ! You must not do that!'

And although she did not move or shrink away she spoke so sadly that somehow that jaunty sailor was baffled; she was a perfect lady! He sat up and behaved himself.

The girl stared through the trees at the lights down in the harbour, and you could not hear a whisper down there, or anywhere else in the world.

She said: 'I was lonely.'

'I bet you was!' was his uncouth reply, and he kept his own arms folded. This was the queerest piece he had met for a long time.

'Please don't be angry,' she said, turning to him.

'No. Sure,' he answered heartily. 'I'd like to know your name, though. Mine's Archy Malin. I'm a sailor.'

'My name?' She gave a sigh. 'It was Freda Listowell.'

'Well, ain't it now?' he quizzed her.

She shook her head.

'Married?' pursued the sailor.

'No.' The question seemed faintly to amuse her.

'You lost it then?'

'Yes,' was the grave reply.

The young man was beginning to enjoy these exchanges. That sort of chitchat was part of the fun of making up to girls like Jane and Katey. This one was a lady—you could not doubt that—and so it surprised him a bit. But all the same, he liked it.

'Freda Listowell! That's a nice name, too good to lose.'

She shivered, the moonlight had grown cold.

'Shall have to help you find it again,' he continued.

'You could not do that.'

'Could I not! Are you staying in this burgh for long?'

'I am not stopping anywhere at all. I must go back soon.'

'You can't get far tonight—it's late. Where are you stopping, then?'

'You would not believe me if I told you.'

'Me! Not! I'd believe you if you said you was an angel from heaven. Unless you've got a car?'

She slowly shook her head.

He began to feel he was not getting on very well with her, after all. Somehow they were making a poor show together. But he could tell she was an actress; it was not the things she said so much as the way she spoke them. Taking a cigarette from a packet, he lit it.

'I've never seen anything like him in my wanderings!' He held the packet towards her indicating the picture of a fathead seaman with whiskers and the word HERO on his hat. 'Have one?' he asked her, but she declined. So he leaned his elbows on his knees and puffed smoke at the ground between his boots. And she had very elegant shoes on, and silk stockings on her fine legs—he couldn't take his eyes off them. But what was she trying to put across? Where did she live then? Without turning, he spoke towards the ground at his feet.

'Are you all right?'

'No,' she replied, and there was despair in her voice that woke an instant sympathy in him. He sat up and faced her.

'What's wrong, Miss Freda? Can I butt in at all?'

For the first time she seemed to relax her grave airs, and echoed: 'Can—you—butt—in!' It almost amused her. 'O no. Thank you, thank you, thank you; but no!'

The refusal was so definite that he could not hope to prevail against it; he could only murmur half apologetically:

'Well, if you wanted my help, I'd do my best. You know—say the word.'

'Ah, I was sure of that!' was the almost caressing rejoinder. 'My dear dear friend—but you—' In agitation she sat up, her hands clasped together slipping out from her cloak. He saw them for the first time, they were gloved. Then she parted her hands, and almost hissed: 'What do you think I am?'

It startled him; there was certainly something the matter with her.

'You'd better let me see you home. Serious, Miss Freda.'

'But I have nowhere to go,' she cried.

'What are you going to do then?'

'Nothing.'

'But you *must* do something.'

Raising her veiled face she gestured with one hand towards the moon, and said:

'I am going to vanish.'

'O, ho!' In a flash of a second the sailor perceived that he was not dealing with an actress at all: she was dotty! She was going to commit suicide! That was what had baffled him—she was a lunatic, lunatic! A pretty fine lot to drop in for!

'You see, I am what you call a ghost!' she solemnly said.

Well, that clinched it; the poor things generally got worse at the time of the moon. He was keeping a wary eye on her; he liked women, got very fond of them, especially nice young women on moonlight nights, but he did not like them mad.

'You don't believe that?' she asked.

He tried to humour her. 'It's a funny thing that I was having an argument about ghosts with a fellow, once before tonight. And now, here you are, the second one that's trying to persuade me. As a matter of fact, take it or leave it, just as you like, I wouldn't believe in ghosts not even if I *saw* one!'

Very calmly she said: 'What do you think I am doing here?'

Archy fidgeted for a moment or two before replying:

'Quite honest then, I never thought you were a ghost. First I thought you were—you know—a nice girl out for a bit of a lark. . . . '

He paused for her comment on this. It was a very cold one.

'Go on,' she said.

'Ah well. Then I thought you were an actress.'

'I'm not.' There was a flash of petulance.

'But then I saw you must be in a bit of trouble of some sort.'

With hesitation she agreed: 'Yes, I am.'

'You know—lost your memory, or. . . . '

'No,' she sharply interposed. 'I've lost my life.'

'Well, something like that,' he said pacifyingly. 'Do you come from . . . or . . . from down there?' He nodded towards the town.

Quietly she answered: 'I come from heaven.'

The poor fellow was almost suffering with bewilderment; a sailor lacks subtlety, and he was adrift, so he almost leaped at his little bit of a joke:

'Ah! That's it! You're an angel—I guessed that.'

'There are no angels in heaven,' cried the girl.

'Ain't!' said he.

'No. I have never seen one there.'

Archy mumbled that that would be a great disappointment to him later on.

'What do you think heaven is?' the lady asked.

He was obliged to admit that he had not up to that moment been able to give very much thought to the matter.

'I can tell you,' she said gravely.

'Do.' She was so patient that somehow he was giving up that notion of her being just mad—and anyway, he did not know how to deal with a lunatic.

'When I died, about three years ago . . . ' she began.

'You know,' the sailor turned laughing towards her, 'you *would* make a blooming good actress!'

Wearily she stirred: 'Listen!'

'What were you before you died?' he jeered; he was not going to let her mesmerize him like that.

'I was young and rich and foolish then. I had only one thought or passion in my life. I doted on clothes, fine clothes. I suppose I must have been mad. Nothing else ever really interested me, though I pretended it did. I lived simply to dress myself in quantities of beautiful garments. I think I was beautiful, too—perhaps you would have thought so . . . '

'Let me see!' Archy made a snatch at her veil.

'No . . . !' There was such a tone in her denial that his marauding arm shrank back on him, and it seemed as if the echo of her cry fluttered for a moment up among the faint stars.

'Take care!' Her gravity quelled him. 'That was my life, that and nothing else: day by day, even hour by hour, to array myself in the richest gowns I could procure. What vanity! And I believed that I was thus honouring my body and delighting my soul. What madness! In everything I did my only thought was of the clothes I might wear, what scope the occasion would give me thus to shine. That was all my joy. Life seemed to have no other care, meaning, or end; no other desire, no other bliss. I poured out fortunes on silk, satin, and brocades, and imagined that by doing so I was a benefactor to all.'

'O, but damn it!' interjected Archy. She stopped him with a gesture and then sank back in the corner of the seat, wholly wrapped in her velvet cloak. The sailor leaned with his arm on the back of the seat and surveyed her very wearily, thinking that if she did not go very soon he would have to clear himself off and leave her to her trouble. He felt like yawning but somehow he did not dare. As far as he could make out she was the picture of misery, and he was veering once more to the belief that she was crazy. Harmless enough, but what could *he* do with a daft woman?

'Then I died, suddenly,' she went. 'Imagine my disgust when I realized, as I soon did, that I was buried in a stupid ugly gown of cheap cotton, much too big for me! Ugh!' The lady shuddered. 'For a long time I seemed to be hanging in a void, like a cloud of matter motionless in some chemical solution, alone and utterly unapproachable. My sight was keen, but I could *see* nothing. All was dim and featureless as though I was staring at a sky dingy with a half dead moon.

'Then my thoughts began to swirl around and come back to me, my worldly thoughts; and though I knew I was dead, a waif of infinity, my thoughts were only of what I had prized in life itself—my wonderful clothes. And while I thought of them, they too began to drift around me, the comforting ghosts of them all—gowns, petticoats, stockings, shoes.'

The sailor sighed, and lit another cigarette. The lady waited until he composed himself again.

'But there they were as real as I was, real to me. Ah, what joy that was! I tore off my hideous cotton shroud and dressed myself in one of those darling frocks. But I soon tired of it. When I took it off it disappeared, and never came back again. I remembered other things I had enjoyed in life, but none of those ever came to me—only the clothes. They had been my ideal, they became my only heaven; in them I resumed the old illusions.'

'Christ!' muttered the sailor. 'I shall! I shall have to clout her in a minute.'

'Pardon?' cried the lady.

'I said: Time's getting on, late you know,' he replied.

In the ensuing silence he could almost *feel* her hurt surprise, so he turned to her quite jocularly:

'Well, you *are* giving me a sermon, Miss Freda. What I'd like to know is how you dropped on *me* like this!'

'They all disappeared after I had worn them once; one by one, they left again. I did not realize that for a long while, and in my joy at getting them back I wore them and changed and wore others, just as I had done in life; but at last all had departed except these you see me in now. When these are gone, I think something strange is going to happen to me. . . . '

'Huh!' said Archy.

' . . . but I cannot tell.'

When she stopped speaking the sailor wriggled his cigarette with his lips; the smoke troubled his nose, and he sniffed.

'There ought to be *something* else, don't you think?' she sorrowfully asked.

There was moonlight in the buckles of her shoes, the leaf patterns lay across her neat legs and graceful body.

'Sure!' he answered consolingly. 'It will be all right in the morning.

Have a good night's sleep, and you'll be as gay as Conky's kitten tomorrow.'

The lady did not speak or move for some minutes, and when the silence became too tiresome the sailor had to ask:

'Well, what are you going to do now?'

'I wish,' she sighed, 'I could be buried very deep, under the floor of the sea.'

'Haw! You'll get over that!' he heartily assured her.

Then she seemed to be summing him up, as if he only irritated her now: 'But I am dead, I tell you. I am nothing but a wraith in the ghosts of my old clothes.'

Her persistence annoyed him; he could not believe she was a lunatic, and this other business was the sort of lark he did not take kindly to.

'O, cheese it, Freda! Where do you live? Come on. You've been trying to put the dreary on me all this time, but I'm not that type of jacko. I'm a sailor, I am. So suppose you give us a kiss and say night-night, and toddle off home like a good girl.'

And yet—he waited for that gesture from her. It did not come.

'You do not believe me?' she asked.

'No. I've been doing my best, and you're a blooming fine actress— aren't you?—but I can't bite in. Can't!'

Up he stood, almost indignant. The girl sat where she was and the sailor lingered. For, to tell the truth, he still did not want to leave her; after all, she *might* be queer, he was still adrift; perhaps if he walked off she would follow him. He had taken but one step away when he heard her voice murmuring. With a frown he listened:

'I could prove it very easily.'

'How?' He swung round.

'By taking off my clothes,' she said.

My! Wasn't that a good one!

'Your clothes off! Here!'

A silent nod was the answer, and it revived at once all his extravagant fancies.

'Aw, now you're talking, Freda!'

He flung himself back on the bench beside her again. 'Will you? Come on!' He knew she was going to do it, he awaited her restlessly. 'What about it?' he urged, glancing up and down the paths. 'It's all right. Come on. There's no one about.'

At last she got up, and as he moved too, she hissed: 'Sit down, you fool!'

For a moment or two she stood there in the path, guarded by the bushes and little trees, fumbling with her clothes, under the cloak. And she was very cunning, because before he knew how it happened all the clothes dropped and lay in a heap there.

And that was all.

There was no slender naked girl awaiting his embrace. Freda Listowell was gone, dissolved, vanished; he had seen nothing of her, not even her hands. Only her ghostly garments lay in the path with the moon shining on them; the cloak and the shoes, the veil, the stockings, flounces, frills, green garters, and a vanity bag with a white comb slipping out of it. So cleanly swift and yet so casual was her proof that he was frightened almost before he knew.

'She was there. She did not move!' he whispered. 'I could pawn my soul on that!'

For a space the doubting sailor dared not rise from the seat; his hands clung to it as a castaway's to a spar, as he turned his fearing eyes to right, to left, and behind him.

'I don't believe it!' he muttered stoutly, and tearing himself away from the bench he cringed in the path.

'Ahoy there!' he whispered. 'Where are you?'

Sternly he straightened himself, and walked erect among the near bushes. She was not there. Nowhere. When he spun round again her clothes had gone too. 'Hoi! Stop it!' he shouted, but he knew she was not hiding—there was nothing of her to hide. With his heart threshing like a flail he breathed appalling air. What was it? He wanted to fly for his life, but could not. His nails were grinding into his palms as he braced himself to grapple with his shocked brain.

'Foo!' he gasped, twining himself round and round, not daring to stand still. 'Foo!' Sweat was blinding him, and thrusting one hand to his pocket he pulled out a handkerchief. It was the perfumed wisp he had found on the seat an hour before. As he caught its scent again, he remembered. He held it out in the moonlight, and stared at it, muttering: 'I don't fancy that. I don't. . . . '

Something invisible in the air plucked it from his fingers.

The Hollow Man

THOMAS BURKE

He came up one of the narrow streets which lead from the docks, and turned into a road whose farther end was gay with the lights of London. At the end of this road he went deep into the lights of London, and sometimes into its shadows. Farther and farther he went from the river, and did not pause until he had reached a poor quarter near the centre.

He made a tall, spare figure, clothed in a black mackintosh. Below this could be seen brown dungaree trousers. A peaked cap hid most of his face; the little that was exposed was white and sharp. In the autumn mist that filled the lighted streets as well as the dark he seemed a wraith, and some of those who passed him looked again, not sure whether they had indeed seen a living man. One or two of them moved their shoulders, as though shrinking from something.

His legs were long, but he walked with the short, deliberate steps of a blind man, though he was not blind. His eyes were open, and he stared straight ahead; but he seemed to see nothing and hear nothing. Neither the mournful hooting of sirens across the black water of the river, nor the genial windows of the shops in the big streets near the centre drew his head to right or left. He walked as though he had no destination in mind, yet constantly, at this corner or that, he turned. It seemed that an unseen hand was guiding him to a given point of whose location he was himself ignorant.

He was searching for a friend of fifteen years ago, and the unseen hand, or some dog-instinct, had led him from Africa to London, and was now leading him, along the last mile of his search, to a certain little eating-house. He did not know that he was going to the eating-house of his friend Nameless, but he did know, from the time he left Africa, that he was journeying towards Nameless, and he now knew that he was very near to Nameless.

Nameless didn't know that his old friend was anywhere near *him*, though, had he observed conditions that evening, he might have wondered why he was sitting up an hour later than usual. He was seated in one of the pews of his prosperous Workmen's Dining-Rooms—a little gold-mine his wife's relations called it—and he was smoking and looking at nothing. He had added up the till and written the copies of the bill of fare for next day, and there was nothing to keep him out of bed after his fifteen hours' attention to business. Had he been asked why he was sitting up later than usual, he would first have answered that he didn't know that he was, and would then have explained, in default of any other explanation, that it was for the purpose of having a last pipe. He was quite unaware that he was sitting up and keeping the door unlatched because a long-parted friend from Africa was seeking him and slowly approaching him, and needed his services. He was quite unaware that he had left the door unlatched at that late hour—half-past eleven—to admit pain and woe.

But even as many bells sent dolefully across the night from their steeples their disagreement as to the point of half-past eleven, pain and woe were but two streets away from him. The mackintosh and dungarees and the sharp white face were coming nearer every moment.

There was silence in the house and in the streets; a heavy silence, broken, or sometimes stressed, by the occasional night-noises—motor horns, back-firing of lorries, shunting at a distant terminus. That silence seemed to envelop the house, but he did not notice it. He did not notice the bells, and he did not even notice the lagging step that approached his shop, and passed—and returned—and passed again—and halted. He was aware of nothing save that he was smoking a last pipe, and he was sitting in somnolence, deaf and blind to anything not in his immediate neighbourhood.

But when a hand was laid on the latch, and the latch was lifted, he did hear that, and he looked up. And he saw the door open, and got up and went to it. And there, just within the door, he came face to face with the thin figure of pain and woe.

To kill a fellow-creature is a frightful thing. At the time the act is committed the murderer may have sound and convincing reasons (to him) for his act. But time and reflection may bring regret; even remorse; and this may live with him for many years. Examined in wakeful hours of the night or early morning, the reasons for the act may shed their cold logic, and may cease to be reasons and become mere excuses. And these naked excuses may strip the murderer and show him to himself as he is. They may begin to hunt his soul, and to run into every little corner of his mind and every little nerve, in search of it.

And if to kill a fellow-creature and to suffer recurrent regret for an act of heated blood is a frightful thing, it is still more frightful to kill a fellow-creature and bury his body deep in an African jungle, and then, fifteen years later, at about midnight, to see the latch of your door lifted by the hand you had stilled and to see the man, looking much as he did fifteen years ago, walk into your home and claim your hospitality.

When the man in mackintosh and dungarees walked into the dining-rooms Nameless stood still; stared; staggered against a table; supported himself by a hand, and said, 'Oh.'

The other man said, 'Nameless.'

Then they looked at each other; Nameless with head thrust forward, mouth dropped, eyes wide; the visitor with a dull, glazed expression. If Nameless had not been the man he was—thick, bovine and costive—he would have flung up his arms and screamed. At that moment he felt the need of some such outlet, but did not know how to find it. The only dramatic expression he gave to the situation was to whisper instead of speak.

Twenty emotions came to life in his head and spine, and wrestled there. But they showed themselves only in his staring eyes and his whisper. His first thought, or rather, spasm, was Ghosts-Indigestion-Nervous-Breakdown. His second, when he saw that the figure was substantial and real, was Impersonation. But a slight movement on the part of the visitor dismissed that.

It was a little habitual movement which belonged only to that man; an unconscious twitching of the third finger of the left hand. He knew then that it was Gopak. Gopak, a little changed, but still, miraculously, thirty-two. Gopak, alive, breathing and real. No ghost. No phantom of the stomach. He was as certain of that as he was that fifteen years ago he had killed Gopak stone-dead and buried him.

The blackness of the moment was lightened by Gopak. In thin, flat tones he asked, 'May I sit down? I'm tired.' He sat down, and said: 'So tired.'

Nameless still held the table. He whispered: 'Gopak. . . . Gopak. . . . But I—I *killed* you. I killed you in the jungle. You were dead. I know you were.'

Gopak passed his hand across his face. He seemed about to cry. 'I know you did. I know. That's all I can remember—about this earth. You killed me.' The voice became thinner and flatter. 'And then they came and—disturbed me. They woke me up. And brought me back.' He sat with shoulders sagged, arms drooping, hands hanging between knees. After the first recognition he did not look at Nameless; he looked at the floor.

'Came and disturbed you?' Nameless leaned forward and whispered the words. 'Woke you up? Who?'

'The Leopard Men.'

'The what?'

'The Leopard Men.' The watery voice said it as casually as if it were saying 'the night watchman.'

'The Leopard Men?' Nameless stared, and his fat face crinkled in an effort to take in the situation of a midnight visitation from a dead man, and the dead man talking nonsense. He felt his blood moving out of its course. He looked at his own hand to see if it was his own hand. He looked at the table to see if it was his table. The hand and the table were facts, and if the dead man was a fact—and he was—his story might be a fact. It seemed anyway as sensible as the dead man's presence. He gave a heavy sigh from the stomach. 'A-ah. . . . The Leopard Men. . . . Yes, I heard about them out there. Tales.'

Gopak slowly wagged his head. 'Not tales. They're real. If they weren't real—I wouldn't be here. Would I?'

Nameless had to admit this. He had heard many tales 'out there' about the Leopard Men, and had dismissed them as jungle yarns. But now, it seemed, jungle yarns had become commonplace fact in a little London shop. The watery voice went on. 'They do it. I saw them. I came back in the middle of a circle of them. They killed a nigger to put his life into me. They wanted a white man—for their farm. So they brought me back. You may not believe it. You wouldn't *want* to believe it. You wouldn't want to—see or know anything like them. And I wouldn't want any man to. But it's true. That's how I'm here.'

'But I left you absolutely dead. I made every test. It was three days before I buried you. And I buried you deep.'

'I know. But that wouldn't make any difference to them. It was a long time after when they came and brought me back. And I'm still dead, you know. It's only my body they brought back.' The voice trailed into a thread. 'And I'm so tired.'

Sitting in his prosperous eating-house Nameless was in the presence of an achieved miracle, but the everyday, solid appointments of the eating-house wouldn't let him fully comprehend it. Foolishly, as he realized when he had spoken, he asked Gopak to explain what had happened. Asked a man who couldn't really be alive to explain how he came to be alive. It was like asking Nothing to explain Everything.

Constantly, as he talked, he felt his grasp on his own mind slipping. The surprise of a sudden visitor at a late hour; the shock of the arrival of a long-dead man; and the realization that this long-dead man was not a wraith, were too much for him.

During the next half-hour he found himself talking to Gopak as to the Gopak he had known seventeen years ago when they were partners. Then he would be halted by the freezing knowledge that he was talking to a dead man, and that a dead man was faintly answering him. He felt that the thing couldn't really have happened, but in the interchange of talk he kept forgetting the improbable side of it, and accepting it. With each recollection of the truth, his mind would clear and settle in one thought—'I've got to get rid of him. How am I going to get rid of him?'

'But how did you get here?'

'I escaped.' The words came slowly and thinly, and out of the body rather than the mouth.

'How.'

'I don't—know. I don't remember anything—except our quarrel. And being at rest.'

'But why come all the way here? Why didn't you stay on the coast?'

'I don't—know. But you're the only man I know. The only man I can remember.'

'But how did you find me?'

'I don't know. But I had to—find you. You're the only man—who can help me.'

'But how can I help you?'

The head turned weakly from side to side. 'I don't—know. But nobody else—can.'

Nameless stared through the window, looking on to the lamplit street and seeing nothing of it. The everyday being which had been his half an hour ago had been annihilated; the everyday beliefs and disbeliefs shattered and mixed together. But some shred of his old sense and his old standards remained. He must handle this situation. 'Well—what you want to do? What you going to do? I don't see how I can help you. And you can't stay here, obviously.' A demon of perversity sent a facetious notion into his head—introducing Gopak to his wife—'This is my dead friend.'

But on his last spoken remark Gopak made the effort of raising his head and staring with the glazed eyes at Nameless. 'But I *must* stay here. There's nowhere else I can stay. I must stay here. That's why I came. You got to help me.'

'But you can't stay here. I got no room. All occupied. Nowhere for you to sleep.'

The wan voice said: 'That doesn't matter. I *don't* sleep.'

'Eh?'

'I *don't* sleep. I haven't slept since they brought me back. I can sit here—till you can think of some way of helping me.'

'But how *can* I?' He again forgot the background of the situation, and began to get angry at the vision of a dead man sitting about the place waiting for him to think of something. 'How *can* I if you don't tell me how?'

'I don't—know. But you got to. You killed me. And I was dead—and comfortable. As it all came from you—killing me—you're responsible for me being—like this. So you got to—help me. That's why I—came to you.'

'But what do you want me to do?'

'I don't—know. I can't—think. But nobody but you can help me. I had to come to you. Something brought me—straight to you. That means that you're the one—that can help me. Now I'm with you, something will—happen to help me. I feel it will. In time you'll—think of something.'

Nameless found his legs suddenly weak. He sat down and stared with a sick scowl at the hideous and the incomprehensible. Here was a dead man in his house—a man he had murdered in a moment of black temper—and he knew in his heart that he couldn't turn the man out. For one thing, he would have been afraid to touch him; he couldn't see himself touching him. For another, faced with the miracle of the presence of a fifteen-years-dead man, he doubted whether physical force or any material agency would be effectual in moving the man.

His soul shivered, as all men's souls shiver at the demonstration of forces outside their mental or spiritual horizon. He had murdered this man, and often, in fifteen years, he had repented the act. If the man's appalling story were true, then he had some sort of right to turn to Nameless. Nameless recognized that, and knew that whatever happened he couldn't turn him out. His hot-tempered sin had literally come home to him.

The wan voice broke into his nightmare. 'You go to rest, Nameless. I'll sit here. You go to rest.' He put his face down to his hands and uttered a little moan. 'Oh, why can't I rest?'

Nameless came down early next morning with a half-hope that Gopak would not be there. But he was there, seated where Nameless had left him last night. Nameless made some tea, and showed him where he might wash. He washed listlessly, and crawled back to his seat, and listlessly drank the tea which Nameless brought to him.

To his wife and the kitchen helpers Nameless mentioned him as an old friend who had had a bit of a shock. 'Shipwrecked and knocked on the head. But quite harmless, and he won't be staying long. He's waiting for admission to a home. A good pal to me in the past, and it's the least I can do to let him stay here a few days. Suffers from sleeplessness and prefers to sit up at night. Quite harmless.'

But Gopak stayed more than a few days. He outstayed everybody. Even when the customers had gone Gopak was still there.

On the first morning of his visit when the regular customers came in at midday, they looked at the odd, white figure sitting vacantly in the first pew, then stared, then moved away. All avoided the pew in which he sat. Nameless explained him to them, but his explanation did not seem to relieve the slight tension which settled on the dining-room. The atmosphere was not so brisk and chatty as usual. Even those who had their backs to the stranger seemed to be affected by his presence.

At the end of the first day Nameless, noticing this, told him that he had arranged a nice corner of the front-room upstairs, where he could sit by the window, and took his arm to take him upstairs. But Gopak feebly shook the hand away, and sat where he was. 'No. I don't want to go. I'll stay here. I'll stay here. I don't want to move.'

And he wouldn't move. After a few more pleadings Nameless realized with dismay that his refusal was definite; that it would be futile to press him or force him; that he was going to sit in that dining-room for ever. He was as weak as a child and as firm as a rock. He continued to sit in that first pew, and the customers continued to avoid it, and to give queer glances at it. It seemed that they half-recognized that he was something more than a fellow who had had a shock.

During the second week of his stay three of the regular customers were missing, and more than one of those that remained made acidly facetious suggestions to Nameless that he park his lively friend somewhere else. He made things too exciting for them; all that whoopee took them off their work, and interfered with digestion. Nameless told them he would be staying only a day or so longer, but they found that this was untrue, and at the end of the second week eight of the regulars had found another place.

Each day, when the dinner-hour came, Nameless tried to get him to take a little walk, but always he refused. He would go out only at night, and then never more than two hundred yards from the shop. For the rest, he sat in his pew, sometimes dozing in the afternoon, at other times staring at the floor. He took his food abstractedly, and never knew whether he had had food or not. He spoke only when questioned, and the burden of his talk was 'I'm so tired.'

One thing only seemed to arouse any light of interest in him; one thing only drew his eyes from the floor. That was the seventeen-year-old daughter of his host, who was known as Bubbles, and who helped with the waiting. And Bubbles seemed to be the only member of the shop and its customers who did not shrink from him.

She knew nothing of the truth about him, but she seemed to

understand him, and the only response he ever gave to anything was to her childish sympathy. She sat and chatted foolish chatter to him—'bringing him out of himself,' she called it—and sometimes he would be brought out to the extent of a watery smile. He came to recognize her step, and would look up before she entered the room. Once or twice in the evening, when the shop was empty, and Nameless was sitting miserably with him, he would ask, without lifting his eyes, 'Where's Bubbles?' and would be told that Bubbles had gone to the pictures or was out at a dance, and would relapse into deeper vacancy.

Nameless didn't like this. He was already visited by a curse which, in four weeks, had destroyed most of his business. Regular customers had dropped off two by two, and no new customers came to take their place. Strangers who dropped in once for a meal did not come again; they could not keep their eyes or their minds off the forbidding, white-faced figure sitting motionless in the first pew. At midday, when the place had been crowded and latecomers had to wait for a seat, it was now two-thirds empty; only a few of the most thick-skinned remained faithful.

And on top of this there was the interest of the dead man in his daughter, an interest which seemed to be having an unpleasant effect. Nameless hadn't noticed it, but his wife had. 'Bubbles don't seem as bright and lively as she was. You noticed it lately? She's getting quiet—and a bit slack. Sits about a lot. Paler than she used to be.'

'Her age, perhaps.'

'No. She's not one of these thin dark sort. No—it's something else. Just the last week or two I've noticed it. Off her food. Sits about doing nothing. No interest. May be nothing—just out of sorts, perhaps. . . . How much longer's that horrible friend of yours going to stay?'

The horrible friend stayed some weeks longer—ten weeks in all—while Nameless watched his business drop to nothing and his daughter get pale and peevish. He knew the cause of it. There was no home in all England like his: no home that had a dead man sitting in it for ten weeks. A dead man brought, after a long time, from the grave, to sit and disturb his customers and take the vitality from his daughter. He couldn't tell this to anybody. Nobody would believe such nonsense. But he *knew* that he was entertaining a dead man, and, knowing that a long-dead man was walking the earth, he could believe in any result of that fact. He could believe almost anything that he would have derided ten weeks ago. His customers had abandoned his shop, not because of the presence of a silent, white-faced man, but because of the presence of a dead-living man. Their minds might not know it, but their blood knew it. And, as his business had been destroyed so, he believed, would his daughter be destroyed. Her blood was not warning her; her blood told her only that this was a long-ago friend of her father's, and she was drawn to him.

It was at this point that Nameless, having no work to do, began to drink. And it was well that he did so. For out of the drink came an idea, and with that idea he freed himself from the curse upon him and his house.

The shop now served scarcely half a dozen customers at midday. It had become ill-kempt and dusty, and the service and the food were bad. Nameless took no trouble to be civil to his few customers. Often, when he was notably under drink, he went to the trouble of being very rude to them. They talked about this. They talked about the decline of his business and the dustiness of the shop and the bad food. They talked about his drinking, and, of course, exaggerated it.

And they talked about the queer fellow who sat there day after day and gave everybody the creeps. A few outsiders, hearing the gossip, came to the dining-rooms to see the queer fellow and the always-tight proprietor; but they did not come again, and there were not enough of the curious to keep the place busy. It went down until it served scarcely two customers a day. And Nameless went down with it into drink.

Then, one evening, out of the drink he fished an inspiration.

He took it downstairs to Gopak, who was sitting in his usual seat, hands hanging, eyes on the floor. 'Gopak—listen. You came here because I was the only man who could help you in your trouble. You listening?'

A faint 'Yes' was his answer.

'Well, now. You told me I'd got to think of something. I've thought of something. . . . Listen. You say I'm responsible for your condition and got to get you out of it, because I killed you. I did. We had a row. You made me wild. You dared me. And what with that sun and the jungle and the insects, I wasn't meself. I killed you. The moment it was done I could 'a cut me right hand off. Because you and me were pals. I could 'a cut me right hand off.'

'I know. I felt that directly it was over. I knew you were suffering.'

'Ah! . . . I have suffered. And I'm suffering now. Well, this is what I've thought. All your present trouble comes from me killing you in that jungle and burying you. An idea came to me. Do you think it would help you—I—if I—if I—killed you again?'

For some seconds Gopak continued to stare at the floor. Then his shoulders moved. Then, while Nameless watched every little response to his idea, the watery voice began. 'Yes. Yes. That's it. That's what I was waiting for. That's why I came here. I can see now. That's why I had to get here. Nobody else could kill me. Only you. I've got to be killed again.

Yes, I see. But nobody else—would be able—to kill me. Only the man who first killed me. . . . Yes, you've found—what we're both—waiting for. Anybody else could shoot me—stab me—hang me—but they couldn't kill me. Only you. That's why I managed to get here and find you.' The watery voice rose to a thin strength. 'That's it. And you must do it. Do it now. You don't want to, I know. But you must. You *must*.'

His head drooped and he stared at the floor. Nameless, too, stared at the floor. He was seeing things. He had murdered a man and had escaped all punishment save that of his own mind, which had been terrible enough. But now he was going to murder him again—not in a jungle but in a city; and he saw the slow points of the result.

He saw the arrest. He saw the first hearing. He saw the trial. He saw the cell. He saw the rope. He shuddered.

Then he saw the alternative—the breakdown of his life—a ruined business, poverty, the poor-house, a daughter robbed of her health and perhaps dying, and always the curse of the dead-living man, who might follow him to the poor-house. Better to end it all, he thought. Rid himself of the curse which Gopak had brought upon him and his family, and then rid his family of himself with a revolver. Better to follow up his idea.

He got stiffly to his feet. The hour was late evening—half-past ten—and the streets were quiet. He had pulled down the shop-blinds and locked the door. The room was lit by one light at the farther end. He moved about uncertainly and looked at Gopak. 'Er—how would you—how shall I—'

Gopak said, 'You did it with a knife. Just under the heart. You must do it that way again.'

Nameless stood and looked at him for some seconds. Then, with an air of resolve, he shook himself. He walked quickly to the kitchen.

Three minutes later his wife and daughter heard a crash, as though a table had been overturned. They called but got no answer. When they came down they found him sitting in one of the pews, wiping sweat from his forehead. He was white and shaking, and appeared to be recovering from a faint.

'Whatever's the matter? You all right?'

He waved them away. 'Yes, I'm all right. Touch of giddiness. Smoking too much, I think.'

'Mmmm. Or drinking. . . . Where's your friend? Out for a walk?'

'No. He's gone off. Said he wouldn't impose any longer, and 'd go and find an infirmary.' He spoke weakly and found trouble in picking words. 'Didn't you hear that bang—when he shut the door?'

'I thought that was you fell down.'

'No. It was him when he went. I couldn't stop him.'

'Mmmm. Just as well, I think.' She looked about her. 'Things seem to
'a gone all wrong since he's been here.'

There was a general air of dustiness about the place. The table-cloths
were dirty, not from use but from disuse. The windows were dim. A long
knife, very dusty, was lying on the table under the window. In a corner by
the door leading to the kitchen, unseen by her, lay a dusty mackintosh
and dungaree, which appeared to have been tossed there. But it was over
by the main door, near the first pew, that the dust was thickest—a long
trail of it—greyish-white dust.

'Reely this place gets more and more slapdash. Just *look* at that dust by
the door. Looks as though somebody's been spilling ashes all over the
place.'

Nameless looked at it, and his hands shook a little. But he answered,
more firmly than before: 'Yes, I know. I'll have a proper clean-up
tomorrow.'

For the first time in ten weeks he smiled at them; a thin, haggard
smile, but a smile.

Et in Sempiternum Pereant

CHARLES WILLIAMS

◄

Lord Arglay came easily down the road. About him the spring was as gaudy as the restraint imposed by English geography ever lets it be. The last village lay a couple of miles behind him; as far in front, he had been told, was a main road on which he could meet a motor bus to carry him near his destination. A casual conversation in a club had revealed to him, some months before, that in a country house of England there were supposed to lie a few yet unpublished legal opinions of the Lord Chancellor Bacon. Lord Arglay, being no longer Chief Justice, and having finished and published his *History of Organic Law*, had conceived that the editing of these papers might provide a pleasant variation upon his present business of studying the more complex parts of the Christian Schoolmen. He had taken advantage of a week-end spent in the neighbourhood to arrange, by the good will of the owner, a visit of inspection; since, as the owner had remarked, with a bitterness due to his financial problems, 'everything that is smoked isn't Bacon.' Lord Arglay had smiled—it hurt him a little to think that he had smiled—and said, which was true enough, that Bacon himself would not have made a better joke.

It was a very deserted part of the country through which he was walking. He had been careful to follow the directions given him, and in fact there were only two places where he could possibly have gone wrong, and at both of them Lord Arglay was certain he had not gone wrong. But he seemed to be taking a long time—a longer time than he had expected. He looked at his watch again, and noted with sharp disapproval of his own judgment that it was only six minutes since he had looked at it last. It had seemed more like sixteen. Lord Arglay frowned. He was usually a good walker, and on that morning he was not conscious of any unusual weariness. His host had offered to send him in a car, but he had declined. For a moment, as he put his watch back, he was almost sorry he had declined. A car would have made short time of this road, and at present his legs seemed to be making rather long time of it. 'Or,' Lord Arglay said aloud, 'making time rather long.' He played a little, as he went on, with the fancy that every road in space had a corresponding measure in time; that it tended, merely of itself, to hasten or delay all those that drove or walked upon it. The nature of some roads, quite apart from their material effectiveness, might urge men to speed, and of others to delay. So that the intentions of all travellers were counterpointed continually by the media they used. The courts, he thought, might reasonably take that into consideration in case of offences against right speed, and a man who accelerated upon one road would be held to have acted under the improper influence of the way, whereas one who did the same on another would be known to have defied and conquered the way.

Lord Arglay just stopped himself looking at his watch again. It was impossible that it should be more than five minutes since he had last done so. He looked back to observe, if possible, how far he had since come. It was not possible; the road narrowed and curved too much. There was a cloud of trees high up behind him; it must have been half an hour ago that he passed through it, yet it was not merely still in sight, but the trees themselves were in sight. He could remark them as trees; he could almost, if he were a little careful, count them. He thought, with some irritation, that he must be getting old more quickly, and more unnoticeably, than he had supposed. He did not much mind about the quickness, but he did mind about the unnoticeableness. It had given him pleasure to watch the various changes which age tended to bring; to be as stealthy and as quick to observe those changes as they were to come upon him—the slower pace, the more meditative voice, the greater reluctance to decide, the inclination to fall back on habit, the desire for the familiar which is the first skirmishing approach of unfamiliar death. He neither welcomed nor grudged such changes; he only observed them with a perpetual interest in the curious nature of the creation. The fantasy of growing old, like the fantasy of growing up, was part of the ineffable sweetness, touched with horror, of existence, itself the lordliest fantasy of all. But now, as he stood looking back over and across the hidden curves of the road, he felt suddenly that time had outmarched and out-twisted him, that it was spreading along the countryside and doubling back on him, so that it troubled and deceived his judgment. In an unexpected and unusual spasm of irritation he put his hand to his watch again. He felt as if it were a quarter of an hour since he had looked at it; very well, making just allowance for his state of impatience, he would expect the actual time to be five minutes. He looked; it was only two.

Lord Arglay made a small mental effort, and almost immediately recognized the effort. He said to himself: 'This is another mark of age. I am losing my sense of duration.' He said also: 'It is becoming an effort to recognize these changes.' Age was certainly quickening its work in him. It approached him now doubly; not only his method of experience, but

his awareness of experience was attacked. His knowledge of it comforted him—perhaps, he thought, for the last time. The knowledge
would go. He would savour it then while he could. Still looking back at
the trees, 'It seems I'm decaying,' Lord Arglay said aloud. 'And that
anyhow is one up against decay. Am I procrastinating? I am, and in the
circumstances procrastination is a proper and pretty game. It is the thief
of time, and quite right too! Why should time have it all its own way?'

He turned to the road again, and went on. It passed now between
open fields; in all those fields he could see no one. It was pasture, but
there were no beasts. There was about him a kind of void, in which he
moved, hampered by this growing oppression of duration. Things *lasted*.
He had exclaimed, in his time, against the too swift passage of the world.
This was a new experience; it was lastingness—almost, he could have
believed, everlastingness. The measure of it was but his breathing, and
his breathing, as it grew slower and heavier, would become the measure
of everlasting labour—the labour of Sisyphus, who pushed his own slow
heart through each infinite moment, and relaxed but to let it beat back
and so again begin. It was the first touch of something Arglay had never
yet known, of simple and perfect despair.

At that moment he saw the house. The road before him curved
sharply, and as he looked he wondered at the sweep of the curve; it
seemed to make a full half-circle and so turn back in the direction that
he had come. At the farthest point there lay before him, tangentially,
another path. The sparse hedge was broken by an opening which was
more than footpath and less than road. It was narrow, even when
compared with the narrowing way by which he had come, yet hard and
beaten as if by the passage of many feet. There had been innumerable
travellers, and all solitary, all on foot. No cars or carts could have taken
that path; if there had been burdens, they had been carried on the
shoulders of their owners. It ran for no long distance, no more than in
happier surroundings might have been a garden path from gate to door.
There, at the end, was the door.

Arglay, at the time, took all this in but half-consciously. His attention
was not on the door but on the chimney. The chimney, in the ordinary
phrase, was smoking. It was smoking effectively and continuously. A
narrow and dense pillar of dusk poured up from it, through which there
glowed every now and then, a deeper undershade of crimson, as if some
trapped genius almost thrust itself out of the moving prison that held it.
The house itself was not much more than a cottage. There was a door,
shut; on the left of it a window, also shut; above, two little attic windows,
shut, and covered within by some sort of dark hanging, or perhaps made
opaque by smoke that filled the room. There was no sign of life

anywhere, and the smoke continued to mount to the lifeless sky. It seemed to Arglay curious that he had not noticed this grey pillar in his approach, that only now when he stood almost in the straight and narrow path leading to the house did it become visible, an exposition of tall darkness reserved to the solitary walkers upon that wearying road.

Lord Arglay was the last person in the world to look for responsibilities. He shunned them by a courteous habit; a responsibility had to present itself with a delicate emphasis before he acceded to it. But when any so impressed itself he was courteous in accepting as in declining; he sought friendship with necessity, and as young lovers call their love fatal, so he turned fatality of life into his love. It seemed to him, as he stood and gazed at the path, the shut door, the smoking chimney, that here perhaps was a responsibility being delicately emphatic. If everyone was out—if the cottage had been left for an hour—ought he to do something? Of course, they might be busy about it within; in which case a thrusting stranger would be inopportune. Another glow of crimson in the pillar of cloud decided him. He went up the path.

As he went he glanced at the little window, but it was blurred by dirt; he could not very well see whether the panes did or did not hide smoke within. When he was so near the threshold that the window had almost passed out of his vision, he thought he saw a face looking out of it—at the extreme edge, nearest the door—and he checked himself, and went back a step to look again. It had been only along the side of his glance that the face, if face it were, had appeared, a kind of sudden white scrawl against the blur, as if it were a mask hung by the window rather than any living person, or as if the glass of the window itself had looked sideways at him, and he had caught the look without understanding its cause. When he stepped back, he could see no face. Had there been a sun in the sky he would have attributed the apparition to a trick of the light, but in the sky over this smoking house there was no sun. It had shone brightly that morning when he started; it had paled and faded and finally been lost to him as he had passed along his road. There was neither sun nor peering face. He stepped back to the threshold, and knocked with his knuckles on the door.

There was no answer. He knocked again and again waited, and as he stood there he began to feel annoyed. The balance of Lord Arglay's mind had not been achieved without the creation of a considerable counter-energy to the violence of Lord Arglay's natural temper. There had been people whom he had once come very near hating, hating with a fury of selfish rage and detestation; for instance, his brother-in-law. His brother-in-law had not been a nice man; Lord Arglay, as he stood by the door and, for no earthly reason, remembered him, admitted it. He admitted, at the same moment, that no lack of niceness on that other's part could excuse any indulgence of vindictive hate on his own, nor could he think why, then and there, he wanted him, wanted to have him merely to hate. His brother-in-law was dead. Lord Arglay almost regretted it. Almost he desired to follow, to be with him, to provoke and torment him, to . . .

Lord Arglay struck the door again. 'There is,' he said to himself, 'entire clarity in the Omnipotence.' It was his habit of devotion, his means of recalling himself into peace out of the angers, greeds, sloths and perversities that still too often possessed him. It operated; the temptation passed into the benediction of the Omnipotence and disappeared. But there was still no answer from within. Lord Arglay laid his hand on the latch. He swung the door, and, lifting his hat with his other hand, looked into the room—a room empty of smoke as of fire, and of all as of both.

Its size and appearance were those of a rather poor cottage, rather indeed a large brick hut than a cottage. It seemed much smaller within than without. There was a fireplace—at least, there was a place for a fire—on his left. Opposite the door, against the right-hand wall, there was a ramshackle flight of wooden steps, going up to the attics, and at its foot, swinging on a broken hinge, a door which gave a way presumably to a cellar. Vaguely, Arglay found himself surprised; he had not supposed that a dwelling of this sort would have a cellar. Indeed, from where he stood, he could not be certain. It might only be a cupboard. But, unwarrantably, it seemed more, a hinted unseen depth, as if the slow slight movement of the broken wooden door measured that labour of Sisyphus, as if the road ran past him and went coiling spirally into the darkness of the cellar. In the room there was no furniture, neither fragment of paper nor broken bit of wood; there was no sign of life, no flame in the grate nor drift of smoke in the air. It was completely and utterly void.

Lord Arglay looked at it. He went back a few steps and looked up again at the chimney. Undoubtedly the chimney was smoking. It was received into a pillar of smoke; there was no clear point where the dark chimney ended and the dark smoke began. House leaned to roof, roof to chimney, chimney to smoke, and smoke went up for ever and ever over those roads where men crawled infinitely through the smallest measurements of time. Arglay returned to the door, crossed the threshold, and stood in the room. Empty of flame, empty of flame's material, holding within its dank air the very opposite of flame, the chill of ancient years, the room lay round him. Lord Arglay contemplated it. 'There's no smoke without fire,' he said aloud. 'Only apparently there is. Thus one lives and learns. Unless indeed this is the place where one lives without learning.'

The phrase, leaving his lips, sounded oddly about the walls and in the corners of the room. He was suddenly revolted by his own chance words—'a place where one lives without learning', where no courtesy or integrity could any more be fined or clarified. The echo daunted him; he made a sharp movement, he took a step aside towards the stairs, and before the movement was complete, was aware of a change. The dank chill became a concentration of dank and deadly heat, pricking at him, entering his nostrils and his mouth. The fantasy of life without knowledge materialized, inimical, in the air, life without knowledge, corrupting life without knowledge, jungle and less than jungle, and though still the walls of the bleak chamber met his eyes, a shell of existence, it seemed that life, withdrawn from all those normal habits of which the useless memory was still drearily sustained by the thin phenomenal fabric, was collecting and corrupting in the atmosphere behind the door he had so rashly passed—outside the other door which swung crookedly at the head of the darker hole within.

He had recoiled from the heat, but not so as to escape it. He had even taken a step or two up the stairs, when he heard from without a soft approach. Light feet were coming up the beaten path to the house. Some other Good Samaritan, Arglay thought, who would be able to keep his twopence in his pocket. For certainly, whatever was the explanation of all this and wherever it lay, in the attics above or in the pit of the cellar below, responsibility was gone. Lord Arglay did not conceive that either he or anyone else need rush about the country in an anxious effort to preserve a house which no one wanted and no one used. Prematurely enjoying the discussion, he waited. Through the doorway someone came in.

It was, or seemed to be, a man, of ordinary height, wearing some kind of loose dark overcoat that flapped about him. His head was bare; so, astonishingly, were his legs and feet. At first, as he stood just inside the door, leaning greedily forward, his face was invisible, and for a moment Arglay hesitated to speak. Then the stranger lifted his face and Arglay uttered a sound. It was emaciated beyond imagination; it was astonishing, at the appalling degree of hunger revealed, that the man could walk or move at all, or even stand as he was now doing, and turn that dreadful skull from side to side. Arglay came down the steps of the stair in one jump; he cried out again, he ran forward, and as he did so the deep burning eyes in the turning face of bone met his full and halted him. They did not see him, or if they saw did not notice; they gazed at him and moved on. Once only in his life had Arglay seen eyes remotely like those;

once, when he had pronounced the death-sentence upon a wretched man who had broken under the long strain of his trial and filled the court with shrieks. Madness had glared at Lord Arglay from that dock, but at least it had looked at him and seen him; these eyes did not. They sought something—food, life, or perhaps only a form and something to hate, and in that energy the stranger moved. He began to run round the room. The bones that were his legs and feet jerked up and down. The head turned from side to side. He ran circularly, round and again round, crossing and recrossing, looking up, down, around, and at last, right in the centre of the room, coming to a halt, where, as if some terrible pain of starvation gripped him, he bent and twisted downward until he squatted grotesquely on the floor. There, squatting and bending, he lowered his head and raised his arm, and as the fantastic black coat slipped back, Arglay saw a wrist, saw it marked with scars. He did not at first think what they were; only when the face and wrist of the figure swaying in its pain came together did he suddenly know. They were teeth-marks; they were bites; the mouth closed on the wrist and gnawed. Arglay cried out and sprang forward, catching the arm, trying to press it down, catching the other shoulder, trying to press it back. He achieved nothing. He held, he felt, he grasped; he could not control. The long limb remained raised, the fierce teeth gnawed. But as Arglay bent, he was aware once more of that effluvia of heat risen round him, and breaking out with the more violence when suddenly the man, if it were man, cast his arm away, and with a jerk of movement rose once more to his feet. His eyes, as the head went back, burned close into Arglay's, who, what with the heat, the eyes, and his sickness at the horror, shut his own against them, and was at the same moment thrown from his balance by the rising form, and sent staggering a step or two away, with upon his face the sensation of a light hot breath, so light that only in the utter stillness of time could it be felt, so hot that it might have been the inner fire from which the pillar of smoke poured outward to the world.

He recovered his balance; he opened his eyes; both motions brought him into a new corner of that world. The odd black coat the thing had worn had disappeared, as if it had been a covering imagined by a habit of mind. The thing itself, a wasted flicker of pallid movement, danced and gyrated in white flame before him. Arglay saw it still, but only now as a dreamer may hear, half-asleep and half-awake, the sound of dogs barking or the crackling of fire in his very room. For he opened his eyes not to such things, but to the thing that on the threshold of this place, some seconds earlier or some years, he had felt and been pleased to feel, to the reality of his hate. It came in a rush within him, a fountain of fire, and without and about him images of the man he hated swept in a thick cloud of burning smoke. The smoke burned his eyes and choked his mouth; he clutched at it, at images within it—at his greedy loves and greedy hates—at the cloud of the sin of his life, yearning to catch but one image and renew again the concentration for which he yearned. He could not. The smoke blinded and stifled him, yet more than stifling or blinding was the hunger for one true thing to lust or hate. He was starving in the smoke, and all the hut was full of smoke, for the hut and the world were smoke, pouring up round him, from him and all like him—a thing once wholly, and still a little, made visible to his corporeal eyes in forms which they recognized, but in itself of another nature. He swung and twisted and crouched. His limbs ached from long wrestling with the smoke, for as the journey to this place had prolonged itself infinitely, so now, though he had no thought of measurement, the clutch of his hands and the growing sickness that invaded him struck through him the sensation of the passage of years and the knowledge of the passage of moments. The fire sank within him, and the sickness grew, but the change could not bring him nearer to any end. The end here was not at the end, but in the beginning. There was no end to this smoke, to this fever and this chill, to crouching and rising and searching, unless the end was now. *Now—now* was the only possible other fact, chance, act. He cried out, defying infinity, '*Now!*'

Before his voice the smoke of his prison yielded, and yielded two ways at once. From where he stood he could see in one place an alteration in that perpetual grey, an alternate darkening and lightening as if two ways, of descent and ascent, met. There was, he remembered, a way in, therefore a path out; he had only to walk along it. But also there was a way still farther in, and he could walk along that. Two doors had swung, to his outer senses, in that small room. From every gate of hell there was a way to heaven, yes, and in every way to heaven there was a gate to deeper hell.

Yet for a moment he hesitated. There was no sign of the phenomenon by which he had discerned the passage of that other spirit. He desired— very strongly he desired—to be of use to it. He desired to offer himself to it, to make a ladder of himself, if that should be desired, by which it might perhaps mount from the nature of the lost, from the dereliction of all minds that refuse living and learning, postponement and irony, whose dwelling is necessarily in their undying and perishing selves. Slowly, unconsciously, he moved his head as if to to seek his neighbour.

He saw, at first he felt, nothing. His eyes returned to that vibrating oblong of an imagined door, the heart of the smoke beating in the smoke. He looked at it; he remembered the way; he was on the point of movement, when the stinging heat struck him again, but this time from behind. It leapt through him; he was seized in it and loosed from it; its rush abandoned him. The torrent of its fiery passage struck the darkening hollow in the walls. At the instant that it struck, there came a small sound; there floated up a thin shrill pipe, too short to hear, too certain to miss, faint and quick as from some single insect in the hedgerow or the field, and yet more than single—a weak wail of multitudes of the lost. The shrill lament struck his ears, and he ran. He cried as he sprang: 'Now is God: now is glory in God,' and as the dark door swung before him it was the threshold of the house that received his flying feet. As he passed, another form slipped by him, slinking hastily into the house, another of the hordes going so swiftly up that straight way, hard with everlasting time; each driven by his own hunger, and each alone. The vision, a face looking in as a face had looked out, was gone. Running still, but more lightly now, and with some communion of peace at heart, Arglay came into the curving road. The trees were all about him; the house was at their heart. He ran on through them; beyond, he saw, he reached, the spring day and the sun. At a little distance a motor bus, gaudy within and without, was coming down the road. The driver saw him. Lord Arglay instinctively made a sign, ran, mounted. As he sat down, breathless and shaken, '*E quindi uscimmo,*' his mind said, '*a riveder le stelle.*'

Bosworth Summit Pound

L. T. C. ROLT

With the exception of the lock-keepers in their lonely cottages by the Cold Bosworth and Canonshanger locks, and of the infrequent boatmen who navigate its narrow, tortuous course, very few people are familiar with the little-used North Midland section of the Great Central Canal. Many have crossed over it and perhaps caught a brief glimpse of its still, reed-fringed waters as they hurried northward by those great main road and rail routes which stride so arrogantly across the Midland Shires. Yet they are seldom sufficiently interested to enquire whither this forgotten water road leads. Again, antiquaries and those who make it their hobby to 'collect' village churches will be familiar with the splendid broach spire of St Peter's, Cold Bosworth, which, standing four-square to the winds of the wolds, is such a prominent local landmark. But when they stand in the nave to admire the remarkable fourteenth-century rood-screen or the delicate tracery of the clerestory windows, they do not realize that the waters of the Great Central Canal lie directly beneath their feet. In fact, the church of St Peter stands upon that great belt of limestone which extends from the Dorset coast to the Yorkshire border, and which here forms the central watershed of England. As a glance at a contoured map will show, the erosion of the small streams which may carry the rain-water from the church roof to the Humber, the Wash or the Bristol Channel has considerably narrowed the ridge at this point. Consequently it was here that the canal engineers decided to cut the watershed by a tunnel over a mile long. Just above the lock called Bosworth Top, and within a few hundred yards of the churchyard wall, the canal disappears underground, but as both lock and tunnel portal are hidden in the thick undergrowth of Bosworth wood, a stranger standing in the churchyard would be unaware of their existence.

Before he leaves the precincts of St Peter's, I would draw the visitor's attention to a tombstone standing on the north side of the churchyard. The stone itself is of no particular merit, while it bears no inscription to attract the eye of the collector of curious epitaphs. It may therefore easily escape notice. Although a frequent visitor to the church, I must confess that I never noticed it myself until my attention was drawn to it by Fawcett's story. It was then that I appreciated that the inscription, though simple, is, after all, somewhat singular. It reads:

Here lies the body of
MARY GRIMSDEN,
of Canonshanger in this parish,
Aged 25 years.

Here lies also the body of
JOHN FORTESCUE LOFTHOUSE
of Coppice Farm, Cold Bosworth.
Died 14th February 1841, aged 31 years.

'In death they were not divided.'

The fact that the date of Mary Grimsden's death is not given might conceivably be due to an error on the part of the village mason, but that two ostensibly unrelated persons should be buried in a common grave and accorded an epitaph usually reserved for those who have enjoyed many years of conjugal felicity should strike the reflective as peculiar.

Henry Fawcett was one of those men who love 'messing about in boats', to use a popular phrase, and as he was a man of independent means with no domestic ties (he was a confirmed bachelor), he was able to indulge his passion to the full throughout his long lifetime. Although I accompanied him on several occasions, even I had no idea of the extent of his voyaging until, after his death, there came into my possession a number of manuscript volumes in which, minutely detailed in his cramped characteristic hand, he had kept a complete record of his travels. From this it appeared that there were few harbours in the Mediterranean or along the north-western seaboard of Europe with which he was not familiar. As may be imagined, the log recorded many adventures, some of them experiences that would have induced many less intrepid sailors to leave the sea for solid earth. There is thus something oddly ironical in the fact that a man who, single-handed, could ride out an equinoctial gale in the Bay of Biscay without a qualm should have been scared almost out of his wits on the narrow landlocked waters of the Great Central Canal at Cold Bosworth in the heart of the English Midlands.

It happened in 1932, on what was fated to be his last voyage. In the autumn of '28, Fawcett had returned to England a sick man. He lay in hospital all that winter, and when at last he was able to get about again he realized bitterly that his sea-going days were over. But he would not leave the water. 'I shall have to stick to fresh water', he told me ruefully. He sold his yawl *Deirdre* and bought one of those long, narrow canal-boats which he proceeded to convert into a comfortable motor-driven house-boat. The last time I saw him was during the winter of '31 when he had a snug berth on the Trent and Mersey Canal. He then seemed in good health and spirits, and told me of his intention to move south in the spring. I had no further news of him until the following June when I heard, with some surprise, that his boat, the *Wildflower*, was up for sale. A week or so afterwards I read the announcement of his death in *The Times*.

Because Fawcett recorded his last voyage in his usual scrupulous manner, and thanks to my intimate knowledge of the district, it has been easy for me to reconstruct the story of his experience at Cold Bosworth. He was accompanied by a friend unknown to me who is referred to in the log as Charles. The journey from the Trent and Mersey to the Great Central was accomplished in good weather and without any untoward incident, and a fine May morning found them beginning the long climb up the Canonshanger locks towards Cold Bosworth summit level. Charles, it appears, had to return to London for a couple of days on business, so it was agreed that when they reached a convenient mooring-point, Fawcett should wait his return. Because it is connected by branch line with Rugby, Cold Bosworth was selected. Fawcett consulted the lock-keeper at Canonshanger as to a convenient mooring and was advised to tie up below Bosworth Top Lock. By midday they had reached the summit, and here they paused for lunch before entering the tunnel.

Navigating a boat through a canal tunnel is always a strange experience, but Fawcett seems to have found the passage of Bosworth tunnel singularly unpleasant. Not only was the narrow cavern of crumbling brickwork as cold and dark as a vault after the warmth and brilliance of the May sunshine, but water streamed from the roof and descended in cascades from the chimneys of the ventilation shafts. He had the utmost difficulty in keeping a straight course, for the damp atmosphere exhaled an evil-smelling mist which obscured the farther end of the tunnel and rendered the headlight on the bow ineffective. All he could see ahead was a lambent white curtain, patterned confusingly with shifting shadows. At one moment he thought he saw Charles leaning dangerously over the gunwale at the bow, and called out, fearing he would strike his head against the tunnel wall. But Charles answered from the aft cabin close at hand and the shadow presently vanished.

At length, a wan disc of daylight appeared and they presently emerged from the mists into the bright sunlight of the short pound between the tunnel mouth and Bosworth Top Lock. The canal here is well sheltered by the slopes of Bosworth Wood. On the one hand, the trees grow down to the water's edge, but on the towing-path side a narrow border of smooth, green turf intervenes. It looks an ideal mooring, and Fawcett wondered why the lock-keeper at Canonshanger should have advised him to lie below the lock. Not only did this appear less inviting, but it was farther from the village. His recommendation seemed even less explicable when, having brought the *Wildflower* alongside the bank, Charles discovered rusty mooring rings buried beneath the turf. Obviously it was here that, in the days of horse-drawn traffic, the horses were detached and led over the hill while the boats were laboriously 'legged' through the tunnel. Now the horse-path has become a little-used footway climbing up the wooded slope towards the village, and in places almost blinded by the thick undergrowth of briar and hazel. It was up this path that Charles set forth half an hour later, just in time to catch the afternoon train from that sleepy station called Cold Bosworth and Marborough Road.

Fawcett was too well accustomed to his own company to feel lonely or at a loss after the departure of his friend. When he had brewed himself a pot of tea he filled his pipe, got out his rod, and sat out on the deck fishing. Though he caught nothing he was well content, for the contemplation of his motionless float was little more than an excuse for the enjoyment of a fine evening. The westering sunlight threw golden, moted rays between trees resplendent with new leaf, and the wood was loud with birdsong. The smoke of Fawcett's pipe made a thin, blue column in the windless air. Yet when the sun left the wood and the shadows began to gather around the mouth of the tunnel it grew chilly and he went below. He cooked himself a liberal supper, wrote up the log for the day and then, with a sigh of contentment, turned in to his comfortable bunk. But for some unaccountable reason he was denied his customary sound sleep. After a fitful doze, during which he tossed and turned uneasily, he suddenly awoke to full consciousness, and the dawn was already breaking before he slept again. Two distracting sounds contributed to this wakefulness. One was a soft, recurrent thudding as though some resilient object, floating in the water, occasionally nudged the hull of the boat. The other was a faint but desolate wailing, rising and falling in mournful, irregular cadences and sounding, now close about the boat and now infinitely far off. It seemed to come from the direction of the tunnel, and though Fawcett could see through his cabin window a pattern of branches in motionless silhouette against the moonlight, he concluded it must be some trick of the wind blowing over the top of one of the ventilation shafts. With the aid of a boat-hook he might, he reflected, dispose of one of these disturbances at all events, yet for some reason he felt singularly disinclined to leave his bed. He excused himself upon the grounds that the night seemed to be remarkably cold for the time of the year.

The following day passed uneventfully. After his uncomfortable night, Fawcett slept late and consequently it was nearly noon when, breakfast disposed of, he set off for Cold Bosworth to replenish his stores at the village shop. On his return, he spent the rest of another glorious afternoon happily engaged upon the numerous small jobs which can always be found on a boat. Charles was due to return the following morning, and this was a good opportunity to get everything ship-shape before they continued their journey. Tomorrow there must be no lying late abed, so he turned in early, and this time fell almost immediately into a deep sleep.

Whether what followed was a dream or not must be left for the reader to judge. He suddenly found himself standing on the stern of the *Wildflower* and peering into the mouth of the tunnel. He had no idea why he was doing so or what he expected to see, for though the moon was bright the blackness of the tunnel was impenetrable. The night was calm and beautiful, the moon-silvered water reflecting dark arabesques of leaf and branch with mirror-like perfection. Yet somehow the whole scene seemed to have become charged with that sense of imminent terror which is the prelude of nightmare. Still he continued to stare wide-eyed into the blackness, seeing nothing and hearing only the hollow echoing plash of the water which dripped from the tunnel roof. But at length he perceived a thickening of the shadows beneath the curving abutment wall, and presently saw a figure, more shade than substance, move down to the margin to crouch and stare into the still water. It moved without sound, and only the face showed pale in the moonlight. For a time, the figure seemed to grope beside the water, and Fawcett knew, without knowing why he knew, that it sought for something which it feared to find. Then with a swift movement which suggested that it had been startled by some sound inaudible to Fawcett, the figure rose and turned to peer intently into the tunnel. It was at this moment that the feeling of ominous expectancy, which all this while had been gathering like a thunder-cloud in Fawcett's mind, suddenly assumed most hideous shape. Something rose out of the water; something monstrous that the reason most vehemently questioned, yet which possessed the semblance of human shape. Mercifully, it could not be clearly seen. The face, if face there was, seemed to be hidden by dark hair as by a veil, but the phosphorescence of corruption dimly suggested a nakedness of obscene distension. The dark watcher on the bank, with a gesture of despair, made to turn away, but stumbled. Upon the instant his fearful antagonist fell upon him with such lithe and intent purpose that the issue of the brief and soundless encounter was never in doubt, and soon the waters had closed over them both.

Now long before this, Fawcett should have awakened with a shout to find himself trembling and sweating in his bed. But he maintains that there was no awakening; that his fear gradually ebbed away until he realized that he was in truth shivering in his pyjamas on the aft deck of the *Wildflower*. I have little doubt that the physical and mental rigours of this experience were at least partly responsible for his early death, for there is no further entry in the log, and I conjecture that it was his friend Charles who took the *Wildflower* on to Horton Junction, where she lay until she was sold.

My recollection of Fawcett convinced me that he had experienced something more than a nightmare accompanied by a risky feat of somnambulism, and it was this conviction which took me to Cold Bosworth. I will not weary the reader with all the details of a search which took me from the lock-keeper at Canonshanger, through the dusty files of the *Marborough Messenger*, to the tomb in the churchyard to which I have already referred.

The lock-keeper at Canonshanger proved to be uncommunicative and sceptical, though he admitted that the summit pound east of the tunnel was said by the boatmen to be 'disturbed' and that on this account they would never tie up there.

Old Tom Okey at Bosworth locks, however, was more loquacious. 'They do say,' he vouchsafed, 'that summit be troubled by a chap what drownded hisself there a long time back,' and it was this observation which was really the starting-point of my research.

The story begins, not with 'the chap what drownded hisself', but with Mary Grimsden. She lived with her widowed mother in a small cottage, pulled down many years ago, which stood on common land on the fringe of Canonshanger woods. They appear to have been of gypsy stock, and Rebecca Grimsden is described as a herbalist. From this and other references I gather that she must have been a formidable old woman who, had she lived in an earlier period, might well have suffered death as a witch. It seems that Mary took after her mother, but this did not prevent young John Lofthouse from falling a victim to her dark good looks. The Lofthouses were substantial yeomen farmers who had held Coppice Farm for generations, so that it is easy to understand why the infatuation of their heir with a cottager of doubtful antecedents and dubious occupation soon set tongues wagging. Eventually, news of the affair reached the ears of his family, and the young man, who by this time may have realized the extent of his folly, undertook to see his Mary no more. Yet rumour hinted that the girl was with child by young John and that she intended by this means to retaliate against her faithless lover and his family. But from this embarrassing eventuality the family of Lofthouse were spared by an unforeseen and surprising circumstance. At dusk on a fine evening in the August of 1840, Mary Grimsden walked out of the little cottage at Canonshanger and never returned. Despite a most extensive search, no trace of her could be found, and though he had forsworn her, it was remarked that John Lofthouse appeared to be deeply affected by her loss. Though old Rebecca Grimsden persisted that she had been the victim of foul play, the village seems to have come to the conclusion that Mary's gypsy blood had got the better of her.

Hardly had the talk aroused by this affair died down when, in February of the following year, on the night of the fourteenth to be exact, it found fresh and startling matter in the disappearance of John Lofthouse. But this time the mystery was soon solved. A local boatman, who had delivered a cargo of lime for Coppice Farm and was working late down the Bosworth locks, claimed to have seen on the tow-path the figure of 'young mister John' walking swiftly and alone in the direction of the tunnel. Acting upon the strength of this evidence, it was decided to drag the canal beginning at the east portal of the tunnel. This led, almost immediately, to a discovery of a most shocking nature. For not only was the body of John Lofthouse recovered, but entangled with it in the grappling irons was another. Because the latter had been long dead, it was unrecognizable, nor was it possible to determine the cause of death. Death in such a form is never pleasant to behold, but this discovery seems to have had a singularly disconcerting effect upon the beholders.

Though the canal had been dragged without result at the time of Mary's disappearance, Rebecca Grimsden identified a ring recovered with the body as having belonged to her daughter. Had it not subsequently been confirmed by other more reliable witnesses, it is doubtful if this evidence of identification would have been admissible for, to judge from her conduct at the inquest, the old woman was out of her mind. Usually grim enough, there is a peculiar quality of the macabre about the account of the proceedings at this inquest. In the first place, when ordered to view the bodies of the deceased, the jury were so affected that proceedings had to be suspended for a time. When the hearing was eventually resumed, Rebecca Grimsden's interruptions made matters worse, for she seemed to be labouring under the ghastly illusion that she was attending her daughter's nuptials. Together with other singular observations, which are not recorded, she kept reiterating that she had fulfilled her promise to provide her daughter with a bridegroom, an assertion which proved so disquieting that the coroner was compelled to order her removal from the court.

Despite evidence that John Lofthouse had become increasingly morose since Mary Grimsden's disappearance, an open verdict was returned in both cases, perhaps in deference to the feelings of the young man's family. Yet why that family should have consented to the burial of their son in a common grave with a gypsy girl, and why they caused to be erected over it so curious a memorial is not explained. I have formed my own conclusion which I prefer not to discuss.

While we shall never know what occurred on that sultry August night so long ago when Mary Grimsden disappeared, I may mention in conclusion a discovery of my own which I consider significant. I was exploring the wood which gives Coppice Farm its name when I came across a circular wall of old brickwork, and, upon investigation, found that it protected the mouth of one of the ventilation shafts of Bosworth tunnel. The wall was not so high that an active man might not thereby rid himself of a heavy and unwelcome burden, and as I leant over the parapet I could hear, as from a well, the drip of water far below.

I returned in the gathering dusk of that winter evening past the east portal of the tunnel and along the towing-path. The water looked black and was very still under the shadow of the trees. Though I would assure the reader that I am not a credulous man, I have to admit that I felt disinclined to stop and look about me, but hurried on, keeping as far as possible from the water's edge, and must confess to a feeling of profound relief when I reached the lower level below the top lock.

An Encounter in the Mist

A. N. L. MUNBY

I am in the fortunate position of having a good deal of leisure. This, however, has its disadvantages. My family is a large one and has never been backward in calling upon my services, and if ever a trustee or an executor is required my name is the first that springs to mind. I assume this is because I have plenty of time on my hands, for I am hardly vain enough to think that I have any aptitude for worldly affairs. But whatever the cause, I not infrequently find myself clearing up the estates and going through the papers of some deceased relative, generally a dull and thankless task. The papers of my late maternal uncle Giles, who died in 1912, looked like proving no exception. He had achieved some small distinction as a geologist in the 'seventies of the last century—I believe his monograph on the fossils of the Middle Chalk was a standard text-book in its day. I had painstakingly arranged for the disposal of his belongings, and had managed to persuade the Natural History Museum at South Kensington to accept eleven large cabinets of geological specimens. His letters and papers I had removed to my flat, and was examining them at my leisure. They were copious and extremely uninteresting, and it was only by exercise of considerable will-power that I persevered to the end. I am exceedingly glad that I did so, for embedded in a diary recording the humdrum affairs of the year 1879 I came upon the narrative of an event unique even in my experience of uncommon events. Uncle Giles obviously appreciated the startling nature of what befell him, for he recorded the incidents in the greatest detail, as one would expect from a man of science. He confined himself, however, to the facts, and failed to comment upon them. The narrative below is reconstructed from the diary, and I have only omitted a number of passages of a geological nature and of no interest to the general reader.

In October 1879 Giles Hampton, then in his middle thirties, was spending a short holiday in Wales. A friend of his, Beverley by name, had recently retired from his business in Liverpool, and had built himself a house in Caernarvonshire, on a lower slope of the Snowdon range. His invitation to stay had been especially welcome as his house was an admirable centre for a number of geological excursions. Giles arrived at Fablan Fawr, as the property was called, on the evening of October 10th. The house was extremely comfortable by the standards of the 'seventies—it possessed, in fact, one of the first bathrooms to be installed in the county. Although its architecture would hardly satisfy modern taste, my uncle waxed enthusiastic over its noble yellow-brick turrets commanding the valley below. It was certainly placed in a splendid setting right at the head of a re-entrant in the hills. From the terrace in front of it one looked down over the Conway Valley, while immediately behind it the mountains proper began; the crest of the range being about seven miles away.

The house lay at the upper extremity of the cultivated zone, and a few hundred yards from the garden began the rocky heather-covered slopes of the hillside.

The weather was good, and for the first week of his stay Giles accompanied Beverley on a number of excursions—on two days they shot, and on others they visited various neighbours and beauty spots in the district. His diary begins to reflect a fear that his social activities will prevent him from making the geological expeditions he had planned. On October 18th, however, his host had business to transact in the local market-town, and Giles took the opportunity to make an all-day excursion to some large slate quarries which lay some ten miles away on the far side of the range of hills. The sky was overcast but gave promise of improvement later when Giles set off after an early breakfast. In his haversack were his luncheon and his geological hammers, and he had received from the groom a minute description of the best route to follow across the range.

It is a commonplace that a journey in hills takes longer than one anticipates, and it was after twelve o'clock when Giles reached his destination. The sun had come out and he was hot and tired, though much encouraged by the interest of the quarries he had come to see. So absorbing did he find them, and so full were the notes he took, that it was not until half-past three that he started on the return journey. By this time the sun had clouded over again and it looked like rain. As he reascended the track into the hills a fine drizzle began to fall which increased as he reached the higher altitudes, and before he had climbed to the crest he was enveloped in a thick mist, which reduced visibility first to a few yards and finally to a few feet only. My uncle had carefully noted various landmarks on his path, and even in the mist was confident of keeping to the right track. The route, however, was ill-defined, being in places little more than a sheep track, and when Giles found himself crossing an unfamiliar stream, he had to confess that he had strayed from the correct path. He retraced his footsteps for nearly half a mile, but failed to return to a point he had noted where the track ran between two prominent rocks. Then indeed he realised that he was lost in earnest.

He sat down for a few moments to consider his position. It was not the prospective discomfort of a night on the hillside that alarmed him, but the certainty that Beverley must be seriously upset by his non-appearance. Above all, he hated making a nuisance of himself. He pictured the assembling of a search party from every cottage on the estate and the upheaval in the well-ordered existence of his host. With this in mind one can appreciate how relieved he was to hear the sound of a dog's bark and footsteps in the mist on the hillside above him—footsteps interspersed with the tapping of a stick. He shouted and a voice in Welsh answered him. From out of the mist came the figure of an old man, with a great collie at his heels. Although old, he bore himself well. He wore a cloak of some dark material which reached to his ankles, but was bareheaded. His hair, which was long and white, framed a red wrinkled face which radiated kindliness and benevolence. He spoke again in Welsh, and when Giles, by his gestures, showed him that he could not understand he smiled reassuringly. Giles indicated that he was lost, which was indeed pretty obvious, and repeated three or four times the name of his friend's estate, Fablan Fawr. The old man smiled again and nodded vigorously; then plunging his hand into the fold of his cloak he brought out a map, which he spread on a stone before him. Beverley's newly built house was not, of course, marked upon it, but it showed clearly the church situated a few hundred yards below it. With a gnarled forefinger the stranger indicated on the map the spot at which they were standing and then traced slowly the track Giles must follow to reach his destination. This he did three times, making sure that my uncle thoroughly understood the route. Then refolding the map, he pressed it into his hearer's hands. Giles tried to refuse the gift, but the old man only laughed and nodded. So thanking him profusely, the lost wayfarer set out along the route he had been shown. Having gone a few yards, he turned and saw the figure standing, dimly discernible in the mist and gathering dusk, watching him. He waved his hand in farewell, took another few steps, and when he next looked round, his guide was invisible.

Giles travelled rapidly to make up for lost time. The mist if anything had become thicker, but the track which he was following was well marked, and by constant reference to the map he made good progress and had soon crossed the ridge and was glad to find himself on the down grade once more. Here the path followed what seemed to be a dry stream-bed, which led him down the hillside at a steep, almost a precipitous angle. With the visibility at only a few feet, it required to be taken cautiously. Suddenly my uncle missed his footing and stumbled— a mishap which in all probability saved his life. In his fall he dislodged a small round rock, which rolled quickly away from him—he heard it gather momentum and go clattering over a few yards of the track; then the sound ceased. Several seconds later he head a crash, hundreds of feet below. The path had led him to the very brink of a sheer drop. Giles experimented with a further stone, with the same result: he looked again at his map, but there could be no mistake; he was sure that he had followed explicitly the course indicated to him. For the first time he became seriously alarmed. He realised the folly of any further move, and sat disconsolately on a boulder. There was nothing for it but to wait and hope that the mist would clear, he thought, and lit his pipe.

It was perhaps an hour later that he heard faint shouts on the hillside below, shouts which he answered with all the power of his lungs. Gradually the voices came nearer and he recognised that of Beverley's coachman. He and the groom had become alarmed for the safety of the guest and had set out to find him. Beverley himself had not yet returned home, for which Giles was profoundly thankful. The two servants escorted my uncle along the top of the cliff to a point where they rejoined the path down to the house, and in not much more than an hour he was changing his wet clothes none the worse for his adventure. Something prompted him to say nothing of his strange encounter on the hillside to his rescuers, nor did he mention this part of the story to his host at dinner-time. He told him, however, that he had strayed in the mist and had found himself on the edge of the cliff.

'You had a damned lucky escape,' said Beverley. 'There have been some nasty accidents in these hills. There was a man killed about four years ago, just before I came here. I believe he was found at the foot of the very cliff where you nearly came to grief.' He turned to the butler. 'You'd remember it, Parry,' he said; 'wasn't that the place?'

'Indeed it was, sir,' replied the butler; 'a gentleman from London he was and buried in the churchyard of the village here. I was in service with Captain Trefor the Fron that time, and he gave us the afternoon off for the funeral. The Reverend Roberts buried him—powerful in prayer he was that day. I've kept a piece from the paper till today—from the *Caernarfon and District Advertiser*. I'll fetch it, if you like, sir.' Beverley assented, and after a few minutes the butler returned with a newspaper cutting. Beverley and my uncle read the trite phrases of the local journalist, dated June 6th, 1875.

'Early on Wednesday morning last the body of a young man was found at the foot of the cliffs near Adwy-yr-Eryron pass, examination of which revealed that the deceased had been dead for some hours. The remains have been identified as being those of John Stephenson, a young legal gentleman of London, who was visiting Llanberis on holiday, and who had set forth on Tuesday morning to explore the splendours of our Cambrian fastness and did not return that night. Wilson Jones, Esq., MP, with the public spirit which characterises his every action, organised a search party, but their efforts were hampered by the inclemency of the elements. It would appear that the deceased wandered from his path in the mist, plunged over the precipice into oblivion, and was thus cut off in his prime. A member of the party who made the sad discovery has informed our correspondent that the unhappy wayfarer had in his possession a long-obsolete map of the hills, upon which was marked the disused track across the ridge, rendered dangerous by the great landslide of 1852, which carried away whole sections of the path, a cataclysmic occurrence that can still be remembered by some of the older members of the community. The use of such a map must be regarded as contributory cause of the catastrophe. Let the future explorers of our barren hills take heed from the sad demise of this young person, and recall the solemn thought, applicable alike to those of high and low degree, that in the midst of life we are in death. A modern, accurate and well-engraved folding map of the area (mounted on linen, with panorama, 1s. 6d.; on paper without panorama, 9d.) can be obtained from the offices of our journal.'

The reference to the obsolete map found on the body excited considerable speculation in my uncle's brain. The coincidence was really too extraordinary to keep to himself and he felt impelled to tell his host the whole story. Beverley was deeply interested. 'Do you remember anything about a map, Parry?' he asked, addressing the butler again.

'Indeed I do, sir,' replied the butler, 'Very old-fashioned it was. The Reverend Roberts has it down at the Vicarage.'

'In that case,' said Beverley, 'would you send down to Mr Roberts, give him my compliments, and ask if it would be convenient for him to come and drink his coffee with us. And ask him if he would be kind enough to bring the map with him.'

The servant hurried off to do his bidding. 'The map given to me is in my pocket,' said Giles. 'I'll go and get it.' He fetched it and having spread it on the table, the two men pored over it. In the mist my uncle had noticed nothing odd about it, but in the brightly lit dining-room it had a very unusual aspect. The engraving had a rude archaic look, the lettering of the place names employed the long 's' and the paper was yellow with age. It was Beverley who first noted the inscription at the foot, engraved in a neat copperplate script—'Madog ap Rhys, 1707.'

The arrival of the vicar put an end to their expressions of surprise and incredulity. He listened with the greatest attention to my uncle's tale and produced from his pocket the duplicate of the map that lay on the table. 'I've always been puzzled how such a map came to be upon the body,' he said. 'It's a very rare piece of engraving. The only other example I know is in the National Library of Wales.'

'And who was Madog ap Rhys?' asked Giles.

'He was a hermit,' replied the vicar, 'who lived up on the hillside. I can show you the remains of his cell. He died in 1720. In those days they were working the lead down in Cwm Cadfan, and the ridge was crossed a great deal more frequently than it is now. Madog ap Rhys made it his special care to seek out lost travellers and guide them to safety, and whenever the mist was down he would wander along the range with his dog. He drew out and had engraved the map which we have before us, to present to wayfarers who had missed their path. There is a local superstition that he is still to be seen on the hillside, but I must confess that until today I have never taken it very seriously.'

Such is the story of my uncle Giles's adventure, and I trust that the reader will agree with me as to its unique quality. Malevolent spirits who lead travellers to their death are common to the folklore of all nations and all periods, but in a very different category is this case of the ghost of a benevolent hermit, who revisited the scene of his former acts of kindness and, with the best intentions in the world, inadvertently sent unsuspecting wanderers to their destruction.

Hand in Glove

ELIZABETH BOWEN

—

Jasmine Lodge was favourably set on a residential, prettily-wooded hillside in the south of Ireland, overlooking a river and, still better, the roofs of a lively garrison town. Around 1904, which was the flowering period of the Miss Trevors, girls could not have had a more auspicious home—the neighbourhood spun merrily round the military. Ethel and Elsie, a spirited pair, garnered the full advantage—no ball, hop, picnic, lawn tennis, croquet or boating party was complete without them; in winter, though they could not afford to hunt, they trimly bicycled to all meets, and on frosty evenings, with their guitars, set off to *soirées*, snug inside their cab in their fur-tipped capes.

They possessed an aunt, a Mrs Varley, *née* Elysia Trevor, a formerly notable local belle, who, drawn back again in her widowhood to what had been the scene of her early triumphs, occupied a back bedroom in Jasmine Lodge. Mrs Varley de Grey had had no luck: her splashing match, in its time the talk of two kingdoms, had ended up in disaster—the well-born captain in a cavalry regiment having gone so far as to blow out his brains in India, leaving behind him nothing but her and debts. Mrs Varley de Grey had returned from India with nothing but seven large trunks crammed with recent finery; and she also had been impaired by shock. This had taken place while Ethel and Elsie, whose father had married late, were still unborn—so it was that, for as long as the girls recalled, their aunt had been the sole drawback to Jasmine Lodge. Their parents had orphaned them, somewhat thoughtlessly, by simultaneously dying of scarlet fever when Ethel was just out and Elsie soon to be—they were therefore left lacking a chaperone and, with their gift for putting everything to some use, propped the aunt up in order that she might play that role. Only when her peculiarities became too marked did they feel it necessary to withdraw her: by that time, however, all the surrounding ladies could be said to compete for the honour of taking into society the sought-after Miss Trevors. From then on, no more was seen or heard of Mrs Varley de Grey. ('Oh, just a trifle unwell, but nothing much!') She remained upstairs, at the back: when the girls were giving one of their little parties, or a couple of officers came to call, the key of her room would be turned in the outer lock.

The girls hung Chinese lanterns from the creepered veranda, and would sit lightly strumming on their guitars. Not less fascinating was their badinage, accompanied by a daring flash of the eyes. They were known as the clever Miss Trevors, not because of any taint of dogmatism or book-learning—no, when a gentleman cried, 'Those girls have brains!' he meant it wholly in admiration—but because of their accomplishments, ingenuity and agility. They took leading parts in theatricals, lent spirit to numbers of drawing-room games, were naughty mimics, and sang duets. Nor did their fingers lag behind their wits—they constructed lampshades, crêpe paper flowers and picturesque hats; and, above all, varied their dresses marvellously—no one could beat them for ideas, nipping, slashing or fitting. Once more allowing nothing to go to waste, they had remodelled the trousseau out of their aunt's trunks, causing sad old tulles and tarlatans, satins and *moiré* taffetas, to appear to have come from Paris only today. They re-stitched spangles, pressed ruffles crisp, and revived many a corsage of squashed silk roses. They went somewhat softly about that task, for the trunks were all stored in the attic immediately over the back room.

They wore their clothes well. 'A pin on either of those two would look smart!' declared other girls. All that they were short of was evening gloves—they had two pairs each, which they had been compelled to buy. *What* could have become of Mrs Varley de Grey's presumably sumptuous numbers of this item, they were unable to fathom, and it was too bad. Had gloves been overlooked in her rush from India?—or, were they here, in that *one* trunk the Trevors could not get at? All other locks had yielded to pulls or pickings, or the sisters found keys to fit them, or they had used the tool-box; but this last stronghold defied them. In that sad little soiled silk sack, always on her person, Mrs Varley de Grey, they became convinced, hoarded the operative keys, along with some frippery rings and brooches—all true emeralds, pearls and diamonds having been long ago, as they knew, sold. Such contrariety on their aunt's part irked them—meanwhile, gaieties bore hard on their existing gloves. Last thing at nights when they came in, last thing in the evenings before they went out, they would manfully dab away at the fingertips. So, it must be admitted that a long whiff of benzine pursued them as they whirled round the ballroom floor.

They were tall and handsome—nothing so soft as pretty, but in those days it was a vocation to be a handsome girl; many of the best marriages had been made by such. They carried themselves imposingly, had good busts and shoulders, waists firm under the whalebone, and straight backs. Their features were striking, their colouring high; low on their foreheads bounced dark mops of curls. Ethel was, perhaps, the dominant one, but both girls were pronounced to be full of character.

Whom, and still more when, did they mean to marry? They had already seen regiments out and in; for quite a number of years, it began to seem, bets in the neighbourhood had been running high. Sympathetic spy-glasses were trained on the conspicuous gateway to Jasmine Lodge; each new cavalier was noted. The only trouble might be, their promoters claimed, that the clever Trevors were always so surrounded they they had not a moment in which to turn or choose. Or otherwise, could it possibly be that the admiration aroused by Ethel and Elsie, and their now institutional place in the local scene, scared out more tender feeling from the masculine breast? It came to be felt, and perhaps by the girls themselves, that, having lingered so long and so puzzlingly, it was up to them to bring off (like their aunt) a *coup*. Society around this garrison town had long plumed itself upon its romantic record; summer and winter, Cupid shot his darts. Lush scenery, the oblivion of all things else bred by the steamy climate, and perpetual gallivanting—all were conducive. Ethel's and Elsie's names, it could be presumed, were by now murmured wherever the Union Jack flew. Nevertheless, it was time they should decide.

Ethel's decision took place late one spring. She set her cap at the second son of an English marquess. Lord Fred had come on a visit, for the fishing, to a mansion some miles down the river from Jasmine Lodge. He first made his appearance, with the rest of the house party, at one of the more resplendent military balls, and was understood to be a man-about-town. The civilian glint of his pince-nez, at once serene and superb, instantaneously wrought, with his great name, on Ethel's heart. She beheld him, and the assembled audience, with approbation, looked on at the moment so big with fate. The truth, it appeared in a flash, was that Ethel, though so condescending with her charms, had not from the first been destined to love a soldier; and that here, after long attrition, her answer was. Lord Fred was, by all, at once signed over to her. For his part, he responded to her attentions quite gladly, though in a somewhat dazed way. If he did not so often dance with her—indeed, how could he, for she was much besought?—he could at least be perceived to gaze. At a swiftly organized river picnic, the next evening, he by consent fell to Ethel's lot—she had spent the foregoing morning snipping and tacking at a remaining muslin of Mrs Varley de Grey's, a very fresh forget-me-not-dotted pattern. The muslin did not survive the evening out, for when the moon should have risen, rain poured into the boats. Ethel's good-humoured drollery carried all before it, and Lord Fred wrapped his blazer around her form.

Next day, more rain; and all felt flat. At Jasmine Lodge, the expectant deck chairs had to be hurried in from the garden, and the small close rooms, with their greeneried windows and plentiful bric-à-brac, gave out a stuffy, resentful, indoor smell. The maid was out; Elsie was lying down with a migraine; so it devolved on Ethel to carry up Mrs Varley de Grey's tea—the invalid set very great store by tea, and her manifestations by door rattlings, sobs and mutters were apt to become disturbing if it did not appear. Ethel, with the not particularly dainty tray, accordingly entered the back room, this afternoon rendered dark by its outlook into a dripping uphill wood. The aunt, her visage draped in a cobweb shawl, was as usual sitting up in bed. '*Aha*,' she at once cried, screwing one eye up and glittering round at Ethel with the other, 'so what's all this in the wind today?'

Ethel, as she lodged the meal on the bed, shrugged her shoulders, saying: 'I'm in a hurry.'

'No doubt you are. The question is, will you get him?'

'Oh, drink your tea!' snapped Ethel, her colour rising.

The old wretch responded by popping a lump of sugar into her cheek, and sucking at it while she fixed her wink on her niece. She then observed: '*I* could tell you a thing or two!'

'We've had enough of *your* fabrications, Auntie.'

'Fabrications!' croaked Mrs Varley de Grey. 'And who's been the fabricator, I'd like to ask? Who's so nifty with the scissors and needle? Who's been going a-hunting in my clothes?'

'Oh, what a fib!' exclaimed Ethel, turning her eyes up. 'Those old musty miserable bundles of things of yours—would Elsie or I consider laying a finger on them?'

Mrs Varley de Grey replied, as she sometimes did, by heaving up and throwing the tray at Ethel. Nought, therefore, but cast-off kitchen china nowadays was ever exposed to risk; and the young woman, not trying to gather the debris up, statuesquely, thoughtfully stood with her arms folded, watching tea steam rise from the carpet. Today, the effort required seemed to have been too much for Aunt Elysia, who collapsed on her pillows, faintly blue in the face. 'Rats in the attic,' she muttered. '*I've* heard them, rats in the attic! Now where's my tea?'

'You've had it,' said Ethel, turning to leave the room. However, she paused to study a photograph in a tarnished, elaborate silver frame. 'Really quite an Adonis, poor Uncle Harry.—From the first glance, you say, he never looked back?'

'My lovely tea,' said her aunt, beginning to sob.

As Ethel slowly put down the photograph, her eyes could be seen to calculate, her mouth hardened and a reflective cast came over her brow.

Step by step, once more she approached the bed, and, as she did so, altered her tune. She suggested, in a beguiling tone: 'You said you could tell me a thing or two . . . ?'

Time went on; Lord Fred, though forever promising, still failed to come quite within Ethel's grasp. Ground gained one hour seemed to be lost the next—it seemed, for example, that things went better for Ethel in the afternoons, in the open air, than at the dressier evening functions. It was when she swept down on him in full plumage that Lord Fred seemed to contract. Could it be that he feared his passions?—she hardly thought so. Or, did her complexion not light up well? When there was a question of dancing, he came so late that her programme already was black with other names, whereupon he would heave a gallant sigh. When they did take the floor together, he held her so far at arm's length, and with his face turned so far away, that when she wished to address him she had to shout—she told herself this must be the London style, but it piqued her, naturally. Next morning, all would be as it was before, with nobody so completely assiduous as Lord Fred—but, through it all, he still never came to the point. And worse, the days of his visit were running out; he would soon be back in the heart of the London Season. 'Will you ever get him, Ethel, now, do you think?' Elsie asked, with trying solicitude, and no doubt the neighbourhood wondered also.

She conjured up all her fascinations. But was something further needed, to do the trick?

It was now that she began to frequent her aunt.

In that dank little back room looking into the hill, proud Ethel humbled herself, to prise out the secret. Sessions were close and long. Elsie, in mystification outside the door, heard the dotty voice of their relative rising, falling, with, now and then, blood-curdling little knowing laughs. Mrs Varley de Grey was back in the golden days. Always, though, of a sudden it would break off, drop back into pleas, whimpers and jagged breathing. No doctor, though she constantly asked for one, had for years been allowed to visit Mrs Varley de Grey—the girls saw no reason for that expense, or for the interference which might follow. Aunt's affliction, they swore, was confined to the head; all she required was quiet, and that she got. Knowing, however, how gossip spreads, they would let no servant near her for more than a minute or two, and then with one of themselves on watch at the door. They had much to bear from the foetid state of her room.

'You don't think you'll kill her, Ethel?' the out-of-it Elsie asked. 'Forever sitting on top of her, as you now do. Can it be healthy, egging her on to talk? What's this attraction, all of a sudden?—whatever's this which has sprung up between you two? She and you are becoming quite hand-in-glove.'

Elsie merely remarked this, and soon forgot: she had her own fish to fry. It was Ethel who had cause to recall the words—for, the afternoon of the very day they were spoken, Aunt Elysia whizzed off on another track, screamed for what was impossible and, upon being thwarted, went into a seizure unknown before. The worst of it was, at the outset her mind cleared—she pushed her shawl back, reared up her unkempt grey head and looked at Ethel, unblinkingly studied Ethel, with a lucid accumulation of years of hate. 'You fool of a gawk,' she said, and with such contempt! 'Coming running to me to know how to trap a man. Could *you* learn, if it was from Venus herself? Wait till I show you beauty.—Bring down those trunks!'

'Oh, Auntie.'

'Bring them down, I say. I'm about to dress myself up.'

'Oh, but I cannot; they're heavy; I'm single-handed.'

'Heavy?—they came here heavy. But there've been rats in the attic.— *I* saw you, swishing downstairs in my *eau-de-nil*!'

'Oh, you dreamed that!'

'Through the crack of the door.—Let me up, then. Let us go where they are, and look—we shall soon see!' Aunt Elysia threw back the bedclothes and began to get up. 'Let's take a look,' she said, 'at the rats' work.' She set out to totter towards the door.

'Oh, but you're not fit!' Ethel protested.

'And when did a doctor say so?' There was a swaying: Ethel caught her in time and, not gently, lugged her back to the bed—and Ethel's mind the whole of this time was whirling, for tonight was the night upon which all hung. Lord Fred's last local appearance was to be, like his first, at a ball: tomorrow he left for London. So it must be tonight, at this ball, or never! How was it that Ethel felt so strangely, wildly confident of the outcome? It was time to begin on her coiffure, lay out her dress. Oh, tonight she would shine as never before! She flung back the bedclothes over the helpless form, heard a clock strike, and hastily turned to go.

'I will be quits with you,' said the voice behind her.

Ethel, in a kimono, hair half done, was in her own room, in front of the open glove drawer, when Elsie came in—home from a tennis party. Elsie acted oddly; she went at once to the drawer and buried her nose in it. 'Oh, my goodness,' she cried, 'it's all too true, and it's awful!'

'What is?' Ethel carelessly asked.

'Ethel dear, would you ever face it out if I were to tell you a certain rumour I heard today at the party as to Lord Fred?'

Ethel turned from her sister, took up the heated tongs and applied more crimps to her natural curliness. She said: 'Certainly; spit it out.'

'Since childhood, he's recoiled from the breath of benzine. He wilts away when it enters the very room!'

'Who says that's so?'

'He confided it to his hostess, who is now spitefully putting it around the country.'

Ethel bit her lip and put down the tongs, while Elsie sorrowfully concluded: 'And your gloves stink, Ethel, as I'm sure do mine.' Elsie then thought it wiser to slip away.

In a minute more, however, she was back, and this time with a still more peculiar air. She demanded: 'In what state did you leave Auntie? She was sounding so very quiet that I peeped in, and I don't care for the looks of her now at all!' Ethel swore, but consented to take a look. She stayed in there in the back room, with Elsie biting her thumb-nail outside the door, for what seemed an ominous length of time—when she did emerge, she looked greenish, but held her head high. The sisters' eyes met. Ethel said, stonily: 'Dozing.'

'You're certain she's *not* . . . ? She *couldn't* ever be—you know?'

'Dozing, I tell you.' Ethel stared Elsie out.

'If she *was* gone,' quavered the frailer sister, 'just think of it—why, we'd never get to the ball!—And a ball that everything hangs on,' she ended up, with a scared but conspiratorial glance at Ethel.

'Reassure yourself. Didn't you hear me say?'

As she spoke Ethel, chiefly from habit, locked her late aunt's door on the outside. The act caused a sort of secret jingle to be heard from inside her fist, and Elsie asked: 'What's that you've got hold of, now?' 'Just a few little keys and trinkets she made me keep,' replied Ethel, disclosing the small bag she had found where she'd looked for it, under the dead one's pillow. 'Scurry on now, Elsie, or you'll never be dressed. Care to make use of my tongs, while they're so splendidly hot?'

Alone at last, Ethel drew in a breath, and, with a gesture of resolution, retied her kimono sash tightly over her corset. She shook the key from the bag and regarded it, murmuring, 'Providential!', then gave a glance upward, towards where the attics were. The late spring sun had set, but an apricot afterglow, not unlike the light cast by a Chinese lantern, crept through the upper storey of Jasmine Lodge. The cessation of all those rustlings, tappings, whimpers and moans from inside Mrs Varley de Grey's room had set up an unfamiliar, somewhat unnerving hush. Not till a whiff of singeing hair announced that Elsie was well employed did Ethel set out on the quest which held all her hopes. Success was imperative—she *must* have gloves. Gloves, gloves . . .

Soundlessly, she set foot on the attic stairs.

Under the skylight, she had to suppress a shriek, for a rat—yes, of all things!—leaped at her out of an empty hatbox; and the rodent gave her a wink before it darted away. Now Ethel and Elsie knew for a certain fact that there never *had* been rats in Jasmine Lodge. However, she continued to steel her nerves, and to push her way to the one inviolate trunk.

All Mrs Varley de Grey's other Indian luggage gaped and yawned at Ethel, void, showing its linings, on end or toppling, forming a barricade around the object of her search—she pushed, pitched and pulled, scowling as the dust flew into her hair. But the last trunk, when it came into view and reach, still had something select and bridal about it: on top, the initials E. V. de G. stared out, quite luminous in a frightening way—for indeed how dusky the attic was! Shadows not only multiplied in the corners but seemed to finger their way up the sloping roof. Silence pierced up through the floor from the room below—and, worst, Ethel had the sensation of being watched by that pair of fixed eyes she had not stayed to close. She glanced this way, that way, backward over her shoulder. But, Lord Fred was at stake!—she knelt down and got to work with the key.

This trunk had two neat brass locks, one left, one right, along the front of the lid. Ethel, after fumbling, opened the first—then, so great was her hurry to know what might be within that she could not wait but slipped her hand in under the lifted corner. She pulled out one pricelessly lacy tip of what must be a bride-veil, and gave a quick laugh— must not this be an omen? She pulled again, but the stuff resisted, almost as though it were being grasped from inside the trunk—she let go, and either her eyes deceived her or the lace began to be drawn back slowly, in again, inch by inch. What was odder was, that the spotless fingertip of a white kid glove appeared for a moment, as though exploring its way out, then withdrew.

Ethel's heart stood still—but she turned to the other lock. Was a giddy attack overcoming her?—for, as she gazed, the entire lid of the trunk seemed to bulge upward, heave and strain, so that the E. V. de G. upon it rippled.

Untouched by the key in her trembling hand, the second lock tore itself open.

She recoiled, while the lid slowly rose—of its own accord.

She should have fled. But oh, how she craved what lay there exposed!—layer upon layer, wrapped in transparent paper, of elbow-length, magnolia-pure white gloves, bedded on the inert folds of the veil. 'Lord Fred,' thought Ethel, 'now you're within my grasp!'

That was her last thought, nor was the grasp to be hers. Down on her knees again, breathless with lust and joy, Ethel flung herself forward on to that sea of kid, scrabbling and seizing. The glove she had seen before was now, however, readier for its purpose. At first it merely pounced after Ethel's fingers, as though making mock of their greedy course; but the hand within it was all the time filling out . . . With one snowy flash through the dusk, the glove clutched Ethel's front hair, tangled itself in her black curls and dragged her head down. She began to choke among the sachets and tissue—then the glove let go, hurled her back, and made its leap at her throat.

It was a marvel that anything so dainty should be so strong. So great, so convulsive was the swell of the force that, during the strangling of Ethel, the seams of the glove split.

In any case, the glove would have been too small for her.

The shrieks of Elsie, upon the attic threshold, began only when all other sounds had died down . . . The ultimate spark of the once-famous cleverness of the Miss Trevors appeared in Elsie's extrication of herself from this awkward mess—for, who was to credit how Ethel came by her end? The sisters' reputation for warmth of heart was to stand the survivor in good stead—for, could those affections nursed in Jasmine Lodge, extending so freely even to the unwell aunt, have culminated in Elsie's setting on Ethel? No. In the end, the matter was hushed up—which is to say, is still talked about even now. Ethel Trevor and Mrs Varley de Grey were interred in the same grave, as everyone understood that they would have wished. What conversation took place under the earth, one does not know.

A Story of Don Juan

V. S. PRITCHETT

—

It is said that on one night of his life Don Juan slept alone, though I think the point has been disputed. Returning to Seville in the spring he was held up, some hours' ride from the city, by the floods of the Quadalquiver, a river as dirty as an old lion after the rains, and was obliged to stay at the *finca* of the Quintero family. The doorway, the walls, the windows of the house were hung with the black and violet draperies of mourning when he arrived there. God rest her soul (the peasants said), the lady of the house was dead. She had been dead a year. The young Quintero was a widower. Nevertheless Quintero took him in and even smiled to see a gallant spattered and drooping in the rain like a sodden cockerel. There was malice in that smile, for Quintero was mad with loneliness and grief; the man who had possessed and discarded all women, was received by a man demented because he had lost only one.

'My house is yours,' said Quintero, speaking the formula. There was bewilderment in his eyes; those who grieve do not find the world and its people either real or believable. Irony inflects the voices of mourners, and there was malice, too, in Quintero's further greetings; for grief appears to put one at an advantage, the advantage (in Quintero's case) being the macabre one that he could receive Juan now without that fear, that terror which Juan brought to the husbands of Seville. It was perfect, Quintero thought, that for once in his life Juan should have arrived at an empty house.

There was not even (as Juan quickly ascertained) a maid, for Quintero was served only by a manservant, being unable any longer to bear the sight of women. This servant dried Don Juan's clothes and in an hour or two brought in a bad dinner, food which stamped up and down in the stomach like people waiting for a coach in the cold. Quintero was torturing his body as well as his mind, and as the familiar pains arrived they agonized him and set him off about his wife. Grief had also made Quintero an actor. His eyes had that hollow, taper-haunted dusk of the theatre as he spoke of the beautiful girl. He dwelled upon their courtship, on details of her beauty and temperament, and how he had rushed her from the church to the marriage bed like a man racing a tray of diamonds through the streets into the safety of a bank vault. The presence of Don Juan turned every man into an artist when he was telling his own love story—one had to tantalize and surpass the great seducer—and Quintero, rolling it all off in the grand manner, could not resist telling that his bride had died on her marriage night.

'Man!' cried Don Juan. He started straight off on stories of his own. But Quintero hardly listened; he had returned to the state of exhaustion and emptiness which is natural to grief. As Juan talked, the madman followed his own thoughts like an actor preparing and mumbling the next entrance; and the thought he had had when Juan had first appeared at his door returned to him: that Juan must be a monster to make a man feel triumphant that his own wife was dead. Half-listening, and indigestion aiding, Quintero felt within himself the total hatred of all the husbands of Seville for this diabolical man. And as Quintero brooded upon this it occurred to him that it was probably not a chance that he had it in his power to effect the most curious revenge on behalf of the husbands of Seville.

The decision was made. The wine being finished Quintero called for his manservant and gave orders to change Don Juan's room.

'For,' said Quintero drily, 'his Excellency's visit is an honour and I cannot allow one who has slept in the most delicately scented room in Spain to pass the night in a chamber which stinks to heaven of goat.'

'The closed room?' said the manservant, astonished that the room which still held the great dynastic marriage bed and which had not been used more than half a dozen times by his master since the lady's death—and then only at the full moon when his frenzy was worst—was to be given to a stranger.

Yet to this room Quintero led his guest and there parted from him with eyes so sparkling with ill-intention that Juan, who was sensitive to this kind of point, understood perfectly that the cat was being let into the cage only because the bird had long ago flown out. The humiliation was unpleasant. Juan saw the night stretching before him like a desert.

What a bed to lie in: so wide, so unutterably vacant, so malignantly inopportune! Juan took off his clothes, snuffed the lamp wick. He lay down conscious that on either side of him lay wastes of sheet, draughty and uninhabited except by the nomadic bug. A desert. To move an arm one inch to the side, to push out a leg, however cautiously, was to enter desolation. For miles and miles the foot might probe, the fingers or the knee explore a friendless Antarctica. Yet to lie rigid and still was to have a foretaste of the grave. And here, too, he was frustrated: for though the wine kept him yawning, that awful food romped in his stomach, jolting him back from the edge of sleep the moment he got there.

There is an art in sleeping alone in a double bed but, naturally, this art was unknown to Juan; he had to learn it. The difficulty is easily solved. If you cannot sleep on one side of the bed, you move over and try the other. Two hours or more must have passed before this occurred to Juan. Sullen-headed he advanced into the desert and the night air lying chill between the sheets flapped, and made him shiver. He stretched out his arm and crawled towards the opposite pillow. Mother of God, the coldness, the more than virgin frigidity of linen! Juan put down his head and, drawing up his knees, he shivered. Soon, he supposed, he would be warm again, but in the meantime, ice could not have been colder. It was unbelievable.

Ice was the word for that pillow and those sheets. Ice. Was he ill? Had the rain chilled him that his teeth must chatter like this and his legs tremble? Far from getting warmer he found the cold growing. Now it was on his forehead and his cheeks, like arms of ice on his body, like legs of ice upon his legs. Suddenly in superstition he got up on his hands and stared down at the pillow in the darkness, threw back the bed-clothes and looked down upon the sheet; his breath was hot, yet blowing against his cheeks was a breath colder than the grave, his shoulders and body were hot, yet limbs of snow were drawing him down; and just as he would have shouted his appalled suspicion, lips like wet ice unfolded upon his own and he sank down to a kiss, unmistakably a kiss, which froze him like a winter.

In his own room Quintero lay listening. His mad eyes were exalted and his ears were waiting. He was waiting for the scream of horror. He knew the apparition. There would be a scream, a tumble, hands fighting for the light, fists knocking at the door. And Quintero had locked the door. But when no scream came, Quintero lay talking to himself, remembering the night the apparition had first come to him and had made him speechless and left him choked and stiff. It would be even better if there were no scream! Quintero lay awake through the night building castle after castle of triumphant revenge and receiving, as he did so, the ovations of the husbands of Seville. 'The stallion is gelded!' At an early hour Quintero unlocked the door and waited downstairs impatiently. He was a wreck after a night like that.

Juan came down at last. He was (Quintero observed) pale. Or was he pale?

'Did you sleep well?' Quintero asked furtively.

'Very well,' Juan replied.

'I do not sleep well in strange beds myself,' Quintero insinuated. Juan smiled and replied that he was more used to strange beds than his own. Quintero scowled.

'I reproach myself: the bed was large,' he said. But the large, Juan said, were necessarily as familiar to him as the strange. Quintero bit his nails. Some noise had been heard in the night—something like a scream, a disturbance. The manservant had noticed it also. Juan answered him that disturbances in the night had indeed bothered him at the beginning of his career, but now he took them in his stride. Quintero dug his nails into the palms of his hands. He brought out the trump.

'I am afraid,' Quintero said, 'it was a cold bed. You must have *frozen*.'

'I am never cold for long,' Juan said, and, unconsciously anticipating the manner of a poem that was to be written in his memory two centuries later, declaimed: 'The blood of Don Juan is hot, for the sun is the blood of Don Juan.'

Quintero watched. His eyes jumped like flies to every movement of his guest. He watched him drink his coffee. He watched him tighten the stirrups of his horse. He watched Juan vault into the saddle. Don Juan was humming and when he went off was singing, was singing in that intolerable tenor of his which was like a cock crow in the olive groves.

Quintero went into the house and rubbed his unshaven chin. Then he went out again to the road where the figure of Don Juan was now only a small smoke of dust between the eucalyptus trees. Quintero went up to the room where Juan had slept and stared at it with accusations and suspicions. He called the manservant.

'I shall sleep here tonight,' Quintero said.

The manservant answered carefully. Quintero was mad again and the moon was still only in its first quarter. The man watched his master during the day looking towards Seville. It was too warm after the rains, the country steamed like a laundry.

And then, when the night came, Quintero laughed at his doubts. He went up to the room and as he undressed he thought of the assurance of those ice-cold lips, those icicle fingers and those icy arms. She had not come last night; oh what fidelity! To think, he would say in his remorse to the ghost, that malice had so disordered him that he had been base and credulous to use the dead for a trick.

Tears were in his eyes as he lay down and for some time he dared not turn on his side and stretch out his hand to touch what, in his disorder, he had been willing to betray. He loathed his heart. He craved—yet how could he hope for it now?—the miracle of recognition and forgiveness. It was this craving which moved him at last. His hands went out. And they were met.

The hands, the arms, the lips moved out of their invisibility and soundlessness towards him. They touched him, they clasped him, they drew him down, but—what was this? He gave a shout, he fought to get away, kicked out and swore; and so the manservant found him wrestling with the sheets, striking out with fists and knees, roaring that he was in hell. Those hands, those lips, those limbs, he screamed, were *burning* him. They were of ice no more. They were of fire.

Cushi

CHRISTOPHER WOODFORDE

Although it is little more than forty miles from London, you would be likely to lose your way in trying to find Rooksgate Green in Hertford-shire. It is hidden away in the chalk hills and is curiously suited to its name. The green is large and is still common ground. There is a pond and there are many geese. Around it are scattered cottages of various sizes and considerable antiquity. A road runs through the green. It is no longer gated, but the gate-posts still remain at each end of the green. Just beyond there is a dilapidated clunch-built church, which is the parish church of Cotterley, although it is nearly three miles from that village. By the church is a very large and ugly red-brick rectory surrounded by tall elms, in which the rooks live noisily. If you visited Rooksgate Green on a cold winter's day, you would be sure that no place in England could be colder; if you visited it in high summer, you would know how hot those chalk uplands can be.

It might not be expected that Rooksgate Green produces much news for the large world around it. Indeed, it seems never to have done so. It once had an important fair, but this has dwindled to a few roundabouts, swings, and stalls which still arrive on the eve of the feast of St John Baptist, under whose patronage Cotterley church was placed. Yet in the year 1939 there was a very strange occurrence which may be recorded in some detail.

Undoubtedly the most striking person in the hamlet was Cushi Holloway. He was probably about sixty years of age. He was short in stature and somewhat lame. He was bald and had a striking face. It was one of those faces which tell of a strong character, an acute brain, but it is very difficult to say whether that character was benevolent or not. Perhaps enigmatic is the best word to describe it. No one had ever seen Cushi, as he was universally called, put out: he was entirely imperturb-able. He lived with his old and rather formidable mother in one of the better cottages on the green, and he was sexton of Cotterley church. He had no other occupation, and the other inhabitants were never able to find out how he and his mother were able to live in reasonable comfort. He spent much time in and about the church, and he was a storehouse of information about its history during the last fifty years. He could remember every visiting preacher, what text he had chosen for his sermon, what the weather was like, and what was the size of the congregation on each occasion.

As a sexton he was invaluable. He was never late. He alone could induce the antiquated stoves to produce sufficient heat to make the church bearable in winter, and he alone could trim the oil lamps so that they did not smoke violently in the middle of the service. No one disputed his claim to dig the neatest grave in the district. Beneath the faded red cushion in his seat in church he stored strange reading matter. There was the current *Old Moore's Almanack*, a recent catalogue issued by a famous firm of seedsmen, and a copy of Struwwelpeter. He knew by heart the number and first line of every hymn in *Hymns Ancient and Modern*.

This last accomplishment expressed itself constantly in a curious way. When Cushi was not in his house, the church, or the churchyard, he would stand for long periods by the pond at the side of the road, acknowledging with a jerk of his head such greetings as came his way. Every car, van, lorry, and tractor that passed was given its appropriate hymn according to its registration number. Thus, a lorry bringing materials to repair The Horse Shoe was '196, Guide me, O Thou great Redeemer' and Mr Johnson's bright new tractor was '392, Forward! be our watchword'. When there were four numerals, the first three or the last three were usually chosen. Cushi rose to new heights when the bishop arrived to conduct a confirmation. The bishop had been told of Cushi's activities in this direction and, after the service, asked what his car number represented.

'What are you, my lord?' was the reply. 'You're two hadvents, you are. "51, Lo! He comes": "52, Great God, what do I see and 'ear?" hup in the pulpit.'

By way of extension, the appropriate number and words might be produced on other occasions. Thus, when the eldest daughter of Mr Hodges, who kept The Stores, married, Cushi produced as a wedding present a large box of chocolates with the remark '109, Sweet the moments, rich in blessing', which might have expressed Cushi's hopes either for her enjoyment of the sweets, or for a successful marriage service, or for happy years of connubial bliss.

At the end of the year 1936 the rector, the Revd Charles French, died. He had been rector of Cotterley for forty-two years and Cushi was deeply affected. His sorrow was not expressed in words, beyond the remark "'E were a good 'un, 'e were,' but it was fully expressed in the care he took over the preparation of Mr French's grave. It was wholly lined with flowers and the heap of earth and chalk thrown out beside it was covered with cut grass.

It was some time before a new appointment was made. Cushi eyed such clergymen as came to inspect the church and rectory, and said nothing. The odd assortment of parsons and lay-readers who conducted the services on Sunday and the few marriages and funerals on week-days added considerably to his store of anecdotes. Eventually the bishop made an appointment which was far from a happy one. The Revd David Evans was being overworked in a huge parish on the outskirts of London and needed rest. He was devoted to forms of worship far 'higher' than Cotterley and Rooksgate Green could ever tolerate or understand. He had grown up in Cardiff, and was wholly ignorant of the ways of an English village. He was somewhat shy, which the villagers mistook for 'offhandedness'. Above all, he made the unpardonable mistake of trying at once to 'wake up' his new flock. If he had won Cushi's approval and support, he might have survived the earlier criticisms, for he was a good and earnest man, but he began by unwittingly dealing blow after blow at his sexton.

The first incident was concerned with Cushi's attendance at Holy Communion. On the second Sunday after his institution Mr Evans said:

'I do not like grumbling about things, Cushi, but I must ask you to desist from making your communion twice. If you communicate at eight o'clock, you must not do so at the later celebration.'

'Mr French, 'e liked me at both 'ouses,' retorted Cushi.

Mr Evans winced.

'I also like to see you at both services,' said he, 'but the Church does not allow any one but a priest to make his communion more than once in a day. And while we are on this subject, I would much prefer that you do not dust the choir stalls with your handkerchief when you are returning from the altar.'

Cushi said nothing.

The second incident was the forbidding by Mr Evans of a very curious custom.

Cushi had what Rooksgate Green people described as 'a wonnerful way with cats'. Indeed, there was something uncanny about it. His cats were always jet black and were named 'Ought One', 'Ought Two', 'Ought Three', and so on. They had been trained, no one knew how, to follow him in a well-ordered line. By custom they were allowed to accompany him to baptisms. During the service the cats sat in a semicircle. Long ago the dumbness of the god-parents had caused Cushi to answer for them. So that the responses were apt to run:

'*Hi* will. Back, Ought Two!'

'*Hi* will. Sit up, Ought Four!'

The Green sharply criticized the rector for the banning of the cats.

They had come to believe that their presence foreshadowed good luck for the newly baptized infants.

A third alteration in Cushi's routine concerned the funerals. In the past, when Mr French pronounced the solemn words 'Earth to earth, ashes to ashes, dust to dust,' Cushi had thrown large lumps of clunch upon the coffin with three resounding thuds. Mr Evans regarded this as irreligious and likely to harrow the feelings of the mourners unnecessarily. In this he was wrong. The people of Rooksgate Green understood the mortality of man better than did the inhabitants of Sedgewillow Lane, Cardiff, and of Borrow Drive, SE18. Nevertheless, Mr Evans persisted in himself dropping a few grains of earth into the grave.

Cushi did not remark upon these changes to other people and it could not be divined how much he minded them, but perhaps signs were not wanting that Mr Evans did not have it quite all his own way. For instance, he wore white linen vestments, whereas Mr French had always worn a surplice and stole. Mr Evans had shown forbearance here, because he liked bright colours suitable to the Church's seasons. Cushi viewed the vestments with a suspicion bred of a very Protestant ancestry. The church was damp, and the vestments could not be left there during the week. They were carried to church each Sunday in a suit-case. Mr Evans asked Cushi to call for them and to lay them out in readiness, and to carry them back afterwards. Mr Evans could not but notice how often they were torn or a button was missing, but he did not feel able to ask Cushi if he had anything to do with it.

Matters continued thus for about a twelvemonth. Mr Evans found that the comparatively large congregations of the first few weeks were dwindling. He commented upon this to his rural dean.

'Don't worry,' replied that worthy, 'it is always the same. They come just once or twice to hear how you preach, and you won't see them again until the harvest festival.'

'I fear that it is going to be a very uphill task,' sighed Mr Evans. 'And you can never tell what they are really thinking.'

'Of course you can't,' said the rural dean cheerfully, 'and you never will know. You are lucky to have that man Cushi Holloway. It is almost impossible to find sextons and grave-diggers nowadays, let alone any one to cut the grass in the churchyard.'

'Am I?' asked Mr Evans, and added doubtfully: 'Yes, I suppose I am.'

It was on his return from his visit to the rural dean that his housekeeper told him that Cushi was ill. Cushi had walked, as his custom was, to the market-town of Arletern and had got drenched with rain on the return journey. Mr Evans called at his cottage after tea and inquired of Mrs Holloway how her son was. He was told politely that

Cushi was 'not very well.' A daily visit produced exactly the same reply and no suggestion that he should go upstairs and see Cushi. On the fifth day Cushi was dead. The undertaker called at the rectory and said that the funeral would be on Thursday at three o'clock with no music. Mr Evans was not a little annoyed.

'Supposing, Mr Spearman,' he said, 'that that day and time are inconvenient for me?'

'Well, sir,' replied Mr Spearman, 'I would manage it somehow if I were you. The people will be very put out if you try to change it. You know how it is in these places.'

Mr Evans was beginning to know how it was in those places, so he fell in with the arrangements with an ill grace.

The whole village turned out for the funeral, some attending the service in church and at the graveside, some going to the church only, and some looking on from a distance, according to a quite indefinable rule. On the next Sunday evening, following local custom, Mr Evans spoke about Cushi before he preached, and after the sermon announced Cushi's favourite hymn: '386. The sower went forth sowing', a hymn for which he had a particular loathing.

On the following day he called upon Mrs Holloway. She opened the door, but did not make room for him to enter. He began to express some sentiments of sympathy. She interrupted him with simple dignity.

'You didn't like my Cushi, and my Cushi couldn't abide you, so it's best to say nothing.'

Mr Evans found the door shut in his face and turned away, more sharply rebuffed than he had ever been in his life before.

It was only a week after this that Mr Evans himself took to his bed. The doctor came and examined him. When he had finished he said that he would call again in the morning. Meanwhile Mr Evans was to lie still, and to take some tablets which must be got from the chemist as soon as possible. At ten o'clock that night he received a message to say that Mr Evans had passed away in his sleep. He was not altogether surprised and was able to tell the coroner that the state of Mr Evans's heart made an inquest unnecessary. Mr Spearman's services were again required. Some long-distance telephone conversations resulted in the arrangement that he should make the best possible unpolished oak coffin, and dispatch the mortal remains of Mr Evans to Cardiff for burial.

The village was comparatively unaffected by the death of Mr Evans. He had not been long amongst them and they had not been impressed by what they had seen of him. The general verdict that ''E wouldn't never 'ave done for the likes of we' was, perhaps, a fair epitaph upon his short ministry at Rooksgate Green.

So matters might have rested. The advent of evacuees, the black-out, the ARP, and Home Guard, and all the restrictions of war were fully occupying their minds. The living of Cotterley was taken by a quiet and inoffensive missionary who had recently returned from India. His parishioners found little to criticize in him save that he was too apt to bring his Indian experiences into his sermons and to cover a small table by the south door of the church with booklets and pamphlets showing the activities and needs of coloured Christians.

It will never be known why some German airman decided to unloose his bombs upon Rooksgate Green. Perhaps a few scattered lights suggested to him that it was a larger and more important place. Be that as it may, he let fall six large bombs. As far as could be immediately discovered in the darkness they had neither killed nor wounded man or beast, although windows and ceilings suffered, especially those of the rectory. It was first discovered by Harry Pitman and Walter Broom that one of the bombs had fallen in the churchyard. When daylight came, they inspected the damage. The bomb had fallen in that part of the churchyard where the most recent burials had taken place. One coffin had been excavated by the missile and its lid had been torn off, exposing the grisly contents. Harry took one glance at it and turned quickly away. Walter was reading the name upon the brass plate on the coffin lid.

'Gawd!' exclaimed he. 'It's old Cushi.'

'No!' replied Walter, going over to look at it.

He spelt out the name.

'You're right, though,' he said, after a pause. 'It's poor old Cushi. Whatever would 'e 'ave said to that, Walt?'

They turned, as if by common consent, to look into the coffin once again. The remains of Cushi Holloway had, by some strange chance, been undisturbed by the explosion. Suddenly Harry Pitman pointed, speechless. Walter Broom looked more intently and then gasped.

'Well, whatever do you make of that?' he asked at length.

'That' was the undoubted fact that within what remained of his arms Cushi was hugging a human skull.

'We can't leave things like this for the women and children to see,' said Harry. 'Do you slip over to the rectory for the key of the churchyard shed. We'll get a couple of shovels and put Cushi back where he belongs. Ask the rector to step back with you. Mebbe 'e'll want to read a bit of a service over 'im.'

The rector came, and saw, and wondered. When the men's work was accomplished and Cushi was safely at rest again, he turned to them.

'How do you think that skull got there?' he asked.

'I can't rightly say,' replied Harry. 'There's something unnatteral 'appened there, rector, you may depend upon it. What do you say, Walt?'

'That's right enough,' said Walter.

'Whose head was it, do you think?' asked the rector.

'It's past telling, as you saw for yourself, sir,' said Harry. 'I wouldn't swear to it, but what hair there was left was just like the Reverend Evans's.' He paused and then continued: 'Yes, I reckon that if you was to go to that cimitary at Cardiff where 'e was put away, and dug 'im up, you'd find 'e ain't got no 'ead.'

'But we will say nothing about this to any one?' suggested the rector.

'That's right,' said Walter as he picked up the shovels. 'It was always best to leave old Cushi to foller 'is own way.'

Bad Company

WALTER DE LA MARE

It is very seldom that one encounters what would appear to be sheer unadulterated evil in a human face; an evil, I mean, active, deliberate, deadly, dangerous. Folly, heedlessness, vanity, pride, craft, meanness, stupidity—yes. But even Iagos in this world are few, and devilry is as rare as witchcraft.

One winter's evening some little time ago, bound on a visit to a friend in London, I found myself on the platform of one of its many sub-terranean railway stations. It is an ordeal that one may undergo as seldom as one can. The glare and glitter, the noise, the very air one breathes affect nerves and spirits. One expects vaguely strange meetings in such surroundings. On this occasion, the expectation was justified. The mind is at times more attentive than the eye. Already tired, and troubled with personal cares and problems, which a little wisdom and enterprise should have refused to entertain, I had seated myself on one of the low, wooden benches to the left of the entrance to the platform, when, for no conscious reason, I was prompted to turn my head in the direction of a fellow traveller, seated across the gangway on the fellow to my bench some few yards away.

What was wrong with him? He was enveloped in a loose cape or cloak, sombre and motionless. He appeared to be wholly unaware of my abrupt scrutiny. And yet I doubt it; for the next moment, although the door of the nearest coach gaped immediately opposite him, he had shuffled into the compartment I had entered myself, and now in its corner, confronted me, all but knee to knee. I could have touched him with my hand. We had, too, come at once into an even more intimate contact than that of touch. Our eyes—his own fixed in a dwelling and lethargic stare—had instantly met, and no less rapidly mine had uncharitably recoiled, not only in misgiving, but in something little short of disgust. The effect resembled that of an acid on milk, and for the time being cast my thoughts into confusion. Yet that one glance had taken him in.

He was old—over seventy. A wide-brimmed rusty and dusty black hat concealed his head—a head fringed with wisps of hair, lank and paper-grey. His loose, jaded cheeks were of the colour of putty; the thin lips above the wide unshaven and dimpled chin showing scarcely a trace of red. The cloak suspended from his shoulders mantled him to his shins. One knuckled, cadaverous, mittened hand clasped a thick ash stick, its handle black and polished with long usage. The only sign of life in his countenance was secreted in his eyes—fixed on mine—hazed and dully glistening, as a snail in winter is fixed to a wall. There was a dull deliberate challenge in them, and, as I fancied, something more than that. They suggested that he had been in wait for me; that for him, it was almost 'well met!'

For minutes together I endeavoured to accept their challenge, to make sure. Yet I realized, fascinated the while, that he was well aware of the futility of this attempt, as a snake is of the restless, fated bird in the branches above its head.

Such a statement, I am aware, must appear wildly exaggerated, but I can only record my impression. It was already latish—much later than I had intended. The passengers came and went, and, whether intentionally or not, none consented to occupy the seat vacant beside him. I fixed my eyes on an advertisement—that of a Friendly Society I remember!—immediately above his head, with the intention of watching him in the field of an eye that I could not persuade to meet his own in full focus again.

He had instantly detected this ingenuous device. By a fraction of an inch he had shifted his grasp upon his stick. So intolerable, at length, became the physical—and psychical—effect of his presence on me that I determined to leave the train at the next station, and there to await the next. And at this precise moment, I was conscious that he had not only withdrawn his eyes but closed them.

I was not so easily to free myself of his company. A glance over my shoulder as, after leaving the train, I turned towards the lift, showed him hastily groping his way out of the carriage. The metal gate clanged. The lift slid upwards and, such is the contrariness of human nature, a faint disappointment followed. One may, for example, be appalled and yet engrossed in reading an account of some act of infamous cruelty.

Concealing myself as best I could at the bookstall, I awaited the next lift-load. Its few passengers having dispersed, he himself followed. In spite of age and infirmity, he *had*, then, ascended alone the spiral staircase. Glancing, it appeared, neither to right nor left, he passed rapidly through the barrier. And yet—*had* he not seen me?

The ticket collector raised his head, opened his mouth, watched his retreating figure, but made no attempt to retrieve *his*. It was dark now—the dark of London. In my absence underground, minute frozen pellets of snow had fallen, whitening the streets and lulling the sound of the traffic. On emerging into the street, he turned in the direction of the next station—my own. Yet again—had he, or had he not, been aware that he was being watched? However that might be, my journey lay his way, and that way my feet directed me; although I was already later than I had intended. I followed him, led on no doubt in part—merely by the effect he had had on me. Some twenty or thirty yards ahead, his dark shapelessness showed—distinct against the whitening pavement.

The waters of the Thames, I was aware, lay on my left. A muffled blast from the siren of a tug announced its presence. Keeping my distance, I followed him on. One lamppost—two—three. At that, he seemed to pause for a moment, as if to listen, momentarily glanced back (as I fancied) and vanished.

When I came up with it, I found that this third lamppost vaguely illuminated the mouth of a narrow, lightless alley between highish walls. It led me, after a while, into another alley, yet dingier. The wall on the left of this was evidently that of a large garden; on the right came a row of nondescript houses, looming up in their neglect against a starless sky.

The first of these houses *appeared* to be occupied. The next two were vacant. Dingy curtains, soot-grey against their snowy window-sills, hung over the next. A litter of paper and refuse—abandoned by the last long gust of wind that must have come whistling round the nearer angle of the house—lay under the broken flight of steps up to a mid-Victorian porch. The small snow clinging to the bricks and to the worn and weathered cement of the wall only added to its gaunt lifelessness.

In the faint hope of other company coming my way, and vowing that I would follow no further than to the outlet of yet another pitch-black and uninviting alley or court—which might indeed prove a dead end—I turned into it. It was then that I observed, in the rays of the lamp over my head, that in spite of the fineness of the snow and the brief time that had elapsed, there seemed to be no trace on its surface of recent footsteps.

A faintly thudding echo accompanied me on my way. I have found it very useful—in the country—always to carry a small electric torch in my greatcoat pocket; but for the time being I refrained from using it. This alley proved not to be blind. Beyond a patch of waste ground, a nebulous, leaden-grey vacancy marked a loop here of the Thames—I decided to go no further; and then perceived a garden gate in the wall to my right. It was ajar, but could not long have been so because no more than an instant's flash of my torch showed marks in the snow of its recent shifting. And yet there was little wind. On the other hand, here was the open river; just a breath of a breeze across its surface might account for this. The cracked and blistered paint was shimmering with a thin coat of rime—of hoar-frost, and as if a finger had just now scrawled it there, a clumsy arrow showed, its 'V' pointing inward. A tramp, an errand-boy, mere accident might have accounted for this. It may indeed have been a mark made some time before on the paint.

I paused in an absurd debate with myself, chiefly I think because I felt some little alarm at the thought of what might follow; yet led on also by the conviction that I had been intended, decoyed to follow. I pushed the gate a little wider open, peered in, and made my way up a woody path beneath ragged unpruned and leafless fruit trees towards the house. The snow's own light revealed a ramshackle flight of steps up to a poor, frenchified sort of canopy above french windows, one-half of their glazed doors ajar. I ascended, and peered into the intense gloom beyond it. And thus and then prepared to retrace my steps as quickly as possible, I called (in tones as near those of a London policeman as I could manage):

'Hello there! Is anything wrong? Is anyone wanted?' After all, I could at least explain to my fellow passenger if he appeared that I found both his gate and his window open; and the house was hardly pleasantly situated.

No answer was returned to me. In doubt and disquietude, but with a conviction that all was not well, I flashed my torch over the walls and furniture of the room and its heavily framed pictures. How could anything be 'well'—with unseen company such as this besieging one's senses! Ease and pleasant companionship, the room may once have been capable of giving; in its dirt, cold, and neglect it showed nothing of that now. I crossed it, paused again in the passage beyond it, and listened. I then entered the room beyond that. Venetian blinds, many of the slats of which had outworn their webbing, and heavy, crimson chenille side-curtains concealed its windows.

The ashes of a fire showed beyond rusty bars of the grate under a black marble mantelpiece. An oil lamp on the table, with a green shade, exuded a stink of paraffin; beyond was a table littered with books and papers; and an overturned chair. There I could see the bent-up old legs, perceptibly lean beneath the trousers, of the occupant of the room. In no doubt of whose remains these were, I drew near, and with bared teeth and icy, trembling fingers, drew back the fold of the cloak that lay over the face. Death has a strange sorcery. A shuddering revulsion of feeling took possession of me. This cold, once genteel, hideous, malignant room—and this!

The skin of the blue loose cheek was drawn tight over the bone; the mouth lay a little open, showing the dislodged false teeth beneath; the dull unspeculative eyes stared out from beneath lowered lids towards the black mouth of the chimney above the fireplace. Vileness and iniquity had left their marks on the lifeless features, and yet it was rather with compassion than with horror and disgust that I stood regarding them. What desolate solitude, what misery must this old man, abandoned to himself, have experienced during the last years of his life; encountering nothing but enmity and the apprehension of his fellow creatures. I am not intending to excuse or even commiserate what I cannot understand, but the almost complete absence of any goodness in the human spirit, cannot but condemn the heart to an appalling isolation. Had he been murdered, or had he come to a violent but natural end? In either case, horror and terror must have supervened.

That I had been enticed, deliberately led on, to this discovery I hadn't the least doubt, extravagant though this, too, may seem. Why? What for?

I could not bring myself to attempt to light the lamp. Besides, in that last vigil, it must have burnt itself out. My torch revealed a stub of candle on the mantelpiece. I lit that. He seemed to have been engaged in writing when the enemy of us all had approached him in silence and had struck him down. A long and unsealed envelope lay on the table. I drew out the contents—a letter and a Will, which had been witnessed some few weeks before, apparently by a tradesman's boy and, possibly, by some derelict charwoman, Eliza Hinks. I knew enough about such things to be sure that the Will was valid and complete. This old man had been evidently more than fairly rich in this world's goods, and reluctant to surrender them. The letter was addressed to his two sisters: 'To my two Sisters, Amelia and Maude.' Standing there in the cold and the silence, and utterly alone—for, if any occupant of the other world had decoyed me there, there was not the faintest hint in consciousness that he or his influence was any longer present with me—I read the vilest letter that has ever come my way. Even in print. It stated that he knew the circumstances of these two remaining relatives—that he was well aware of their poverty and physical conditions. One of them, it seemed, was afflicted with Cancer. He then proceeded to explain that, although they should by the intention of their mother have had a due share in her property and in the money she had left, it rejoiced him to think that his withholding of this knowledge must continually have added to their wretchedness. Why he so hated them was only vaguely suggested.

The Will he had enclosed with the letter left all that he died possessed of to—of all human establishments that need it least—the authorities of Scotland Yard. It was to be devoted, it ran, to the detection of such evil-doers as are ignorant or imbecile enough to leave their misdemeanours and crimes detectable.

It is said that confession is good for the soul. Well then, as publicly as possible, I take this opportunity of announcing that, there and then, I made a little heap of envelope, letter and Will on the hearth and put a match to them. When every vestige of the paper had been consumed, I stamped the ashes down. I had touched nothing else. I would leave the vile, jaded, forsaken house to reveal its own secret; and I might ensure that that would not be long delayed.

What continues to perplex me is that so far as I can see no other agency but that of this evil old recluse himself had led me to my discovery. Why? Can it have been with this very intention? I stooped down and peeped and peered narrowly in under the lowered lids in the light of my torch, but not the feeblest flicker, remotest signal—or faintest syllabling echo of any message rewarded me. Dead fish are less unseemly.

And yet. Well—we are all of us, I suppose, at any extreme *capable* of remorse and not utterly shut against repentance. Is it possible that this priceless blessing is not denied us even when all that's earthly else appear to have come to an end?

The Bottle of 1912

SIMON RAVEN

—

In the Spring of 1947 I returned, you might say, from the dead. Never
mind what I had been doing. I suppose you would call me a spy; I had
penetrated into a world so remote that it was a long time before I learned
of the end of the war, and even longer before my task was done and I
could make my way back, by slow and careful stages, to the Head-
quarters in Delhi. Here they were in the fever which precedes
departure, for India would be independent in a few months; and besides
being thus preoccupied, they were rather embarrassed to see me.

'We didn't expect to see *you* again,' said Stetson accusingly; 'we gave
you up last summer.'

'It all took longer than we thought.'

'Evidently. How long will it take you to make out your report?'

'A week . . . ten days. And then I suppose I can go home?'

'Yes,' said Stetson, 'you can go home.'

'By the way,' I said, 'you should have all my mail here. I gave this as my
holding address.'

'We did have it. But we sent it off to your next of kin when we ceased
to expect you back. A married sister in Kent, I think?'

'That's right.'

'You'll just have to wait a few days longer for your bills. After all,
you've waited some years already. . . . '

Yes, I thought: four years. Ever since 1943, when I left England
reported to Stetson, and went off into the hills. A few days more would
hardly matter. But I should like to have read the letters from my sister; to
have heard the news of her husband and my little nephew and the farm
in Kent. And there was another thing—something that had not really
occurred to me in the mountains but was obvious now that I was back in
the familiar world: my sister would think I was dead. Or at best missing.
In 1946 she would have received the parcel with my mail in it, along with
a polite letter from Stetson—' . . . Very much regret . . . has failed to
report back . . . must reluctantly conclude . . . '; so that for all I knew
there was a tablet bearing my name on the church wall by now. How
awkward it was coming back from the dead. No wonder Stetson had
been so put out. But it would be easier with my sister: I would not shock

her with a cable but would send her a long, soothing letter. She wouldn't have time to reply, but that didn't matter. She would have been prepared . . . and gently. I would tell her to keep my mail and to expect me in about ten days—I should be flown home, Stetson said—and that I should warn her as soon as I reached London.

So I wrote to my sister; then I settled to my report for Stetson; and nine days later I left by air for home.

And so now at last I was to see them all again—the only family I had. My sister Anne, Richard her husband, my nephew (and my godson) Robin. Robin had been five when I left in 1943, a merry, bubbling infant; now he would be nine, gravely dressed in grey shorts and knee-stockings, rather reserved, I anticipated, in his smart prep. school blazer. Very different from the trusting baby who had trotted round the room in his blue pyjamas on my last night at home.

'Robin can stay up a little longer,' Anne had said. 'This is a special occasion.'

'Yes,' said Richard; 'we must have a bottle of the 1912.'

On any special occasion, grave or gay, Richard would open a bottle or two of the famous 1912. There had been, Richard would say, no year to equal it. If only his father had realized soon enough and bought more. . . . I remembered how, on that distant evening in 1943, he had said:

'I've only a dozen left now. But I shall save a bottle for the day you come back.'

'When *will* Uncle Jonathan come back?' asked Robin.

'Quite soon,' I said.

'How soon is quite soon?'

'When the war's over. The time will pass very quickly.'

'Sometimes it does,' said Robin reflectively, 'sometimes not. What makes the time go so slow and then suddenly fast?'

'You'll be busy,' I said, 'busy learning things at school. Time always goes fast for busy people.'

'Will *you* be busy, Uncle Jonathan?'

'I expect so.'

'So the time will go fast for both of us till Uncle Jonathan comes home again. Robin is very glad,' said Robin.

Then he gave me a hug and a kiss and was taken away to bed by Anne.

'The Government is going to take this place over as a hospital,' Richard had said later, gently tilting the decanter of 1912 over my glass. 'I'm not really too upset. It's very difficult for Anne just now with no servants and Robin at a demanding age. It's next August they're coming, I think.'

'Where will you live?'

'I'm having a sort of flat done up over the stables. It wasn't easy to arrange—the work permits and so on were endless—but they agreed finally because I shall still be farming the land. It'll be quite comfortable and I shall still be living more or less in my own home. And if things go well after the war, perhaps we can move back.'

'Government concerns are like women. Easy to get into a house, impossible to get out.'

Richard laughed.

'We want no cynicism from departing heroes,' he said.

Then Anne rejoined us.

'Robin is asleep,' she said. 'He put Uncle Jonathan before Mummy and Daddy in his prayers tonight. Afterwards he told me it was just this once, because Uncle Jonathan was going away to the war.'

And two big tears had rolled slowly down her cheeks.

This, then, was the family to which I was returning after so long. My sister Anne, her gentle husband with his cherished acres of Kentish soil, and my nephew Robin—now, I must suppose, an unknown quantity. And, of course, the last bottle of 1912. How wonderful it would be to sit with them all again, above the stables or perhaps in the old house itself, hearing Richard's quiet voice tell of the crops or the summer's cricket, persuading Robin to take me back into his life and to talk of his school and his friends, and drinking the noblest of all wines from Anne's beautiful glass. I was not ashamed that I thought almost as much of the wine as of the people I loved, for that bottle of wine had become a symbol to me as the years went on. It was the symbol of my return; when it appeared, cradled in Richard's careful hands, it would be a sign that the years of pain were finally done and that at last and for ever I was home. What more seemly offering to the returning soldier and what more fitting object for his thoughts? Wine, that maketh glad the heart of a man.

My aeroplane was punctual, but in London I came up against a mild difficulty. I had promised in my letter from Delhi to warn Anne as soon as I reached England. Enquiring from the telephone exchange, I found that Richard's house was now listed as —— Hospital, and that they had no number for Richard himself, whom I must presume was still living with Anne above the stables. That Richard should not be listed was really natural enough, because at the time when he had had the stables done up to live in, neither love nor money could procure private telephones and this, according to the exchange, was still the case. But how to warn Anne? I toyed with the idea of ringing the Hospital and asking them to take over a message, but did not fancy talking to some sniffish Matron who would make me feel she was being put upon. In the end I dictated a wire, incurring some expense by making it elaborately plain in the address that the recipient lived in an annexe of the Hospital. I should be arriving by train, I told Anne, at nine-thirty that night.

There was no one to meet at the station (no petrol? had that wretched wire misfired after all my trouble?), so I took a taxi to the gate of the park where, having only a small case, I yielded to a sentimental impulse and paid off the driver. I would walk up the drive, I thought, at once delaying and giving spice to the arrival I had dreamed of so often. Although it had been dark some time, there was a fair three-quarter moon and I could relish the familiar trees and hedges. At first I was surprised to find myself walking, not on gravel, but on concrete; then I remembered that government hospitals have money to spend. I hoped they had not spent too much, for I cared little for alteration, let it be in a cause that was never so excellent. On the whole I was reassured. There were two or three shapeless huts in the fields on either side, but perhaps Richard would find them useful when the hospital left or be able to remove them. And as I approached the house, I saw that its low and graceful front, long and white and welcoming, was the same as ever; save for a couple of ambulances parked at the bottom of the steps nothing indicated disturbance or even change. Inside, of course . . . . But I could hear about that later. Now I must go to my family. To the bottle of 1912. I turned along a wall, went through a door, stepped into the stable yard. And there to greet me, with his head sticking out of a window above the stables, was my nephew Robin.

'Uncle Jonathan,' he called, 'Uncle Jonathan.'

'Robin,' I said, 'oh, Robin.'

'I knew you were coming,' he called.

'You had my telegram all right?'

'I knew you were coming. Go through that door in front of you and up the stairs. I'm in the first room at the top.'

I opened the door and, with some difficulty, picked my way up the narrow and uncarpeted stairway. War-time work, I thought; shoddy. But there was nothing shoddy or uncomfortable about the room in which I found my nephew. There was a polished table and a bright fire. Robin himself was standing near the window, behind a beautifully covered sofa which I remembered from the house in the old days. He had grown up splendidly, my godson. Straight fair hair, a round, honest face with a clear if slightly pale complexion. Bright eyes. A sound, well-proportioned build, suggesting that he was ten or eleven rather than nine. Robin had always been big for his age. He made a handsome figure

standing there behind the sofa in his blue pyjamas, allowed to wait up—
how else on such a night—to welcome his uncle home.

'I've waited so long for you to come,' he said, 'to welcome you back
from the war. And then today they told me you were coming.'

'I took a lot of trouble to address the telegram right,' I said.

Then I waited for him to come to me. He did not move. Boys of nine
dislike demonstration, I thought, they don't want to be kissed and
mauled about even by mothers and long-lost uncles. He is shy, reserved,
as I knew he would be. Let him come in his own time.

'Where are Mummy and Daddy?' I asked.

'I always knew you were all right,' he said; 'I knew you would come
back.'

I could wait no longer.

'Then come and shake hands with me, Robin. Let me have a look at
you.'

Still he did not move.

'I knew you would come back. The wine is ready for you.'

He pointed to a small side table. On it stood a decanter, gleaming,
purple, imperial, and by it one of Anne's most beautiful glasses, into
which some wine had already been poured.

'The 1912?' I asked. 'The last bottle?'

'Yes, Uncle Jonathan. The last bottle. Now you must drink.'

'But where are Mummy and Daddy? I must wait for them.'

'They don't want you to wait, Uncle Jonathan.'

'Then surely you will drink with me, Robin? You are a big chap now.
A small glass won't hurt you.'

'No, thank you, Uncle Jonathan. But you must drink.'

So I lifted the full glass that stood on the table and raised it in front of
my face.

'To you, Robin,' I said: 'to my nephew and godson, who has grown
into such a fine boy.'

'Thank you, Uncle Jonathan,' he said.

I sipped the wine. For a moment the magnificent flavour, first deep
and distant, then rich, then subtly apologetic for its richness, bringing
the assurance that life was good and God was merciful, was there as it
always had been. Then I was alone in a cold, bare room, with only the
moon to shine on the cracked and filthy glass in my hand and with a taste
of vinegar and ashes on my tongue.

At the reception desk of the hospital they gave me my bundle of letters,
the letters which had followed me to Delhi and had been sent back to my
next of kin in Kent. There were only a few from Anne and Richard, and

one scrawl in capitals from Robin, at the bottom of the pile. Above these there was the buff envelope, and the sheet of thin war-time paper inside it, which told how they had all three been killed, in the late summer of 1943, when a braking ambulance skidded off the gravel drive and crashed into them where they stood by the park gate.

The Cicerones

ROBERT AICKMAN

John Trant entered the Cathedral of St Bavon at almost exactly
11.30.

An unexpected week's holiday having come his way, he was spending
it in Belgium, because Belgium was near and it was late in the season,
and because he had never been there. Trant, who was unmarried
(though one day he intended to marry), was travelling alone, but he
seldom felt lonely at such times because he believed that his solitude was
optional and regarded it rather as freedom. He was thirty-two and saw
himself as quite ordinary, except perhaps in this very matter of travel,
which he thought he took more seriously and systematically than most.
The hour at which he entered the Cathedral was important, because he
had been inconvenienced in other towns by the irritating continental
habit of shutting tourist buildings between 12.00 and 2.00, even big
churches. In fact, he had been in two minds as to whether to visit the
Cathedral at all with so little time in hand. One could not even count
upon the full half-hour, because the driving out of visitors usually began
well before the moment of actual closure. It was a still morning, very still
but overcast. Men were beginning to wait, one might say, for the year
finally to die.

The thing that struck Trant most as he entered the vast building was
how silent it seemed to be within; how empty. Other Belgian cathedrals
had contained twenty or thirty scattered people praying, or anyway
kneeling; priests importantly on the move, followed by acolytes; and, of
course, Americans. There had always been dingy bustle, ritual action,
and neck-craning. Here there seemed to be no one; other, doubtless,
than the people in the tombs. Trant again wondered whether the
informed did not know that it was already too late to go in.

He leant against a column at the west end of the nave as he always did,
and read the history of the cathedral in his Blue Guide. He chose this
position in order that when he came to the next section to be perused,
the architectual summary, he could look about him to the best advantage. He usually found, none the less, that he soon had to move if he
were to follow what the guide book had to say, as the architecture of few
cathedrals can be apprehended, even in outline, by a newcomer from a

single point. So it was now: Trant found that he was losing the thread, and decided he would have to take up the guide book's trail. Before doing so, he looked around him for a moment. The Cathedral seemed still to be quite empty. It was odd, but a very pleasant change.

Trant set out along the south aisle of the nave, holding the guide book like a breviary. 'Carved oak pulpit,' said the guide book, 'with marble figures, all by Laurent Delvaux.' Trant had observed it vaguely from afar, but as, looking up from the book, he began consciously to think about it, he saw something extraordinary. Surely there was a figure in the pulpit, not standing erect, but slumped forward over the preacher's cushion? Trant could see the top of a small, bald head with a deep fringe, almost a halo, of white hair; and, on each side, widespread arms, with floppy hands. Not that it appeared to be a priest: the figure was wearing neither white nor black, but on the contrary, bright colours, several of them. Though considerably unnerved, Trant went forward, passed the next column, in the arcade between the nave and the aisle, and looked again, through the next bay. He saw at once that there was nothing: at least there was only a litter of minor vestments and scripts in coloured bindings.

Trant heard a laugh. He turned. Behind him stood a slender, brown-haired young man in a grey suit.

'Excuse me,' said the young man. 'I saw it myself so don't be frightened.' He spoke quite clearly, but had a vague foreign accent.

'It was terrifying,' said Trant. 'Out of this world.'

'Yes. Out of this world, as you say. Did you notice the hair?'

'I did indeed.' The young man had picked on the very detail which had perturbed Trant the most. 'What did you make of it?'

'Holy, holy, holy,' said the young man in his foreign accent; then smiled and sauntered off westwards. Trant was *almost* sure that this was what he had said. The hair of the illusory figure in the pulpit had, at the time, reminded Trant of the way in which nimbuses are shown in certain old paintings; with wide bars or strips of light linking an outer misty ring with the sacred head. The figure's white hair had seemed to project in just such spikes.

Trant pulled himself together and reached the south transept, hung high with hatchments. He sought out 'Christ among the Doctors', 'The masterpiece of Frans Pourbus the Elder', the guide book remarked, and set himself to identifying the famous people said to be depicted in it, including the Duke of Alva, Vigilius ab Ayatta, and even the Emperor Charles V himself.

In the adjoining chapel, 'The Martyrdom of St Barbara' by De Crayer proved to be covered with a cloth, another irritating continental habit, as

Trant had previously discovered. As there seemed to be no one about, Trant lifted a corner of the cloth, which was brown and dusty, like so many things in Belgian cathedrals, and peered beneath. It was difficult to make out very much, especially as the light was so poor.

'Let me help,' said a transatlantic voice at Trant's back. 'Let me take it right off, and then you'll see something, believe me.'

Again it was a young man, but this time a red-haired cheerful looking youth in a green windcheater.

The youth not only removed the cloth, but turned on an electric light.

'Thank you,' said Trant.

'Now have a good look.'

Trant looked. It was an extremely horrible scene.

'Oh, boy.' Trant had no desire to look any longer. 'Thank you all the same,' he said, apologizing for his repulsion.

'What a circus those old saints were,' commented the transatlantic youth, as he replaced the worn cloth.

'I suppose they received their reward in heaven,' suggested Trant.

'You bet they did,' said the youth, with a fervour that Trant couldn't quite fathom. He turned off the light. 'Be seeing you.'

'I expect so,' said Trant smiling.

The youth said no more, but put his hands in his pockets, and departed whistling towards the south door. Trant himself would not have cared to whistle so loudly in a foreign church.

As all the world knows, the most important work of art in the Cathedral of St Bavon is the 'Adoration' by the mysterious van Eyck or van Eycks, singular or plural. Nowadays the picture is hung in a small, curtained-off chapel leading from the south choir ambulatory; and most strangers must pay to see it. When Trant reached the chapel, he saw the notice at the door, but, hearing nothing, as elsewhere, supposed the place to be empty. Resenting mildly the demand for a fee, as Protestants do, he took the initiative and gently lifted the dark red curtain.

The chapel, though still silent, was not empty at all. On the contrary, it was so full that Trant could have gone no further inside, even had he dared.

There were two kinds of people in the chapel. In front were several rows of men in black. They knelt shoulder to shoulder, heads dropped, hip-bone against hip-bone, in what Trant took to be silent worship. Behind them, packed in even more tightly, was a group, even a small crowd, of funny old Belgian women, fat, ugly, sexless, and bossy, such as Trant had often seen in other places both devotional and secular. The old women were not kneeling but sitting. All the same, they seemed eerily rapt. Strangest of all was their motionless silence. Trant had seen such groups everywhere in Belgium, but never, never silent, very far from it. Not a single one of this present group seemed even to be aware that he was there: something equally unusual with a people so given to curiosity.

And in this odd setting not the least strange thing was the famous picture itself, with its enigmatic monsters, sibyls, and walking allegories, and its curiously bright, other-world colours: a totality doubtless interpretable in terms of Freud, but, all the same, as dense as an oriental carpet, and older than Adam and Eve, who stand beside. Trant found the picture all too cognate to the disconcerting devotees.

He let fall the curtain and went on his way, distinctly upset.

Two chapels further around, he came upon the 'Virgin Glorified' by Liemakere. Here a choir-boy in a red cassock was polishing the crucifix on the altar. Already, he had thin black hair and a grey, watchful face.

'Onze lieve Vrouw,' said the choir-boy, explaining the picture to Trant.

'Yes,' said Trant. 'Thank you.'

It occurred to him that polishing was odd work for a choir-boy. Perhaps this was not a choir-boy at all, but some other kind of young servitor. The idea of being shortly ejected from the building returned to Trant's mind. He looked at his watch. It had stopped. It still showed 11.28.

Trant shook the watch against his ear, but there were no recovering ticks. He saw that the polishing boy (he was at work on the pierced feet) wore a watch also, on a narrow black strap. Trant gesticulated again. The boy shook his head more violently. Trant could not decide whether the boy's own watch was broken, or whether, conceivably, he thought that Trant was trying to take it from him. Then, all in seconds, it struck Trant that, whatever else there was about the boy he certainly did not appear alarmed. Far from it. He seemed as aloof as if he were already a priest, and to be refusing to tell Trant the time on principle; almost implying, as priests presume to do, that he was refusing for the other's good. Trant departed from the chapel containing Liemakere's masterpiece rather quickly.

How much time had he left?

In the next chapel was Rubens's vast altarpiece of St Bavon distributing all his goods among the poor.

In the next was the terrifying 'Martyrdom of Saint Livinus' by Seghers.

After one more chapel, Trant had reached the junction of the north transept and the choir. The choir was surrounded by a heavy and impenetrable screen of black marble, like a cage for the imperial lions.

The guide book recommended the four tombs of past bishops which were said to be inside; but Trant, peering through the stone bars, could hardly see even outlines. He shifted from end to end of the choir steps seeking a viewpoint where the light might be better. It was useless. In the end, he tried the handle of the choir gate. The gate had given every appearance of being locked, but in fact it opened at once when Trant made the attempt. He tiptoed into the dark enclosure and thought he had better shut the gate behind him. He was not sure that he was going to see very much of the four tombs even now; but there they were, huge boxes flanking the high altar, like dens for the lions.

He stood at the steps of the altar itself, leaning across the marble rails, the final barricade, trying to read one of the Latin inscriptions. In such an exercise Trant made it a matter of principle not lightly to admit defeat. He craned his neck and screwed up his eyes until he was half-dazed; capturing the antique words one at a time, and trying to construe them. The matter of the cathedral shutting withdrew temporarily to the back of his mind. Then something horrible seemed to happen; or rather two things, one after the other. Trant thought, first, that the stone panel he was staring at so hard, seemed somehow to move; and then that a hand had appeared round one upper corner of it. It seemed to Trant a curiously small hand.

Trant decided, almost calmly, to see it out. There must obviously be an explanation, and anything like flight would make him look ridiculous, as well as leaving the mystery unsolved. An explanation there was; the stone opened further, and from within emerged a small, fair-haired child.

'Hullo,' said the child, looking at Trant across the black marble barrier and smiling.

'Hullo,' said Trant. 'You speak very good English.'

'I *am* English,' said the child. It was wearing a dark brown garment open at the neck, and dark brown trousers, but Trant could not quite decide whether it was a boy or a girl. From the escapade a boy seemed likelier, but there was something about the child which was more like a girl, Trant thought.

'Should you have been in there?'

'I always go in.'

'Aren't you afraid?'

'No one could be afraid of Bishop Triest. He gave us those candle-sticks.' The child pointed to four copper objects; which seemed to Trant to offer no particular confirmation of the child's logic.

'Would *you* like to go in?' enquired the child politely.

'No, thank you,' said Trant.

'Then I'll just shut up.' The child heaved the big stone slab into place. It was a feat of strength all the more remarkable in that Trant noticed that the child seemed to limp.

'Do you live here?' asked Trant.

'Yes,' said the child, and, child-like, said no more.

It limped forward, climbed the altar rail, and stood beside Trant, looking up at him. Trant found it difficult to assess how old it was.

'Would you like to see one of the other bishops?'

'No thank you,' said Trant.

'I think you ought to see a bishop,' said the child quite gravely.

'I'd rather not,' said Trant smiling.

'There may not be another chance.'

'I expect not,' said Trant, still smiling. He felt it was best to converse with the child at its own level, and make no attempt at adult standards of flat questioning and conventionalized reference.

'Then I'll take you to the crypt,' said the child.

The crypt was the concluding item in the guide book. Entered from just by the north-western corner of the choir, it was, like the 'Adoration', a speciality, involving payment. Trant had rather assumed that he would not get round to it.

'Shall I have time?' he asked, looking instinctively at his stopped watch, still showing 11.28.

'Yes,' said the child, as before.

The child limped ahead, opened the choir-gate, and held it for Trant, his inscriptions unread, to pass through. The child closed the gate, and led the way to the crypt entry, looking over its shoulder to see that Trant was following. In the rather better light outside the choir, Trant saw that its hair was a wonderful mass of silky gold; its face almost white, with the promise of fine bones; its lips unusually full and red.

'This is called the crossing,' said the child informatively. Trant knew that the term was sometimes applied to the intersection of nave and transepts.

'Or the narthex, I believe,' he said, plunging in order to show who was the grown-up.

The child, not unnaturally, looked merely puzzled.

There was still no one else visible in the cathedral.

They began to descend the crypt stairs, the child holding on to the iron handrail, because of its infirmity. There was a table at the top, obviously for the collection of the fee, but deserted. Trant did not feel called upon to comment.

In the crypt, slightly to his surprise, many of the lights were on.

Probably the custodian had forgotten to turn them off when he or she had hurried forth to eat.

The guide book described the crypt as 'large', but it was much larger than Trant had expected. The stairs entered it at one corner, and columns seemed to stretch away like trees into the distance. They were built in stones of different colours, maroon, purple, green, grey, gold; and they often bore remains of painting as well, which also spread over areas of the vaulted stone roof and weighty walls. In the soft patchy light, the place was mysterious and beautiful; and all the more so because the whole area could not be seen simultaneously. With the tide of centuries the stone-paved floor had become rolling and uneven, but agreeably so. There were occasional showcases and objects on pedestals, and there was a gentle perfume of incense. As Trant entered, all was silence. He even felt for a moment that there was something queer about the silence; that only sounds of another realm moved in it, and that the noises of this world, of his own arrival for example, were in a different dimension and irrelevant. He stood, a little awed, and listened for a moment to the nothingness.

The child stood too, or rather rested against a pillar. It was smiling again, though very slightly. Perhaps it smiled like this all the time, as if always happy.

Trant thought more than ever that it might be a girl. By this time it was rather absurd not to be sure, but by this time it was more than before difficult to ask.

'Bishop Triest's clothes,' said the child, pointing. They were heavy vestments, hanging, enormously embroidered, in a glass cabinet.

'Saint Livinus's ornament,' said the child, and crossed itself. Trant did not know quite what to make of the ornament.

'Animals,' said the child. It was an early book of natural history, written by a monk, and even the opened page showed some very strange ones.

The child was now beginning positively to dart about in its eagerness, pointing out item after item.

'Shrine of Saint Marcarius,' said the child, not crossing itself, presumably because the relic was absent.

'Abbot Hughenois's clothes.' They were vestments again, and very much like Triest's vestments, Trant thought.

'What's that?' asked Trant, taking the initiative and pointing. Right on the other side of the crypt, as it seemed, and now visible to Trant for the first time through the forest of soft coloured columns, was something which appeared to be winking and gleaming with light.

'That's at the end,' replied the child. 'You'll be there soon.'

Soon indeed, at this hour, thought Trant: if in fact we're not thrown out first.

'Via Dolorosa,' said the child, pointing to a picture. It was a gruesome scene, painted very realistically, as if the artist had been a bystander at the time; and it was followed by another which was even more gruesome and at least equally realistic.

'Calvary,' explained the child.

They rounded a corner with a stone wall on the left, the forest of columns on the right. The two parts of a diptych came into view, of which Trant had before seen only the discoloured reverse.

'The blessed and the lost,' said the child, indicating, superfluously, which was which.

Trant thought that the pictures and frescoes were becoming more and more morbid, but supposed that this feeling was probably the result of their cumulative impact. In any case, there could not be much more.

But there were still many things to be seen. In due course they came to a group of pictures hanging together.

'The sacrifice of three blessed martyrs,' said the child. Each of the martyrs had died in a different way: by roasting on a very elaborate gridiron; by disembowelling; and by some process involving a huge wheel. The paintings, unlike some of the others, were extraordinarily well preserved. The third of the martyrs was a young woman. She had been martyred naked and was of great and still living beauty. Next to her hung a further small picture, showing a saint carrying his own skin. Among the columns to the right, was an enormous black cross. At a little distance, the impaled figure looked lifelike in the extreme.

The child was still skipping in front, making so light of its disability that Trant could not but be touched. They turned another corner. At the end of the ambulatory ahead was the gleaming, flashing object that Trant had noticed from the other side of the crypt. The child almost ran on, ignoring the intervening sights, and stood by the object, waiting for Trant to catch up. The child's head was sunk, but Trant could see that it was looking at him from under its fair, silky eyelashes.

This time the child said nothing, and Trant could only stare.

The object was a very elaborate, jewelled reliquary of the renaissance. It was presumably the jewels which had seemed to give off the flashing lights, because Trant could see no lights now. At the centre of the reliquary was a transparent vertical tube or cylinder. It was only about an inch high, and probably made of crystal. Just visible inside it was a short black thread, almost like the mercury in a minute thermometer; and at the bottom of the tube was, Trant noticed, a marked discoloration.

The child was still standing in the same odd position; now glancing sideways at Trant, now glancing away. It was perhaps smiling a little more broadly, but its head was sunk so low that Trant could not really see. Its whole posture and behaviour suggested that there was something about the reliquary which Trant should be able to see for himself. It was almost as if the child were timing him, to see how long he took.

Time, thought Trant, yet again; and now with a start. The reliquary was so fascinating that he had managed somehow almost to forget about time. He looked away and along the final ambulatory, which ran to the foot of the staircase by which he had descended. While he had been examining the reliquary, someone else had appeared in the crypt. A man stood in the centre of the passage, a short distance from Trant. Or not exactly a man: it was, Trant realized, the acolyte in the red cassock, the boy who had been polishing the brass feet. Trant had no doubt that he had come to hurry him out.

Trant bustled off, full of unreasonable guilt, without even properly thanking his child guide. But when he reached the boy in the cassock, the boy silently stretched out his arms to their full length and seemed, on the contrary, to bar his passage.

It was rather absurd; and especially as one could so readily turn right and weave a way out through the Gothic columns.

Trant, in fact, turned his head in that direction, simply upon instinct. But, in the bay to his right, stood the youth from across the Atlantic in the green windcheater. He had the strangest of expressions (unlike the boy in the cassock, who seemed the same dull peasant as before); and as soon as Trant caught his eye, he too raised his arms to their full extent, as the boy had done.

There was still one more free bay. Trant retreated a step or two, but then saw among the shadows within (which seemed to be deepening) the man in the grey suit with the vague foreign accent. His arms were going up even as Trant sighted him, but when their eyes met (though Trant could not see his face very well) he did something the others had not done. He laughed.

And in the entrance to the other ambulatory, through which Trant had just come and down which the child had almost run, bravely casting aside its affliction, stood that same child, now gazing upwards again, and indeed looking quite radiant, as it spread its arms almost as a bird taking flight.

Trant heard the great clock of the cathedral strike twelve. In the crypt, the tone of the bell was lost: there was little more to be distinguished than twelve great thuds, almost as if cannon were being discharged. The twelve strokes of the hour took a surprisingly long time to complete.

In the meantime, and just beside the reliquary, a small door had opened, in the very angle of the crypt. Above it was a small but exquisite and well preserved alabaster keystone showing a soul being dragged away on a hook by a demon. Trant had hardly noticed the door before, as people commonly overlook the working details of a place which is on show, the same details that those who work the place look to first.

In the door, quite filling it, was the man Trant believed himself to have seen in the pulpit soon after he had first entered the great building. The man looked bigger now, but there were the same bald head, the same resigned hands, the same multicoloured garments. It was undoubtedly the very person, but in some way enlarged or magnified; and the curious fringe of hair seemed more luminous than ever.

'You must leave now,' said the man kindly but firmly. 'Follow me.'

The four figures encircling Trant began to shut in on him until their extended finger-tips were almost touching.

His questions went quite unanswered, his protests quite unheard; especially after everyone started singing.

Soft Voices at Passenham

T. H. WHITE

The Professor said: 'Very few people ever see ghosts, because they are localized. Now Passenham is a good locality for ghosts, near Stony Stratford. They have more ghosts there than ratepayers.'

'All these supernatural stories,' said the Countess coldly, 'boil down to hearsay in the end. Even the Holy Ghost has always struck me as being a great deal less definite than the other members of the Trinity. Have you ever seen one of the creatures yourself?'

'At Passenham I attended a sort of concert with several of them. Ghosts are fond of music, and will go anywhere to hear it.'

'Did you actually see one?'

'No,' replied the Professor with reluctance.

'I suppose you'll have to tell the story if your mind is set on it.'

'I don't tell stories to amuse myself,' said the Professor in dignified tones.

'Of course you do, Jacky. Don't be so pompous. You know perfectly well that you consider nobody's interests in that matter except your own. And, what is more, you make them up as you go along.'

The Professor smiled a pleased smile.

'It is the creative urge,' he said. 'But this one is deadly true.'

'I believe you.'

'Why, of course it's true. Passenham is a real place. You can look it up in any map of the shire. How could I invent stories about a real place? For that matter, you can go there and see for yourself.'

'Thank you for nothing,' said the Countess. 'Who wants to go and see a ghost, anyway? Horrid creatures smelling of mould!'

'Mould,' repeated the Professor with relish. 'Mould. Well may you say mould. It is not only music that ghosts are fond of, but also mist. Music and mist. Damp. Humidity. The watery air that makes things go mouldy: go soft and cold and wet and furry. Toadstools, you know, and that steep pervasive cellar air, and the bleached delicate green-blue fur between the chinks. The silent damp rots their bodies away to bones, and I suppose they need the same thing to build them up again before they walk. There is something solid about humidity, something ecto-plasmic with which to compose a soft and putrid body visible to men.'

'I think you're horrid,' said the Countess.

'I was trying to explain about Passenham,' explained the Professor. 'It lies low and flat, on the banks of the Ouse. The Ouse is a very haunted stream really, as you can imagine from its name. Silent, green and slimy, it goes slow and cold through the flooded winter landscape: bearing with it the bodies of drowned maidens, goggle-eyed in mid-water, attended by sluggish perch and muddy roach and a few staring, garbage-eating trout. The ironic pike lie frozen in the water, and the stream itself scarcely seems to move. Even the mill wheels no longer turn, mill wheels which used to collect their harvest of suicides (expectant country lasses who, lacking a father to their children, chose silence in the dank water rather than the horrible susurrus of the village tongues). There was Nancy Webb, for instance, at Passenham Mill. She goes through it once a year with a dreadful shriek, carrying her child in her arms, and her bones crackle in the great wheel like a firework squibs. The river makes nothing of this. Ouse by name, say the inhabitants, and ooze by nature. Shake not thy oozy locks at me.'

'Gory,' said the Countess.

'But oozy is just as good. Those are pearls that were her eyes. Few people realize the beauty of Shakespeare's description. They think of pearls as precious jewels worn by distinguished dowagers at first nights. But they are white stones really, the pale viscous secretion of oysters: a dead, wall-eyed colour particularly suitable for the eyes of corpses under the sea. A boiled haddock has much the same look.'

'Could we leave Nancy Webb to her grave?'

'Certain, for she is the least of my ghosts at Passenham. I mention her only because she happens to inhabit the Ouse, and the Ouse is necessary to any description of the village. The mists, you see, come from it.

'Music and mists. The village lies there by the riverside, flat and secluded. It has very few inhabitants now; live inhabitants, I mean, for the dead ones come and go in the mist. Mist into mist, they throng the bridle paths and saunter between the hedgerows. The man who drives the new maids out from Stony Stratford to the big house always says to them, as he drops them at the door, "I'll be back for you in a month, miss. They never stay longer than that." Indeed, the only man not frightened of ghosts is old Fowley the sexton. He, when the spirits are more than usually troublesome in November, has been known to walk down the village street brandishing a scythe and exclaiming to the white air: "I'll larn 'em to come a-plaguing decent people, what have been at the trouble of burying on 'em." '

'What sort of ghosts do they have in particular at Passenham?'

'Oh, all sorts and conditions. And they find many curious things. The farmer there has a big barn. It's a beautiful thing, ancient, with enormous rafters. They got up to the rafters one day and found a skeleton there, all cramped up, wedged between the beams and the roof. Under the hearthstone in the rectory they dug up two men. Strange doings there must have been, in a strange place, hidden always in the cold mists of the Ouse.'

'Murders, I suppose?'

'Oh, yes. Murders and things like that. There were the three louts of Calverton, who slit an old lady's throat for her money, but were caught in Beachampton Grove and hanged behind Calverton Church on a tree. You can still see a carving of them, cut deep outside the church wall.'

'It sounds an unfriendly community.'

'You might say so. But the ghosts are friendly, of course. Not so much friendly as sociable. They seem to have a liking for company, just as all people do in mists. The fog makes you feel lonely, cut off from your fellow beings, so that when you do see a figure looming up out of the silence it is natural to fall into step beside him. The old sexton would often find somebody walking at his shoulder, but he never paid much heed. He had a kind of acquaintance with them, I suppose, having rumbled the earth down on to most of their coffins. In fact, old Fowley treated them very much like rabbits: a nuisance if they got into the garden and nibbled the vegetables, but nothing more. On the whole the ghosts were respectful towards Fowley. He ignored them in rather a pointed way, and this made them feel inferior. It is galling to be cut by anybody, and to be positively sent to Coventry, as he had done with all the shire ghosts, must have made them feel very small beer. The only time Fowley was ever frightened himself—and then it was more a case of being startled—was on a Sunday night in December. He was verger and general factotum, and he was ringing the church bell for service. He had a lanthorn with him in the belfry, and it blew out, for it was a stormy night. He let go the bell rope to light the lanthorn, and the bell went on ringing. This surprised him, so he took hold of the rope again in the dark: but there was a hand under his own on the rope, a skeleton hand, rather frigid and slippery, and a faint musty smell in the belfry.

'Then there was Robert Bannister, the huntsman. The Whaddon and the Grafton are often over there; sometimes the Bicester. Nobody minds the thunder of the horses' hoofs during the daytime, the earth-shaking music as the cavalry goes by. But it is not nice at night to hear the galloping iron hoofs behind you on a lonely road: possibly just a real horse that has got out of a field by a gate being left open, but possibly not. Would a real horse gallop at midnight, in the pitch dark? And why does it not come nearer? They have put a heavy stone on Bannister in the churchyard to keep him down; but, bless you, as old Fowley says, he doesn't sleep many months together. He rides with his whole pack of hounds in full cry, making a lovely music which sounds more terrible in the darkness, and marks to ground by his grave. He broke his neck out hunting, and was dragged home dead by a frightened horse with his foot in the stirrup. So now he rides like that, a rattling skeleton behind a fiery horse, and the neck is out of joint. It is a fine sight, with the pealing of the hounds and the jolting of the bones, on a roaring north-westerly night of windy December.'

'Preserve us!' exclaimed the Countess, putting some more logs on the fire.

'There is a coach, of course, for which the lodge gates open on their rusty hinges, and many another unfortunate wanderer, our of step with time. The place is infested with 'em, in Fowley's phrase; but they won't never hurt ye, man, so long as ye doan't get too much sulphur down your chest as they go by.'

'There is a coach over Cheltenham way,' said the Countess weakly, 'that drives at motorists round one of the bends. People always swerve and go into the ditch; but you don't see it if you put your hat on your knee.'

'Indeed,' said the Professor. 'But I was going to tell you about my concert.'

'This conversation,' said the Countess, 'is making me feel chilly.'

'It is the damp,' said the Professor.

'Go on, then, if you must.'

'I used to know the Vicar of Passenham, a fellow called Brown. Reverent Brown, old Fowley used to call him. He was a stout, hearty fellow that hunted two days a week and preached his sermons out of the *Cambridge Review*. He used to pooh-pooh these ghosts to keep his courage up, and he never let the verger talk about their doings in his presence. A nice fellow in every way, who could generally offer a mount to his friends, and I was in the habit of going down to his vicarage for a day with the Grafton now and then. He put me up one January, a wet cold month that was more like the fill-dyke of February than the snowy Christmas cards which we are disposed to remember. Even the Ouse had begun to move a bit, it was so full. A misty February, but then it is always fog at Passenham.

'I recollect that Reverent Brown was looking a bit overwrought when I got down to him, but he said nothing about it, and we had a good day's hunt on Saturday. I made a point of going to church whenever he did—after all, it is only polite when you are staying with a clergyman, and besides, I enjoyed the services in Passenham Church. The oil lamps burned in a kind of halo on the Sunday evening, and the wet fog outside was kept at bay by a primitive heating apparatus that was tended by old Fowley. I liked the bells of Passenham also. They rang out over the water meadows, calling in visitors out of the night. There never was much of a living congregation, but the church did not feel lonely.

'It was a pleasant and unpretentious service, although Brown looked and spoke like a worn man. I read one of the lessons myself, a bit out of an epistle by St Paul, ill-punctuated as usual. St Paul never could put a verb into a sentence. I stumbled through it somehow, and the post-mistress played "The Lord's my Shepherd" on the harmonium, and we chanted along after her in the best voice we might. It was music of a sort: better, I suppose, than the silence of the grave.'

'Cold,' said the Countess.

'Yes,' said the Professor. 'In the grave it must be very cold. You could feel all the wet graves about the church, listening as they huddled round it for shelter: the stone graves of the notables, and the headstones cocked sideways to hear better, and the mere grassy oblongs of forgotten toil. It was a well-attended service.

'When Brown had finished he came out of the vestry in his daily clothes and told me to carry off old Fowley to the vicarage for a glass of whisky. It was a raw night, he said, smiling wanly at the old man, for a gentleman to be out in who would never be able to dig his own grave. He himself was feeling like a little music, and would follow us after he had played a couple of hymns. He was tired, he said, and wanted some dull music to settle down. He sat himself at the harmonium as he was speaking; and I went off with the verger, rejoicing in the proximity of a warm drink.

'Fowley's conversation was always original. The vicar, it seemed, had been quite wrong about digging one's own grave. The sexton had dug his own twenty years ago, and trimmed it every Saturday since. This led us naturally to talk of ghosts, and the old fellow told me that they were particularly partial to church bells; would swarm about them, indeed, like bees, during the foggy months. Bells and music, something harmonious to vary the silence of death: anything to pass away the secret tonelessness of earth and stars. Just then we heard the vicar launch out into the "Dead March" in *Saul*.

' "Foolhardiness!" remarked old Fowley, shaking his head.

'Ghosts, he told me, had been charmed by the music of Orpheus, who had brought one of them, called Dinah, back from the grave. King Orphew, he added, pronouncing the name in a different way, was a god of the dark himself, as his Greek name testified.

'By this time I was feeling that the conversation had gone far enough. I changed it by remarking that the congregation had been small that night.

' "We had the usuals," said old Fowley.

' "Do you get bigger gatherings," I asked, "at any other season of the year? At harvest festivals, for instance, or Christmas Day?"

' "The harvest here is a big 'un," said Fowley, "and we gets 'em most about All Soul's Day."

'It was at this point that we heard the vicar wading into the "Danse Macabre". Tum-tum, ter-Tum-tum. What on earth could have persuaded him to start that garish and unecclesiastical melody? I remarked wildly to the sexton that Reverent Brown seemed to have an interesting taste in music.

' "The Nine Tailors," replied Fowley, "soothes us all to sleep."

' "The present one," said I, "is scarcely a soothing tune."

' "Perhaps," said Fowley, "it is intended for to waken of 'em."

' "But the inhabitants of Passenham would scarcely be in bed by now?"

' "They likes to air their beds."

' "What I like," said I, 'about the country is the feather beds."

' "They all likes to sleep soft," said Mr Fowley.

' "Only they are difficult to get out of."

' "Difficult to get out of, and difficult to get in. Them that folds their hands to hold flowers, has to have bigger 'uns, for it makes their elbows stick out."

'Reverent Brown was playing Tennyson's funeral hymn. The long moving chords came out of the little church with a strangely quavering intonation. I finished up my whisky.

' "I was never very good," said I, "at getting up in the morning."

' "It's music as wakens you best. The curfew bell wakens some on 'em, as the cock-crow puts 'em to sleep, and the music of a trumpet will waken all of 'em on the Last Day.

' "That," added Mr Fowley, 'is all they have left to 'em. That and the music of the spheres."

'He left me at this point alone with the whisky bottle, and I could not help pouring myself another stiff tumbler as I waited for the vicar. I was alone in the vicarage, as the maids were out for the evening, and I wandered nervously from one damp room to another: from the moth-eaten antlers in the hall, where a small lamp burned, to the cold beef and pickles laid out for the grace to be said over them in the dining-room. I could not help thinking of the music outside in the reeds of the Ouse, the desolate Pan-piping with which the god of nature used to terrify the ancients, and of all the other ghostly music in the world: the military bands coming back out of the battle, thronged with ghosts, and the pipes in the glen, populating it. At midnight, too, when the dead are supposed to rise, the clocks are playing their longest chimes. All the time the vicar's harmonies kept coming over in shreds from the church porch, and it was getting very late for supper.

'It was an hour before I went over to the church, and the music was still going on. I whistled to keep my spirits up as I crossed the graveyard, but stopped in the middle of a bar as I ran into the sexton. He was sitting on a square tomb looking up at the windows, which were dark, and remarked on perceiving me: "Them as whistles at Passenham fetches 'em round." I stopped whistling at once.

' "Is he playing in the dark?" I asked.

'Mr Fowley nodded to the windows.

'I made an effort, and suggested: "I think we ought to go in and fetch him out to his supper."

' "Them doors," said Mr Fowley,' "is locked."

' "Does the vicar usually play in the dark and lock himself in?"

' "He hasn't got no keys," said Mr Fowley, without turning his head.

'I need not weary you, as I exhausted myself, with a full experience of that long winter night. The least I could do was to stay up outside the church. I sat with old Fowley on the square gravestone, with the bottle of whisky between us, and listened to the infernal concert. The sexton talked in snatches through the fog. King David, he told me, charmed the ghosts that fluttered round King Saul by playing on his harp: the Bible prophets summoned their familiars by psaltery, timbrel and pipe: Elisha sought spirits by making a minstrel play, and thereby discovered water in the desert: the devil, who was the greatest of the spirits, doted upon the fiddle, to which he danced on the witch's sabbath, while the Sanctus bell summoned his opposite angel into church. All the time, as the background to the horrid conversation, we could hear the harmonium ploughing its hymns. It exhausted the hymn book long before dawn, and went off into a ghastly memorization of the *Students' Song Book*. "The Londonderry Air" sank to "Linden Lea", to the "Minstrel Boy". Soon we were in "The Vicar of Bray", "John Peel", "The Bay of Biscay", "Down Among the Dead Men" (which was encored), and eventually "Mademoiselle from Armentières". Through the whole night the melancholy breathings agonized behind the locked doors, whined for "Loch Lomond", jigged with a ghastly bonhomie through Gilbert and Sullivan. It was still dark when the cock crew, and the doors opened to the accompaniment of "God Save the King".

'We never saw anything come out. Only, after a bit, there was the vicar in the wet dawn: a drawn and speechless man, peering out of the porch. He never spoke, poor fellow, and is now in Stone asylum. I suppose they must have come to his first notes, come and stood round him in the dark, and made him go on. I dare say he never dared to look over his shoulder, but only went on frozenly with his music. Hair really does stand on end, you know, as you can see if you get yourself sufficiently charged with electricity. When he stopped, the pedals went on moving of their own accord; and the pages were turned over for him. He plays now continually in the asylum. "Music," as Mr Fowley quoted to me when they took him away, "when soft voices die, vibrates in the memory." '

NOTES

THE following notes give publication details of the individual stories and copyright information where applicable, together with brief biographical information about an author where this was felt to be relevant. Many ghost stories first appeared in magazines and periodicals, and where this information is known to the present editors it has been indicated; otherwise first publication in book form is given. Place of publication is London unless otherwise stated.

'The Tapestried Chamber; or, The Lady in the Sacque' by Sir Walter Scott (1771-1832), first published in *The Keepsake* (1829).

'The Phantom Coach' by Amelia B. Edwards (1831-92), first published in Charles Dickens's *All the Year Round* (Christmas Number, 1864).

'Squire Toby's Will. A Ghost Story' by Joseph Sheridan Le Fanu (1814-73), first published in *Temple Bar*, 22 (January 1868); reprinted for the first time in *Madame Crowl's Ghost and Other Tales of Mystery*, ed. M. R. James (Bell & Sons, 1923). This tale was considered by James to be among the best ghost stories in the English language.

'The Shadow in the Corner' by Mary Elizabeth Braddon (1835-1915), first published in *All the Year Round* (Extra Summer Number, 1879).

'The Upper-Berth' by Francis Marion Crawford (1854-1909), first published in *Unwin's Annual 1886: The Broken Shaft*; the story also appeared (with Crawford's 'By the Waters of Paradise') in the inaugural volume of T. F. Unwin's Autonym Library and was reprinted in *Uncanny Tales* (T. Fisher Unwin, 1911).

'A Wicked Voice' by Vernon Lee (pseudonym of Violet Paget, 1856-1935), from *Hauntings. Fantastic Stories* (Heinemann, 1889 for 1890).

'The Judge's House' by Bram Stoker (1847-1912), first published in *Holly Leaves*, Christmas number of the *Illustrated Sporting and Dramatic Life* (5 December 1891); reprinted in *Dracula's Guest, and Other Weird Stories* (Routledge, 1914). The story develops ideas from Le Fanu's 'An Account of Some Strange Disturbances in Aungier Street' (*Dublin University Magazine*, December 1853), the earlier form of Le Fanu's 'Mr Justice Harbottle' (*Belgravia*, January 1872).

'Man-Size in Marble' by Edith Nesbit (Mrs Hubert Bland, 1858-1924), author of the children's classic *The Railway Children* (1906); from *Grim Tales* (Innes, 1893).

'The Roll-Call of the Reef' by Sir Arthur Quiller-Couch (1863-1944), from *Wandering Heath. Stories, Studies, and Sketches* (Cassell, 1895).

'The Friends of the Friends' by Henry James (1843-1916), first published as 'The Way It Came' in the *Chap Book* (May 1896) and *Chapman's Magazine of Fiction* (May 1896); reprinted in *Embarrassments* (1896), retitled 'The Friends of the Friends' in *The Novels and Tales of Henry James* (New York edn., 1907-9).

'The Red Room' by Herbert George Wells (1866-1946), first published in *The Idler* (March 1896); reprinted in *The Plattner Story, and Others* (1897). Reprinted by permission of A. P. Watt Ltd. and the Literary Executors of the Estate of H. G. Wells.

'The Monkey's Paw' by William Wymark Jacobs (1863-1943), first published in *Harper's Monthly Magazine* (September 1902); reprinted in *The Lady of the Barge* (Harper, 1902). Reprinted by permission of the Society of Authors as the literary representative of the Estate of W. W. Jacobs.

'The Lost Ghost' by Mary E. Wilkins (later Wilkins-Freeman, 1852-1930), from *The Wind in the Rose-Bush and Other Stories of the Supernatural* (John Murray, 1903).

' "Oh, Whistle, and I'll Come to You, My Lad" ' by Montague Rhodes James (1862-1936), from *Ghost Stories of an Antiquary* (Edward Arnold, 1904). Reprinted in *The Ghost Stories of M. R. James* and used by permission of Edward Arnold (Publishers) Ltd. James was one of the most distinguished scholars of his generation and from 1905-18 was Provost of King's College, Cambridge, with which institution several writers of ghost stories were to be associated.

'The Empty House' by Algernon Blackwood (1869-1951), from *The Empty House and Other Ghost Stories* (Eveleigh Nash, 1906). Reprinted by permission of A. P. Watt Ltd. and Mrs Sheila Reeves.

'The Cigarette Case' by Oliver Onions (George Oliver Onions, 1873-1961), from *Widdershins* (Secker, 1911). Reprinted by permission of A. P. Watt Ltd., Arthur Oliver, and William R. Oliver.

'Rose Rose' by Barry Pain (pseudonym of Eric Odell, 1864-1928), from *Stories in Grey* (T. Werner Laurie [1911]). The volume was undated: Pain himself gave the date as 1912, but the *British Library General Catalogue of Printed Books* has 1911.

'The Confession of Charles Linkworth' by Edward Frederic Benson (1867-1940), from *The Room in the Tower and Other Stories* (Mills and Boon, 1912). Reprinted by permission of A. P. Watt Ltd. on behalf of the Executors of the Estate of K. S. P. McDowall. Benson knew M. R. James at Cambridge through his elder brother Arthur (A.C.) Benson, prolific author (including some ghost stories) and Master of Magdalene College, Cambridge, 1915-25. E. F. Benson is now chiefly remembered for his 'Mapp and Lucia' stories. The third Benson brother, Robert Hugh, also wrote ghost stories (see Select Bibliography).

'On the Brighton Road' by Richard Middleton (1882-1911), from *The Ghost Ship and Other Stories* (T. Fisher Unwin, 1912), introduction by Arthur Machen.

'Bone to His Bone' by Edmund Gill Swain (1861-1938), from *The Stoneground Ghost Tales. Compiled From the Recollections of the Reverend Roland Batchel, Vicar of the Parish* (Cambridge: Heffer, 1912). Reprinted by permission of

W. Heffer & Sons Ltd. Swain was Chaplain of King's College, Cambridge, and a friend of M. R. James, to whom *The Stoneground Ghost Tales* were dedicated.

'The True History of Anthony Ffryar' by Arthur Gray ('Ingulphus', 1852-1940), from *Tedious Brief Tales of Granta and Gramarye* (Cambridge: Heffer, 1919). Reprinted by permission of W. Heffer & Sons Ltd. Gray was Master of Jesus College, Cambridge, 1912-40 and was a noted historian of Cambridge.

'The Taipan' by William Somerset Maugham (1874-1965), from *On a Chinese Screen* (Heinemann, 1922). Reprinted in *The Complete Short Stories of W. Somerset Maugham*. Copyright 1922 by Doubleday & Company, Inc. Used by permission of Doubleday & Company, Inc., A. P. Watt Ltd., the Executors of the Estate of W. Somerset Maugham, and William Heinemann Ltd.

'The Victim' by May Sinclair (1863-1946), first published in *The Criterion*, Vol.1, No.1 (Oct. 1922); reprinted in *Uncanny Stories* (Hutchinson, 1923). © May Sinclair. Reprinted by kind permission of Curtis Brown on behalf of the author.

'A Visitor From Down Under' by Leslie Poles Hartley (1895-1972), first published in *The Ghost Book*, ed. Lady Cynthia Asquith (Hutchinson, 1926); reprinted in *The Travelling Grave* (Sauk City: Arkham House, 1948; London: James Barrie, 1951). Reprinted by permission of Century Hutchinson Ltd.

'Fullcircle' by John Buchan (1875-1940), from *The Runagates Club* (Hodder & Stoughton, 1928). Reprinted by permission of A. P. Watt Ltd. and the Rt. Hon. Lord Tweedsmuir.

'The Clock' by William Fryer Harvey (1885-1937), from *The Beast with Five Fingers and Other Stories* (Dent, 1928). Reprinted by permission of J. M. Dent & Sons Ltd.

'Old Man's Beard' by Herbert Russell Wakefield (1888-1964), from *Old Man's Beard. Fifteen Disturbing Tales* (Geoffrey Bles, 1929).

'Mr Jones' by Edith Wharton (1862-1937), from *Certain People* Appleton, (1930). Reprinted in *The Ghost Stories of Edith Wharton* and used by permission of Constable Publishers. In the US in *The Collected Short Stories of Edith Wharton*. Copyright 1928 The Curtis Publishing Co.; copyright renewed © 1956. Copyright © 1968 William R. Tyler. Reprinted with the permission of Charles Scribner's Sons.

'Smee' by Alfred McLellan Burrage ('Ex-Private X', 1889-1956), from *Someone in the Room* (Jarrolds, 1931).

'The Little Ghost' by (Sir) Hugh Walpole (1884-1941), first published in *When Churchyards Yawn*, ed. Lady Cynthia Asquith (Hutchinson, 1931); reprinted in *All Souls' Night* (Macmillan, 1933). Reprinted by permission of Sir Rupert Hart-Davis.

'Ahoy, Sailor Boy!' by Alfred Edgar Coppard (1878-1957), from *Dunky Fitlow. Tales* (Cape, 1933). Reprinted by permission of David Higham Associates Ltd.

'The Hollow Man' by Thomas Burke 1886-1945, from *Night-Pieces. Eighteen Tales* (Constable, 1935). Reprinted by permission of John Farquharson Ltd.

'Et in Sempiternum Pereant' by Charles Walter Stansby Williams (1886-1945), first published in the *London Mercury*, 3, 194 (December 1935). Reprinted by permission of David Higham Associates Ltd.

'Bosworth Summit Pound' by Lionel Thomas Caswell Rolt (1910-74), from *Sleep No More. Twelve Stories of the Supernatural* (Constable, 1948). Reprinted by permisssion of Mrs S. M. Rolt. Rolt was an authority on the inland waterways of Britain.

'An Encounter in the Mist' by Alan Noel Latimer Munby (1913-74), from *The Alabaster Hand and Other Ghost Stories* (Dennis Dobson, 1949). Reprinted by permission of Dobson Books Ltd. Munby was Librarian of King's College, Cambridge, from 1947 to 1974; the stories in *The Alabaster Hand* were written between 1943 and 1945 when Munby was a prisoner of war at Eichstätt in Upper Franconia. Like Swain's *The Stoneground Ghost Tales*, Munby's volume was dedicated (in Latin) to M. R. James.

'Hand in Glove' by Elizabeth Bowen (1899-1973), first published in *The Second Ghost Book*, ed. Lady Cynthia Asquith (James Barrie, 1952), for which she wrote an excellent introduction; reprinted in *The Collected Stories of Elizabeth Bowen* (Cape, 1980), which contains all her supernatural stories except 'The Claimant' (from *The Third Ghost Book*, 1955). Copyright © 1981 by Curtis Brown Ltd., Literary Executors of the Estate of Elizabeth Bowen. Reprinted by permission of Alfred A. Knopf, Inc., Jonathan Cape Ltd., and the Estate of Elizabeth Bowen.

'A Story of Don Juan' by (Sir) Victor Sawdon Pritchett (1900-), first published in *The Second Ghost Book*, ed. Lady Cynthia Asquith (James Barrie, 1952). Copyright 1950 by V. S. Pritchett. Reprinted from *More Collected Stories*, by V. S. Pritchett, by permission of Random House, Inc., and Chatto & Windus.

'Cushi' by Christopher Woodforde (1907-62), from *A Pad in the Straw* (Dent, 1952). Reprinted by permission of J. M. Dent & Sons Ltd. Woodforde was a lecturer in modern history at New College, Oxford.

'Bad Company' by Walter de la Mare (1873-1956), from *A Beginning and Other Stories* (Faber, 1955). Reprinted by permission of the Literary Trustees of Walter de la Mare and the Society of Authors as their representative.

'The Bottle of 1912' by Simon Arthur Noel Raven (1927-), from *The Compleat Imbiber. An Entertainment*, ed. Cyril Ray (1961), 105-11, © Simon Raven 1961. Reprinted by kind permission of Curtis Brown on behalf of the author. The first *Compleat Imbiber* was published in 1957 as part of the centenary of W. & A. Gilbey Ltd., Distillers and Wine Shippers.

'The Cicerones' by Robert Fordyce Aickman (1914-81), from *Sub Rosa* (Gollancz, 1968). Reprinted by permission of the Leslie Gardner Literary Agency Ltd. on behalf of the Estate of Robert Aickman. The story had first appeared in the anthology *Travellers by Night*, ed. August Derleth (Arkham House, 1967; Gollancz, 1968). Aickman investigated the famous 'haunted' house, Borley Rectory, in 1943.

'Soft Voices at Passenham' by Terence Hanbury White (1906-64); though written in the 1930s, it was published for the first time in *The Maharajah and Other Stories*, collected and edited by Kurth Sprague (Macdonald, 1981). Reprinted by permission of David Higham Associates Ltd. It is similar to some of the stories in White's *Gone to Ground* (Collins, 1935).

While every effort has been made to secure permission, we may have failed in a few cases to trace the copyright holder. We apologize for any apparent negligence.

SELECT BIBLIOGRAPHY

COLLECTIONS

Aickman, Robert, *We Are For the Dark* [with Elizabeth Jane Howard] (1951).
—, *Dark Entries* (1964).
—, *Powers of Darkness* (1966).
—, *Sub Rosa* (1968).
—, *Cold Hand in Mine* (1975).
—, *Tales of Love and Death* (1977).
—, *Intrusions. Strange Tales* (1980).
—, *Night Voices. Strange Stories* (1985).

Asquith, Lady Cynthia, *What Dreams May Come* (1951) [revised edn. of *This Mortal Coil*, 1947].

Benson, A. C., *The Hill of Trouble* (1903).
—, *The Isles of Sunset* (1904).
—, *Basil Netherby* (1927).

Benson E. F., *The Room in the Tower* (1912).
—, *Visible and Invisible* (1923).
—, *Spook Stories* (1928).
—, *More Spook Stories* (1934).

Benson, R. H., *A Mirror of Shalott* (1907).

Blackwood, Algernon, *The Empty House* (1906).
—, *The Listener* (1907).
—, *John Silence. Physician Extraordinary* (1908).
—, *Day and Night Stories* (1917).
—, *Tales of the Uncanny and Supernatural* (1949).

Bowen, Marjorie, *Dark Ann and Other Stories* (1927).
—, *The Last Bouquet* (1933).
—, *The Bishop of Hell* (1949).
—, *Kecksies* (1976).

Broster, D. K., *Couching at the Door* (1942).

Broughton, Rhoda, *Twilight Stories* (1879) [enlarged edn. of *Tales For Christmas Eve*, 1873].

Bulwer-Lytton, Sir Edward, 'The Haunters and the Haunted', *Blackwood's Magazine* (1859).

Burke, Thomas, *Night-Pieces* (1935).

Burrage, A. M. ['Ex-Private X'], *Some Ghost Stories* (1927).
—, *Someone in the Room* (1931).
—, *Between the Minute and the Hour* [selection by A. Skene] (1967).

Caldecott, Sir Andrew, *Not Exactly Ghosts* (1947).

Collins, Wilkie, see *Tales of Terror and the Supernatural*, ed. H. Van Thal (1972).

Coppard, A. E., various: see *The Collected Tales of A. E. Coppard* (1948).

Crawford, F. Marion, *Uncanny Tales* (1911).

de la Mare, Walter, various: see *Ghost Stories* (Folio Society, 1956).

Donovan, Dick [J. E. Preston-Muddock], *Stories Weird and Wonderful* (1889).

Gift, Theo [Dora Havers], *Not For the Night-Time* (1889).

Gray, Arthur ['Ingulphus'], *Tedious Brief Tales of Granta and Gramarye* (1919).

Hartley, L. P., *Night Fears* (1924).
—, *The Travelling Grave* (USA, 1948: UK, 1951).
—, *Collected Short Stories* (1968).

Harvey, W. F., *The Beast with Five Fingers* (1928).
—, *Midnight Tales* [selection ed. Maurice Richardson] (1946).

Hodgson, William Hope, *Carnacki, The Ghost-Finder* (1913).

Hunt, Violet, *Tales of the Uneasy* (1911).
—, *More Tales of the Uneasy* (1925).

Irwin, Margaret, *Madame Fears the Dark* (1935).

Jackson, T. G., *Six Ghost Stories* (1919).

James, Henry, see *The Ghostly Tales of Henry James*, ed. Leon Edel (1948).

James, M. R., *Ghost Stories of an Antiquary* (1904).
—, *More Ghost Stories of an Antiquary* (1911).
—, *A Thin Ghost, and Others* (1919).
—, *A Warning to the Curious* (1925).
—, *Collected Ghost Stories* (1931).

John, Jasper [Rosalie Muspratt)], *Sinister Stories* (1930).
—, *Tales of Terror* (1931).

Kneale, Nigel, *Tomato Cain* (1949).

Lawrence, Margery, *The Terraces of Night* (1932).

Lee, Vernon [Violet Paget], *Hauntings* (1890).

Le Fanu, J. S., *Ghost Stories and Tales of Mystery* (1851).
—, *In a Glass Darkly* (1872).
—, *The Purcell Papers* (1880).
—, *The Watcher and Other Weird Stories* (1894).
—, *A Chronicle of Golden Friars and Other Stories* (1896).
—, *Madam Crowl's Ghost and Other Tales of Mystery*, ed. M. R. James (1923).
—, *Best Ghost Stories of J. S. Le Fanu*, ed. E. F. Bleiler (1964).

Malden, R. H., *Nine Ghosts* (1943).

Marsh, Richard, *The Seen and the Unseen* (1900).

Metcalfe, John, *The Smoking Leg* (1925).
—, *Judas and Other Stories* (1931).

Molesworth, Mary, *Four Ghost Stories* (1888).
—, *Uncanny Tales* (1896).

Munby, A. N. L., *The Alabaster Hand* (1949).

Nesbit, E., *Grim Tales* (1893).
—, *Fear* (1910).

Oliphant, Margaret, *Stories of the Seen and Unseen* (1889).

Onions, Oliver, *Widdershins* (1911).
—, *Ghosts in Daylight* (1924).
—, *Collected Ghost Stories* (1935).
—, *Bells Rung Backwards* (1953).

Pain, Barry [Eric Odell], *Stories in the Dark* (1901).
—, *Stories in Grey* (1911).

Pater, Roger [Gilbert Roger Hudlestone], *Mystic Voices* (1923).

Quiller-Couch, Sir Arthur, *Wandering Heath* (1895).
—, *Old Fires and Profitable Ghosts* (1900).

Riddell, J. H., *Weird Stories* (1884).

Rolt, L. T. C., *Sleep No More* (1948).

Sinclair, May, *Uncanny Stories* (1923).

Swain, E. G., *The Stoneground Ghost Tales* (1912).

Wakefield, H. Russell, *They Return at Evening* (1928).
—, *Old Man's Beard* (1929)
—, *Imagine a Man in a Box* (1931).
—, *The Clock Strikes Twelve* (1940).
—, *Strayers From Sheol* (1961).
—, *Ghost Stories* [selection] (1932).
—, *Best Ghost Stories of H. Russell Wakefield*, ed. Richard Dalby (1978).

Walpole, Hugh, *All Souls' Night* (1933).

Wharton, Edith, *Tales of Men and Ghosts* (1910).
—, *Ghosts* (1937).
—, *The Ghost Stories of Edith Wharton* (1973).

Wilkins [later Wilkins-Freeman], Mary E., *The Wind in the Rose-Bush* (1903).
—, *Collected Ghost Stories* (1974).

ANTHOLOGIES

There follows a small selection only of the many anthologies of ghost stories that have been published over the past fifty years.

Aickman, Robert (ed.), *The Fontana Book of Great Ghost Stories*, vols. 1-8 (1964-72) [vols. 9-20 (1973-84) ed. R. Chetwynd-Hayes].

Asquith, Lady Cynthia (ed.), *The Ghost Book* (1926).
—, *Shudders* (1929).
—, *When Churchyards Yawn* (1931).
—, *The Second Ghost Book* (1952).
—, *The Third Ghost Book* (1955) [the *Ghost Book* series revived after Cynthia

Asquith's death, in 1965, by James Turner, Rosemary Timperley, and Aidan Chambers].

[Birkin, Charles (ed.)], *The Creeps Omnibus* (1935).

Bowen, Marjorie (ed.), *Great Tales of Horror* (1933).

—, *More Great Tales of Horror* (1935).

Bull, R. C. (ed.), *Perturbed Spirits* (1954).

Century of Creepy Stories, A, (1934) [anonymous compilation drawing on Cynthia Asquith's *The Ghost Book*, *Shudders*, and *When Churchyards Yawn* (q.v.); see also WALPOLE].

Collins, V. H. (ed.), *Ghosts and Marvels* (Oxford, 1924) [introduction by M. R. James].

—, *More Ghosts and Marvels* (Oxford, 1927).

Cuddon, J. A. (ed.), *The Penguin Book of Ghost Stories* (1984).

Dalby, Richard (ed.), *The Sorceress in Stained Glass* (1971).

Dale, Harrison (ed.), *Great Ghost Stories* (1930).
—, *More Great Ghost Stories* (1932).

Danby, Mary (ed.), *65 Great Tales of the Supernatural* (1979).
—, *65 Great Spine Chillers* (1985).

de la Mare, Colin (ed.), *They Walk Again* (1931); reprinted many times as *The Ghost Book*.

Derleth, August (ed.), *Travellers by Night* (1967).

Fraser, Phyllis, and Wise, H. A. (eds.), *Great Tales of Terror and the Supernatural* (USA, 1944; UK, 1947).

Laing, Alexander (ed.), *The Haunted Omnibus* (1937).

Lamb, Hugh (ed.), *A Tide of Terror* (1972).
—, *A Wave of Fear* (1973).
—, *Victorian Tales of Terror* (1974).
—, *Terror by Gaslight* (1975).
—, *Return From the Grave* (1976).
—, *The Taste of Fear* (1976).
—, *Victorian Nightmares* (1977).

Netherwood, Bryan A. (ed.), *Medley Macabre* (1966).

Ridler, Anne (ed.), *Best Ghost Stories* (1945).

Search, Pamela (ed.), *The Supernatural in the English Short Story* (1959).

Summers, Montague (ed.), *The Supernatural Omnibus* (1931).
—, *Victorian Ghost Stories* (1934).

Walpole, Hugh (ed.), *A Second Century of Creepy Stories* (1937).

BIOGRAPHY AND CRITICISM

Ashley, Mike, *Who's Who in Horror and Fantasy Fiction* (1977).

Bleiler, E. F. (ed.), *Supernatural Fiction Writers*, 2 vols. (New York, 1985).

Briggs, Julia, *Night Visitors. The Rise and Fall of the English Ghost Story* (1977).

Browne, Nelson, *Sheridan Le Fanu* (1951).

Cox, Michael, *M. R. James. An Informal Portrait* (Oxford, 1983, 1986).
—, 'The Malice of Inanimate Objects', *Ghosts and Scholars* 6 (1984), 1-5.
—, introduction to *M. R. James: 'Casting the Runes', and Other Stories* (Oxford, 1987).

Ellis, S. M., 'The Ghost Story and Its Exponents', *The Fortnightly Review* (December 1923); reprinted in *Mainly Victorian* (1925).
—, *Wilkie Collins, Le Fanu, and Others* (1931).

Gunn, Peter, *Vernon Lee. Violet Paget 1856-1935* (1964).

Jackson, Rosemary, *Fantasy. The Literature of Subversion* (1981).

James, M. R., introduction to V. H. Collins (ed.), *Ghosts and Marvels* (Oxford, 1924).
—, 'Some Remarks on Ghost Stories', *The Bookman* (December 1929), 169-72; reprinted in Michael Cox (ed.), *M. R. James: 'Casting the Runes', and Other Stories* (Oxford, 1987).

Lang, Andrew, 'The Comparative Study of Ghost Stories', *Nineteenth Century* (April 1885), 623-32.

Lovecraft, H. P., *Supernatural Horror in Literature* (New York, 1945); reprinted, with an introduction by E. F. Bleiler, 1973.

McCormack, W. J., *Sheridan Le Fanu and Victorian Ireland* (Oxford, 1980).

Manlove, C. N., *Modern Fantasy. Five Studies* (Cambridge, 1975).
—, *The Impulse of Fantasy Literature* (1983).

Penzoldt, Peter, *The Supernatural in Fiction* (1952).

Prickett, Stephen, *Victorian Fantasy* (1979).

Scarborough, Dorothy, *The Supernatural in Modern English Fiction* (1917).

Scott, Sir Walter, 'On the Supernatural in Fictitious Composition', *Foreign Quarterly Review*, (1817), 60-98; reprinted in *Walter Scott: On Novelists and Fiction*, ed. J. Williams (1968).

Sullivan, Jack, *Elegant Nightmares. The English Ghost Story from Le Fanu to Blackwood* (Ohio University Press, 1978).

Summers, Montague, introduction to *The Supernatural Omnibus* (1931).

BIBLIOGRAPHIES

Bleiler, E. F., *The Checklist of Science-Fiction and Supernatural Fiction* (1978).

Locke, George, *A Spectrum of Fantasy* (1980).

Schlobin, Roger C., *The Literature of Fantasy. A Comprehensive, Annotated Bibliography* (1979).

Tuck, Donald H., *The Encyclopaedia of Science Fiction and Fantasy*, 3 vols. (Chicago, 1974, 1978, 1982).